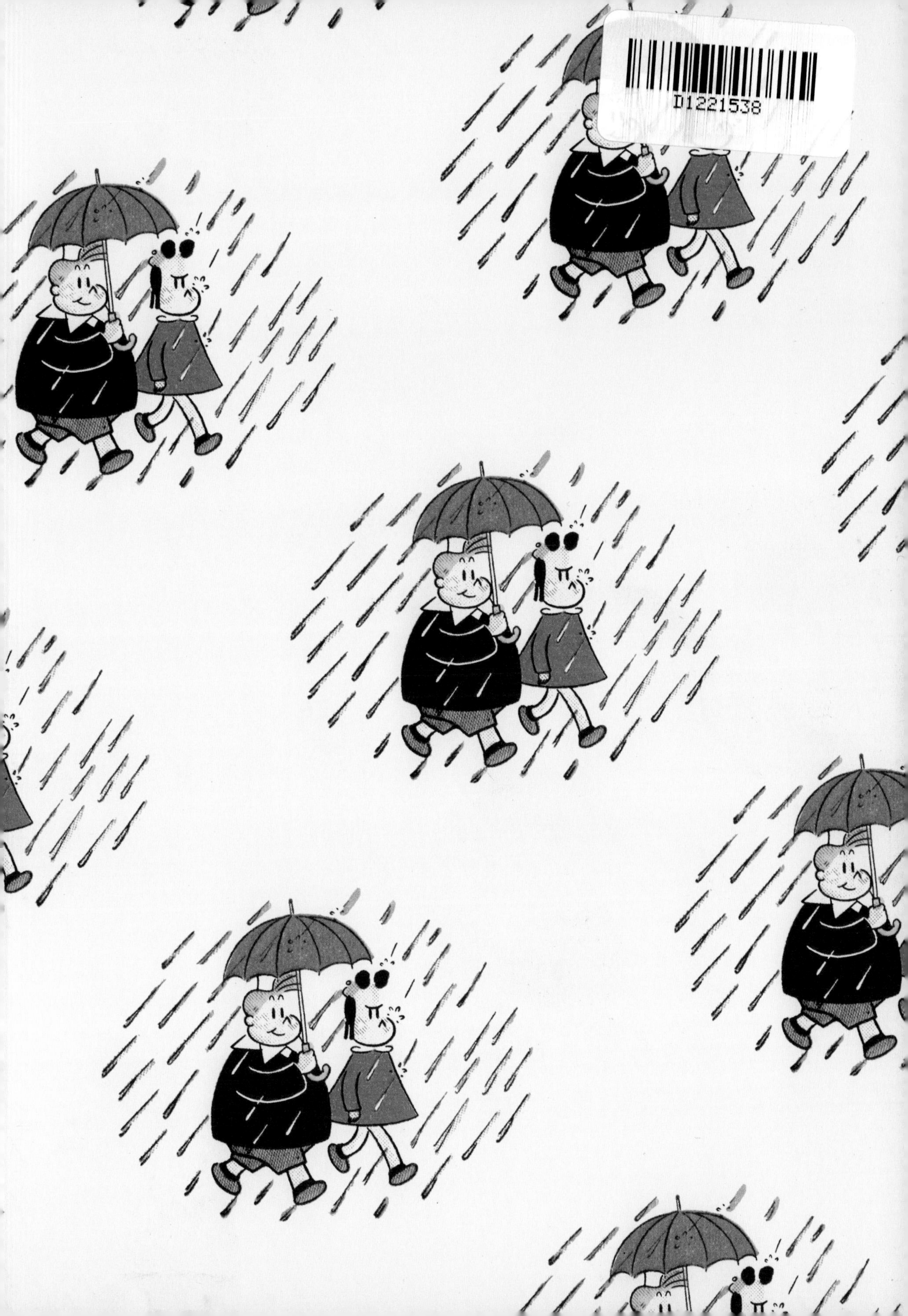

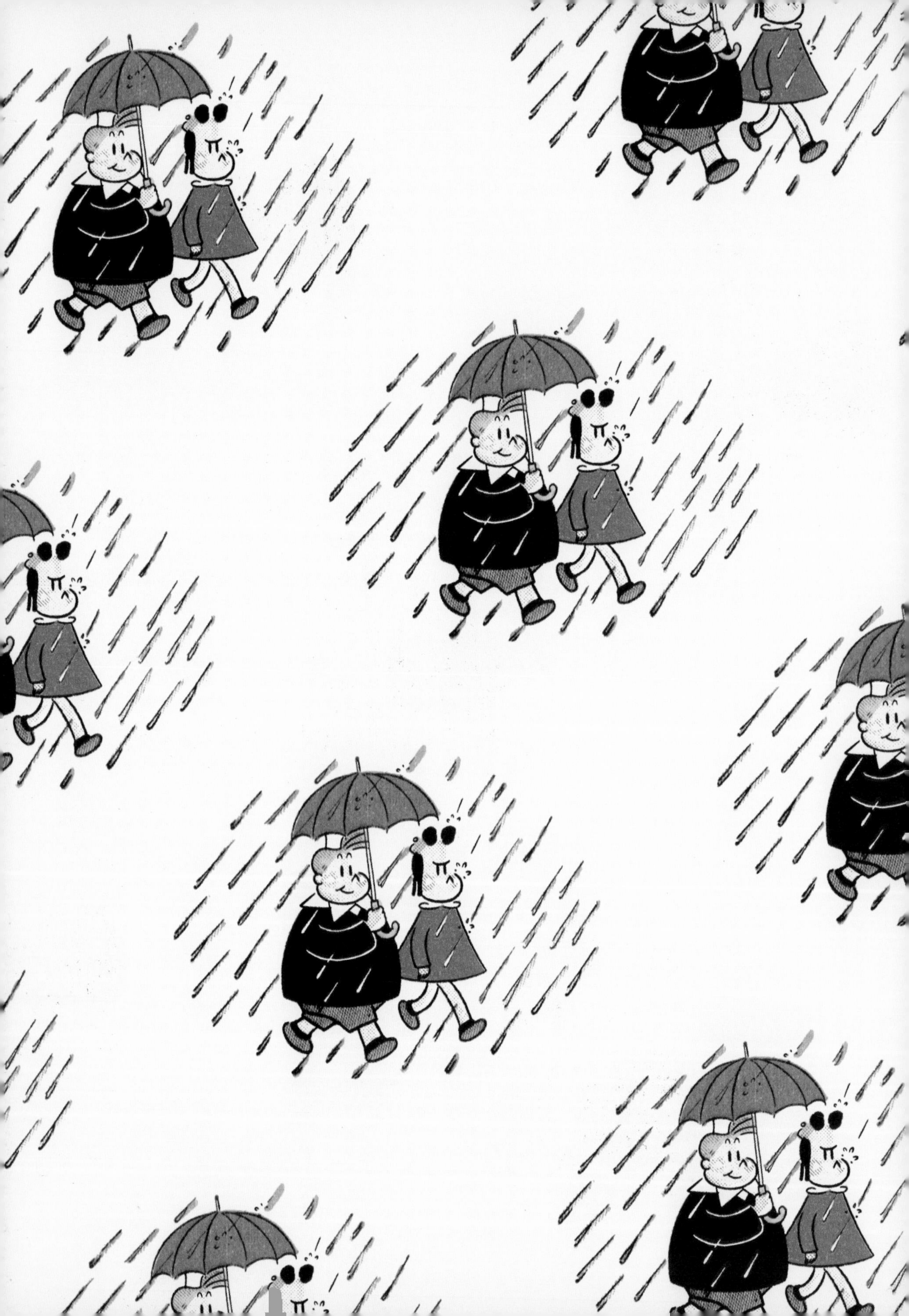

Marge's *Little Lulu*

Working Girl

John Stanley

Edited by Frank Young and Tom Devlin

Drawn & Quarterly

Introduction

I grew up in the golden age of comics: the 1940s, and most particularly the five years immediately after the end of World War II. Comics were one of the main sources of entertainment for children then: there was not yet much television, and although there were Saturday matinees, most films were for adults. On Saturday mornings groups of children would congregate around the stashes of comics that had been collected to have comic-book orgies. The comics were read and re-read; they were also traded.

Among those collected and traded at our place were *Little Lulu*s. They were read by boys as well as girls—bratty kids were universally appealing to bratty kids, which all of us were some of the time in those years when kids were allowed to roam freely as long as they came home before dark. The things Lulu and her pals and frenemies got up to behind the backs of their oblivious parents were close to our own experiences, and being able to think your way out of a tight spot you'd got yourself into was a skill we all wished to have.

But Lulu had a special significance for me, because she had curls and so did I. Curly hair went in and out of fashion—Twiggy was to get revenge on behalf of the straight-haired in the late 1960s—but in the Shirley-Temple-dominated 1940s, curls were at a premium, and it was horrifying for me to witness the Torquemada-like tortures inflicted on my friends' heads by their mothers: the hair was twisted up in damp rags and secured with bobby pins at night, producing, in the morning, a few limp spirals of hair that would quickly wilt. Whereas Lulu and I were all set! Soon I would surely get a job selling that new consumer item, Kleenex, just like her. (This failed to happen.)

But Lulu had a few other things going for her in my eyes. She was little, as was I, but this did not stop her for an instant. The eternal problem of the boys' clubhouse—not being let into it, that is—was treated by her, by and large, with a phnuh. She had other and better things to do, and anyway she—being the title character—was smarter, so there. And, in an age somewhat devoid of female title characters, she was the title character. One could therefore be little, and a girl, and *nonetheless* the title character. Move over, Jane Eyre!

But most of all Lulu was a story-teller. The episodes I remember most clearly were those in which Lulu resorts to tale-spinning in order to soothe the savage breast of the pesky and persistent Alvin. Her tales featured a poor little girl identical to Lulu who picked beebleberries and sold them, but frequently ran afoul of a wicked witch called Hazel. (Witch Hazel: get it? Lulu was not averse to puns.) Witch Hazel was a

formidable adversary, but the *Little Lulu* avatar always won out in the end through a mixture of inventiveness, deviousness, and trickery—joining a long list of female heroines from folk tales and epics—and, more recently, novels—who have done the same. Lulu also indulged in a certain amount of snooping—hiding in the bushes and eavesdropping—and is thus in the line of famous female spies and detectives, from Sally the Sleuth to Josephine Baker. She is brave but not stupid: when in doubt, she runs away very fast. All of these are qualities to be admired.

Little Lulu made her stories up as she went along, which was the approach my brother and I took to the serial narratives we were in the habit of concocting, taking turns as we got tired. Like us, Lulu frequently left off in mid-story, thus leaving Alvin clamouring for more. It was a good exercise in the value of Suspense. Lulu is thus in the lineage of female wordspinners that includes Scheherazade, giving us the equation: Scheherazade is to the Sultan as Little Lulu is to Alvin. It's a stretch, I know, but what the heck.

I loved the beebleberry stories as a child. Any berry you couldn't identify became a beebleberry, and so it remains to this very day. The difference is that Lulu's beebleberries were edible, whereas you should never eat my kind of beebleberries until you find out what they are. At which point they cease to be beebleberries.

Little Lulu never grew up. Like Peter Pan, another child trickster, she remained little. But I did grow up, more or less, eventually, though not enough to become tall. What would Bigger Lulu have been like, I now wonder? I prefer to think she would have been a writer of some kind; certainly a story-teller.

As one of those myself, I am frequently asked about my influences.

I haven't yet cited Little Lulu, but I will do so now. What were the life lessons taught to me by this diminutive but curly-headed prankster?

1. It's okay to have curls.
2. It's okay to be short.
3. It's okay to be female.
4. Story-telling is a skill, and putting beebleberries, witches or witch-substitutes, and suspense into the mixture definitely leavens the lump.
5. If you hide in the bushes and eavesdrop, you can learn some very useful things. Just don't sneeze.

So here's to Little Lulu! Thanks to her for many hours of entertainment and instruction, and long may the beebleberries flourish.

marge's Little Lulu

WHEN ARE YOU GETTING YOUR WINGS, LULU?
I GUESS MY MOTHER'S GOT 'EM FINISHED BY NOW
I BET I'LL LOOK LIKE SOMETHIN' IN MY PIRATE COSTUME
I'LL LOOK LIKE SOMETHIN' AWFUL IN THAT SISSY THING I HAVE TO WEAR
SO LONG, LULU... I'LL CALL FOR YOU LATER
S'LONG
IF TH' KIDS SEE ME IN THAT COSTUME, I'LL NEVER LIVE IT DOWN
LULU! YOUR COSTUME IS ALMOST READY ♫ ♫
YOU'RE GOING TO BE THE MOST POPULAR GIRL AT ELSIE JONES'S BIRTHDAY PARTY TODAY
OH, SURE

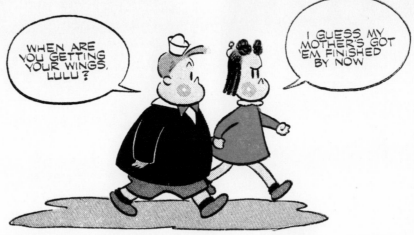

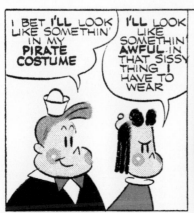

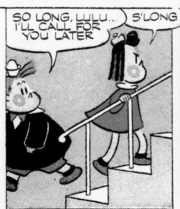

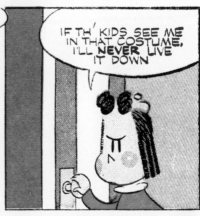

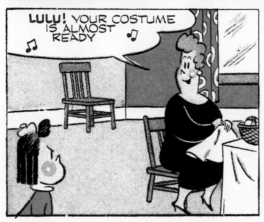

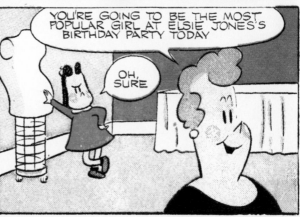

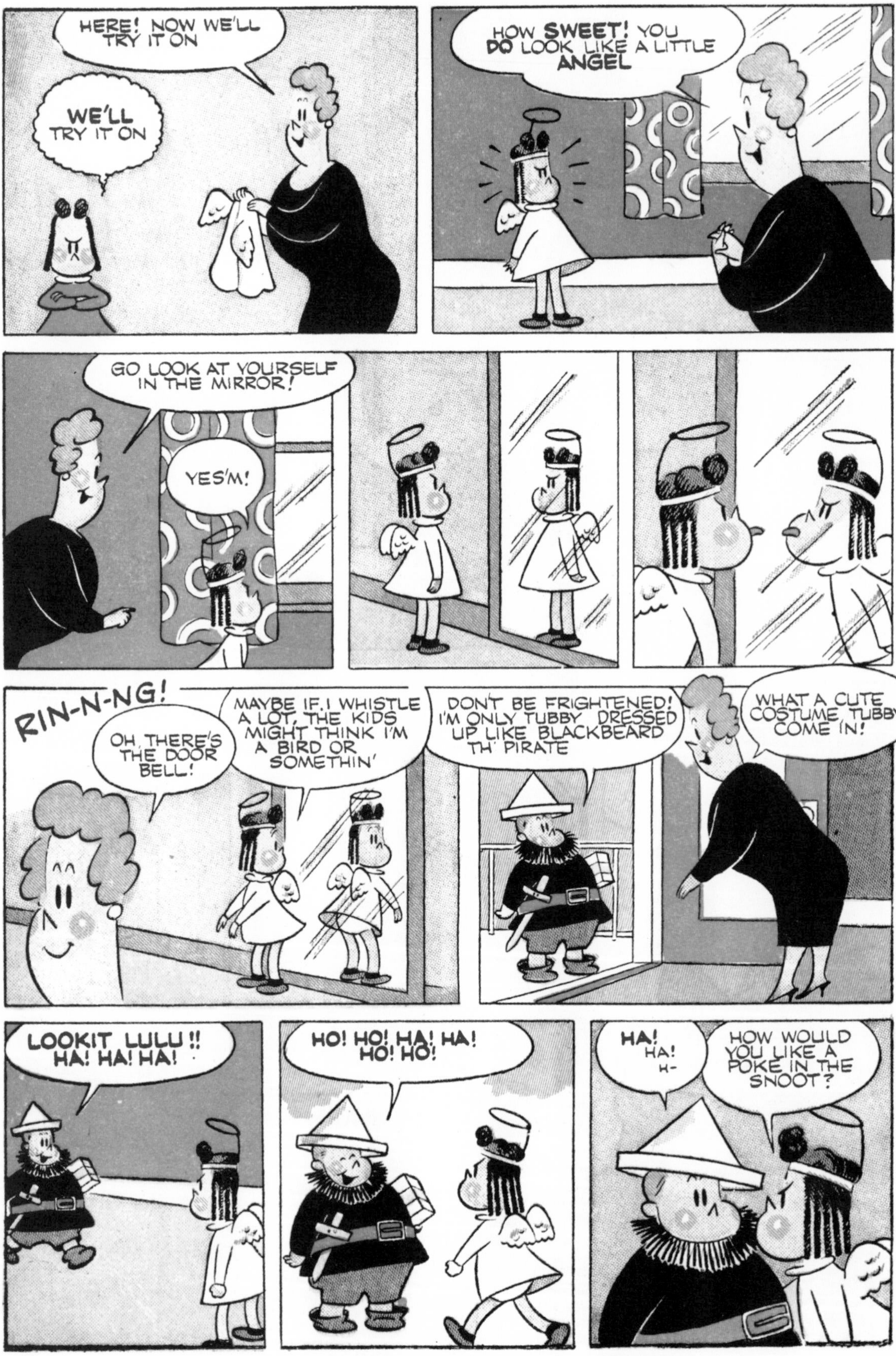
HERE! NOW WE'LL TRY IT ON
WE'LL TRY IT ON
HOW SWEET! YOU DO LOOK LIKE A LITTLE ANGEL
GO LOOK AT YOURSELF IN THE MIRROR!
YES'M!
RIN-N-NG!
OH, THERE'S THE DOOR BELL!
MAYBE IF I WHISTLE A LOT, THE KIDS MIGHT THINK I'M A BIRD OR SOMETHIN'
DON'T BE FRIGHTENED! I'M ONLY TUBBY DRESSED UP LIKE BLACKBEARD TH' PIRATE
WHAT A CUTE COSTUME TUBBY... COME IN!
LOOKIT LULU!! HA! HA! HA!
HO! HO! HA! HA! HO! HO!
HA! HA! H-
HOW WOULD YOU LIKE A POKE IN THE SNOOT?

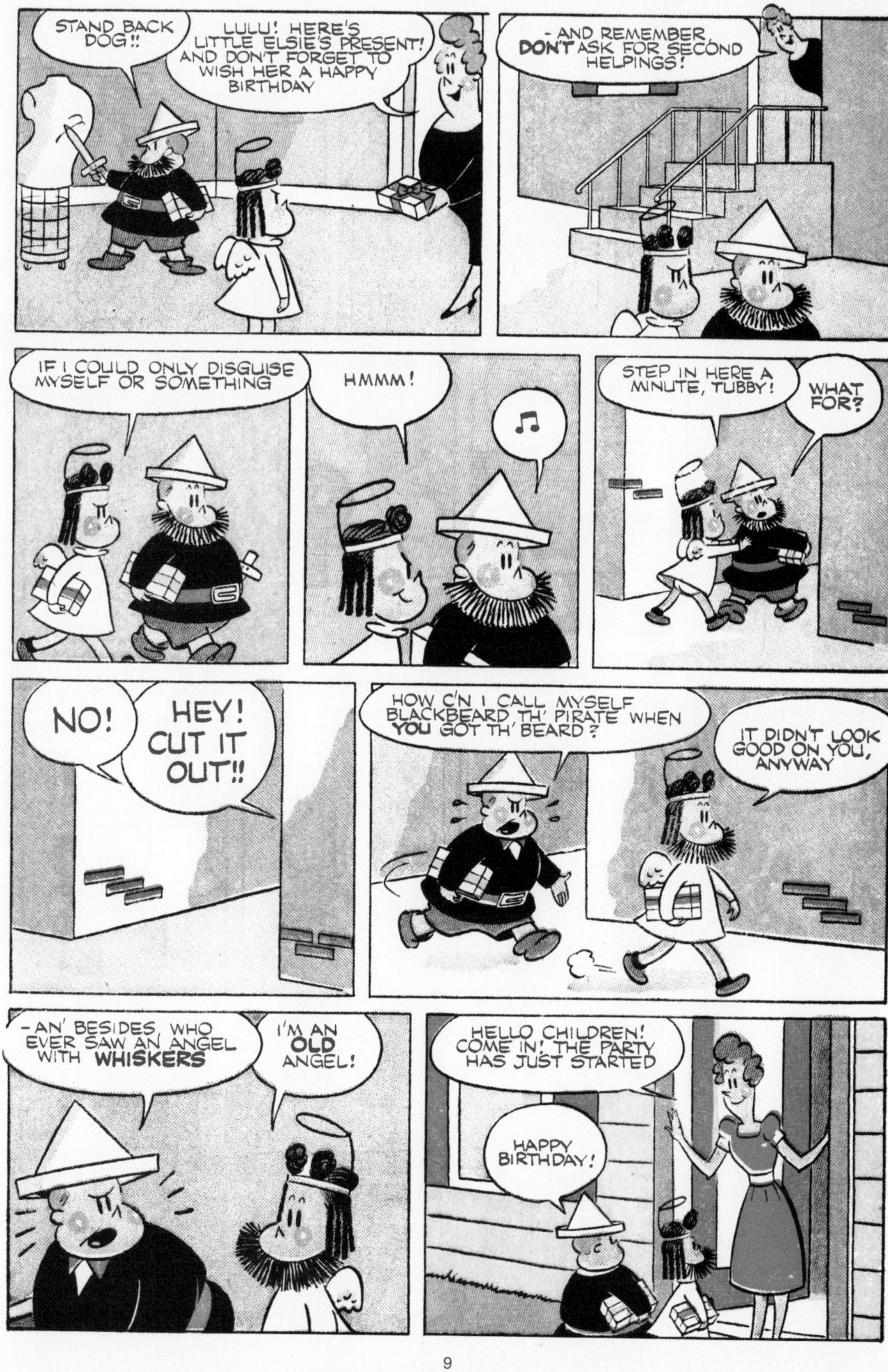
STAND BACK DOG!!
LULU! HERE'S LITTLE ELSIE'S PRESENT! AND DON'T FORGET TO WISH HER A HAPPY BIRTHDAY
- AND REMEMBER, DON'T ASK FOR SECOND HELPINGS!
IF I COULD ONLY DISGUISE MYSELF OR SOMETHING
HMMM!
STEP IN HERE A MINUTE, TUBBY!
WHAT FOR?
NO!
HEY! CUT IT OUT!!
HOW C'N I CALL MYSELF BLACKBEARD TH' PIRATE WHEN YOU GOT TH' BEARD?
IT DIDN'T LOOK GOOD ON YOU, ANYWAY
- AN' BESIDES, WHO EVER SAW AN ANGEL WITH WHISKERS
I'M AN OLD ANGEL!
HELLO CHILDREN! COME IN! THE PARTY HAS JUST STARTED
HAPPY BIRTHDAY!

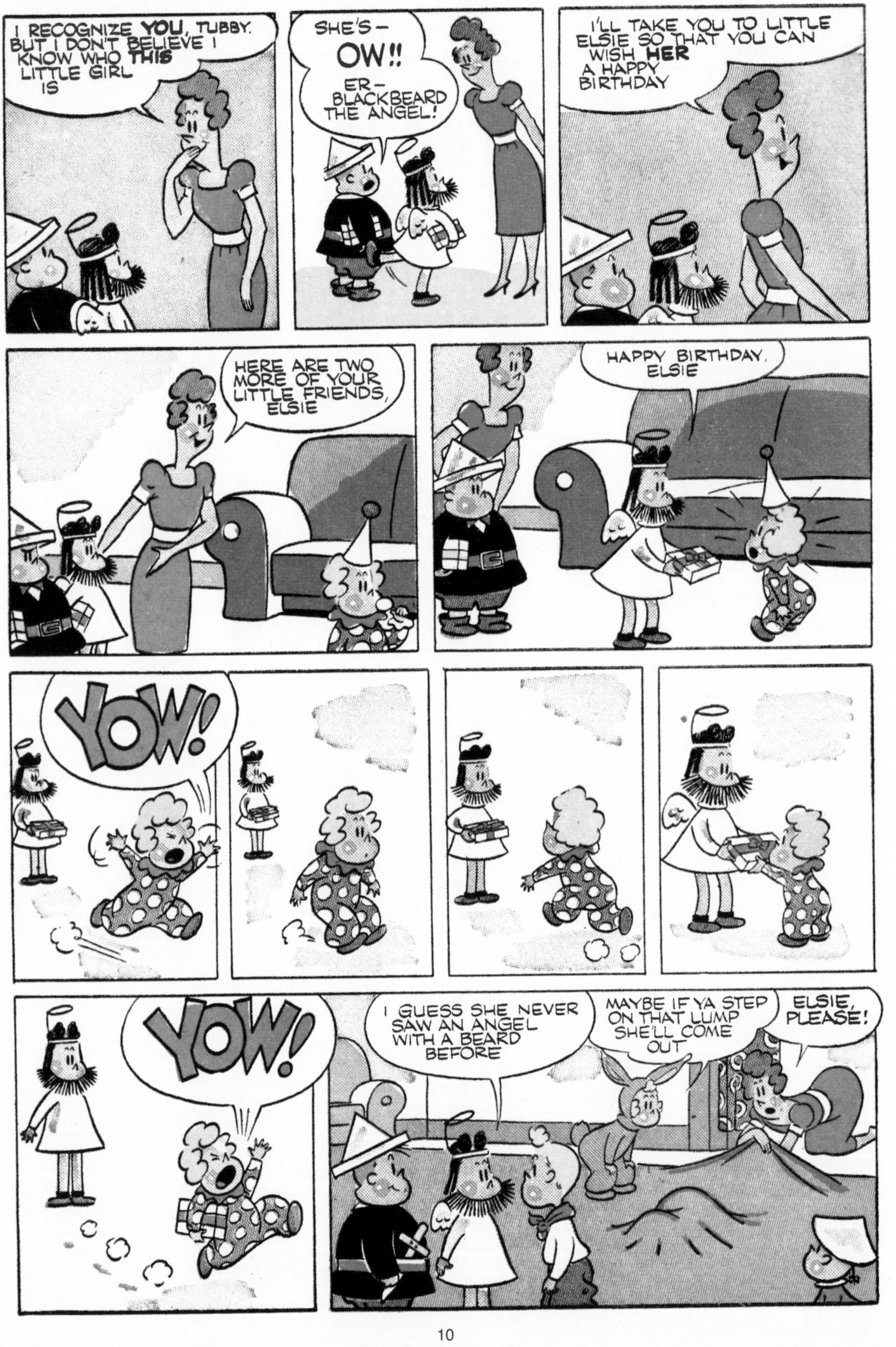
I RECOGNIZE YOU, TUBBY. BUT I DON'T BELIEVE I KNOW WHO THIS LITTLE GIRL IS
SHE'S— OW!! ER— BLACKBEARD THE ANGEL!
I'LL TAKE YOU TO LITTLE ELSIE SO THAT YOU CAN WISH HER A HAPPY BIRTHDAY
HERE ARE TWO MORE OF YOUR LITTLE FRIENDS, ELSIE
HAPPY BIRTHDAY, ELSIE
YOW!
YOW!
I GUESS SHE NEVER SAW AN ANGEL WITH A BEARD BEFORE
MAYBE IF YA STEP ON THAT LUMP SHE'LL COME OUT
ELSIE, PLEASE!

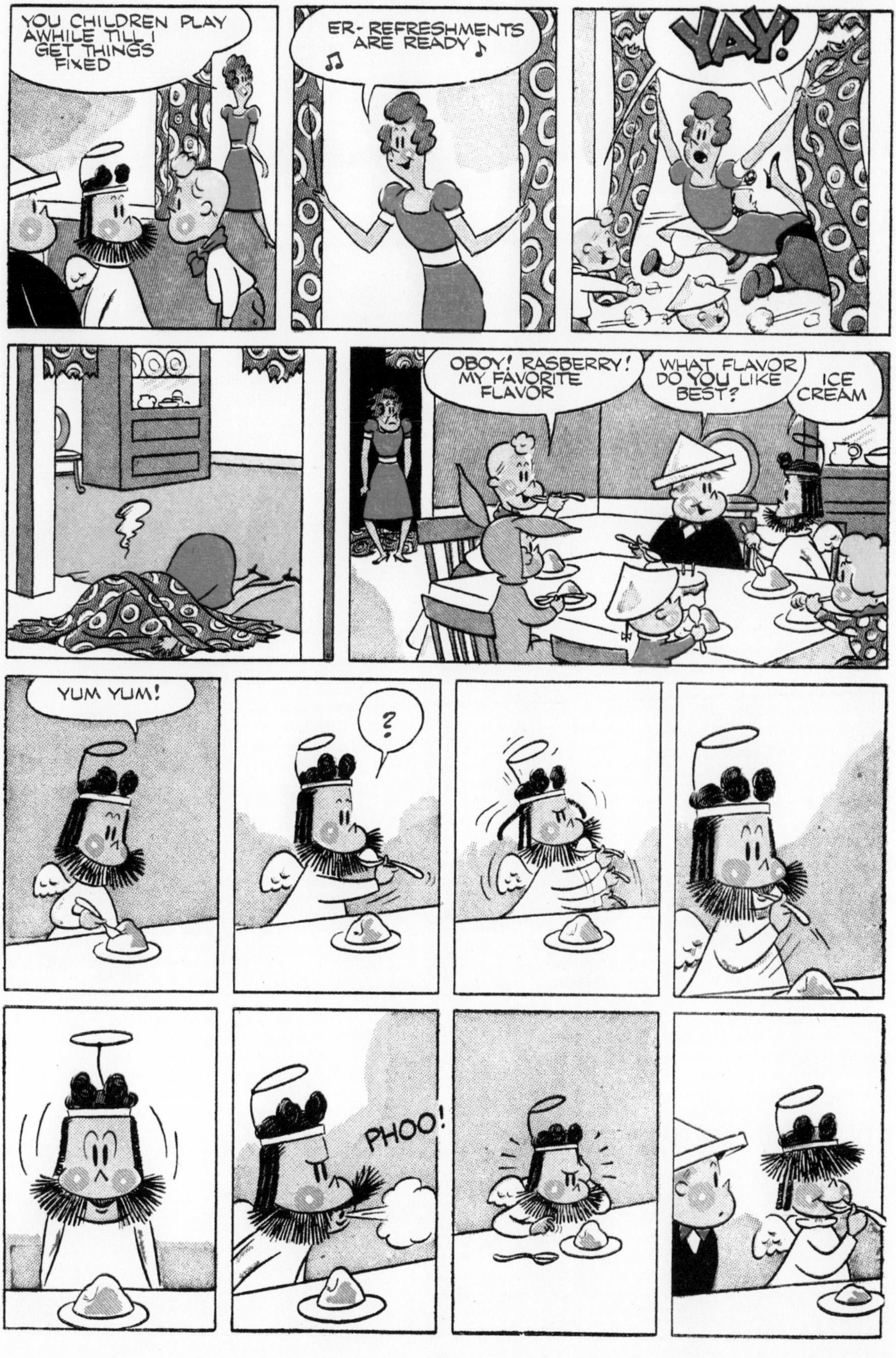
YOU CHILDREN PLAY AWHILE TILL I GET THINGS FIXED
ER- REFRESHMENTS ARE READY ♪
YAY!
OBOY! RASBERRY! MY FAVORITE FLAVOR
WHAT FLAVOR DO YOU LIKE BEST?
ICE CREAM
YUM YUM!
?
PHOO!

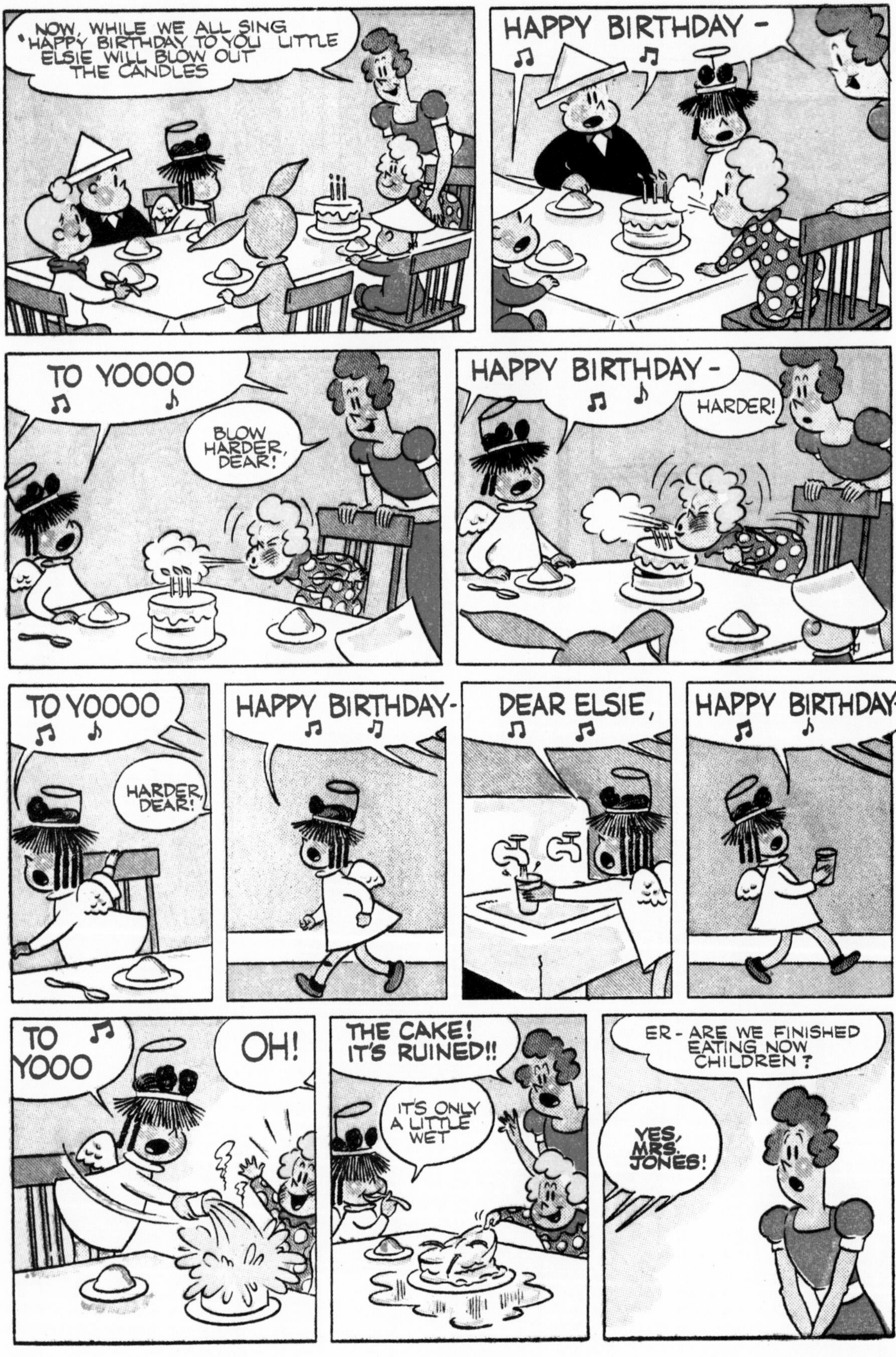
NOW, WHILE WE ALL SING "HAPPY BIRTHDAY TO YOU" LITTLE ELSIE WILL BLOW OUT THE CANDLES
HAPPY BIRTHDAY -
TO YOOOO
BLOW HARDER, DEAR!
HAPPY BIRTHDAY -
HARDER!
TO YOOOO
HARDER, DEAR!
HAPPY BIRTHDAY-
DEAR ELSIE,
HAPPY BIRTHDAY-
TO YOOO
OH!
THE CAKE! IT'S RUINED!!
IT'S ONLY A LITTLE WET
ER - ARE WE FINISHED EATING NOW CHILDREN ?
YES, MRS. JONES!

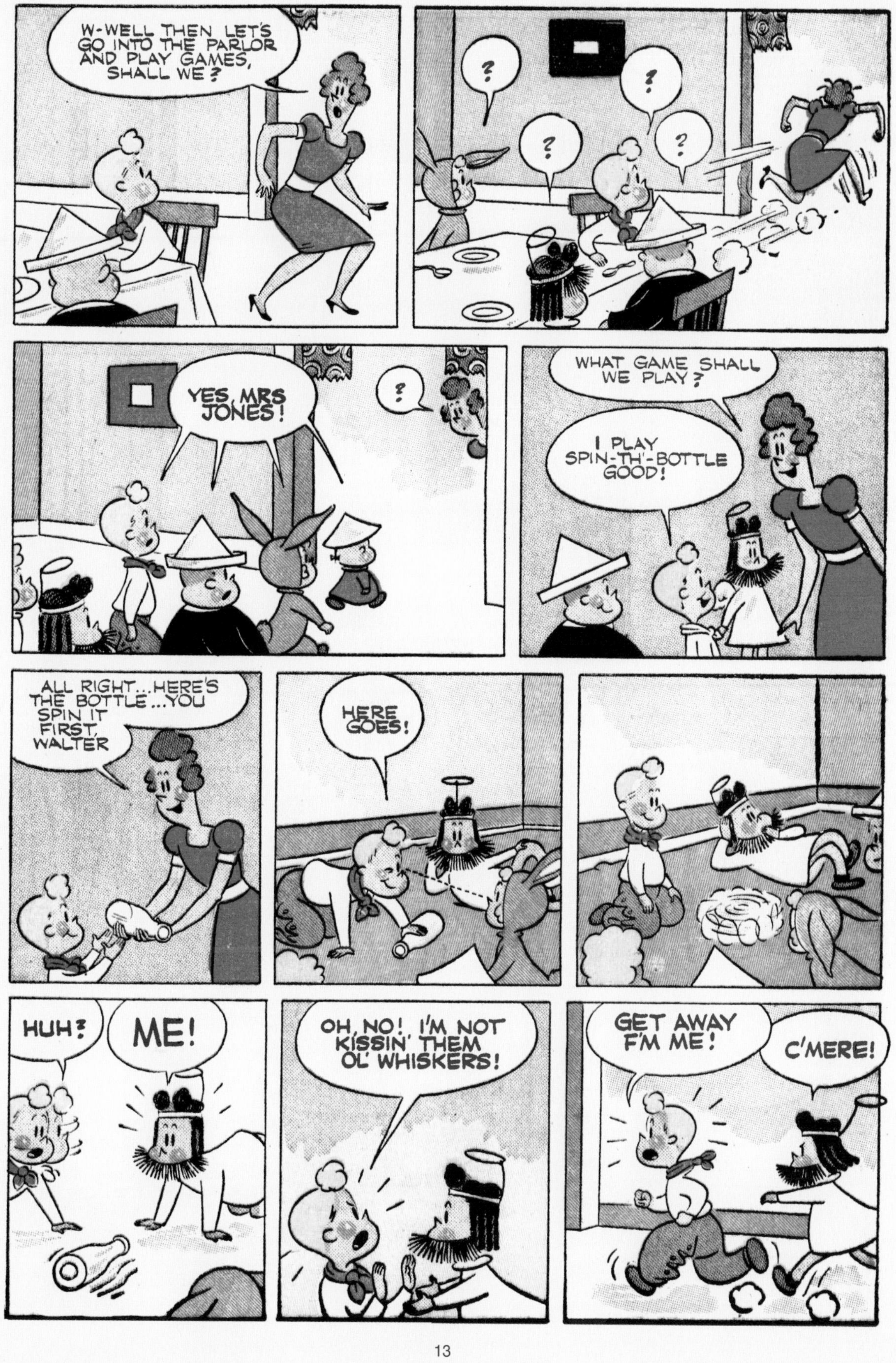
W-WELL THEN LET'S GO INTO THE PARLOR AND PLAY GAMES, SHALL WE?
?
?
?
?
YES, MRS JONES!
?
WHAT GAME SHALL WE PLAY?
I PLAY SPIN-TH'-BOTTLE GOOD!
ALL RIGHT...HERE'S THE BOTTLE...YOU SPIN IT FIRST, WALTER
HERE GOES!
HUH?
ME!
OH, NO! I'M NOT KISSIN' THEM OL' WHISKERS!
GET AWAY F'M ME!
C'MERE!

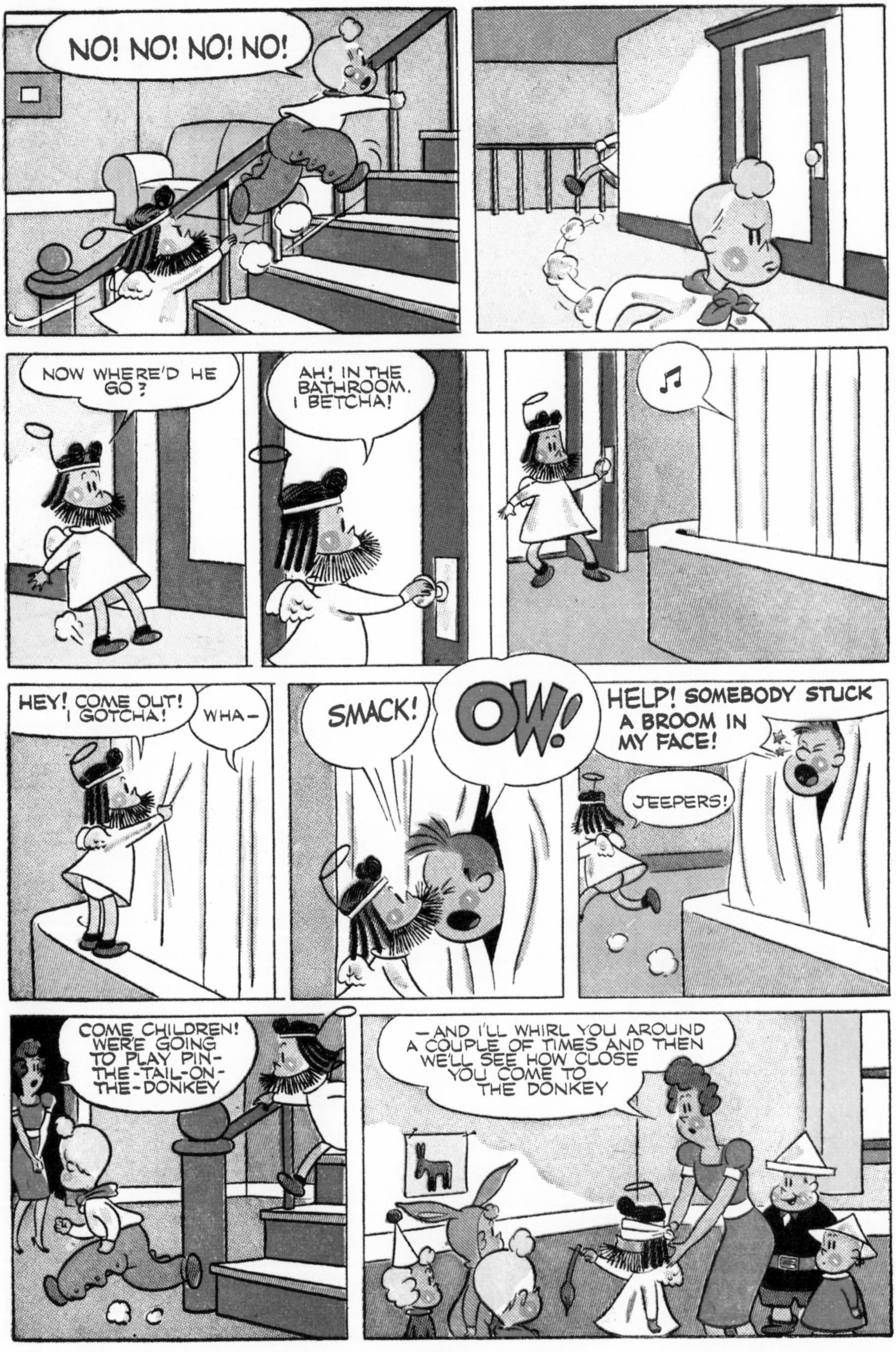
NO! NO! NO! NO!
NOW WHERE'D HE GO?
AH! IN THE BATHROOM, I BETCHA!
♫
HEY! COME OUT! I GOTCHA!
WHA-
SMACK!
OW!
HELP! SOMEBODY STUCK A BROOM IN MY FACE!
JEEPERS!
COME CHILDREN! WE'RE GOING TO PLAY PIN-THE-TAIL-ON-THE-DONKEY
—AND I'LL WHIRL YOU AROUND A COUPLE OF TIMES AND THEN WE'LL SEE HOW CLOSE YOU COME TO THE DONKEY

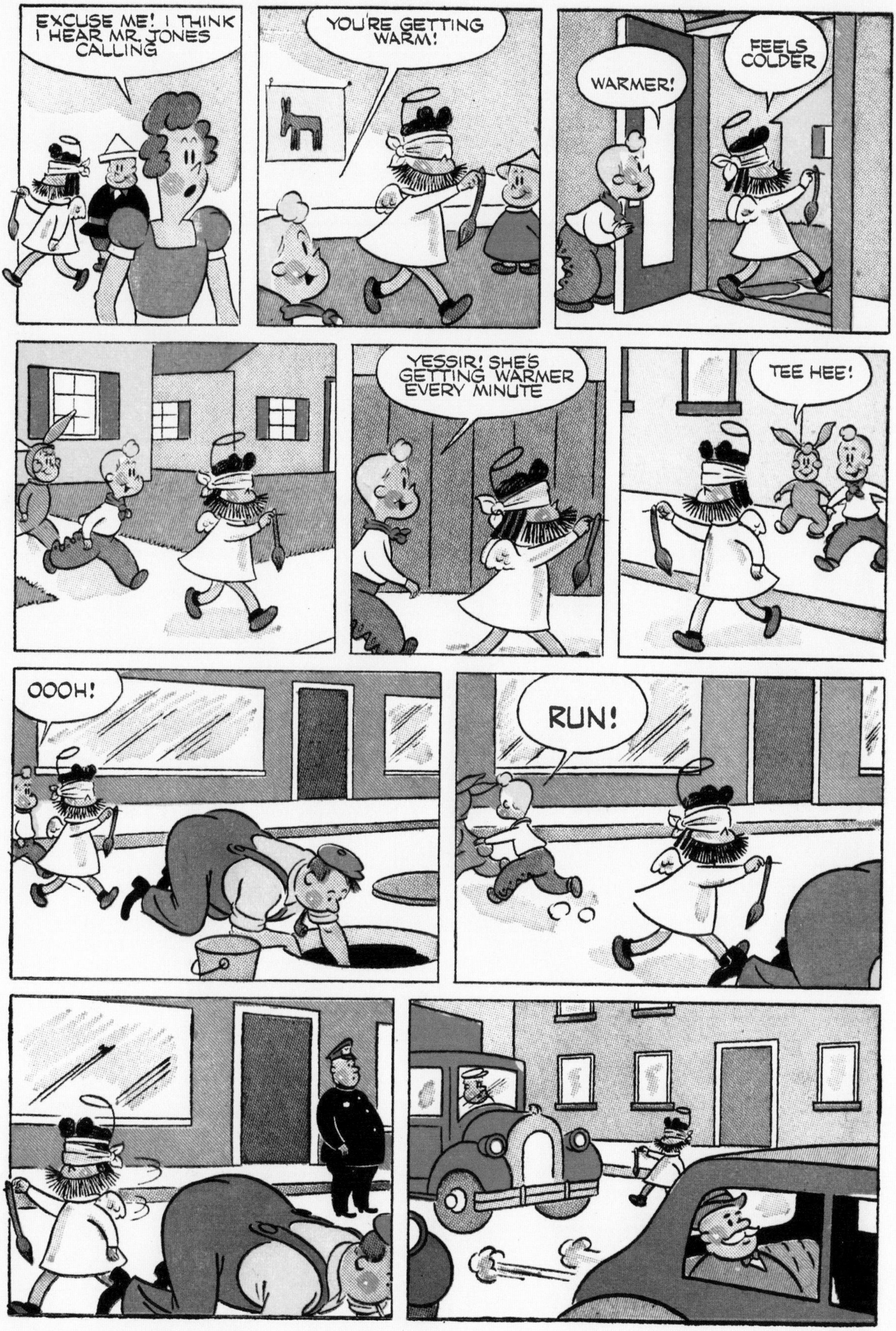
EXCUSE ME! I THINK I HEAR MR. JONES CALLING
YOU'RE GETTING WARM!
WARMER!
FEELS COLDER
YESSIR! SHE'S GETTING WARMER EVERY MINUTE
TEE HEE!
OOOH!
RUN!

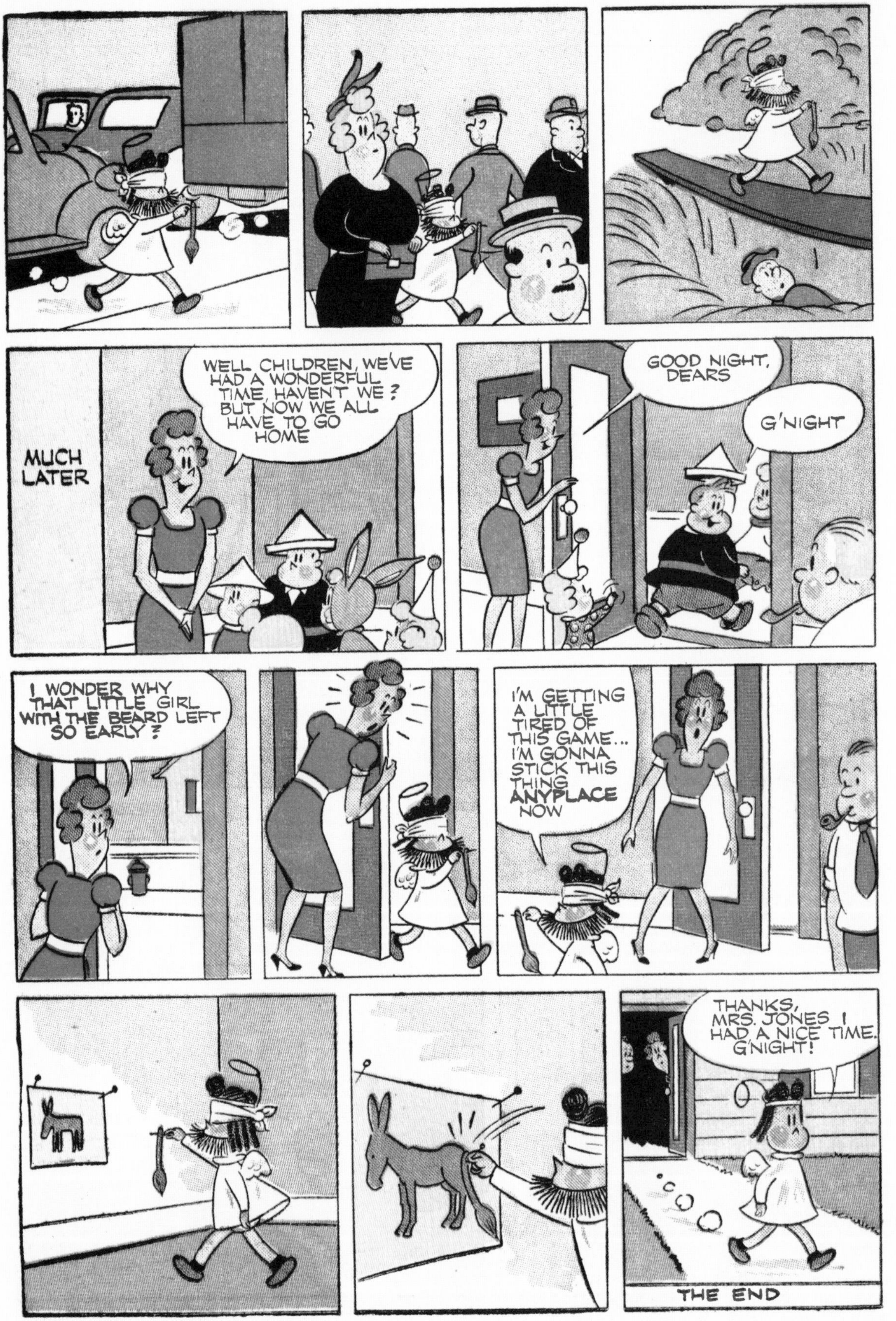

MUCH LATER
WELL CHILDREN, WE'VE HAD A WONDERFUL TIME, HAVEN'T WE? BUT NOW WE ALL HAVE TO GO HOME
GOOD NIGHT, DEARS
G'NIGHT
I WONDER WHY THAT LITTLE GIRL WITH THE BEARD LEFT SO EARLY?
I'M GETTING A LITTLE TIRED OF THIS GAME... I'M GONNA STICK THIS THING ANYPLACE NOW
THANKS, MRS. JONES! I HAD A NICE TIME. G'NIGHT!
THE END

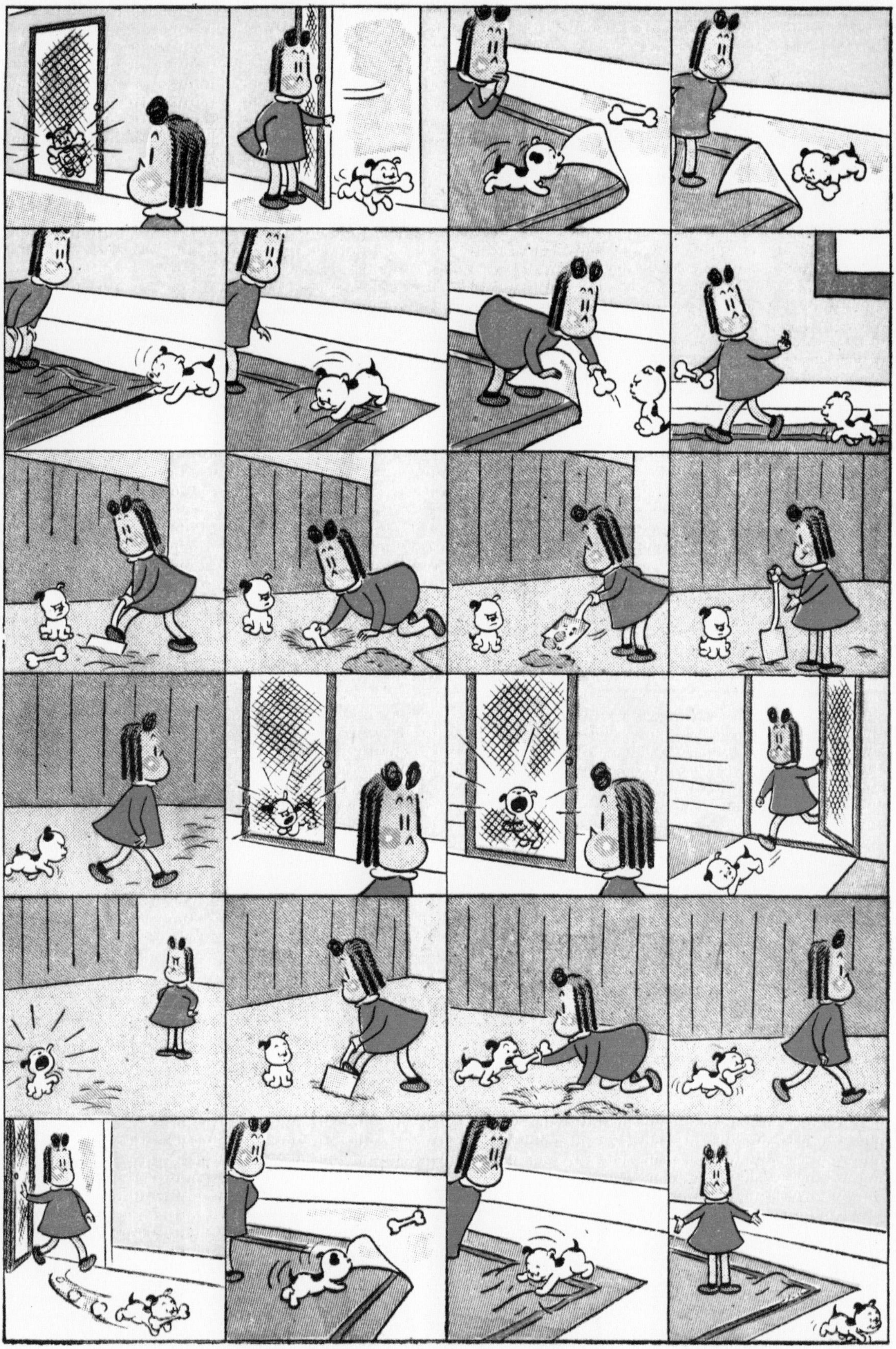

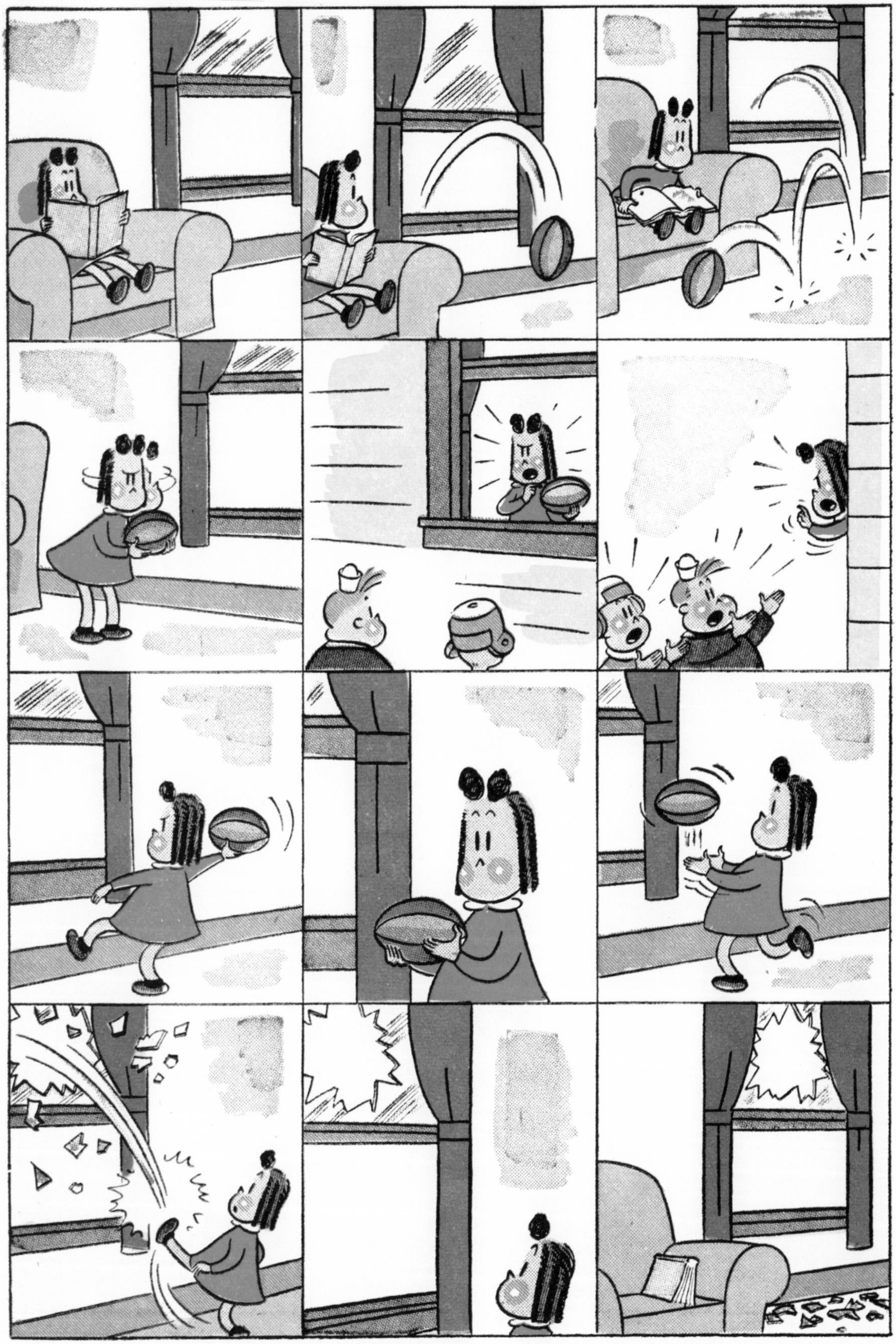

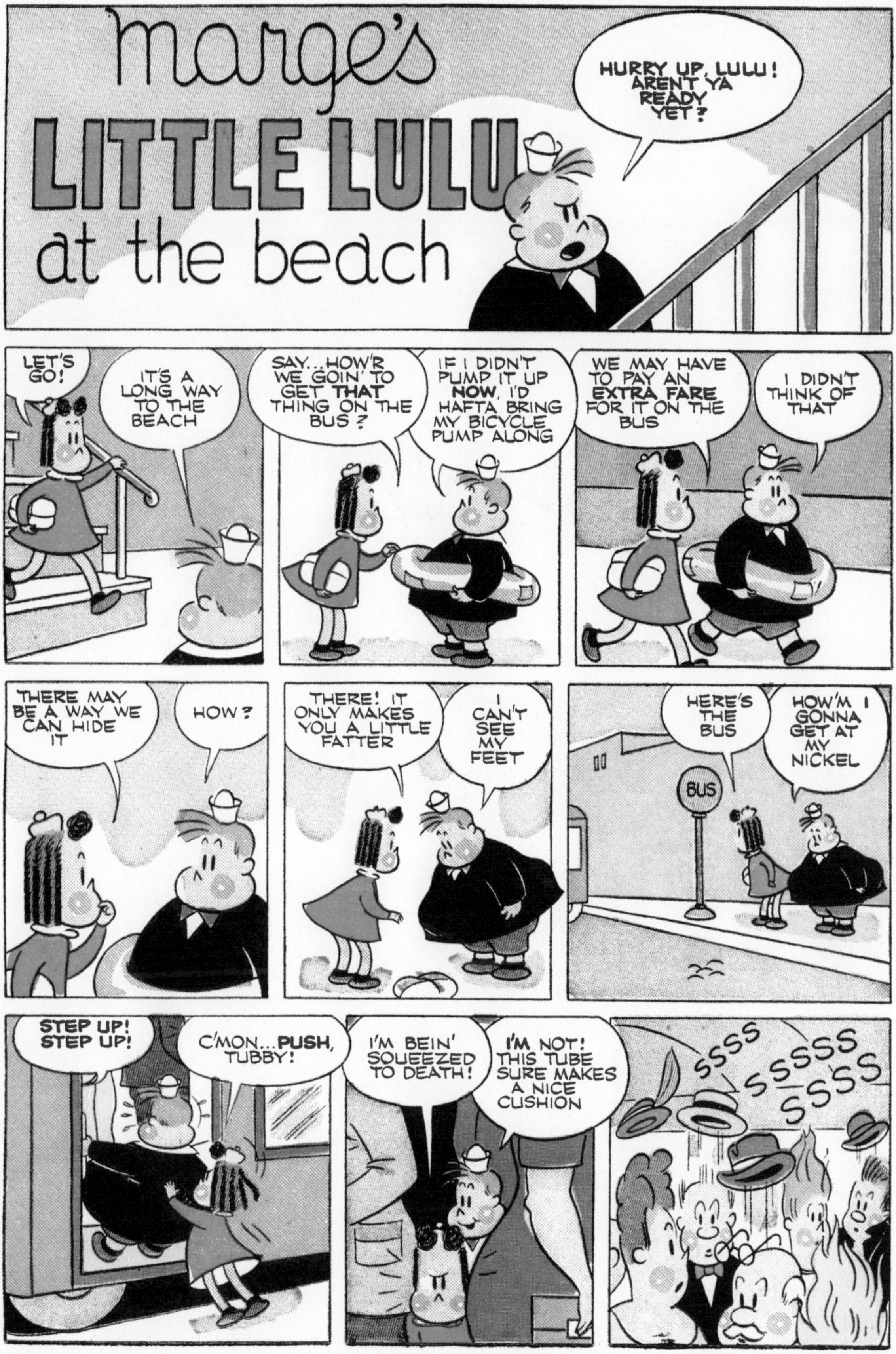
marge's
LITTLE LULU
at the beach
HURRY UP, LULU! AREN'T YA READY YET?
LET'S GO!
IT'S A LONG WAY TO THE BEACH
SAY... HOW'R WE GOIN' TO GET THAT THING ON THE BUS?
IF I DIDN'T PUMP IT UP NOW, I'D HAFTA BRING MY BICYCLE PUMP ALONG
WE MAY HAVE TO PAY AN EXTRA FARE FOR IT ON THE BUS
I DIDN'T THINK OF THAT
THERE MAY BE A WAY WE CAN HIDE IT
HOW?
THERE! IT ONLY MAKES YOU A LITTLE FATTER
I CAN'T SEE MY FEET
BUS
HERE'S THE BUS
HOW'M I GONNA GET AT MY NICKEL
STEP UP! STEP UP!
C'MON... PUSH, TUBBY!
I'M BEIN' SQUEEZED TO DEATH!
I'M NOT! THIS TUBE SURE MAKES A NICE CUSHION
SSSS SSSSS SSSS

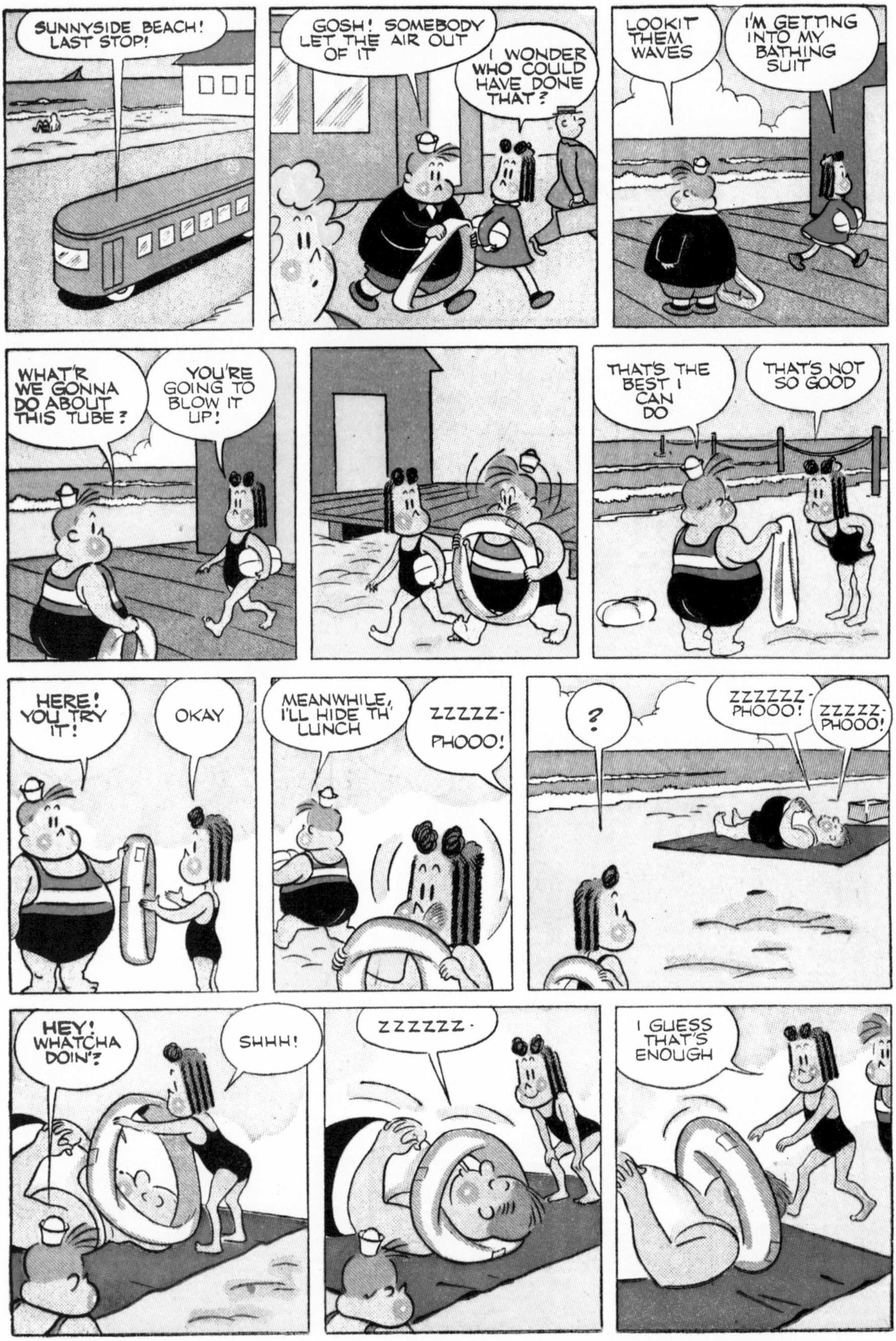
SUNNYSIDE BEACH! LAST STOP!
GOSH! SOMEBODY LET THE AIR OUT OF IT
I WONDER WHO COULD HAVE DONE THAT?
LOOKIT THEM WAVES
I'M GETTING INTO MY BATHING SUIT
WHAT'R WE GONNA DO ABOUT THIS TUBE?
YOU'RE GOING TO BLOW IT UP!
THAT'S THE BEST I CAN DO
THAT'S NOT SO GOOD
HERE! YOU TRY IT!
OKAY
MEANWHILE, I'LL HIDE TH' LUNCH
ZZZZZ-PHOOO!
?
ZZZZZZ-PHOOO!
ZZZZZ-PHOOO!
HEY! WHATCHA DOIN'?
SHHH!
ZZZZZZ-
I GUESS THAT'S ENOUGH

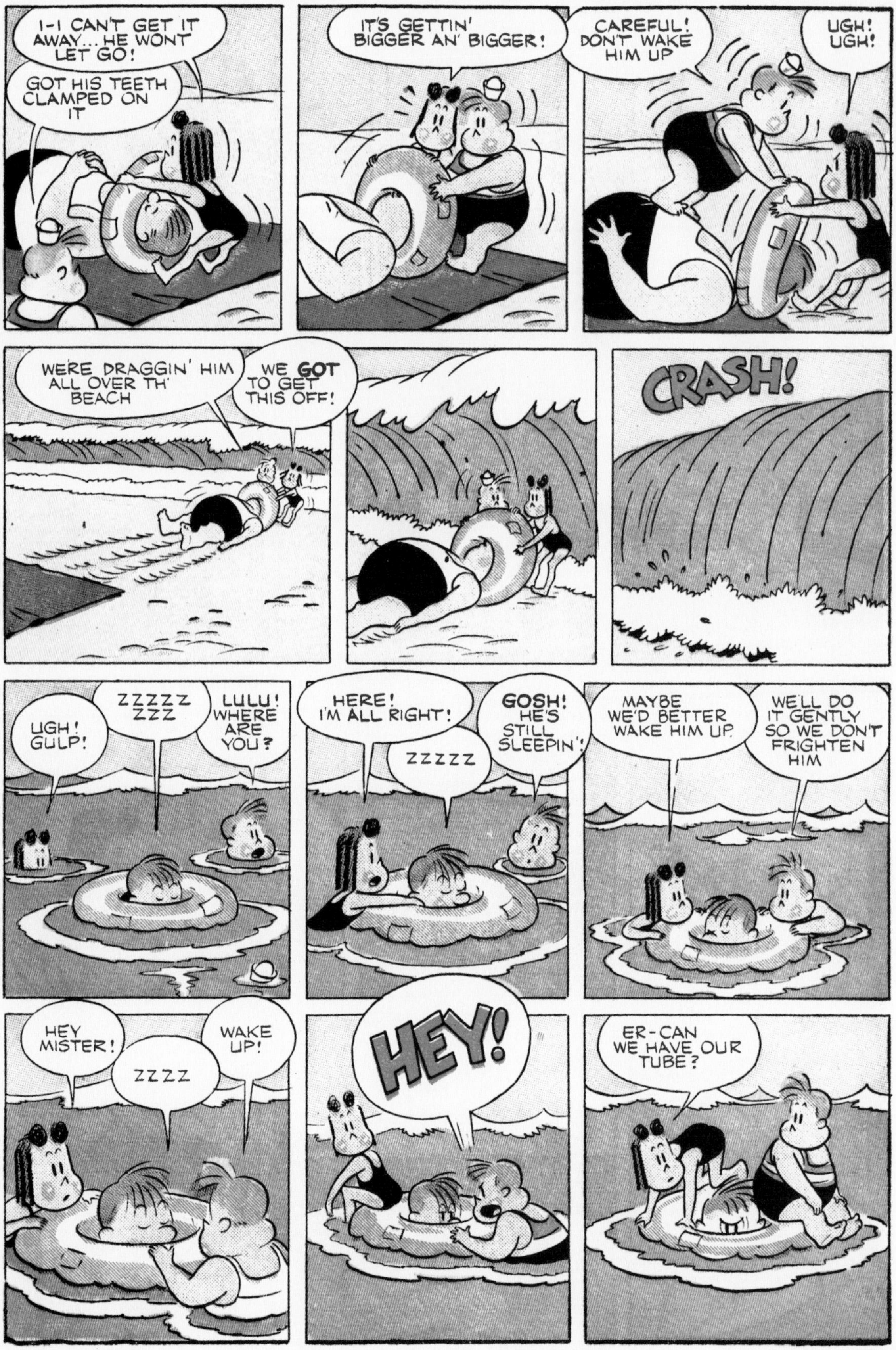
I-I CAN'T GET IT AWAY... HE WONT LET GO!
GOT HIS TEETH CLAMPED ON IT
IT'S GETTIN' BIGGER AN' BIGGER!
CAREFUL! DON'T WAKE HIM UP
UGH! UGH!
WE'RE DRAGGIN' HIM ALL OVER TH' BEACH
WE GOT TO GET THIS OFF!
CRASH!
UGH! GULP!
ZZZZZ ZZZ
LULU! WHERE ARE YOU?
HERE! I'M ALL RIGHT!
ZZZZZ
GOSH! HE'S STILL SLEEPIN'!
MAYBE WE'D BETTER WAKE HIM UP.
WE'LL DO IT GENTLY SO WE DON'T FRIGHTEN HIM
HEY MISTER!
ZZZZ
WAKE UP!
HEY!
ER-CAN WE HAVE OUR TUBE?

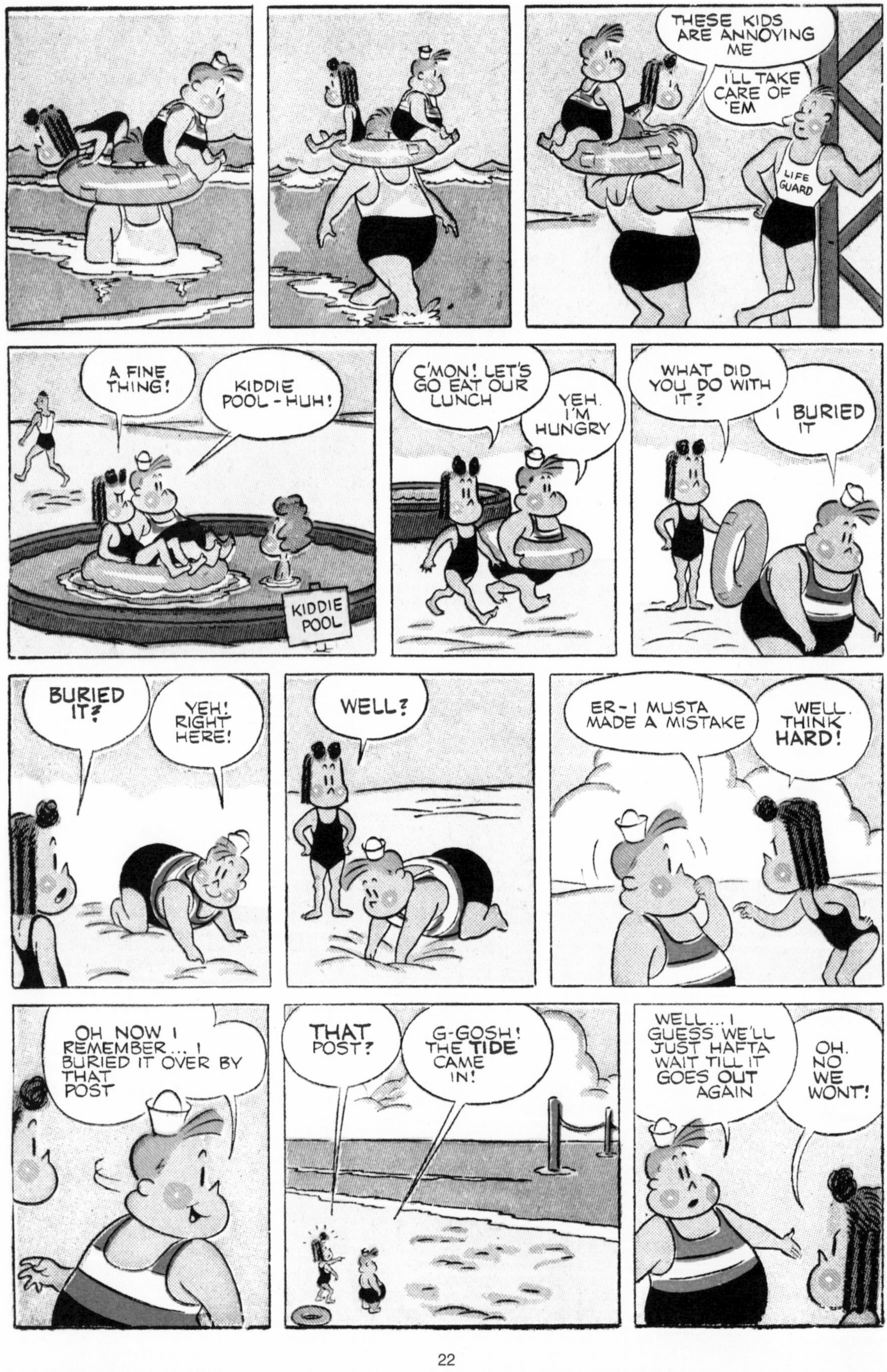

THESE KIDS ARE ANNOYING ME
I'LL TAKE CARE OF 'EM
LIFE GUARD
A FINE THING!
KIDDIE POOL - HUH!
KIDDIE POOL
C'MON! LET'S GO EAT OUR LUNCH
YEH. I'M HUNGRY
WHAT DID YOU DO WITH IT?
I BURIED IT
BURIED IT?
YEH! RIGHT HERE!
WELL?
ER- I MUSTA MADE A MISTAKE
WELL. THINK HARD!
OH NOW I REMEMBER... I BURIED IT OVER BY THAT POST
THAT POST?
G-GOSH! THE TIDE CAME IN!
WELL... I GUESS WE'LL JUST HAFTA WAIT TILL IT GOES OUT AGAIN
OH. NO WE WONT!

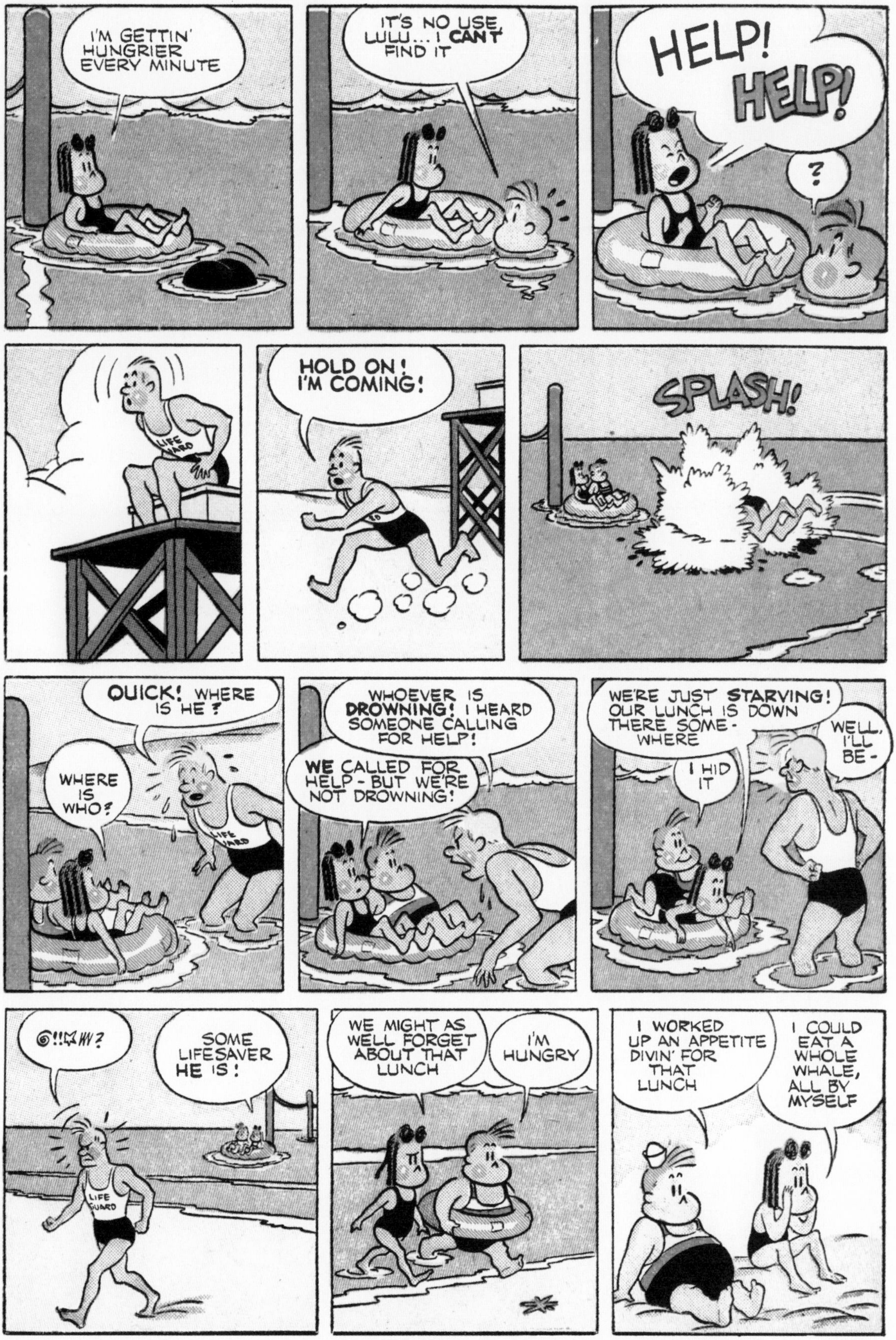

I'M GETTIN' HUNGRIER EVERY MINUTE
IT'S NO USE, LULU... I CAN'T FIND IT
HELP! HELP!
?
HOLD ON! I'M COMING!
SPLASH!
QUICK! WHERE IS HE?
WHERE IS WHO?
WHOEVER IS DROWNING! I HEARD SOMEONE CALLING FOR HELP!
WE CALLED FOR HELP - BUT WE'RE NOT DROWNING!
WE'RE JUST STARVING! OUR LUNCH IS DOWN THERE SOME-WHERE
I HID IT
WELL, I'LL BE-
SOME LIFESAVER HE IS!
WE MIGHT AS WELL FORGET ABOUT THAT LUNCH
I'M HUNGRY
I WORKED UP AN APPETITE DIVIN' FOR THAT LUNCH
I COULD EAT A WHOLE WHALE, ALL BY MYSELF

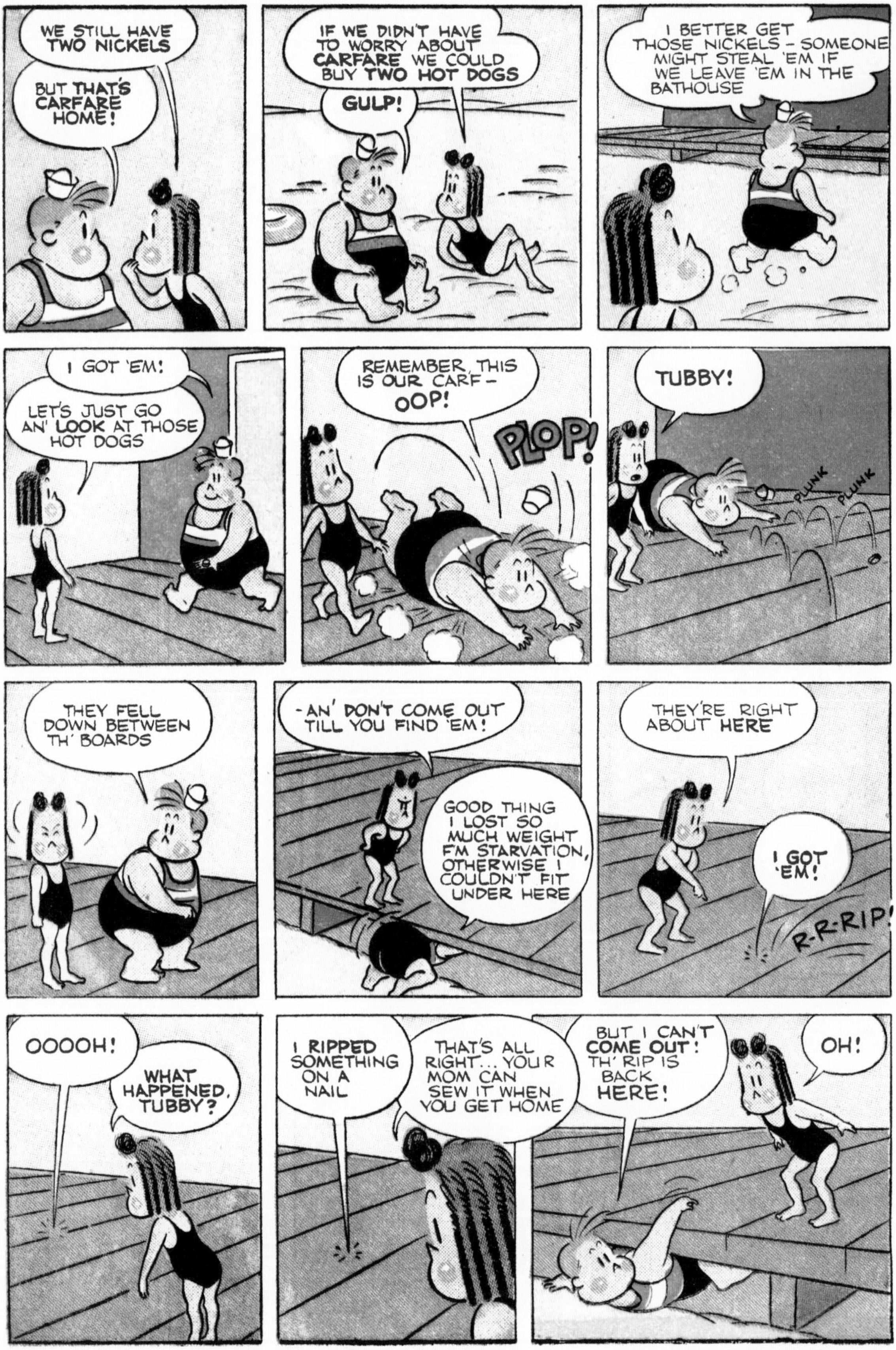
WE STILL HAVE TWO NICKELS
BUT THAT'S CARFARE HOME!
IF WE DIDN'T HAVE TO WORRY ABOUT CARFARE WE COULD BUY TWO HOT DOGS
GULP!
I BETTER GET THOSE NICKELS - SOMEONE MIGHT STEAL 'EM IF WE LEAVE 'EM IN THE BATHOUSE
I GOT 'EM!
LET'S JUST GO AN' LOOK AT THOSE HOT DOGS
REMEMBER, THIS IS OUR CARF - OOP!
PLOP!
TUBBY!
PLUNK
PLUNK
THEY FELL DOWN BETWEEN TH' BOARDS
- AN' DON'T COME OUT TILL YOU FIND 'EM!
GOOD THING I LOST SO MUCH WEIGHT I'M STARVATION, OTHERWISE I COULDN'T FIT UNDER HERE
THEY'RE RIGHT ABOUT HERE
I GOT 'EM!
R-R-RIP!
OOOOH!
WHAT HAPPENED, TUBBY?
I RIPPED SOMETHING ON A NAIL
THAT'S ALL RIGHT... YOUR MOM CAN SEW IT WHEN YOU GET HOME
BUT I CAN'T COME OUT! TH' RIP IS BACK HERE!
OH!

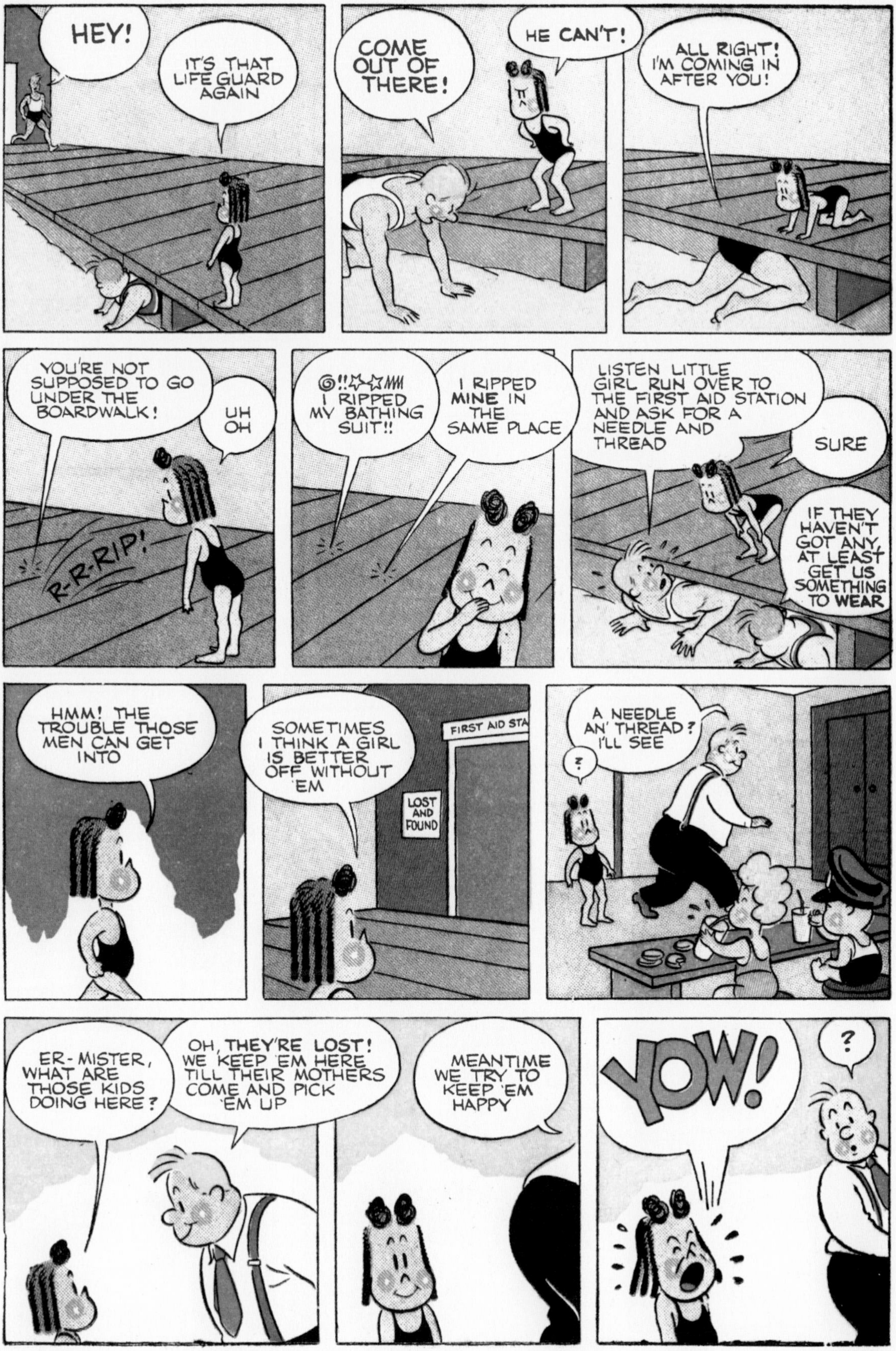
HEY!
IT'S THAT LIFE GUARD AGAIN
COME OUT OF THERE!
HE CAN'T!
ALL RIGHT! I'M COMING IN AFTER YOU!
YOU'RE NOT SUPPOSED TO GO UNDER THE BOARDWALK!
UH OH
R-R-RIP!
I RIPPED MY BATHING SUIT!!
I RIPPED MINE IN THE SAME PLACE
LISTEN LITTLE GIRL RUN OVER TO THE FIRST AID STATION AND ASK FOR A NEEDLE AND THREAD
SURE
IF THEY HAVEN'T GOT ANY, AT LEAST GET US SOMETHING TO WEAR
HMM! THE TROUBLE THOSE MEN CAN GET INTO
SOMETIMES I THINK A GIRL IS BETTER OFF WITHOUT 'EM
FIRST AID STA
LOST AND FOUND
A NEEDLE AN' THREAD? I'LL SEE
?
ER-MISTER, WHAT ARE THOSE KIDS DOING HERE?
OH, THEY'RE LOST! WE KEEP 'EM HERE TILL THEIR MOTHERS COME AND PICK 'EM UP
MEANTIME WE TRY TO KEEP 'EM HAPPY
YOW!
?

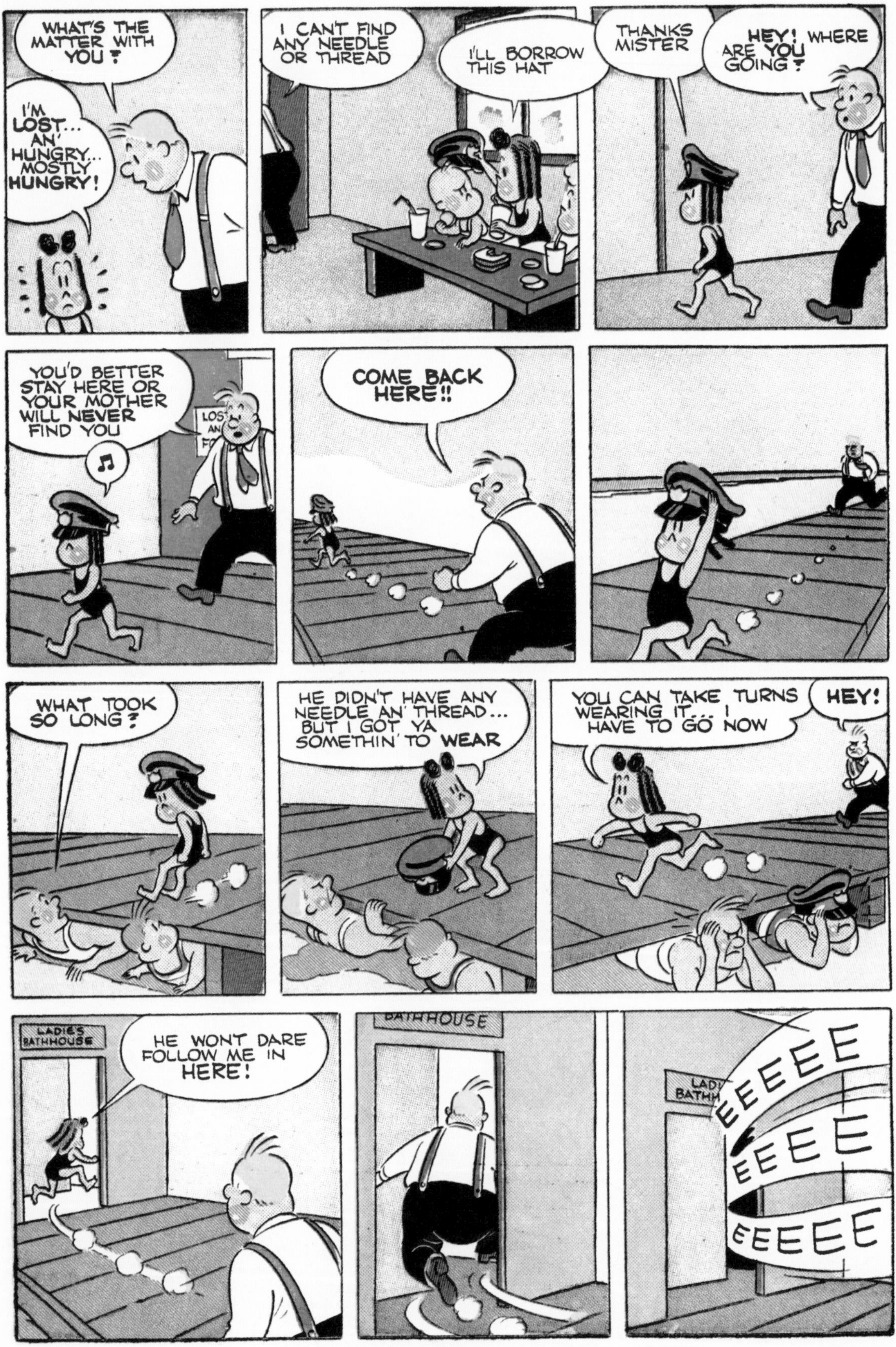
WHAT'S THE MATTER WITH YOU ?
I'M LOST... AN' HUNGRY... MOSTLY HUNGRY!
I CAN'T FIND ANY NEEDLE OR THREAD
I'LL BORROW THIS HAT
THANKS MISTER
HEY! WHERE ARE YOU GOING ?
YOU'D BETTER STAY HERE OR YOUR MOTHER WILL NEVER FIND YOU
♫
COME BACK HERE!!
WHAT TOOK SO LONG ?
HE DIDN'T HAVE ANY NEEDLE AN' THREAD... BUT I GOT YA SOMETHIN' TO WEAR
YOU CAN TAKE TURNS WEARING IT... I HAVE TO GO NOW
HEY!
LADIES BATHHOUSE
HE WON'T DARE FOLLOW ME IN HERE!
BATHHOUSE
EEEEE
EEEE
EEEEE

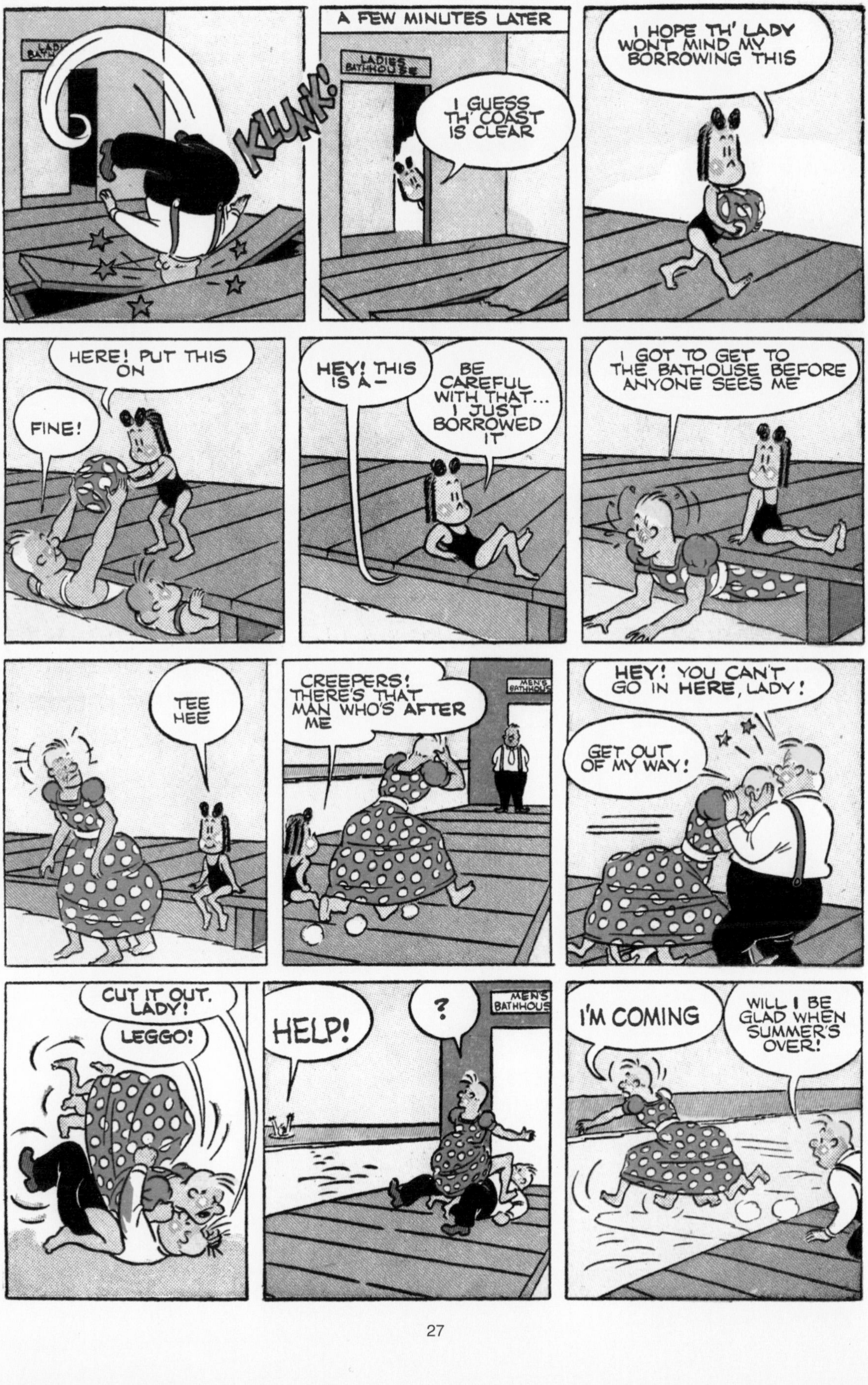
KLUNK!
A FEW MINUTES LATER
LADIES BATHHOUSE
I GUESS TH' COAST IS CLEAR
I HOPE TH' LADY WONT MIND MY BORROWING THIS
HERE! PUT THIS ON
FINE!
HEY! THIS IS A—
BE CAREFUL WITH THAT... I JUST BORROWED IT
I GOT TO GET TO THE BATHOUSE BEFORE ANYONE SEES ME
TEE HEE
CREEPERS! THERE'S THAT MAN WHO'S AFTER ME
HEY! YOU CAN'T GO IN HERE, LADY!
GET OUT OF MY WAY!
CUT IT OUT, LADY!
LEGGO!
HELP!
?
I'M COMING
WILL I BE GLAD WHEN SUMMER'S OVER!

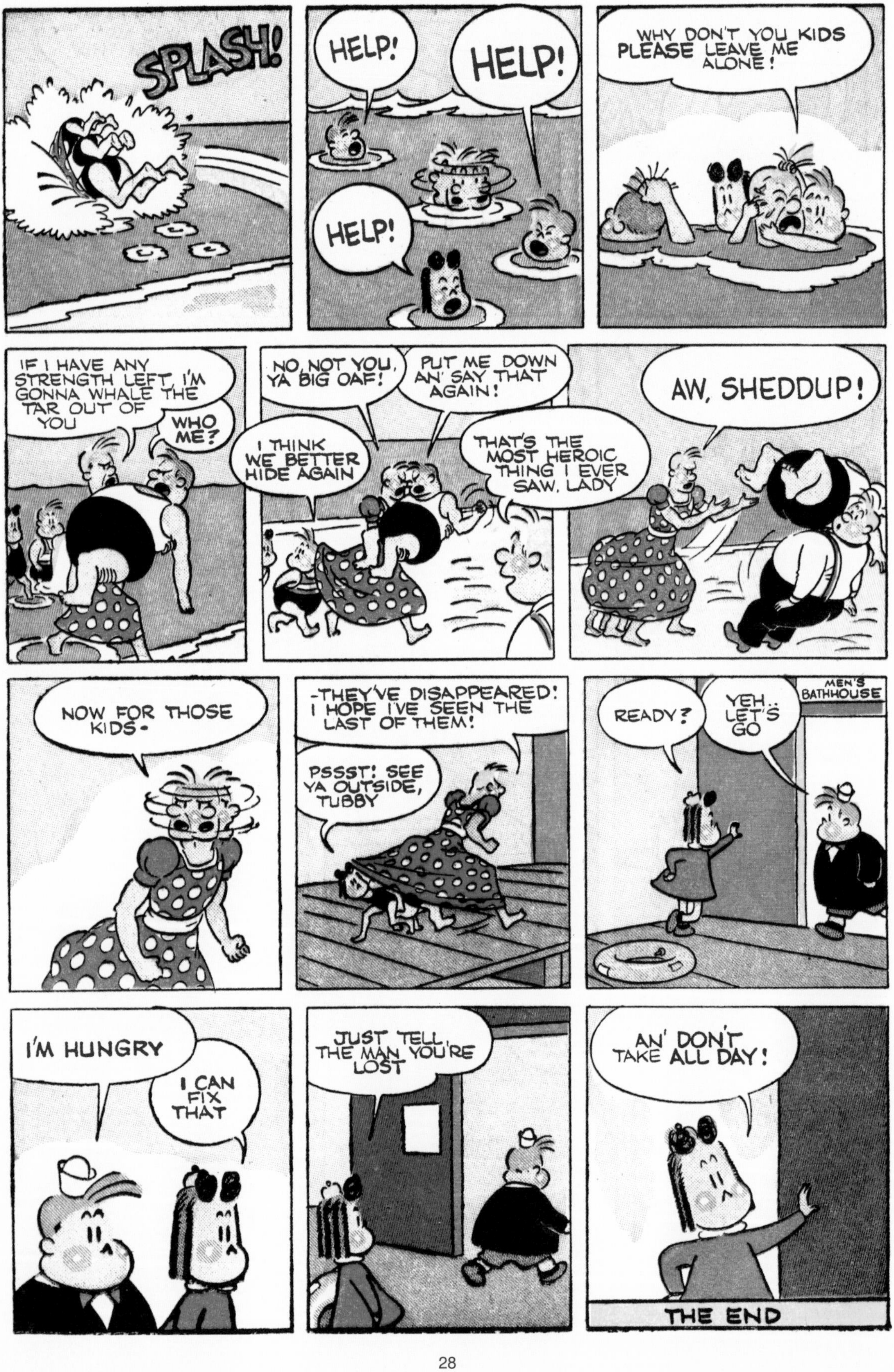
SPLASH!
HELP!
HELP!
HELP!
WHY DON'T YOU KIDS PLEASE LEAVE ME ALONE!
IF I HAVE ANY STRENGTH LEFT, I'M GONNA WHALE THE TAR OUT OF YOU
WHO ME?
NO, NOT YOU, YA BIG OAF!
PUT ME DOWN AN' SAY THAT AGAIN!
I THINK WE BETTER HIDE AGAIN
THAT'S THE MOST HEROIC THING I EVER SAW, LADY
AW, SHEDDUP!
NOW FOR THOSE KIDS-
-THEY'VE DISAPPEARED! I HOPE I'VE SEEN THE LAST OF THEM!
PSSST! SEE YA OUTSIDE, TUBBY
MEN'S BATHHOUSE
READY?
YEH.. LET'S GO
I'M HUNGRY
I CAN FIX THAT
JUST TELL THE MAN YOU'RE LOST
AN' DON'T TAKE ALL DAY!
THE END

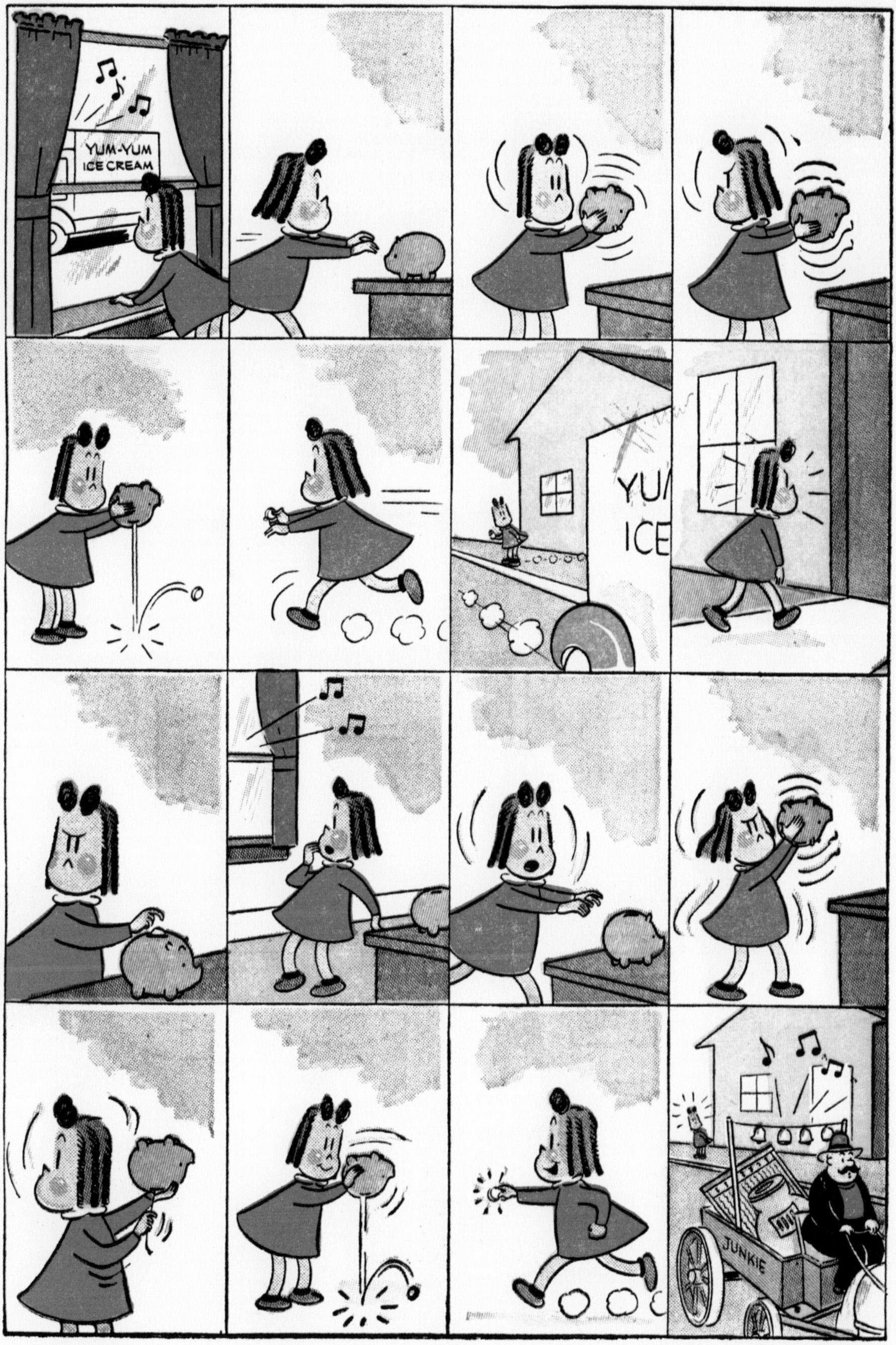

YUM-YUM
ICE CREAM
YUM
ICE
JUNKIE

Marge's

LITTLE LULU

minds Alvin

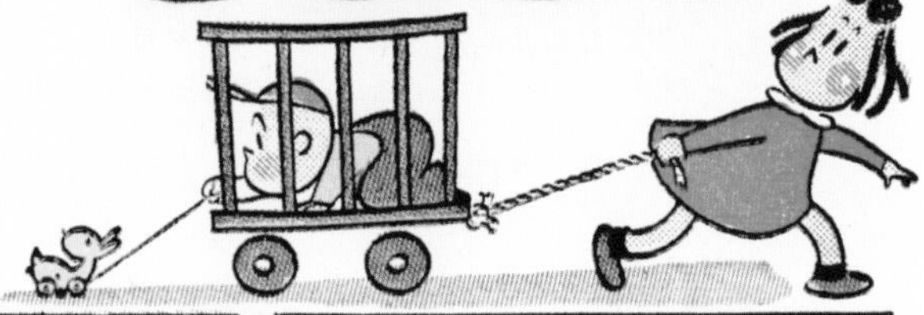

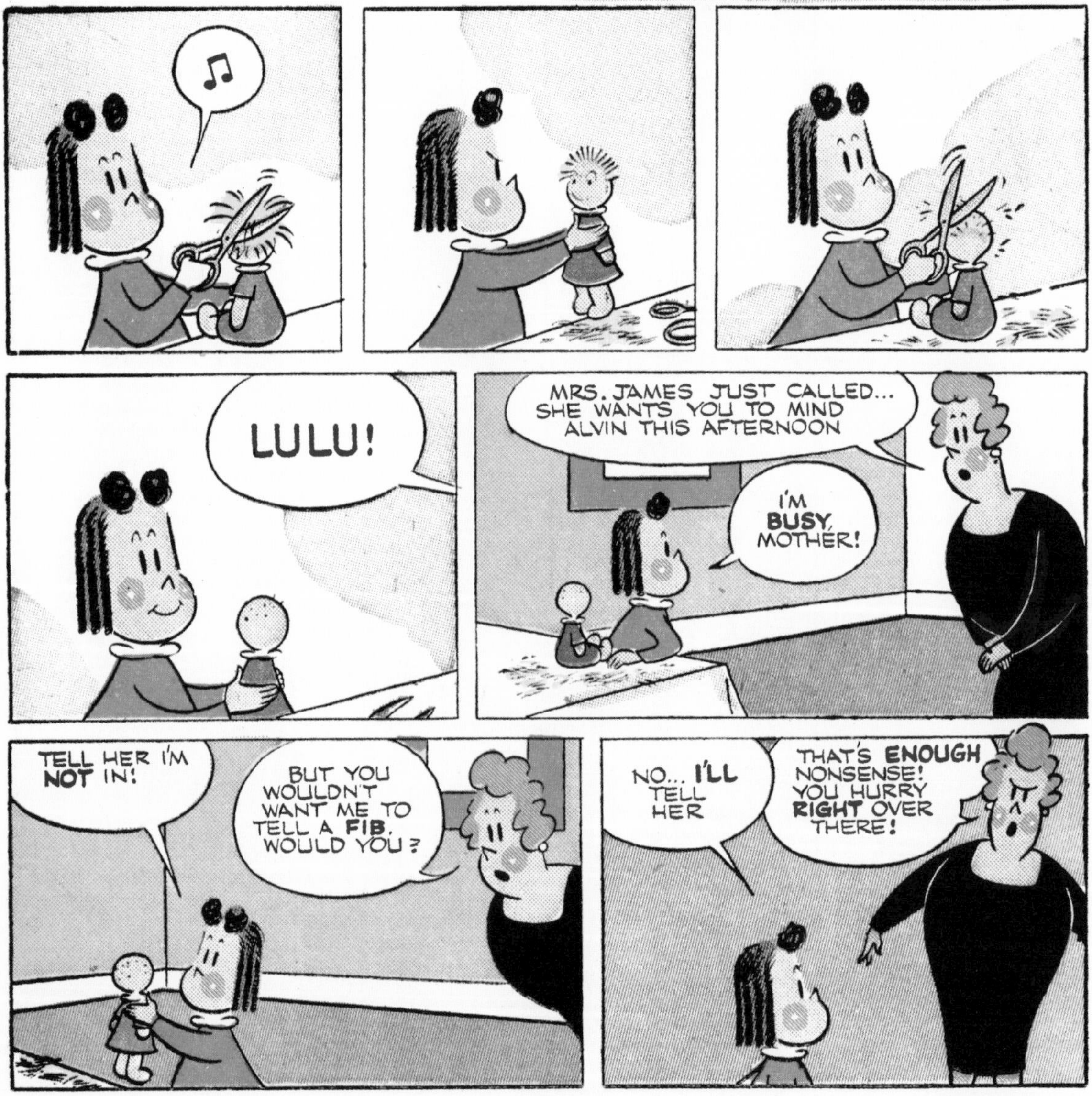

♫
LULU!
MRS. JAMES JUST CALLED... SHE WANTS YOU TO MIND ALVIN THIS AFTERNOON
I'M **BUSY**, MOTHER!
TELL HER I'M **NOT** IN!
BUT YOU WOULDN'T WANT ME TO TELL A **FIB**, WOULD YOU?
NO... **I'LL** TELL HER
THAT'S **ENOUGH** NONSENSE! YOU HURRY **RIGHT** OVER THERE!

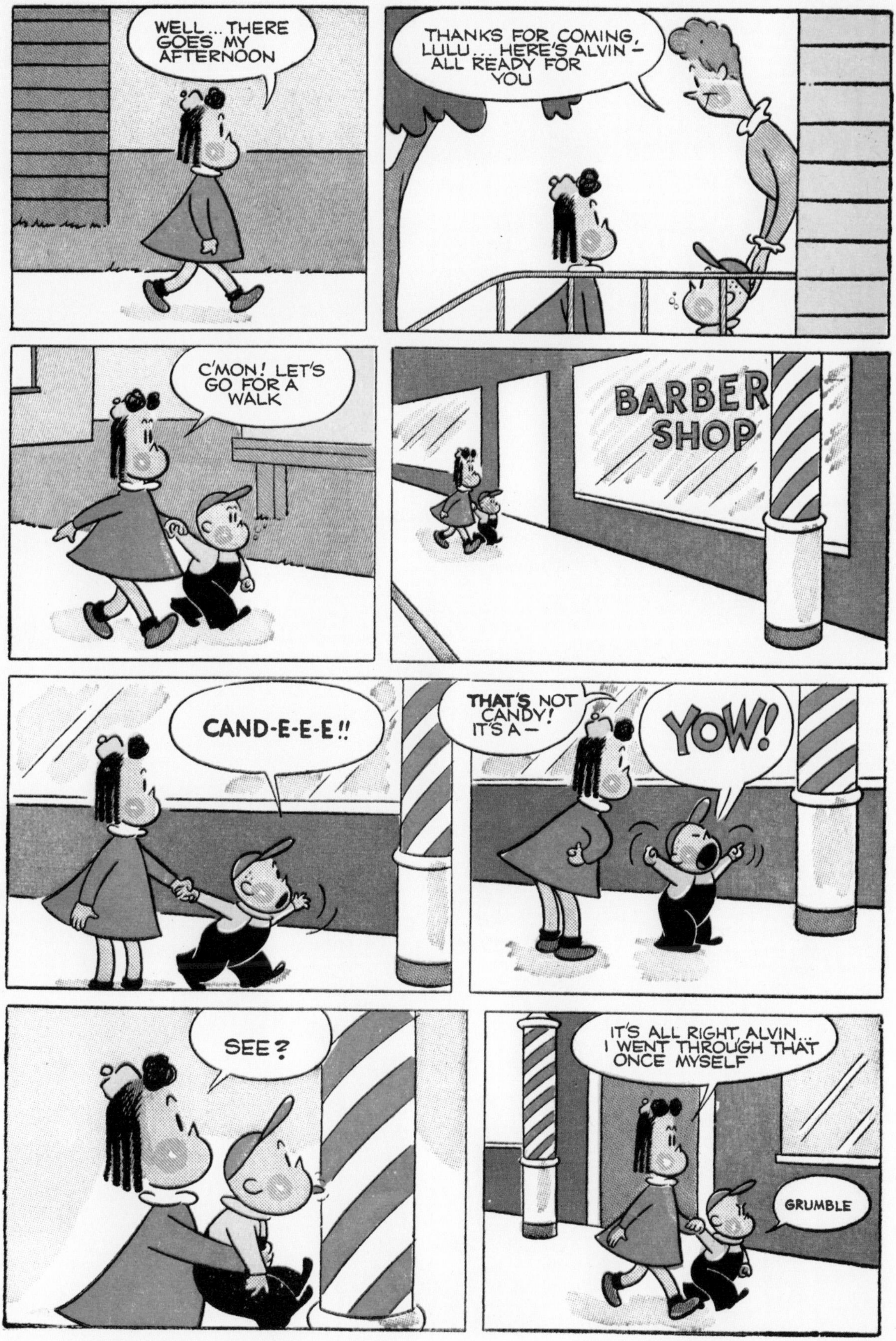
WELL... THERE GOES MY AFTERNOON
THANKS FOR COMING, LULU... HERE'S ALVIN — ALL READY FOR YOU
C'MON! LET'S GO FOR A WALK
BARBER SHOP
CAND-E-E-E!!
THAT'S NOT CANDY! IT'S A —
YOW!
SEE?
IT'S ALL RIGHT ALVIN... I WENT THROUGH THAT ONCE MYSELF
GRUMBLE

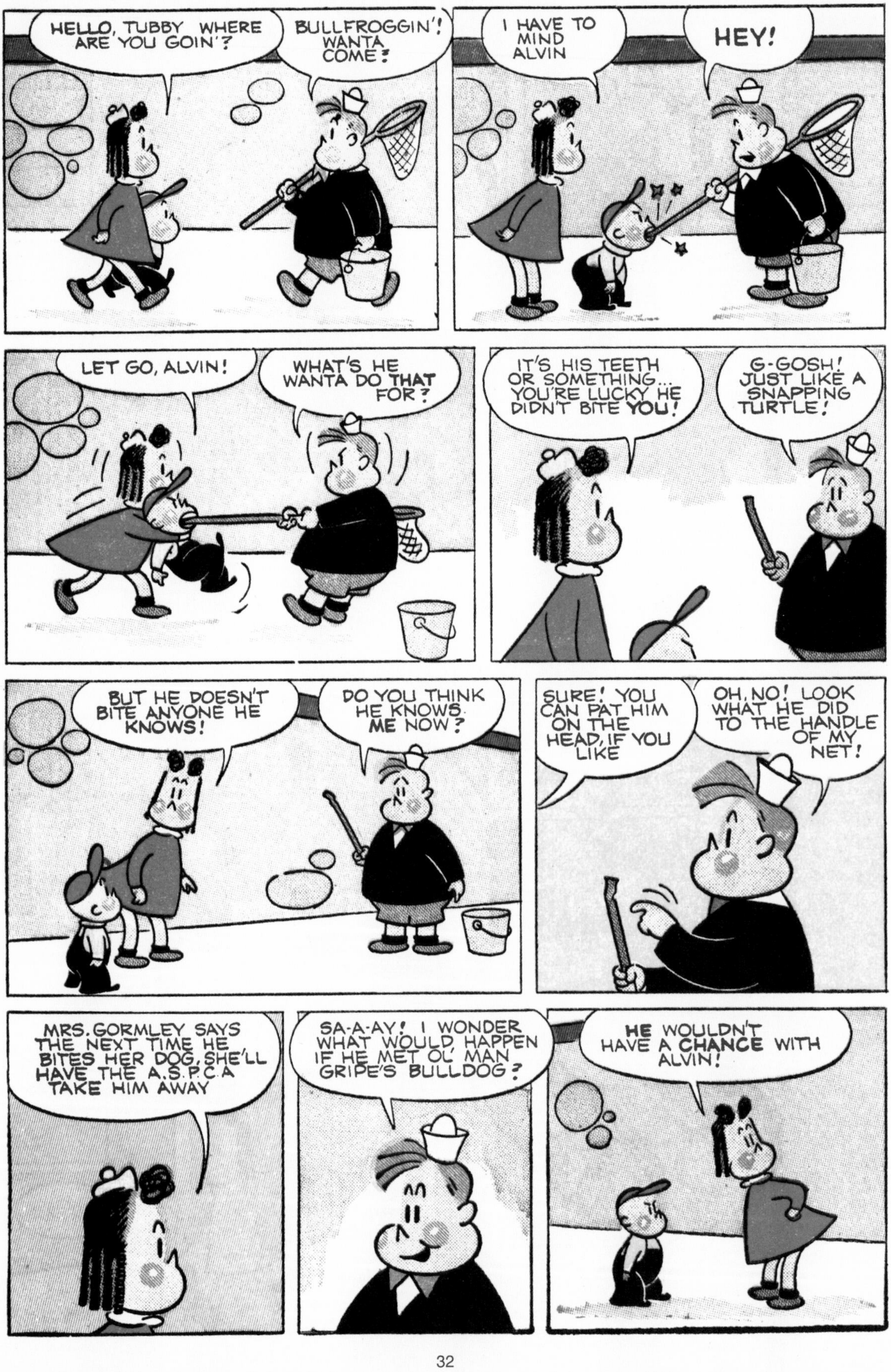
HELLO, TUBBY WHERE ARE YOU GOIN'?
BULLFROGGIN'! WANTA COME?
I HAVE TO MIND ALVIN
HEY!
LET GO, ALVIN!
WHAT'S HE WANTA DO THAT FOR?
IT'S HIS TEETH OR SOMETHING... YOU'RE LUCKY HE DIDN'T BITE YOU!
G-GOSH! JUST LIKE A SNAPPING TURTLE!
BUT HE DOESN'T BITE ANYONE HE KNOWS!
DO YOU THINK HE KNOWS ME NOW?
SURE! YOU CAN PAT HIM ON THE HEAD, IF YOU LIKE
OH, NO! LOOK WHAT HE DID TO THE HANDLE OF MY NET!
MRS. GORMLEY SAYS THE NEXT TIME HE BITES HER DOG, SHE'LL HAVE THE A.S.P.C.A TAKE HIM AWAY
SA-A-AY! I WONDER WHAT WOULD HAPPEN IF HE MET OL' MAN GRIPE'S BULLDOG?
HE WOULDN'T HAVE A CHANCE WITH ALVIN!

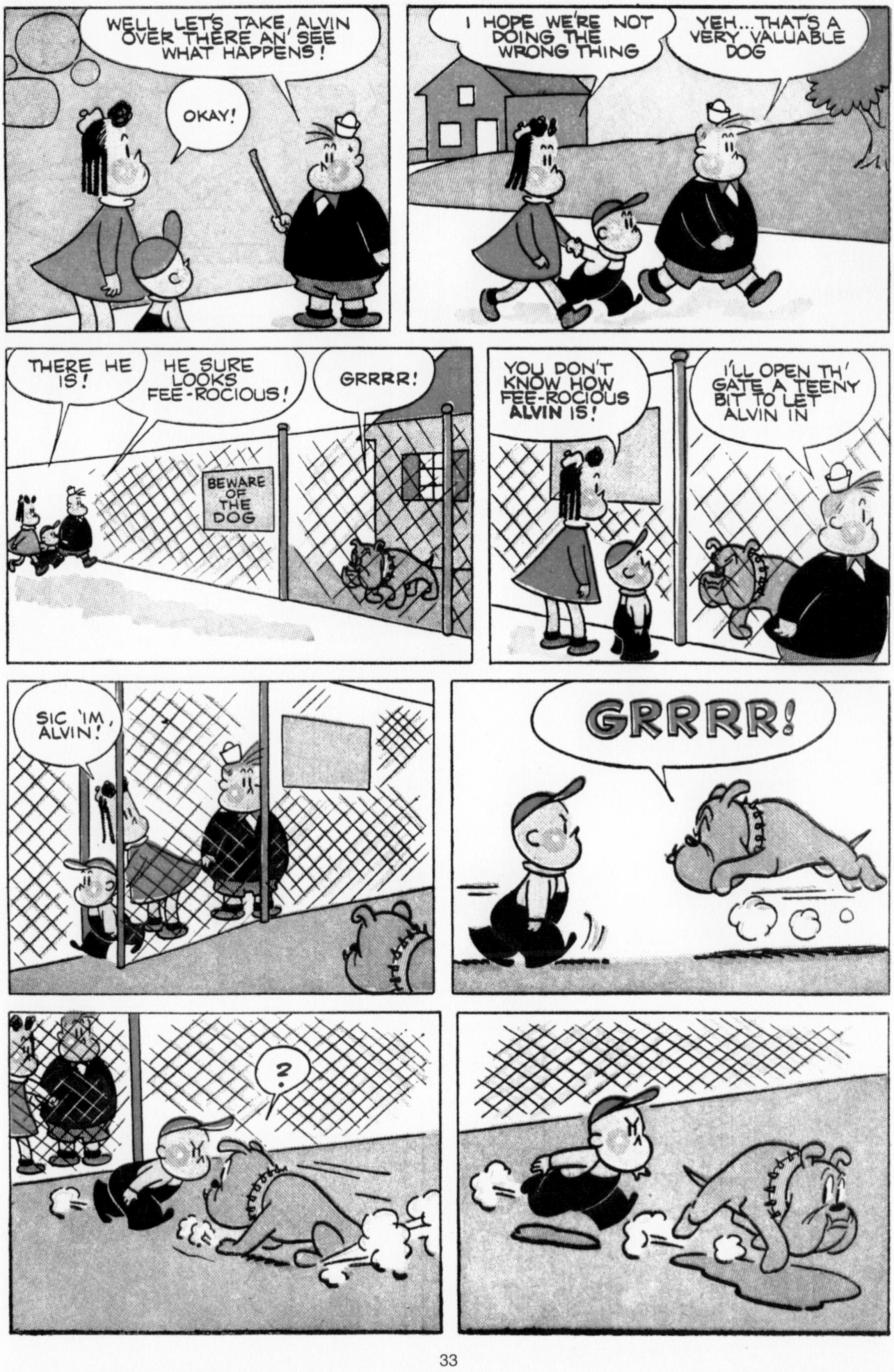

WELL, LET'S TAKE ALVIN OVER THERE AN' SEE WHAT HAPPENS!
OKAY!
I HOPE WE'RE NOT DOING THE WRONG THING
YEH... THAT'S A VERY VALUABLE DOG
THERE HE IS!
HE SURE LOOKS FEE-ROCIOUS!
GRRRR!
BEWARE OF THE DOG
YOU DON'T KNOW HOW FEE-ROCIOUS ALVIN IS!
I'LL OPEN TH' GATE A TEENY BIT TO LET ALVIN IN
SIC 'IM, ALVIN!
GRRRR!
?

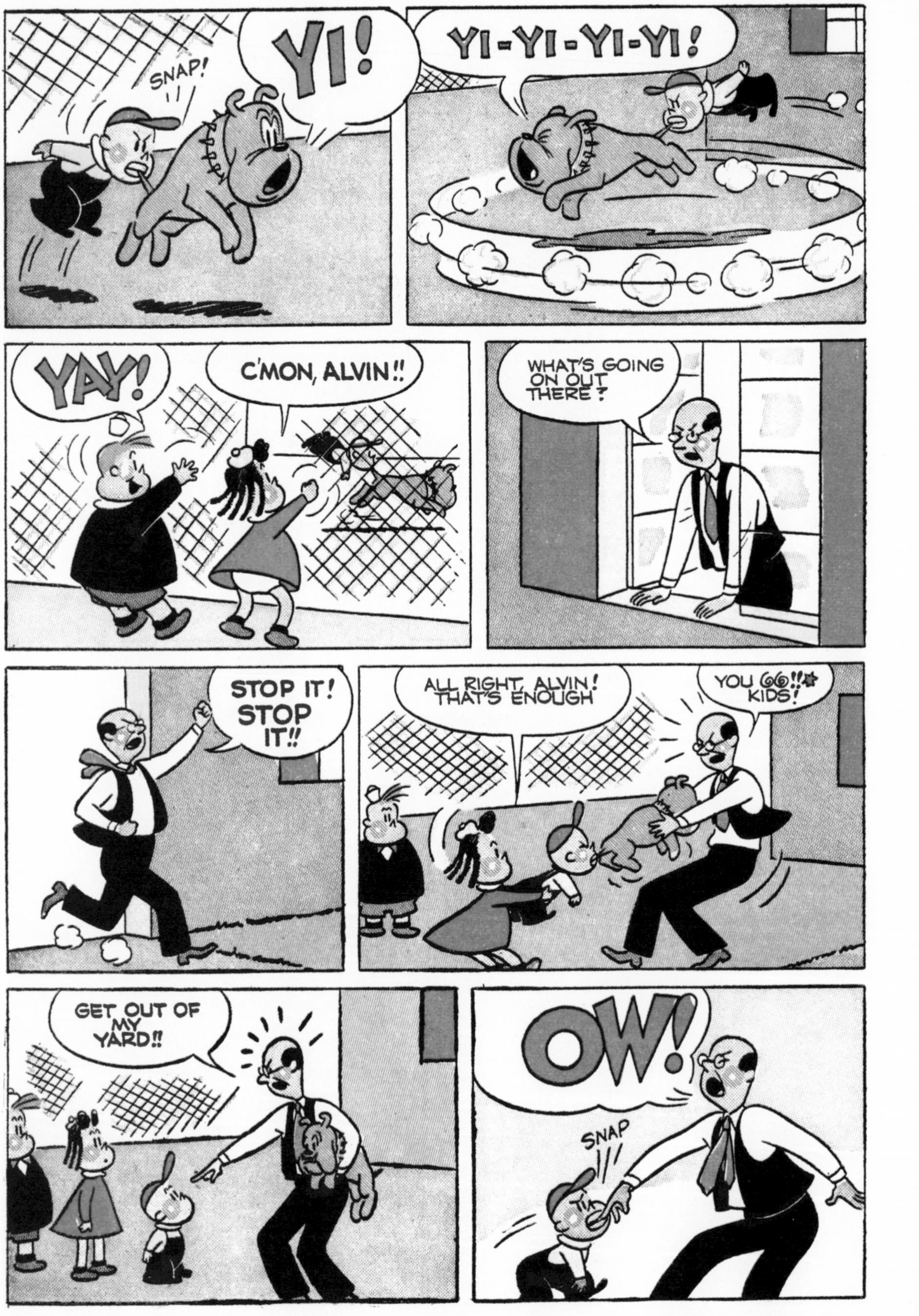
SNAP!
YI!
YI-YI-YI-YI!
YAY!
C'MON, ALVIN!!
WHAT'S GOING ON OUT THERE?
STOP IT! STOP IT!!
ALL RIGHT, ALVIN! THAT'S ENOUGH
YOU @@!!* KIDS!
GET OUT OF MY YARD!!
OW!
SNAP

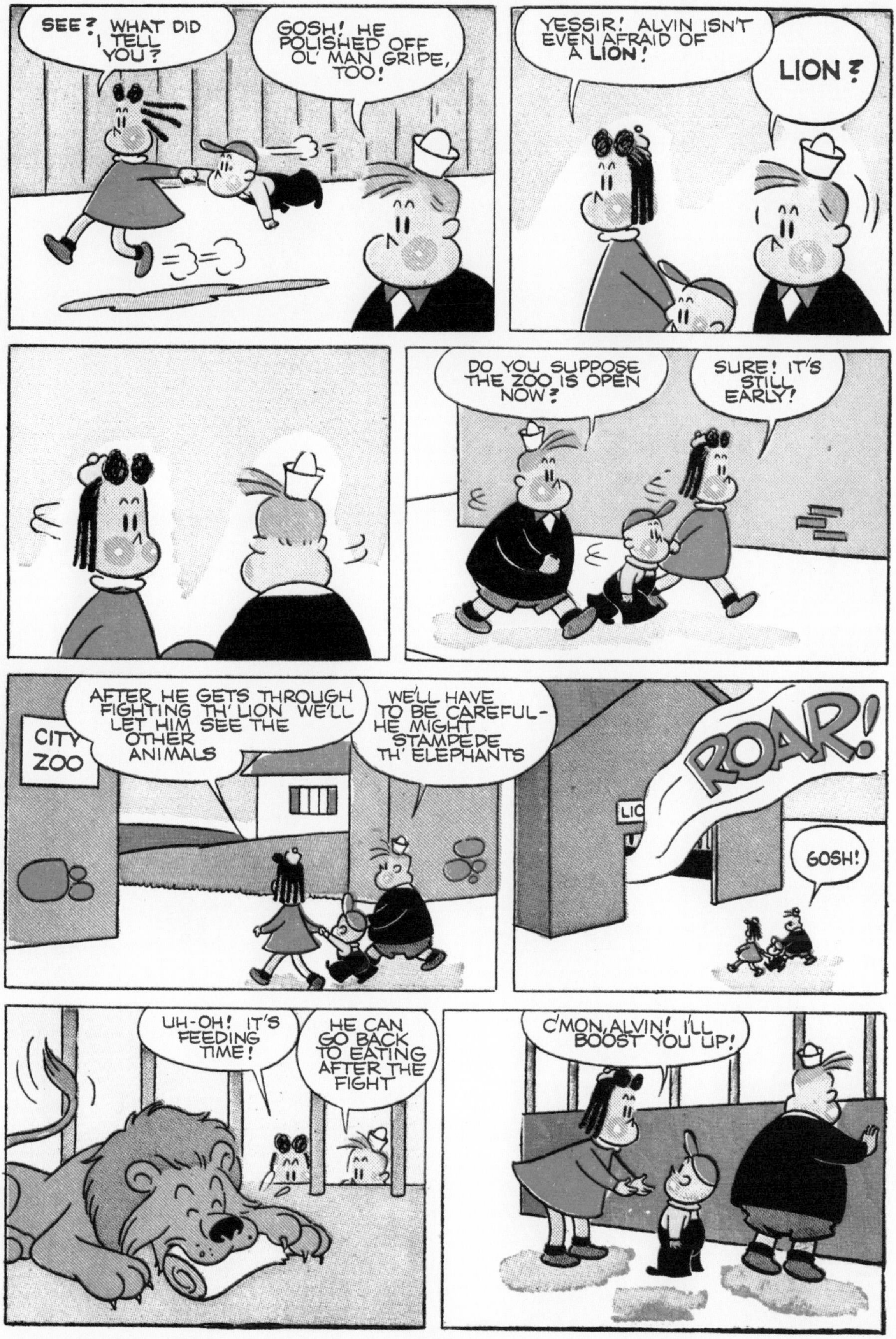
SEE? WHAT DID I TELL YOU?
GOSH! HE POLISHED OFF OL' MAN GRIPE, TOO!
YESSIR! ALVIN ISN'T EVEN AFRAID OF A LION!
LION?
DO YOU SUPPOSE THE ZOO IS OPEN NOW?
SURE! IT'S STILL EARLY!
CITY ZOO
AFTER HE GETS THROUGH FIGHTING TH' LION WE'LL LET HIM SEE THE OTHER ANIMALS
WE'LL HAVE TO BE CAREFUL-HE MIGHT STAMPEDE TH' ELEPHANTS
ROAR!
GOSH!
UH-OH! IT'S FEEDING TIME!
HE CAN GO BACK TO EATING AFTER THE FIGHT
C'MON, ALVIN! I'LL BOOST YOU UP!

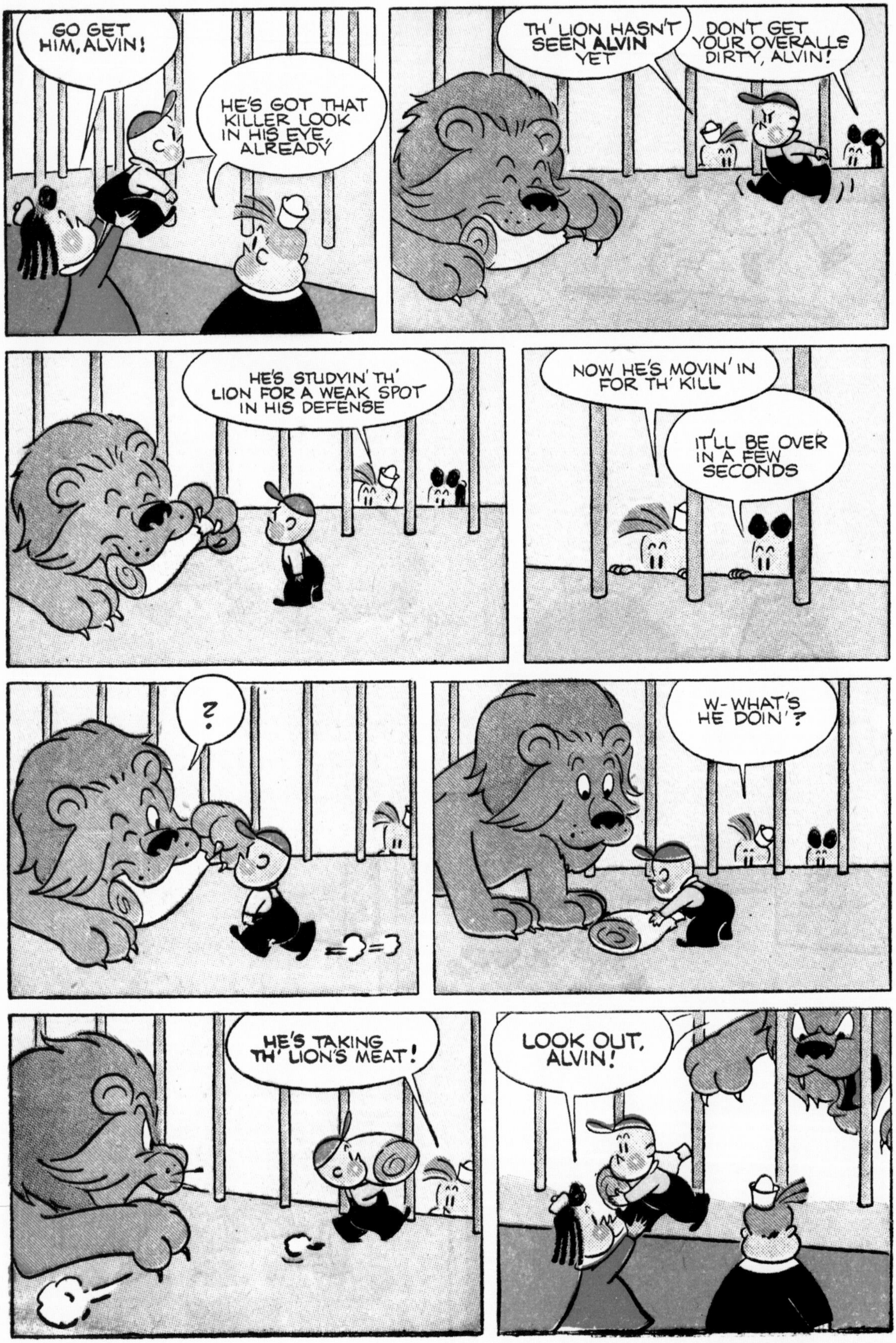
GO GET HIM, ALVIN!
HE'S GOT THAT KILLER LOOK IN HIS EYE, ALREADY
TH' LION HASN'T SEEN ALVIN YET
DON'T GET YOUR OVERALLS DIRTY, ALVIN!
HE'S STUDYIN' TH' LION FOR A WEAK SPOT IN HIS DEFENSE
NOW HE'S MOVIN' IN FOR TH' KILL
IT'LL BE OVER IN A FEW SECONDS
?
W-WHAT'S HE DOIN'?
HE'S TAKING TH' LION'S MEAT!
LOOK OUT, ALVIN!

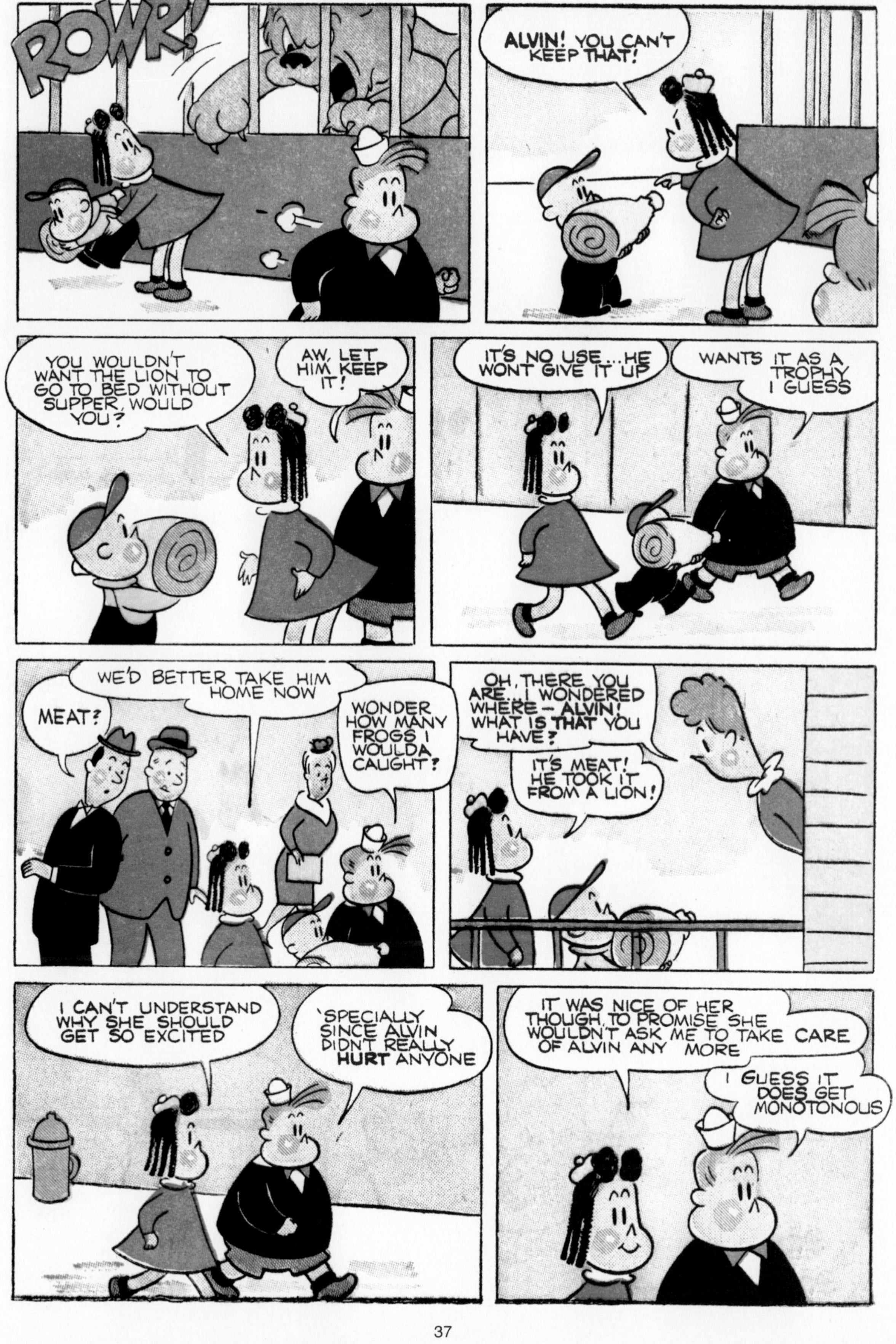
ROWR!
ALVIN! YOU CAN'T KEEP THAT!
YOU WOULDN'T WANT THE LION TO GO TO BED WITHOUT SUPPER, WOULD YOU?
AW, LET HIM KEEP IT!
IT'S NO USE... HE WONT GIVE IT UP
WANTS IT AS A TROPHY I GUESS
WE'D BETTER TAKE HIM HOME NOW
MEAT?
WONDER HOW MANY FROGS I WOULDA CAUGHT?
OH, THERE YOU ARE... I WONDERED WHERE – ALVIN! WHAT IS THAT YOU HAVE?
IT'S MEAT! HE TOOK IT FROM A LION!
I CAN'T UNDERSTAND WHY SHE SHOULD GET SO EXCITED
'SPECIALLY SINCE ALVIN DIDN'T REALLY HURT ANYONE
IT WAS NICE OF HER THOUGH, TO PROMISE SHE WOULDN'T ASK ME TO TAKE CARE OF ALVIN ANY MORE
I GUESS IT DOES GET MONOTONOUS

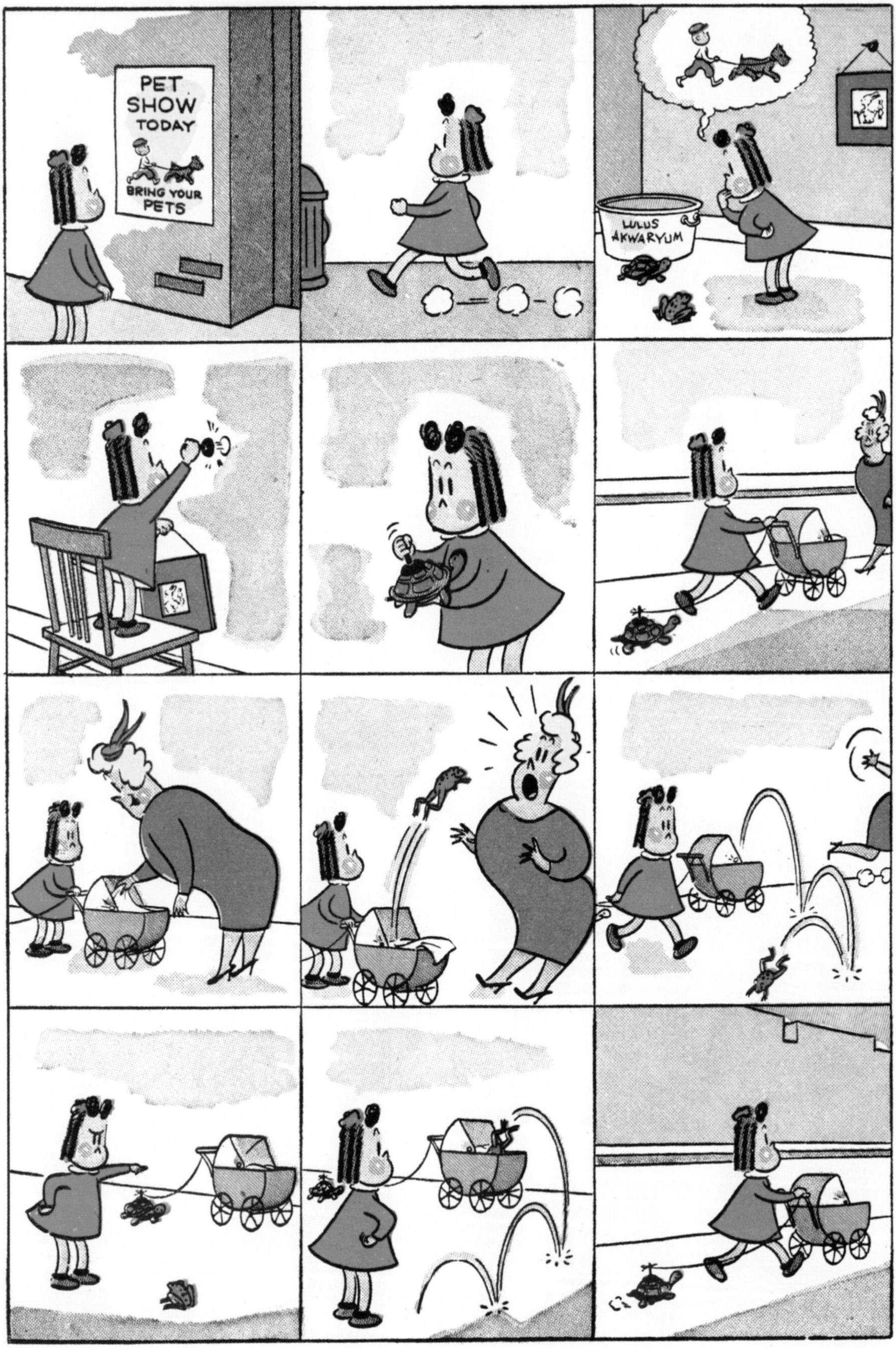
PET SHOW TODAY
BRING YOUR PETS
LULUS AKWARYUM

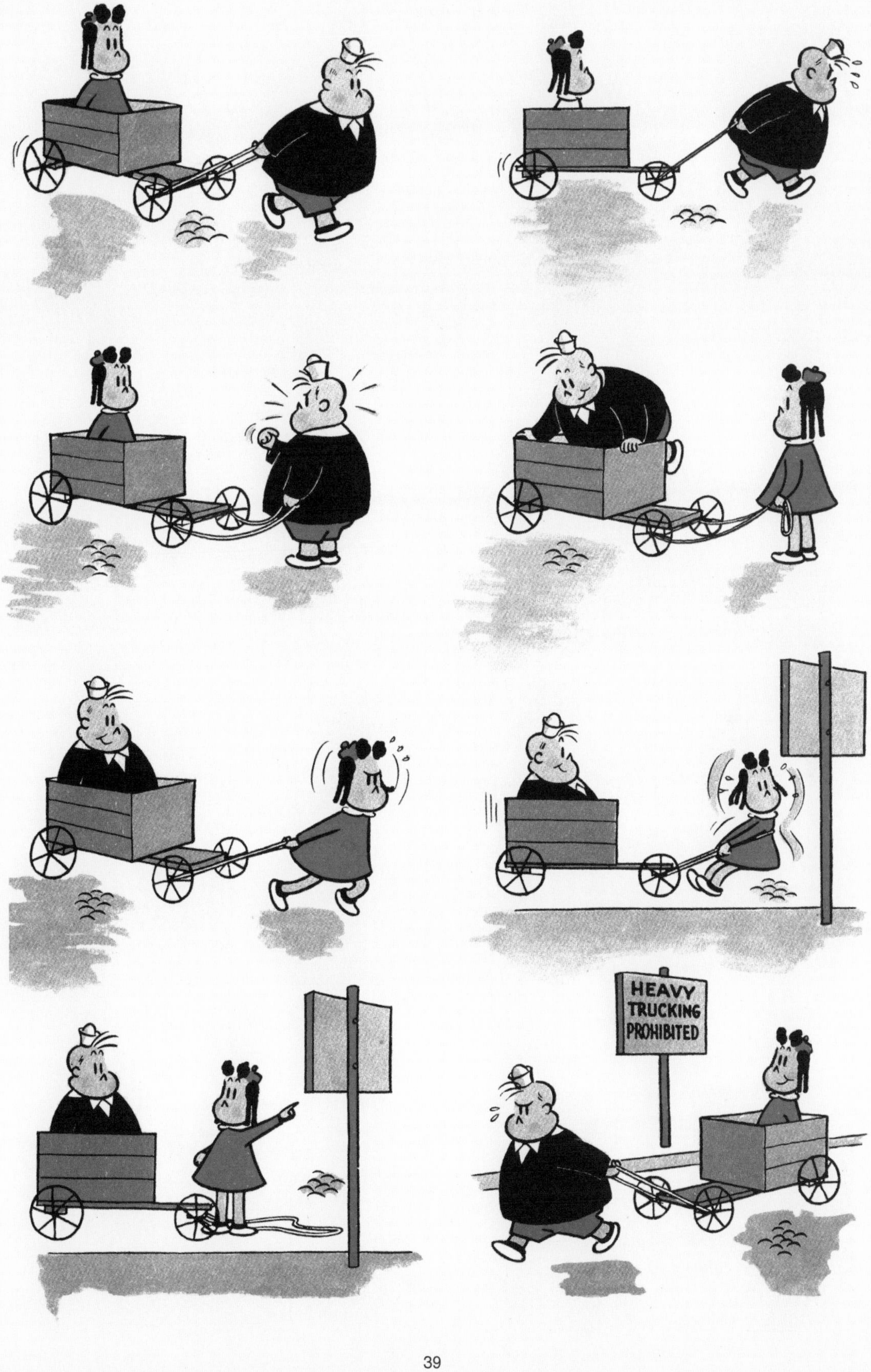
HEAVY
TRUCKING
PROHIBITED

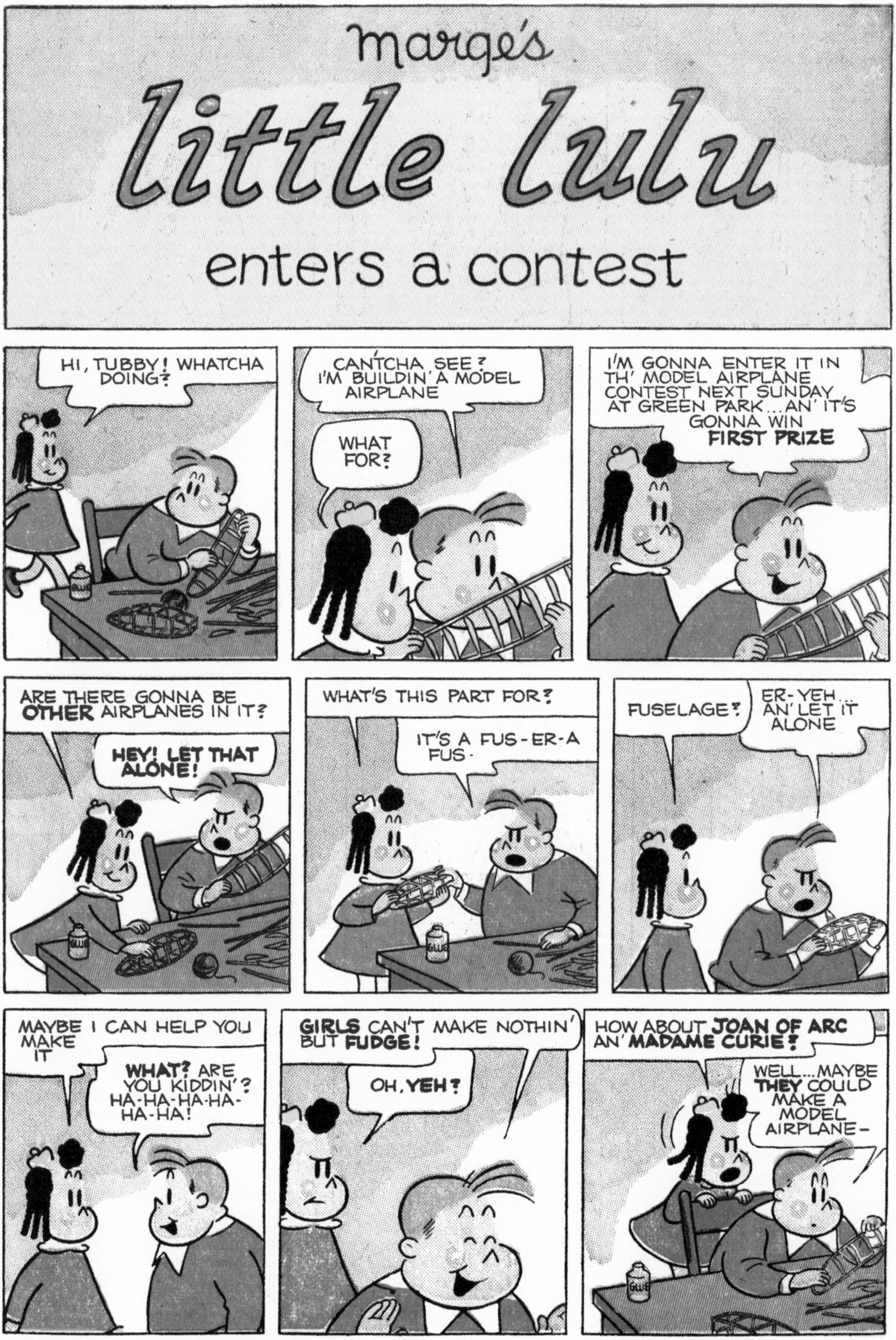
marge's
little lulu
enters a contest
HI, TUBBY! WHATCHA DOING?
CAN'TCHA SEE? I'M BUILDIN' A MODEL AIRPLANE
WHAT FOR?
I'M GONNA ENTER IT IN TH' MODEL AIRPLANE CONTEST NEXT SUNDAY AT GREEN PARK... AN' IT'S GONNA WIN FIRST PRIZE
ARE THERE GONNA BE OTHER AIRPLANES IN IT?
HEY! LET THAT ALONE!
WHAT'S THIS PART FOR?
IT'S A FUS-ER-A FUS-
FUSELAGE?
ER-YEH... AN' LET IT ALONE
MAYBE I CAN HELP YOU MAKE IT
WHAT? ARE YOU KIDDIN'? HA-HA-HA-HA-HA-HA!
GIRLS CAN'T MAKE NOTHIN' BUT FUDGE!
OH, YEH?
HOW ABOUT JOAN OF ARC AN' MADAME CURIE?
WELL... MAYBE THEY COULD MAKE A MODEL AIRPLANE-

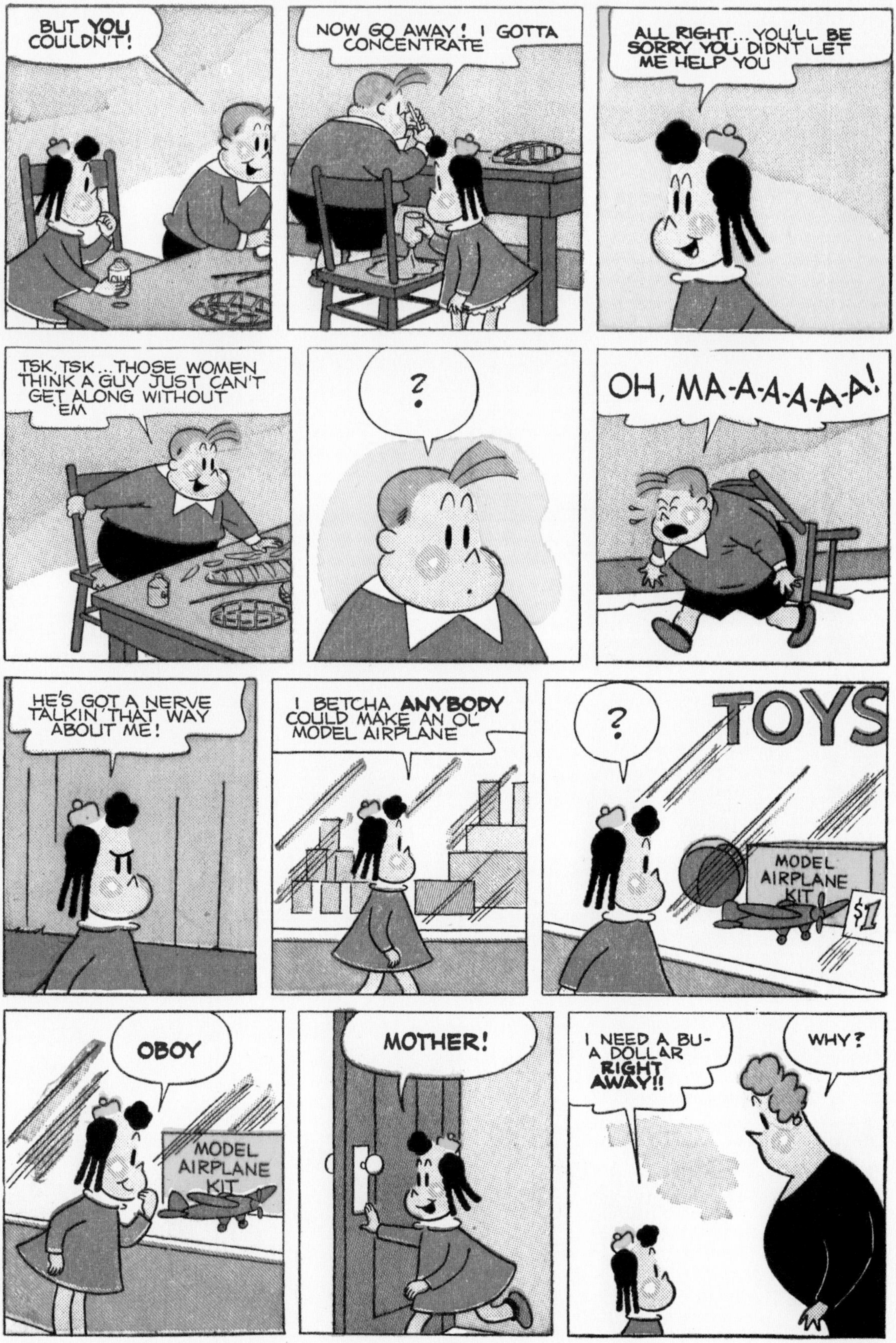
BUT YOU COULDN'T!
NOW GO AWAY! I GOTTA CONCENTRATE
ALL RIGHT... YOU'LL BE SORRY YOU DIDN'T LET ME HELP YOU
TSK, TSK... THOSE WOMEN THINK A GUY JUST CAN'T GET ALONG WITHOUT 'EM
?
OH, MA-A-A-A-A-A!
HE'S GOT A NERVE TALKIN' THAT WAY ABOUT ME!
I BETCHA ANYBODY COULD MAKE AN OL' MODEL AIRPLANE
?
TOYS
MODEL AIRPLANE KIT
$1
OBOY
MODEL AIRPLANE KIT
MOTHER!
I NEED A BU- A DOLLAR RIGHT AWAY!!
WHY?

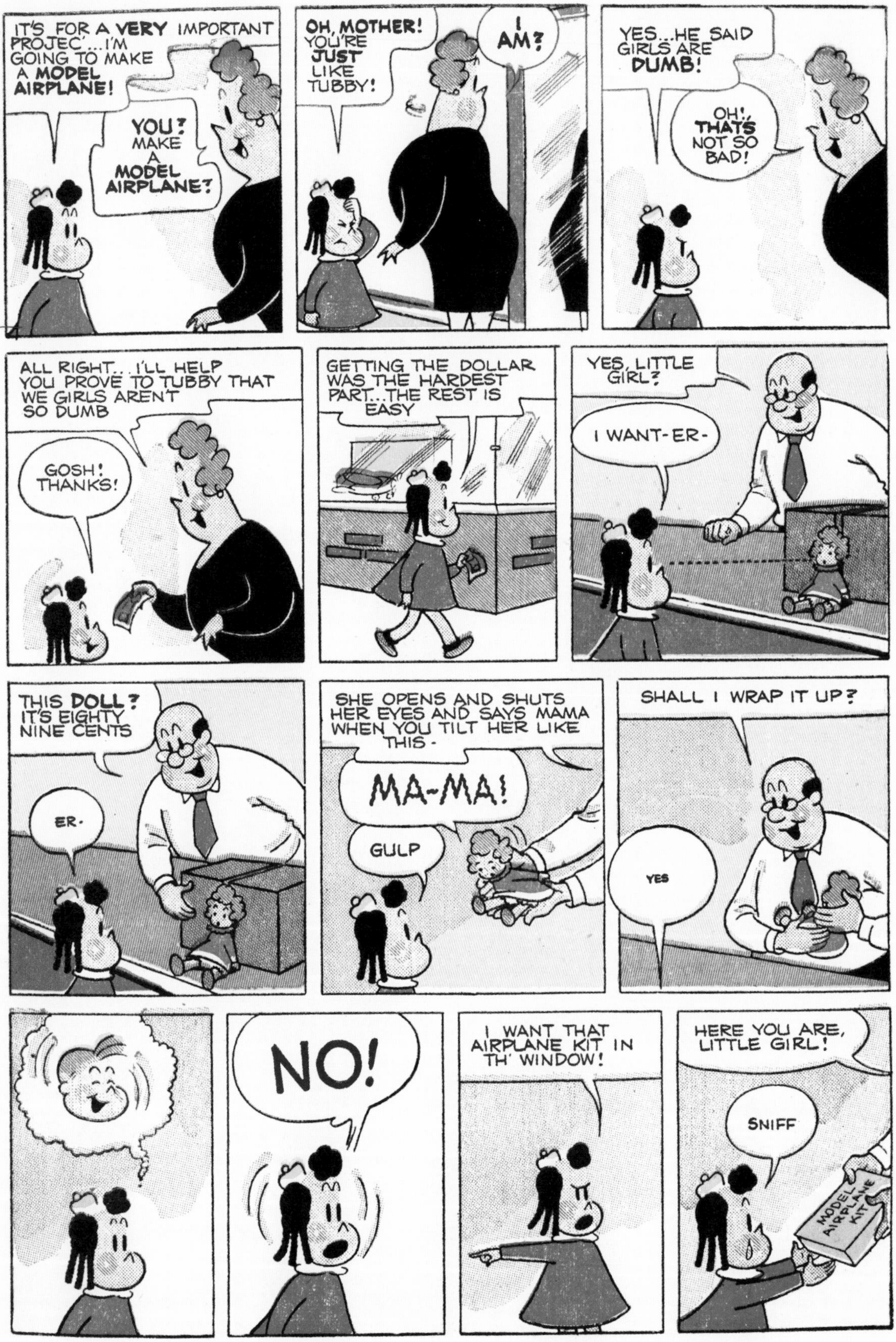
IT'S FOR A **VERY** IMPORTANT PROJEC'... I'M GOING TO MAKE A **MODEL AIRPLANE**!
YOU? MAKE A **MODEL AIRPLANE?**
OH, MOTHER! YOU'RE **JUST** LIKE TUBBY!
I **AM?**
YES... HE SAID GIRLS ARE **DUMB**!
OH!, **THAT'S** NOT SO BAD!
ALL RIGHT... I'LL HELP YOU PROVE TO TUBBY THAT WE GIRLS AREN'T SO DUMB
GOSH! THANKS!
GETTING THE DOLLAR WAS THE HARDEST PART... THE REST IS EASY
YES, LITTLE GIRL?
I WANT-ER-
THIS **DOLL?** IT'S EIGHTY NINE CENTS
ER-
SHE OPENS AND SHUTS HER EYES AND SAYS MAMA WHEN YOU TILT HER LIKE THIS-
MA-MA!
GULP
SHALL I WRAP IT UP?
YES
NO!
I WANT THAT AIRPLANE KIT IN TH' WINDOW!
HERE YOU ARE, LITTLE GIRL!
SNIFF
MODEL AIRPLANE KIT

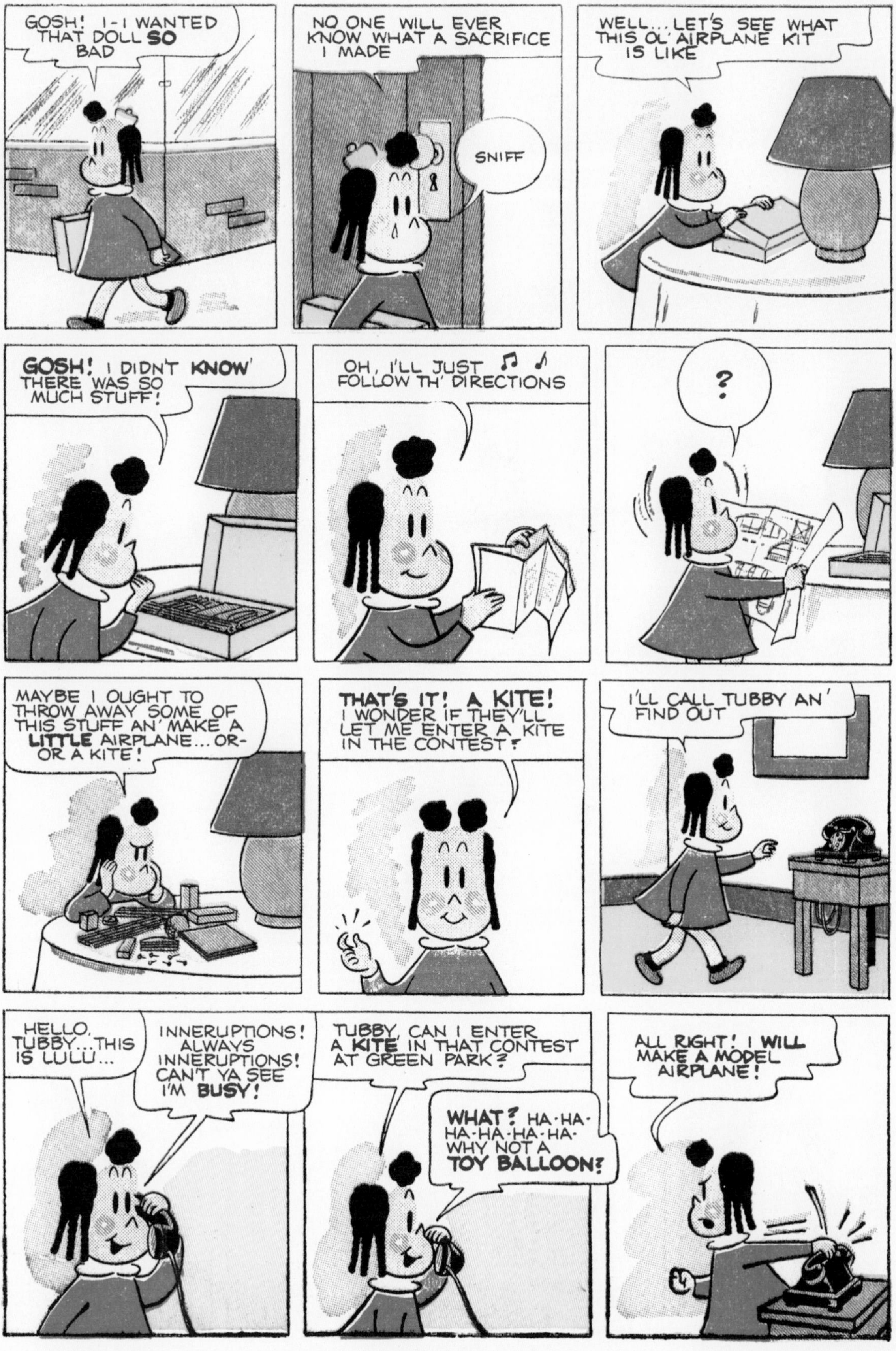
GOSH! I-I WANTED THAT DOLL **SO** BAD
NO ONE WILL EVER KNOW WHAT A SACRIFICE I MADE
SNIFF
WELL... LET'S SEE WHAT THIS OL' AIRPLANE KIT IS LIKE
GOSH! I DIDN'T **KNOW** THERE WAS SO MUCH STUFF!
OH, I'LL JUST ♫ ♪ FOLLOW TH' DIRECTIONS
?
MAYBE I OUGHT TO THROW AWAY SOME OF THIS STUFF AN' MAKE A **LITTLE** AIRPLANE... OR- OR A KITE!
THAT'S IT! A KITE! I WONDER IF THEY'LL LET ME ENTER A KITE IN THE CONTEST?
I'LL CALL TUBBY AN' FIND OUT
HELLO, TUBBY... THIS IS LULU...
INNERUPTIONS! ALWAYS INNERUPTIONS! CAN'T YA SEE I'M **BUSY**!
TUBBY, CAN I ENTER A **KITE** IN THAT CONTEST AT GREEN PARK?
WHAT? HA-HA-HA-HA-HA-HA- WHY NOT A **TOY BALLOON?**
ALL **RIGHT!** I **WILL** MAKE A MODEL AIRPLANE!

A BOTTLE OF GLUE AND A COUPLE OF GOOD CRIES LATER

'S FUNNY... I USED ALL TH' STUFF BUT IT DOESN'T LOOK RIGHT

IT PROBABLY **FLYS** GOOD THOUGH

I BETTER TRY IT **INDOORS** FIRST 'CAUSE IT MIGHT FLY AWAY AN' GET LOST

THERE IT—

GOES

PROPELLER'S PROB'LY STUCK

I'LL FIX THAT IN A JIFFY

RRRRR

SMACK!

HEY! STOP IT!

RRRR

QUIT IT, WILLYA?

WHEW!

DON'T YOU KNOW ME? I'M YOUR **MOTHER!**

44

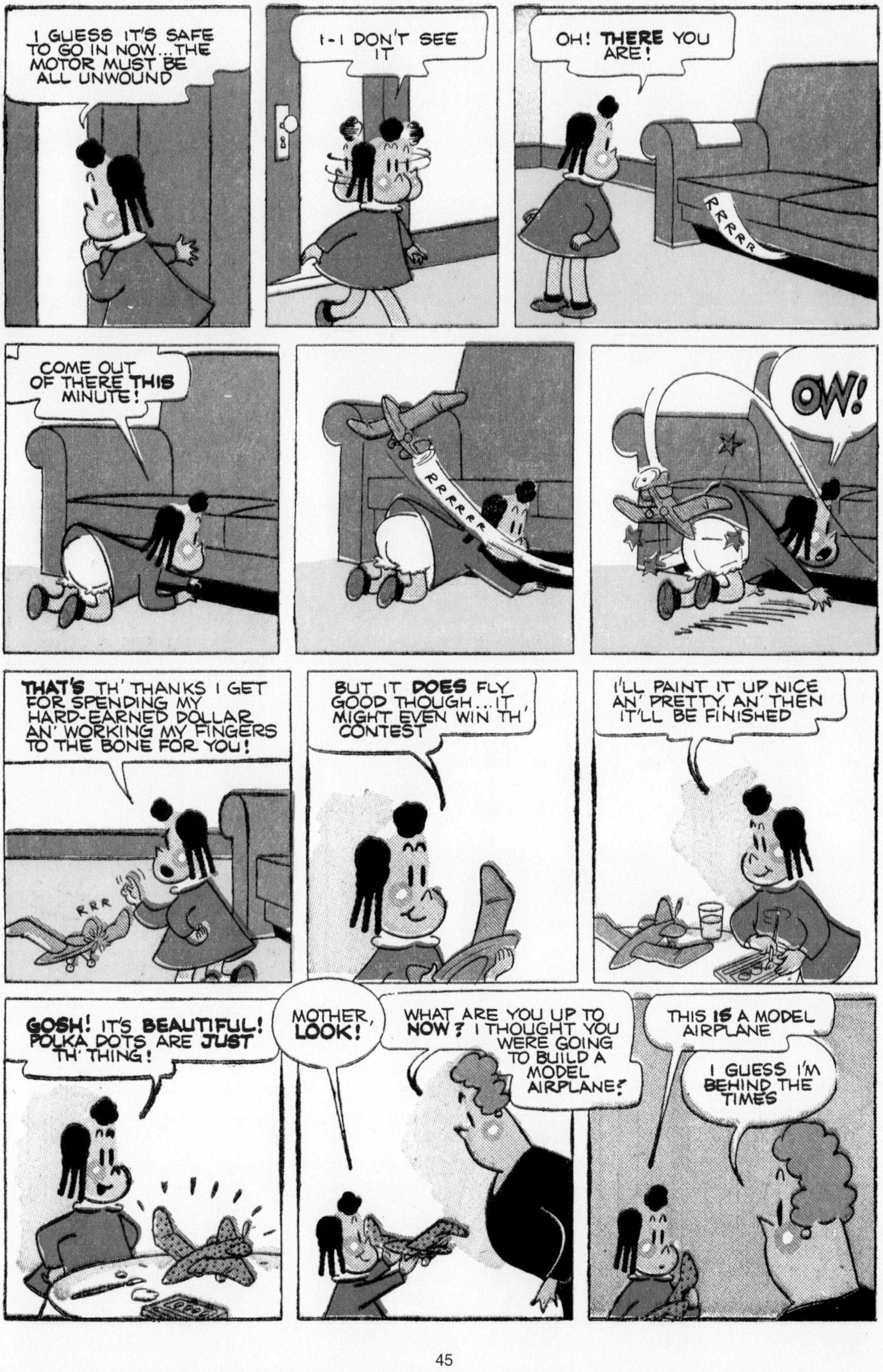

I GUESS IT'S SAFE TO GO IN NOW... THE MOTOR MUST BE ALL UNWOUND
I-I DON'T SEE IT
OH! THERE YOU ARE!
RRRRR
COME OUT OF THERE THIS MINUTE!
RRRRRRR
OW!
THAT'S TH' THANKS I GET FOR SPENDING MY HARD-EARNED DOLLAR AN' WORKING MY FINGERS TO THE BONE FOR YOU!
RRR
BUT IT DOES FLY GOOD THOUGH... IT MIGHT EVEN WIN TH' CONTEST
I'LL PAINT IT UP NICE AN' PRETTY, AN' THEN IT'LL BE FINISHED
GOSH! IT'S BEAUTIFUL! POLKA DOTS ARE JUST TH' THING!
MOTHER, LOOK!
WHAT ARE YOU UP TO NOW? I THOUGHT YOU WERE GOING TO BUILD A MODEL AIRPLANE?
THIS IS A MODEL AIRPLANE
I GUESS I'M BEHIND THE TIMES

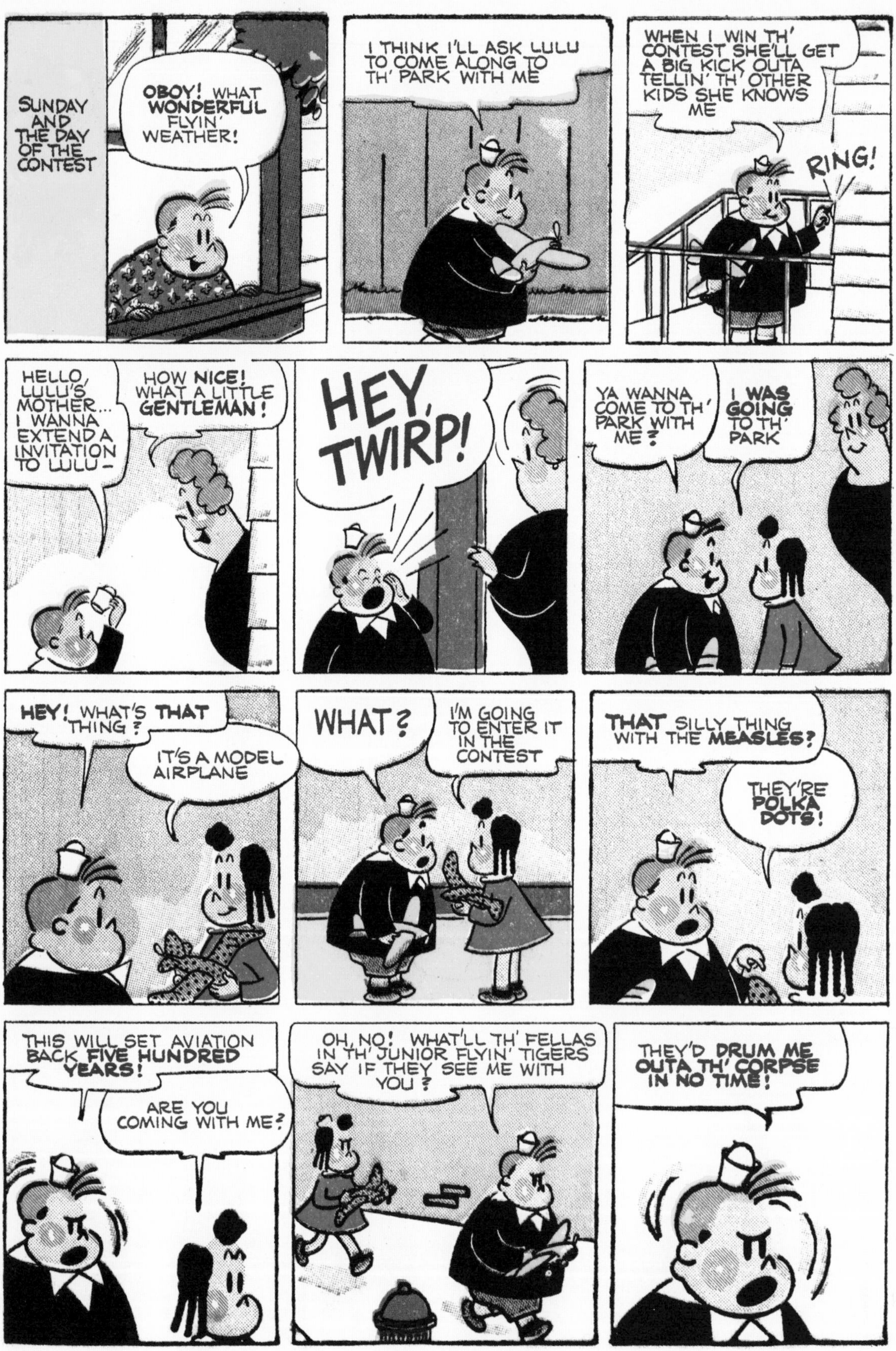
SUNDAY AND THE DAY OF THE CONTEST
OBOY! WHAT WONDERFUL FLYIN' WEATHER!
I THINK I'LL ASK LULU TO COME ALONG TO TH' PARK WITH ME
WHEN I WIN TH' CONTEST SHE'LL GET A BIG KICK OUTA TELLIN' TH' OTHER KIDS SHE KNOWS ME
RING!
HELLO, LULU'S MOTHER... I WANNA EXTEND A INVITATION TO LULU—
HOW NICE! WHAT A LITTLE GENTLEMAN!
HEY, TWIRP!
YA WANNA COME TO TH' PARK WITH ME?
I WAS GOING TO TH' PARK
HEY! WHAT'S THAT THING?
IT'S A MODEL AIRPLANE
WHAT?
I'M GOING TO ENTER IT IN THE CONTEST
THAT SILLY THING WITH THE MEASLES?
THEY'RE POLKA DOTS!
THIS WILL SET AVIATION BACK FIVE HUNDRED YEARS!
ARE YOU COMING WITH ME?
OH, NO! WHAT'LL TH' FELLAS IN TH' JUNIOR FLYIN' TIGERS SAY IF THEY SEE ME WITH YOU?
THEY'D DRUM ME OUTA TH' CORPSE IN NO TIME!

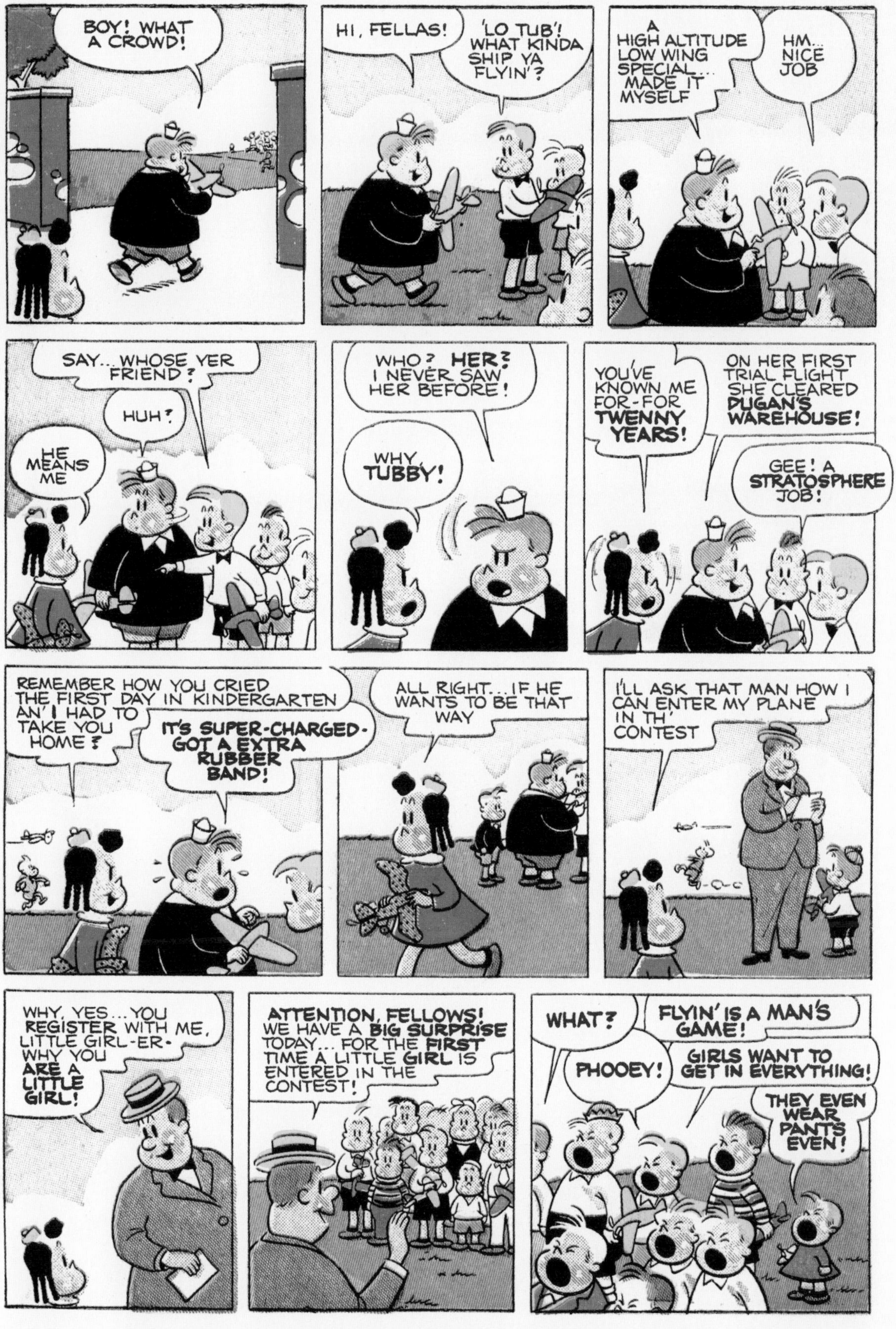
BOY! WHAT A CROWD!
HI, FELLAS!
'LO TUB'! WHAT KINDA SHIP YA FLYIN'?
A HIGH ALTITUDE LOW WING SPECIAL... MADE IT MYSELF
HM... NICE JOB
SAY... WHOSE YER FRIEND?
HUH?
HE MEANS ME
WHO? HER? I NEVER SAW HER BEFORE!
WHY, TUBBY!
YOU'VE KNOWN ME FOR-FOR TWENNY YEARS!
ON HER FIRST TRIAL FLIGHT SHE CLEARED DUGAN'S WAREHOUSE!
GEE! A STRATOSPHERE JOB!
REMEMBER HOW YOU CRIED THE FIRST DAY IN KINDERGARTEN AN' I HAD TO TAKE YOU HOME?
IT'S SUPER-CHARGED-GOT A EXTRA RUBBER BAND!
ALL RIGHT... IF HE WANTS TO BE THAT WAY
I'LL ASK THAT MAN HOW I CAN ENTER MY PLANE IN TH' CONTEST
WHY, YES... YOU REGISTER WITH ME, LITTLE GIRL-ER-WHY YOU ARE A LITTLE GIRL!
ATTENTION, FELLOWS! WE HAVE A BIG SURPRISE TODAY... FOR THE FIRST TIME A LITTLE GIRL IS ENTERED IN THE CONTEST!
WHAT?
FLYIN' IS A MAN'S GAME!
PHOOEY!
GIRLS WANT TO GET IN EVERYTHING!
THEY EVEN WEAR PANTS EVEN!

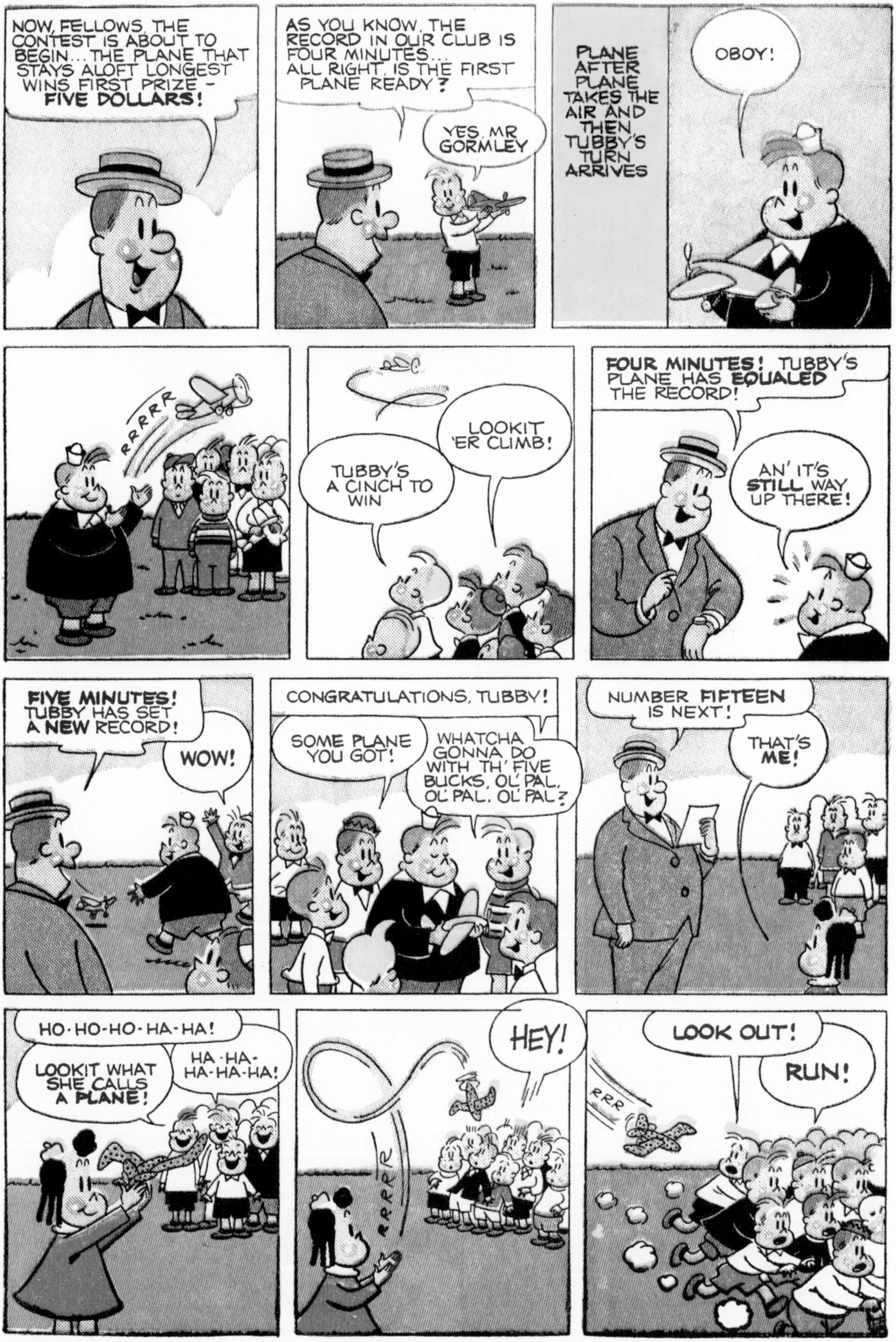

NOW, FELLOWS, THE CONTEST IS ABOUT TO BEGIN... THE PLANE THAT STAYS ALOFT LONGEST WINS FIRST PRIZE - FIVE DOLLARS!
AS YOU KNOW, THE RECORD IN OUR CLUB IS FOUR MINUTES... ALL RIGHT, IS THE FIRST PLANE READY?
YES, MR GORMLEY
PLANE AFTER PLANE TAKES THE AIR AND THEN TUBBY'S TURN ARRIVES
OBOY!
RRRRR
TUBBY'S A CINCH TO WIN
LOOKIT 'ER CLIMB!
FOUR MINUTES! TUBBY'S PLANE HAS EQUALED THE RECORD!
AN' IT'S STILL WAY UP THERE!
FIVE MINUTES! TUBBY HAS SET A NEW RECORD!
WOW!
CONGRATULATIONS, TUBBY!
SOME PLANE YOU GOT!
WHATCHA GONNA DO WITH TH' FIVE BUCKS, OL' PAL, OL' PAL, OL' PAL?
NUMBER FIFTEEN IS NEXT!
THAT'S ME!
HO-HO-HO-HA-HA!
LOOKIT WHAT SHE CALLS A PLANE!
HA-HA-HA-HA-HA!
HEY!
RRRRR
LOOK OUT!
RUN!
RRR

GIT OUTA MY WAY!!
RRRRRRRR
HA-HA-HA-HA-HA-HA-HO-HO-HO-HO-HO-
HA-HA-HA ULP!
RRRR
YOU BETTER DUCK, MR GORMLEY!
HEY!
RRRRRRR
HOW LONG IS MY PLANE IN THE AIR NOW, MR GORMLEY?
FIVE MINUTES!
CUTTITOUT! DON'T YOU KNOW ME YET?
RRRR
MOVE OVER!
RRRRRRR
BOYS, THE LITTLE GIRL'S-ER-PLANE WAS IN THE AIR SIX MINUTES!
SO SHE WINS THE FIVE DOLLARS!
GEE THANKS!
A FEW MINUTES LATER
THE DOLL? CHANGED YOUR MIND, EH?
THE END

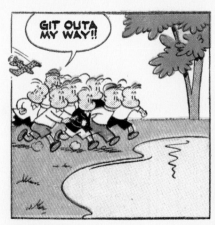

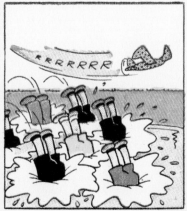

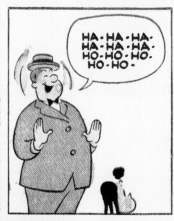

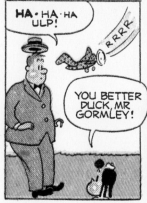

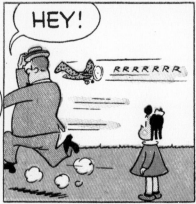

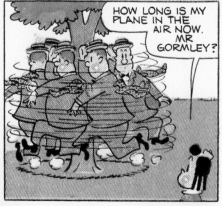

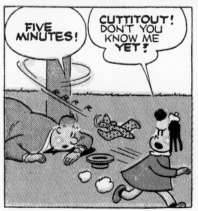

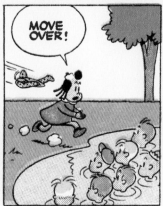

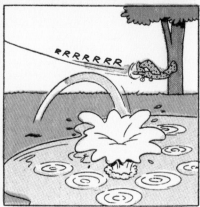

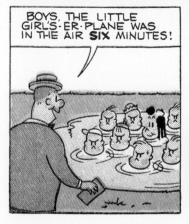

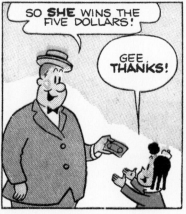

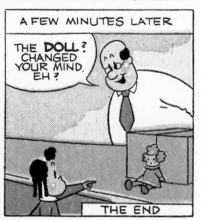

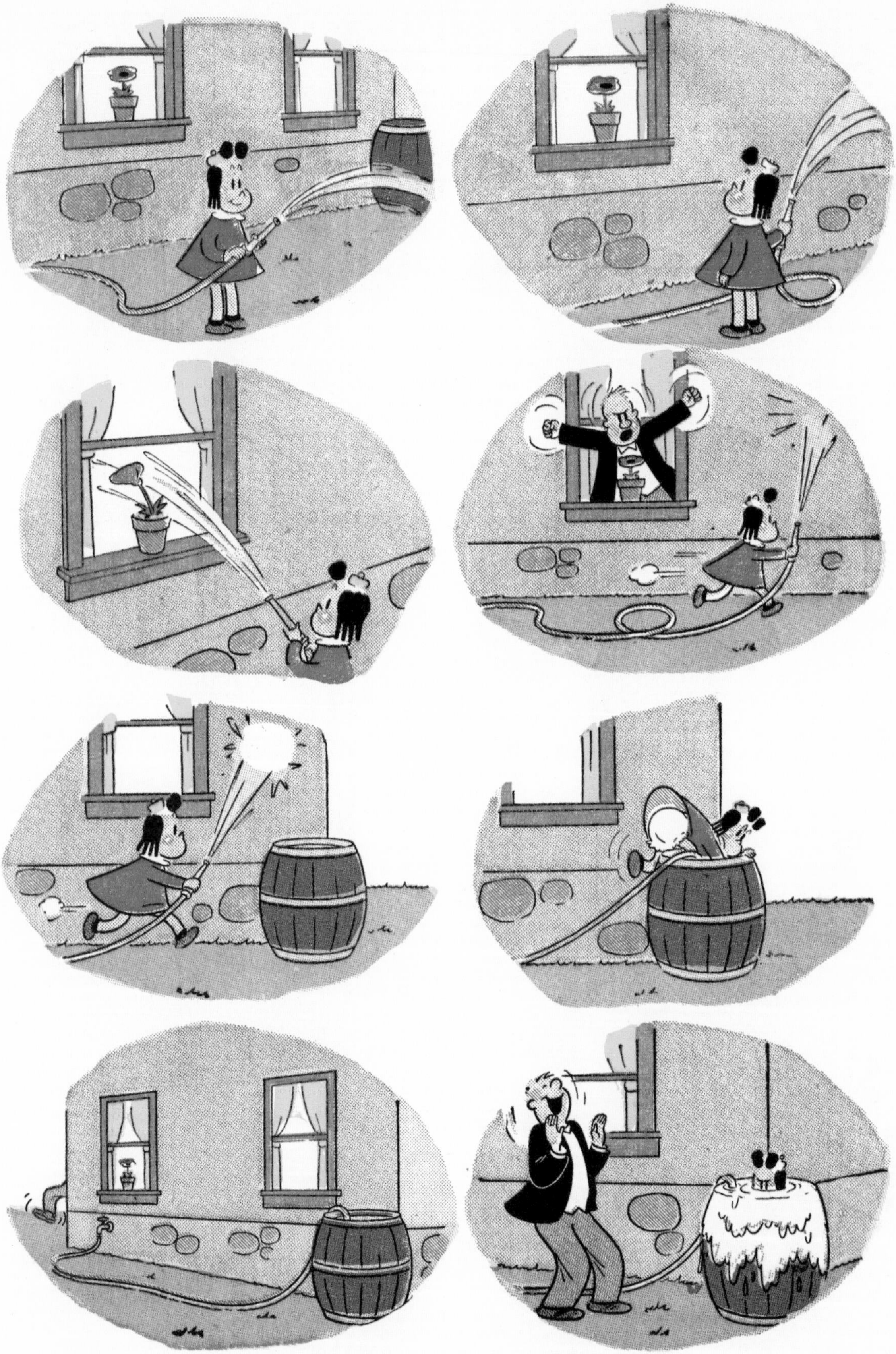

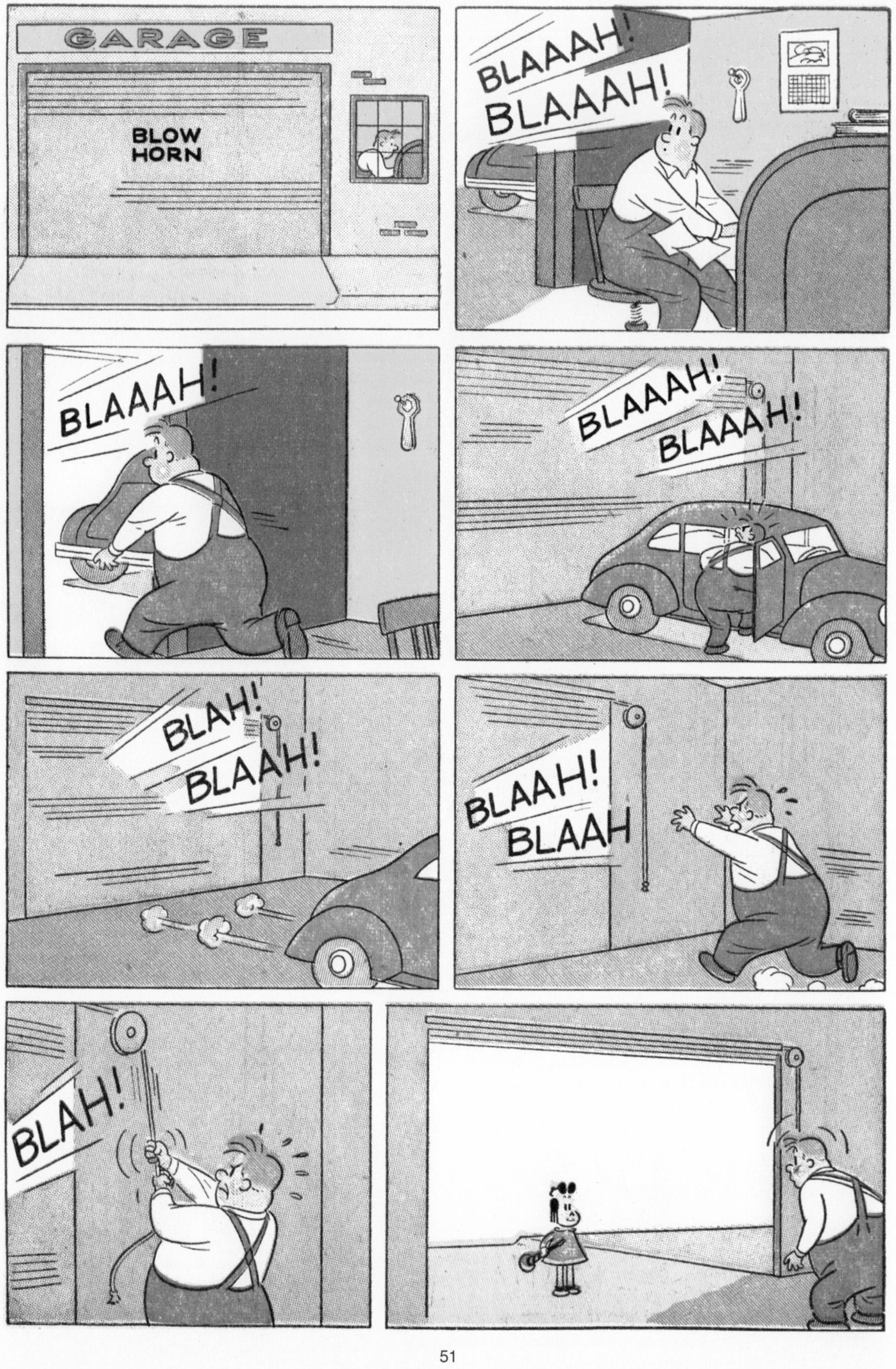
GARAGE
BLOW HORN
BLAAAH!
BLAAAH!
BLAAAH!
BLAAAH!
BLAAAH!
BLAH!
BLAAH!
BLAAH!
BLAAH
BLAH!

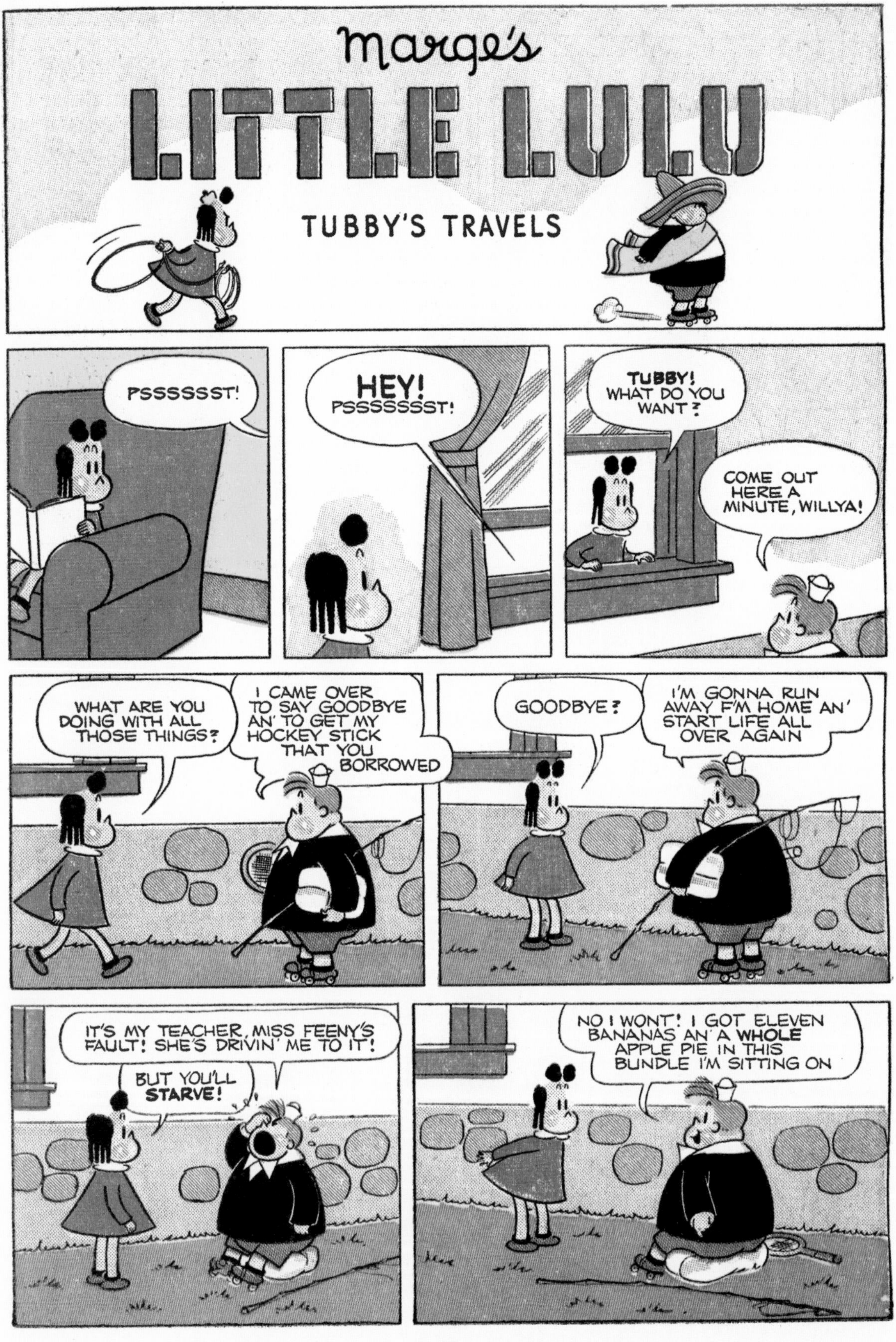
marge's
LITTLE LULU
TUBBY'S TRAVELS
PSSSSSST!
HEY!
PSSSSSSST!
TUBBY!
WHAT DO YOU WANT?
COME OUT HERE A MINUTE, WILLYA!
WHAT ARE YOU DOING WITH ALL THOSE THINGS?
I CAME OVER TO SAY GOODBYE AN' TO GET MY HOCKEY STICK THAT YOU BORROWED
GOODBYE?
I'M GONNA RUN AWAY F'M HOME AN' START LIFE ALL OVER AGAIN
IT'S MY TEACHER, MISS FEENY'S FAULT! SHE'S DRIVIN' ME TO IT!
BUT YOU'LL **STARVE!**
NO I WONT! I GOT ELEVEN BANANAS AN' A **WHOLE** APPLE PIE IN THIS BUNDLE I'M SITTING ON

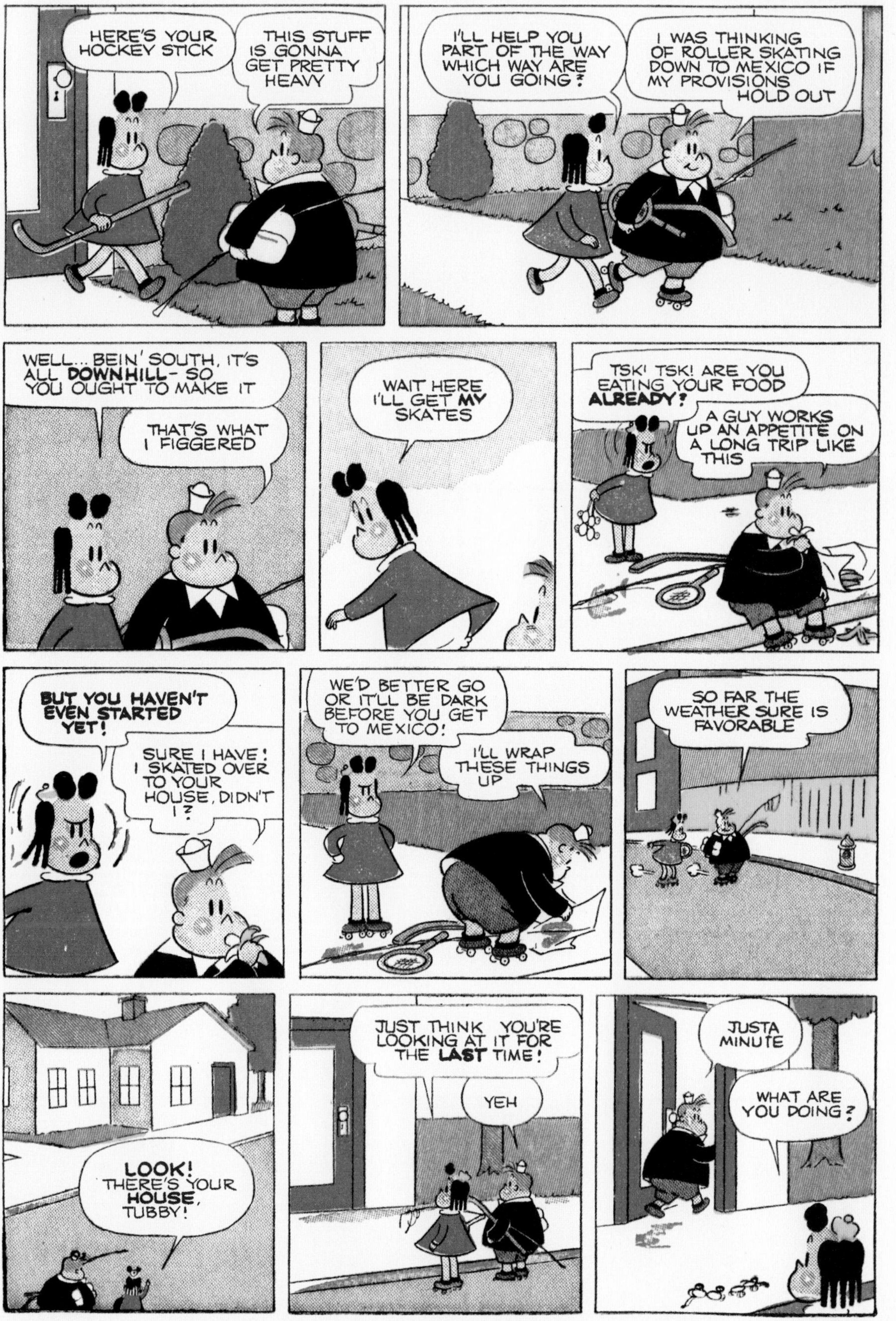
HERE'S YOUR HOCKEY STICK
THIS STUFF IS GONNA GET PRETTY HEAVY
I'LL HELP YOU PART OF THE WAY WHICH WAY ARE YOU GOING?
I WAS THINKING OF ROLLER SKATING DOWN TO MEXICO IF MY PROVISIONS HOLD OUT
WELL... BEIN' SOUTH, IT'S ALL **DOWNHILL**- SO YOU OUGHT TO MAKE IT
THAT'S WHAT I FIGGERED
WAIT HERE I'LL GET **MY** SKATES
TSK! TSK! ARE YOU EATING YOUR FOOD **ALREADY?**
A GUY WORKS UP AN APPETITE ON A LONG TRIP LIKE THIS
BUT YOU HAVEN'T EVEN STARTED YET!
SURE I HAVE! I SKATED OVER TO YOUR HOUSE, DIDN'T I?
WE'D BETTER GO OR IT'LL BE DARK BEFORE YOU GET TO MEXICO!
I'LL WRAP THESE THINGS UP
SO FAR THE WEATHER SURE IS FAVORABLE
LOOK! THERE'S YOUR **HOUSE**, TUBBY!
JUST THINK YOU'RE LOOKING AT IT FOR THE **LAST** TIME!
YEH
JUSTA MINUTE
WHAT ARE YOU DOING?

H-HE'S PROB'LY GOING TO TAKE ONE **LAST LOOK** AT HIS MOTHER- B- BECAUSE -

HE'LL NEVER SEE HER AGAIN!

SNIFF

I DIDN'T THINK I'D BE ABLE TO CARRY THIS BOX OF FUDGE - BUT NOW THAT **YOU'RE** GOING TO HELP ME -

OH!

THIS FUDGE WILL COME IN HANDY IF I HAVE TO TRADE WITH THE NATIVES OR SOMETHING

TUBBY! YOU'LL **NEVER** GET TO MEXICO **THIS** WAY!

OKAY! I'M READY!

I CAN'T GO ANY FARTHER WITH YOU ... I HAVE TO DO MY HOMEWORK

HA! HA! HA! **THAT'S** SOMETHING I DON'T HAVE TO WORRY ABOUT!

G'BYE!

THANKS FOR HELPING ME! I'LL SEND YOU A CARD FROM MEXICO

POOR TUBBY! I'M AFRAID HE WON'T BE ABLE TO TAKE CARE OF HIMSELF

HE'LL HAVE TO LIVE WITH TRAMPS AN' BE CHASED BY DOGS -

AN' SLEEP OUT IN THE COLD AN' HAVE NO FRIENDS

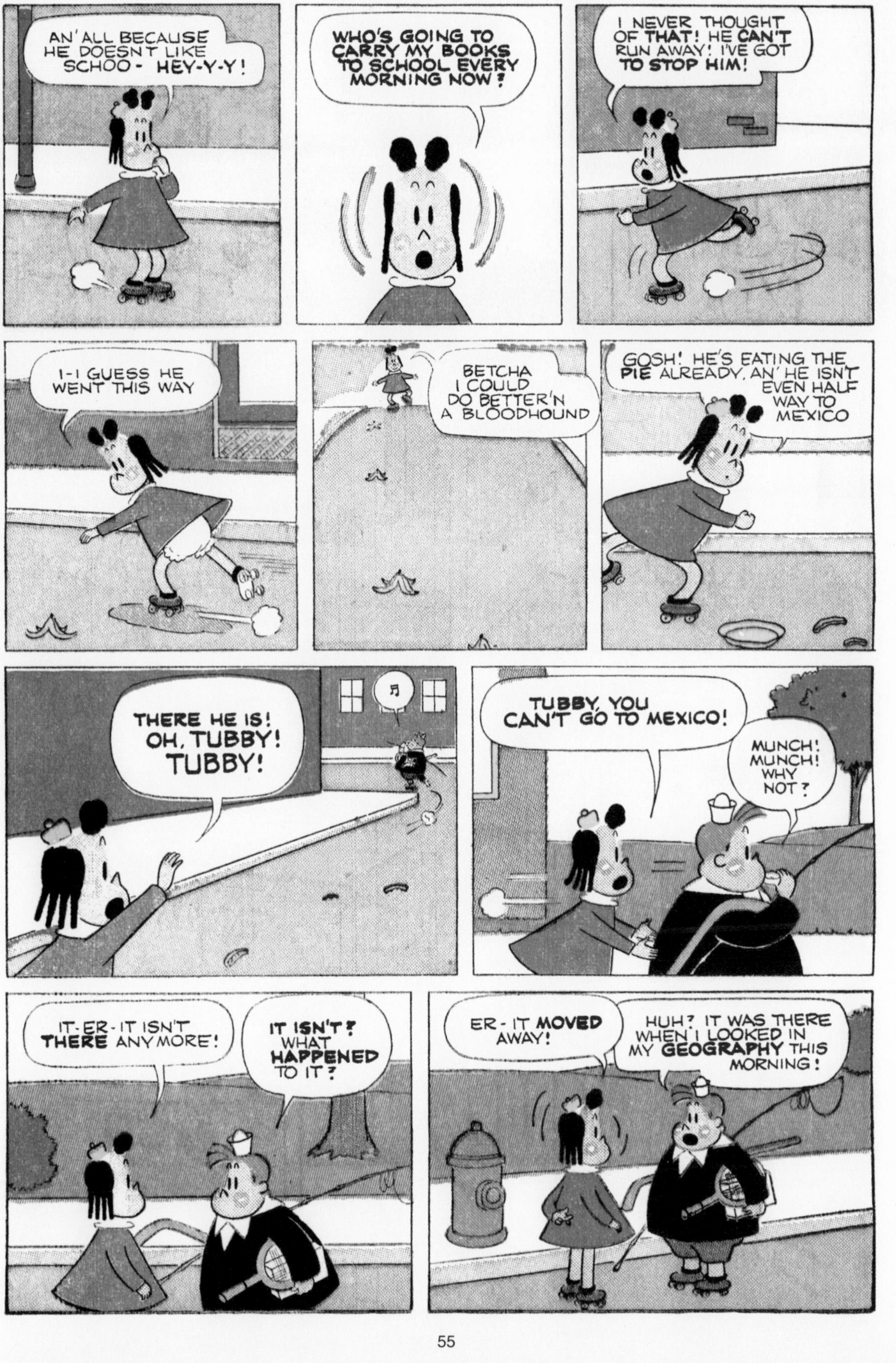
AN' ALL BECAUSE HE DOESN'T LIKE SCHOO - HEY-Y-Y!
WHO'S GOING TO CARRY MY BOOKS TO SCHOOL EVERY MORNING NOW?
I NEVER THOUGHT OF THAT! HE CAN'T RUN AWAY! I'VE GOT TO STOP HIM!
I-I GUESS HE WENT THIS WAY
BETCHA I COULD DO BETTER'N A BLOODHOUND
GOSH! HE'S EATING THE PIE ALREADY, AN' HE ISN'T EVEN HALF WAY TO MEXICO
THERE HE IS! OH, TUBBY! TUBBY!
TUBBY, YOU CAN'T GO TO MEXICO!
MUNCH! MUNCH! WHY NOT?
IT-ER-IT ISN'T THERE ANYMORE!
IT ISN'T? WHAT HAPPENED TO IT?
ER-IT MOVED AWAY!
HUH? IT WAS THERE WHEN I LOOKED IN MY GEOGRAPHY THIS MORNING!

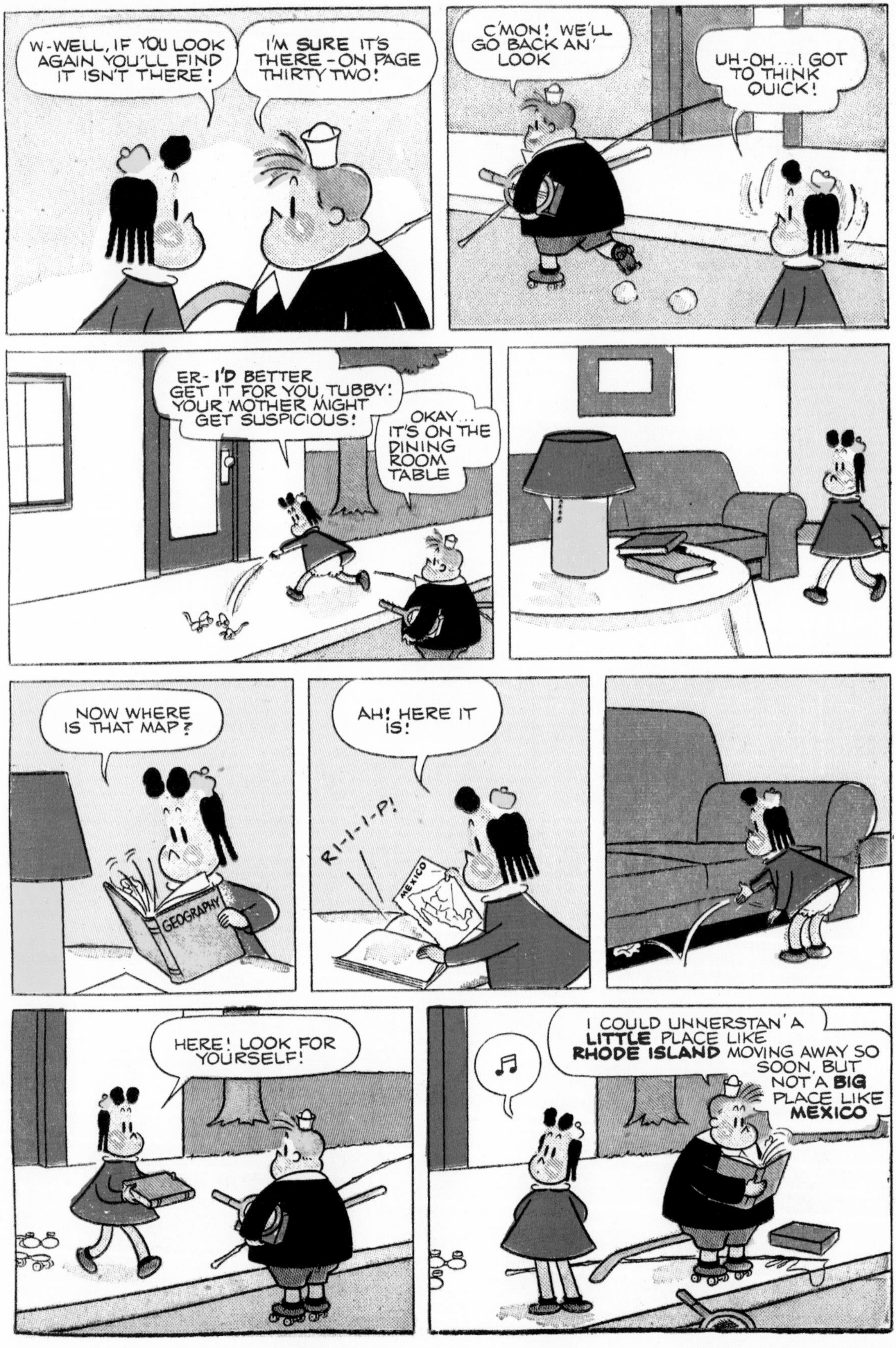
W-WELL, IF YOU LOOK AGAIN YOU'LL FIND IT ISN'T THERE!
I'M SURE IT'S THERE - ON PAGE THIRTY TWO!
C'MON! WE'LL GO BACK AN' LOOK
UH-OH... I GOT TO THINK QUICK!
ER- I'D BETTER GET IT FOR YOU, TUBBY! YOUR MOTHER MIGHT GET SUSPICIOUS!
OKAY... IT'S ON THE DINING ROOM TABLE
NOW WHERE IS THAT MAP?
AH! HERE IT IS!
R-I-I-I-P!
GEOGRAPHY
MEXICO
HERE! LOOK FOR YOURSELF!
I COULD UNNERSTAN' A LITTLE PLACE LIKE RHODE ISLAND MOVING AWAY SO SOON, BUT NOT A BIG PLACE LIKE MEXICO

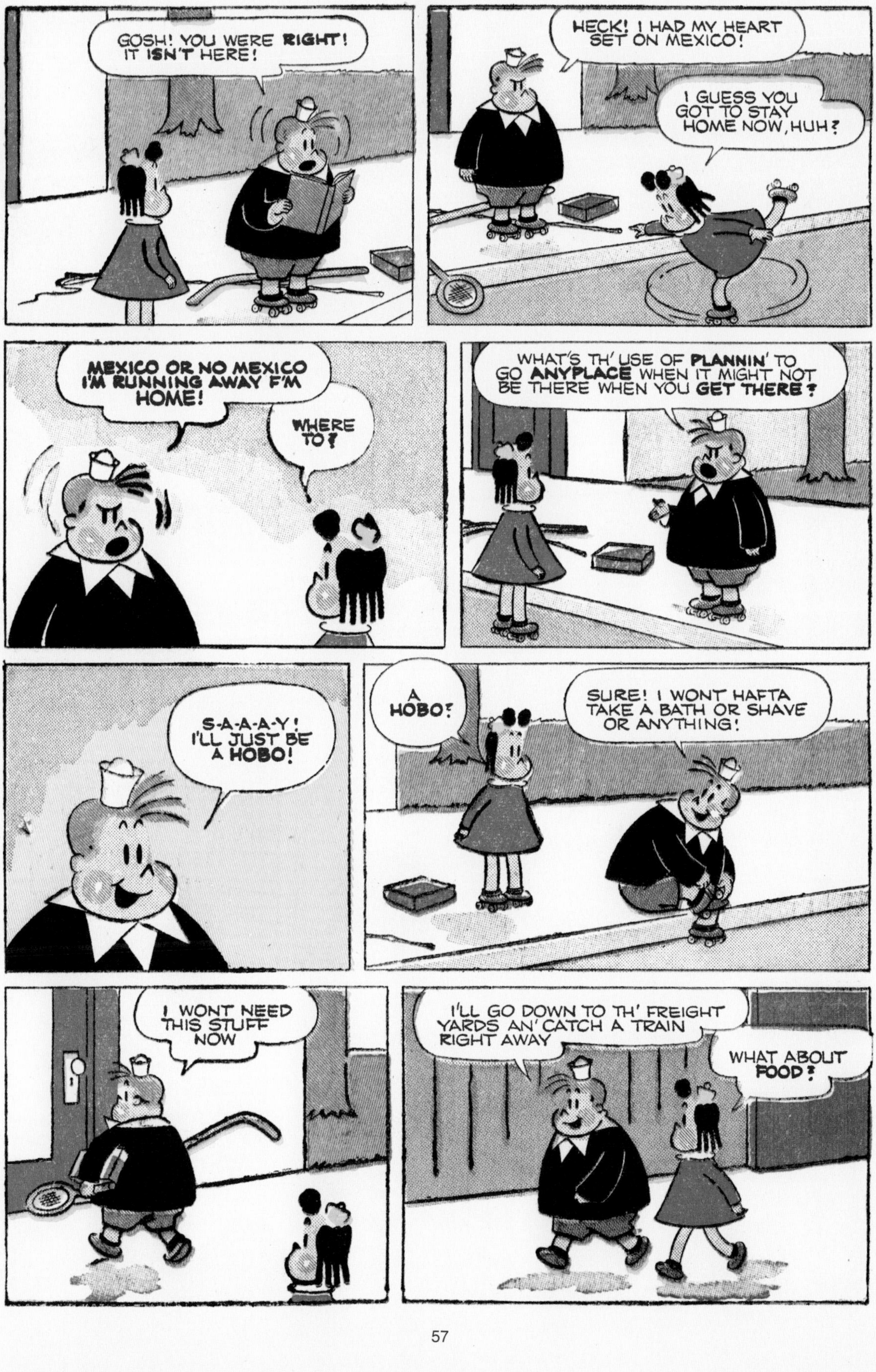
GOSH! YOU WERE RIGHT! IT ISN'T HERE!
HECK! I HAD MY HEART SET ON MEXICO!
I GUESS YOU GOT TO STAY HOME NOW, HUH?
MEXICO OR NO MEXICO I'M RUNNING AWAY F'M HOME!
WHERE TO?
WHAT'S TH' USE OF PLANNIN' TO GO ANYPLACE WHEN IT MIGHT NOT BE THERE WHEN YOU GET THERE?
S-A-A-A-Y! I'LL JUST BE A HOBO!
A HOBO?
SURE! I WONT HAFTA TAKE A BATH OR SHAVE OR ANYTHING!
I WONT NEED THIS STUFF NOW
I'LL GO DOWN TO TH' FREIGHT YARDS AN' CATCH A TRAIN RIGHT AWAY
WHAT ABOUT FOOD?

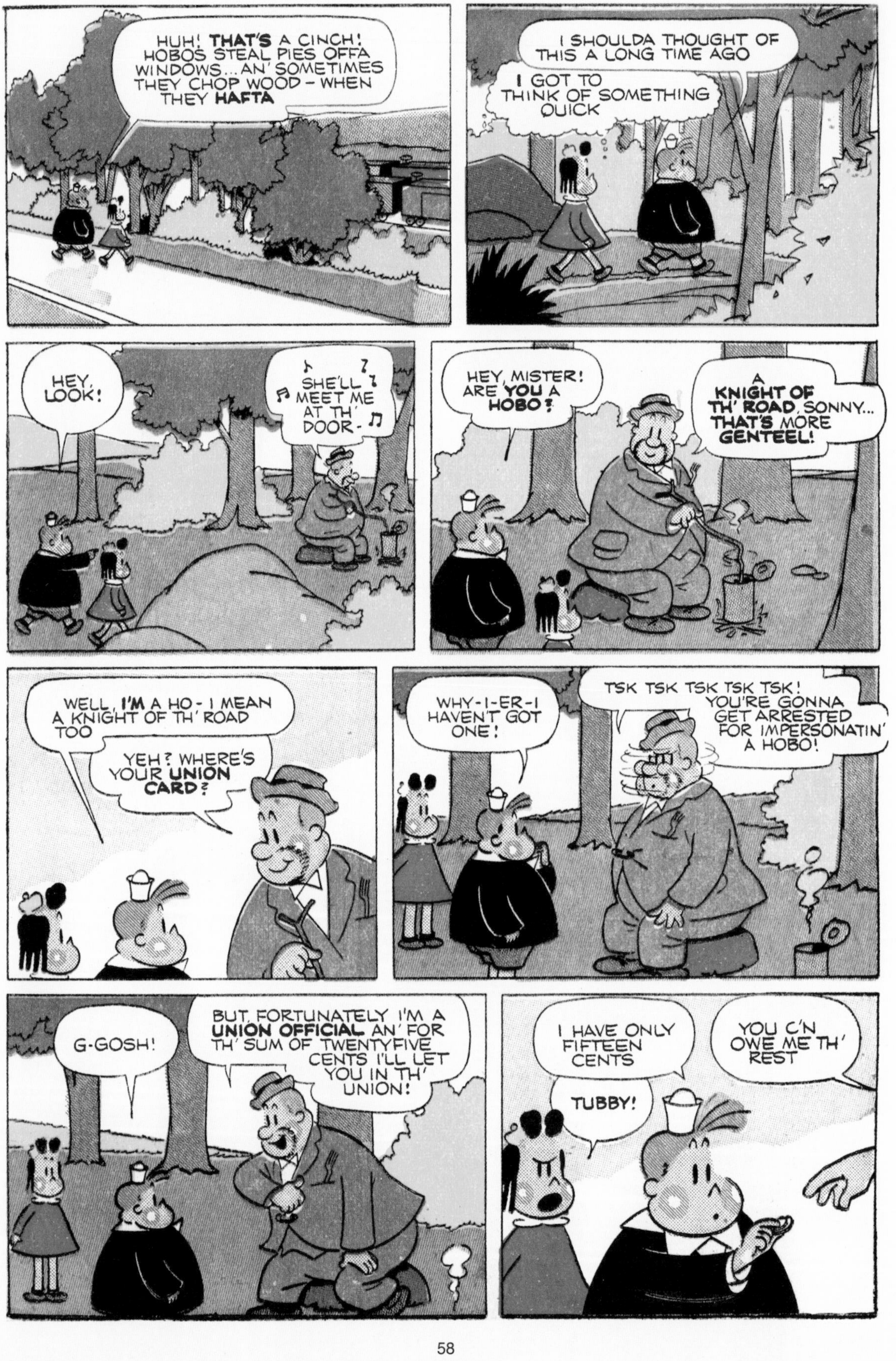
HUH! THAT'S A CINCH! HOBOS STEAL PIES OFFA WINDOWS...AN' SOMETIMES THEY CHOP WOOD – WHEN THEY HAFTA
I SHOULDA THOUGHT OF THIS A LONG TIME AGO
I GOT TO THINK OF SOMETHING QUICK
HEY, LOOK!
SHE'LL MEET ME AT TH' DOOR-
HEY, MISTER! ARE YOU A HOBO?
A KNIGHT OF TH' ROAD, SONNY... THAT'S MORE GENTEEL!
WELL, I'M A HO- I MEAN A KNIGHT OF TH' ROAD TOO
YEH? WHERE'S YOUR UNION CARD?
WHY-I-ER-I HAVEN'T GOT ONE!
TSK TSK TSK TSK TSK! YOU'RE GONNA GET ARRESTED FOR IMPERSONATIN' A HOBO!
G-GOSH!
BUT, FORTUNATELY I'M A UNION OFFICIAL AN' FOR TH' SUM OF TWENTYFIVE CENTS I'LL LET YOU IN TH' UNION!
I HAVE ONLY FIFTEEN CENTS
TUBBY!
YOU C'N OWE ME TH' REST

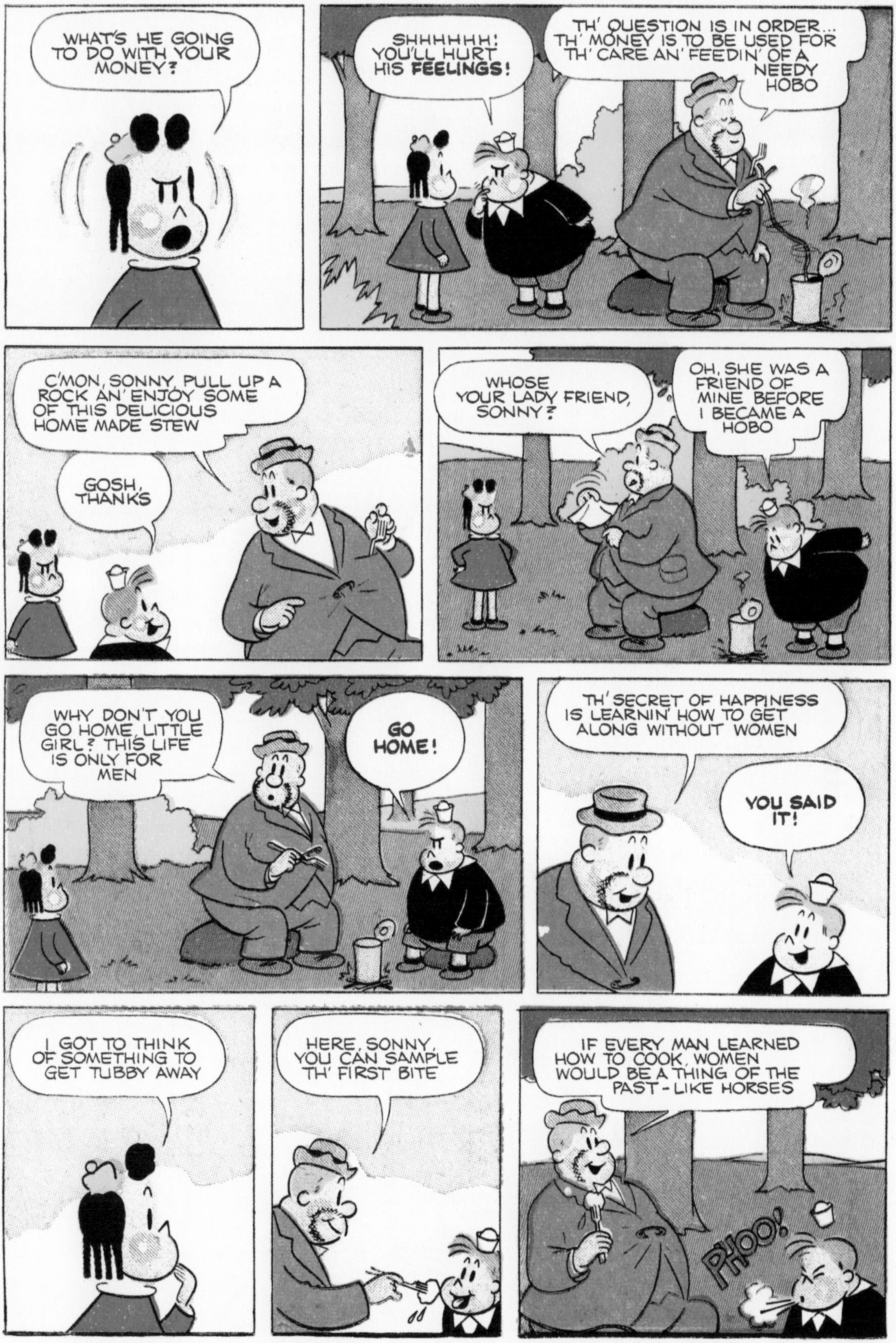
WHAT'S HE GOING TO DO WITH YOUR MONEY?
SHHHHHH! YOU'LL HURT HIS FEELINGS!
TH' QUESTION IS IN ORDER... TH' MONEY IS TO BE USED FOR TH' CARE AN' FEEDIN' OF A NEEDY HOBO
C'MON, SONNY, PULL UP A ROCK AN' ENJOY SOME OF THIS DELICIOUS HOME MADE STEW
GOSH, THANKS
WHOSE YOUR LADY FRIEND, SONNY?
OH, SHE WAS A FRIEND OF MINE BEFORE I BECAME A HOBO
WHY DON'T YOU GO HOME, LITTLE GIRL? THIS LIFE IS ONLY FOR MEN
GO HOME!
TH' SECRET OF HAPPINESS IS LEARNIN' HOW TO GET ALONG WITHOUT WOMEN
YOU SAID IT!
I GOT TO THINK OF SOMETHING TO GET TUBBY AWAY
HERE, SONNY, YOU CAN SAMPLE TH' FIRST BITE
IF EVERY MAN LEARNED HOW TO COOK, WOMEN WOULD BE A THING OF THE PAST - LIKE HORSES
PHOO!

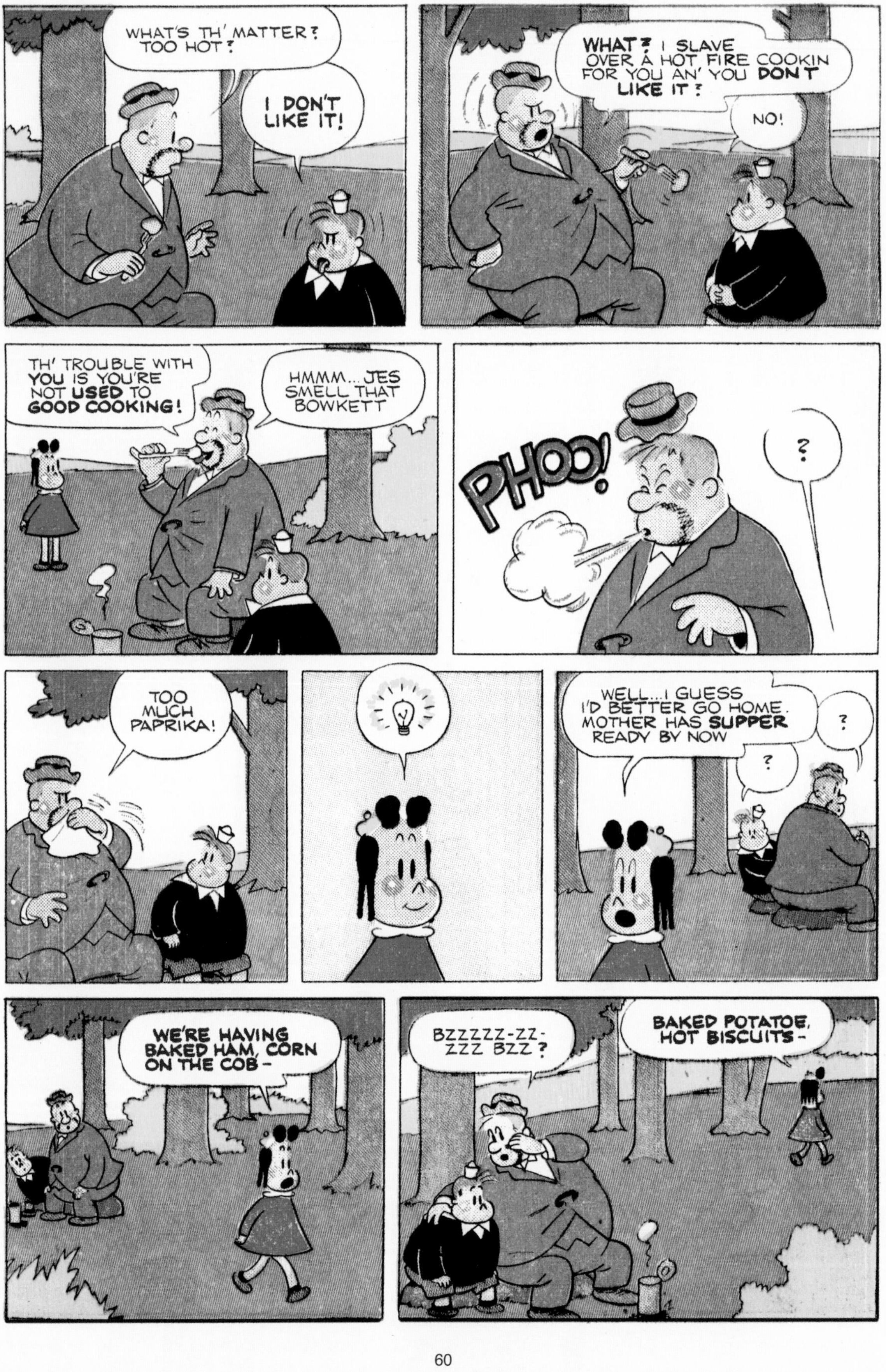
WHAT'S TH' MATTER? TOO HOT?
I DON'T LIKE IT!
WHAT? I SLAVE OVER A HOT FIRE COOKIN FOR YOU AN' YOU DON'T LIKE IT?
NO!
TH' TROUBLE WITH YOU IS YOU'RE NOT USED TO GOOD COOKING!
HMMM... JES SMELL THAT BOWKETT
PHOO!
?
TOO MUCH PAPRIKA!
WELL... I GUESS I'D BETTER GO HOME. MOTHER HAS SUPPER READY BY NOW
?
?
WE'RE HAVING BAKED HAM, CORN ON THE COB –
BZZZZZ-ZZ-ZZZ BZZ?
BAKED POTATOE, HOT BISCUITS –

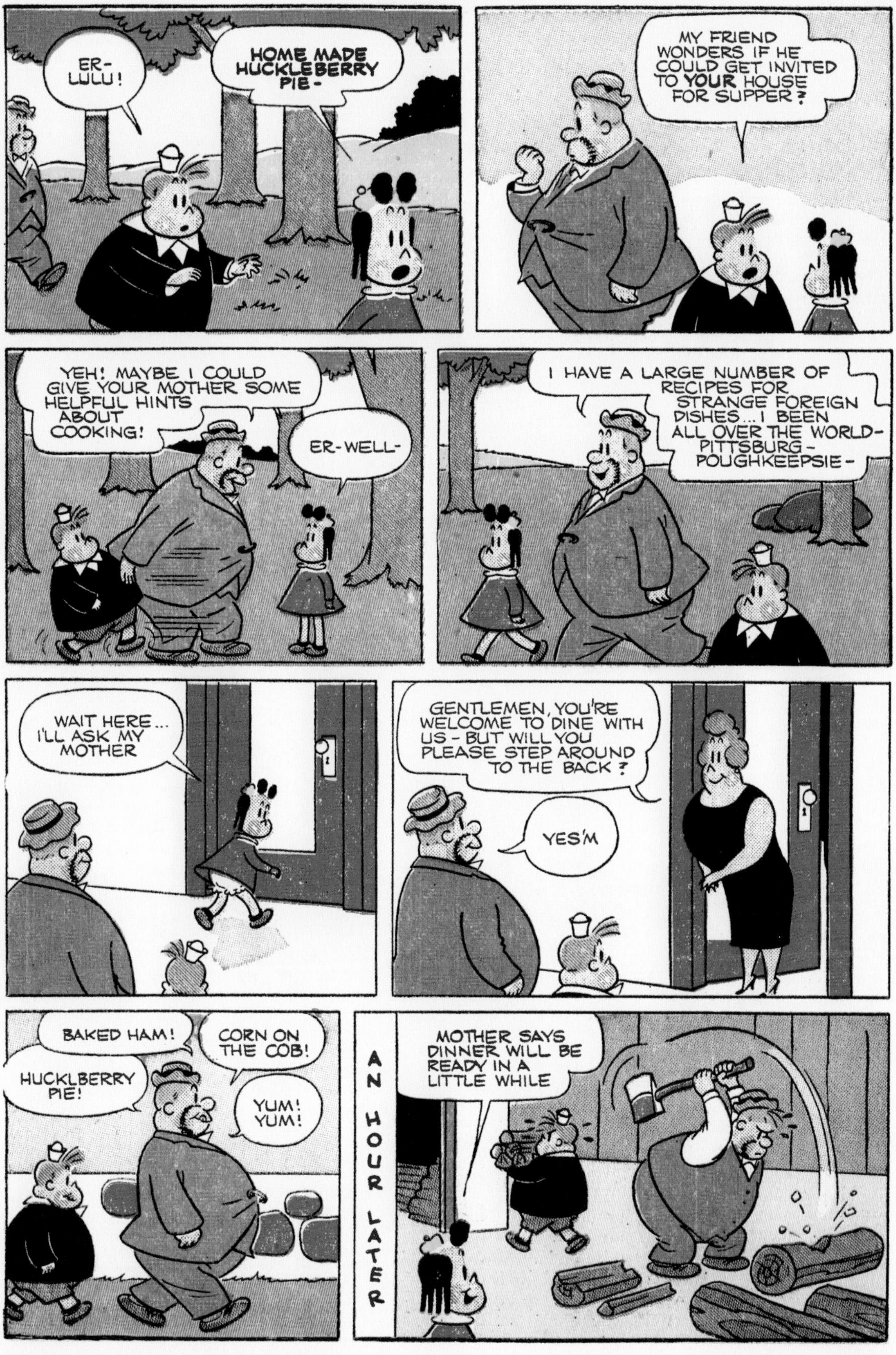
ER-LULU!
HOME MADE HUCKLEBERRY PIE-
MY FRIEND WONDERS IF HE COULD GET INVITED TO YOUR HOUSE FOR SUPPER?
YEH! MAYBE I COULD GIVE YOUR MOTHER SOME HELPFUL HINTS ABOUT COOKING!
ER-WELL-
I HAVE A LARGE NUMBER OF RECIPES FOR STRANGE FOREIGN DISHES... I BEEN ALL OVER THE WORLD-PITTSBURG-POUGHKEEPSIE-
WAIT HERE... I'LL ASK MY MOTHER
GENTLEMEN, YOU'RE WELCOME TO DINE WITH US - BUT WILL YOU PLEASE STEP AROUND TO THE BACK?
YES'M
BAKED HAM!
HUCKLBERRY PIE!
CORN ON THE COB!
YUM! YUM!
AN HOUR LATER
MOTHER SAYS DINNER WILL BE READY IN A LITTLE WHILE

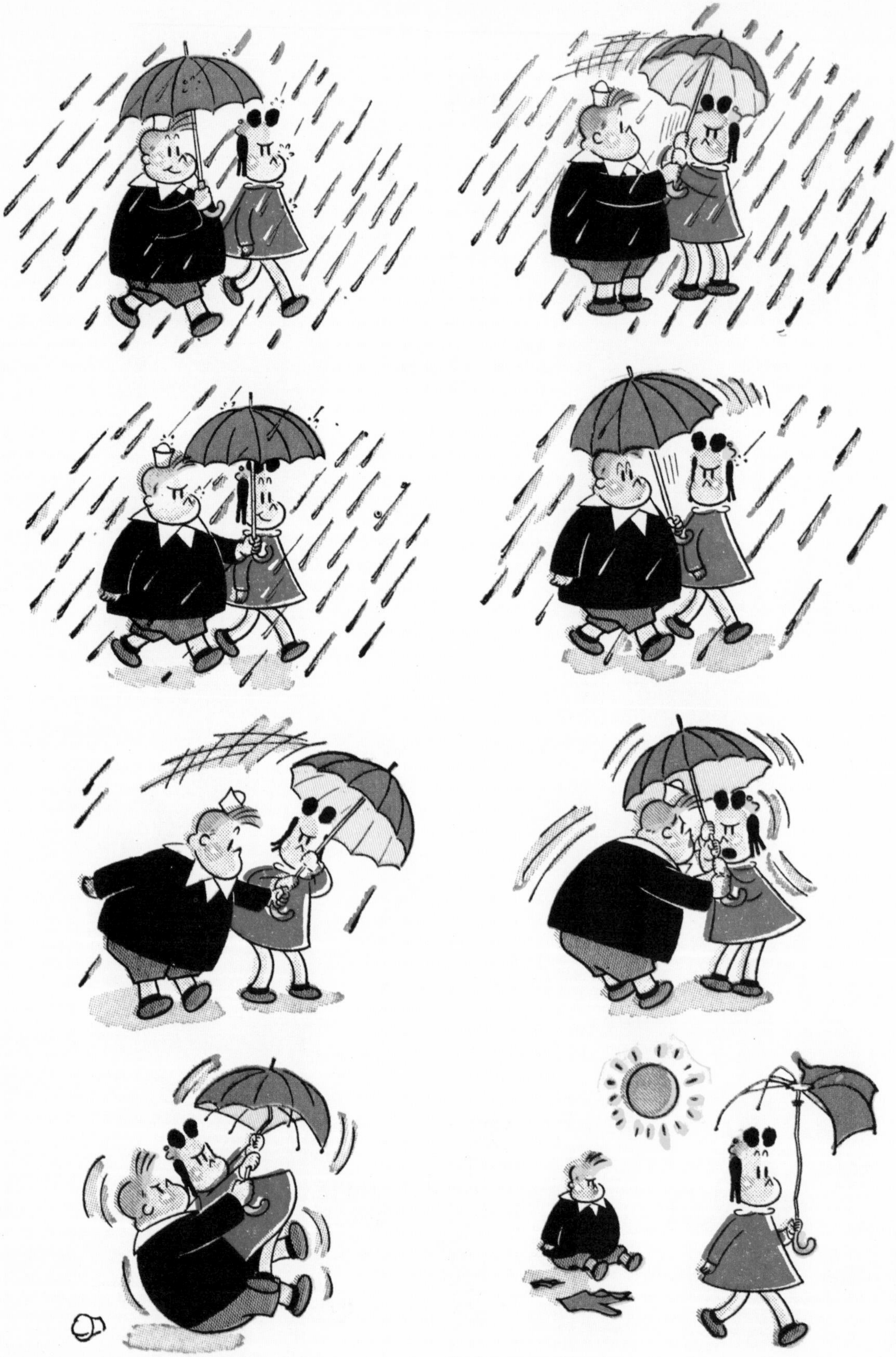

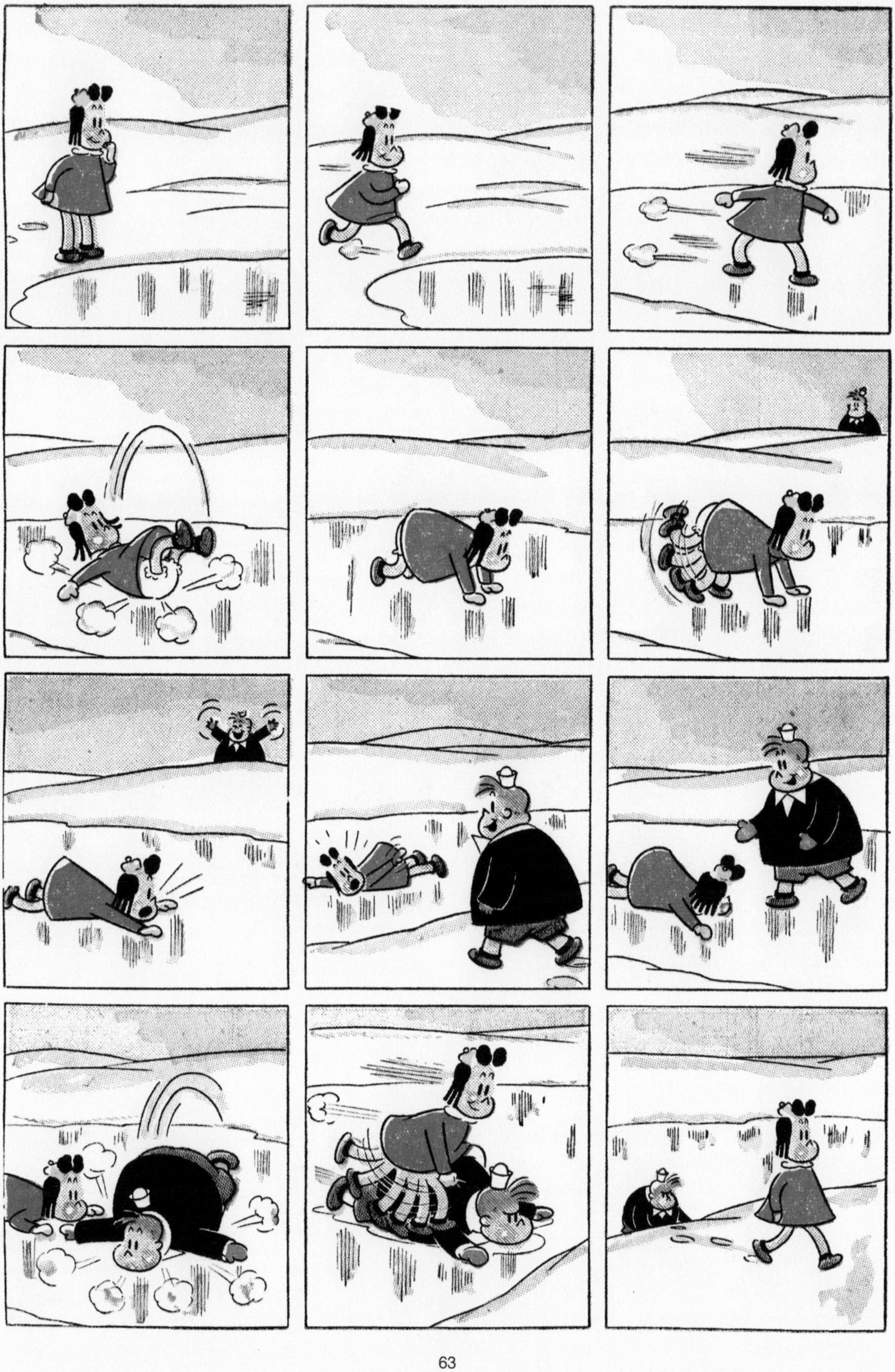

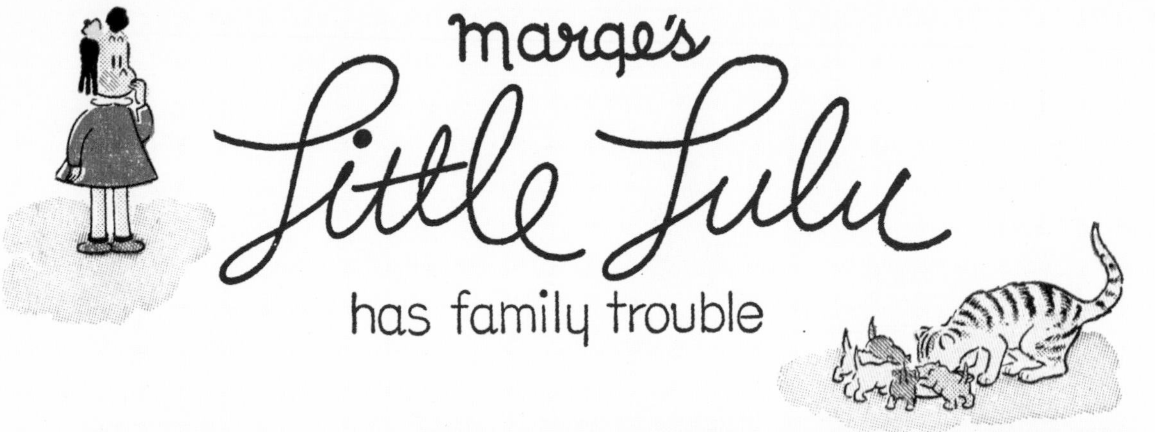
marge's
Little Lulu
has family trouble

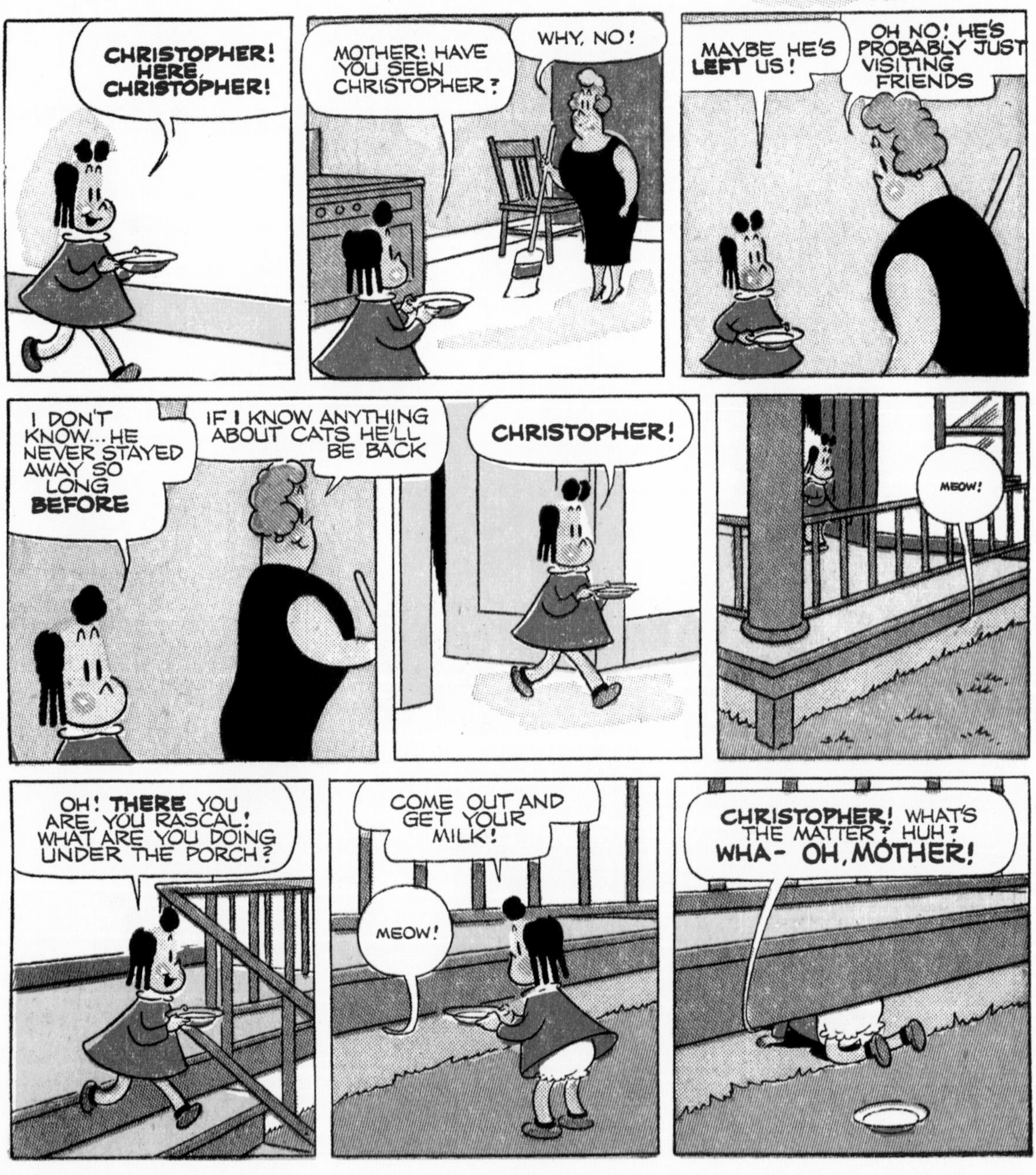
CHRISTOPHER! HERE, CHRISTOPHER!
MOTHER! HAVE YOU SEEN CHRISTOPHER?
WHY, NO!
MAYBE HE'S LEFT US!
OH NO! HE'S PROBABLY JUST VISITING FRIENDS
I DON'T KNOW... HE NEVER STAYED AWAY SO LONG BEFORE
IF I KNOW ANYTHING ABOUT CATS HE'LL BE BACK
CHRISTOPHER!
MEOW!
OH! THERE YOU ARE, YOU RASCAL! WHAT ARE YOU DOING UNDER THE PORCH?
COME OUT AND GET YOUR MILK!
MEOW!
CHRISTOPHER! WHAT'S THE MATTER? HUH? WHA- OH, MOTHER!

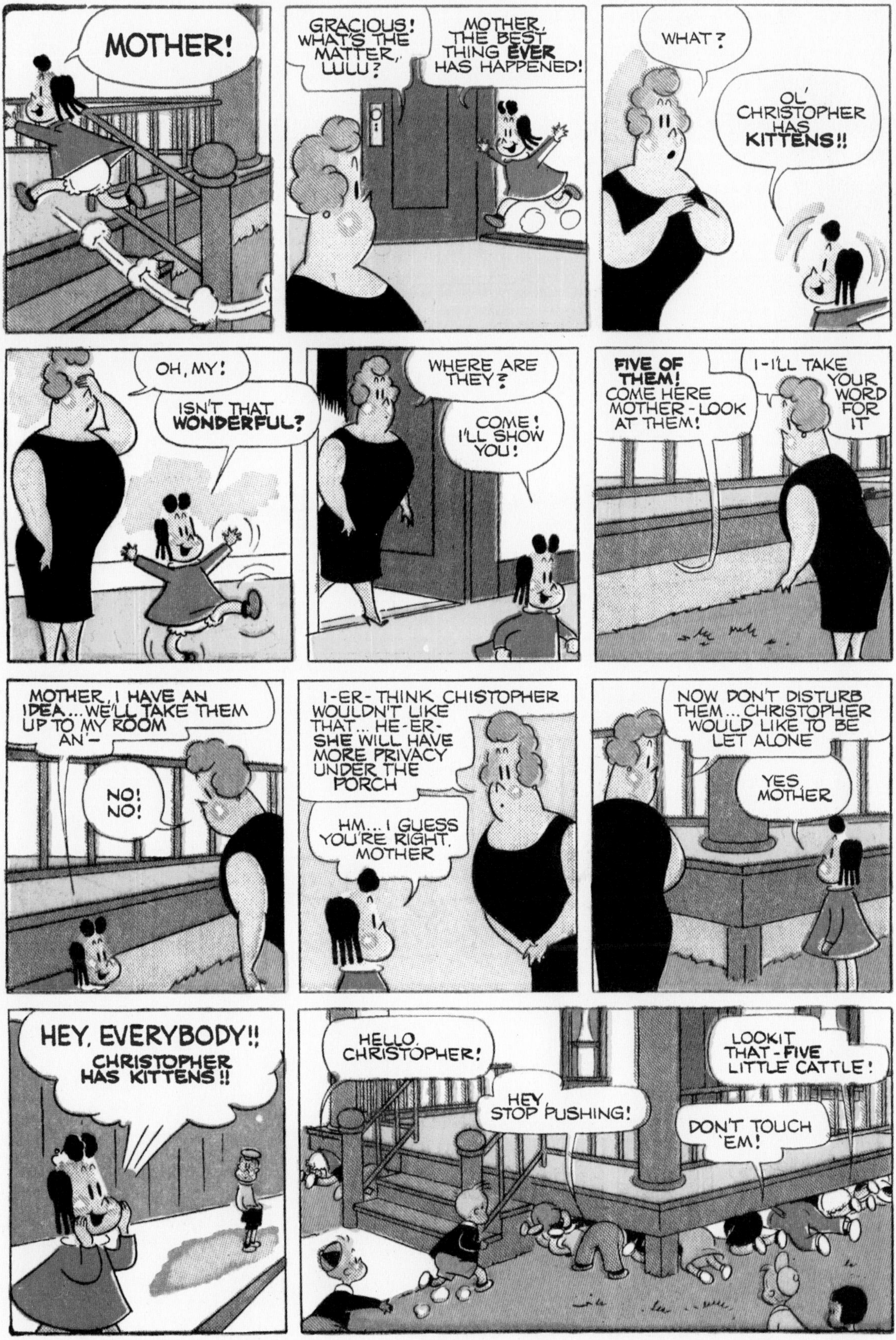
MOTHER!
GRACIOUS! WHAT'S THE MATTER, LULU?
MOTHER, THE BEST THING EVER HAS HAPPENED!
WHAT?
OL' CHRISTOPHER HAS KITTENS!!
OH, MY!
ISN'T THAT WONDERFUL?
WHERE ARE THEY?
COME! I'LL SHOW YOU!
FIVE OF THEM! COME HERE MOTHER - LOOK AT THEM!
I-I'LL TAKE YOUR WORD FOR IT
MOTHER, I HAVE AN IDEA... WE'LL TAKE THEM UP TO MY ROOM AN'—
NO! NO!
I-ER-THINK CHISTOPHER WOULDN'T LIKE THAT... HE-ER-SHE WILL HAVE MORE PRIVACY UNDER THE PORCH
HM... I GUESS YOU'RE RIGHT, MOTHER
NOW DON'T DISTURB THEM... CHRISTOPHER WOULD LIKE TO BE LET ALONE
YES, MOTHER
HEY, EVERYBODY!! CHRISTOPHER HAS KITTENS!!
HELLO, CHRISTOPHER!
HEY, STOP PUSHING!
LOOKIT THAT - FIVE LITTLE CATTLE!
DON'T TOUCH 'EM!

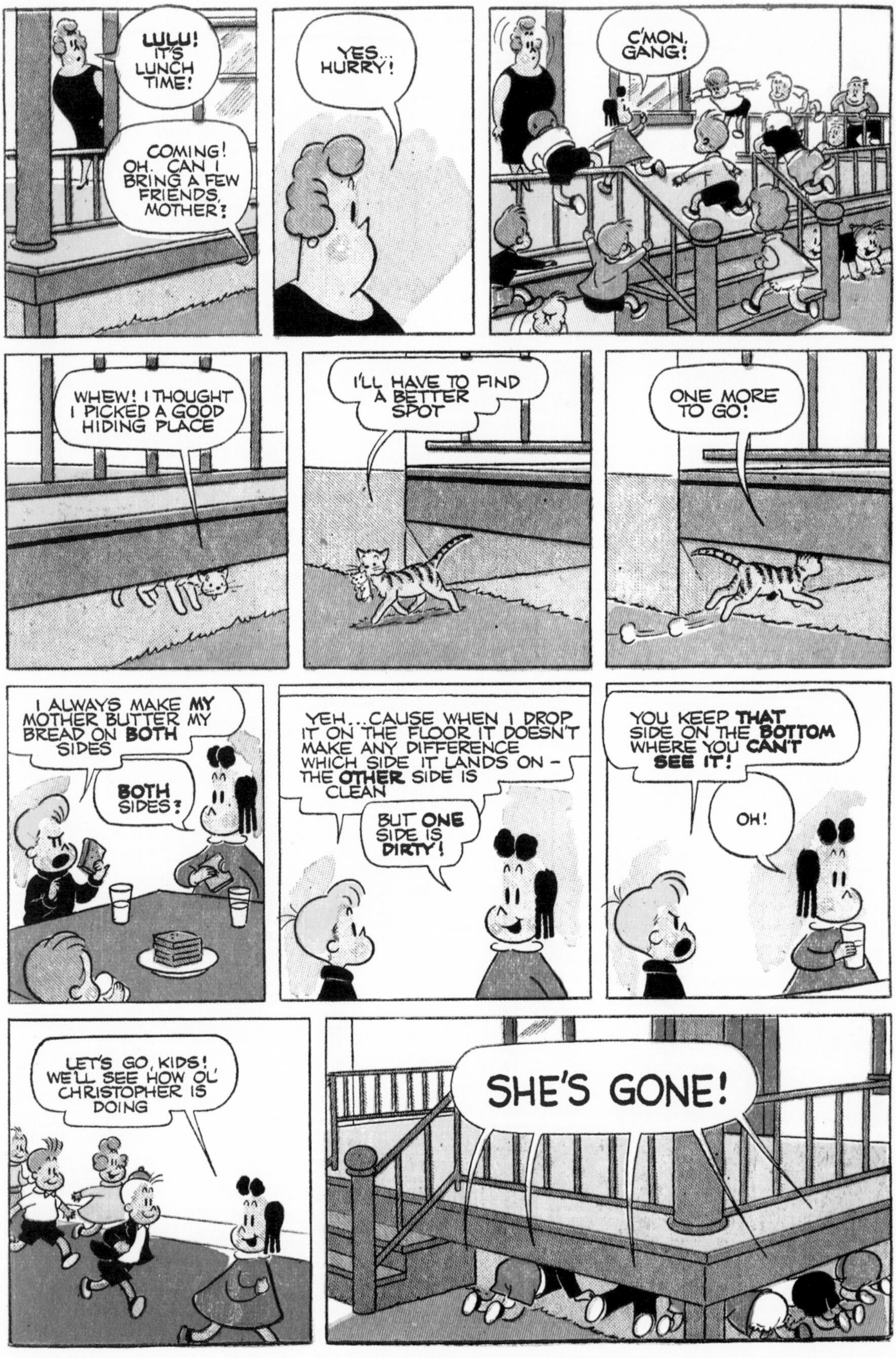
LULU! IT'S LUNCH TIME!
COMING! OH. CAN I BRING A FEW FRIENDS, MOTHER?
YES... HURRY!
C'MON, GANG!
WHEW! I THOUGHT I PICKED A GOOD HIDING PLACE
I'LL HAVE TO FIND A BETTER SPOT
ONE MORE TO GO!
I ALWAYS MAKE MY MOTHER BUTTER MY BREAD ON BOTH SIDES
BOTH SIDES?
YEH...CAUSE WHEN I DROP IT ON THE FLOOR IT DOESN'T MAKE ANY DIFFERENCE WHICH SIDE IT LANDS ON – THE OTHER SIDE IS CLEAN
BUT ONE SIDE IS DIRTY!
YOU KEEP THAT SIDE ON THE BOTTOM WHERE YOU CAN'T SEE IT!
OH!
LET'S GO, KIDS! WE'LL SEE HOW OL' CHRISTOPHER IS DOING
SHE'S GONE!

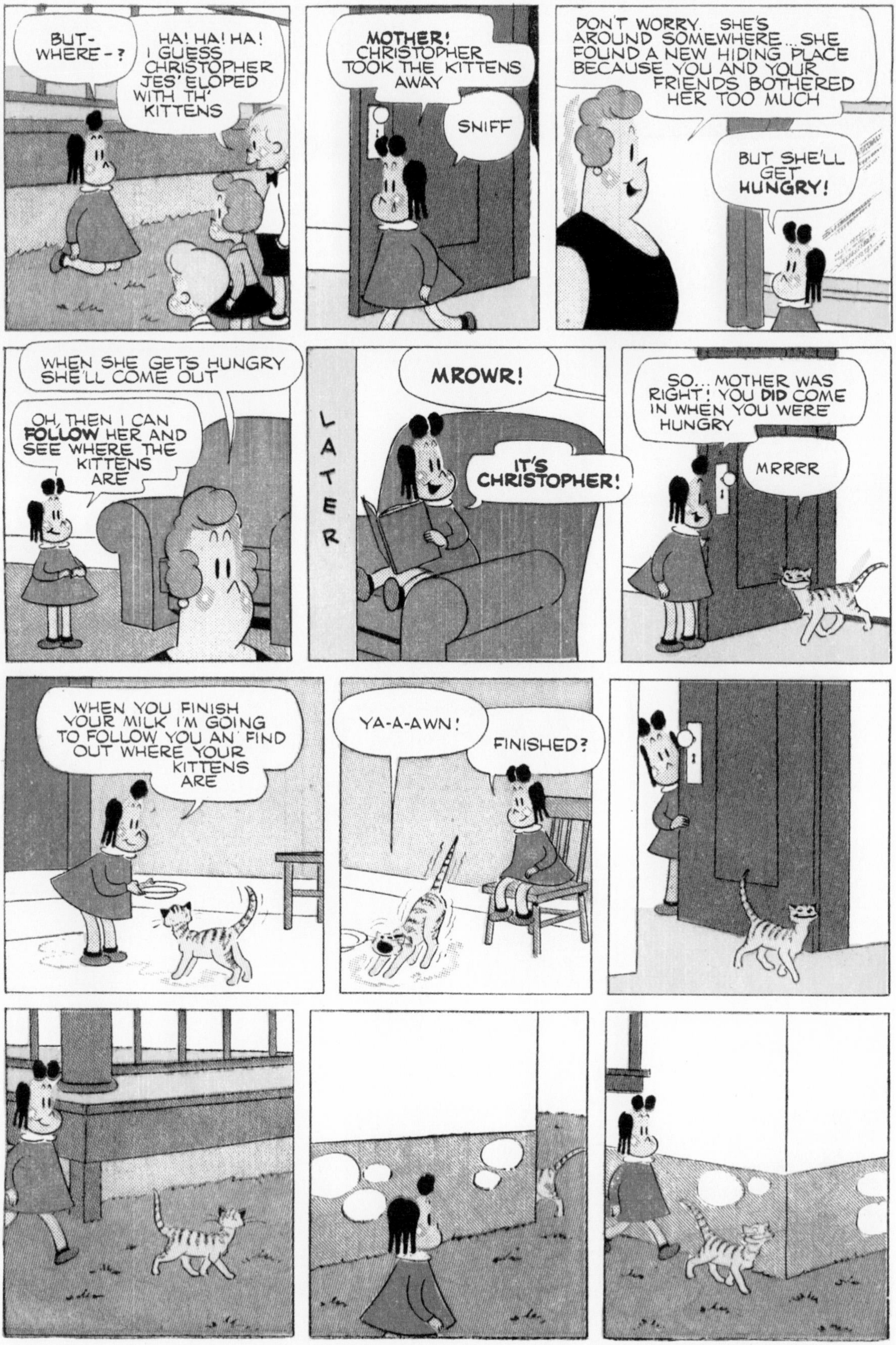
BUT- WHERE - ?
HA! HA! HA! I GUESS CHRISTOPHER JES' ELOPED WITH TH' KITTENS
MOTHER! CHRISTOPHER TOOK THE KITTENS AWAY
SNIFF
DON'T WORRY. SHE'S AROUND SOMEWHERE... SHE FOUND A NEW HIDING PLACE BECAUSE YOU AND YOUR FRIENDS BOTHERED HER TOO MUCH
BUT SHE'LL GET **HUNGRY!**
WHEN SHE GETS HUNGRY SHE'LL COME OUT
OH, THEN I CAN **FOLLOW** HER AND SEE WHERE THE KITTENS ARE
LATER
MROWR!
IT'S CHRISTOPHER!
SO... MOTHER WAS RIGHT! YOU **DID** COME IN WHEN YOU WERE HUNGRY
MRRRR
WHEN YOU FINISH YOUR MILK I'M GOING TO FOLLOW YOU AN' FIND OUT WHERE YOUR KITTENS ARE
YA-A-AWN!
FINISHED?

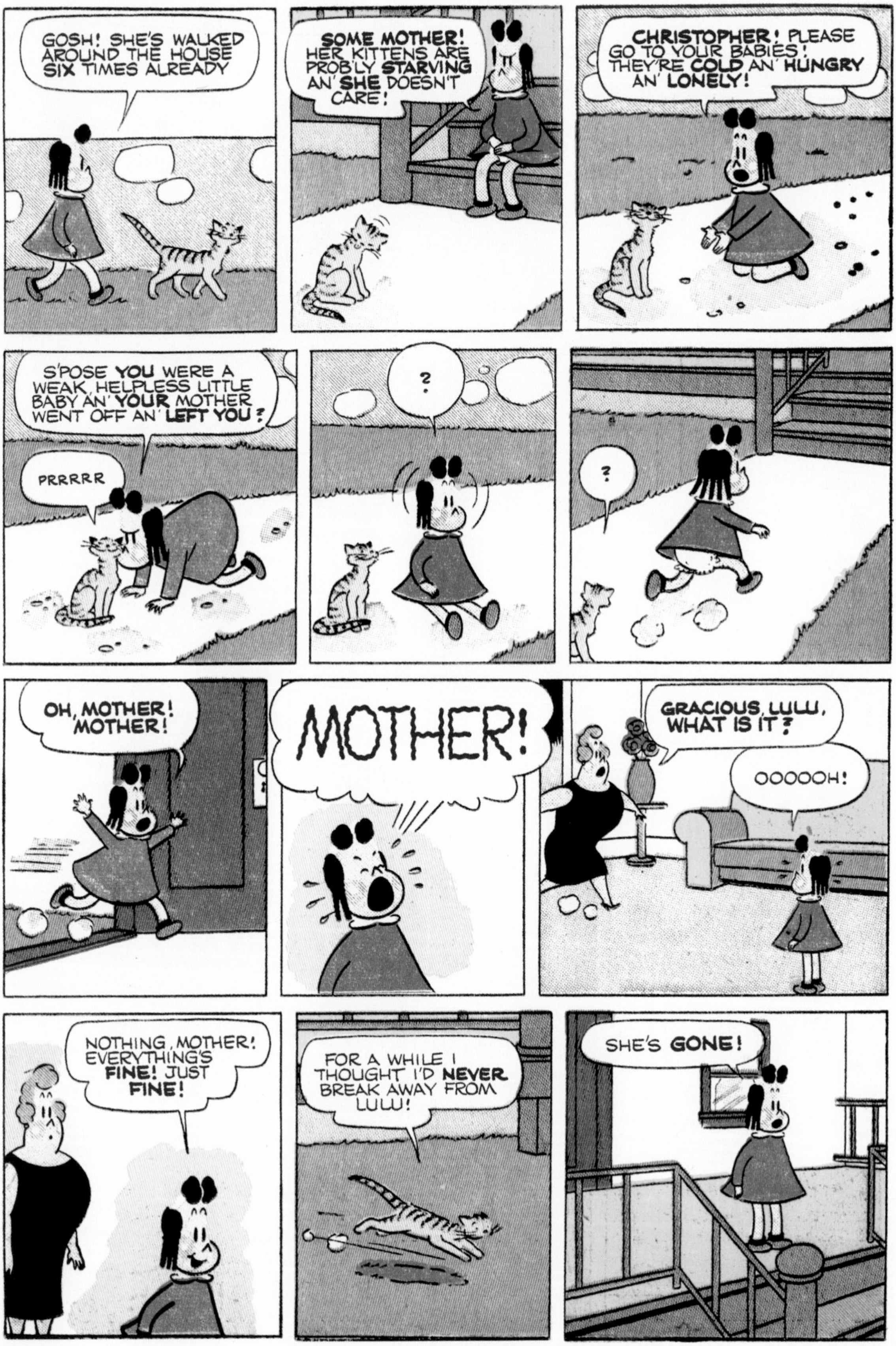

GOSH! SHE'S WALKED AROUND THE HOUSE SIX TIMES ALREADY
SOME MOTHER! HER KITTENS ARE PROB'LY STARVING AN' SHE DOESN'T CARE!
CHRISTOPHER! PLEASE GO TO YOUR BABIES! THEY'RE COLD AN' HUNGRY AN' LONELY!
S'POSE YOU WERE A WEAK, HELPLESS LITTLE BABY AN' YOUR MOTHER WENT OFF AN' LEFT YOU?
PRRRRR
?
?
OH, MOTHER! MOTHER!
MOTHER!
GRACIOUS, LULU, WHAT IS IT?
OOOOOH!
NOTHING, MOTHER! EVERYTHING'S FINE! JUST FINE!
FOR A WHILE I THOUGHT I'D NEVER BREAK AWAY FROM LULU!
SHE'S GONE!

A FEW WEEKS GO BY AND **LULU** **STILL** HASN'T DISCOVERED WHERE CHRISTOPHER HAS HIDDEN HIS - ER - HER KITTENS

MEOWR!

IT'S CHRISTOPHER! I GUESS SHE'S HUNGRY

I SURE WOULD **LOVE** TO KNOW WHERE THOSE KITTENS ARE

I—

WOW!

MOTHER! LOOK!!

MOTHER! AREN'T THEY **BEAUTIFUL**?

FIVE OF THEM!

YES! DON'T YOU WISH IT WAS A **HUNDRED**?

ER - YOU KNOW YOU WILL HAVE TO START FINDING **HOMES** FOR THEM SOON

HOMES? WHY, THEY **HAVE** A HOME!

I - ER - I'M AFRAID WE **CAN'T** KEEP THEM! BUT THERE ARE OTHER PEOPLE WHO LIKE CATS TOO - AND YOU WILL HAVE TO BE GENEROUS AND GIVE THEM ONE

YOU CAN KEEP ONE FOR YOURSELF

B - BUT I'LL **NEVER** BE ABLE TO LOOK CHRISTOPHER IN THE FACE AGAIN!

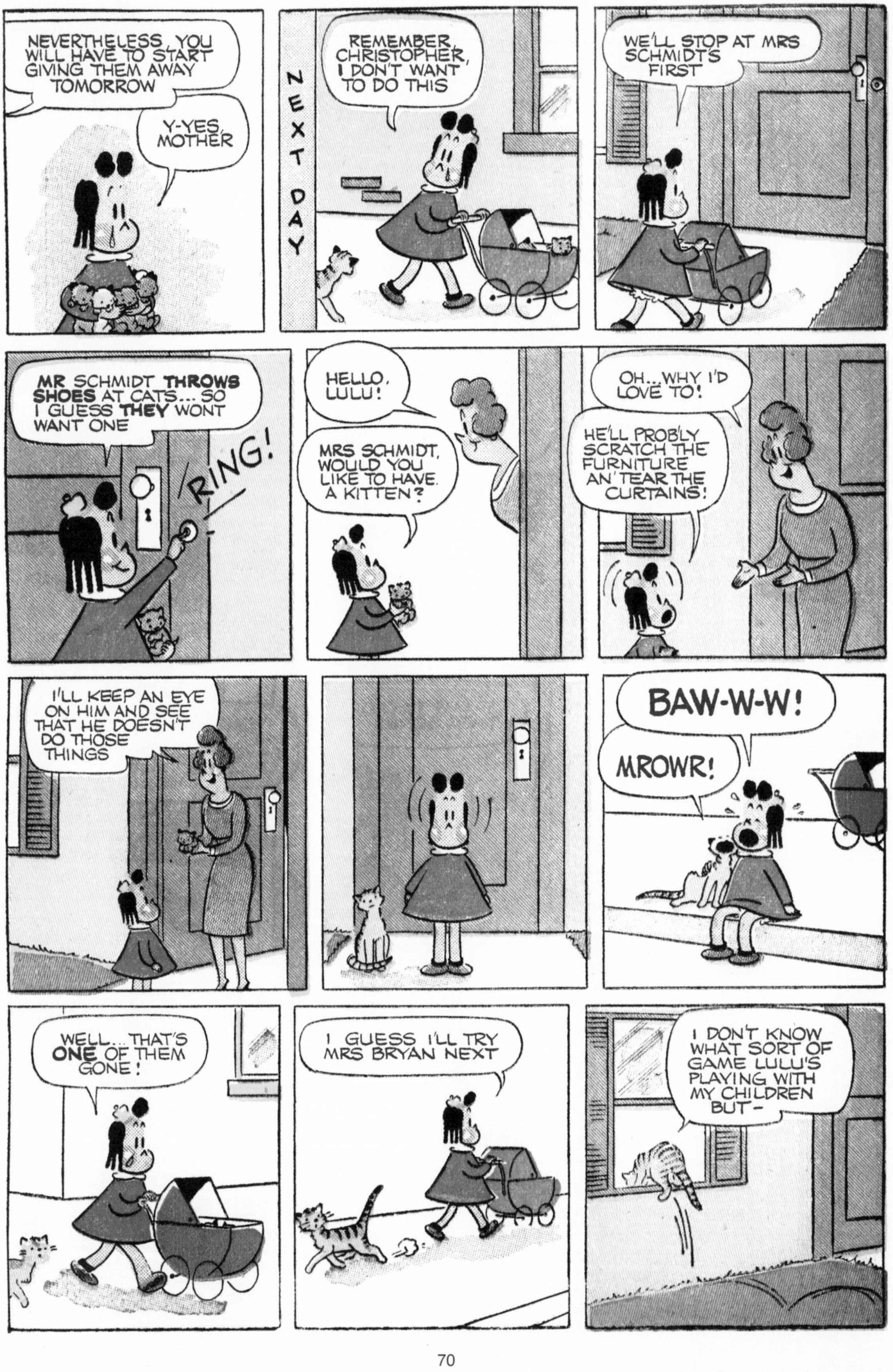
NEVERTHELESS, YOU WILL HAVE TO START GIVING THEM AWAY TOMORROW
Y-YES, MOTHER
NEXT DAY
REMEMBER, CHRISTOPHER, I DON'T WANT TO DO THIS
WE'LL STOP AT MRS SCHMIDT'S FIRST
MR SCHMIDT THROWS SHOES AT CATS... SO I GUESS THEY WONT WANT ONE
RING!
HELLO, LULU!
MRS SCHMIDT, WOULD YOU LIKE TO HAVE A KITTEN?
OH... WHY I'D LOVE TO!
HE'LL PROB'LY SCRATCH THE FURNITURE AN' TEAR THE CURTAINS!
I'LL KEEP AN EYE ON HIM AND SEE THAT HE DOESN'T DO THOSE THINGS
BAW-W-W!
MROWR!
WELL... THAT'S ONE OF THEM GONE!
I GUESS I'LL TRY MRS BRYAN NEXT
I DON'T KNOW WHAT SORT OF GAME LULU'S PLAYING WITH MY CHILDREN BUT–

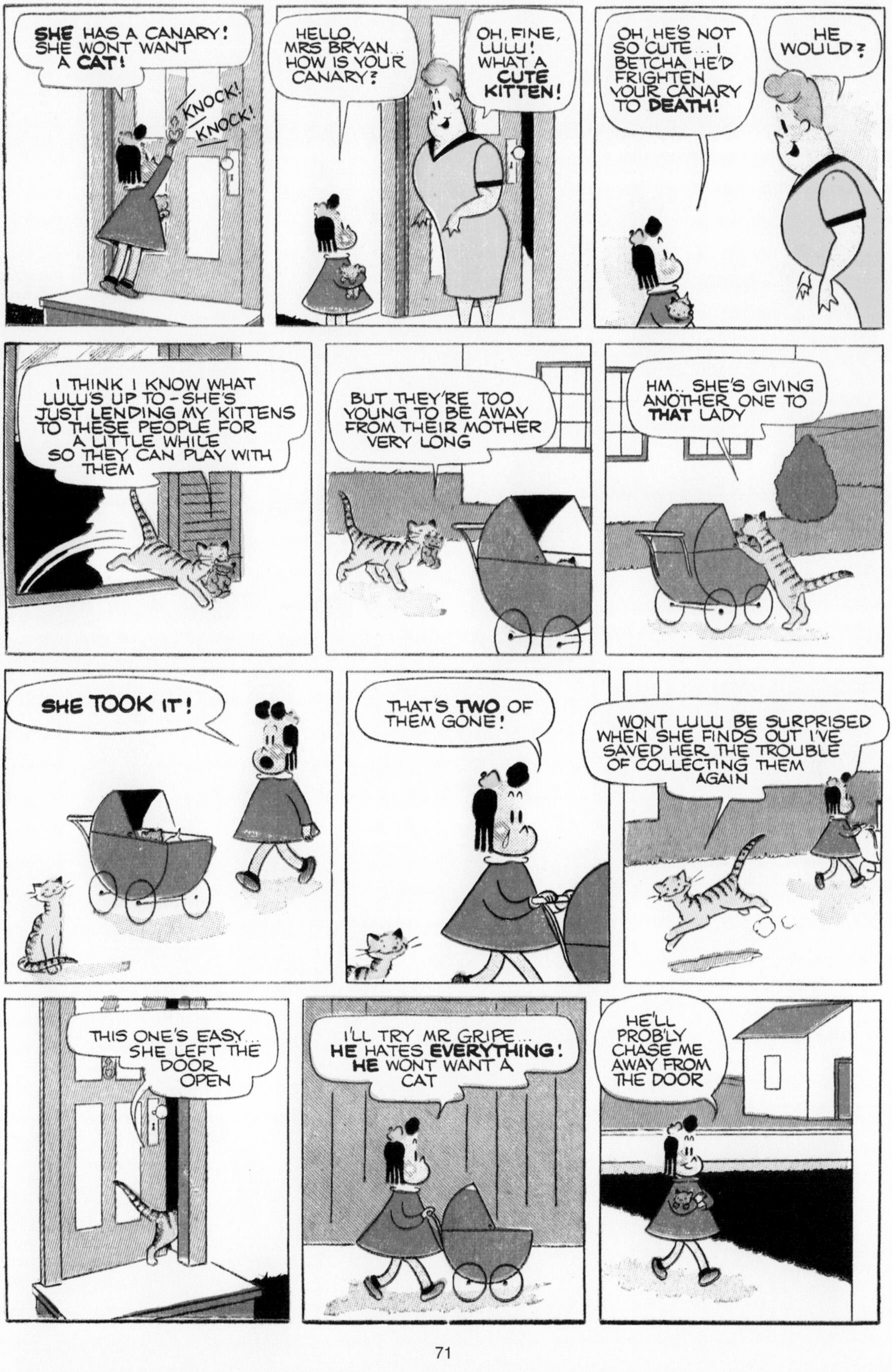

SHE HAS A CANARY! SHE WONT WANT A CAT!
KNOCK! KNOCK!
HELLO, MRS BRYAN... HOW IS YOUR CANARY?
OH, FINE, LULU! WHAT A CUTE KITTEN!
OH, HE'S NOT SO CUTE... I BETCHA HE'D FRIGHTEN YOUR CANARY TO DEATH!
HE WOULD?
I THINK I KNOW WHAT LULU'S UP TO - SHE'S JUST LENDING MY KITTENS TO THESE PEOPLE FOR A LITTLE WHILE SO THEY CAN PLAY WITH THEM
BUT THEY'RE TOO YOUNG TO BE AWAY FROM THEIR MOTHER VERY LONG
HM.. SHE'S GIVING ANOTHER ONE TO THAT LADY
SHE TOOK IT!
THAT'S TWO OF THEM GONE!
WONT LULU BE SURPRISED WHEN SHE FINDS OUT I'VE SAVED HER THE TROUBLE OF COLLECTING THEM AGAIN
THIS ONE'S EASY... SHE LEFT THE DOOR OPEN
I'LL TRY MR GRIPE... HE HATES EVERYTHING! HE WONT WANT A CAT
HE'LL PROB'LY CHASE ME AWAY FROM THE DOOR

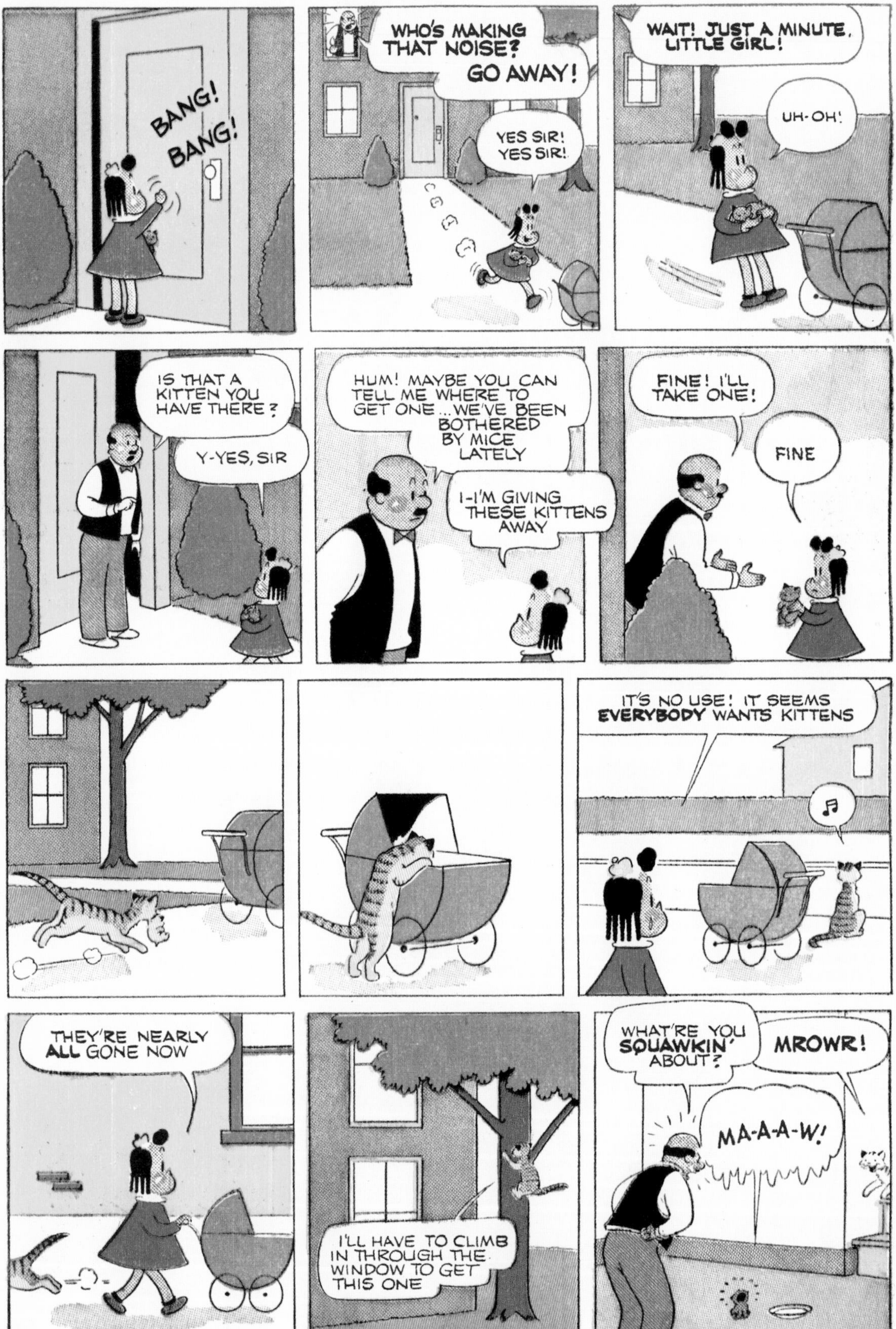
BANG!
BANG!
WHO'S MAKING THAT NOISE?
GO AWAY!
YES SIR! YES SIR!
WAIT! JUST A MINUTE, LITTLE GIRL!
UH-OH!
IS THAT A KITTEN YOU HAVE THERE?
Y-YES, SIR
HUM! MAYBE YOU CAN TELL ME WHERE TO GET ONE ... WE'VE BEEN BOTHERED BY MICE LATELY
I-I'M GIVING THESE KITTENS AWAY
FINE! I'LL TAKE ONE!
FINE
IT'S NO USE! IT SEEMS EVERYBODY WANTS KITTENS
THEY'RE NEARLY ALL GONE NOW
I'LL HAVE TO CLIMB IN THROUGH THE WINDOW TO GET THIS ONE
WHAT'RE YOU SQUAWKIN' ABOUT?
MROWR!
MA-A-A-W!

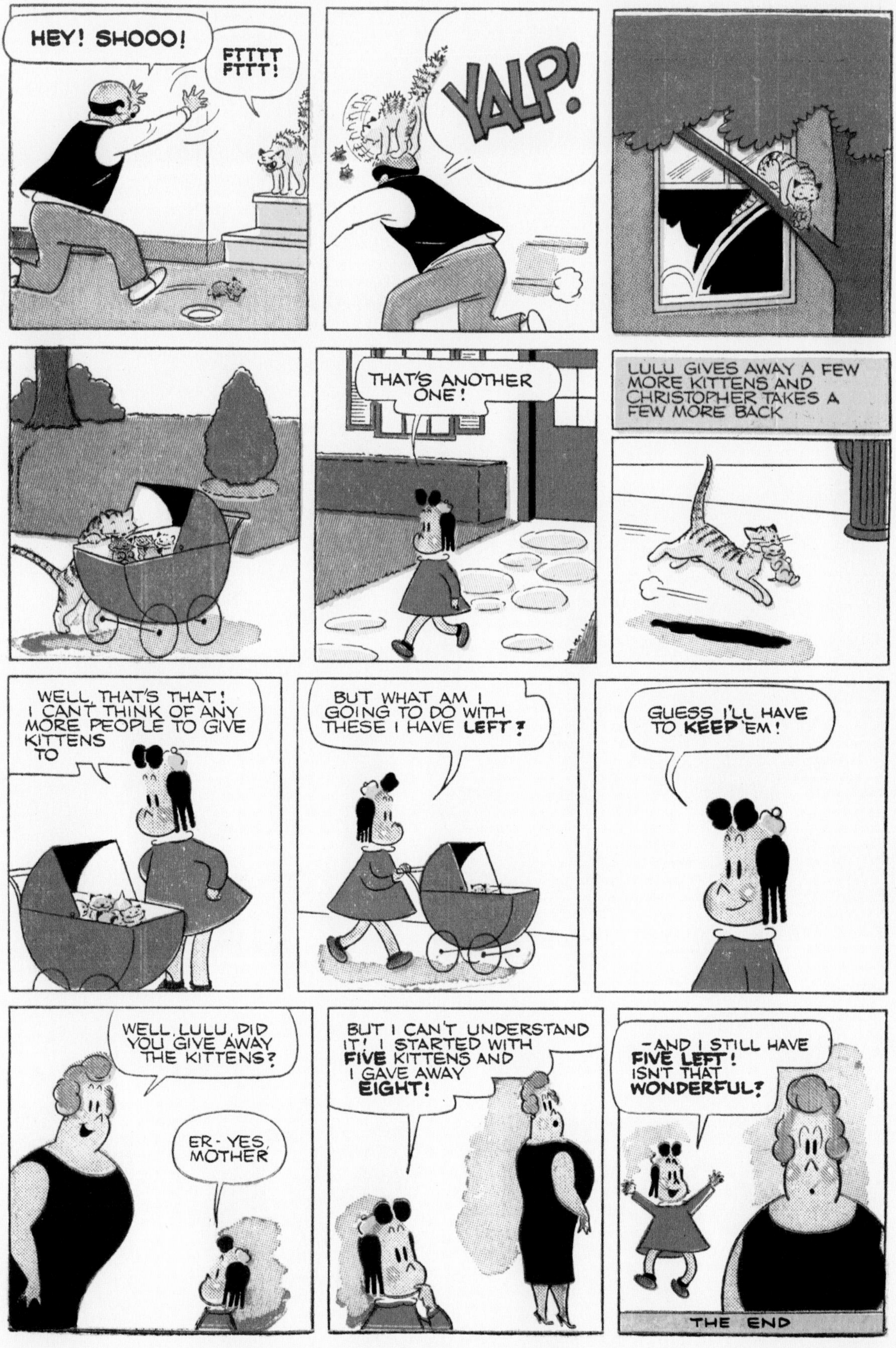
HEY! SHOOO!
FTTTT FTTT!
YALP!
THAT'S ANOTHER ONE!
LULU GIVES AWAY A FEW MORE KITTENS AND CHRISTOPHER TAKES A FEW MORE BACK
WELL, THAT'S THAT! I CAN'T THINK OF ANY MORE PEOPLE TO GIVE KITTENS TO
BUT WHAT AM I GOING TO DO WITH THESE I HAVE LEFT?
GUESS I'LL HAVE TO KEEP 'EM!
WELL, LULU, DID YOU GIVE AWAY THE KITTENS?
ER- YES, MOTHER
BUT I CAN'T UNDERSTAND IT! I STARTED WITH FIVE KITTENS AND I GAVE AWAY EIGHT!
-AND I STILL HAVE FIVE LEFT! ISN'T THAT WONDERFUL?
THE END

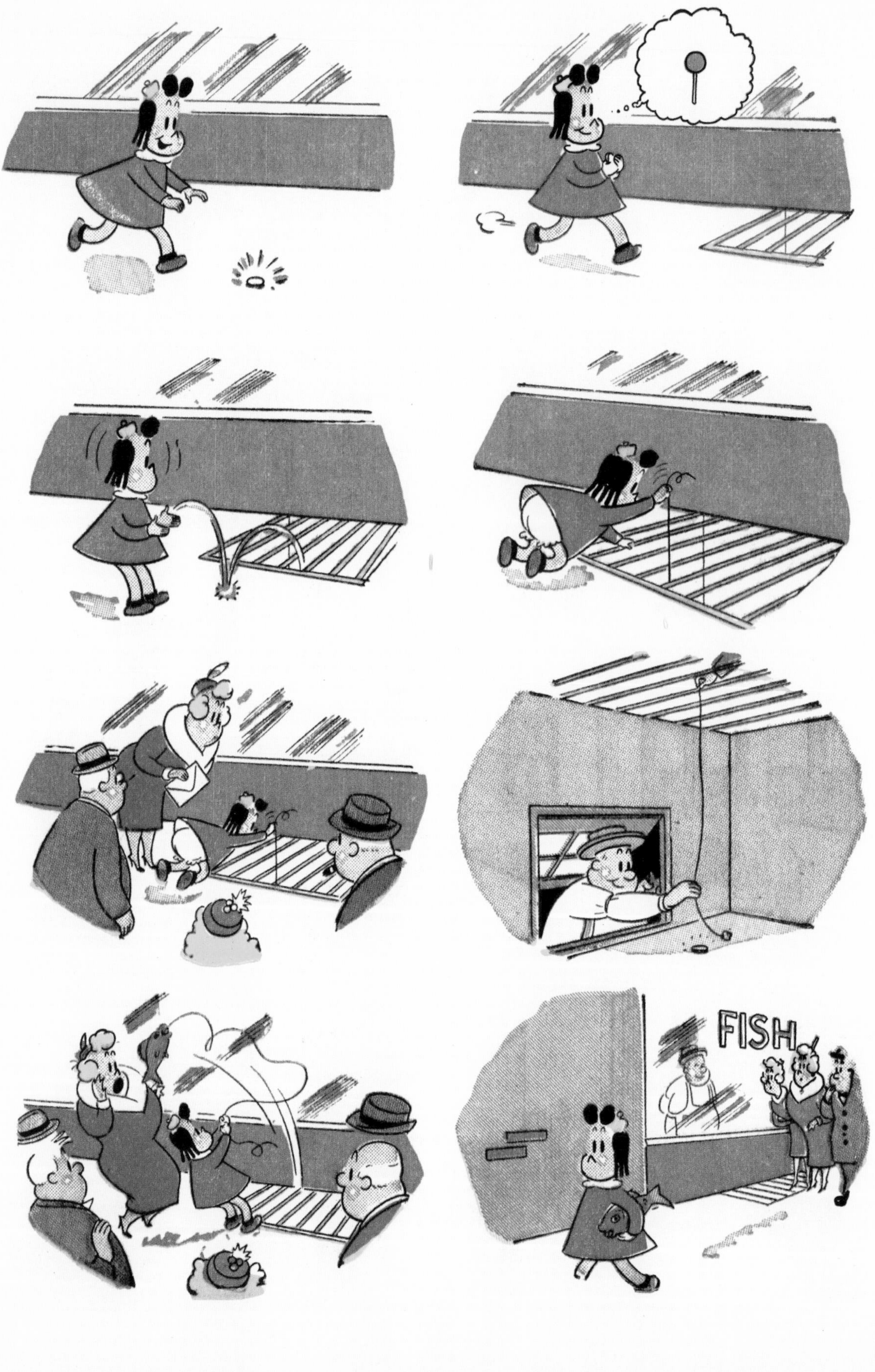
FISH

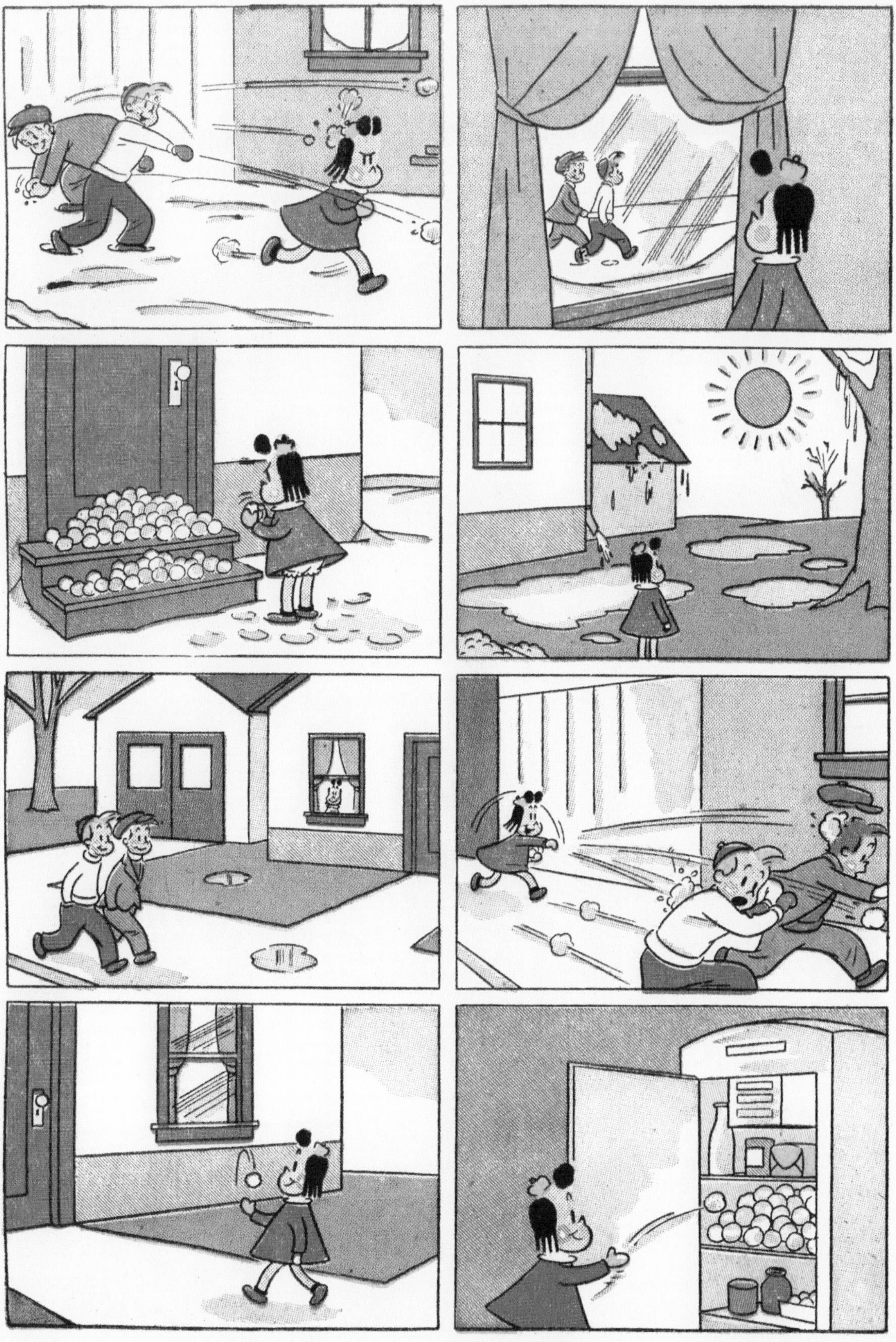

marge's LITTLE LULU

GOES ON A PICNIC

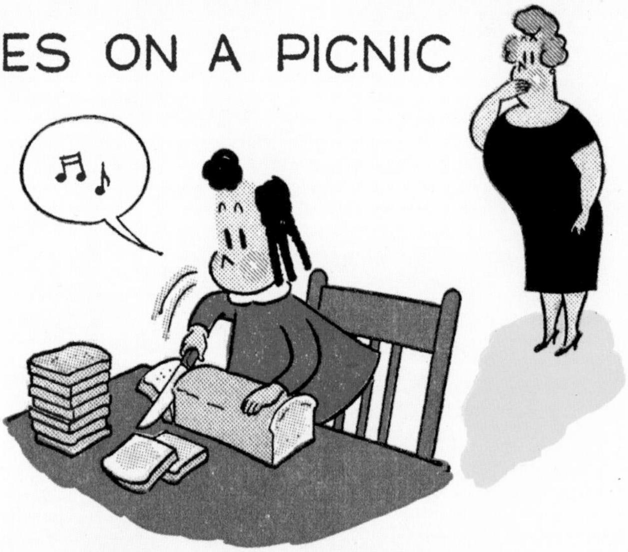

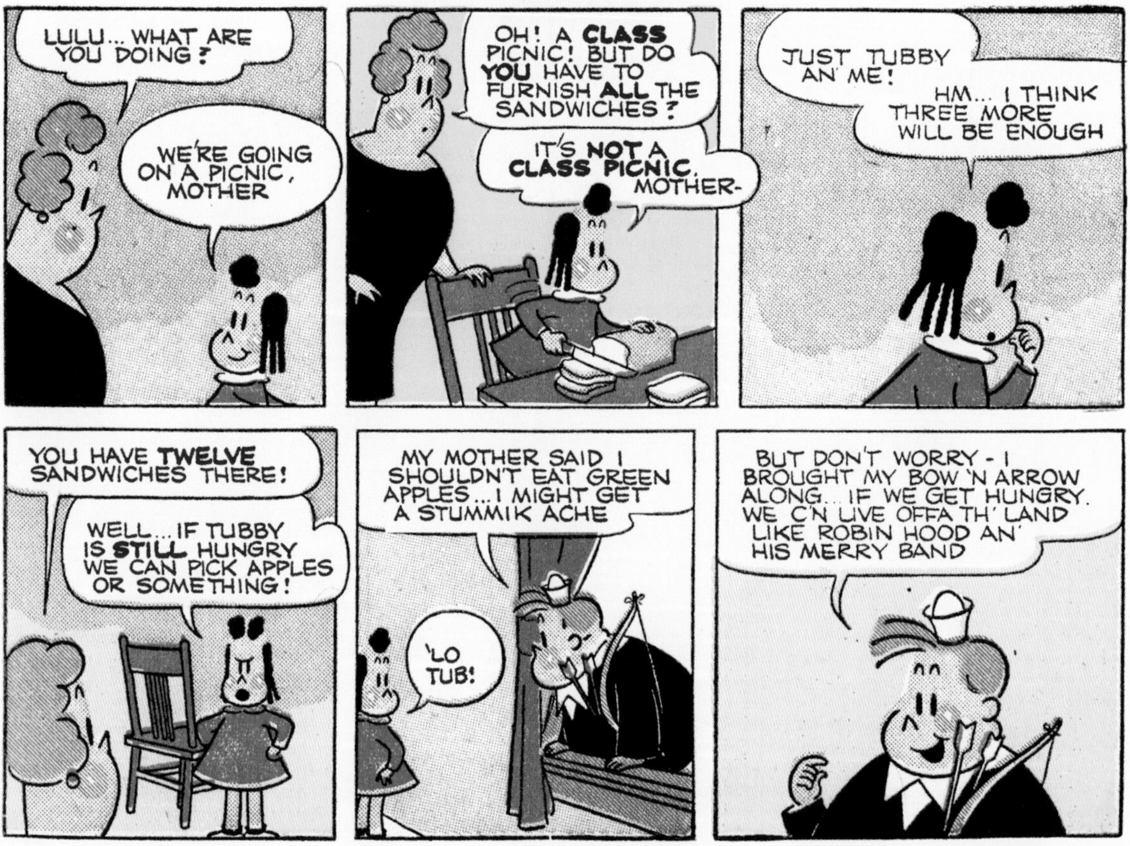

LULU... WHAT ARE YOU DOING?
WE'RE GOING ON A PICNIC, MOTHER
OH! A **CLASS** PICNIC! BUT DO **YOU** HAVE TO FURNISH **ALL** THE SANDWICHES?
IT'S **NOT** A **CLASS PICNIC**, MOTHER-
JUST TUBBY AN' ME!
HM... I THINK THREE MORE WILL BE ENOUGH
YOU HAVE **TWELVE** SANDWICHES THERE!
WELL... IF TUBBY IS **STILL** HUNGRY WE CAN PICK APPLES OR SOMETHING!
MY MOTHER SAID I SHOULDN'T EAT GREEN APPLES... I MIGHT GET A STUMMIK ACHE
'LO TUB!
BUT DON'T WORRY - I BROUGHT MY BOW 'N ARROW ALONG... IF WE GET HUNGRY, WE C'N LIVE OFFA TH' LAND LIKE ROBIN HOOD AN' HIS MERRY BAND

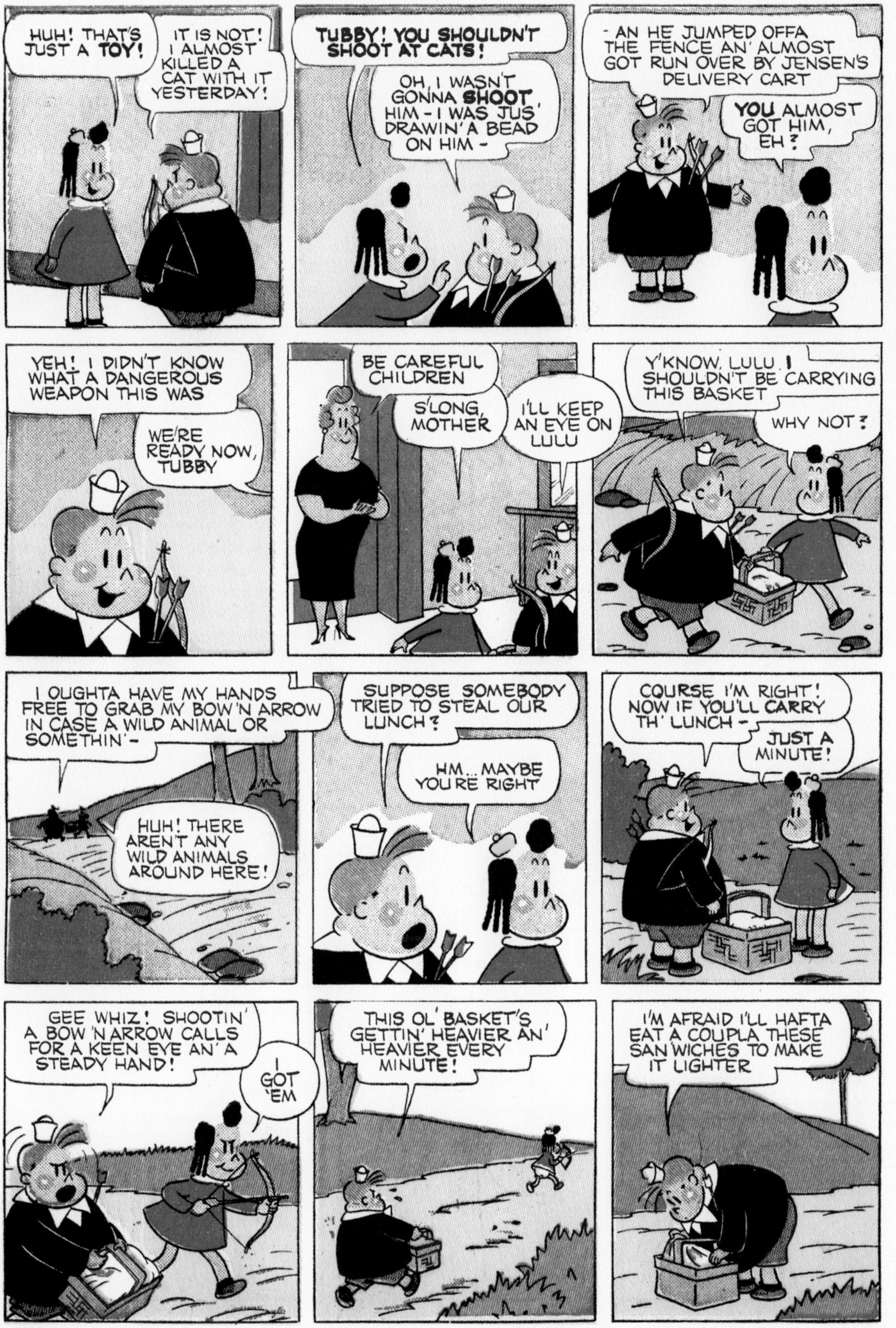

HUH! THAT'S JUST A TOY!
IT IS NOT! I ALMOST KILLED A CAT WITH IT YESTERDAY!
TUBBY! YOU SHOULDN'T SHOOT AT CATS!
OH, I WASN'T GONNA SHOOT HIM - I WAS JUS' DRAWIN' A BEAD ON HIM -
- AN HE JUMPED OFFA THE FENCE AN' ALMOST GOT RUN OVER BY JENSEN'S DELIVERY CART
YOU ALMOST GOT HIM, EH?
YEH! I DIDN'T KNOW WHAT A DANGEROUS WEAPON THIS WAS
WE'RE READY NOW, TUBBY
BE CAREFUL CHILDREN
S'LONG, MOTHER
I'LL KEEP AN EYE ON LULU
Y'KNOW, LULU, I SHOULDN'T BE CARRYING THIS BASKET
WHY NOT?
I OUGHTA HAVE MY HANDS FREE TO GRAB MY BOW 'N ARROW IN CASE A WILD ANIMAL OR SOMETHIN' -
HUH! THERE AREN'T ANY WILD ANIMALS AROUND HERE!
SUPPOSE SOMEBODY TRIED TO STEAL OUR LUNCH?
HM... MAYBE YOU'RE RIGHT
COURSE I'M RIGHT! NOW IF YOU'LL CARRY TH' LUNCH -
JUST A MINUTE!
GEE WHIZ! SHOOTIN' A BOW 'N ARROW CALLS FOR A KEEN EYE AN' A STEADY HAND!
I GOT 'EM
THIS OL' BASKET'S GETTIN' HEAVIER AN' HEAVIER EVERY MINUTE!
I'M AFRAID I'LL HAFTA EAT A COUPLA THESE SAN'WICHES TO MAKE IT LIGHTER

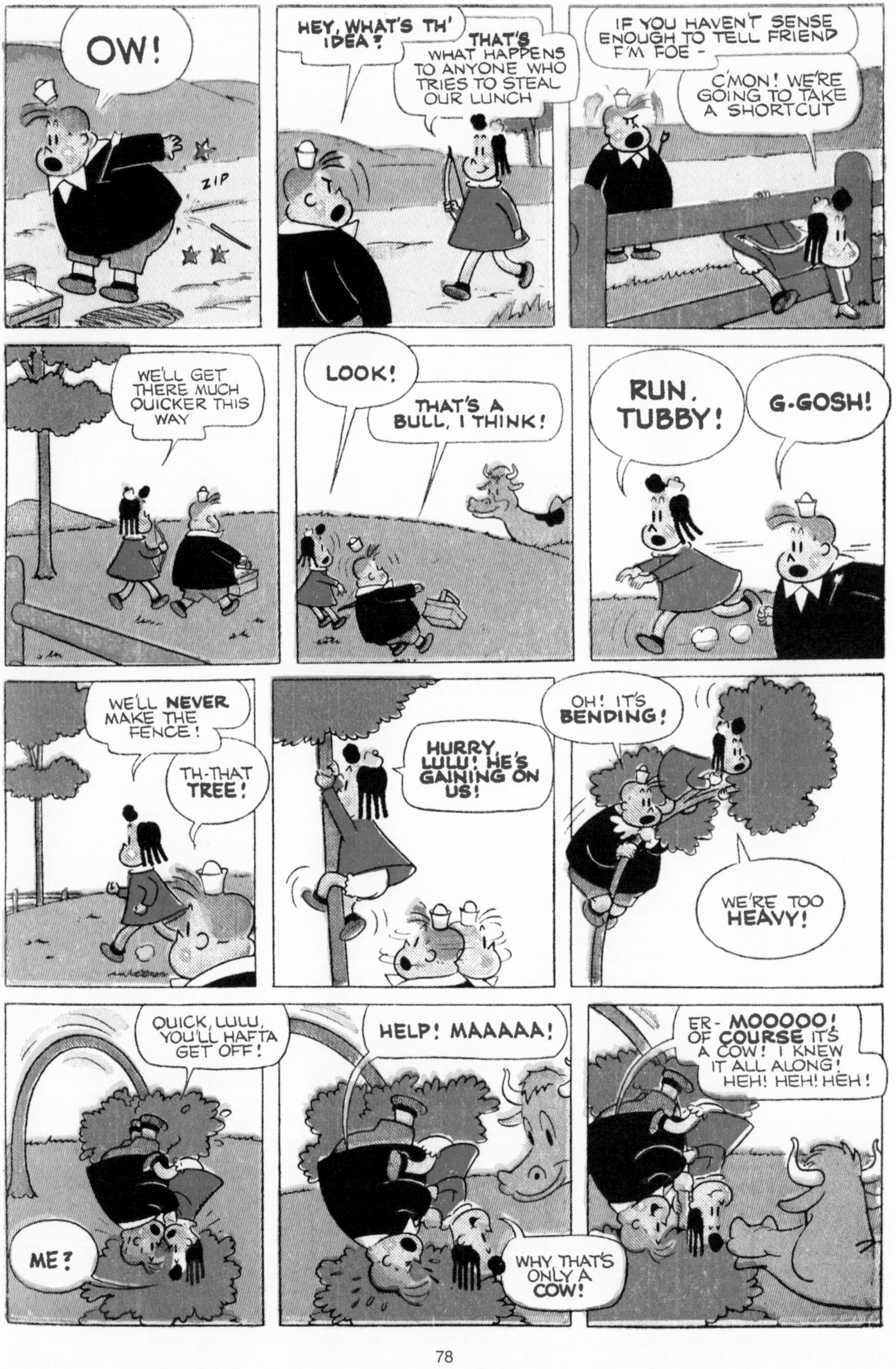

OW!
ZIP
HEY, WHAT'S TH' IDEA?
THAT'S WHAT HAPPENS TO ANYONE WHO TRIES TO STEAL OUR LUNCH
IF YOU HAVEN'T SENSE ENOUGH TO TELL FRIEND F'M FOE -
C'MON! WE'RE GOING TO TAKE A SHORTCUT
WE'LL GET THERE MUCH QUICKER THIS WAY
LOOK!
THAT'S A BULL, I THINK!
RUN, TUBBY!
G-GOSH!
WE'LL NEVER MAKE THE FENCE!
TH-THAT TREE!
HURRY, LULU! HE'S GAINING ON US!
OH! IT'S BENDING!
WE'RE TOO HEAVY!
QUICK, LULU, YOU'LL HAFTA GET OFF!
ME?
HELP! MAAAAA!
WHY THAT'S ONLY A COW!
ER- MOOOOO! OF COURSE IT'S A COW! I KNEW IT ALL ALONG! HEH! HEH! HEH!

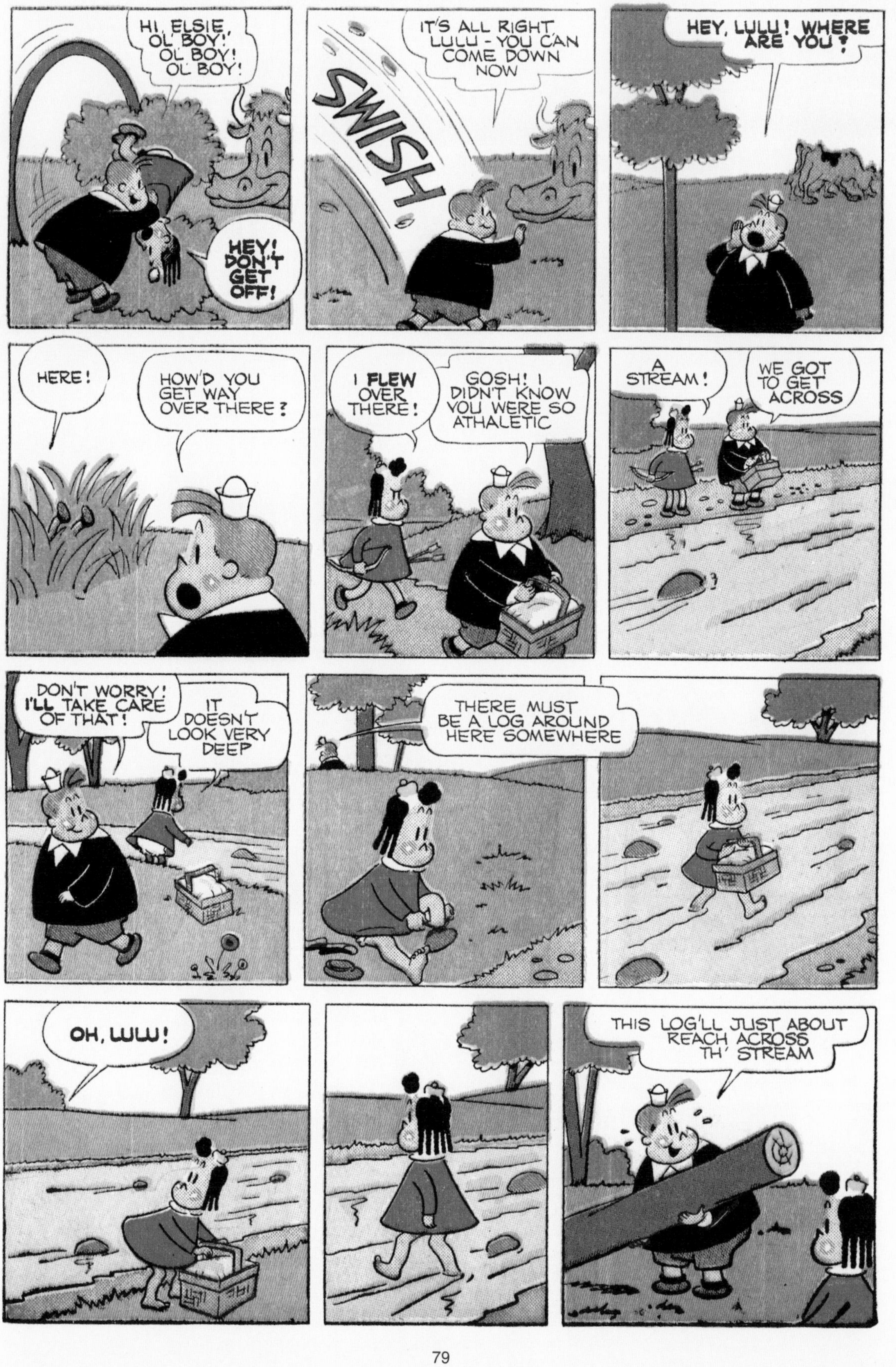

HI, ELSIE, OL' BOY! OL' BOY! OL' BOY!
HEY! DON'T GET OFF!
SWISH
IT'S ALL RIGHT LULU - YOU CAN COME DOWN NOW
HEY, LULU! WHERE ARE YOU?
HERE!
HOW'D YOU GET WAY OVER THERE?
I FLEW OVER THERE!
GOSH! I DIDN'T KNOW YOU WERE SO ATHALETIC
A STREAM!
WE GOT TO GET ACROSS
DON'T WORRY! I'LL TAKE CARE OF THAT!
IT DOESN'T LOOK VERY DEEP
THERE MUST BE A LOG AROUND HERE SOMEWHERE
OH, LULU!
THIS LOG'LL JUST ABOUT REACH ACROSS TH' STREAM

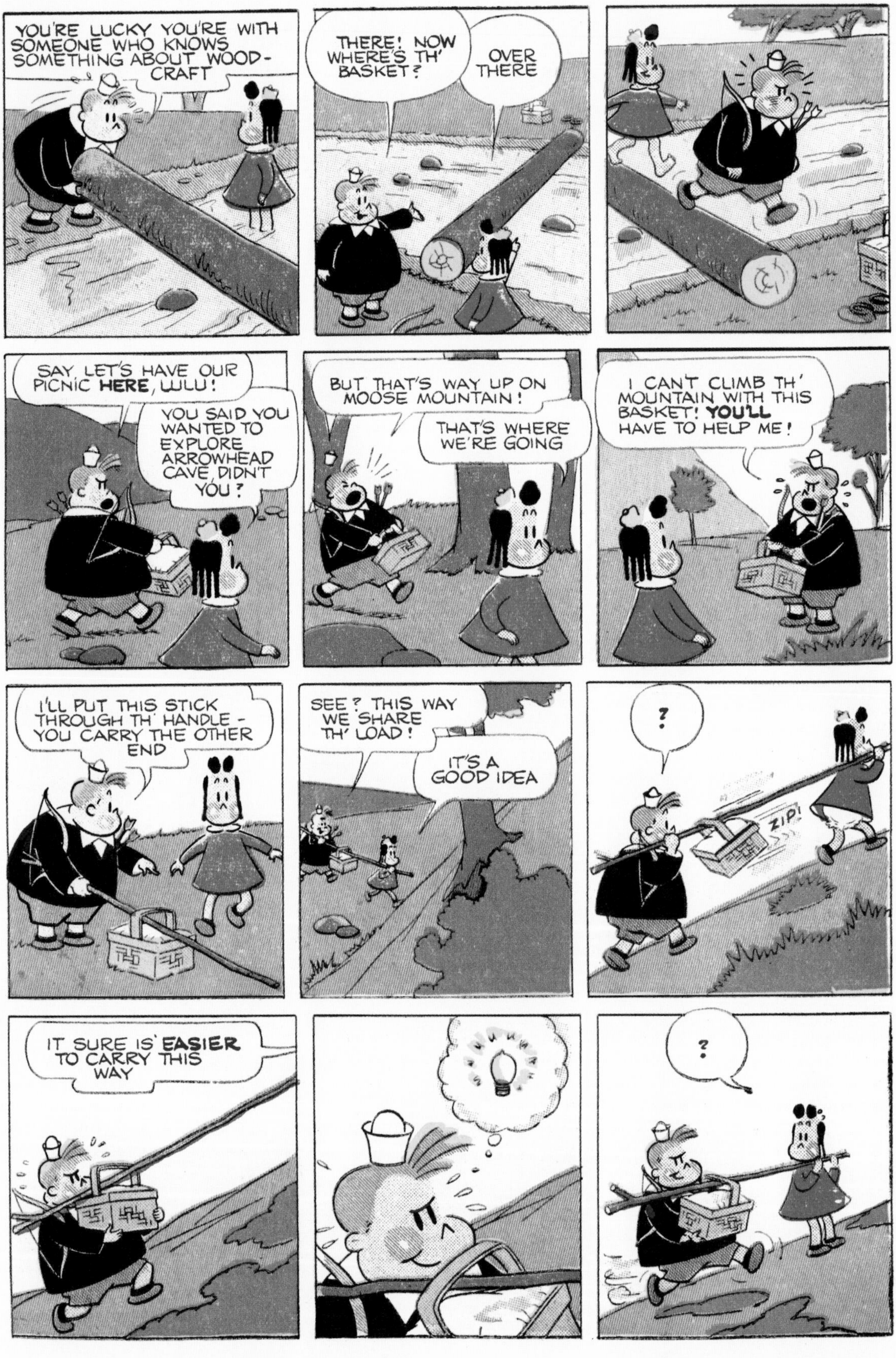
YOU'RE LUCKY YOU'RE WITH SOMEONE WHO KNOWS SOMETHING ABOUT WOOD-CRAFT
THERE! NOW WHERE'S TH' BASKET?
OVER THERE
SAY, LET'S HAVE OUR PICNIC **HERE**, LULU!
YOU SAID YOU WANTED TO EXPLORE ARROWHEAD CAVE, DIDN'T YOU?
BUT THAT'S WAY UP ON MOOSE MOUNTAIN!
THAT'S WHERE WE'RE GOING
I CAN'T CLIMB TH' MOUNTAIN WITH THIS BASKET! **YOU'LL** HAVE TO HELP ME!
I'LL PUT THIS STICK THROUGH TH' HANDLE - YOU CARRY THE OTHER END
SEE? THIS WAY WE SHARE TH' LOAD!
IT'S A GOOD IDEA
?
ZIP!
IT SURE IS **EASIER** TO CARRY THIS WAY
?

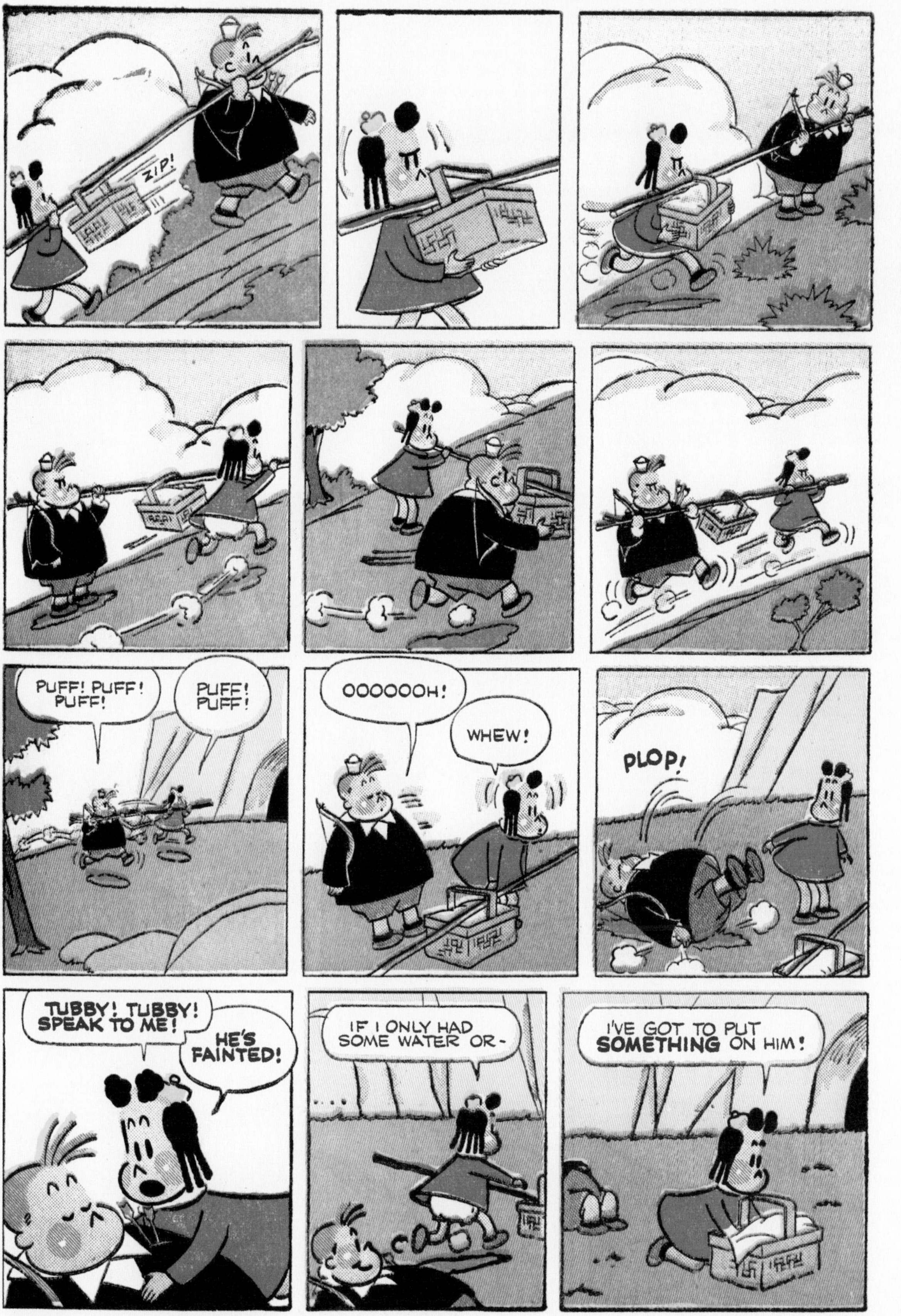

ZIP!
PUFF! PUFF! PUFF!
PUFF! PUFF!
OOOOOOH!
WHEW!
PLOP!
TUBBY! TUBBY! SPEAK TO ME!
HE'S FAINTED!
IF I ONLY HAD SOME WATER OR-
I'VE GOT TO PUT SOMETHING ON HIM!

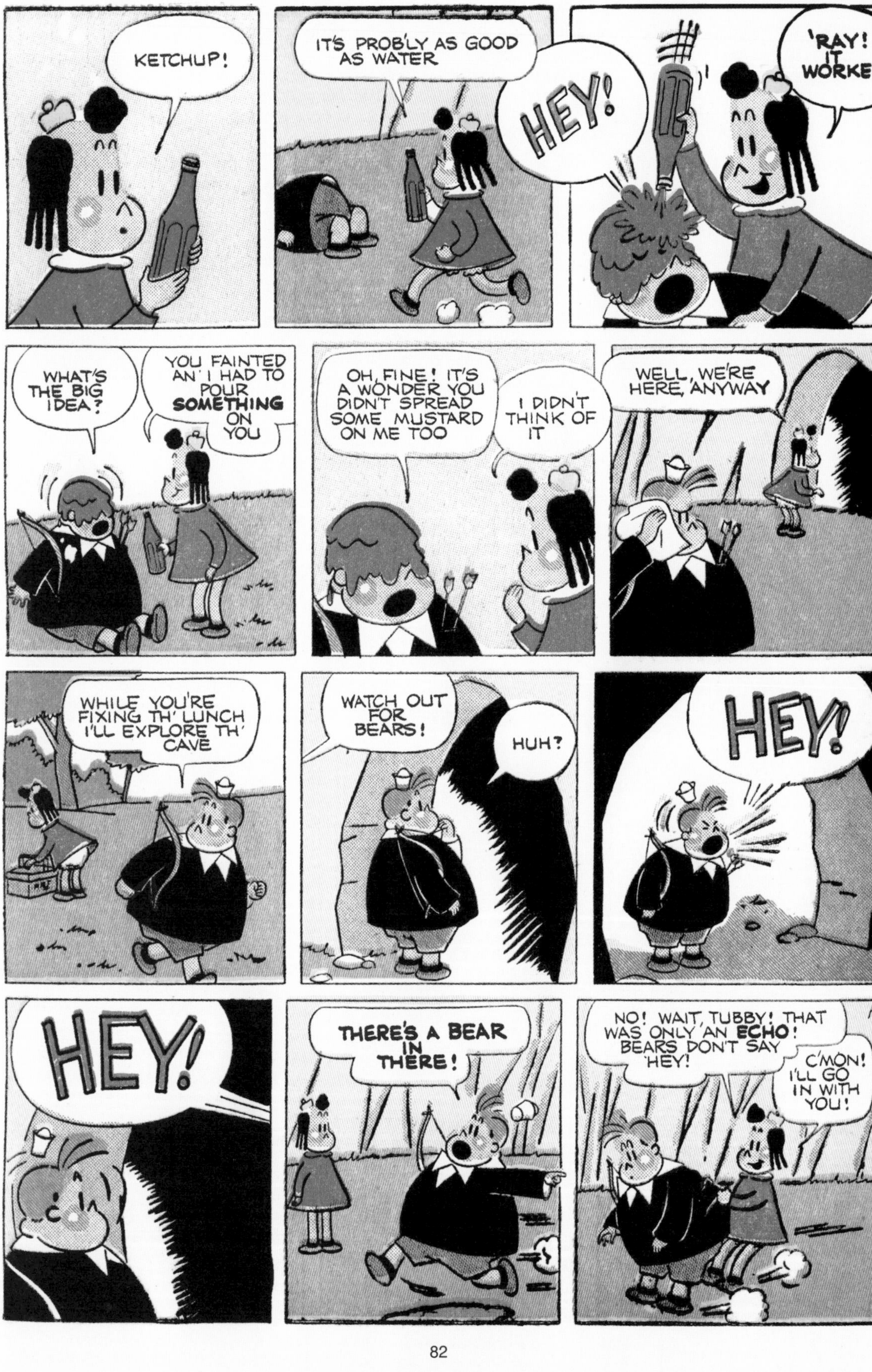

KETCHUP!
IT'S PROB'LY AS GOOD AS WATER
HEY!
'RAY! IT WORKED!
WHAT'S THE BIG IDEA?
YOU FAINTED AN' I HAD TO POUR **SOMETHING** ON YOU
OH, FINE! IT'S A WONDER YOU DIDN'T SPREAD SOME MUSTARD ON ME TOO
I DIDN'T THINK OF IT
WELL, WE'RE HERE, ANYWAY
WHILE YOU'RE FIXING TH' LUNCH I'LL EXPLORE TH' CAVE
WATCH OUT FOR BEARS!
HUH?
HEY!
HEY!
THERE'S A BEAR IN THERE!
NO! WAIT, TUBBY! THAT WAS ONLY AN **ECHO**! BEARS DON'T SAY 'HEY!
C'MON! I'LL GO IN WITH YOU!

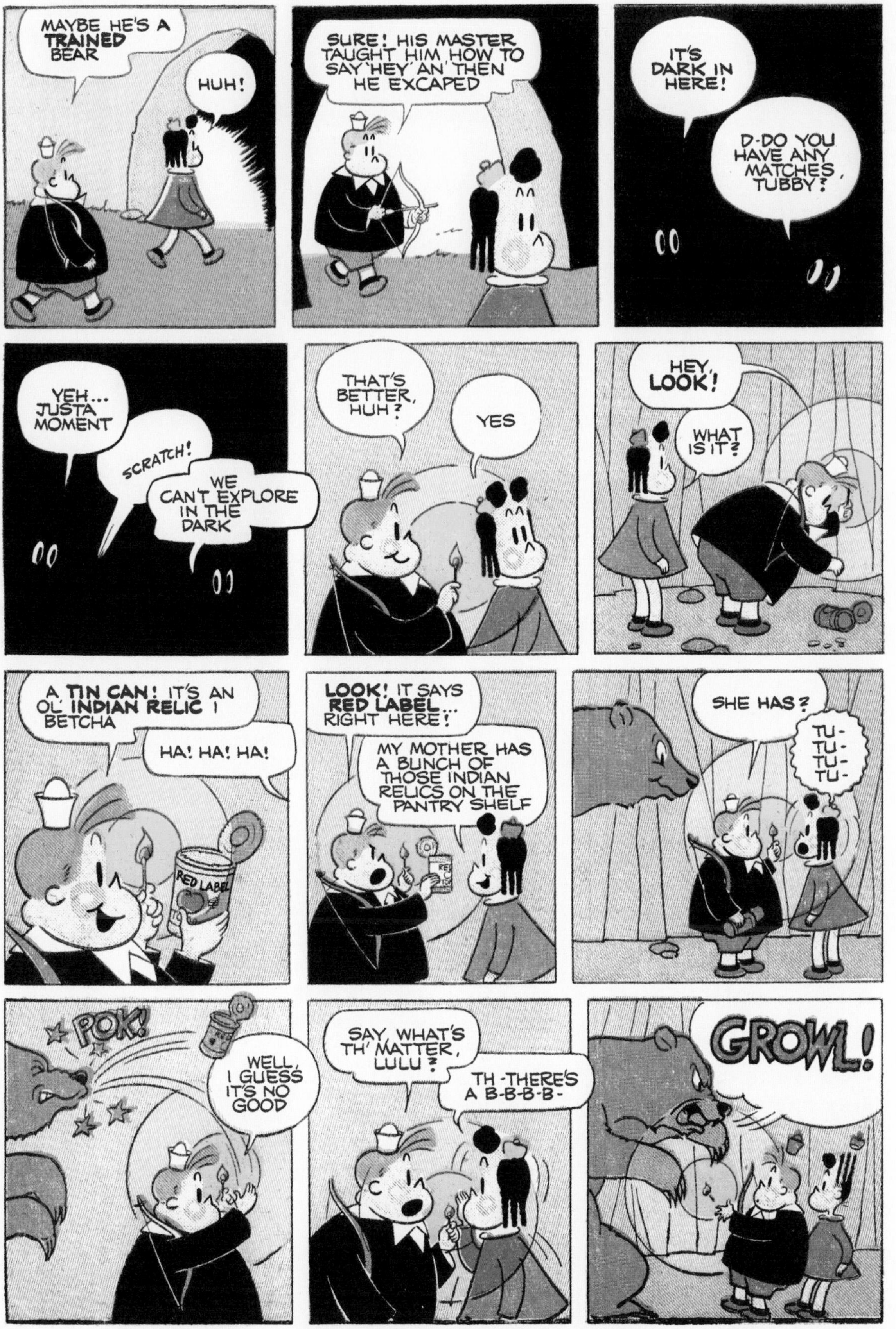
MAYBE HE'S A TRAINED BEAR
HUH!
SURE! HIS MASTER TAUGHT HIM HOW TO SAY 'HEY' AN' THEN HE EXCAPED
IT'S DARK IN HERE!
D-DO YOU HAVE ANY MATCHES, TUBBY?
YEH... JUSTA MOMENT
SCRATCH!
WE CAN'T EXPLORE IN THE DARK
THAT'S BETTER, HUH?
YES
HEY, LOOK!
WHAT IS IT?
A TIN CAN! IT'S AN OL' INDIAN RELIC I BETCHA
HA! HA! HA!
RED LABEL
LOOK! IT SAYS RED LABEL... RIGHT HERE!
MY MOTHER HAS A BUNCH OF THOSE INDIAN RELICS ON THE PANTRY SHELF
SHE HAS?
TU-TU-TU-TU-
POK!
WELL, I GUESS IT'S NO GOOD
SAY, WHAT'S TH' MATTER, LULU?
TH-THERE'S A B-B-B-B-
GROWL!

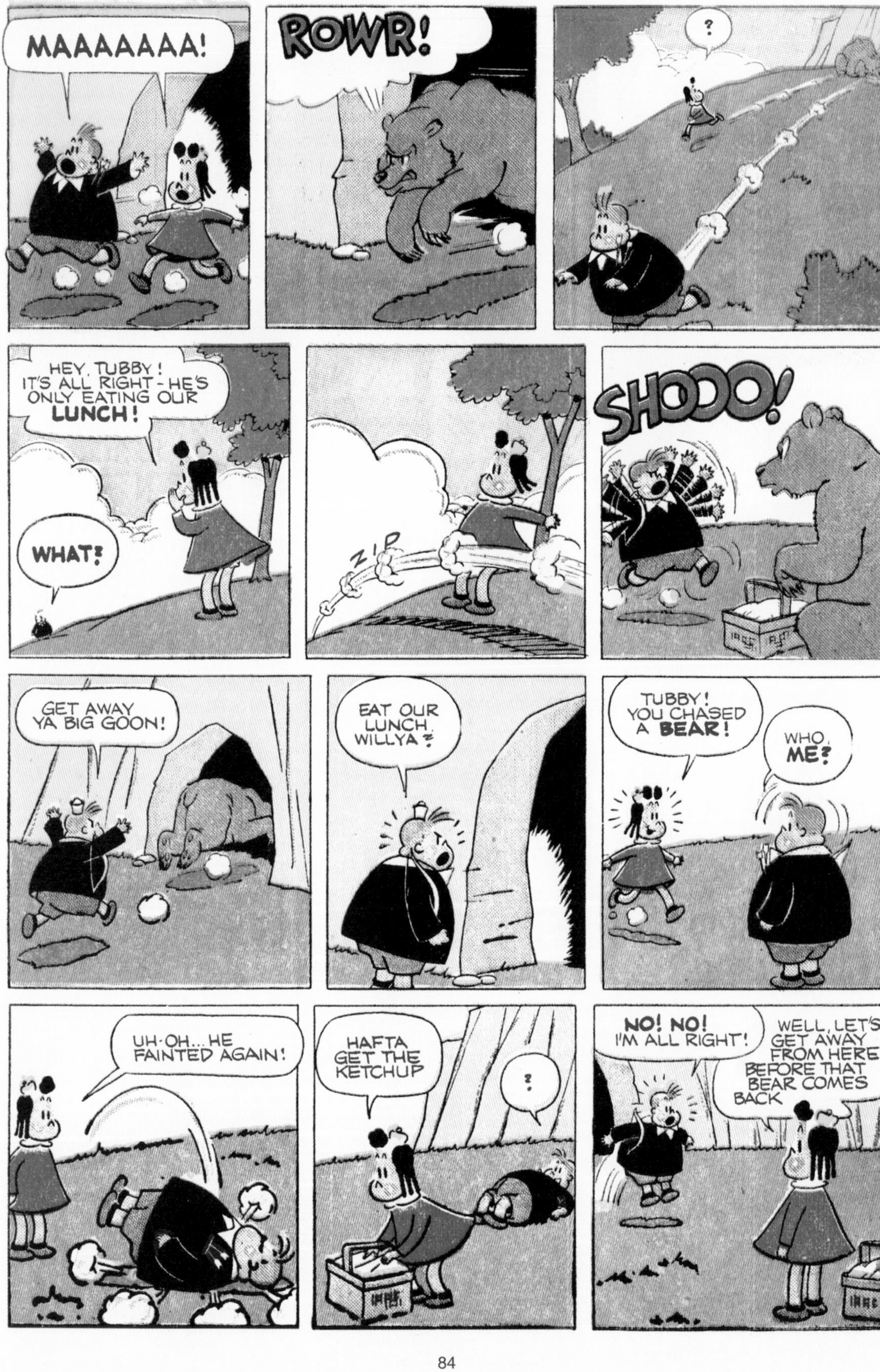

MAAAAAAA!
ROWR!
?
HEY, TUBBY! IT'S ALL RIGHT - HE'S ONLY EATING OUR **LUNCH!**
WHAT?
ZIP
SHOOO!
GET AWAY YA BIG GOON!
EAT OUR LUNCH, WILLYA?
TUBBY! YOU CHASED A **BEAR!**
WHO, **ME?**
UH-OH... HE FAINTED AGAIN!
HAFTA GET THE KETCHUP
?
NO! NO! I'M ALL RIGHT!
WELL, LET'S GET AWAY FROM HERE BEFORE THAT BEAR COMES BACK

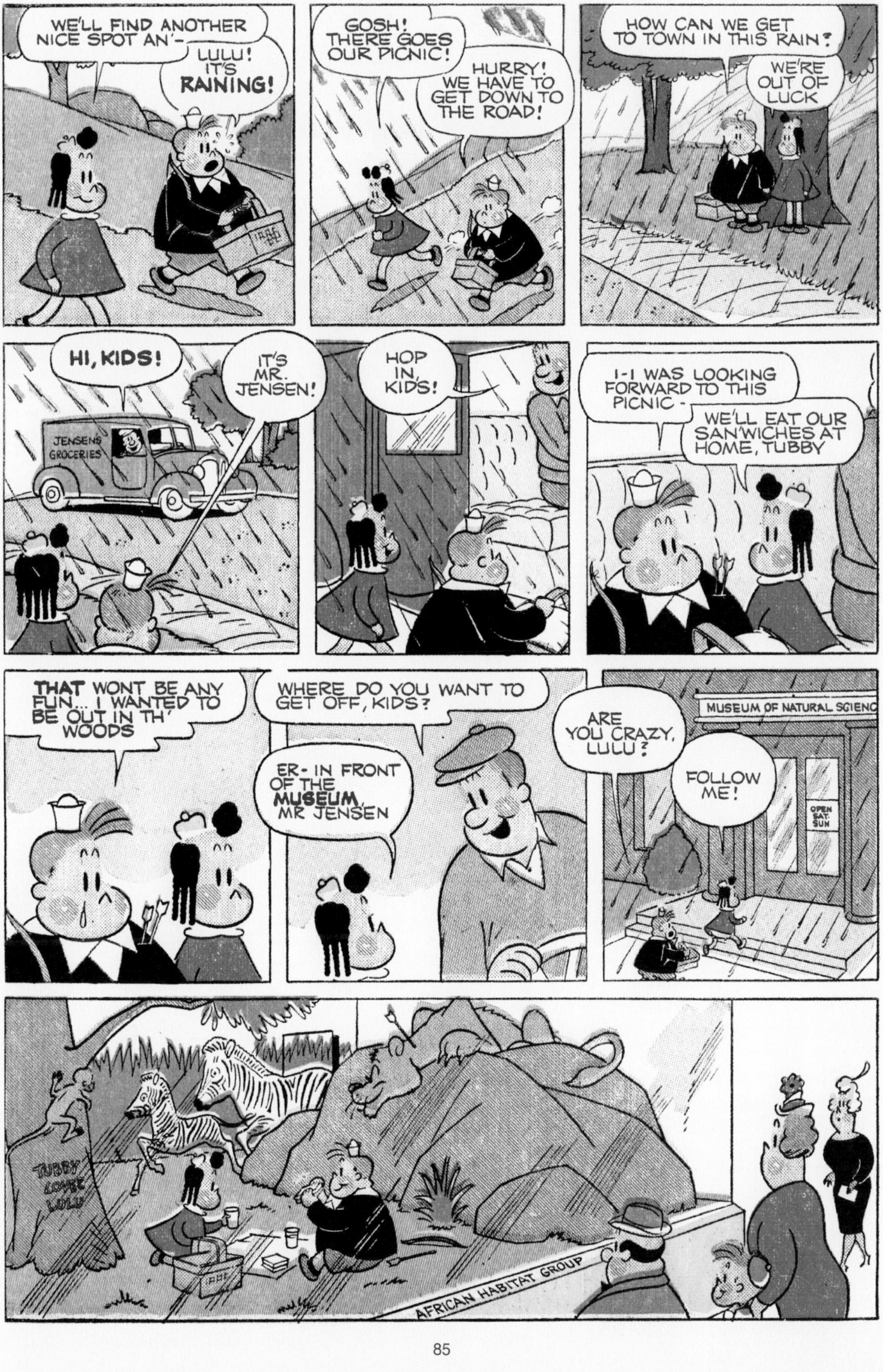

WE'LL FIND ANOTHER NICE SPOT AN'-
LULU! IT'S RAINING!
GOSH! THERE GOES OUR PICNIC!
HURRY! WE HAVE TO GET DOWN TO THE ROAD!
HOW CAN WE GET TO TOWN IN THIS RAIN?
WE'RE OUT OF LUCK
HI, KIDS!
JENSENS GROCERIES
IT'S MR. JENSEN!
HOP IN, KIDS!
I-I WAS LOOKING FORWARD TO THIS PICNIC -
WE'LL EAT OUR SAN'WICHES AT HOME, TUBBY
THAT WONT BE ANY FUN... I WANTED TO BE OUT IN TH' WOODS
WHERE DO YOU WANT TO GET OFF, KIDS?
ER- IN FRONT OF THE MUSEUM, MR JENSEN
MUSEUM OF NATURAL SCIENC
ARE YOU CRAZY, LULU?
FOLLOW ME!
OPEN SAT SUN
TUBBY LOVES LULU
AFRICAN HABITAT GROUP

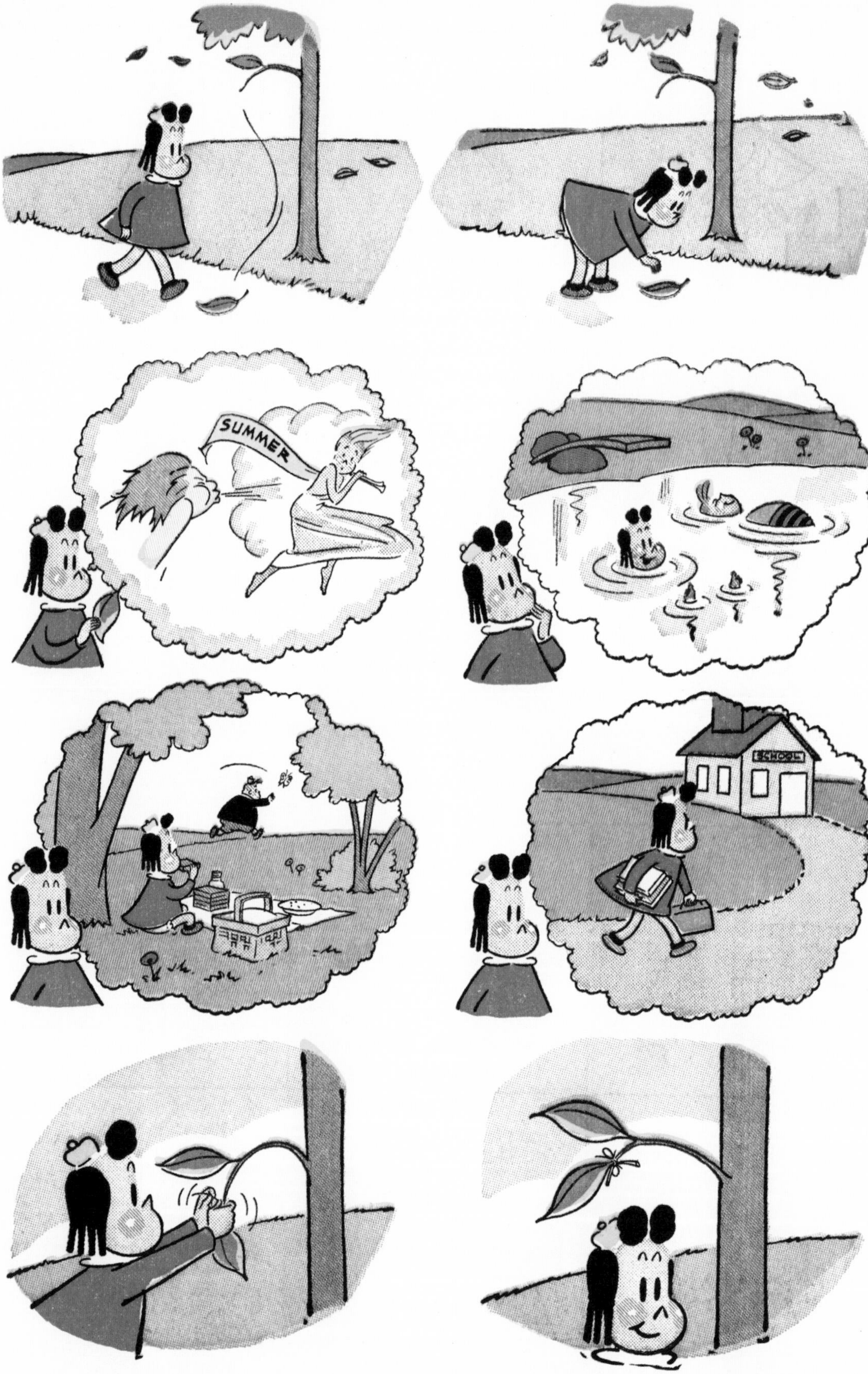
SUMMER
SCHOOL

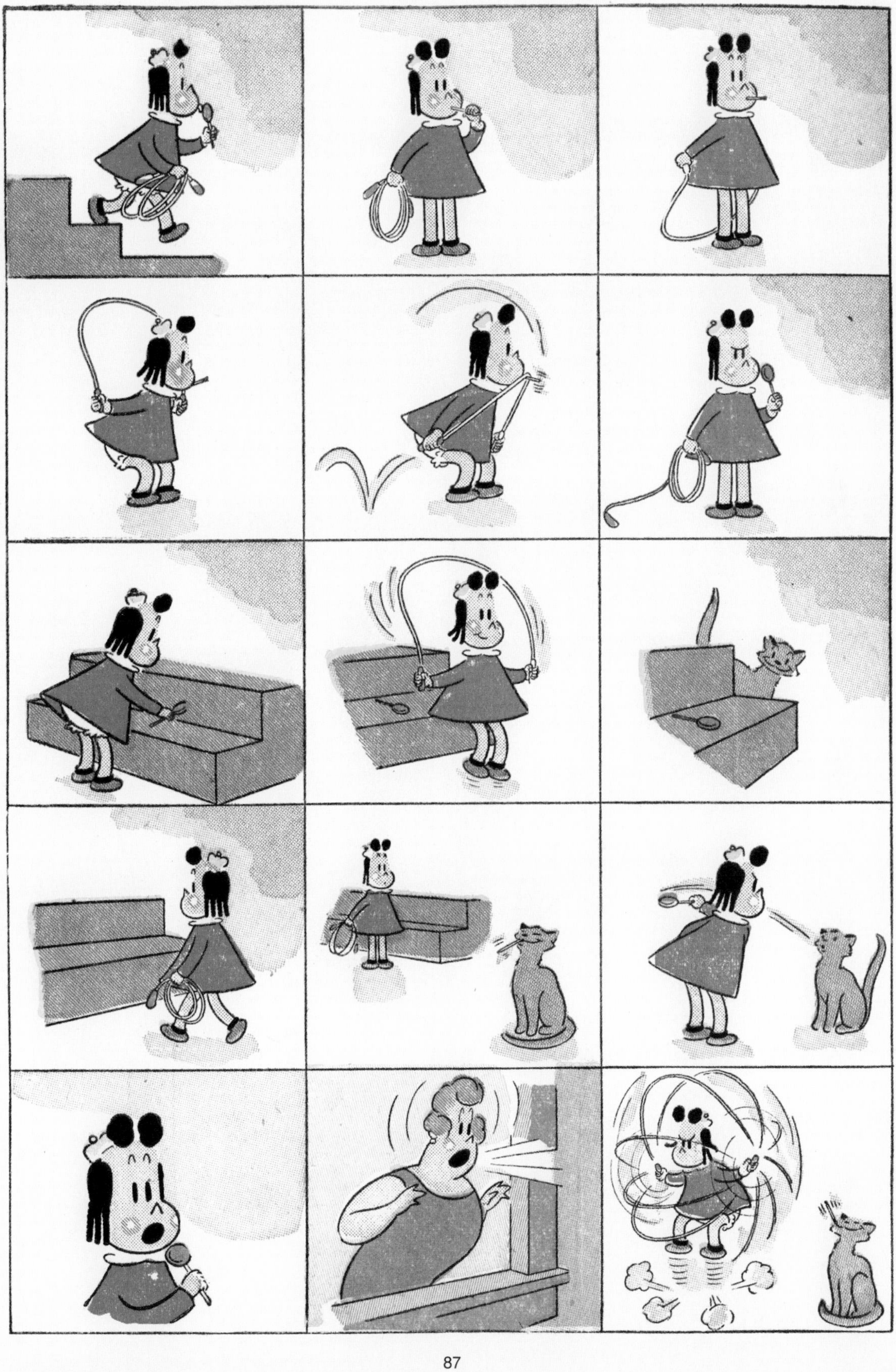

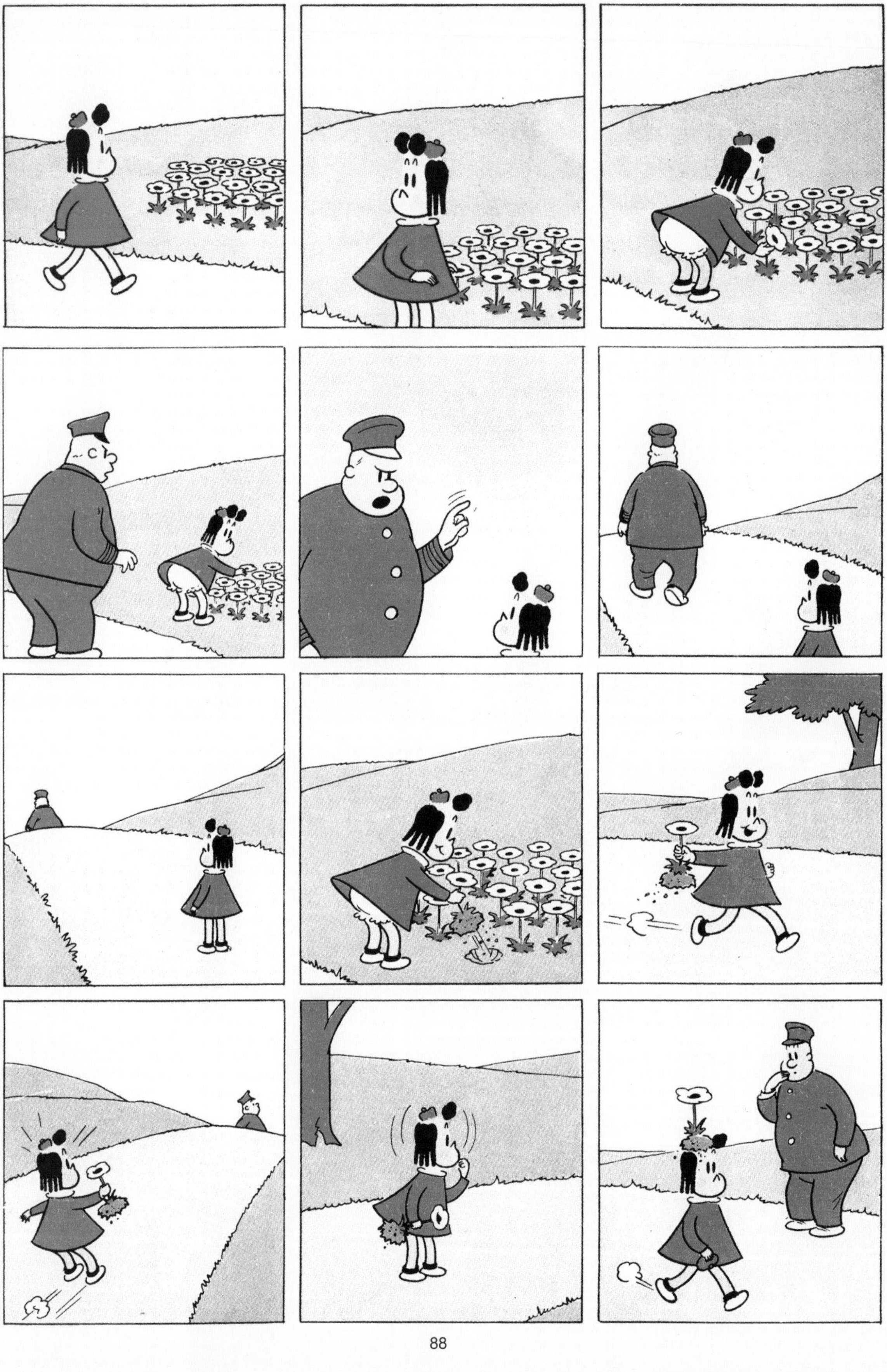

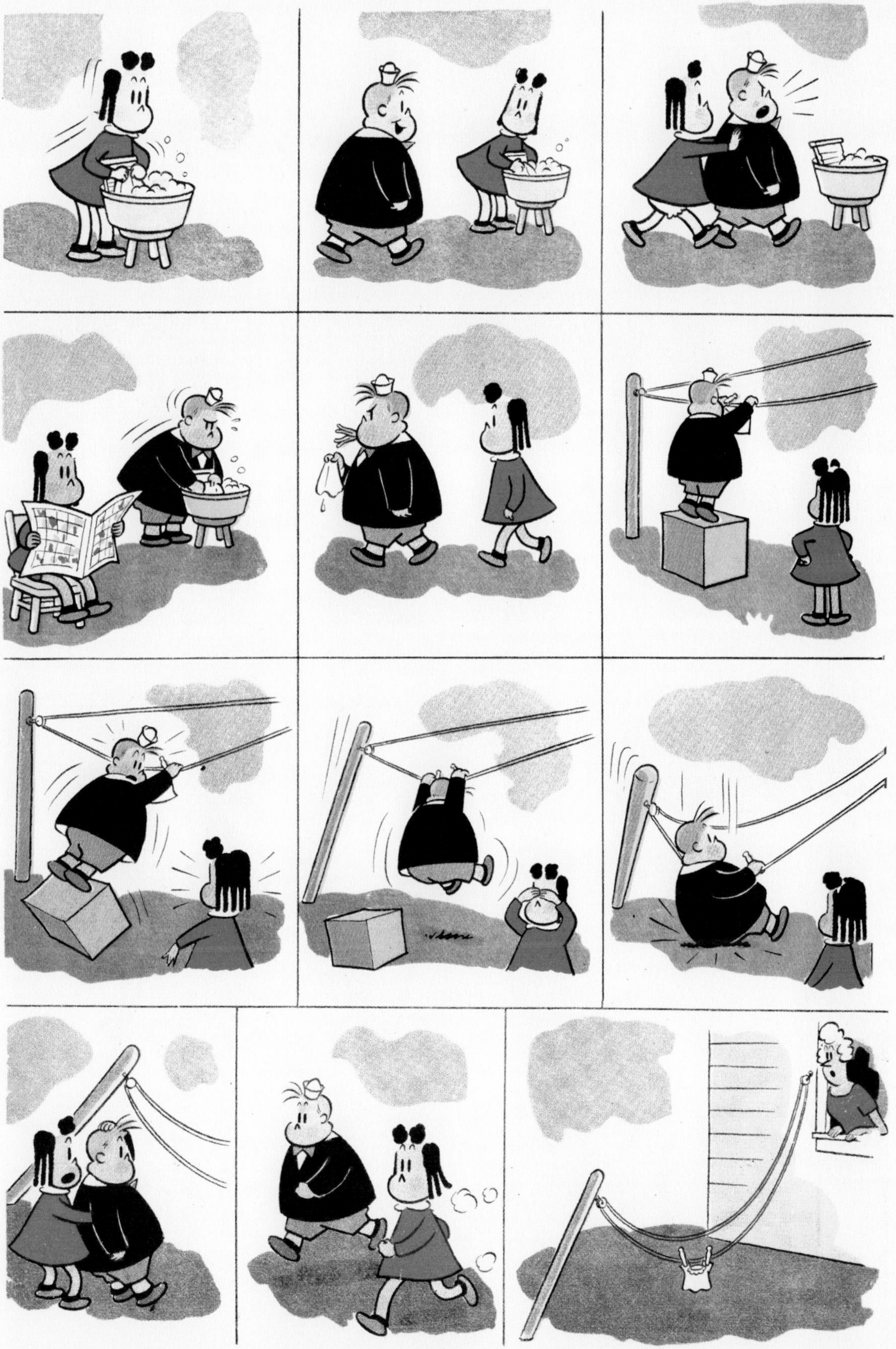

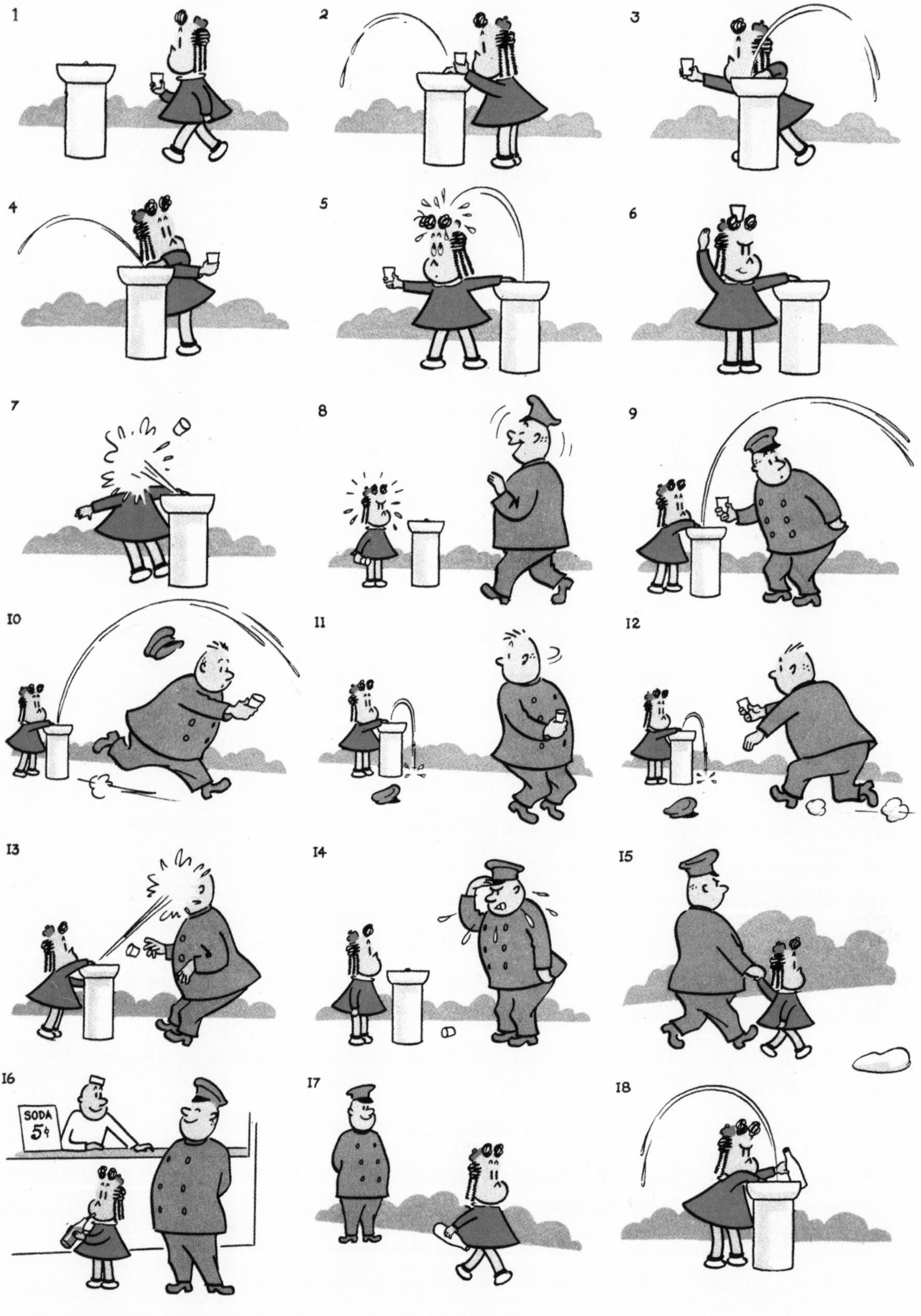
SODA
5¢

marge's

LITTLE LULU

TREASURE HUNT

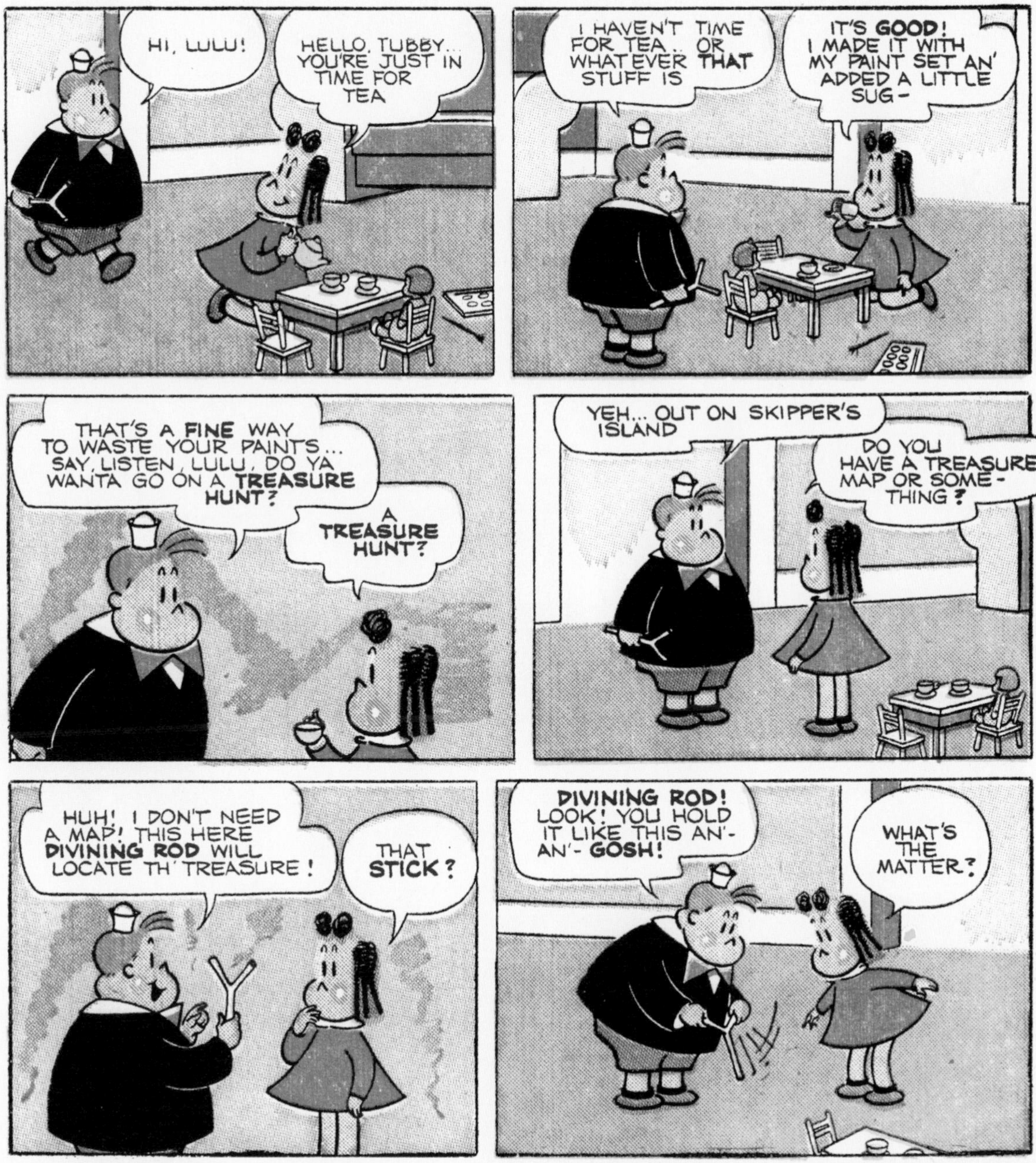

HI, LULU!
HELLO, TUBBY... YOU'RE JUST IN TIME FOR TEA
I HAVEN'T TIME FOR TEA.. OR WHATEVER THAT STUFF IS
IT'S GOOD! I MADE IT WITH MY PAINT SET AN' ADDED A LITTLE SUG-
THAT'S A FINE WAY TO WASTE YOUR PAINTS... SAY, LISTEN, LULU, DO YA WANTA GO ON A TREASURE HUNT?
A TREASURE HUNT?
YEH... OUT ON SKIPPER'S ISLAND
DO YOU HAVE A TREASURE MAP OR SOME-THING?
HUH! I DON'T NEED A MAP! THIS HERE DIVINING ROD WILL LOCATE TH' TREASURE!
THAT STICK?
DIVINING ROD! LOOK! YOU HOLD IT LIKE THIS AN'- AN'- GOSH!
WHAT'S THE MATTER?

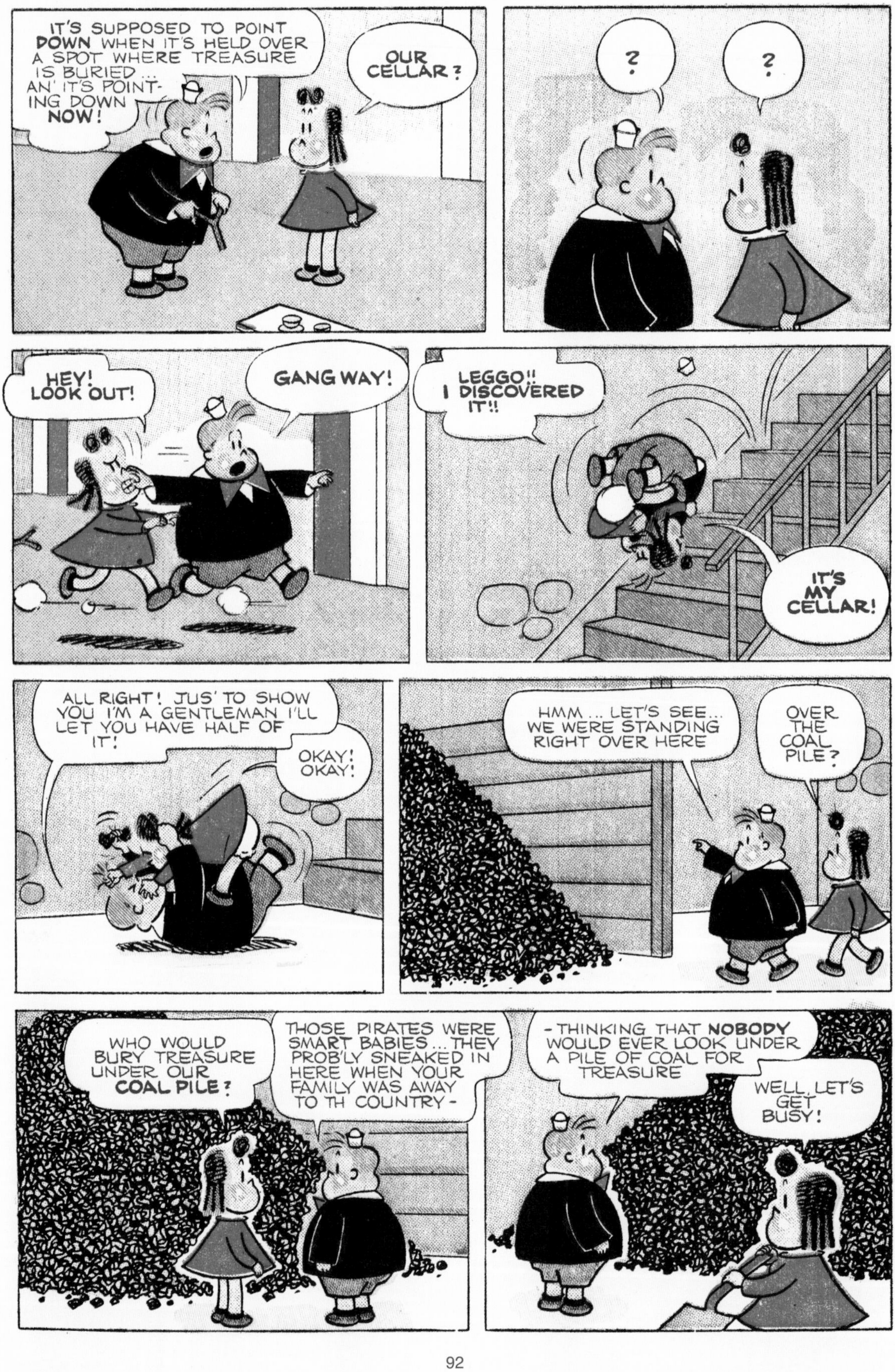
IT'S SUPPOSED TO POINT DOWN WHEN IT'S HELD OVER A SPOT WHERE TREASURE IS BURIED... AN' IT'S POINTING DOWN NOW!
OUR CELLAR?
?
?
HEY! LOOK OUT!
GANG WAY!
LEGGO!! I DISCOVERED IT!!
IT'S MY CELLAR!
ALL RIGHT! JUS' TO SHOW YOU I'M A GENTLEMAN I'LL LET YOU HAVE HALF OF IT!
OKAY! OKAY!
HMM... LET'S SEE... WE WERE STANDING RIGHT OVER HERE
OVER THE COAL PILE?
WHO WOULD BURY TREASURE UNDER OUR COAL PILE?
THOSE PIRATES WERE SMART BABIES... THEY PROB'LY SNEAKED IN HERE WHEN YOUR FAMILY WAS AWAY TO TH COUNTRY -
- THINKING THAT NOBODY WOULD EVER LOOK UNDER A PILE OF COAL FOR TREASURE
WELL, LET'S GET BUSY!

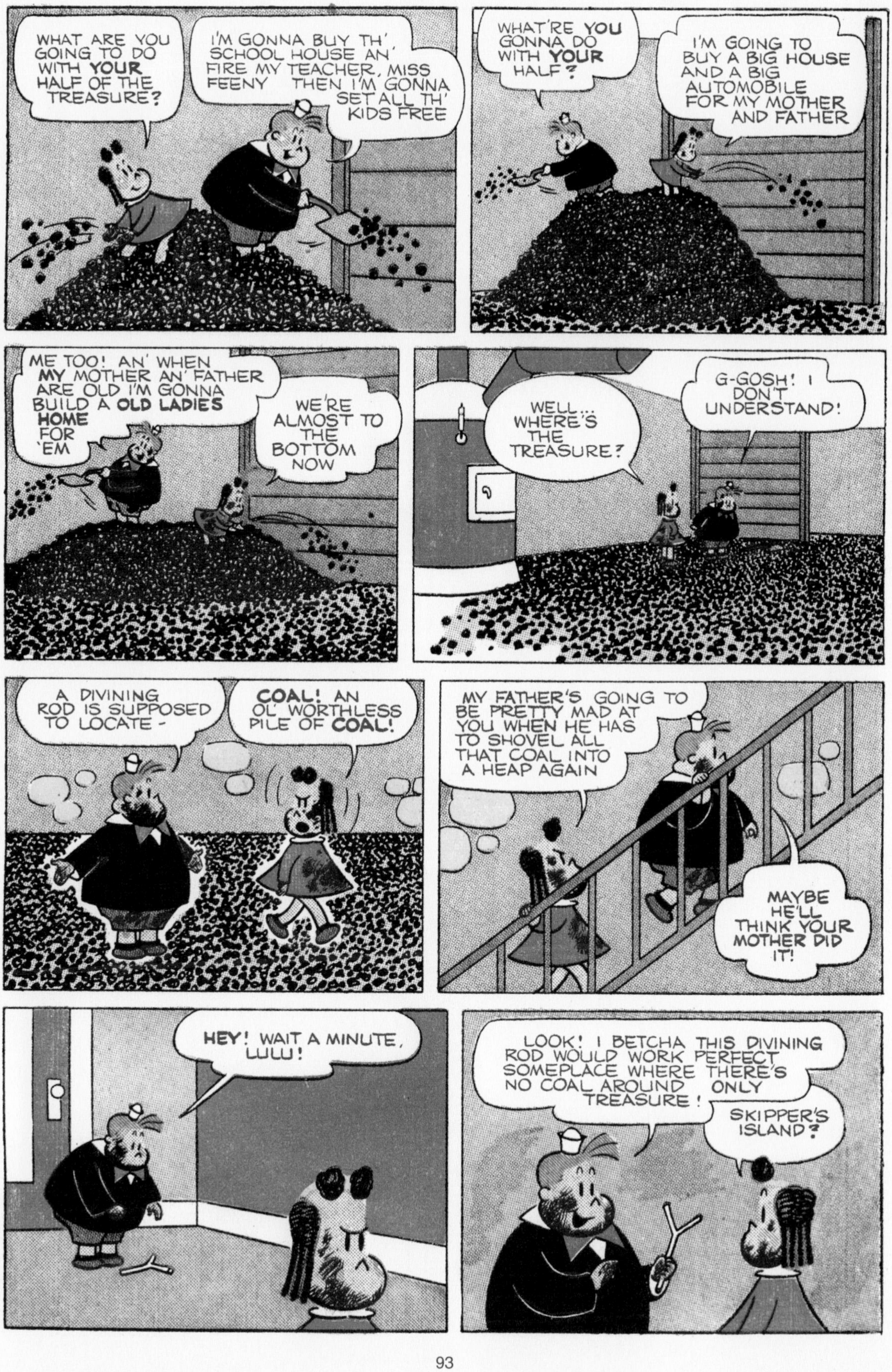

WHAT ARE YOU GOING TO DO WITH YOUR HALF OF THE TREASURE?
I'M GONNA BUY TH' SCHOOL HOUSE AN' FIRE MY TEACHER, MISS FEENY THEN I'M GONNA SET ALL TH' KIDS FREE
WHAT'RE YOU GONNA DO WITH YOUR HALF?
I'M GOING TO BUY A BIG HOUSE AND A BIG AUTOMOBILE FOR MY MOTHER AND FATHER
ME TOO! AN' WHEN MY MOTHER AN' FATHER ARE OLD I'M GONNA BUILD A OLD LADIES HOME FOR 'EM
WE'RE ALMOST TO THE BOTTOM NOW
WELL... WHERE'S THE TREASURE?
G-GOSH! I DON'T UNDERSTAND!
A DIVINING ROD IS SUPPOSED TO LOCATE -
COAL! AN OL' WORTHLESS PILE OF COAL!
MY FATHER'S GOING TO BE PRETTY MAD AT YOU WHEN HE HAS TO SHOVEL ALL THAT COAL INTO A HEAP AGAIN
MAYBE HE'LL THINK YOUR MOTHER DID IT!
HEY! WAIT A MINUTE, LULU!
LOOK! I BETCHA THIS DIVINING ROD WOULD WORK PERFECT SOMEPLACE WHERE THERE'S NO COAL AROUND ONLY TREASURE!
SKIPPER'S ISLAND?

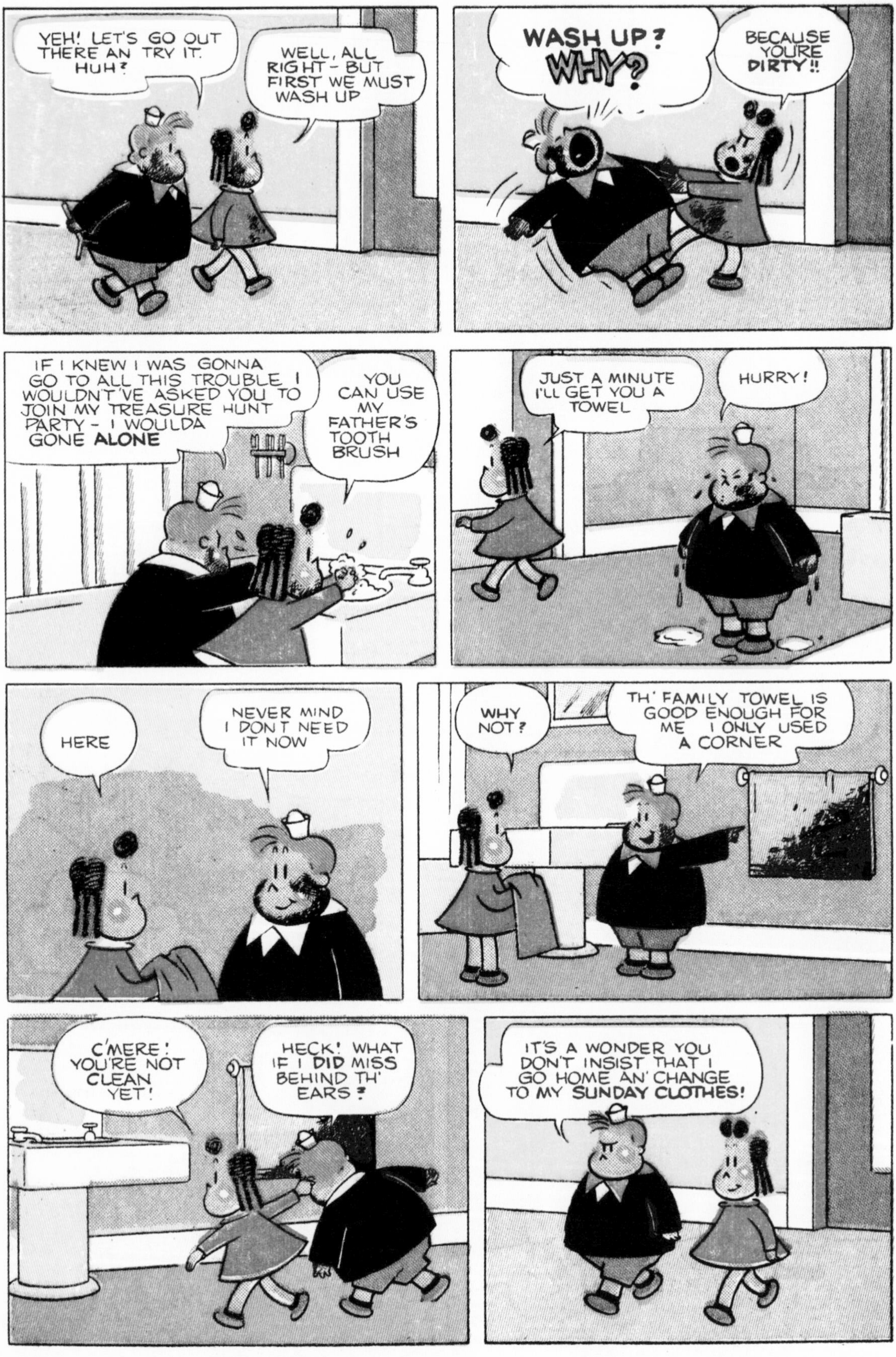
YEH! LET'S GO OUT THERE AN TRY IT. HUH?
WELL, ALL RIGHT - BUT FIRST WE MUST WASH UP
WASH UP? WHY?
BECAUSE YOU'RE DIRTY!!
IF I KNEW I WAS GONNA GO TO ALL THIS TROUBLE I WOULDN'T'VE ASKED YOU TO JOIN MY TREASURE HUNT PARTY - I WOULDA GONE ALONE
YOU CAN USE MY FATHER'S TOOTH BRUSH
JUST A MINUTE I'LL GET YOU A TOWEL
HURRY!
HERE
NEVER MIND I DON'T NEED IT NOW
WHY NOT?
TH' FAMILY TOWEL IS GOOD ENOUGH FOR ME I ONLY USED A CORNER
C'MERE! YOU'RE NOT CLEAN YET!
HECK! WHAT IF I DID MISS BEHIND TH' EARS?
IT'S A WONDER YOU DON'T INSIST THAT I GO HOME AN' CHANGE TO MY SUNDAY CLOTHES!

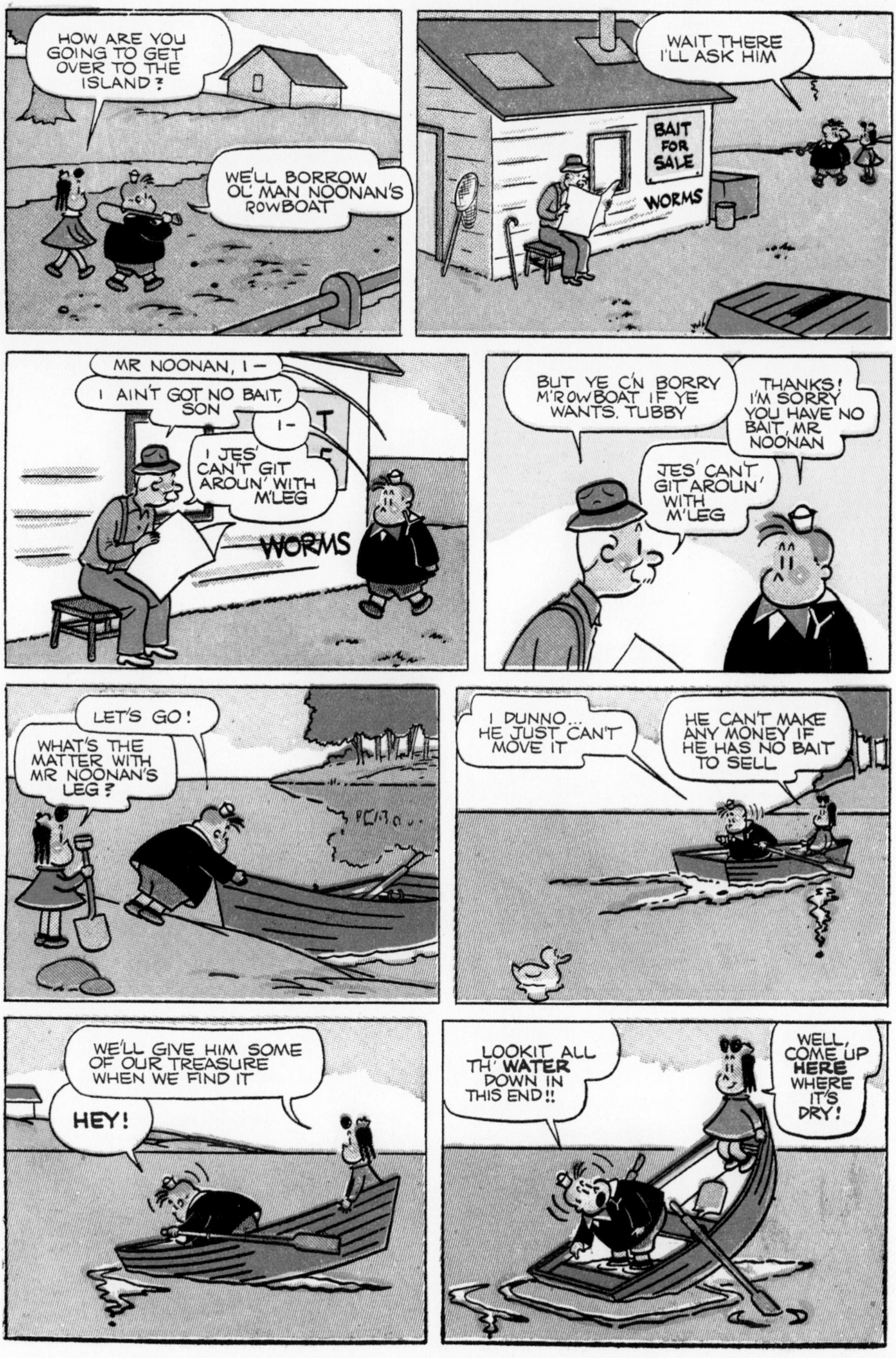
HOW ARE YOU GOING TO GET OVER TO THE ISLAND?
WE'LL BORROW OL' MAN NOONAN'S ROWBOAT
WAIT THERE I'LL ASK HIM
BAIT FOR SALE
WORMS
MR NOONAN, I—
I AIN'T GOT NO BAIT, SON
I—
I JES' CAN'T GIT AROUN' WITH M'LEG
WORMS
BUT YE C'N BORRY M'ROWBOAT IF YE WANTS, TUBBY
JES' CAN'T GIT AROUN' WITH M'LEG
THANKS! I'M SORRY YOU HAVE NO BAIT, MR NOONAN
LET'S GO!
WHAT'S THE MATTER WITH MR NOONAN'S LEG?
I DUNNO... HE JUST CAN'T MOVE IT
HE CAN'T MAKE ANY MONEY IF HE HAS NO BAIT TO SELL
WE'LL GIVE HIM SOME OF OUR TREASURE WHEN WE FIND IT
HEY!
LOOKIT ALL TH' WATER DOWN IN THIS END!!
WELL, COME UP HERE WHERE IT'S DRY!

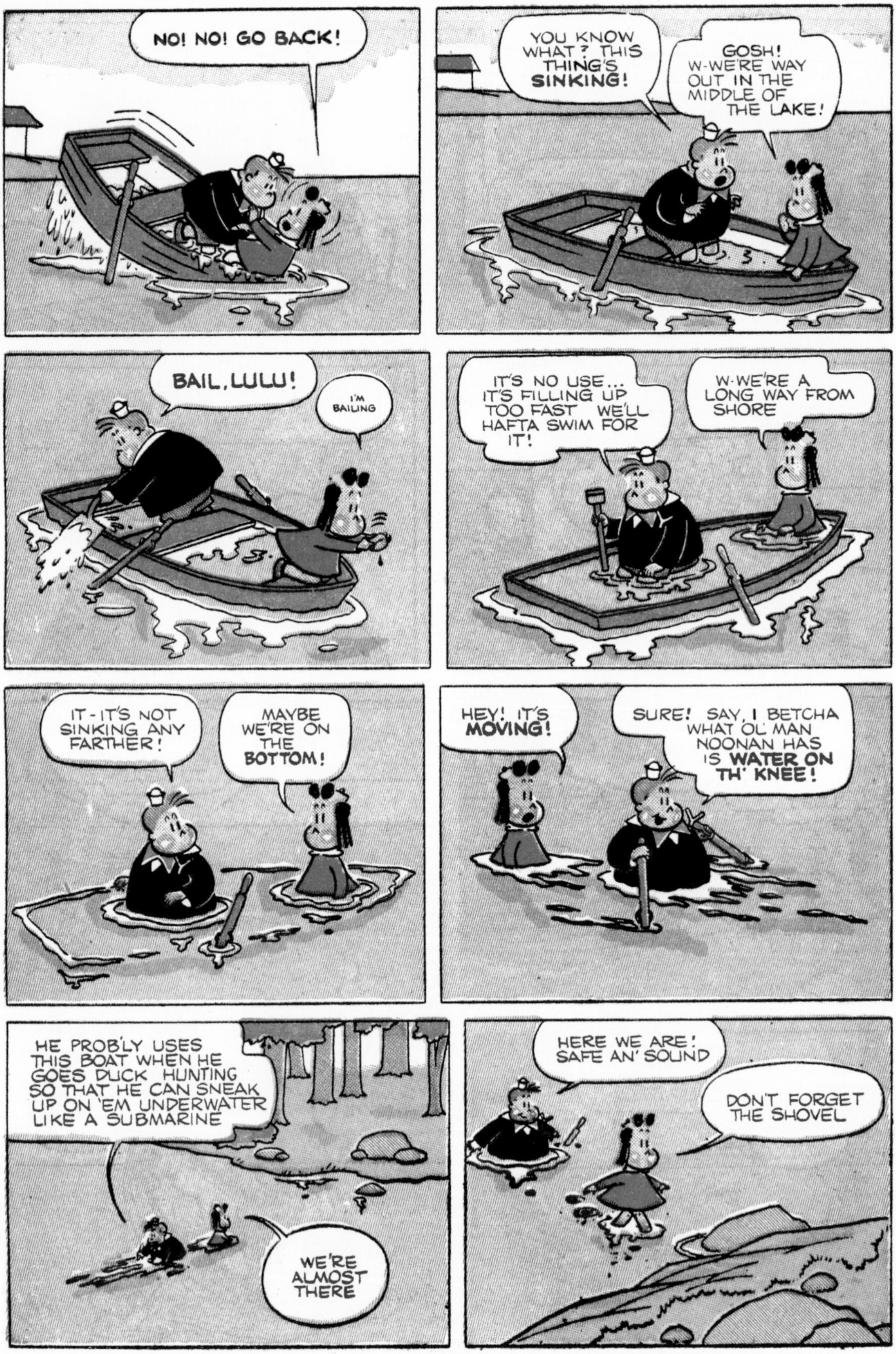
NO! NO! GO BACK!
YOU KNOW WHAT? THIS THING'S SINKING!
GOSH! W-WE'RE WAY OUT IN THE MIDDLE OF THE LAKE!
BAIL, LULU!
I'M BAILING
IT'S NO USE... IT'S FILLING UP TOO FAST WE'LL HAFTA SWIM FOR IT!
W-WE'RE A LONG WAY FROM SHORE
IT-IT'S NOT SINKING ANY FARTHER!
MAYBE WE'RE ON THE BOTTOM!
HEY! IT'S MOVING!
SURE! SAY, I BETCHA WHAT OL' MAN NOONAN HAS IS WATER ON TH' KNEE!
HE PROB'LY USES THIS BOAT WHEN HE GOES DUCK HUNTING SO THAT HE CAN SNEAK UP ON 'EM UNDERWATER LIKE A SUBMARINE
WE'RE ALMOST THERE
HERE WE ARE! SAFE AN' SOUND
DON'T FORGET THE SHOVEL

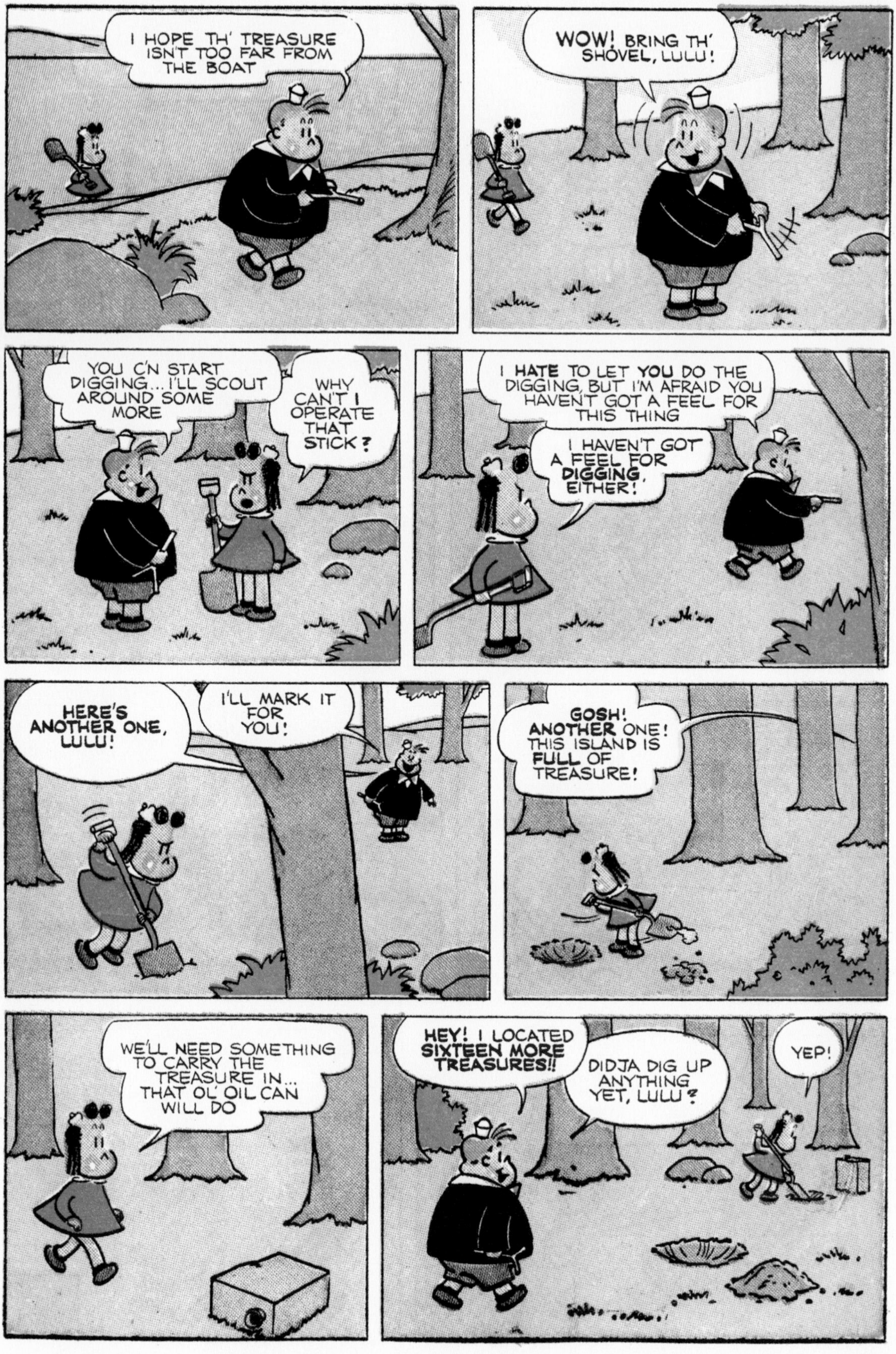

I HOPE TH' TREASURE ISN'T TOO FAR FROM THE BOAT
WOW! BRING TH' SHOVEL, LULU!
YOU C'N START DIGGING... I'LL SCOUT AROUND SOME MORE
WHY CAN'T I OPERATE THAT STICK?
I HATE TO LET YOU DO THE DIGGING, BUT I'M AFRAID YOU HAVEN'T GOT A FEEL FOR THIS THING
I HAVEN'T GOT A FEEL FOR DIGGING, EITHER!
HERE'S ANOTHER ONE, LULU!
I'LL MARK IT FOR YOU!
GOSH! ANOTHER ONE! THIS ISLAND IS FULL OF TREASURE!
WE'LL NEED SOMETHING TO CARRY THE TREASURE IN... THAT OL' OIL CAN WILL DO
HEY! I LOCATED SIXTEEN MORE TREASURES!!
DIDJA DIG UP ANYTHING YET, LULU?
YEP!

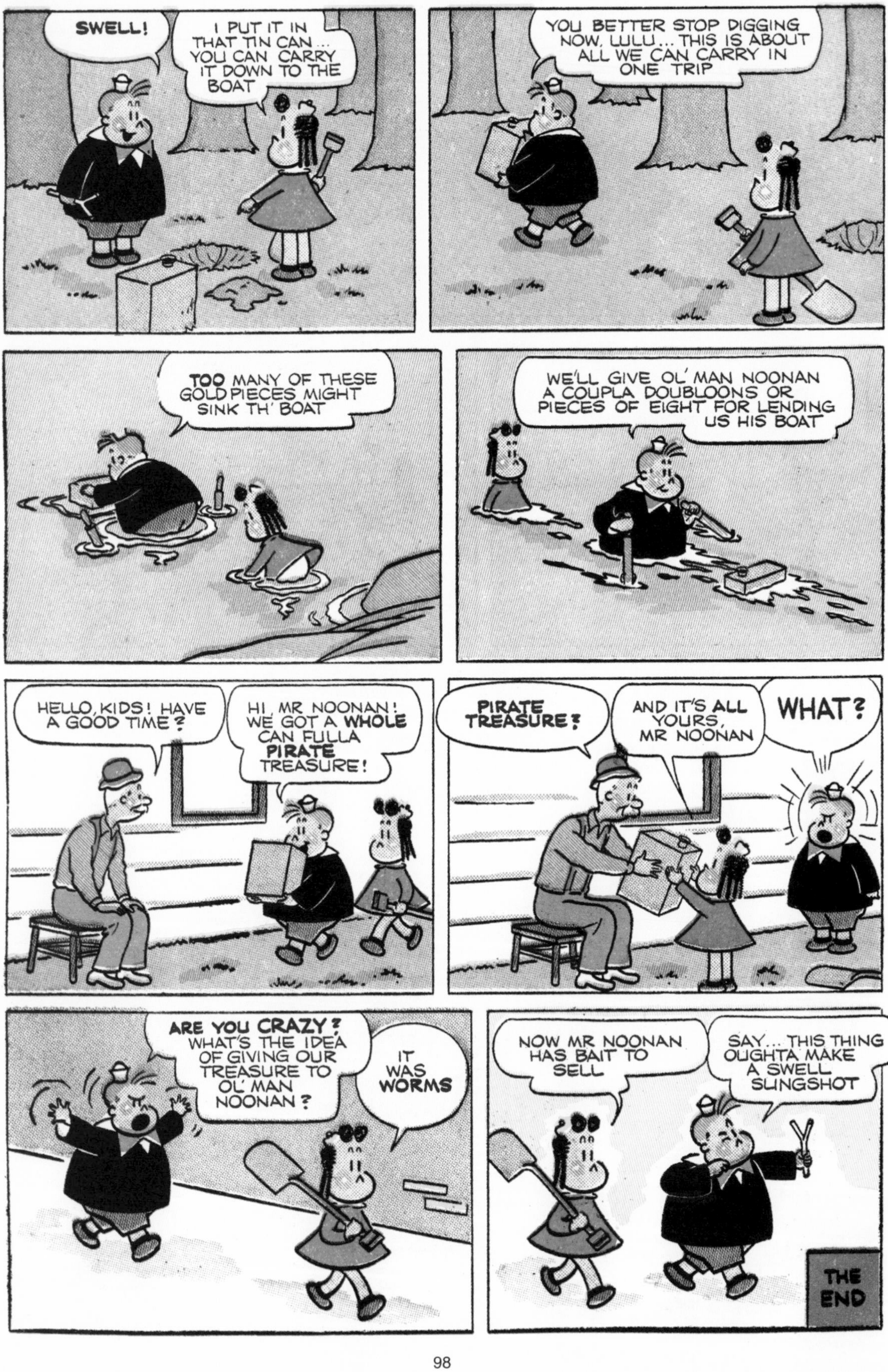

SWELL!
I PUT IT IN THAT TIN CAN... YOU CAN CARRY IT DOWN TO THE BOAT
YOU BETTER STOP DIGGING NOW, LULU... THIS IS ABOUT ALL WE CAN CARRY IN ONE TRIP
TOO MANY OF THESE GOLD PIECES MIGHT SINK TH' BOAT
WE'LL GIVE OL' MAN NOONAN A COUPLA DOUBLOONS OR PIECES OF EIGHT FOR LENDING US HIS BOAT
HELLO, KIDS! HAVE A GOOD TIME?
HI, MR NOONAN! WE GOT A WHOLE CAN FULLA PIRATE TREASURE!
PIRATE TREASURE?
AND IT'S ALL YOURS, MR NOONAN
WHAT?
ARE YOU CRAZY? WHAT'S THE IDEA OF GIVING OUR TREASURE TO OL' MAN NOONAN?
IT WAS WORMS
NOW MR NOONAN HAS BAIT TO SELL
SAY... THIS THING OUGHTA MAKE A SWELL SLINGSHOT
THE END

marge's

LITTLE LULU

"HE CAN'T HURT US"

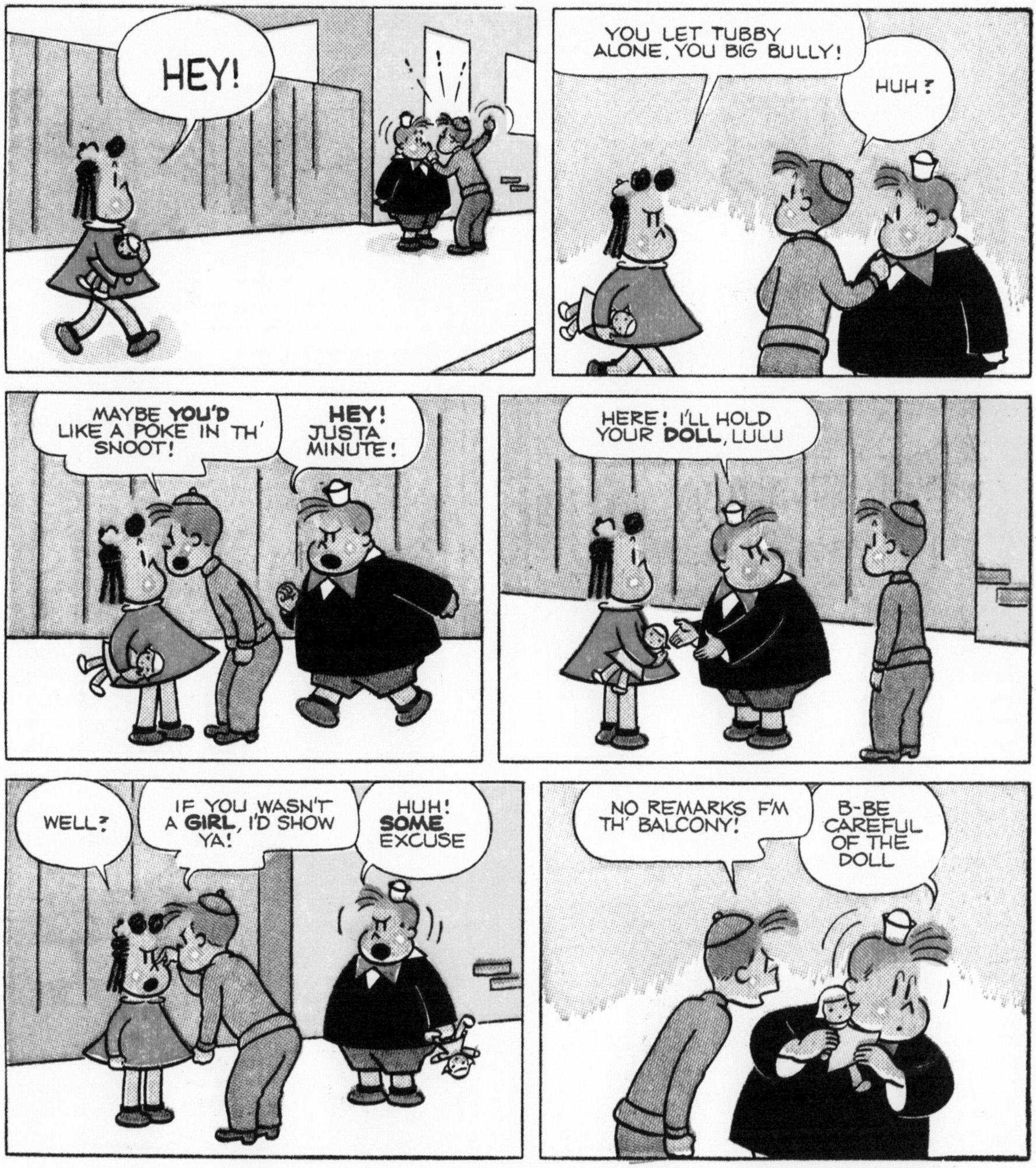
HEY!
YOU LET TUBBY ALONE, YOU BIG BULLY!
HUH?
MAYBE YOU'D LIKE A POKE IN TH' SNOOT!
HEY! JUSTA MINUTE!
HERE! I'LL HOLD YOUR DOLL, LULU
WELL?
IF YOU WASN'T A GIRL, I'D SHOW YA!
HUH! SOME EXCUSE
NO REMARKS F'M TH' BALCONY!
B-BE CAREFUL OF THE DOLL

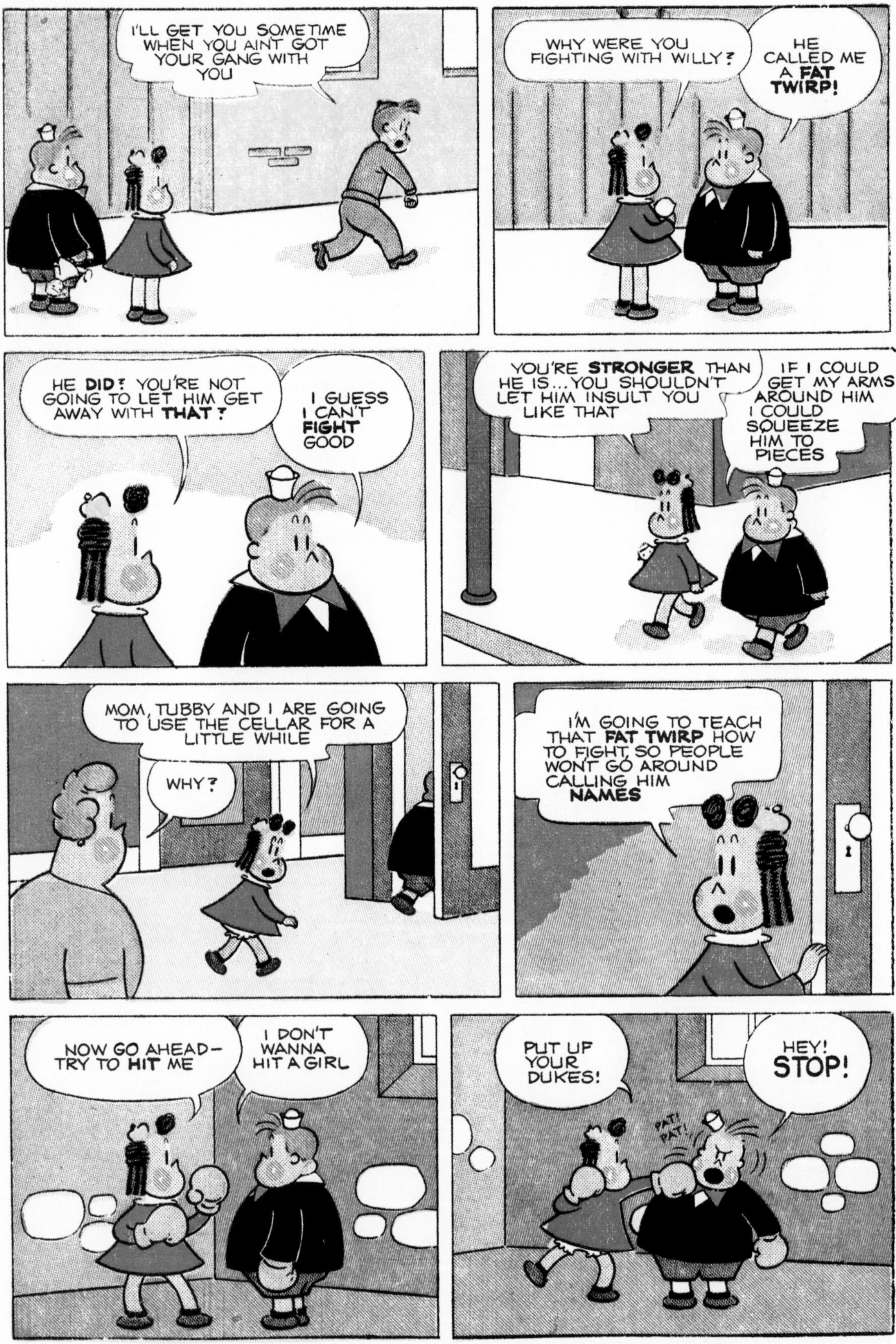
I'LL GET YOU SOMETIME WHEN YOU AINT GOT YOUR GANG WITH YOU
WHY WERE YOU FIGHTING WITH WILLY?
HE CALLED ME A FAT TWIRP!
HE DID? YOU'RE NOT GOING TO LET HIM GET AWAY WITH THAT?
I GUESS I CAN'T FIGHT GOOD
YOU'RE STRONGER THAN HE IS... YOU SHOULDN'T LET HIM INSULT YOU LIKE THAT
IF I COULD GET MY ARMS AROUND HIM I COULD SQUEEZE HIM TO PIECES
MOM, TUBBY AND I ARE GOING TO USE THE CELLAR FOR A LITTLE WHILE
WHY?
I'M GOING TO TEACH THAT FAT TWIRP HOW TO FIGHT, SO PEOPLE WON'T GO AROUND CALLING HIM NAMES
NOW GO AHEAD-TRY TO HIT ME
I DON'T WANNA HIT A GIRL
PUT UP YOUR DUKES!
PAT! PAT!
HEY! STOP!

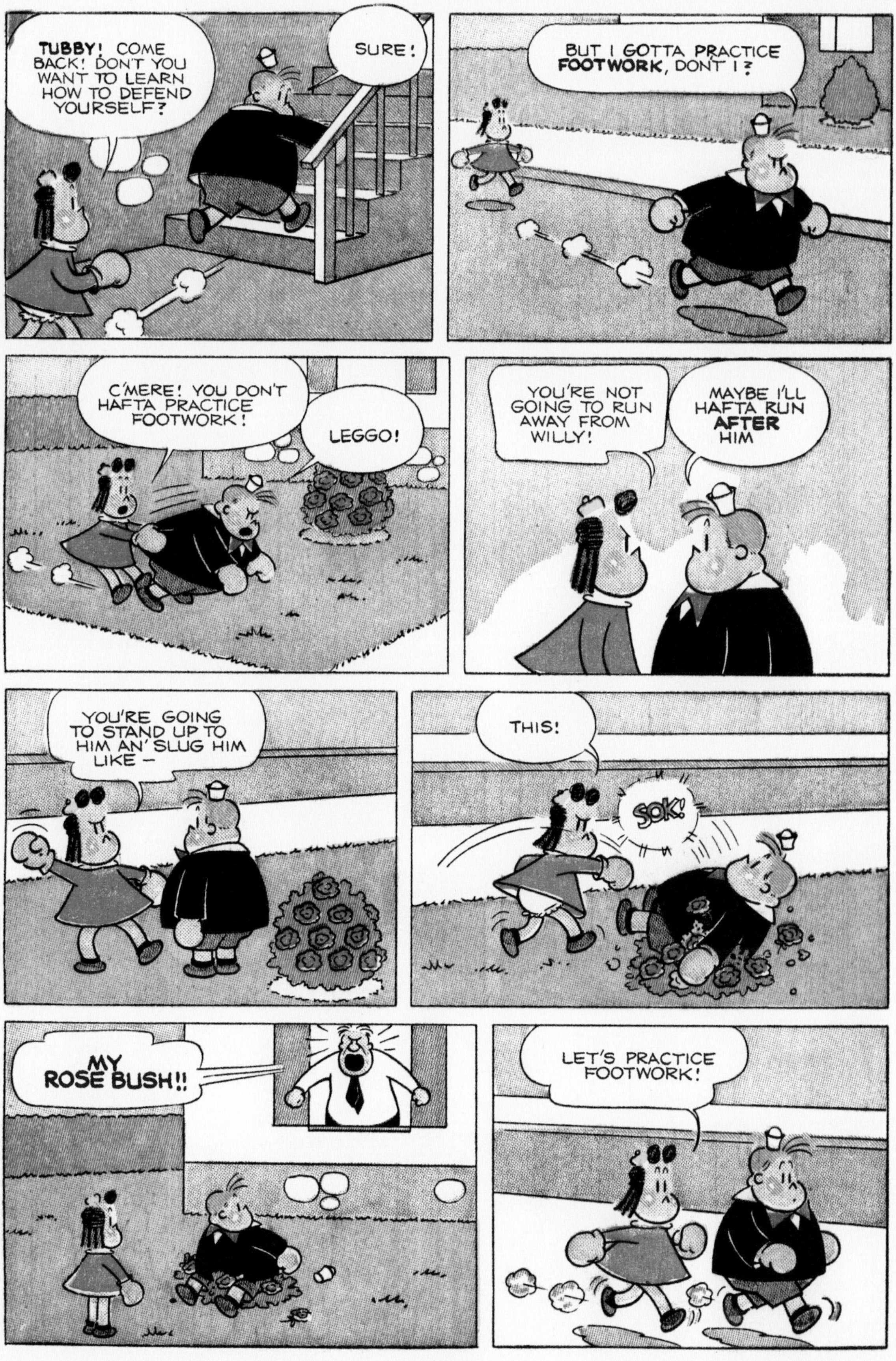
TUBBY! COME BACK! DON'T YOU WANT TO LEARN HOW TO DEFEND YOURSELF?
SURE!
BUT I GOTTA PRACTICE FOOTWORK, DON'T I?
C'MERE! YOU DON'T HAFTA PRACTICE FOOTWORK!
LEGGO!
YOU'RE NOT GOING TO RUN AWAY FROM WILLY!
MAYBE I'LL HAFTA RUN AFTER HIM
YOU'RE GOING TO STAND UP TO HIM AN' SLUG HIM LIKE –
THIS!
SOK!
MY ROSE BUSH!!
LET'S PRACTICE FOOTWORK!

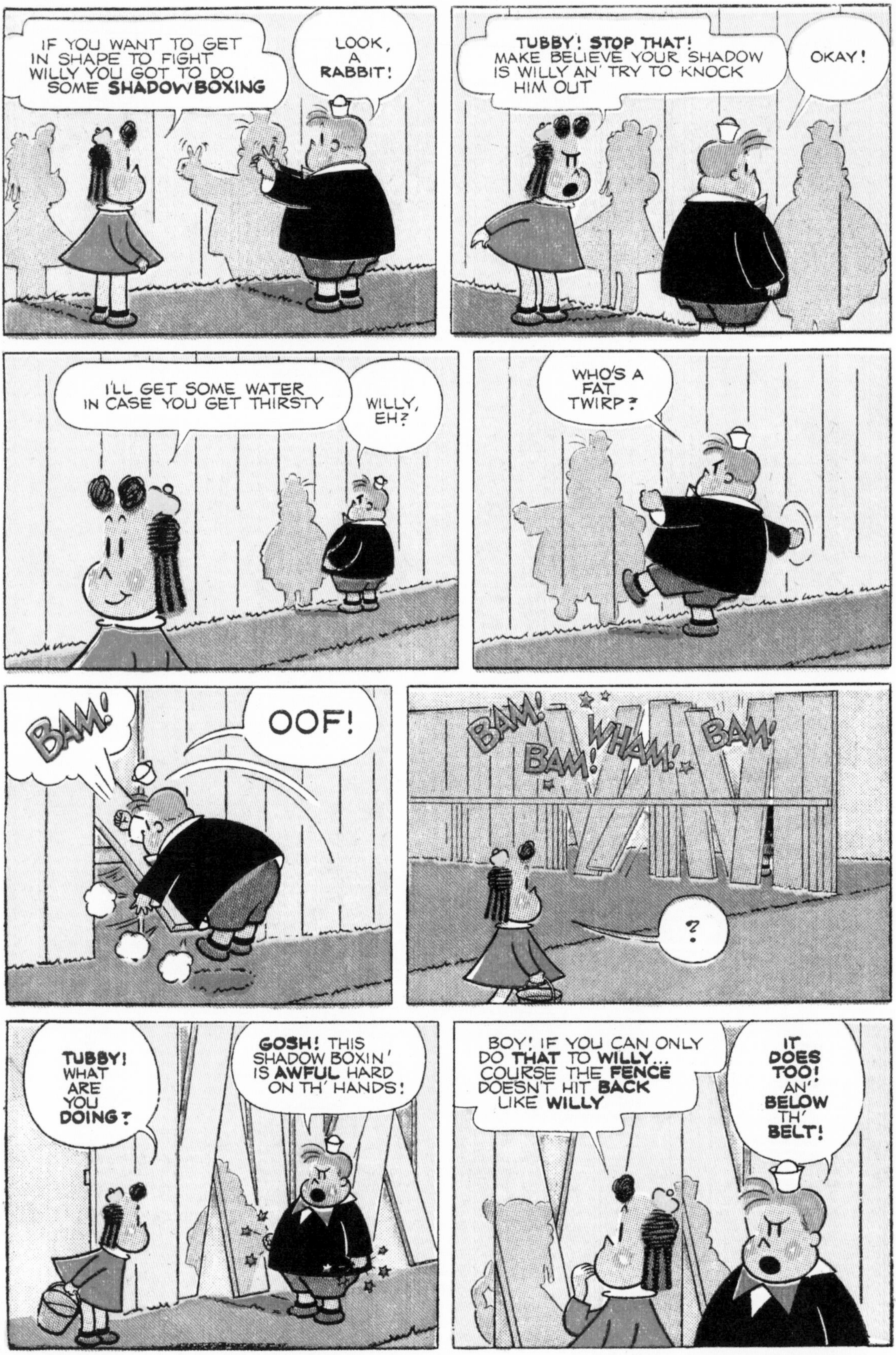
IF YOU WANT TO GET IN SHAPE TO FIGHT WILLY YOU GOT TO DO SOME **SHADOWBOXING**
LOOK, A **RABBIT**!
TUBBY! STOP THAT! MAKE BELIEVE YOUR SHADOW IS WILLY AN' TRY TO KNOCK HIM OUT
OKAY!
I'LL GET SOME WATER IN CASE YOU GET THIRSTY
WILLY, EH?
WHO'S A FAT TWIRP?
BAM!
OOF!
BAM!
BAM!
WHAM!
BAM!
?
TUBBY! WHAT ARE YOU **DOING**?
GOSH! THIS SHADOW BOXIN' IS **AWFUL** HARD ON TH' HANDS!
BOY! IF YOU CAN ONLY DO **THAT** TO **WILLY**... COURSE THE **FENCE** DOESN'T HIT **BACK** LIKE **WILLY**
IT DOES TOO! AN' **BELOW** TH' **BELT!**

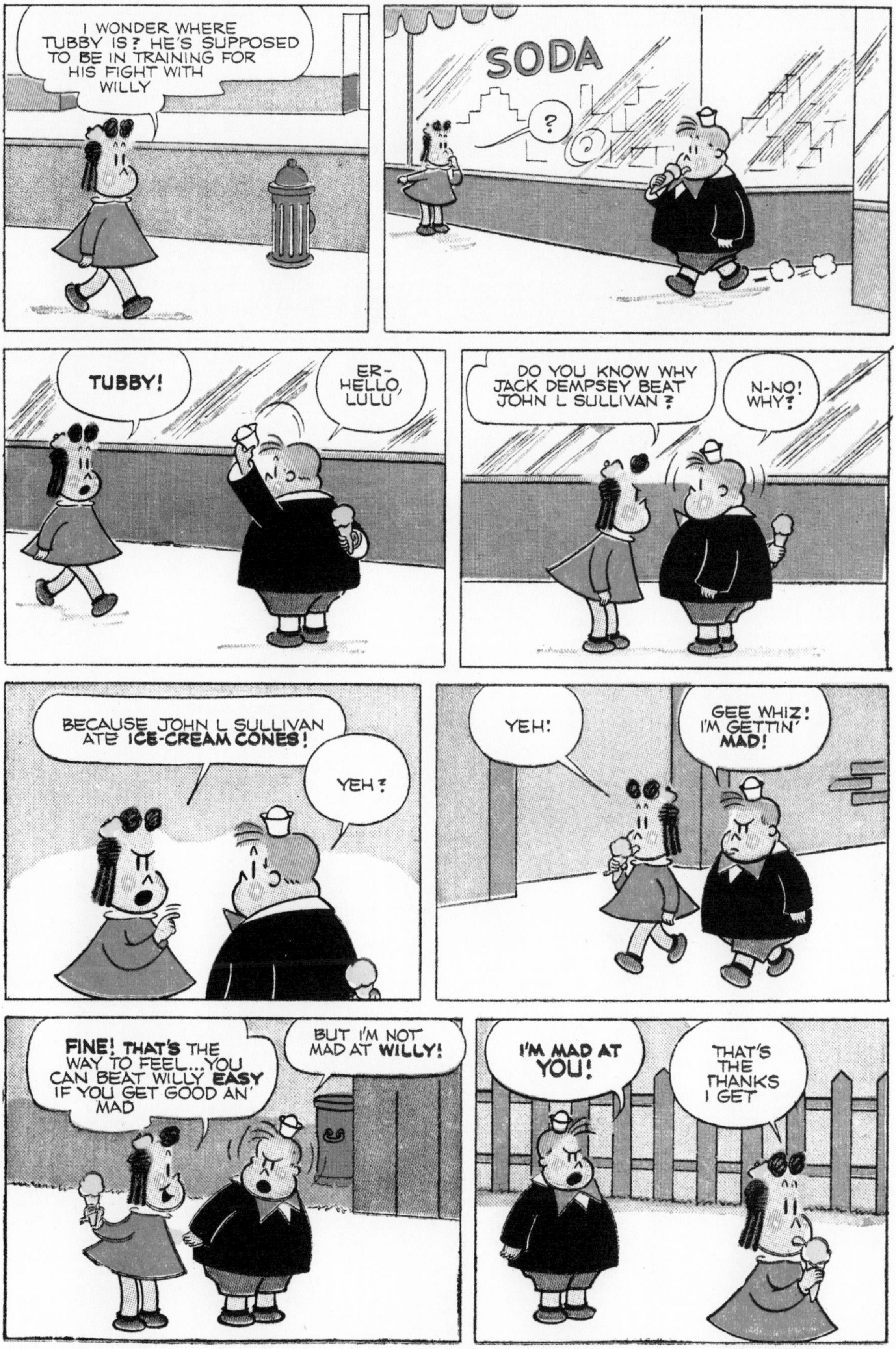
I WONDER WHERE TUBBY IS? HE'S SUPPOSED TO BE IN TRAINING FOR HIS FIGHT WITH WILLY
SODA
?
TUBBY!
ER- HELLO, LULU
DO YOU KNOW WHY JACK DEMPSEY BEAT JOHN L SULLIVAN?
N-NO! WHY?
BECAUSE JOHN L SULLIVAN ATE ICE-CREAM CONES!
YEH?
YEH!
GEE WHIZ! I'M GETTIN' MAD!
FINE! THAT'S THE WAY TO FEEL...YOU CAN BEAT WILLY EASY IF YOU GET GOOD AN' MAD
BUT I'M NOT MAD AT WILLY!
I'M MAD AT YOU!
THAT'S THE THANKS I GET

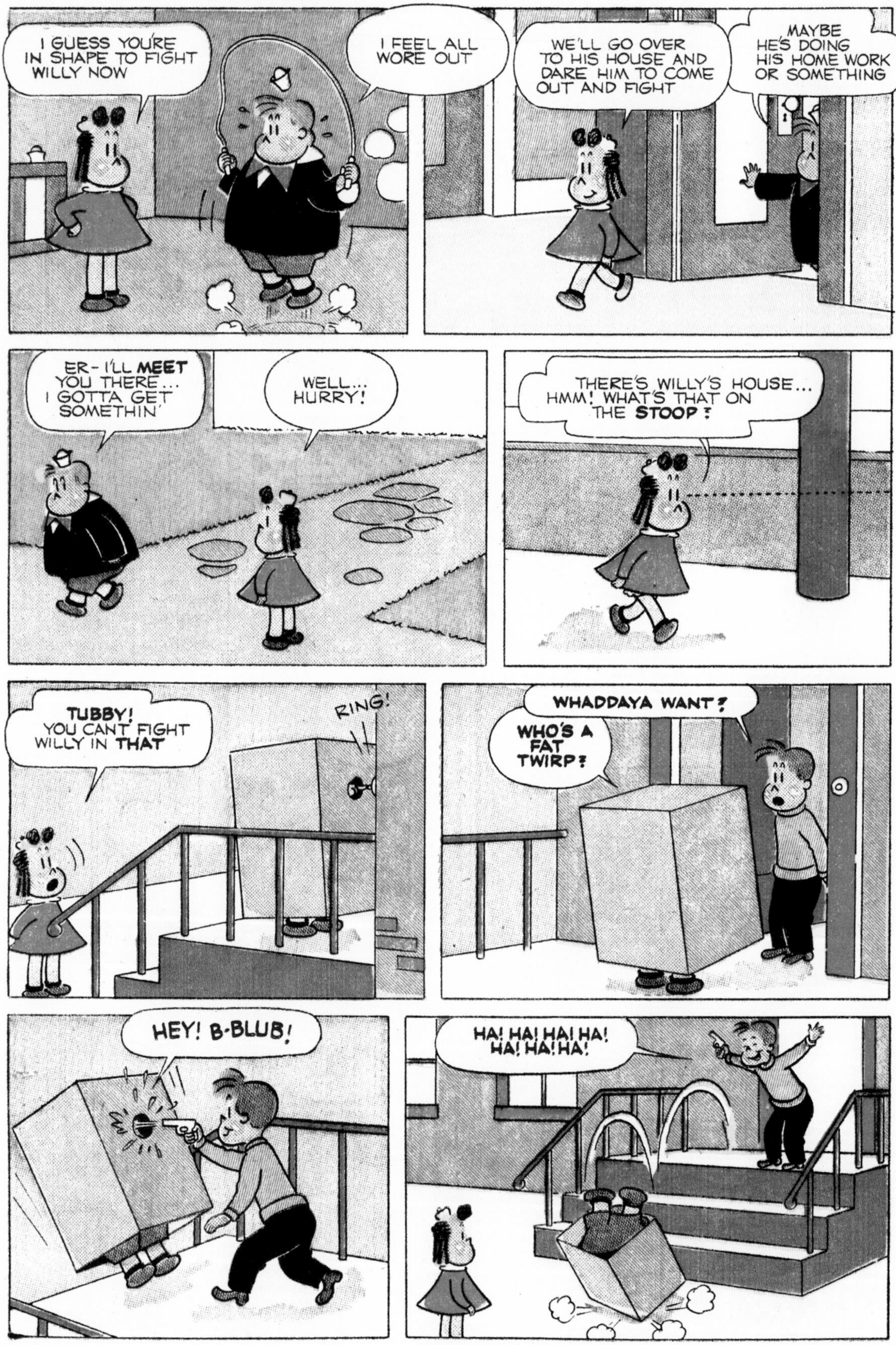

I GUESS YOU'RE IN SHAPE TO FIGHT WILLY NOW
I FEEL ALL WORE OUT
WE'LL GO OVER TO HIS HOUSE AND DARE HIM TO COME OUT AND FIGHT
MAYBE HE'S DOING HIS HOME WORK OR SOMETHING
ER- I'LL MEET YOU THERE... I GOTTA GET SOMETHIN'
WELL... HURRY!
THERE'S WILLY'S HOUSE... HMM! WHAT'S THAT ON THE STOOP?
TUBBY! YOU CAN'T FIGHT WILLY IN THAT
RING!
WHADDAYA WANT?
WHO'S A FAT TWIRP?
HEY! B-BLUB!
HA! HA! HA! HA! HA! HA! HA!

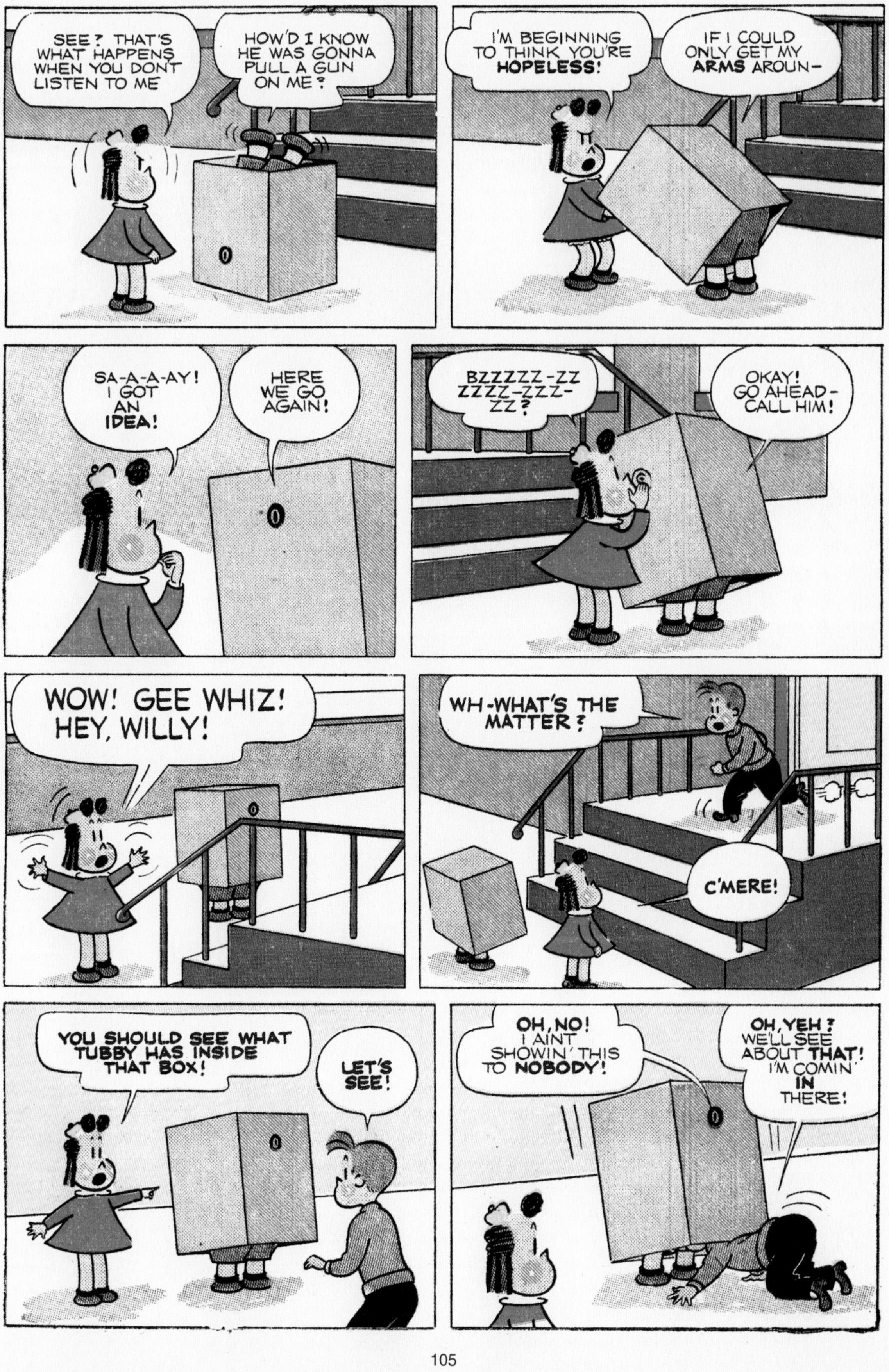
SEE? THAT'S WHAT HAPPENS WHEN YOU DON'T LISTEN TO ME
HOW'D I KNOW HE WAS GONNA PULL A GUN ON ME?
I'M BEGINNING TO THINK YOU'RE **HOPELESS**!
IF I COULD ONLY GET MY **ARMS** AROUN-
SA-A-A-AY! I GOT AN **IDEA**!
HERE WE GO AGAIN!
BZZZZZ-ZZ ZZZZ-ZZZ-ZZ?
OKAY! GO AHEAD-CALL HIM!
WOW! GEE WHIZ! HEY, WILLY!
WH-WHAT'S THE MATTER?
C'MERE!
YOU SHOULD SEE WHAT TUBBY HAS INSIDE THAT BOX!
LET'S SEE!
OH, NO! I AINT SHOWIN' THIS TO **NOBODY**!
OH, YEH? WE'LL SEE ABOUT **THAT**! I'M COMIN' **IN** THERE!

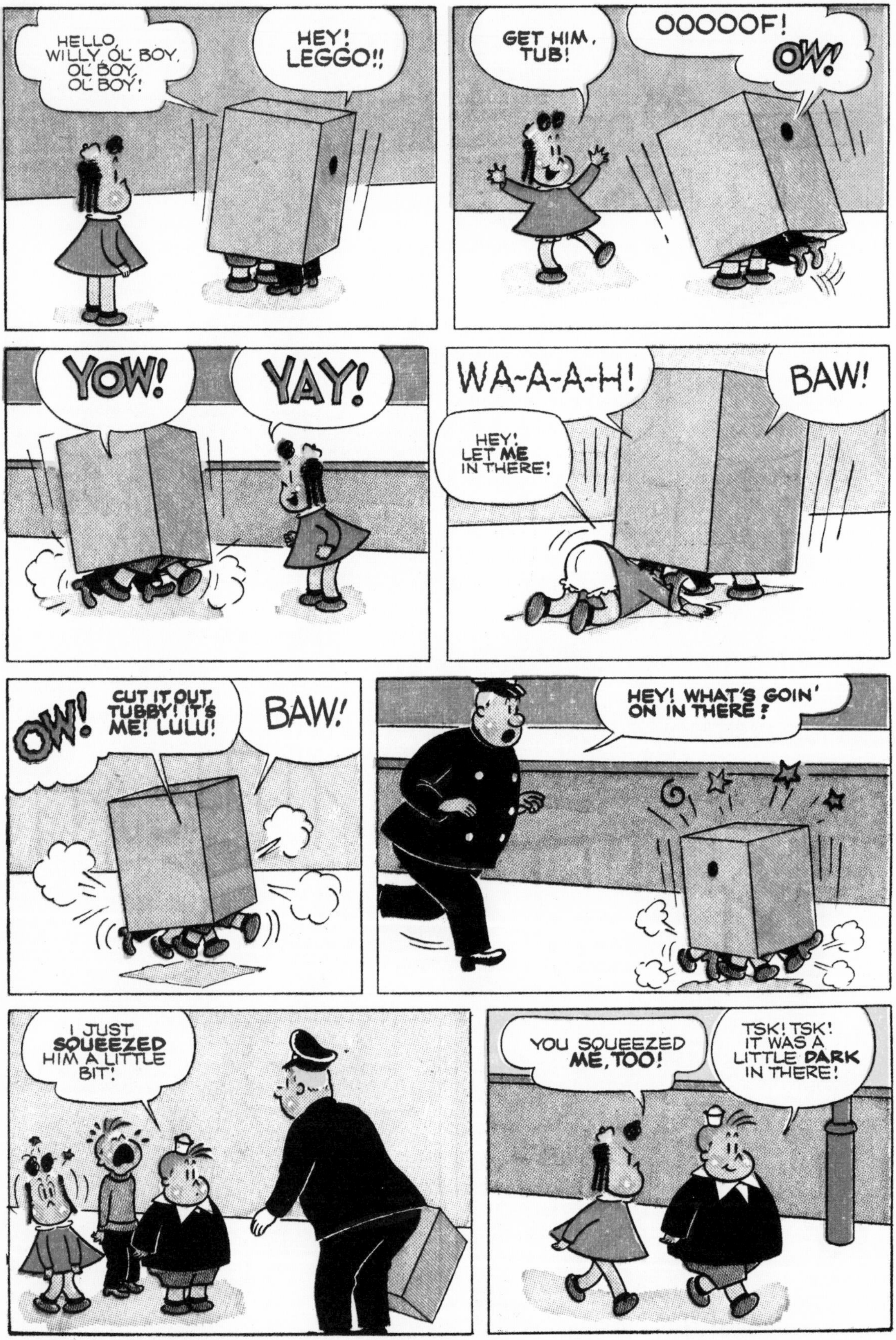
HELLO, WILLY, OL' BOY, OL' BOY, OL' BOY!
HEY! LEGGO!!
GET HIM, TUB!
OOOOOF!
OW!
YOW!
YAY!
WA-A-A-H!
HEY! LET ME IN THERE!
BAW!
OW!
CUT IT OUT, TUBBY! IT'S ME! LULU!
BAW!
HEY! WHAT'S GOIN' ON IN THERE?
I JUST SQUEEZED HIM A LITTLE BIT!
YOU SQUEEZED ME, TOO!
TSK! TSK! IT WAS A LITTLE DARK IN THERE!

marge's

LITTLE LULU

STUFF AN' NONSENSE

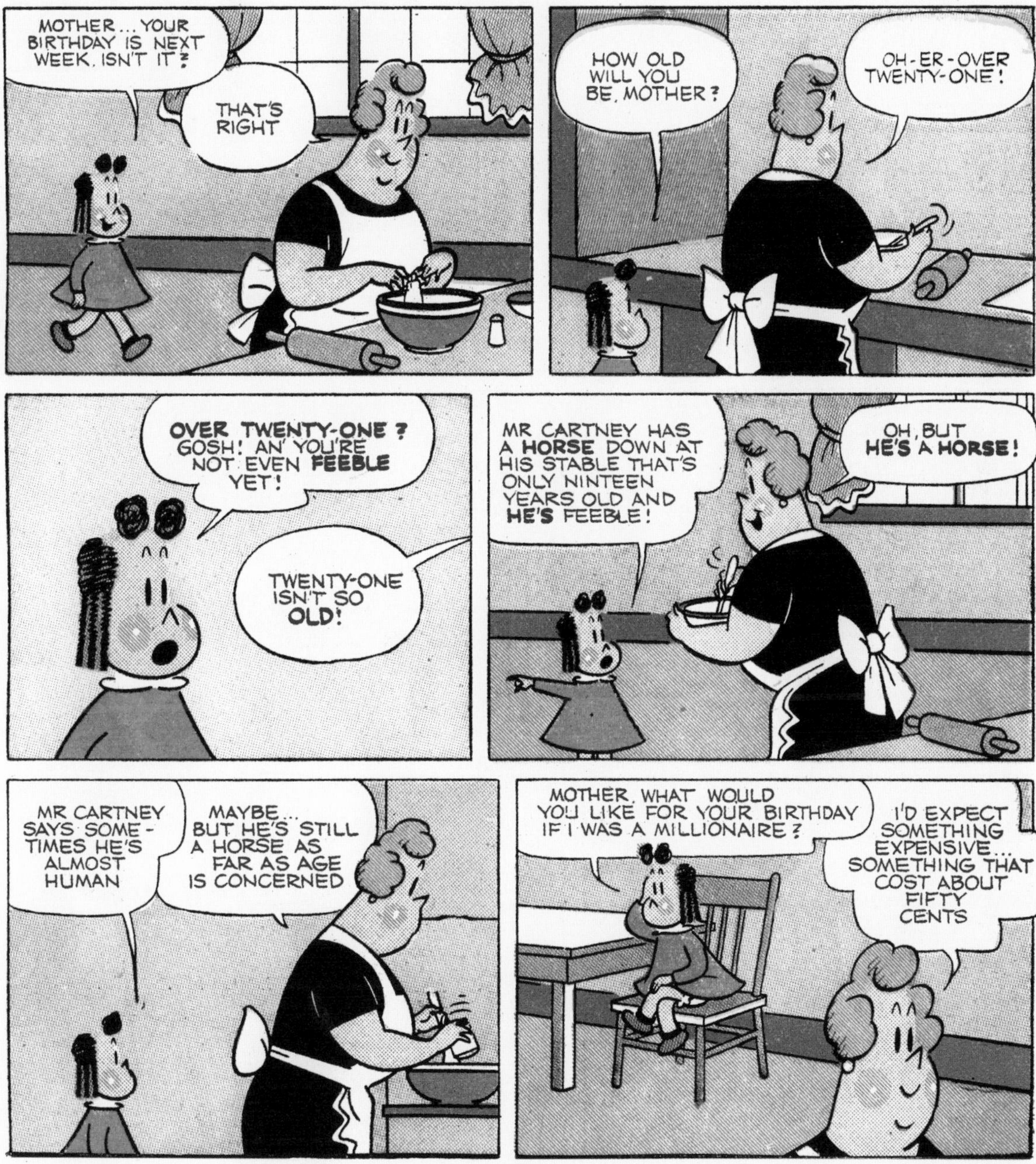
MOTHER... YOUR BIRTHDAY IS NEXT WEEK, ISN'T IT?
THAT'S RIGHT
HOW OLD WILL YOU BE, MOTHER?
OH-ER-OVER TWENTY-ONE!
OVER TWENTY-ONE? GOSH! AN' YOU'RE NOT EVEN FEEBLE YET!
TWENTY-ONE ISN'T SO OLD!
MR CARTNEY HAS A HORSE DOWN AT HIS STABLE THAT'S ONLY NINTEEN YEARS OLD AND HE'S FEEBLE!
OH, BUT HE'S A HORSE!
MR CARTNEY SAYS SOME-TIMES HE'S ALMOST HUMAN
MAYBE... BUT HE'S STILL A HORSE AS FAR AS AGE IS CONCERNED
MOTHER, WHAT WOULD YOU LIKE FOR YOUR BIRTHDAY IF I WAS A MILLIONAIRE?
I'D EXPECT SOMETHING EXPENSIVE... SOMETHING THAT COST ABOUT FIFTY CENTS

WELL SUPPOSE I WASN'T A MILLIONAIRE? SUPPOSE I WAS POOR?
THEN I'D BE SATISFIED WITH A BIG KISS
I WOULDN'T BE SATISFIED WITH A BIG KISS FOR MY BIRTHDAY
BETCHA THERE'S AT LEAST FIFTY CENTS IN MY PIGGY BANK
RATTLE! RATTLE!
LULU! LET THAT BANK ALONE!!
RATTLE! RATTLE! RAT
I'VE TOLD YOU NOT TO LET ME CATCH YOU TAKING MONEY OUT OF YOUR BANK!
YES, MOTHER
RATTLE! RATTLE! RATTLE!
LULU!
RATTLE! RATTLE!

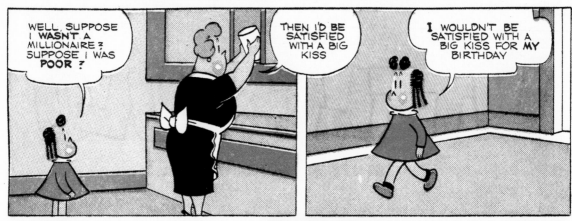

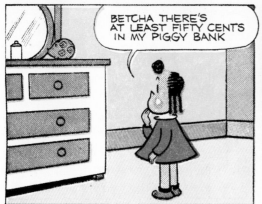

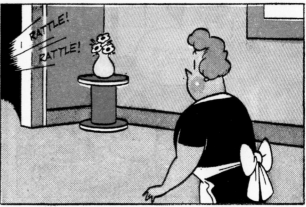

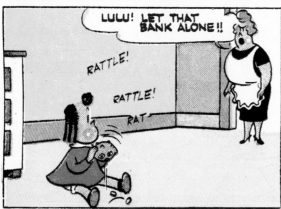

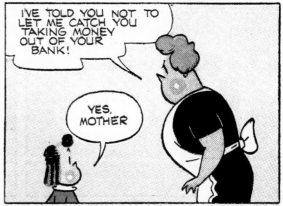

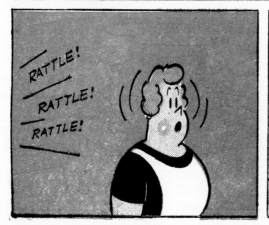

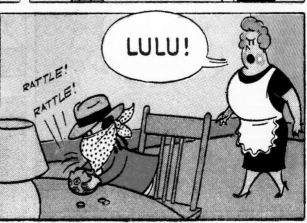

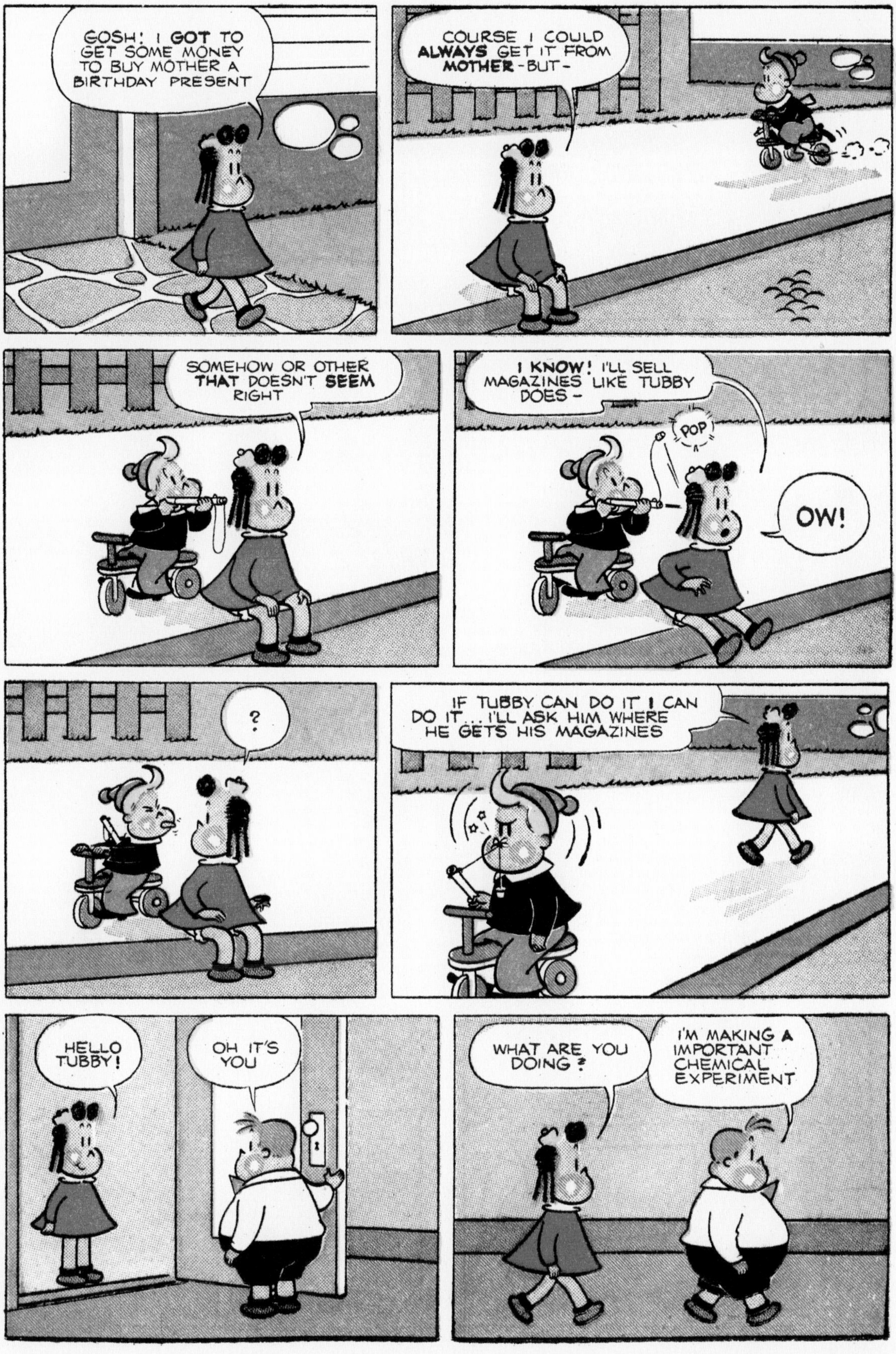
GOSH! I GOT TO GET SOME MONEY TO BUY MOTHER A BIRTHDAY PRESENT
COURSE I COULD ALWAYS GET IT FROM MOTHER-BUT-
SOMEHOW OR OTHER THAT DOESN'T SEEM RIGHT
I KNOW! I'LL SELL MAGAZINES LIKE TUBBY DOES-
POP
OW!
?
IF TUBBY CAN DO IT I CAN DO IT... I'LL ASK HIM WHERE HE GETS HIS MAGAZINES
HELLO TUBBY!
OH IT'S YOU
WHAT ARE YOU DOING?
I'M MAKING A IMPORTANT CHEMICAL EXPERIMENT

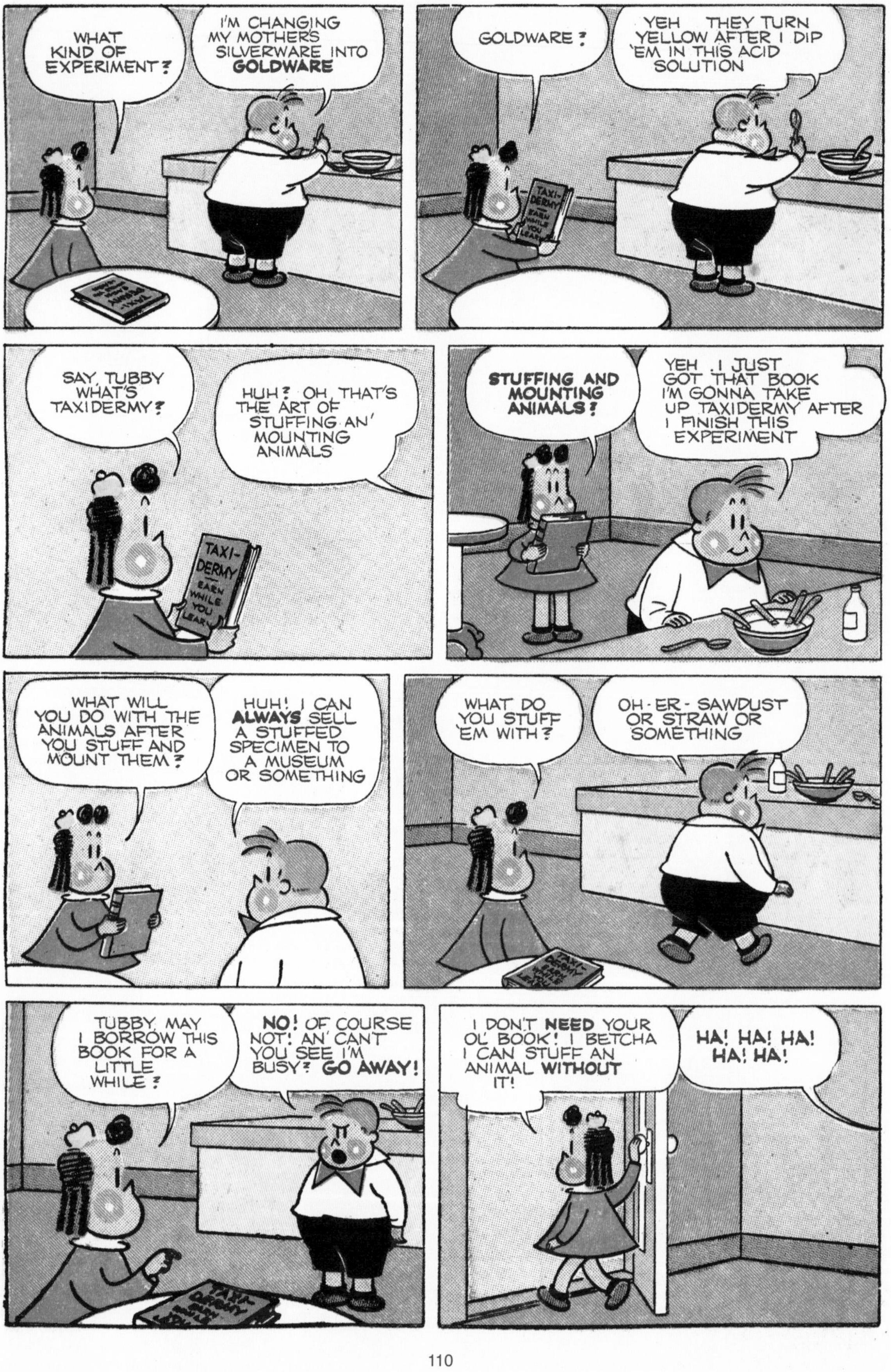
WHAT KIND OF EXPERIMENT?
I'M CHANGING MY MOTHER'S SILVERWARE INTO **GOLDWARE**
GOLDWARE?
YEH THEY TURN YELLOW AFTER I DIP 'EM IN THIS ACID SOLUTION
SAY, TUBBY WHAT'S TAXIDERMY?
HUH? OH, THAT'S THE ART OF STUFFING AN' MOUNTING ANIMALS
TAXI- DERMY
STUFFING AND MOUNTING ANIMALS?
YEH . I JUST GOT THAT BOOK I'M GONNA TAKE UP TAXIDERMY AFTER I FINISH THIS EXPERIMENT
WHAT WILL YOU DO WITH THE ANIMALS AFTER YOU STUFF AND MOUNT THEM?
HUH! I CAN **ALWAYS** SELL A STUFFED SPECIMEN TO A MUSEUM OR SOMETHING
WHAT DO YOU STUFF 'EM WITH?
OH-ER-SAWDUST OR STRAW OR SOMETHING
TUBBY, MAY I BORROW THIS BOOK FOR A LITTLE WHILE?
NO! OF COURSE NOT! AN' CAN'T YOU SEE I'M BUSY? **GO AWAY!**
I DON'T **NEED** YOUR OL' BOOK! I BETCHA I CAN STUFF AN ANIMAL **WITHOUT** IT!
HA! HA! HA! HA! HA!

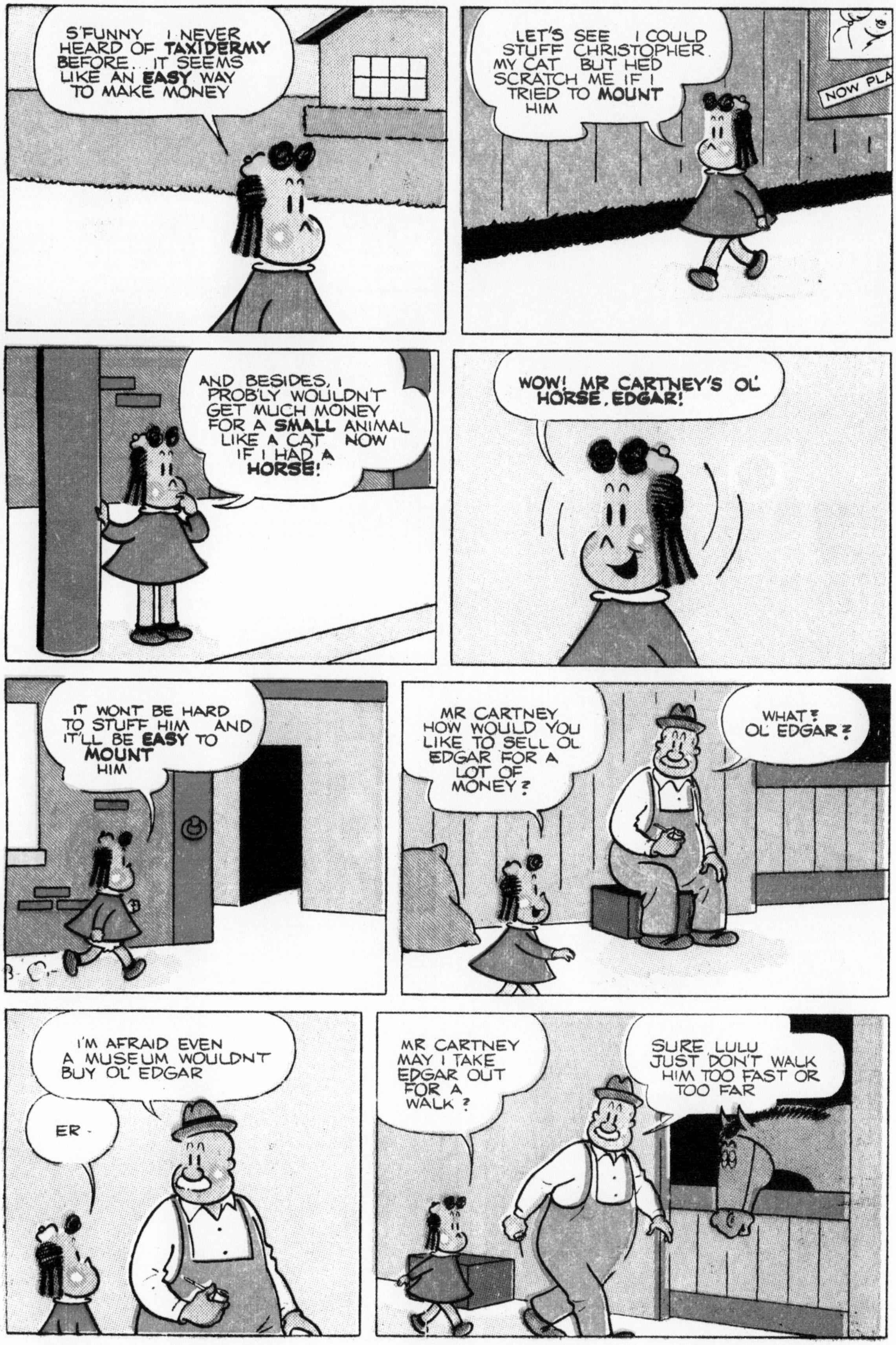
S'FUNNY I NEVER HEARD OF TAXIDERMY BEFORE... IT SEEMS LIKE AN EASY WAY TO MAKE MONEY
LET'S SEE I COULD STUFF CHRISTOPHER MY CAT BUT HED SCRATCH ME IF I TRIED TO MOUNT HIM
NOW PLA
AND BESIDES, I PROB'LY WOULDN'T GET MUCH MONEY FOR A SMALL ANIMAL LIKE A CAT NOW IF I HAD A HORSE!
WOW! MR CARTNEY'S OL' HORSE, EDGAR!
IT WONT BE HARD TO STUFF HIM AND IT'LL BE EASY TO MOUNT HIM
MR CARTNEY HOW WOULD YOU LIKE TO SELL OL EDGAR FOR A LOT OF MONEY?
WHAT? OL' EDGAR?
I'M AFRAID EVEN A MUSEUM WOULDNT BUY OL' EDGAR
ER -
MR CARTNEY MAY I TAKE EDGAR OUT FOR A WALK?
SURE LULU JUST DON'T WALK HIM TOO FAST OR TOO FAR

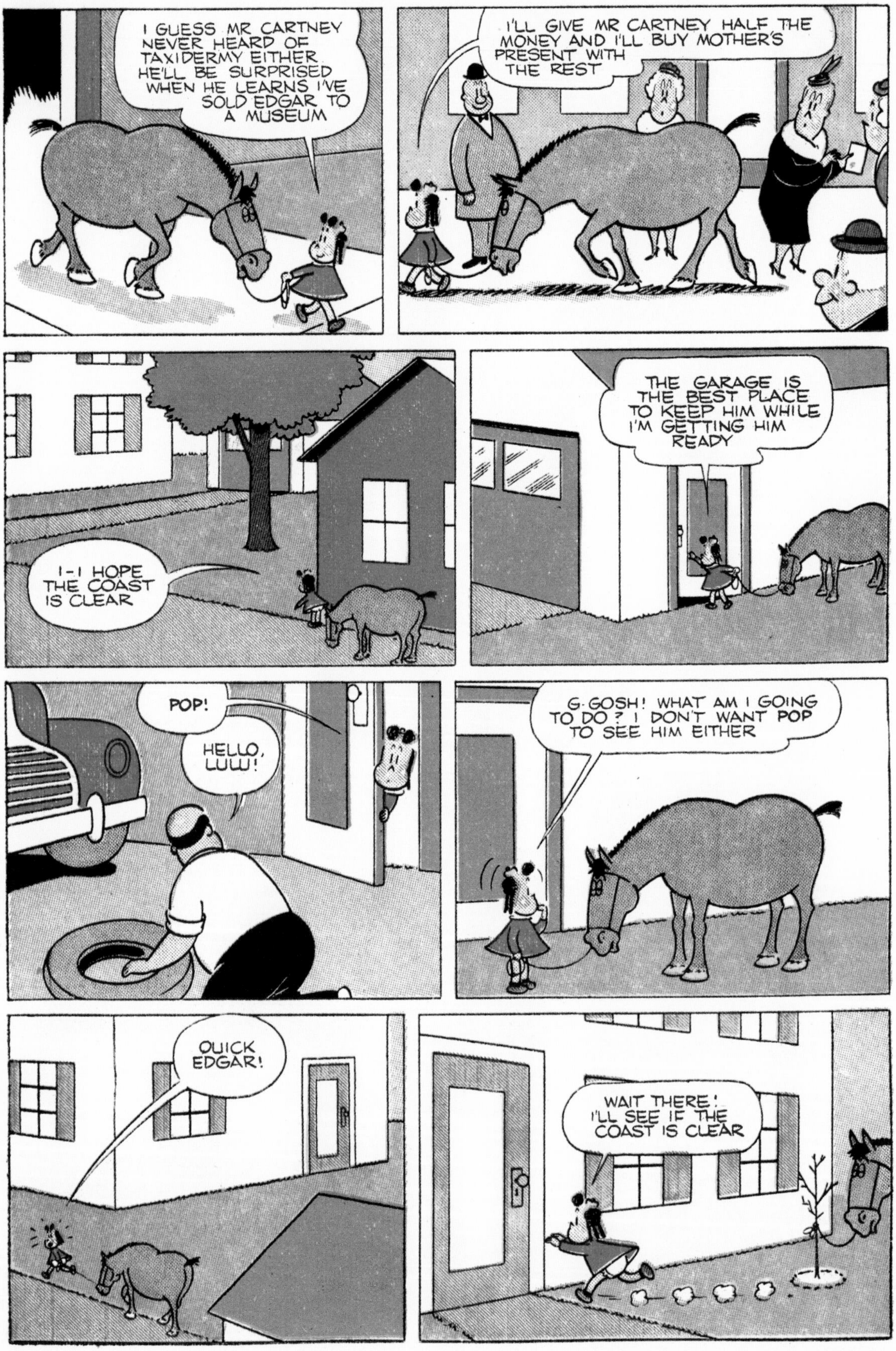
I GUESS MR CARTNEY NEVER HEARD OF TAXIDERMY EITHER HE'LL BE SURPRISED WHEN HE LEARNS I'VE SOLD EDGAR TO A MUSEUM
I'LL GIVE MR CARTNEY HALF THE MONEY AND I'LL BUY MOTHER'S PRESENT WITH THE REST
I-I HOPE THE COAST IS CLEAR
THE GARAGE IS THE BEST PLACE TO KEEP HIM WHILE I'M GETTING HIM READY
POP!
HELLO, LULU!
G-GOSH! WHAT AM I GOING TO DO? I DON'T WANT POP TO SEE HIM EITHER
QUICK EDGAR!
WAIT THERE! I'LL SEE IF THE COAST IS CLEAR

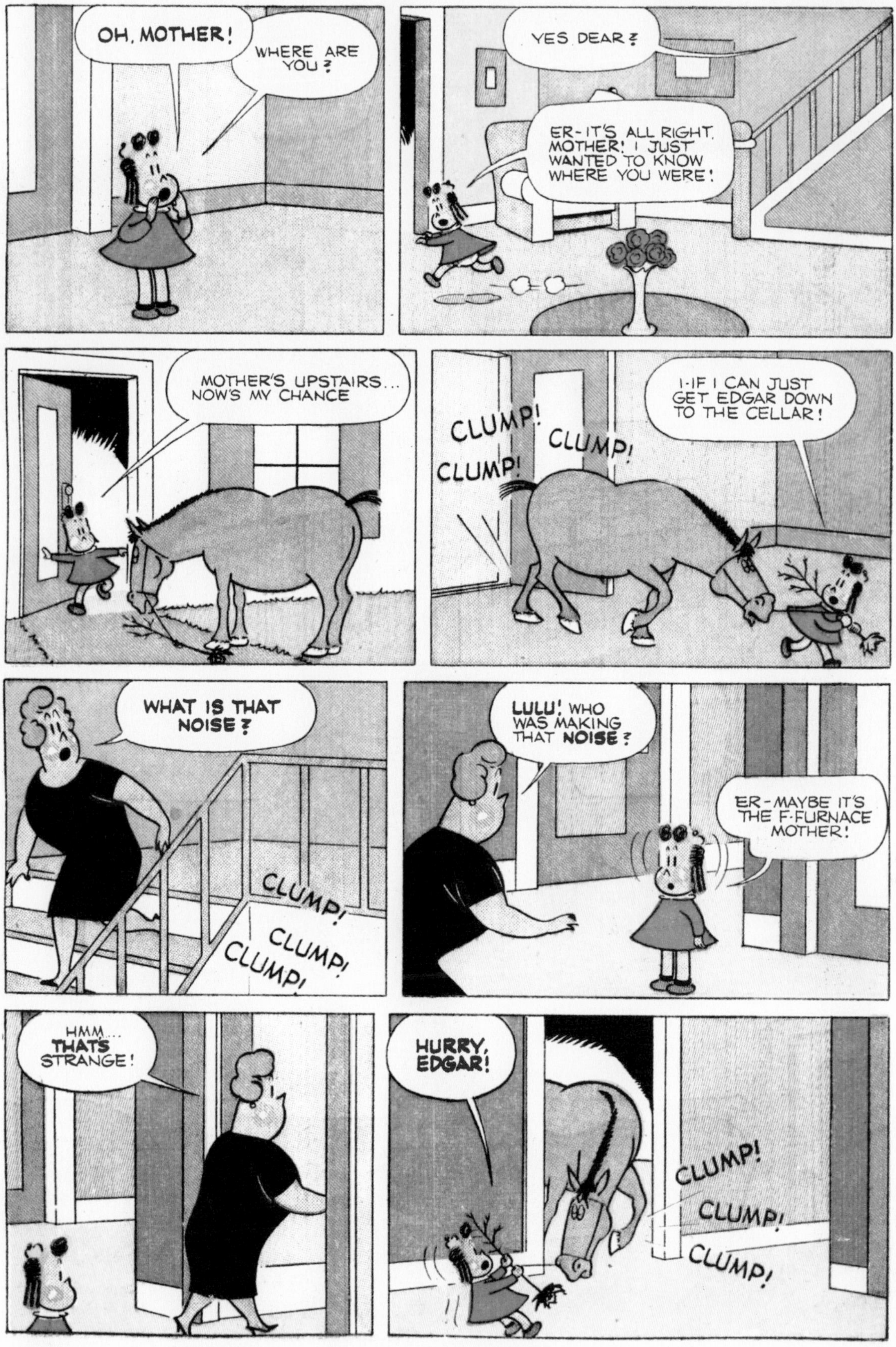
OH, MOTHER!
WHERE ARE YOU?
YES DEAR?
ER-IT'S ALL RIGHT, MOTHER! I JUST WANTED TO KNOW WHERE YOU WERE!
MOTHER'S UPSTAIRS... NOW'S MY CHANCE
CLUMP!
CLUMP!
CLUMP!
I-IF I CAN JUST GET EDGAR DOWN TO THE CELLAR!
WHAT IS THAT NOISE?
CLUMP!
CLUMP!
CLUMP!
LULU! WHO WAS MAKING THAT NOISE?
ER-MAYBE IT'S THE F-FURNACE MOTHER!
HMM... THATS STRANGE!
HURRY, EDGAR!
CLUMP!
CLUMP!
CLUMP!

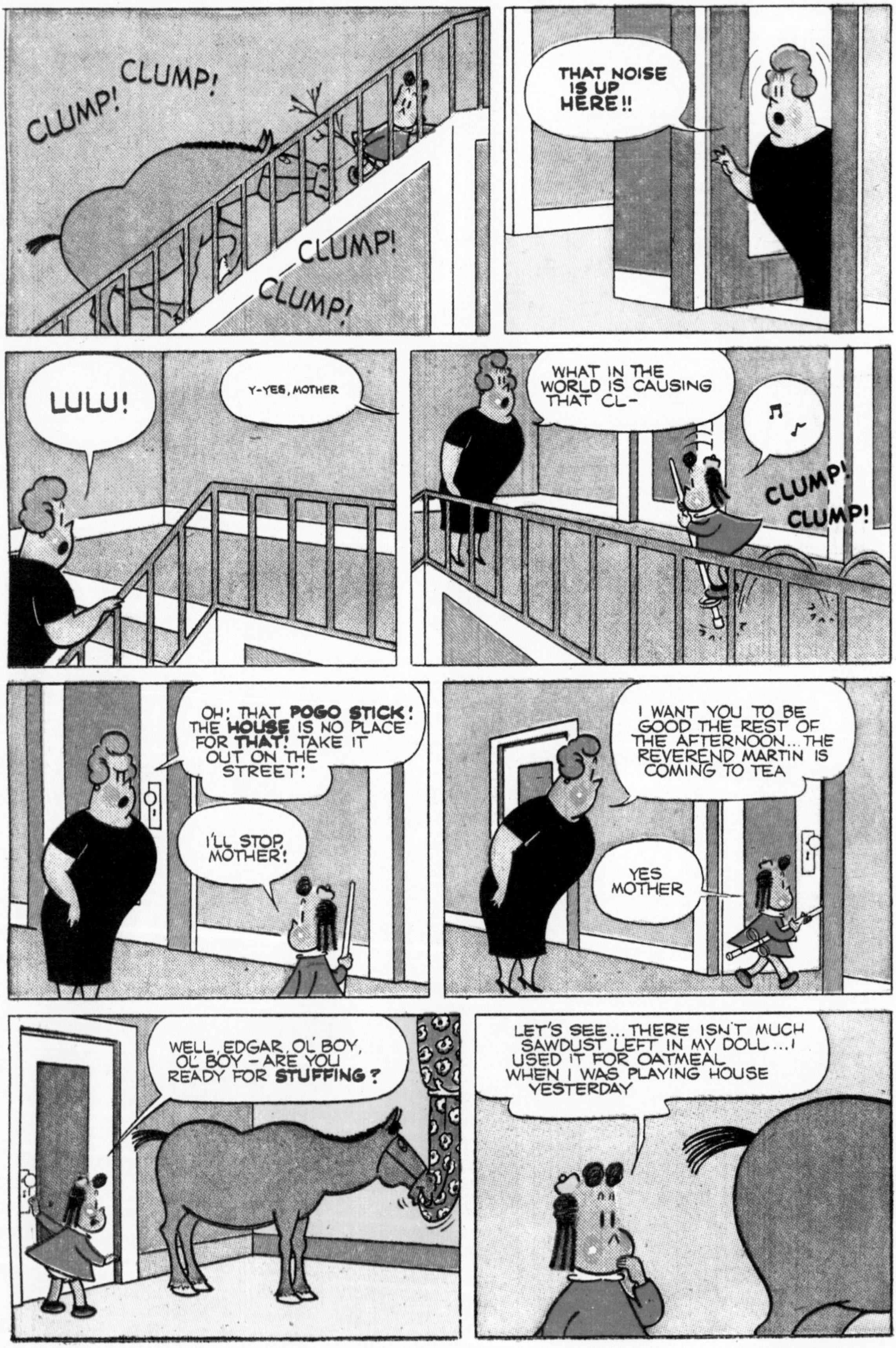

CLUMP! CLUMP!
CLUMP!
CLUMP!
THAT NOISE IS UP HERE!!
LULU!
Y-YES, MOTHER
WHAT IN THE WORLD IS CAUSING THAT CL-
CLUMP!
CLUMP!
OH! THAT POGO STICK! THE HOUSE IS NO PLACE FOR THAT! TAKE IT OUT ON THE STREET!
I'LL STOP, MOTHER!
I WANT YOU TO BE GOOD THE REST OF THE AFTERNOON...THE REVEREND MARTIN IS COMING TO TEA
YES MOTHER
WELL, EDGAR, OL' BOY, OL' BOY - ARE YOU READY FOR STUFFING?
LET'S SEE...THERE ISN'T MUCH SAWDUST LEFT IN MY DOLL...I USED IT FOR OATMEAL WHEN I WAS PLAYING HOUSE YESTERDAY

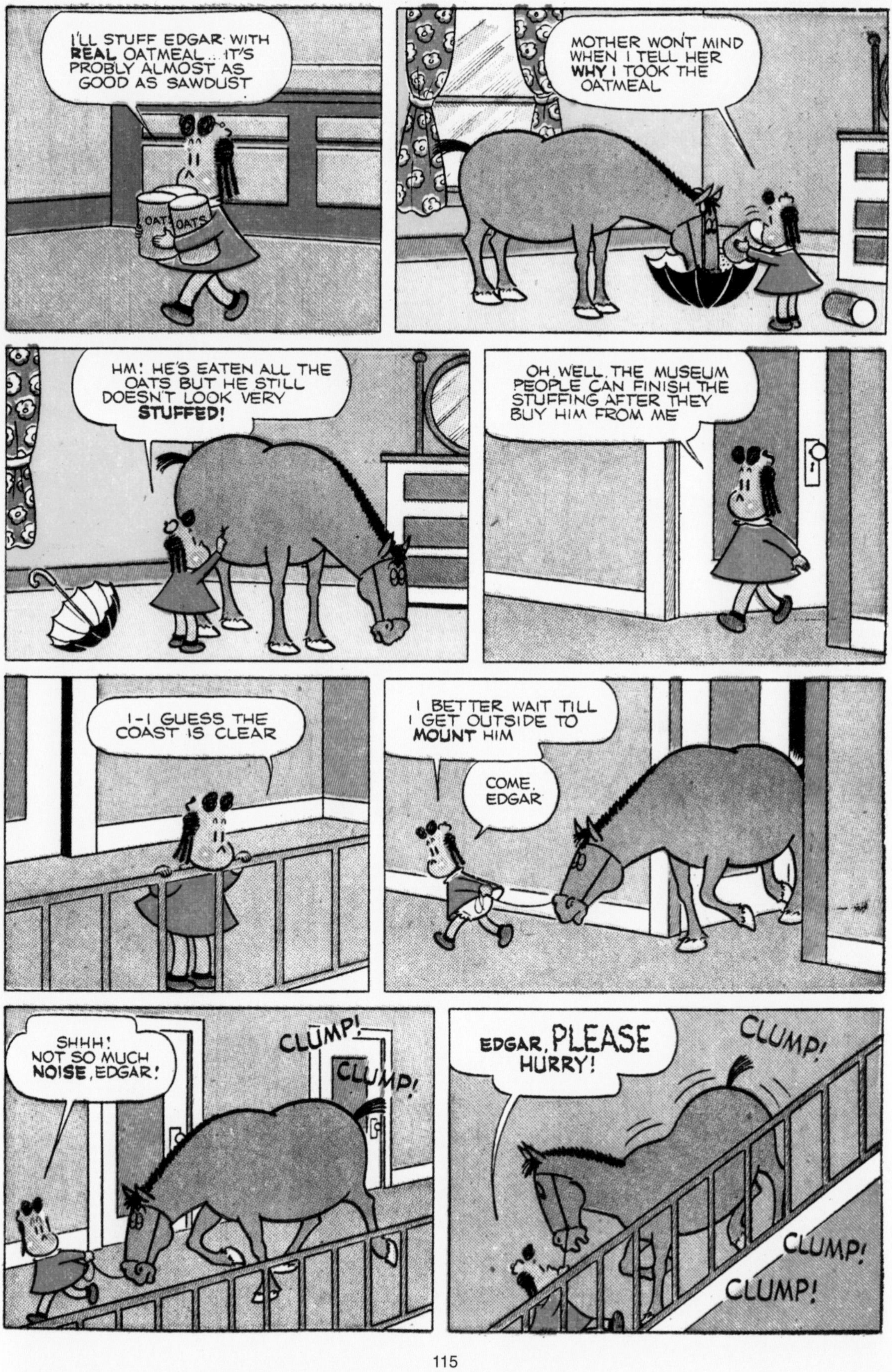
I'LL STUFF EDGAR WITH REAL OATMEAL... IT'S PROBLY ALMOST AS GOOD AS SAWDUST
OATS
OATS
MOTHER WON'T MIND WHEN I TELL HER WHY I TOOK THE OATMEAL
HM! HE'S EATEN ALL THE OATS BUT HE STILL DOESN'T LOOK VERY STUFFED!
OH, WELL, THE MUSEUM PEOPLE CAN FINISH THE STUFFING AFTER THEY BUY HIM FROM ME
I-I GUESS THE COAST IS CLEAR
I BETTER WAIT TILL I GET OUTSIDE TO MOUNT HIM
COME, EDGAR
SHHH! NOT SO MUCH NOISE, EDGAR!
CLUMP!
CLUMP!
EDGAR, PLEASE HURRY!
CLUMP!
CLUMP!
CLUMP!

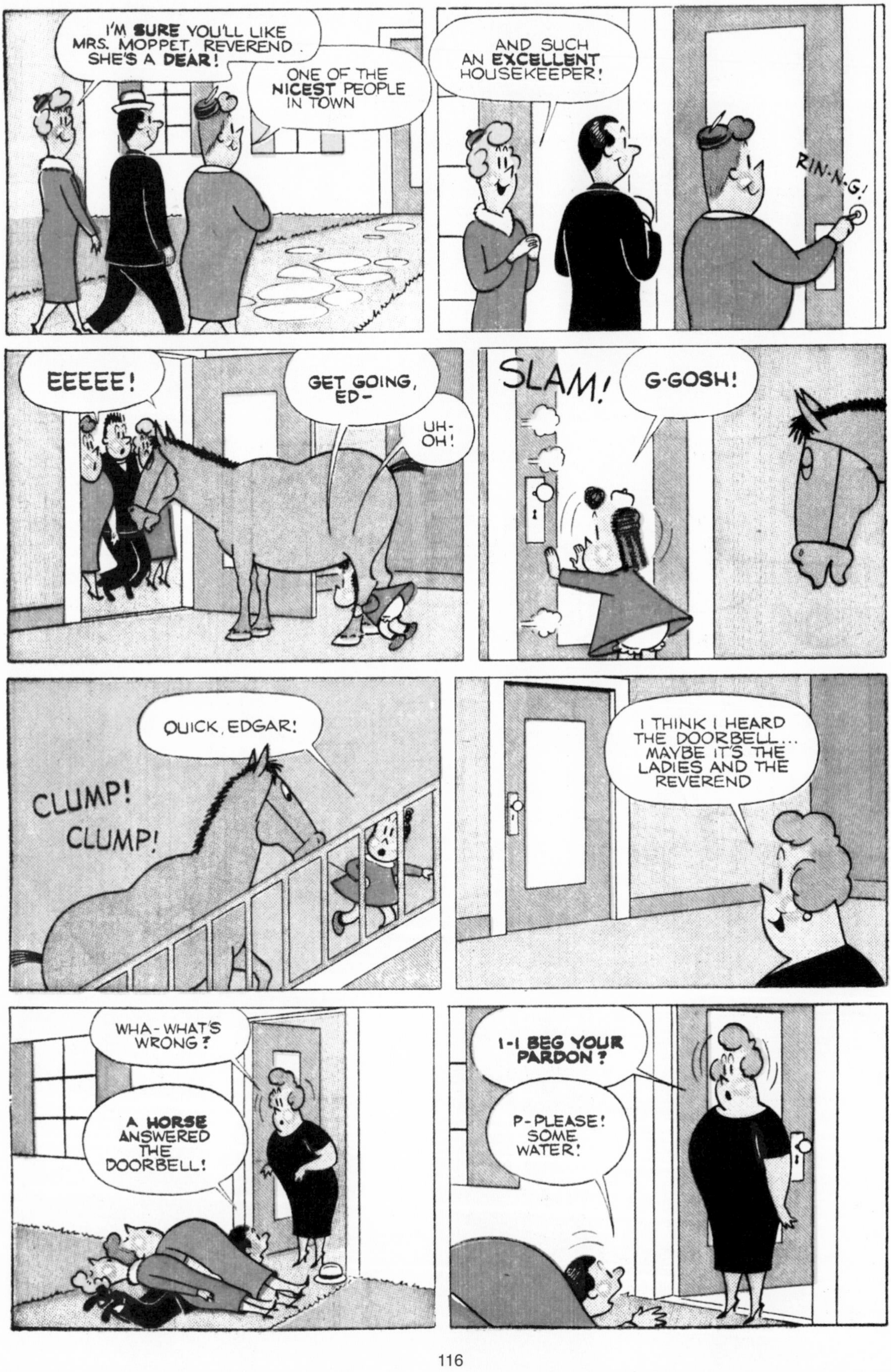
I'M SURE YOU'LL LIKE MRS. MOPPET, REVEREND. SHE'S A DEAR!
ONE OF THE NICEST PEOPLE IN TOWN
AND SUCH AN EXCELLENT HOUSEKEEPER!
RIN-N-G!
EEEEE!
GET GOING, ED-
UH-OH!
SLAM!
G-GOSH!
QUICK, EDGAR!
CLUMP! CLUMP!
I THINK I HEARD THE DOORBELL... MAYBE IT'S THE LADIES AND THE REVEREND
WHA-WHAT'S WRONG?
A HORSE ANSWERED THE DOORBELL!
I-I BEG YOUR PARDON?
P-PLEASE! SOME WATER!

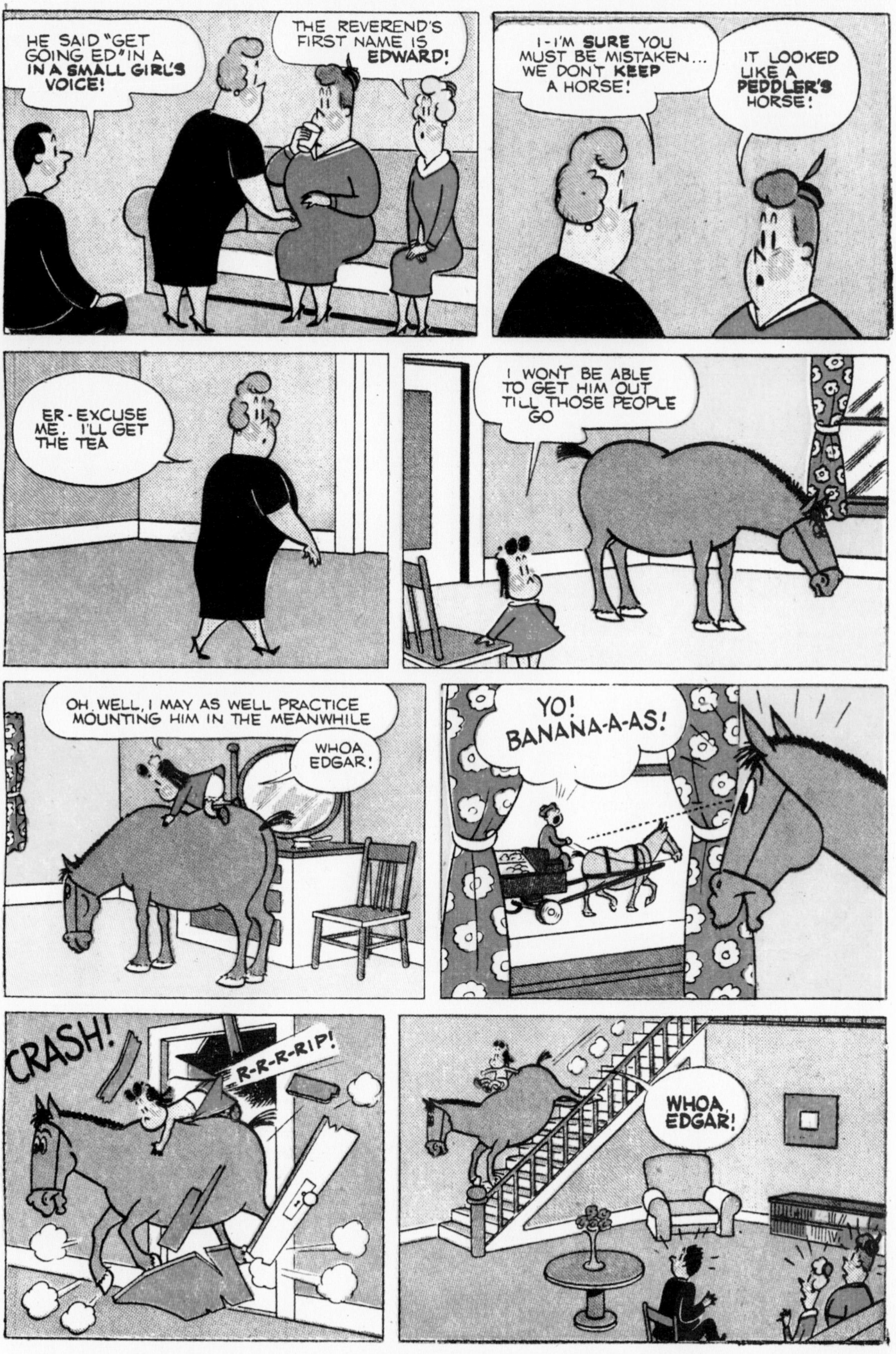

HE SAID "GET GOING ED" IN A IN A SMALL GIRL'S VOICE!
THE REVEREND'S FIRST NAME IS EDWARD!
I-I'M SURE YOU MUST BE MISTAKEN... WE DON'T KEEP A HORSE!
IT LOOKED LIKE A PEDDLER'S HORSE!
ER-EXCUSE ME. I'LL GET THE TEA
I WON'T BE ABLE TO GET HIM OUT TILL THOSE PEOPLE GO
OH WELL, I MAY AS WELL PRACTICE MOUNTING HIM IN THE MEANWHILE
WHOA EDGAR!
YO! BANANA-A-AS!
CRASH!
R-R-R-RIP!
WHOA, EDGAR!

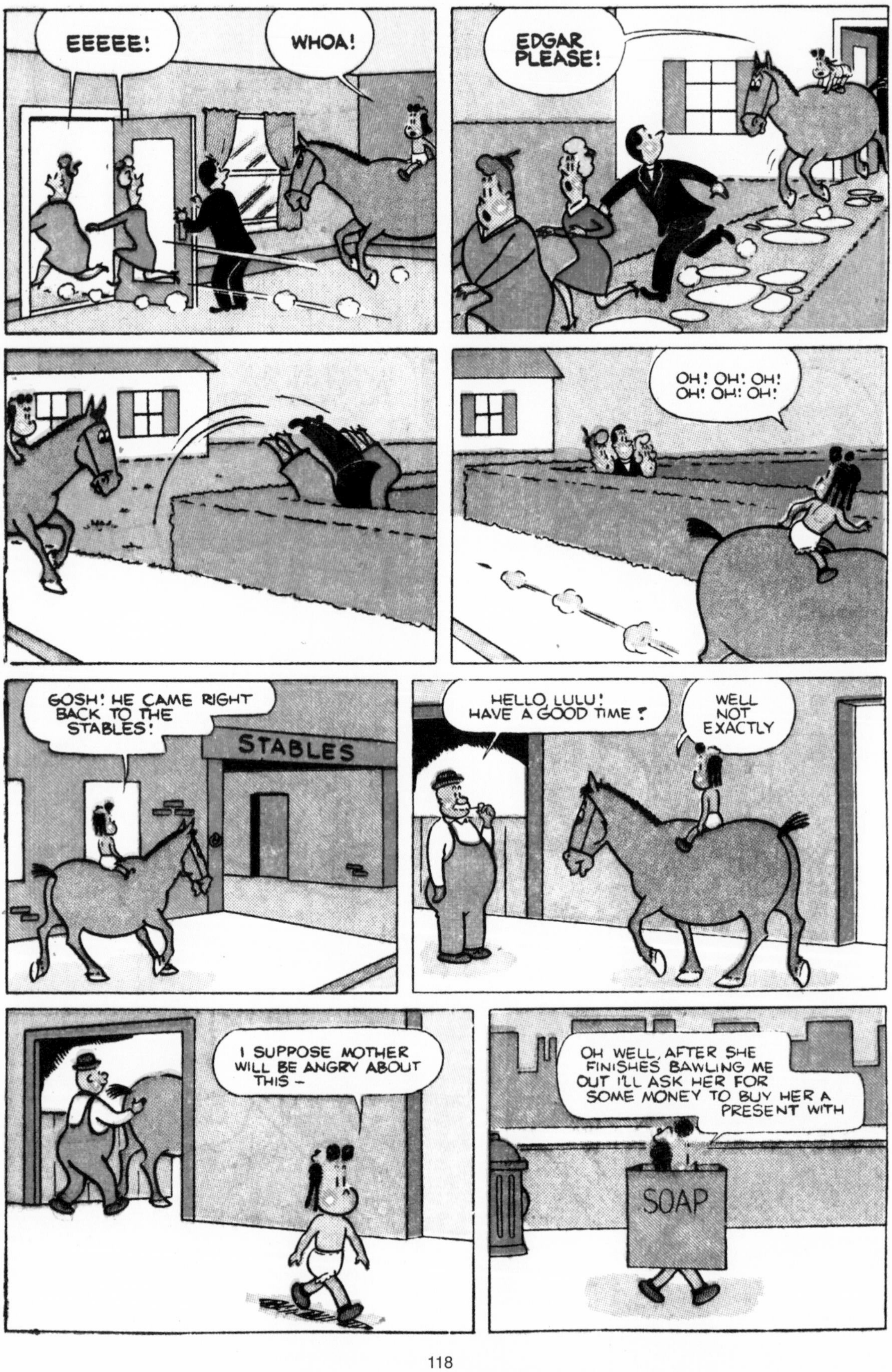
EEEEE!
WHOA!
EDGAR PLEASE!
OH! OH! OH! OH! OH! OH!
GOSH! HE CAME RIGHT BACK TO THE STABLES!
STABLES
HELLO LULU! HAVE A GOOD TIME ?
WELL NOT EXACTLY
I SUPPOSE MOTHER WILL BE ANGRY ABOUT THIS -
OH WELL, AFTER SHE FINISHES BAWLING ME OUT I'LL ASK HER FOR SOME MONEY TO BUY HER A PRESENT WITH
SOAP

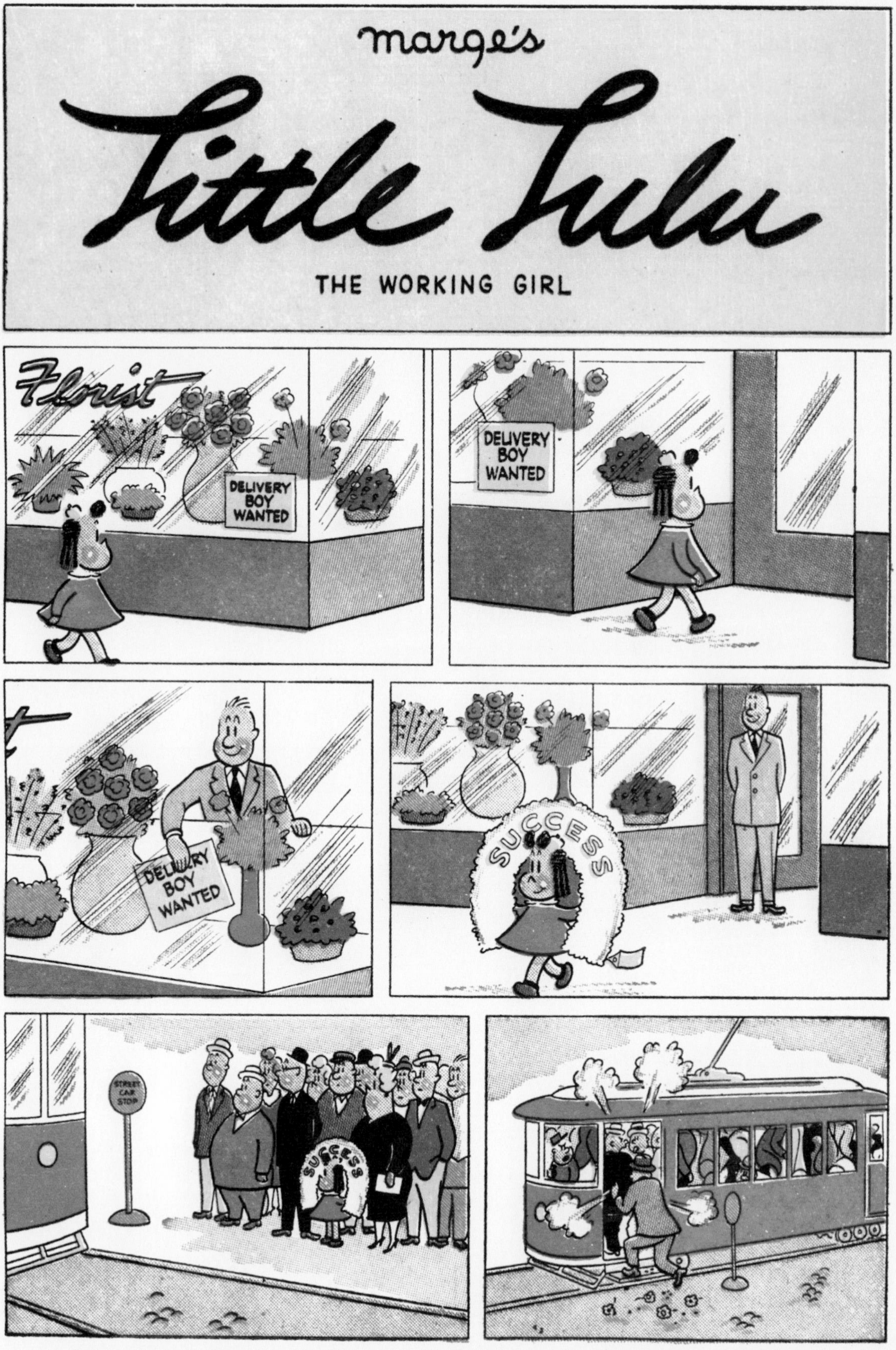
marge's
Little Lulu
THE WORKING GIRL
Florist
DELIVERY BOY WANTED
DELIVERY BOY WANTED
DELIVERY BOY WANTED
SUCCESS
STREET CAR STOP
SUCCESS

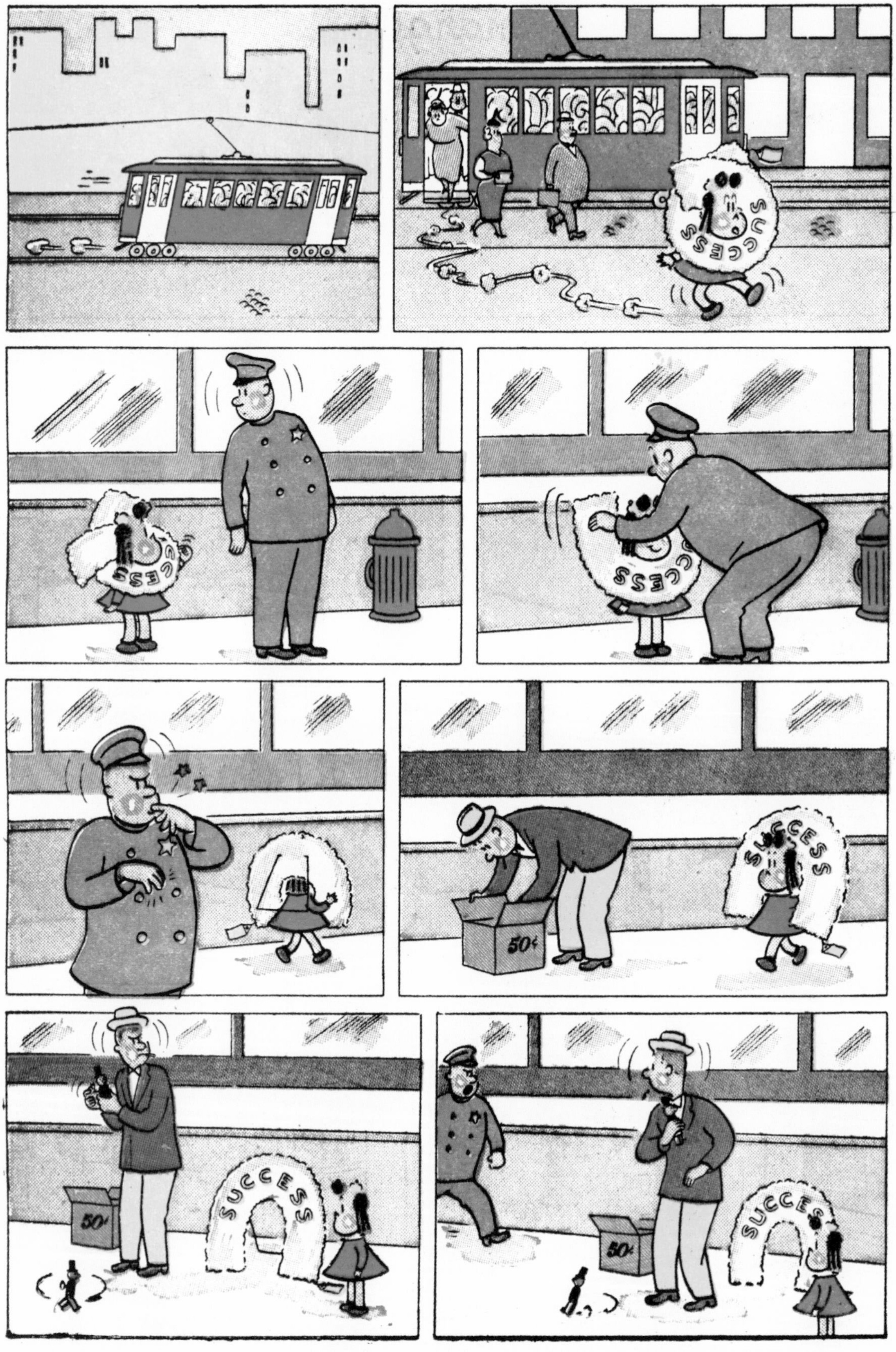
SUCCESS
50¢

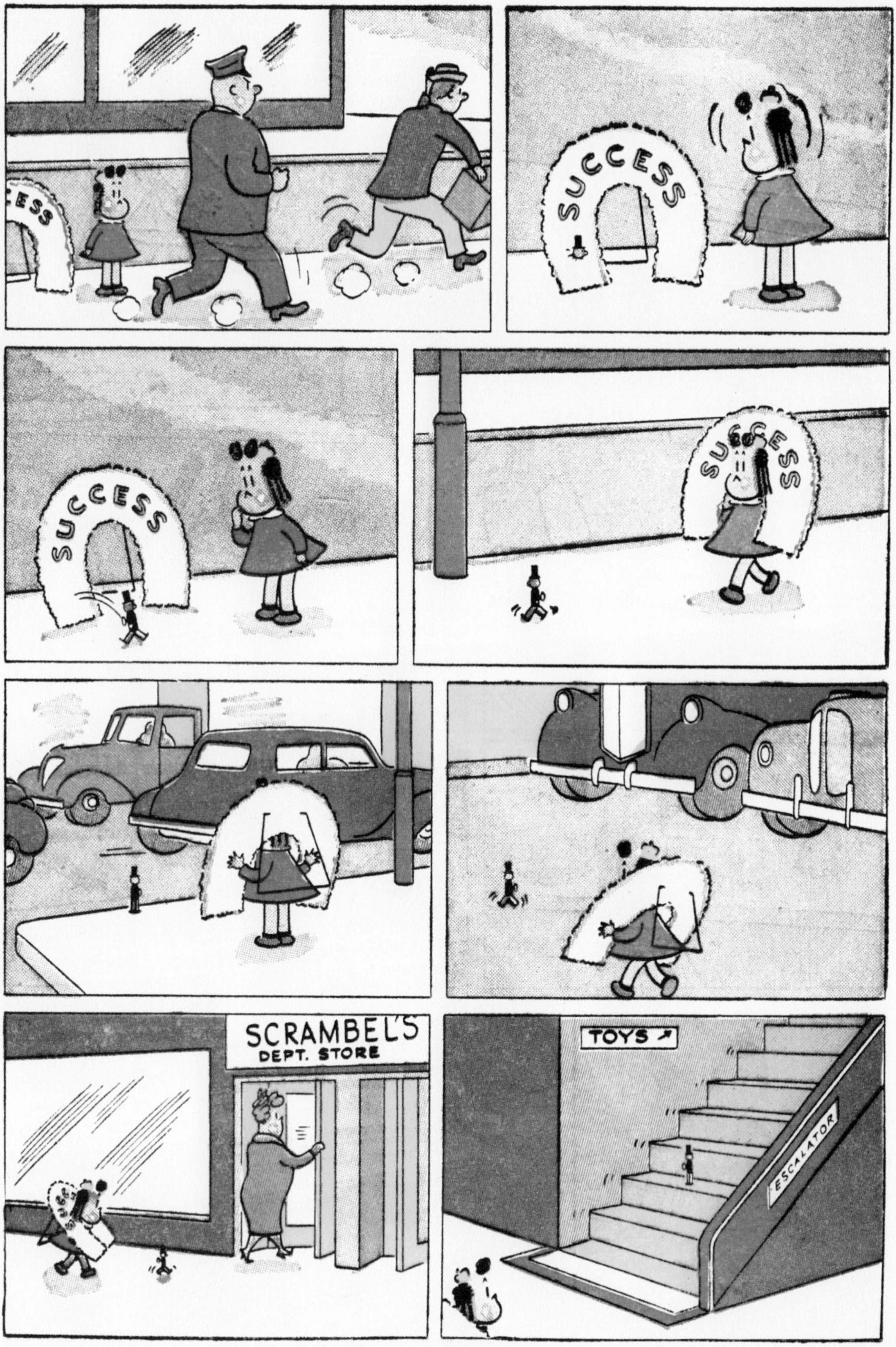
CESS
SUCCESS
SUCCESS
SUCCESS
SCRAMBEL'S
DEPT. STORE
TOYS
ESCALATOR

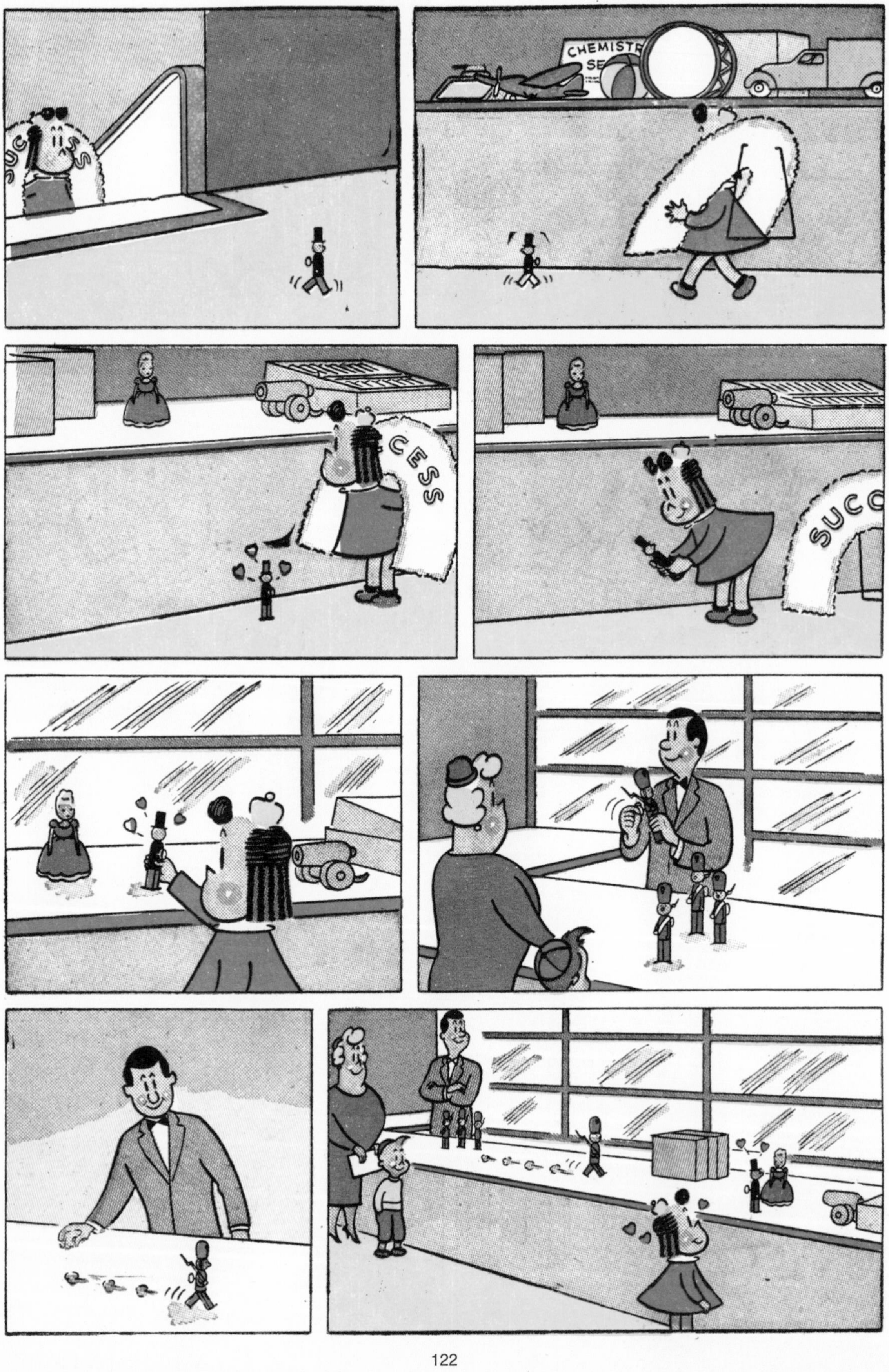
CHEMISTR
SE
CESS
SUCC

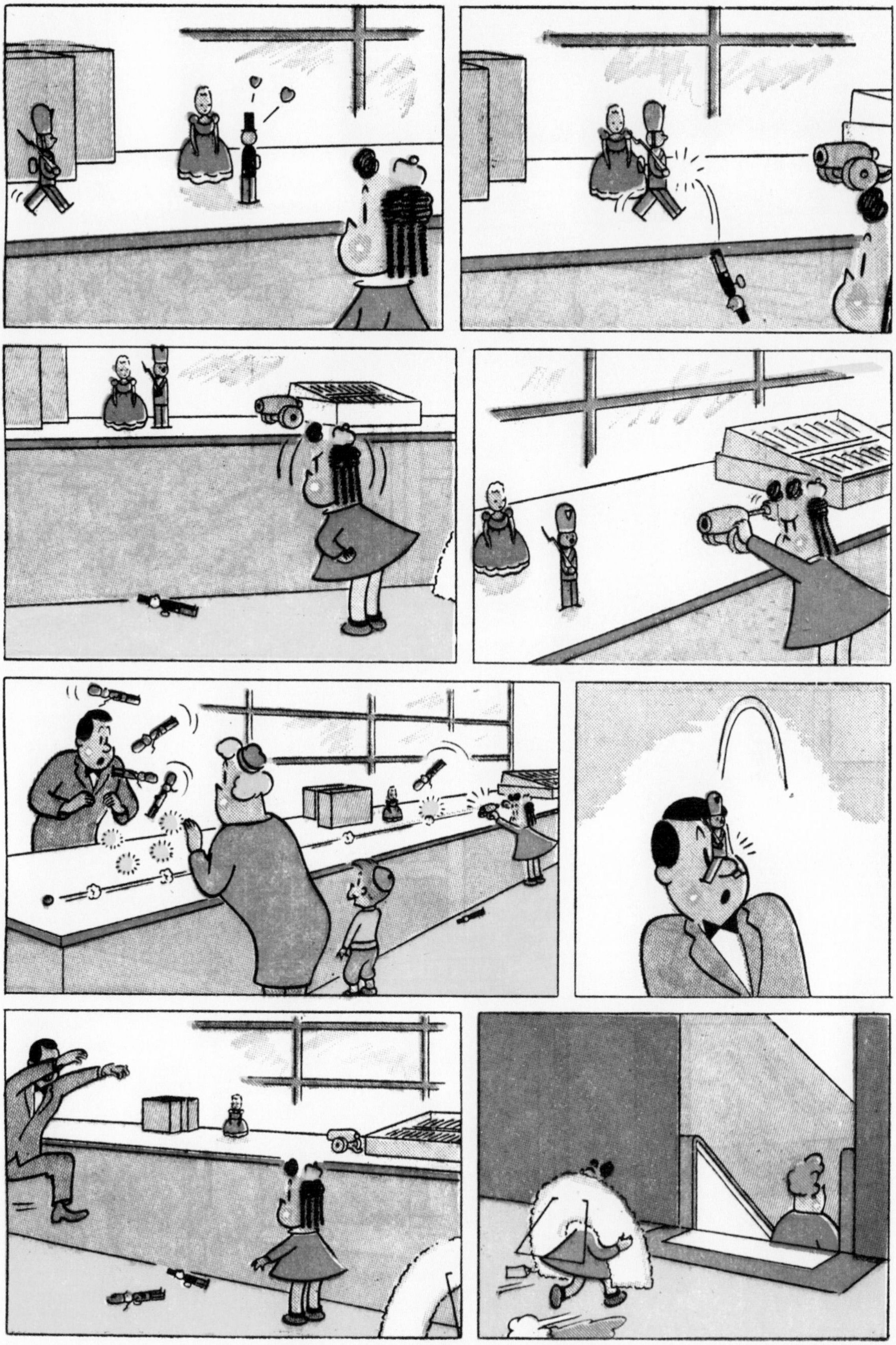

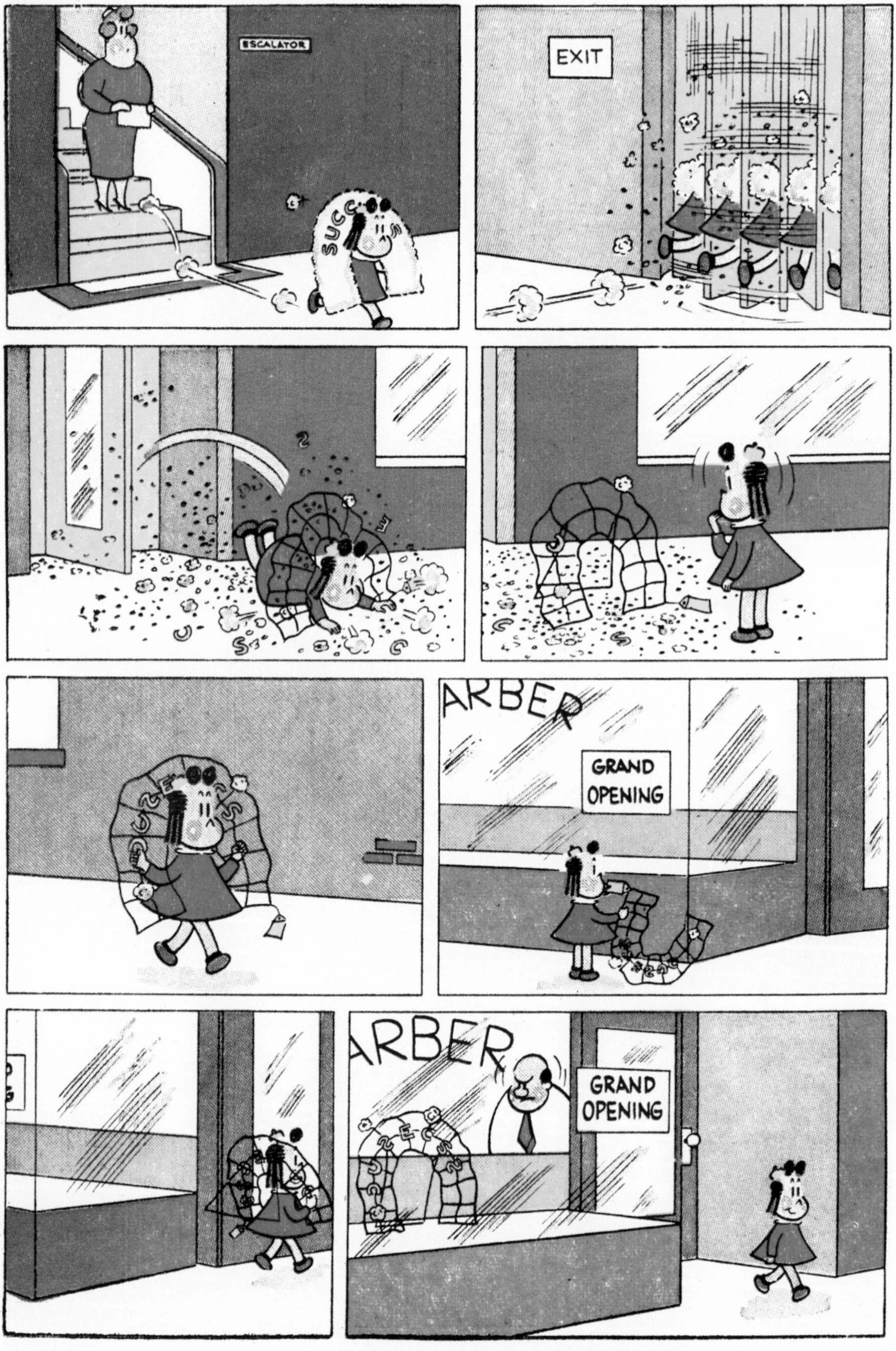
ESCALATOR
EXIT
ARBER
GRAND OPENING
ARBER
GRAND OPENING

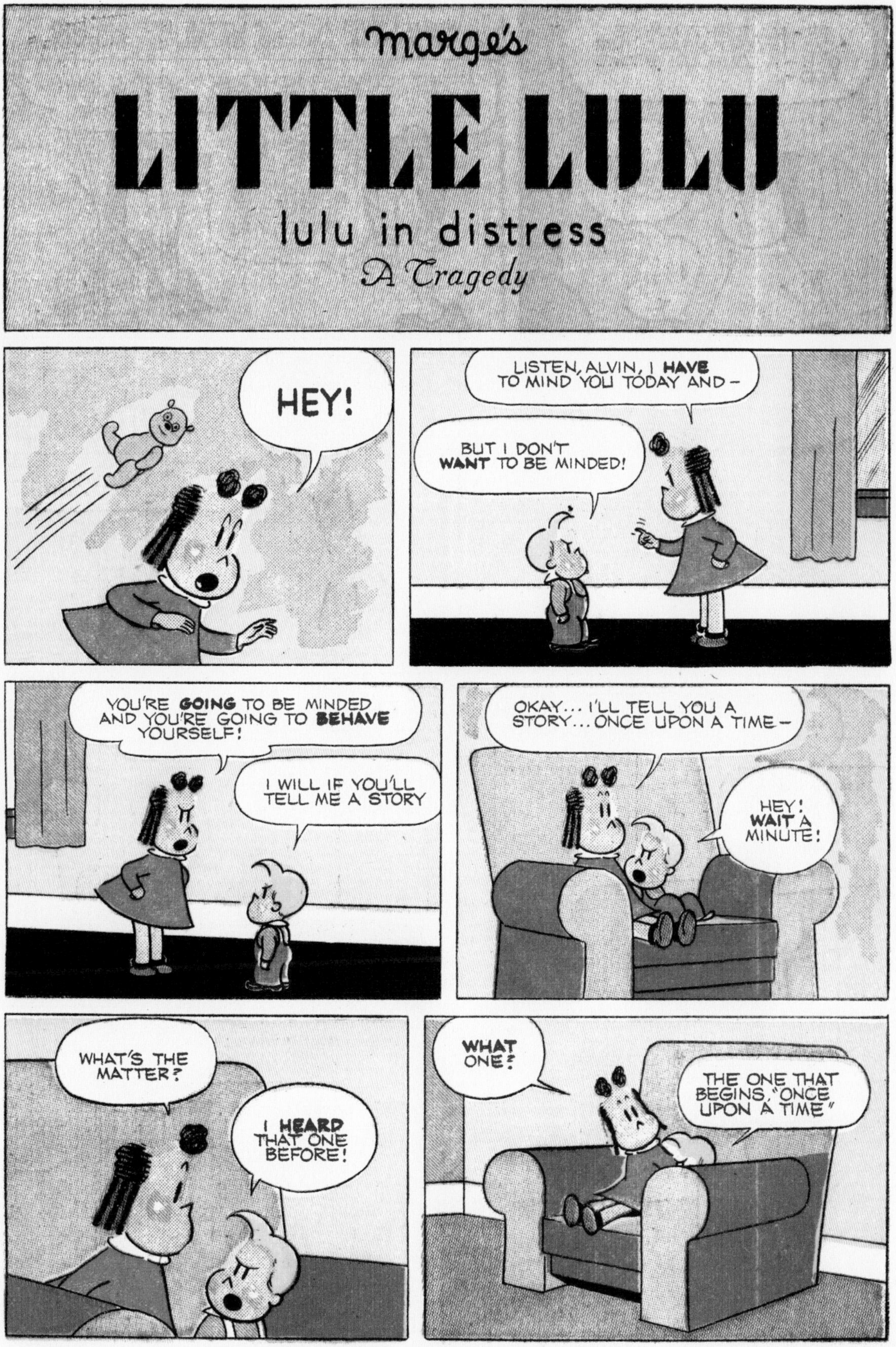
marge's
LITTLE LULU
lulu in distress
A Tragedy
HEY!
LISTEN, ALVIN, I HAVE TO MIND YOU TODAY AND –
BUT I DON'T WANT TO BE MINDED!
YOU'RE GOING TO BE MINDED AND YOU'RE GOING TO BEHAVE YOURSELF!
I WILL IF YOU'LL TELL ME A STORY
OKAY... I'LL TELL YOU A STORY... ONCE UPON A TIME –
HEY! WAIT A MINUTE!
WHAT'S THE MATTER?
I HEARD THAT ONE BEFORE!
WHAT ONE?
THE ONE THAT BEGINS, "ONCE UPON A TIME"

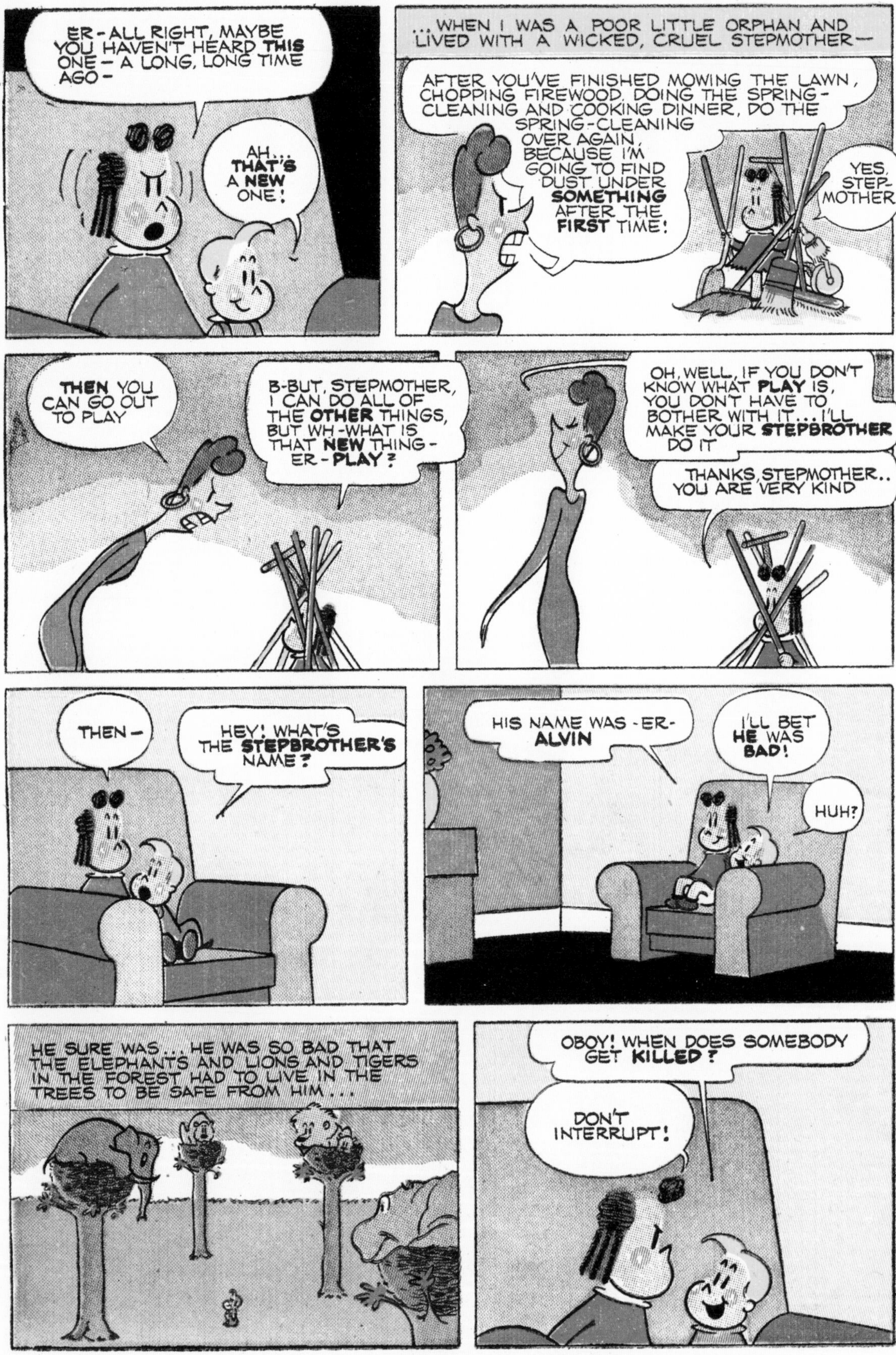
ER-ALL RIGHT, MAYBE YOU HAVEN'T HEARD THIS ONE - A LONG, LONG TIME AGO-
AH... THAT'S A NEW ONE!
...WHEN I WAS A POOR LITTLE ORPHAN AND LIVED WITH A WICKED, CRUEL STEPMOTHER—
AFTER YOU'VE FINISHED MOWING THE LAWN, CHOPPING FIREWOOD, DOING THE SPRING-CLEANING AND COOKING DINNER, DO THE SPRING-CLEANING OVER AGAIN, BECAUSE I'M GOING TO FIND DUST UNDER SOMETHING AFTER THE FIRST TIME!
YES, STEP-MOTHER
THEN YOU CAN GO OUT TO PLAY
B-BUT, STEPMOTHER, I CAN DO ALL OF THE OTHER THINGS, BUT WH-WHAT IS THAT NEW THING-ER-PLAY?
OH, WELL, IF YOU DON'T KNOW WHAT PLAY IS, YOU DON'T HAVE TO BOTHER WITH IT... I'LL MAKE YOUR STEPBROTHER DO IT
THANKS, STEPMOTHER.. YOU ARE VERY KIND
THEN—
HEY! WHAT'S THE STEPBROTHER'S NAME?
HIS NAME WAS-ER-ALVIN
I'LL BET HE WAS BAD!
HUH?
HE SURE WAS... HE WAS SO BAD THAT THE ELEPHANTS AND LIONS AND TIGERS IN THE FOREST HAD TO LIVE IN THE TREES TO BE SAFE FROM HIM...
OBOY! WHEN DOES SOMEBODY GET KILLED?
DON'T INTERRUPT!

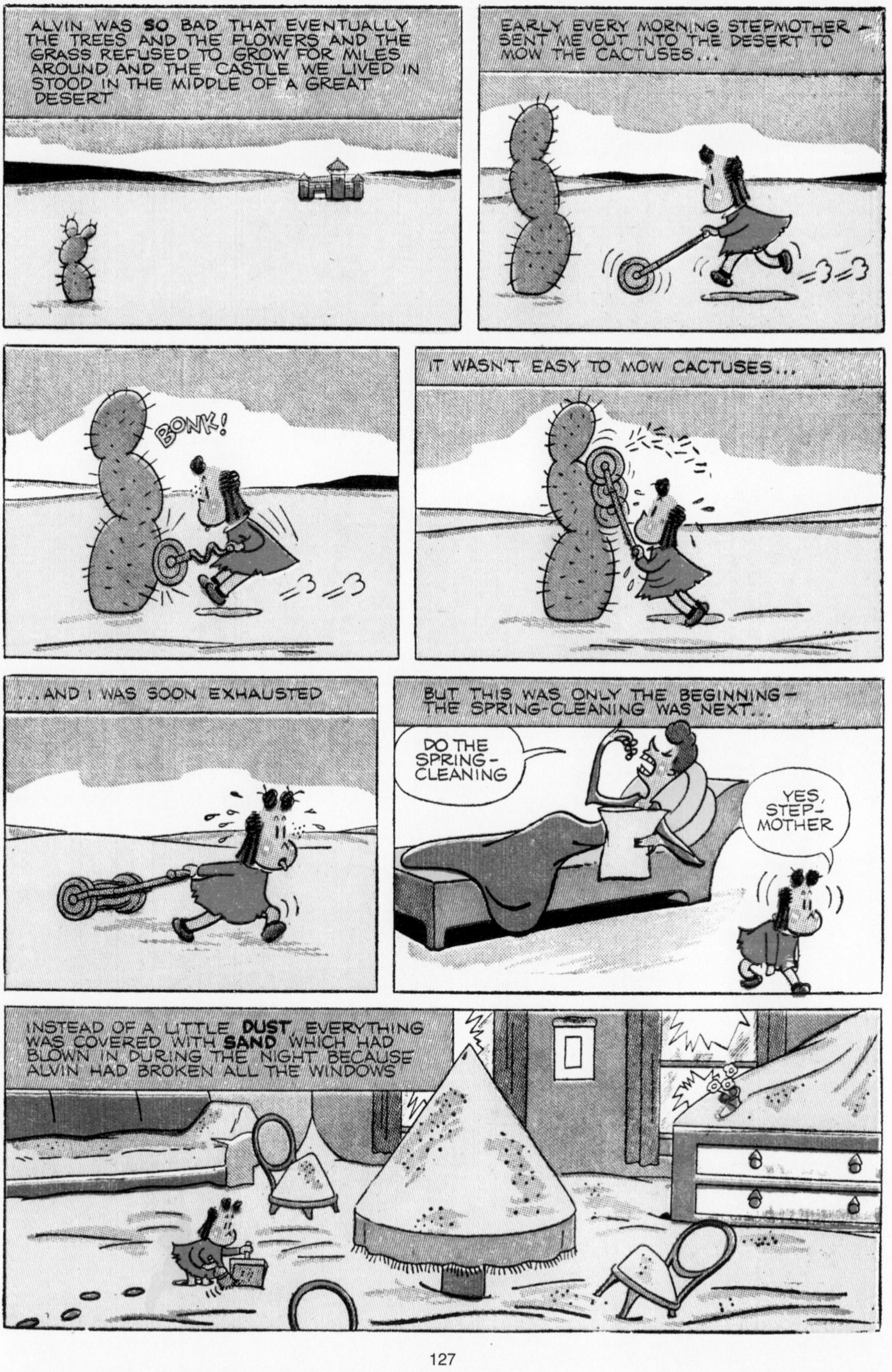
ALVIN WAS SO BAD THAT EVENTUALLY THE TREES AND THE FLOWERS AND THE GRASS REFUSED TO GROW FOR MILES AROUND AND THE CASTLE WE LIVED IN STOOD IN THE MIDDLE OF A GREAT DESERT
EARLY EVERY MORNING STEPMOTHER SENT ME OUT INTO THE DESERT TO MOW THE CACTUSES...
BONK!
IT WASN'T EASY TO MOW CACTUSES...
...AND I WAS SOON EXHAUSTED
BUT THIS WAS ONLY THE BEGINNING – THE SPRING-CLEANING WAS NEXT...
DO THE SPRING-CLEANING
YES, STEP-MOTHER
INSTEAD OF A LITTLE DUST EVERYTHING WAS COVERED WITH SAND WHICH HAD BLOWN IN DURING THE NIGHT BECAUSE ALVIN HAD BROKEN ALL THE WINDOWS

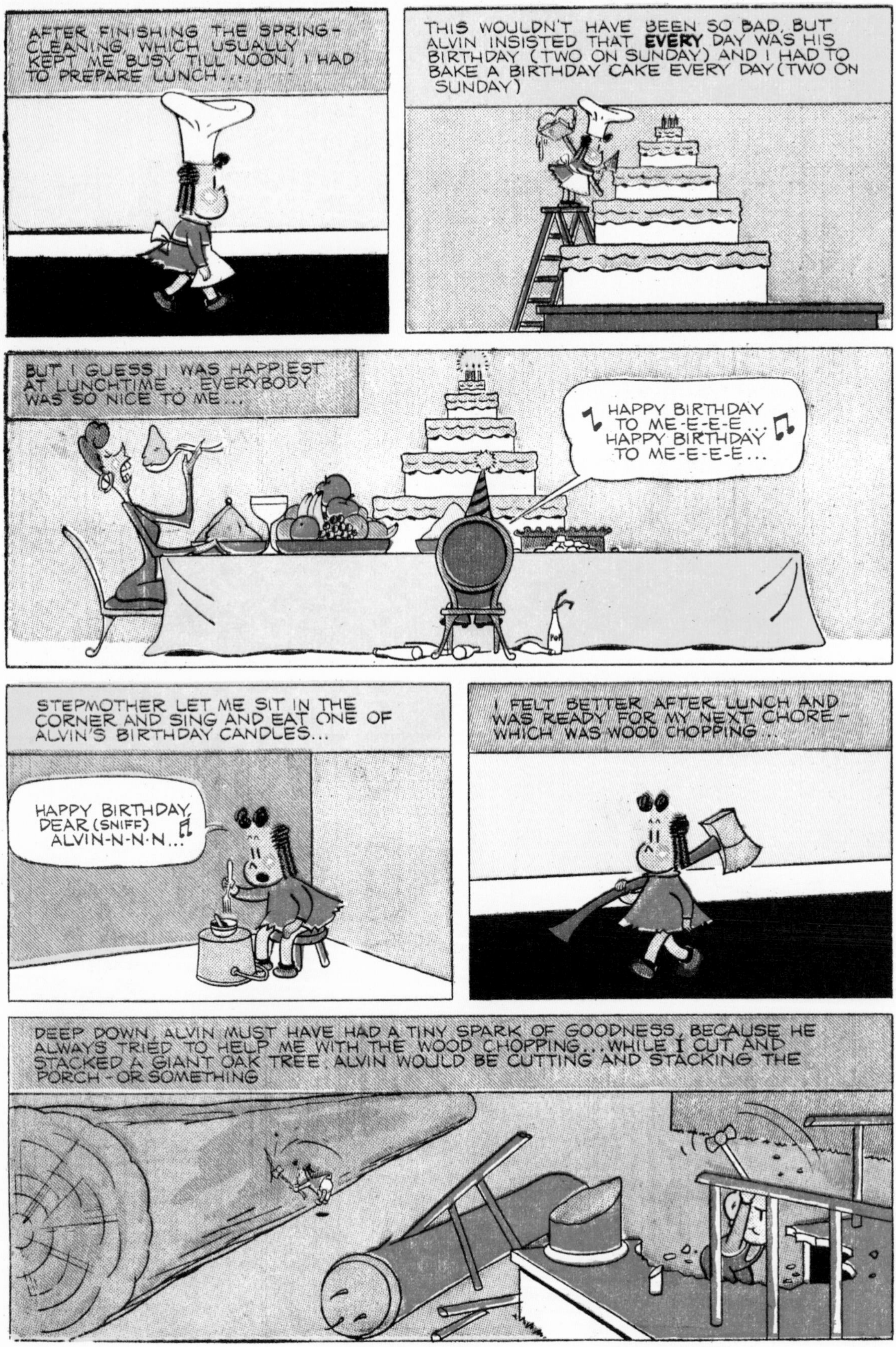
AFTER FINISHING THE SPRING-CLEANING, WHICH USUALLY KEPT ME BUSY TILL NOON, I HAD TO PREPARE LUNCH...
THIS WOULDN'T HAVE BEEN SO BAD, BUT ALVIN INSISTED THAT **EVERY** DAY WAS HIS BIRTHDAY (TWO ON SUNDAY) AND I HAD TO BAKE A BIRTHDAY CAKE EVERY DAY (TWO ON SUNDAY)
BUT I GUESS I WAS HAPPIEST AT LUNCHTIME... EVERYBODY WAS SO NICE TO ME...
HAPPY BIRTHDAY TO ME-E-E-E... HAPPY BIRTHDAY TO ME-E-E-E...
STEPMOTHER LET ME SIT IN THE CORNER AND SING AND EAT ONE OF ALVIN'S BIRTHDAY CANDLES...
HAPPY BIRTHDAY, DEAR (SNIFF) ALVIN-N-N-N...
I FELT BETTER AFTER LUNCH AND WAS READY FOR MY NEXT CHORE - WHICH WAS WOOD CHOPPING...
DEEP DOWN, ALVIN MUST HAVE HAD A TINY SPARK OF GOODNESS, BECAUSE HE ALWAYS TRIED TO HELP ME WITH THE WOOD CHOPPING...WHILE I CUT AND STACKED A GIANT OAK TREE, ALVIN WOULD BE CUTTING AND STACKING THE PORCH - OR SOMETHING

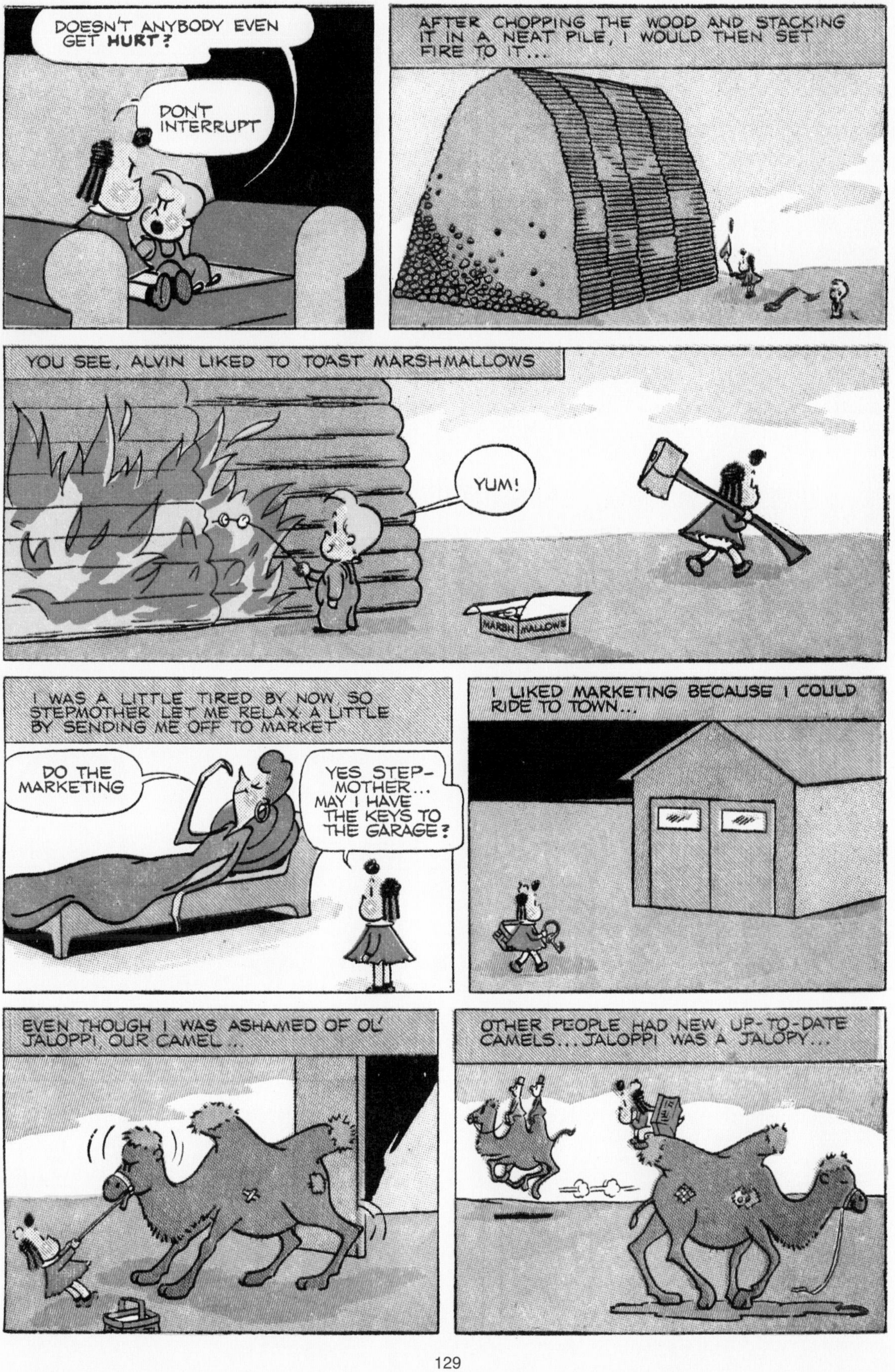
DOESN'T ANYBODY EVEN GET HURT?
DON'T INTERRUPT
AFTER CHOPPING THE WOOD AND STACKING IT IN A NEAT PILE, I WOULD THEN SET FIRE TO IT...
YOU SEE, ALVIN LIKED TO TOAST MARSHMALLOWS
YUM!
MARSH MALLOWS
I WAS A LITTLE TIRED BY NOW, SO STEPMOTHER LET ME RELAX A LITTLE BY SENDING ME OFF TO MARKET
DO THE MARKETING
YES STEP-MOTHER... MAY I HAVE THE KEYS TO THE GARAGE?
I LIKED MARKETING BECAUSE I COULD RIDE TO TOWN...
EVEN THOUGH I WAS ASHAMED OF OL' JALOPPI, OUR CAMEL...
OTHER PEOPLE HAD NEW, UP-TO-DATE CAMELS... JALOPPI WAS A JALOPY...

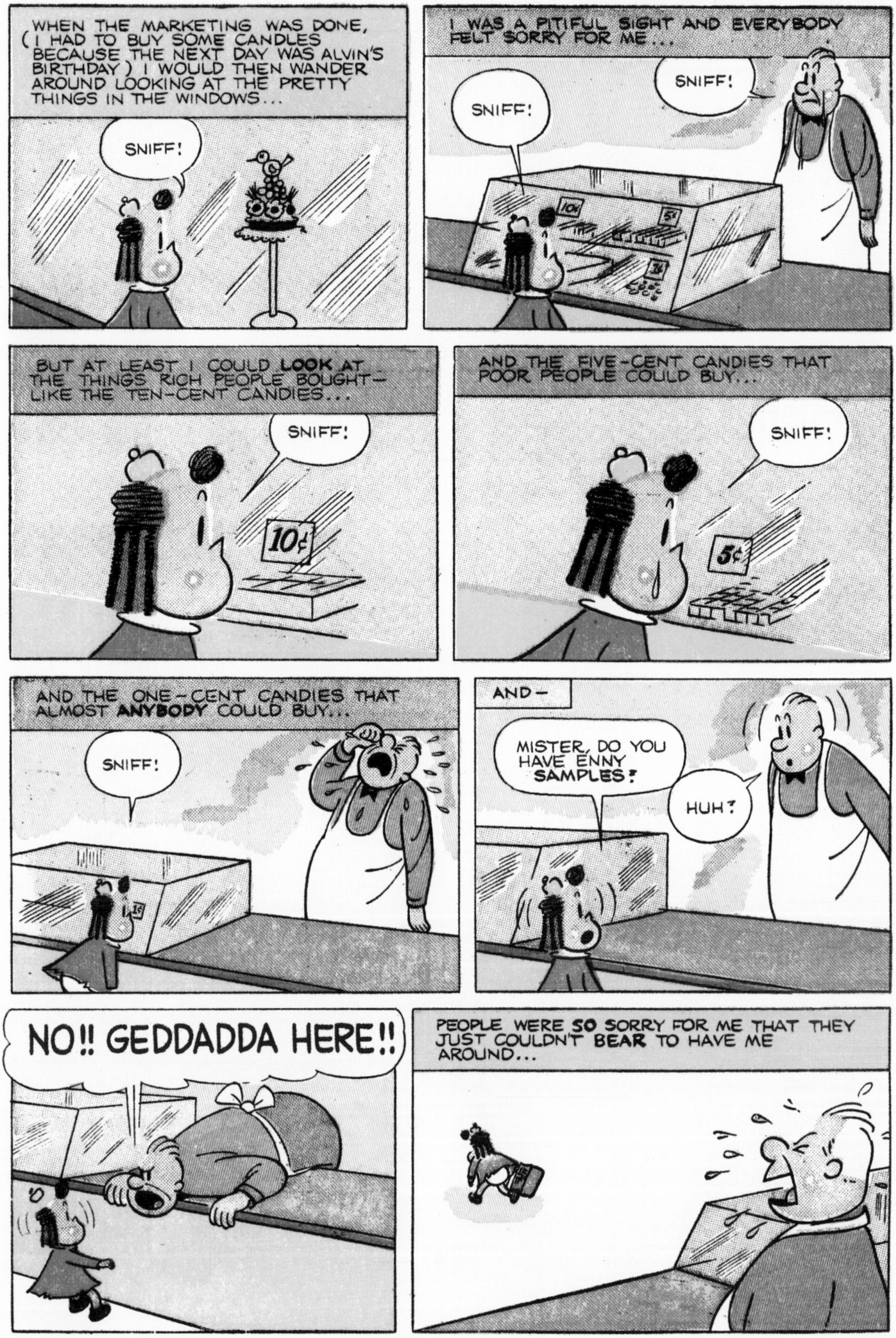
WHEN THE MARKETING WAS DONE, (I HAD TO BUY SOME CANDLES BECAUSE THE NEXT DAY WAS ALVIN'S BIRTHDAY) I WOULD THEN WANDER AROUND LOOKING AT THE PRETTY THINGS IN THE WINDOWS...
SNIFF!
I WAS A PITIFUL SIGHT AND EVERYBODY FELT SORRY FOR ME...
SNIFF!
SNIFF!
BUT AT LEAST I COULD LOOK AT THE THINGS RICH PEOPLE BOUGHT— LIKE THE TEN-CENT CANDIES...
SNIFF!
10¢
AND THE FIVE-CENT CANDIES THAT POOR PEOPLE COULD BUY...
SNIFF!
5¢
AND THE ONE-CENT CANDIES THAT ALMOST ANYBODY COULD BUY...
SNIFF!
AND—
MISTER, DO YOU HAVE ENNY SAMPLES?
HUH?
NO!! GEDDADDA HERE!!
PEOPLE WERE SO SORRY FOR ME THAT THEY JUST COULDN'T BEAR TO HAVE ME AROUND...

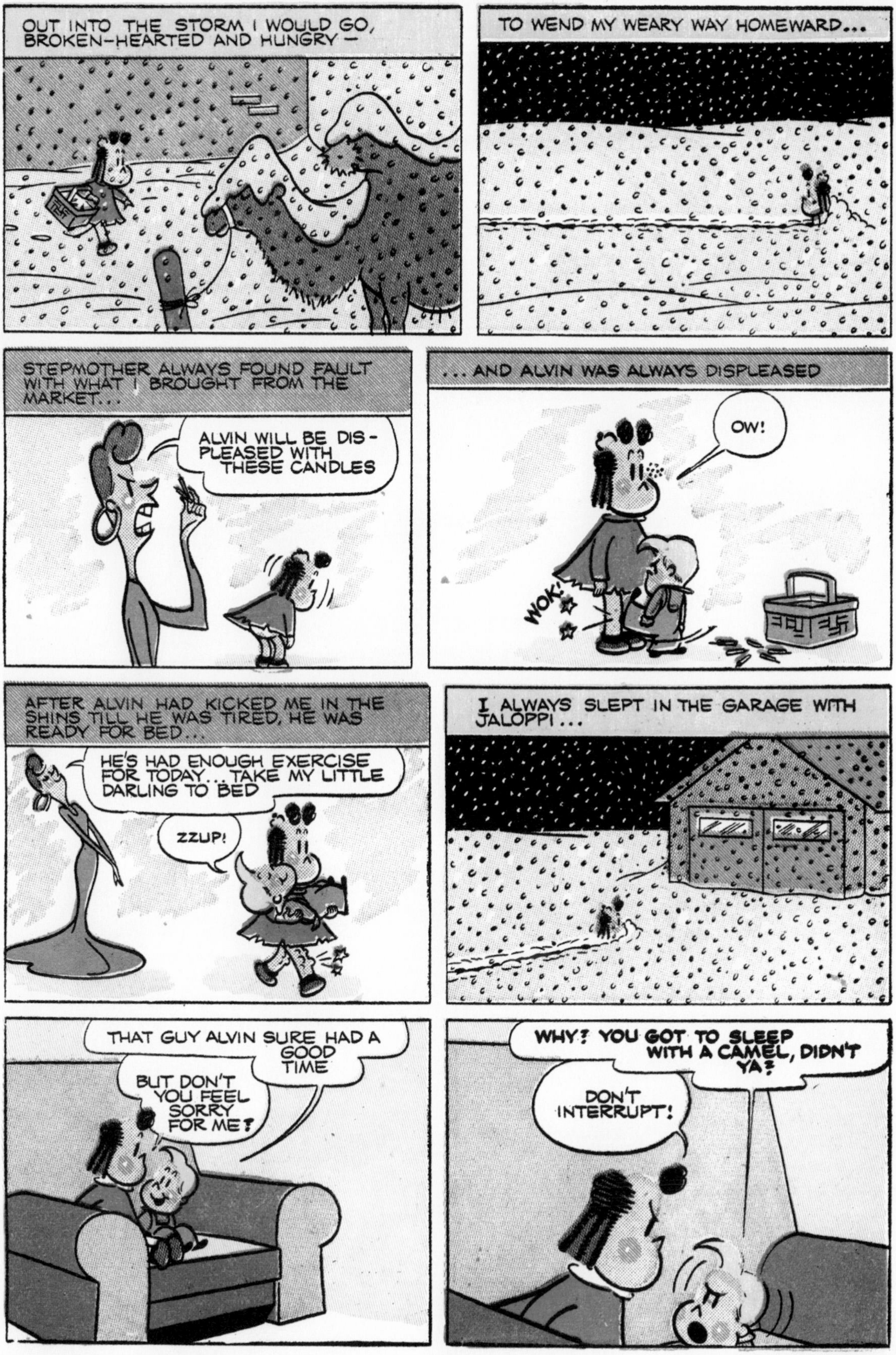

OUT INTO THE STORM I WOULD GO, BROKEN-HEARTED AND HUNGRY —
TO WEND MY WEARY WAY HOMEWARD...
STEPMOTHER ALWAYS FOUND FAULT WITH WHAT I BROUGHT FROM THE MARKET...
ALVIN WILL BE DIS-PLEASED WITH THESE CANDLES
...AND ALVIN WAS ALWAYS DISPLEASED
OW!
WOK!
AFTER ALVIN HAD KICKED ME IN THE SHINS TILL HE WAS TIRED, HE WAS READY FOR BED...
HE'S HAD ENOUGH EXERCISE FOR TODAY...TAKE MY LITTLE DARLING TO BED
ZZUP!
I ALWAYS SLEPT IN THE GARAGE WITH JALOPPI...
THAT GUY ALVIN SURE HAD A GOOD TIME
BUT DON'T YOU FEEL SORRY FOR ME?
WHY? YOU GOT TO SLEEP WITH A CAMEL, DIDN'T YA?
DON'T INTERRUPT!

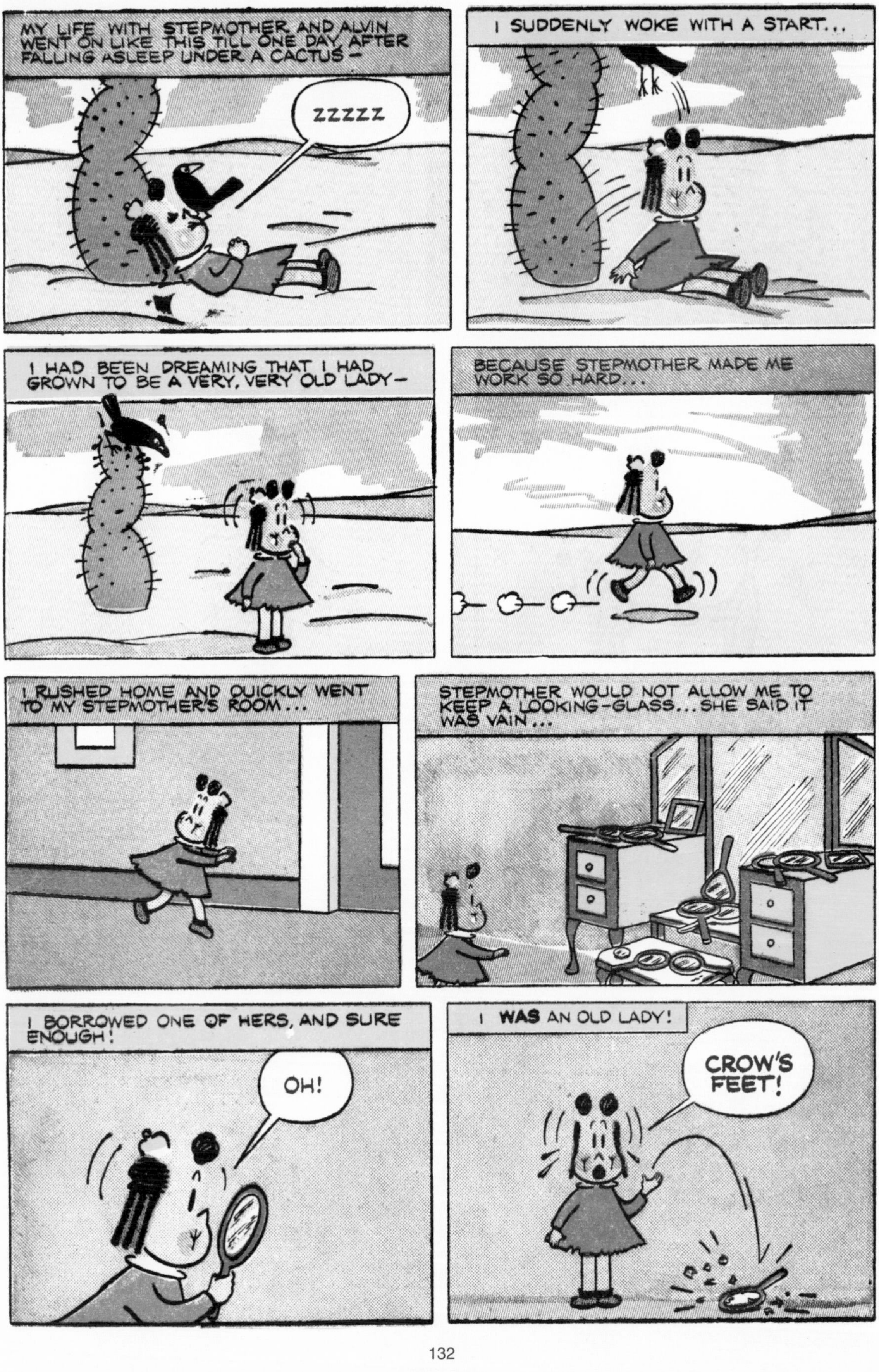
MY LIFE WITH STEPMOTHER AND ALVIN WENT ON LIKE THIS TILL ONE DAY, AFTER FALLING ASLEEP UNDER A CACTUS—
ZZZZZ
I SUDDENLY WOKE WITH A START...
I HAD BEEN DREAMING THAT I HAD GROWN TO BE A VERY, VERY OLD LADY—
BECAUSE STEPMOTHER MADE ME WORK SO HARD...
I RUSHED HOME AND QUICKLY WENT TO MY STEPMOTHER'S ROOM...
STEPMOTHER WOULD NOT ALLOW ME TO KEEP A LOOKING-GLASS... SHE SAID IT WAS VAIN...
I BORROWED ONE OF HERS, AND SURE ENOUGH!
OH!
I **WAS** AN OLD LADY!
CROW'S FEET!

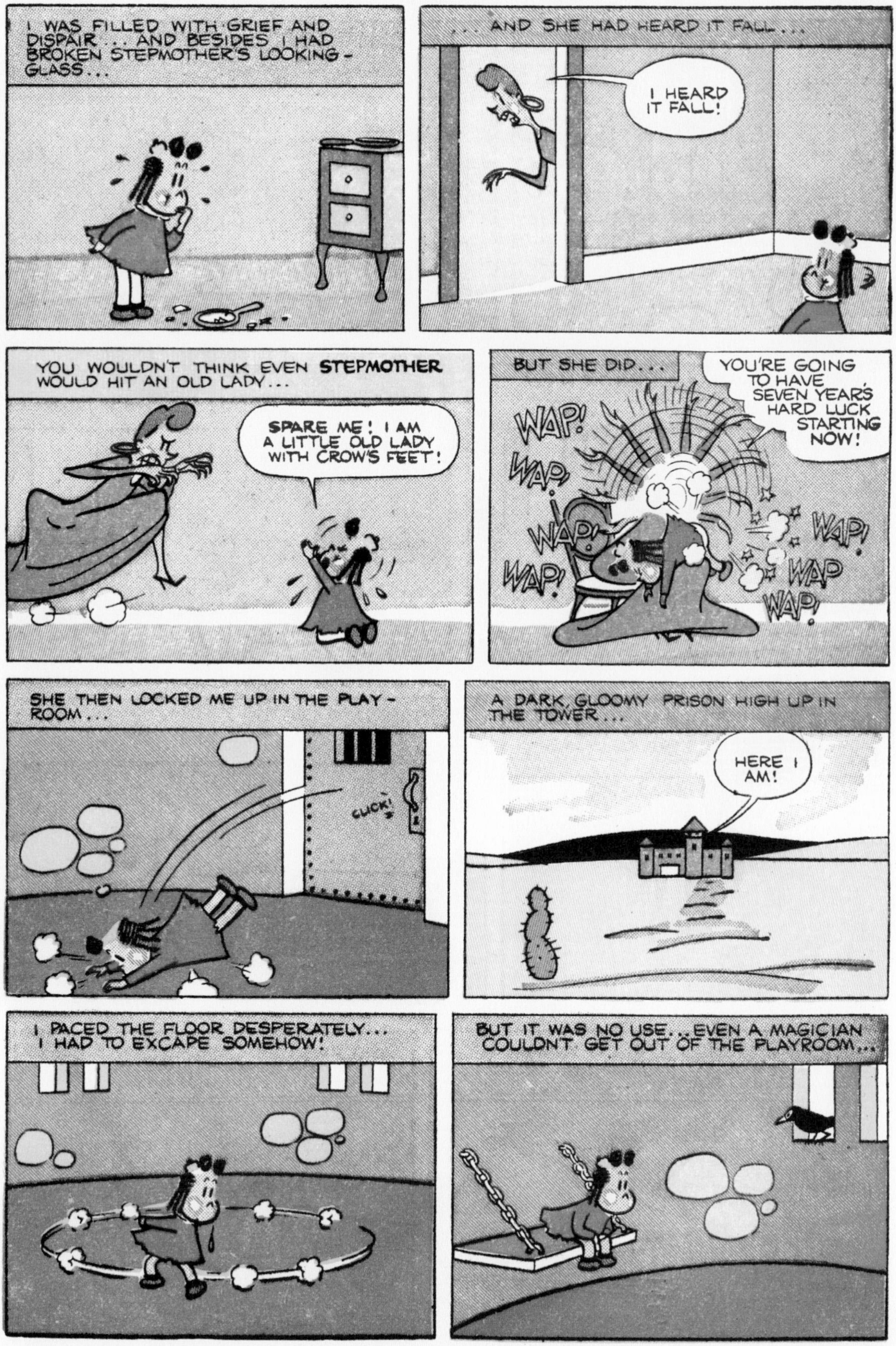

I WAS FILLED WITH GRIEF AND DISPAIR ... AND BESIDES I HAD BROKEN STEPMOTHER'S LOOKING-GLASS ...
... AND SHE HAD HEARD IT FALL ...
I HEARD IT FALL!
YOU WOULDN'T THINK EVEN STEPMOTHER WOULD HIT AN OLD LADY ...
SPARE ME! I AM A LITTLE OLD LADY WITH CROW'S FEET!
BUT SHE DID ...
YOU'RE GOING TO HAVE SEVEN YEAR'S HARD LUCK STARTING NOW!
WAP! WAP! WAP! WAP! WAP! WAP WAP!
SHE THEN LOCKED ME UP IN THE PLAY-ROOM ...
CLICK!
A DARK, GLOOMY PRISON HIGH UP IN THE TOWER ...
HERE I AM!
I PACED THE FLOOR DESPERATELY ... I HAD TO EXCAPE SOMEHOW!
BUT IT WAS NO USE ... EVEN A MAGICIAN COULDN'T GET OUT OF THE PLAYROOM ...

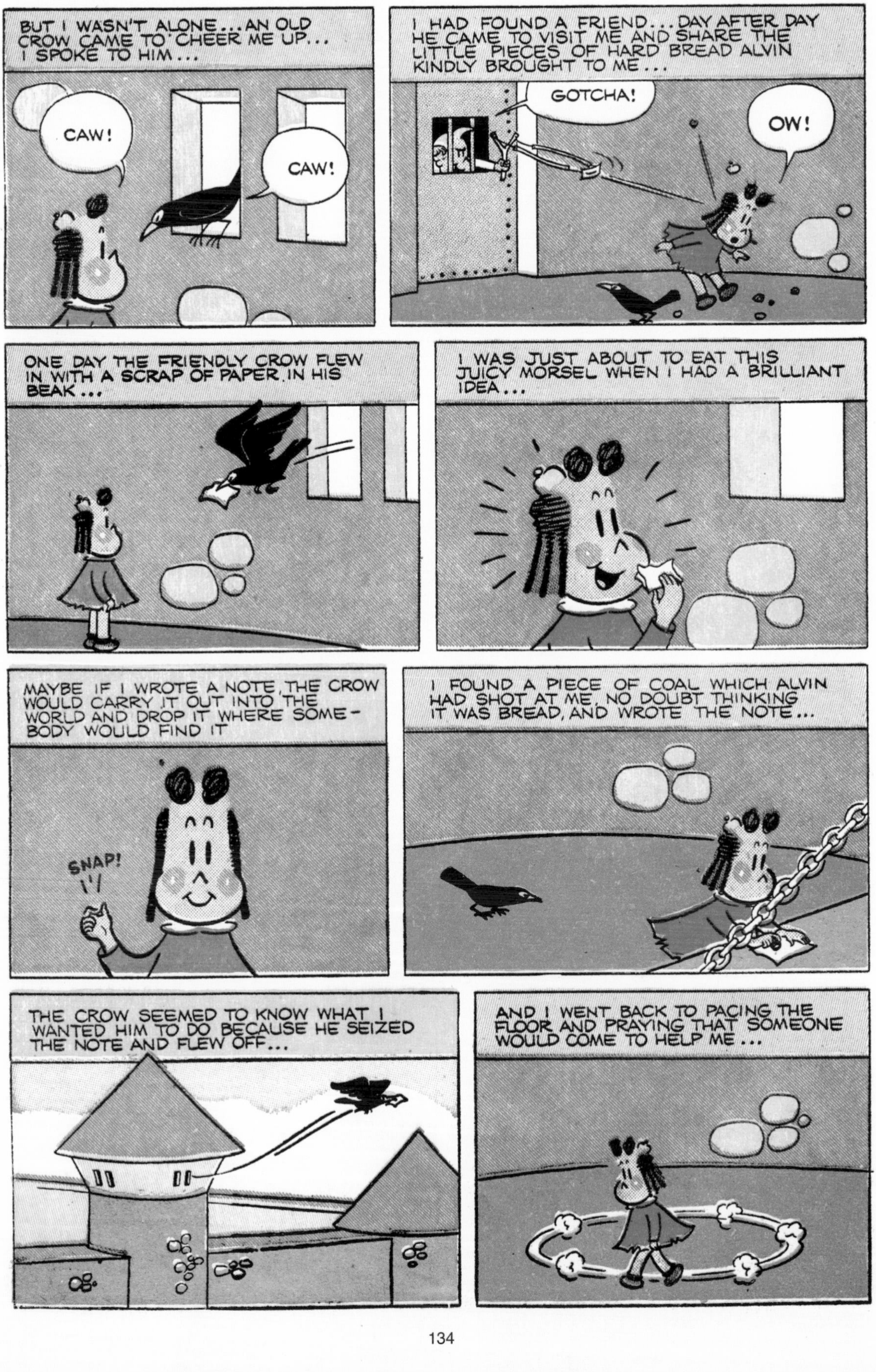
BUT I WASN'T ALONE... AN OLD CROW CAME TO CHEER ME UP... I SPOKE TO HIM...
CAW!
CAW!
I HAD FOUND A FRIEND... DAY AFTER DAY HE CAME TO VISIT ME AND SHARE THE LITTLE PIECES OF HARD BREAD ALVIN KINDLY BROUGHT TO ME...
GOTCHA!
OW!
ONE DAY THE FRIENDLY CROW FLEW IN WITH A SCRAP OF PAPER IN HIS BEAK...
I WAS JUST ABOUT TO EAT THIS JUICY MORSEL WHEN I HAD A BRILLIANT IDEA...
MAYBE IF I WROTE A NOTE, THE CROW WOULD CARRY IT OUT INTO THE WORLD AND DROP IT WHERE SOME-BODY WOULD FIND IT
SNAP!
I FOUND A PIECE OF COAL WHICH ALVIN HAD SHOT AT ME, NO DOUBT THINKING IT WAS BREAD, AND WROTE THE NOTE...
THE CROW SEEMED TO KNOW WHAT I WANTED HIM TO DO BECAUSE HE SEIZED THE NOTE AND FLEW OFF...
AND I WENT BACK TO PACING THE FLOOR AND PRAYING THAT SOMEONE WOULD COME TO HELP ME...

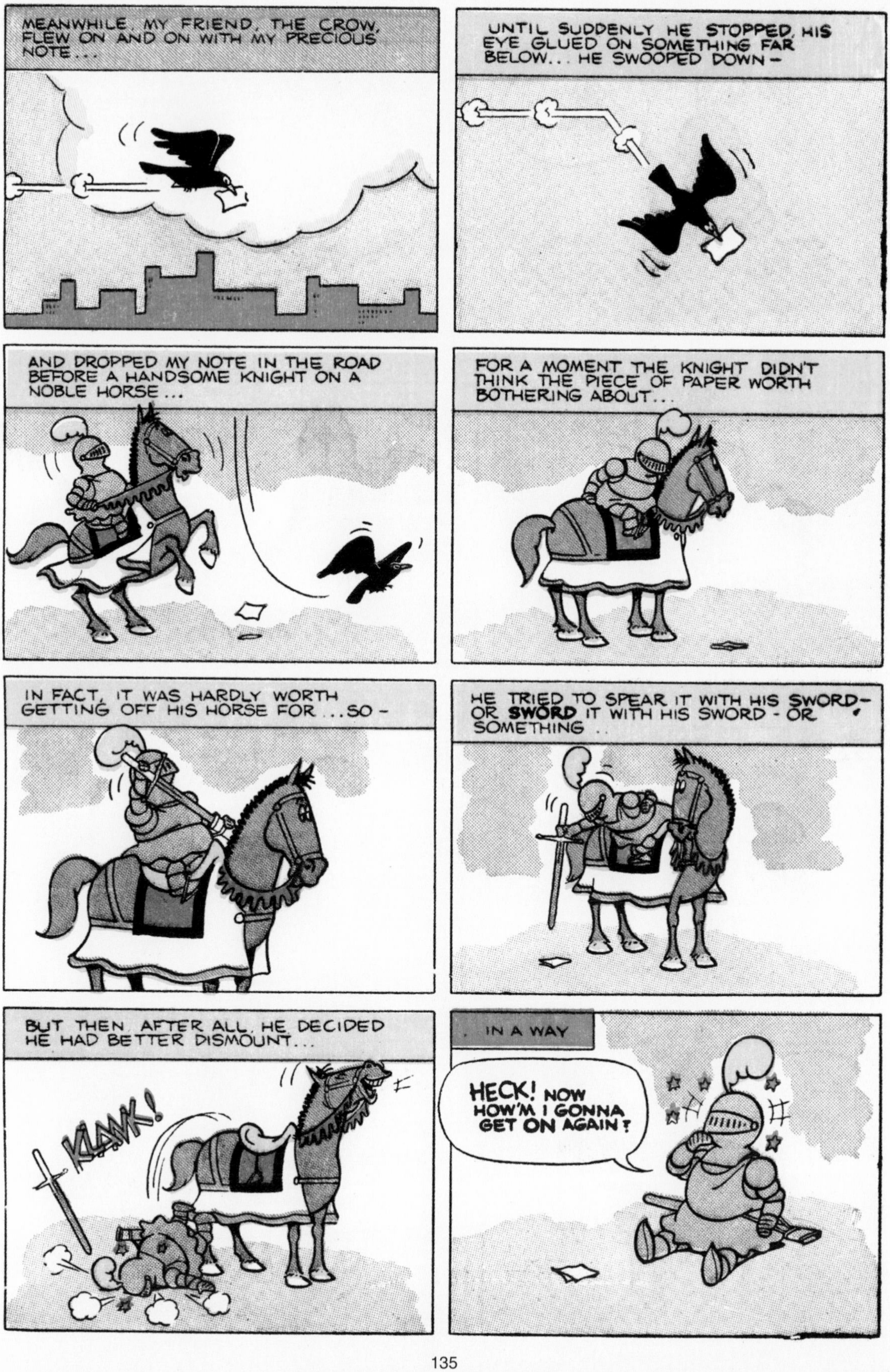
MEANWHILE, MY FRIEND, THE CROW, FLEW ON AND ON WITH MY PRECIOUS NOTE...
UNTIL SUDDENLY HE STOPPED, HIS EYE GLUED ON SOMETHING FAR BELOW... HE SWOOPED DOWN -
AND DROPPED MY NOTE IN THE ROAD BEFORE A HANDSOME KNIGHT ON A NOBLE HORSE...
FOR A MOMENT THE KNIGHT DIDN'T THINK THE PIECE OF PAPER WORTH BOTHERING ABOUT...
IN FACT, IT WAS HARDLY WORTH GETTING OFF HIS HORSE FOR ...SO -
HE TRIED TO SPEAR IT WITH HIS SWORD - OR **SWORD** IT WITH HIS SWORD - OR SOMETHING ..
BUT THEN, AFTER ALL, HE DECIDED HE HAD BETTER DISMOUNT...
KLANK!
. IN A WAY
HECK! NOW HOW'M I GONNA GET ON AGAIN?

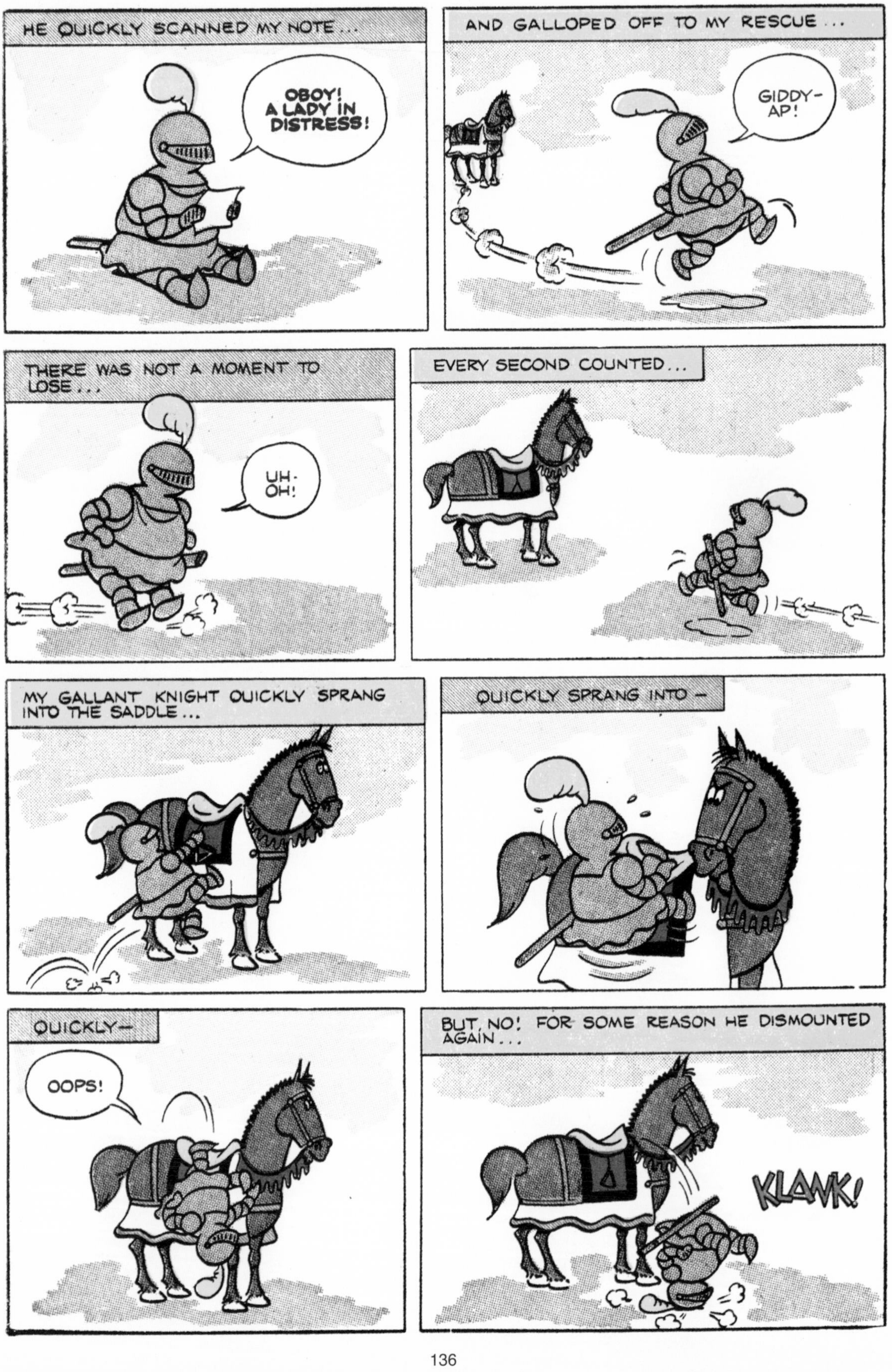
HE QUICKLY SCANNED MY NOTE...
OBOY! A LADY IN DISTRESS!
AND GALLOPED OFF TO MY RESCUE...
GIDDY-AP!
THERE WAS NOT A MOMENT TO LOSE...
UH-OH!
EVERY SECOND COUNTED...
MY GALLANT KNIGHT QUICKLY SPRANG INTO THE SADDLE...
QUICKLY SPRANG INTO—
QUICKLY—
OOPS!
BUT, NO! FOR SOME REASON HE DISMOUNTED AGAIN...
KLANK!

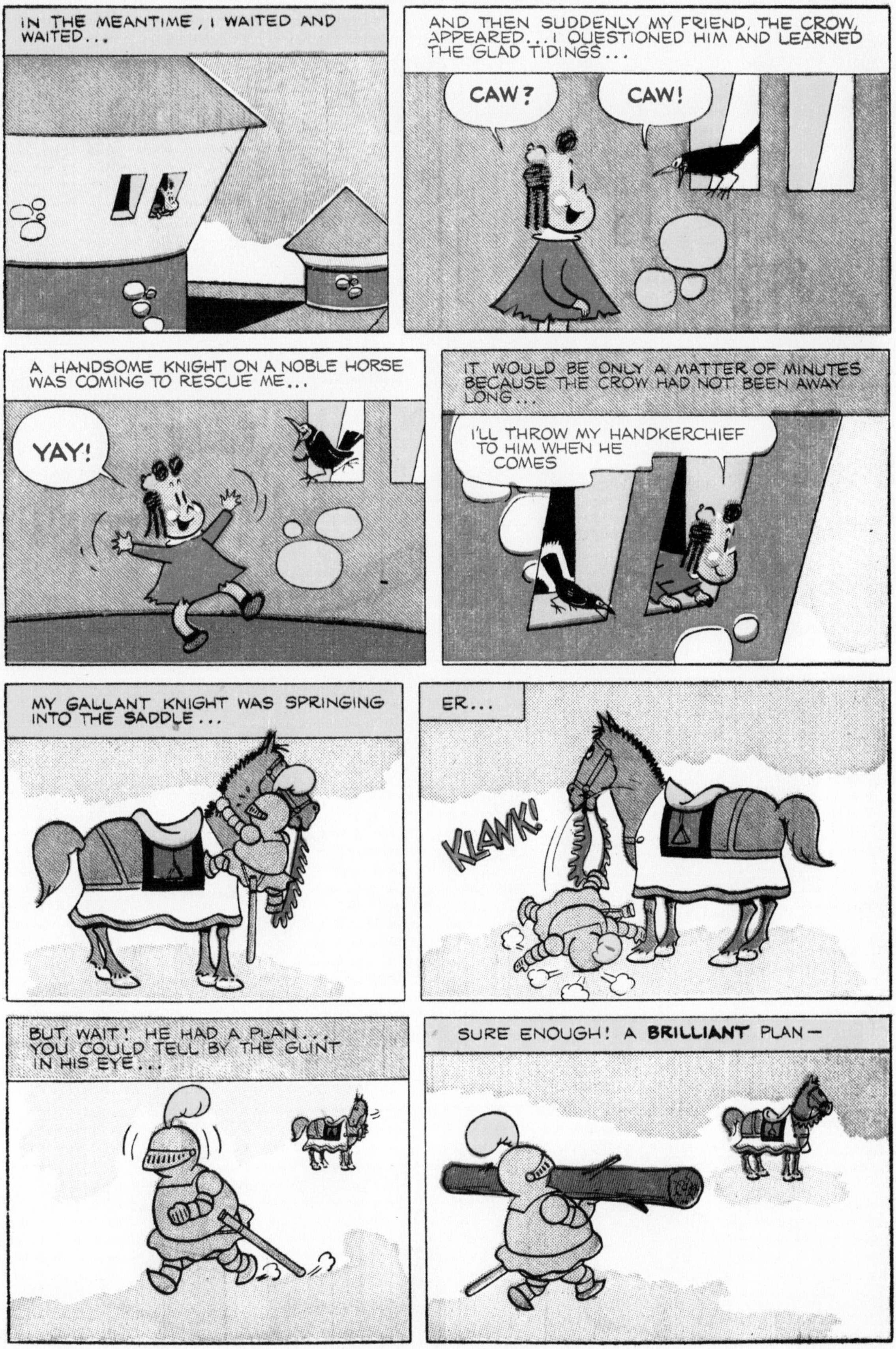
IN THE MEANTIME, I WAITED AND WAITED...
AND THEN SUDDENLY MY FRIEND, THE CROW, APPEARED... I QUESTIONED HIM AND LEARNED THE GLAD TIDINGS...
CAW?
CAW!
A HANDSOME KNIGHT ON A NOBLE HORSE WAS COMING TO RESCUE ME...
YAY!
IT WOULD BE ONLY A MATTER OF MINUTES BECAUSE THE CROW HAD NOT BEEN AWAY LONG...
I'LL THROW MY HANDKERCHIEF TO HIM WHEN HE COMES
MY GALLANT KNIGHT WAS SPRINGING INTO THE SADDLE...
ER...
KLANK!
BUT, WAIT! HE HAD A PLAN... YOU COULD TELL BY THE GLINT IN HIS EYE...
SURE ENOUGH! A BRILLIANT PLAN—

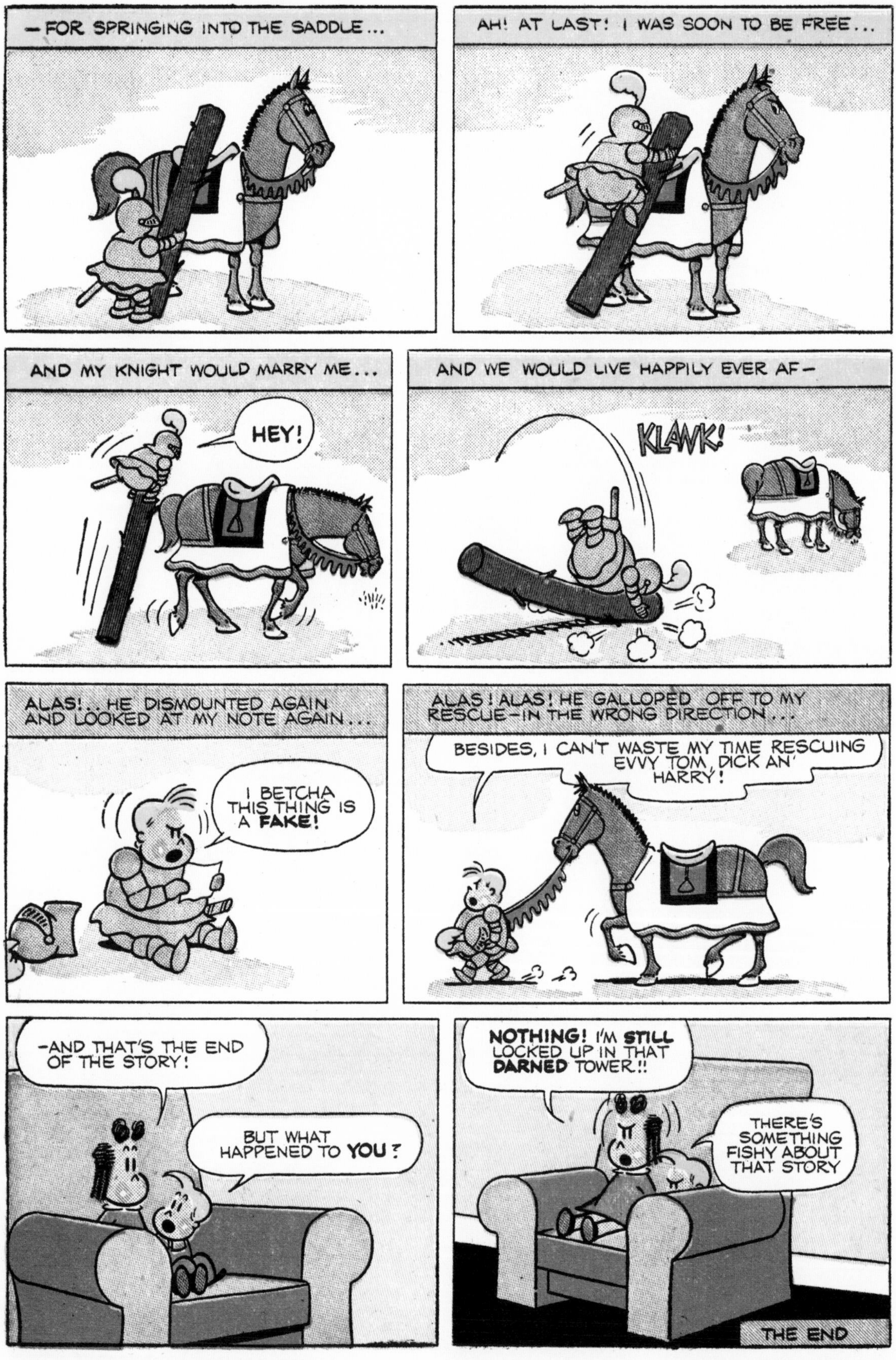
—FOR SPRINGING INTO THE SADDLE...
AH! AT LAST! I WAS SOON TO BE FREE...
AND MY KNIGHT WOULD MARRY ME...
HEY!
AND WE WOULD LIVE HAPPILY EVER AF—
KLANK!
ALAS!...HE DISMOUNTED AGAIN AND LOOKED AT MY NOTE AGAIN...
I BETCHA THIS THING IS A FAKE!
ALAS! ALAS! HE GALLOPED OFF TO MY RESCUE—IN THE WRONG DIRECTION...
BESIDES, I CAN'T WASTE MY TIME RESCUING EVVY TOM, DICK AN' HARRY!
—AND THAT'S THE END OF THE STORY!
BUT WHAT HAPPENED TO YOU?
NOTHING! I'M STILL LOCKED UP IN THAT DARNED TOWER!!
THERE'S SOMETHING FISHY ABOUT THAT STORY
THE END

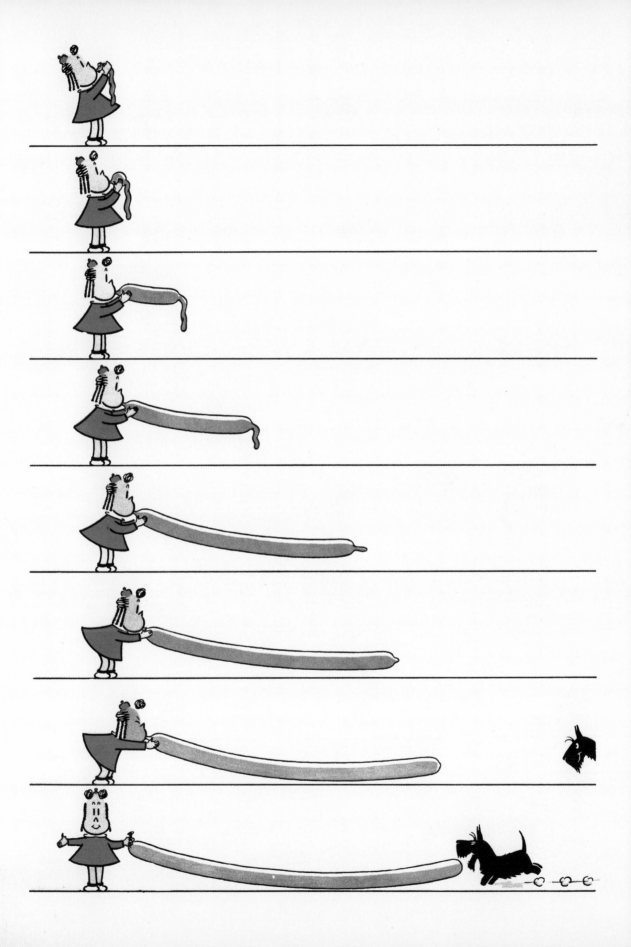

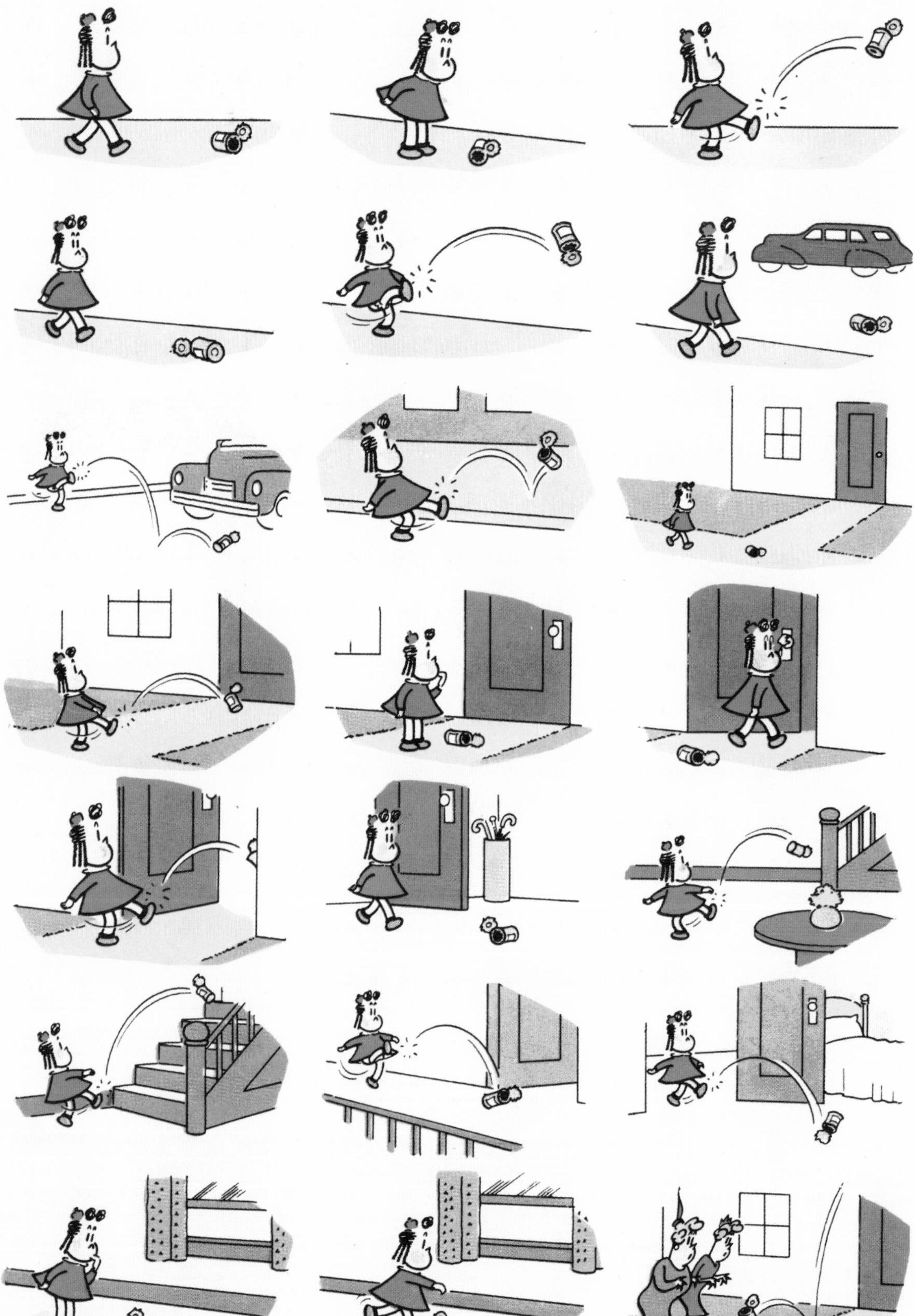

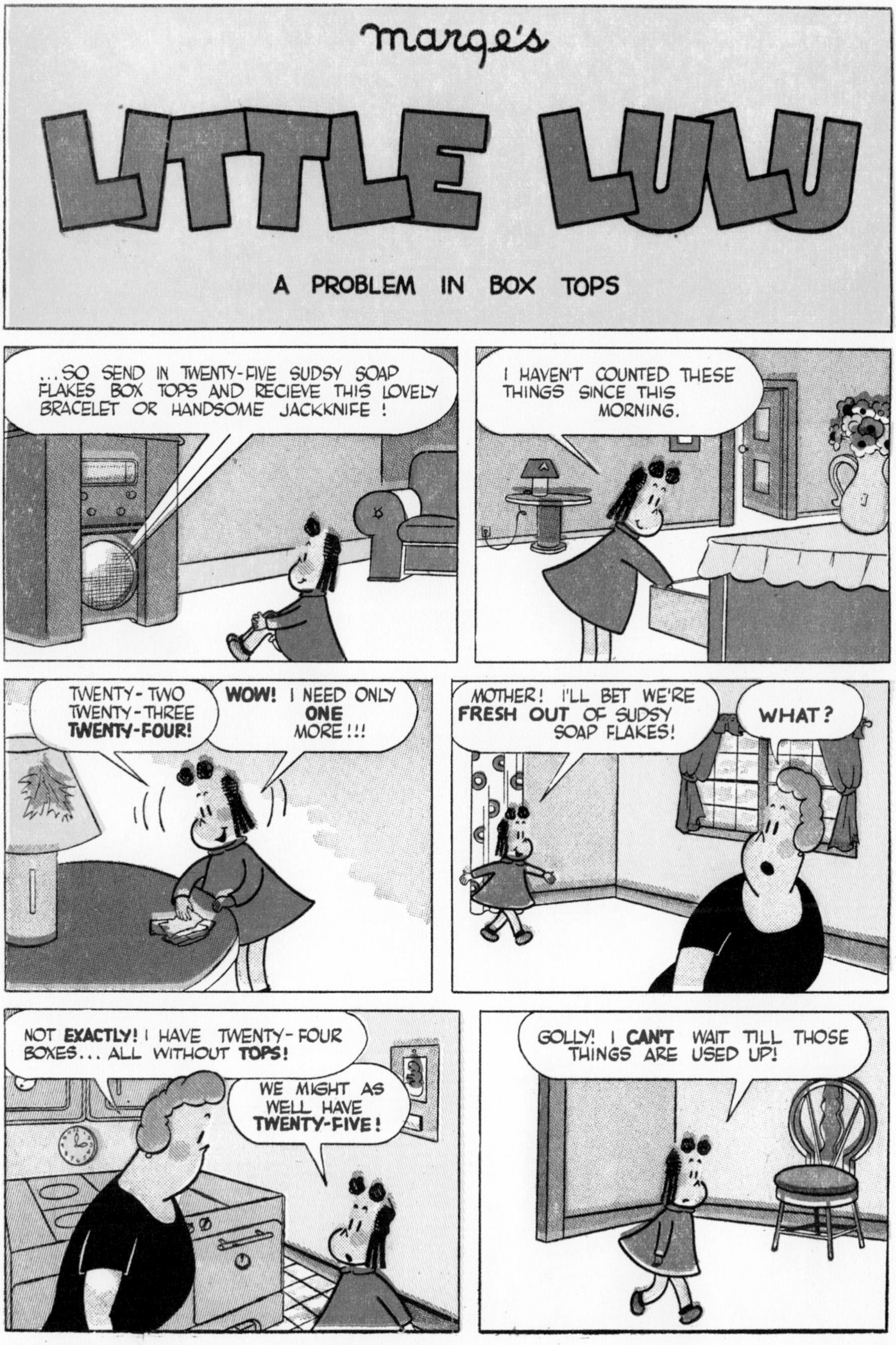
marge's
LITTLE LULU
A PROBLEM IN BOX TOPS
...SO SEND IN TWENTY-FIVE SUDSY SOAP FLAKES BOX TOPS AND RECIEVE THIS LOVELY BRACELET OR HANDSOME JACKKNIFE!
I HAVEN'T COUNTED THESE THINGS SINCE THIS MORNING.
TWENTY-TWO TWENTY-THREE TWENTY-FOUR!
WOW! I NEED ONLY ONE MORE!!!
MOTHER! I'LL BET WE'RE FRESH OUT OF SUDSY SOAP FLAKES!
WHAT?
NOT EXACTLY! I HAVE TWENTY-FOUR BOXES... ALL WITHOUT TOPS!
WE MIGHT AS WELL HAVE TWENTY-FIVE!
GOLLY! I CAN'T WAIT TILL THOSE THINGS ARE USED UP!

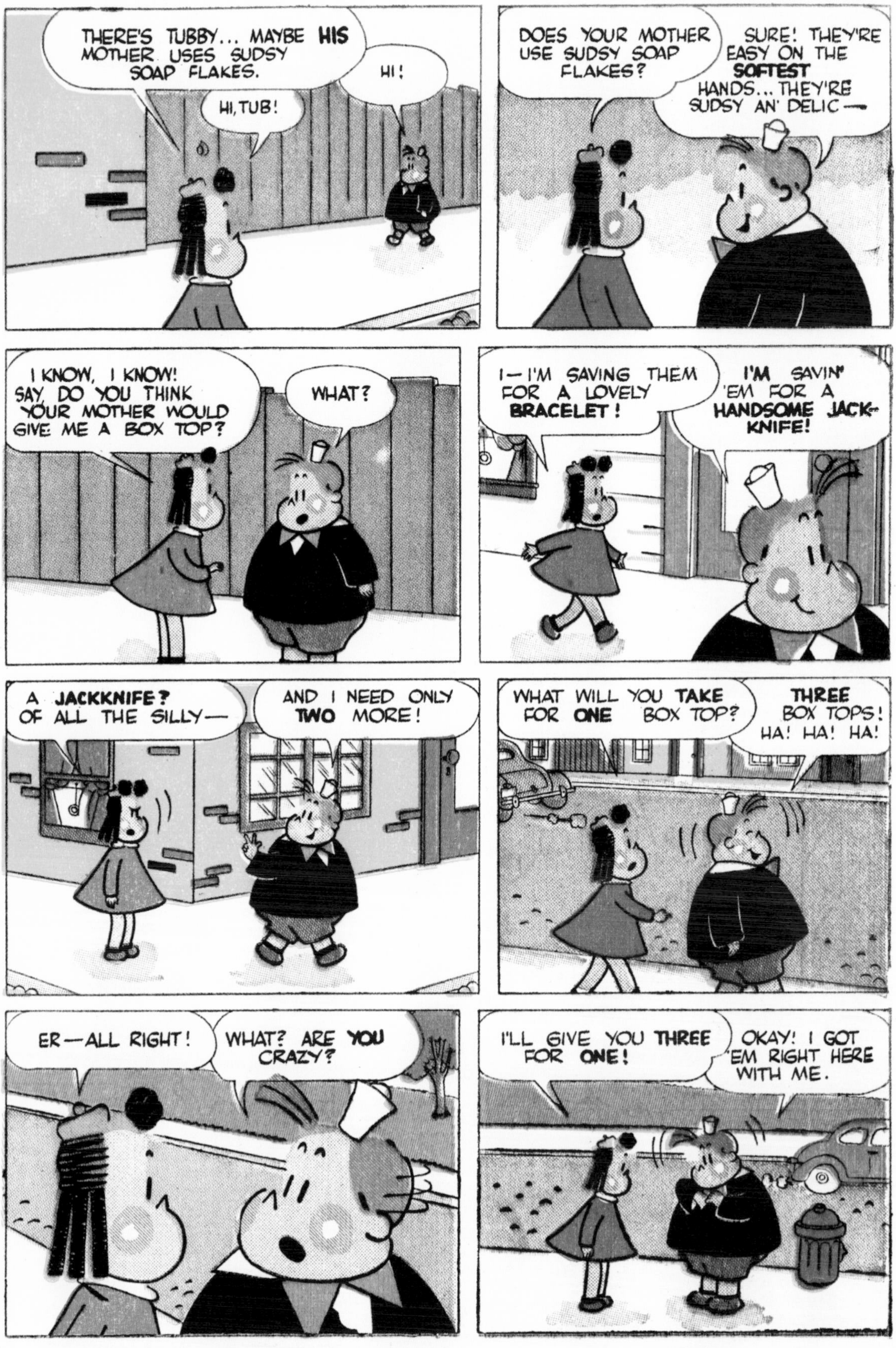
THERE'S TUBBY... MAYBE HIS MOTHER USES SUDSY SOAP FLAKES.
HI!
HI, TUB!
DOES YOUR MOTHER USE SUDSY SOAP FLAKES?
SURE! THEY'RE EASY ON THE SOFTEST HANDS... THEY'RE SUDSY AN' DELIC—
I KNOW, I KNOW! SAY, DO YOU THINK YOUR MOTHER WOULD GIVE ME A BOX TOP?
WHAT?
I—I'M SAVING THEM FOR A LOVELY BRACELET!
I'M SAVIN' 'EM FOR A HANDSOME JACK-KNIFE!
A JACKKNIFE? OF ALL THE SILLY—
AND I NEED ONLY TWO MORE!
WHAT WILL YOU TAKE FOR ONE BOX TOP?
THREE BOX TOPS! HA! HA! HA!
ER—ALL RIGHT!
WHAT? ARE YOU CRAZY?
I'LL GIVE YOU THREE FOR ONE!
OKAY! I GOT 'EM RIGHT HERE WITH ME.

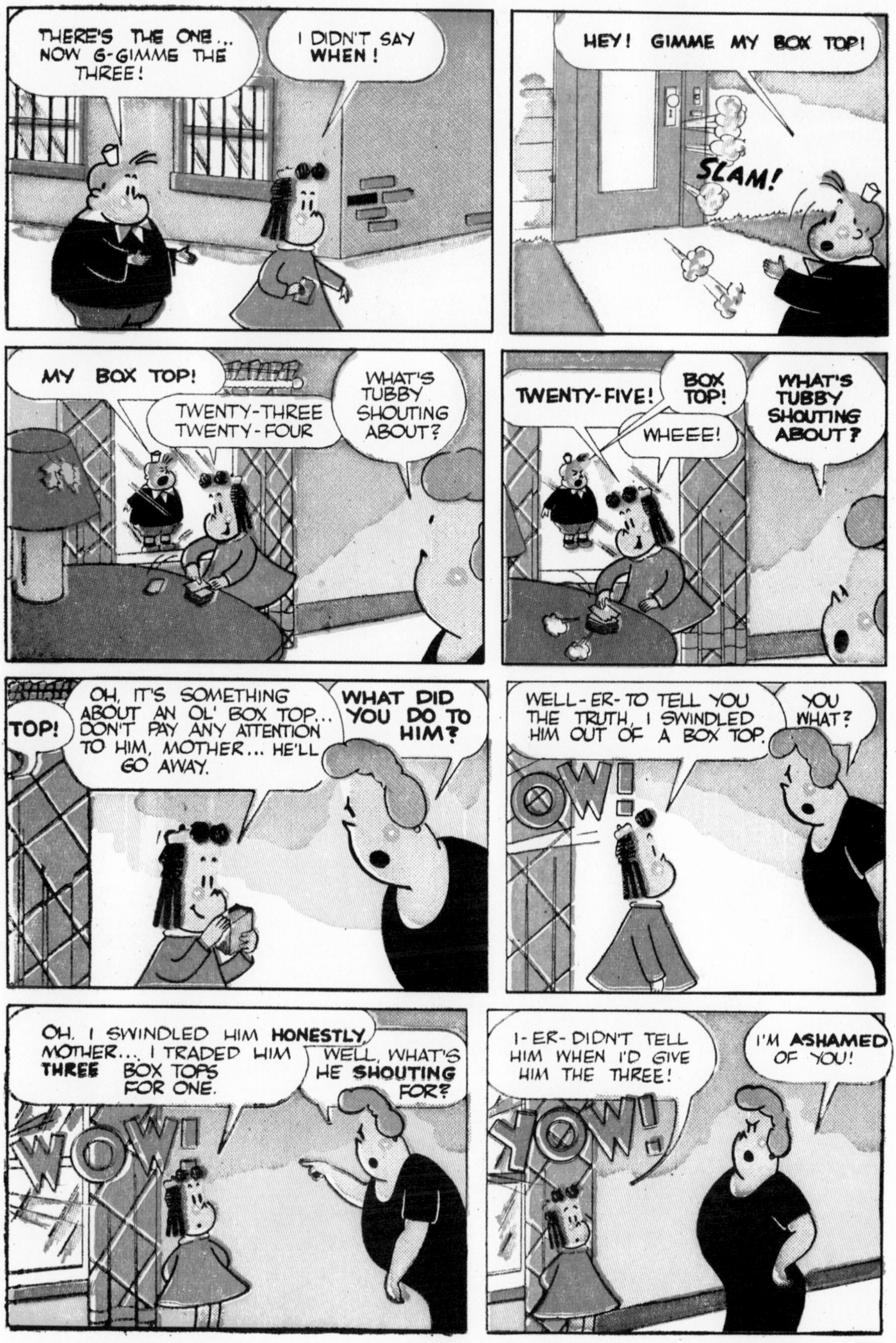
THERE'S THE ONE... NOW G-GIMME THE THREE!
I DIDN'T SAY WHEN!
HEY! GIMME MY BOX TOP!
SLAM!
MY BOX TOP!
TWENTY-THREE TWENTY-FOUR
WHAT'S TUBBY SHOUTING ABOUT?
TWENTY-FIVE!
BOX TOP!
WHEEE!
WHAT'S TUBBY SHOUTING ABOUT?
TOP!
OH, IT'S SOMETHING ABOUT AN OL' BOX TOP... DON'T PAY ANY ATTENTION TO HIM, MOTHER... HE'LL GO AWAY.
WHAT DID YOU DO TO HIM?
WELL-ER-TO TELL YOU THE TRUTH, I SWINDLED HIM OUT OF A BOX TOP.
YOU WHAT?
OW!
OH, I SWINDLED HIM HONESTLY, MOTHER... I TRADED HIM THREE BOX TOPS FOR ONE.
WELL, WHAT'S HE SHOUTING FOR?
WOW!
I-ER-DIDN'T TELL HIM WHEN I'D GIVE HIM THE THREE!
I'M ASHAMED OF YOU!
YOW!

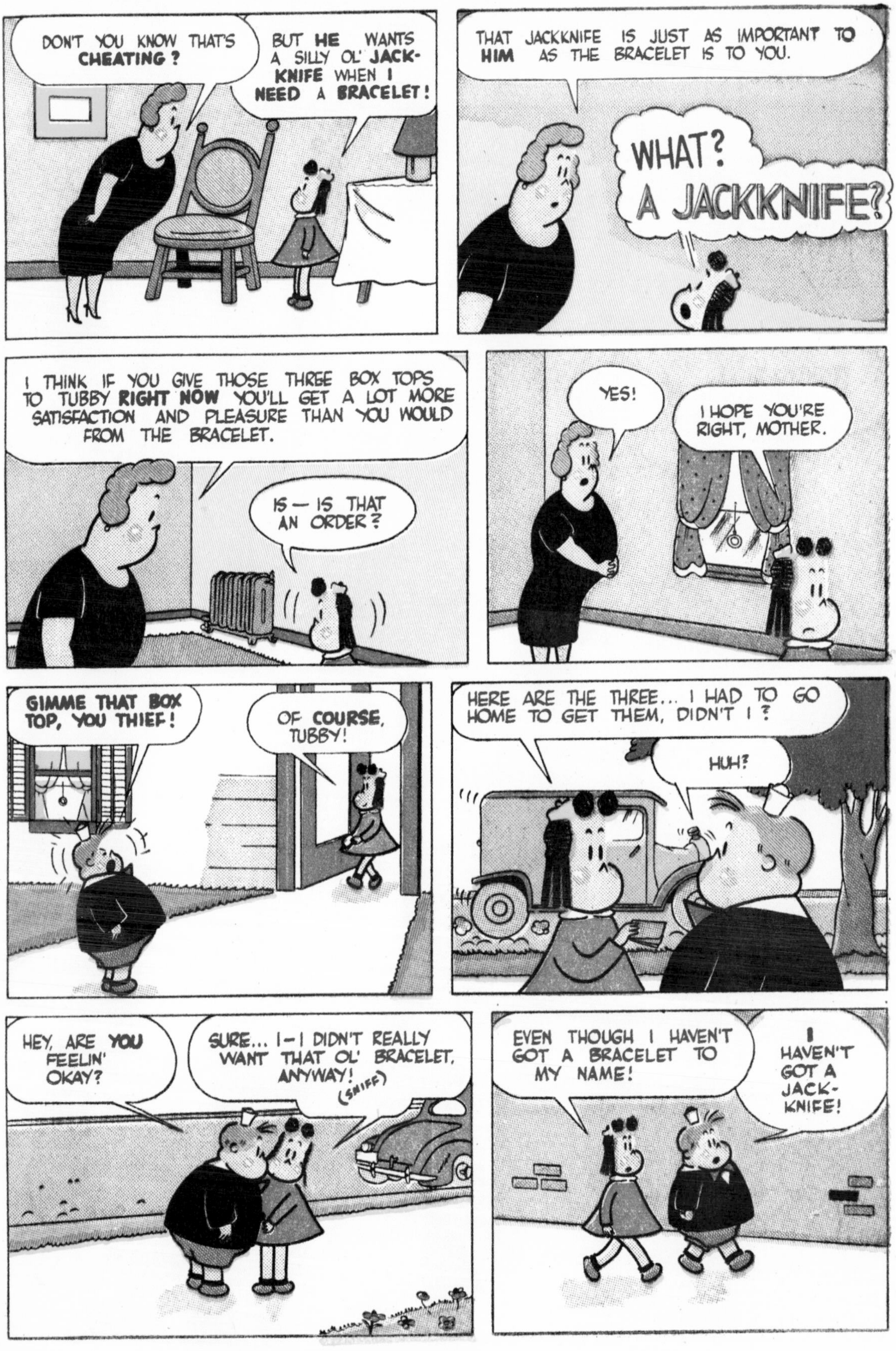
DON'T YOU KNOW THAT'S CHEATING?
BUT HE WANTS A SILLY OL' JACK-KNIFE WHEN I NEED A BRACELET!
THAT JACKKNIFE IS JUST AS IMPORTANT TO HIM AS THE BRACELET IS TO YOU.
WHAT? A JACKKNIFE?
I THINK IF YOU GIVE THOSE THREE BOX TOPS TO TUBBY RIGHT NOW YOU'LL GET A LOT MORE SATISFACTION AND PLEASURE THAN YOU WOULD FROM THE BRACELET.
IS — IS THAT AN ORDER?
YES!
I HOPE YOU'RE RIGHT, MOTHER.
GIMME THAT BOX TOP, YOU THIEF!
OF COURSE, TUBBY!
HERE ARE THE THREE... I HAD TO GO HOME TO GET THEM, DIDN'T I?
HUH?
HEY, ARE YOU FEELIN' OKAY?
SURE... I-I DIDN'T REALLY WANT THAT OL' BRACELET, ANYWAY!
(SNIFF)
EVEN THOUGH I HAVEN'T GOT A BRACELET TO MY NAME!
I HAVEN'T GOT A JACK-KNIFE!

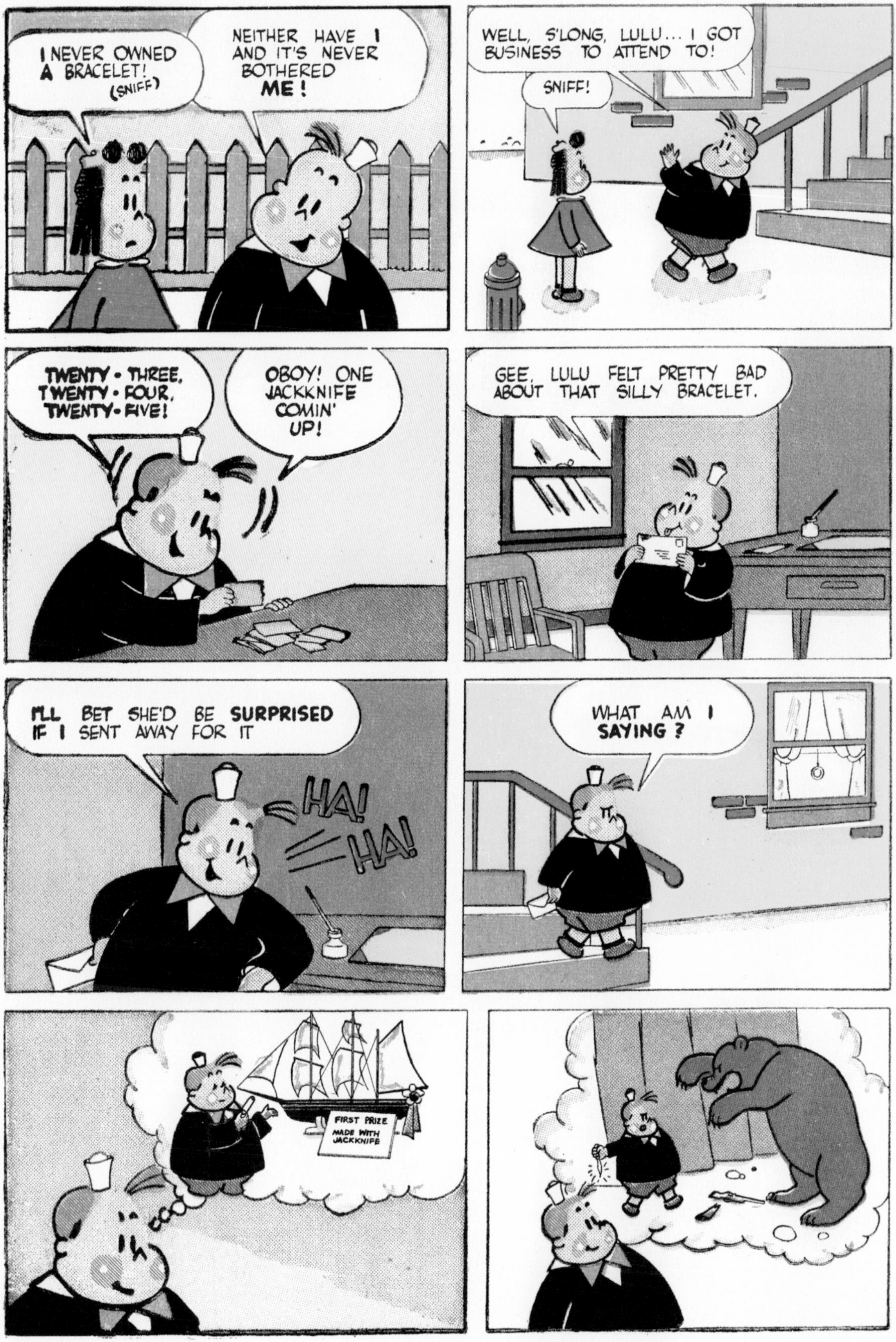

I NEVER OWNED A BRACELET! (SNIFF)
NEITHER HAVE I AND IT'S NEVER BOTHERED ME!
WELL, S'LONG, LULU... I GOT BUSINESS TO ATTEND TO!
SNIFF!
TWENTY - THREE, TWENTY - FOUR, TWENTY - FIVE!
OBOY! ONE JACKKNIFE COMIN' UP!
GEE, LULU FELT PRETTY BAD ABOUT THAT SILLY BRACELET.
I'LL BET SHE'D BE SURPRISED IF I SENT AWAY FOR IT
HA! HA!
WHAT AM I SAYING?
FIRST PRIZE
MADE WITH JACKKNIFE

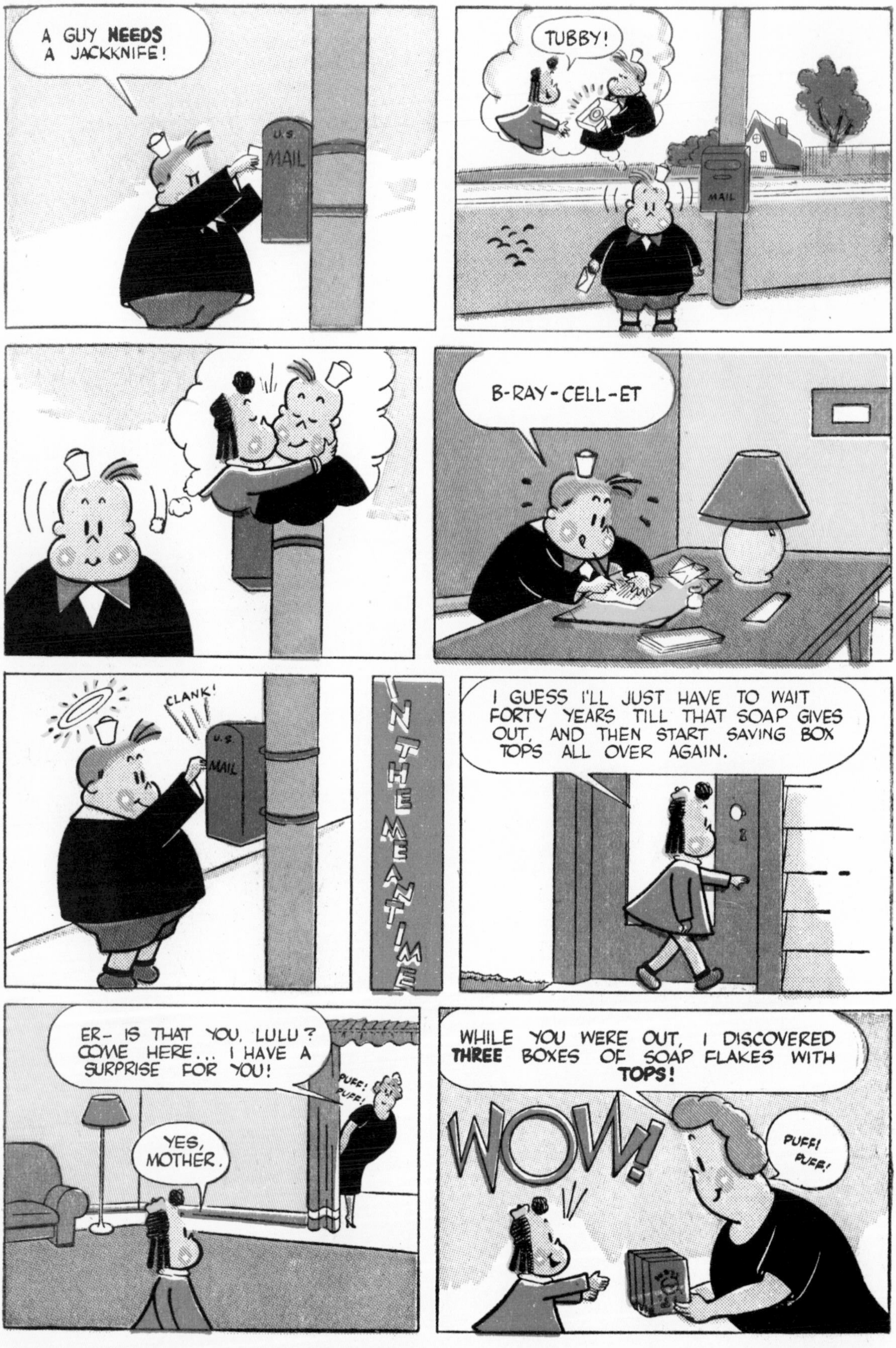
A GUY NEEDS A JACKKNIFE!
U.S. MAIL
TUBBY!
MAIL
B-RAY-CELL-ET
CLANK!
U.S. MAIL
IN THE MEANTIME
I GUESS I'LL JUST HAVE TO WAIT FORTY YEARS TILL THAT SOAP GIVES OUT, AND THEN START SAVING BOX TOPS ALL OVER AGAIN.
ER– IS THAT YOU, LULU? COME HERE... I HAVE A SURPRISE FOR YOU!
PUFF! PUFF!
YES, MOTHER.
WHILE YOU WERE OUT, I DISCOVERED THREE BOXES OF SOAP FLAKES WITH TOPS!
WOW!
PUFF! PUFF!

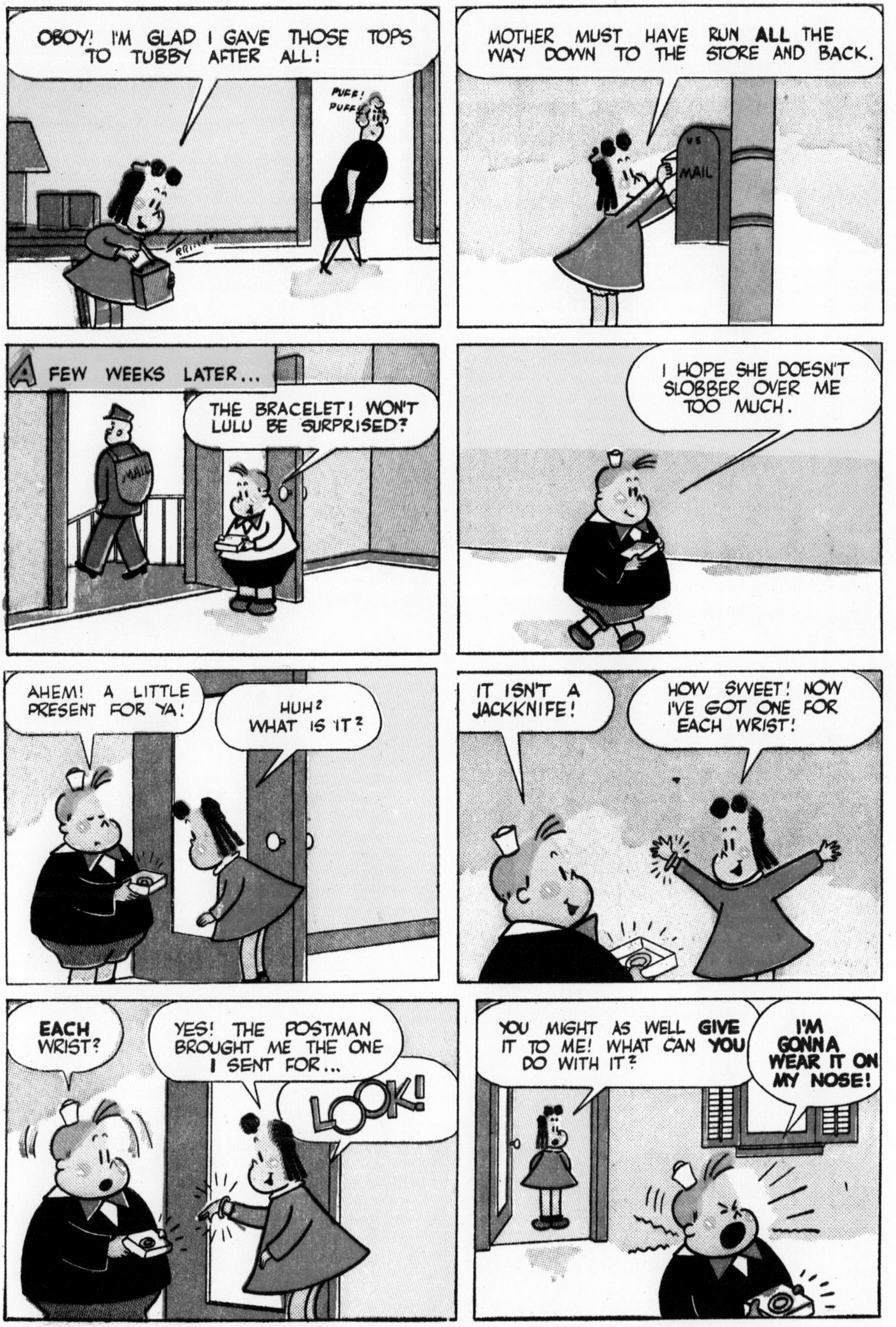
OBOY! I'M GLAD I GAVE THOSE TOPS TO TUBBY AFTER ALL!
PUFF! PUFF!
MOTHER MUST HAVE RUN ALL THE WAY DOWN TO THE STORE AND BACK.
MAIL
A FEW WEEKS LATER...
THE BRACELET! WON'T LULU BE SURPRISED?
MAIL
I HOPE SHE DOESN'T SLOBBER OVER ME TOO MUCH.
AHEM! A LITTLE PRESENT FOR YA!
HUH? WHAT IS IT?
IT ISN'T A JACKKNIFE!
HOW SWEET! NOW I'VE GOT ONE FOR EACH WRIST!
EACH WRIST?
YES! THE POSTMAN BROUGHT ME THE ONE I SENT FOR...
LOOK!
YOU MIGHT AS WELL GIVE IT TO ME! WHAT CAN YOU DO WITH IT?
I'M GONNA WEAR IT ON MY NOSE!

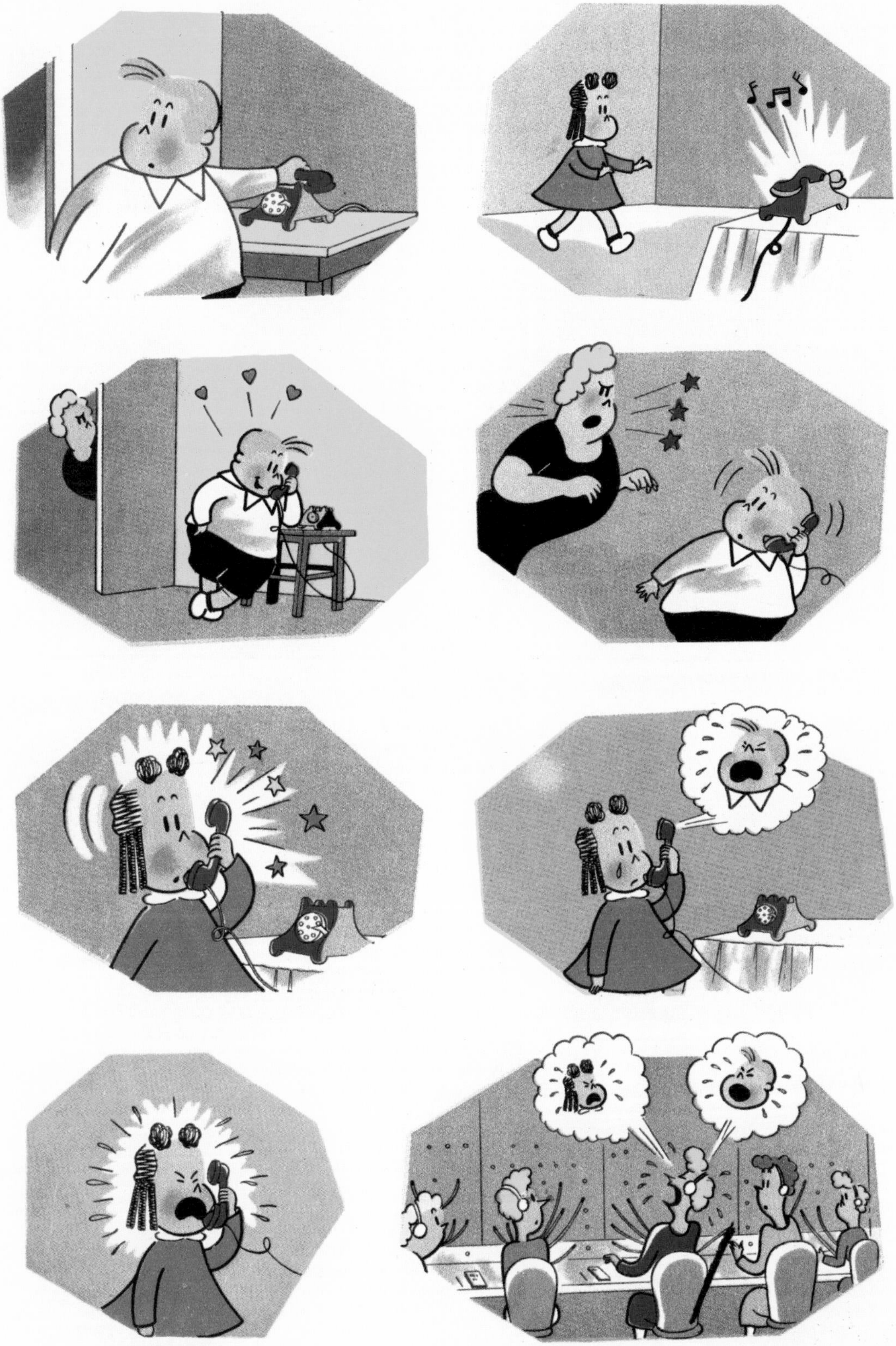

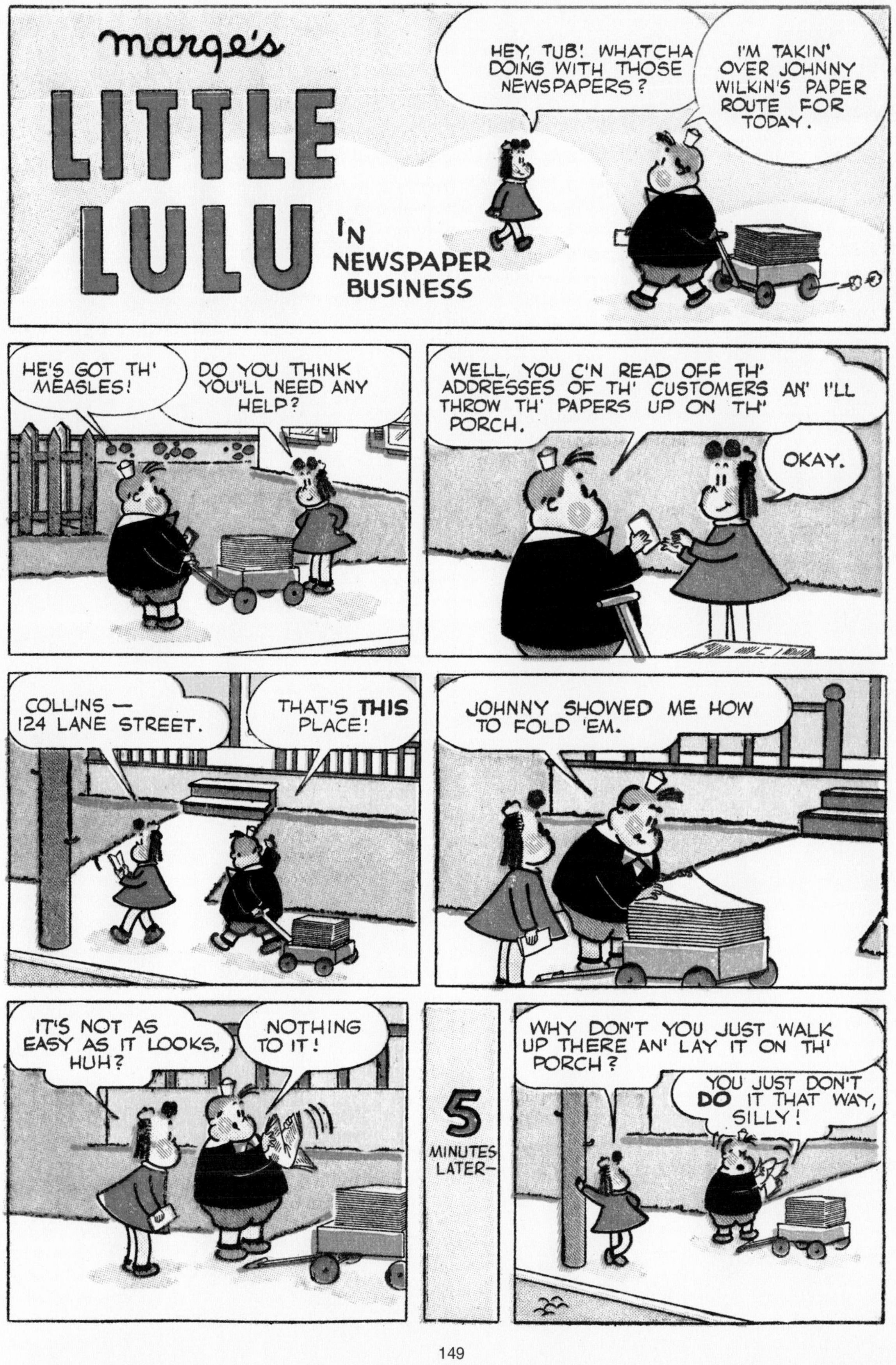
marge's
LITTLE LULU
IN NEWSPAPER BUSINESS
HEY, TUB! WHATCHA DOING WITH THOSE NEWSPAPERS?
I'M TAKIN' OVER JOHNNY WILKIN'S PAPER ROUTE FOR TODAY.
HE'S GOT TH' MEASLES!
DO YOU THINK YOU'LL NEED ANY HELP?
WELL, YOU C'N READ OFF TH' ADDRESSES OF TH' CUSTOMERS AN' I'LL THROW TH' PAPERS UP ON TH' PORCH.
OKAY.
COLLINS — 124 LANE STREET.
THAT'S **THIS** PLACE!
JOHNNY SHOWED ME HOW TO FOLD 'EM.
IT'S NOT AS EASY AS IT LOOKS, HUH?
NOTHING TO IT!
5 MINUTES LATER—
WHY DON'T YOU JUST WALK UP THERE AN' LAY IT ON TH' PORCH?
YOU JUST DON'T **DO** IT THAT WAY, SILLY!

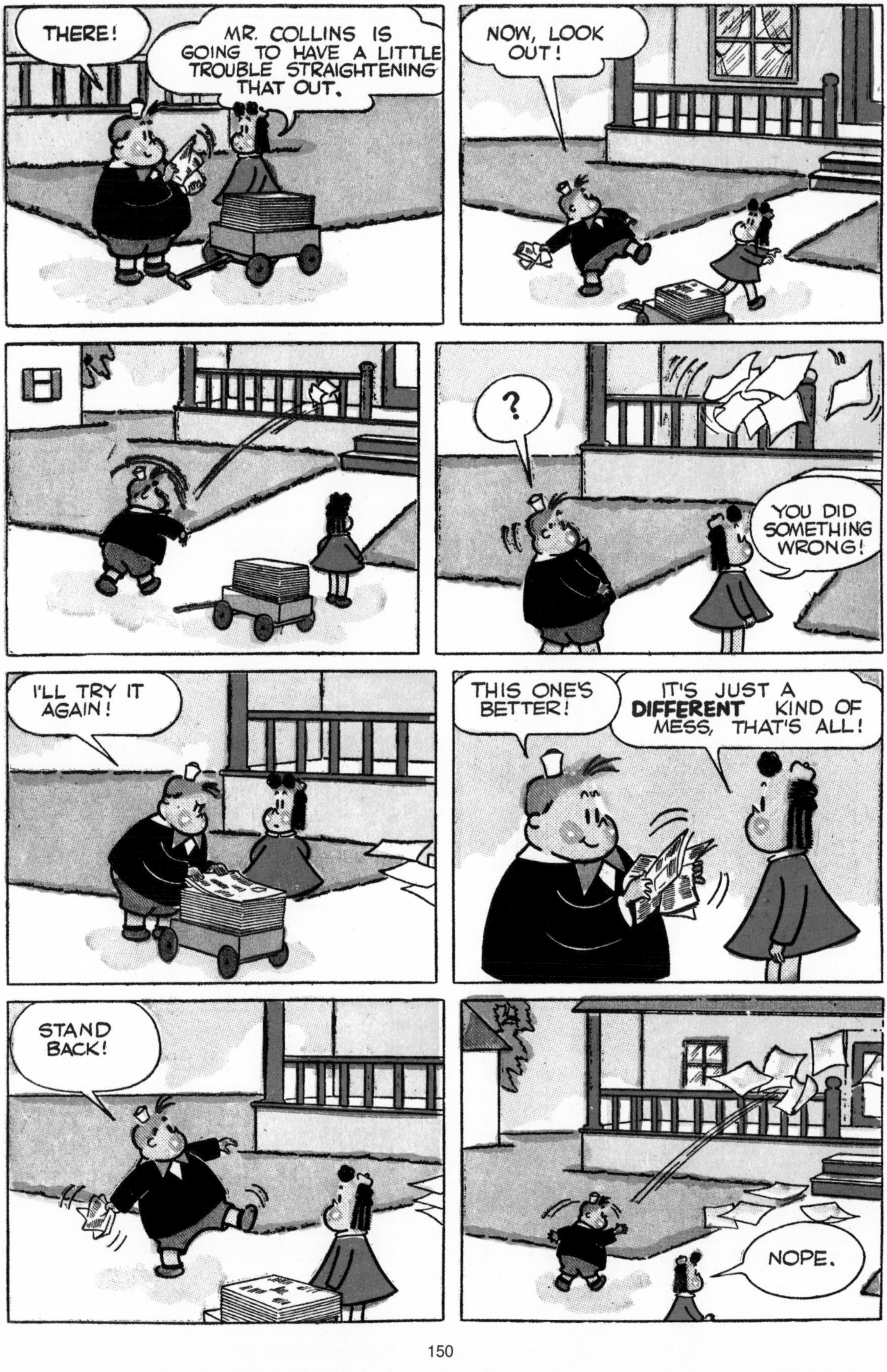
THERE!
MR. COLLINS IS GOING TO HAVE A LITTLE TROUBLE STRAIGHTENING THAT OUT.
NOW, LOOK OUT!
?
YOU DID SOMETHING WRONG!
I'LL TRY IT AGAIN!
THIS ONE'S BETTER!
IT'S JUST A **DIFFERENT** KIND OF MESS, THAT'S ALL!
STAND BACK!
NOPE.

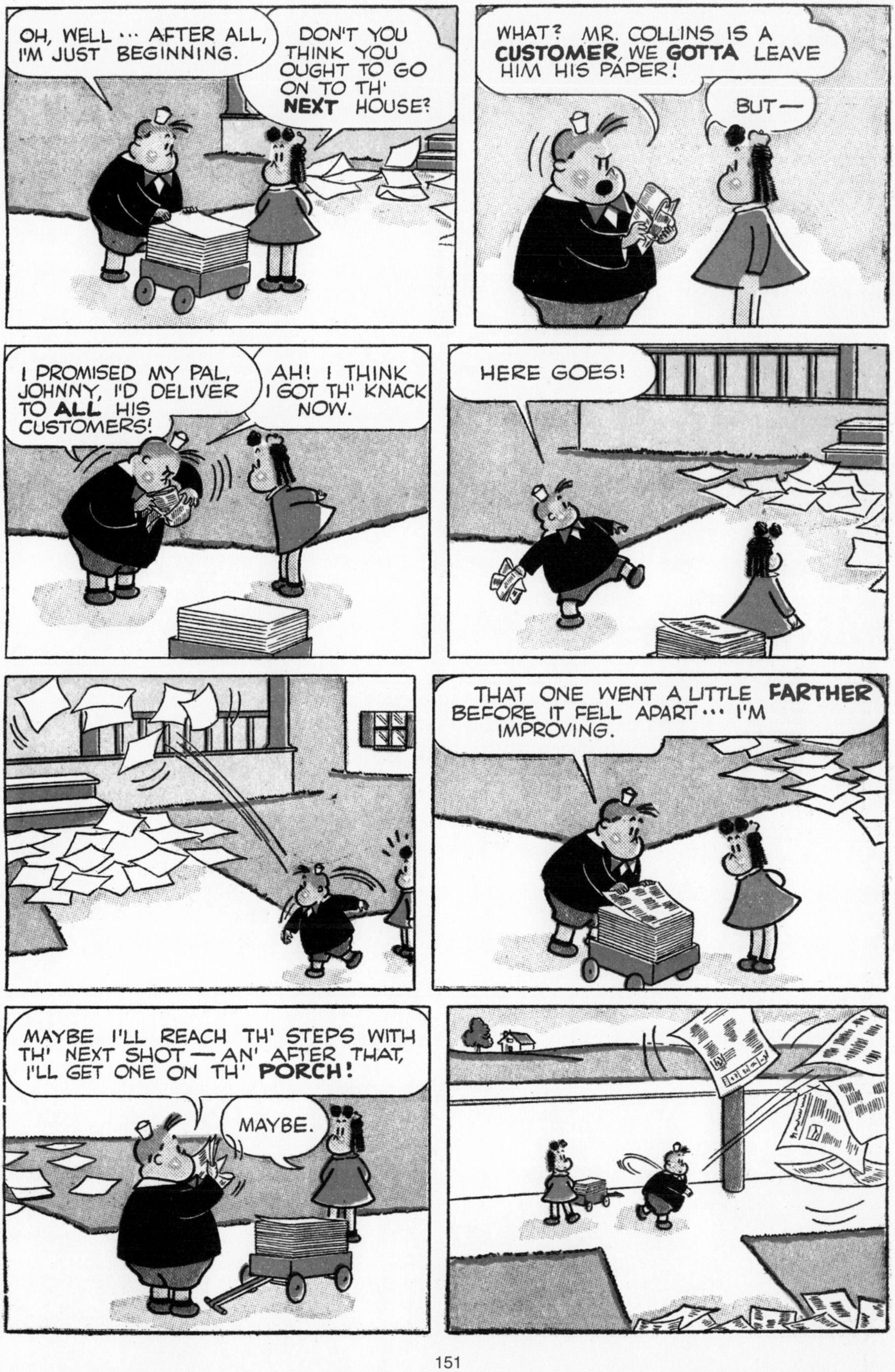
OH, WELL ··· AFTER ALL, I'M JUST BEGINNING.
DON'T YOU THINK YOU OUGHT TO GO ON TO TH' **NEXT** HOUSE?
WHAT? MR. COLLINS IS A **CUSTOMER**, WE **GOTTA** LEAVE HIM HIS PAPER!
BUT—
I PROMISED MY PAL, JOHNNY, I'D DELIVER TO **ALL** HIS CUSTOMERS!
AH! I THINK I GOT TH' KNACK NOW.
HERE GOES!
THAT ONE WENT A LITTLE **FARTHER** BEFORE IT FELL APART ··· I'M IMPROVING.
MAYBE I'LL REACH TH' STEPS WITH TH' NEXT SHOT — AN' AFTER THAT, I'LL GET ONE ON TH' **PORCH**!
MAYBE.

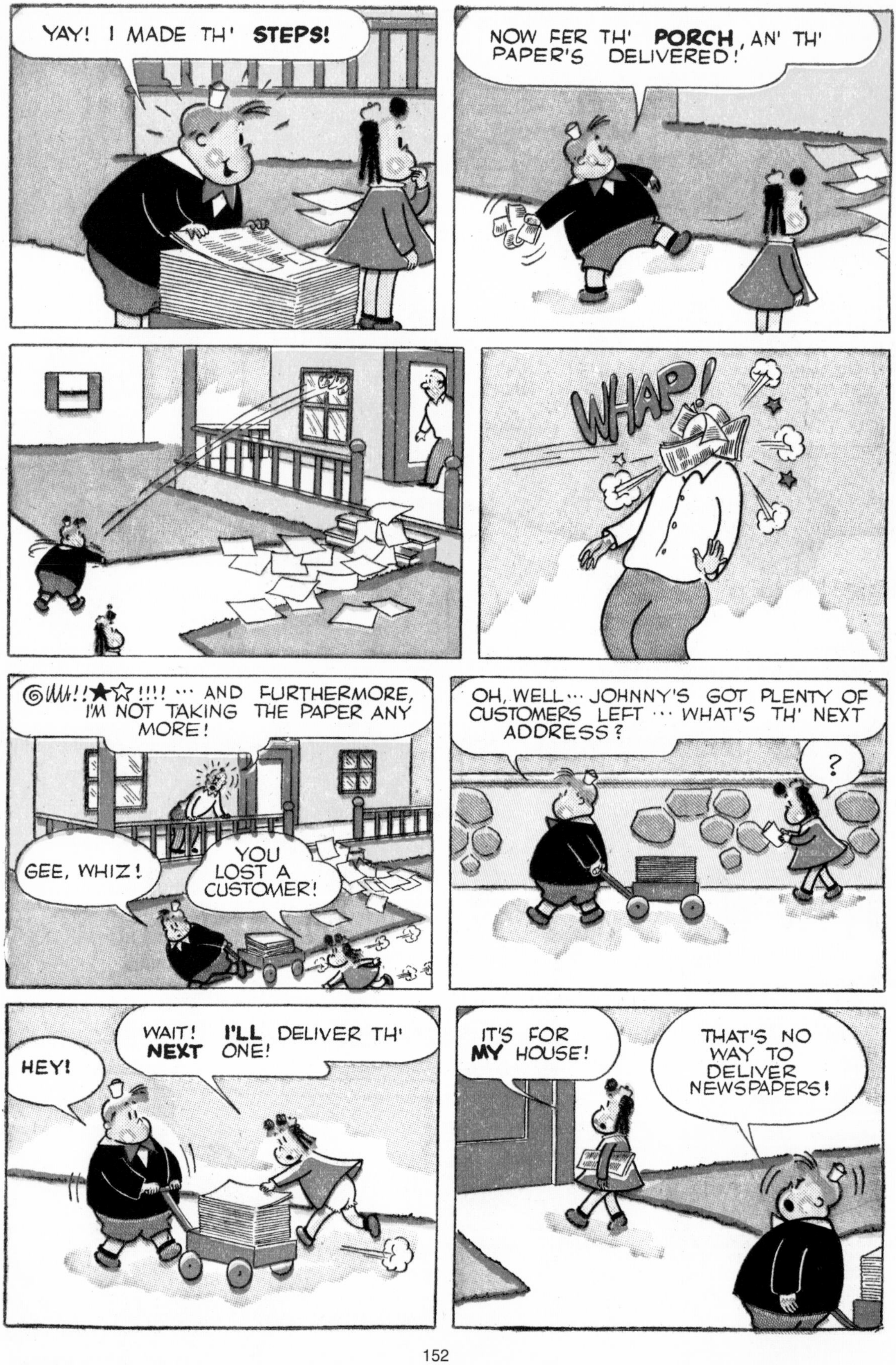
YAY! I MADE TH' STEPS!
NOW FER TH' PORCH, AN' TH' PAPER'S DELIVERED!
WHAP!
!!!! ... AND FURTHERMORE, I'M NOT TAKING THE PAPER ANY MORE!
GEE, WHIZ!
YOU LOST A CUSTOMER!
OH, WELL... JOHNNY'S GOT PLENTY OF CUSTOMERS LEFT ... WHAT'S TH' NEXT ADDRESS?
?
HEY!
WAIT! I'LL DELIVER TH' NEXT ONE!
IT'S FOR MY HOUSE!
THAT'S NO WAY TO DELIVER NEWSPAPERS!

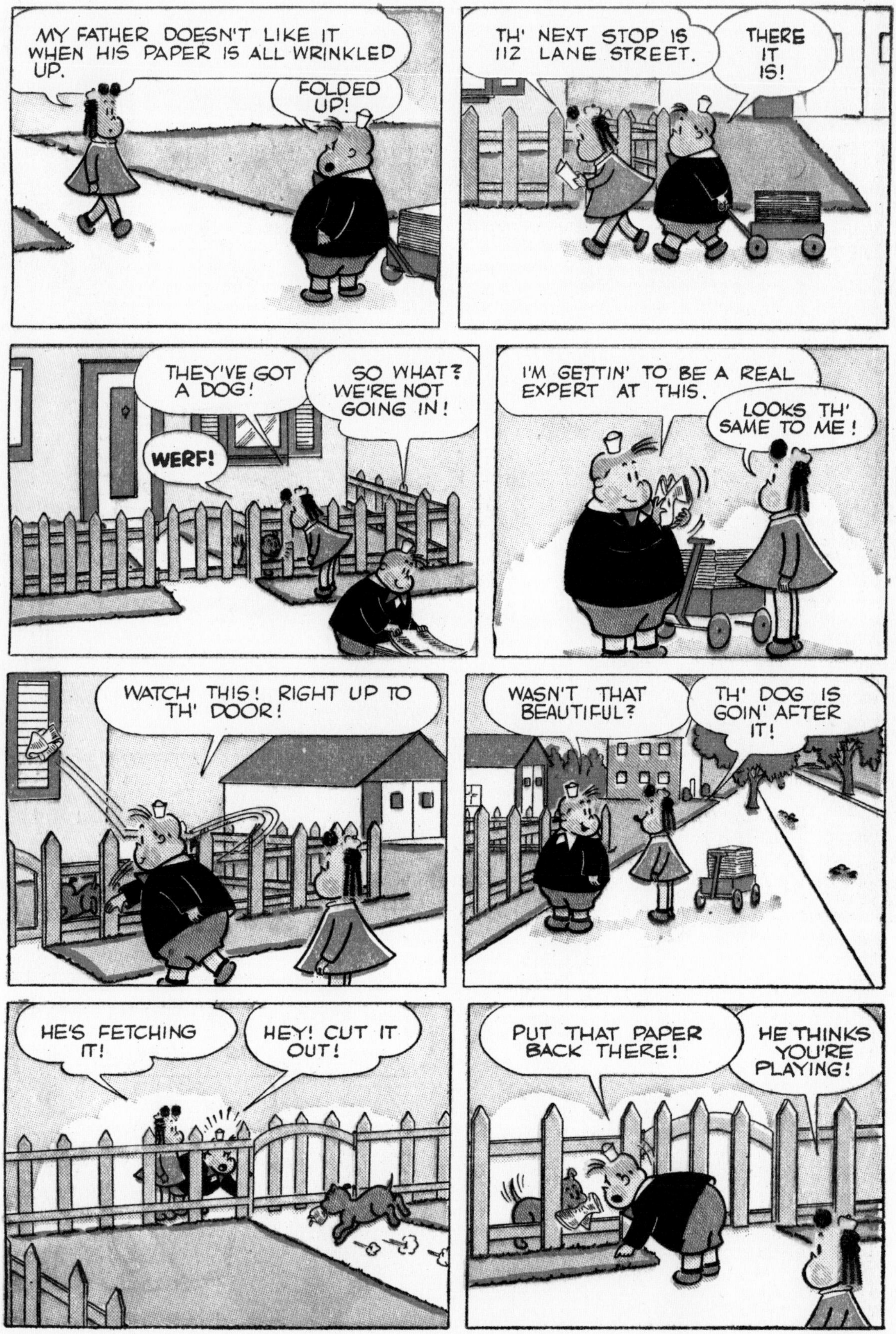
MY FATHER DOESN'T LIKE IT WHEN HIS PAPER IS ALL WRINKLED UP.
FOLDED UP!
TH' NEXT STOP IS 112 LANE STREET.
THERE IT IS!
THEY'VE GOT A DOG!
SO WHAT? WE'RE NOT GOING IN!
WERF!
I'M GETTIN' TO BE A REAL EXPERT AT THIS.
LOOKS TH' SAME TO ME!
WATCH THIS! RIGHT UP TO TH' DOOR!
WASN'T THAT BEAUTIFUL?
TH' DOG IS GOIN' AFTER IT!
HE'S FETCHING IT!
HEY! CUT IT OUT!
PUT THAT PAPER BACK THERE!
HE THINKS YOU'RE PLAYING!

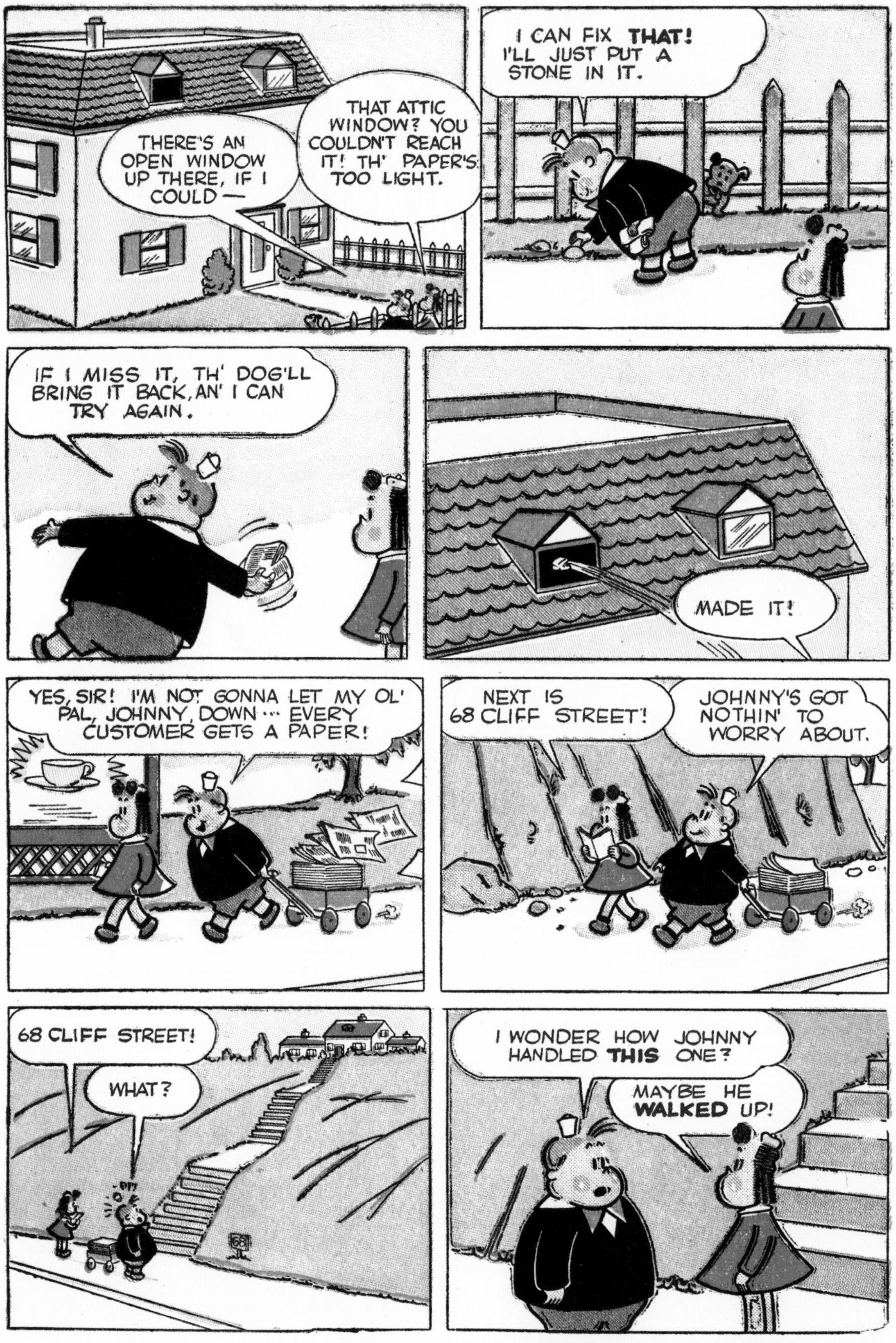
THERE'S AN OPEN WINDOW UP THERE, IF I COULD—
THAT ATTIC WINDOW? YOU COULDN'T REACH IT! TH' PAPER'S TOO LIGHT.
I CAN FIX THAT! I'LL JUST PUT A STONE IN IT.
IF I MISS IT, TH' DOG'LL BRING IT BACK, AN' I CAN TRY AGAIN.
MADE IT!
YES, SIR! I'M NOT GONNA LET MY OL' PAL, JOHNNY, DOWN ··· EVERY CUSTOMER GETS A PAPER!
NEXT IS 68 CLIFF STREET!
JOHNNY'S GOT NOTHIN' TO WORRY ABOUT.
68 CLIFF STREET!
WHAT?
68
I WONDER HOW JOHNNY HANDLED THIS ONE?
MAYBE HE WALKED UP!

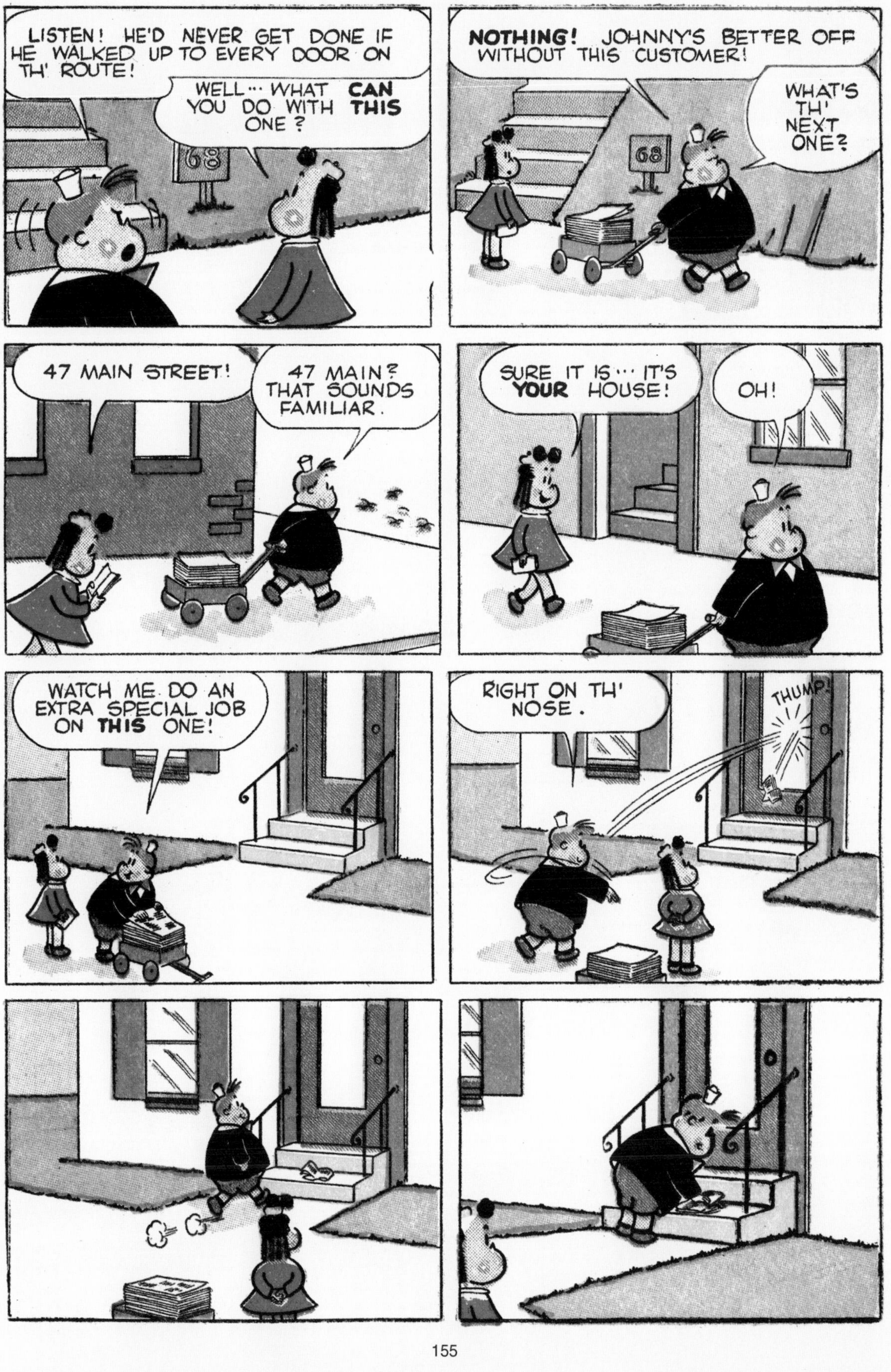
LISTEN! HE'D NEVER GET DONE IF HE WALKED UP TO EVERY DOOR ON TH' ROUTE!
WELL... WHAT CAN YOU DO WITH THIS ONE?
68
NOTHING! JOHNNY'S BETTER OFF WITHOUT THIS CUSTOMER!
WHAT'S TH' NEXT ONE?
68
47 MAIN STREET!
47 MAIN? THAT SOUNDS FAMILIAR.
SURE IT IS... IT'S YOUR HOUSE!
OH!
WATCH ME DO AN EXTRA SPECIAL JOB ON THIS ONE!
RIGHT ON TH' NOSE.
THUMP!

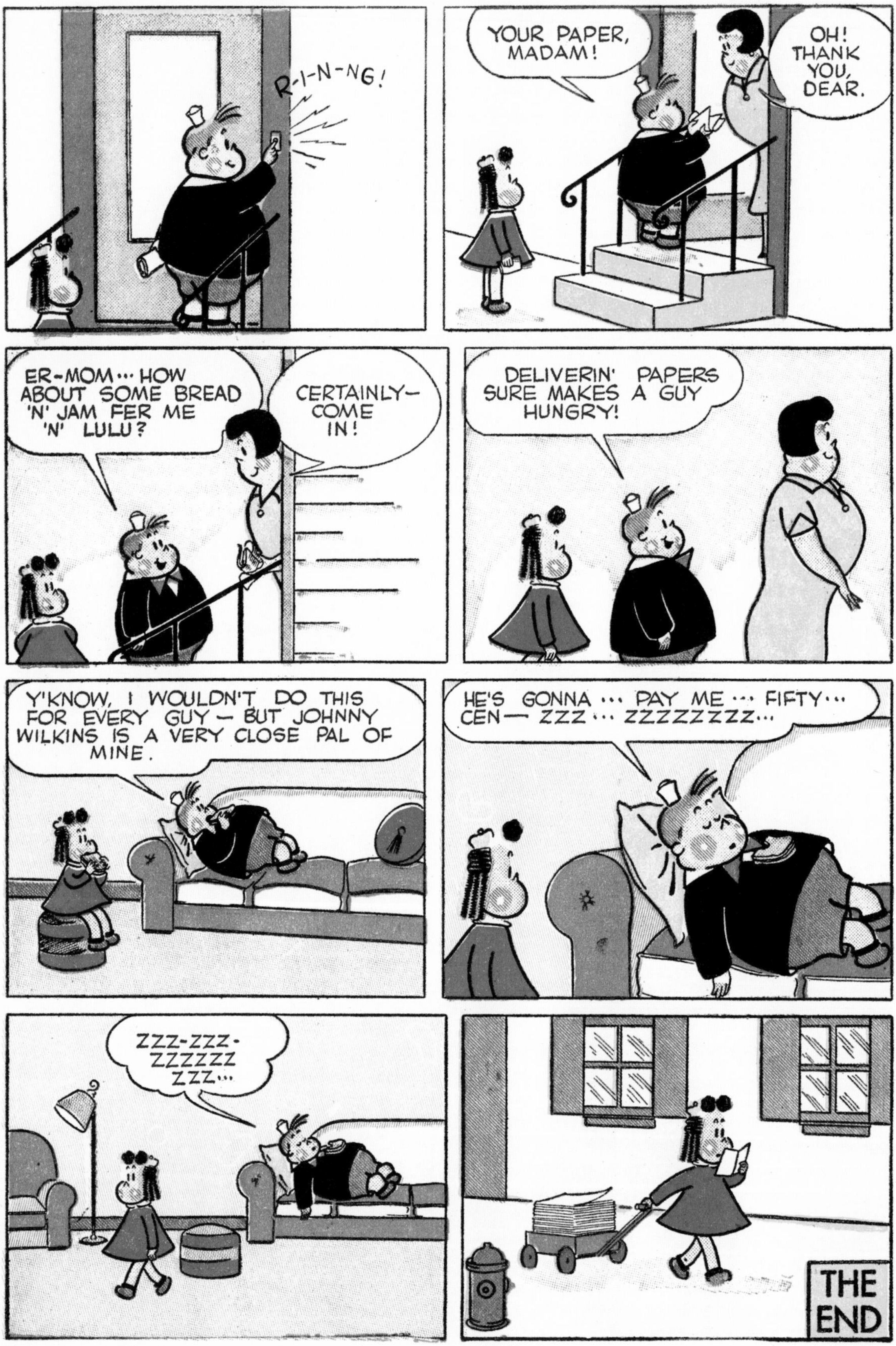
R-I-N-NG!
YOUR PAPER, MADAM!
OH! THANK YOU, DEAR.
ER-MOM... HOW ABOUT SOME BREAD 'N' JAM FER ME 'N' LULU?
CERTAINLY— COME IN!
DELIVERIN' PAPERS SURE MAKES A GUY HUNGRY!
Y'KNOW, I WOULDN'T DO THIS FOR EVERY GUY — BUT JOHNNY WILKINS IS A VERY CLOSE PAL OF MINE.
HE'S GONNA ... PAY ME ... FIFTY... CEN— ZZZ ... ZZZZZZZZ...
ZZZ-ZZZ-ZZZZZZ ZZZ...
THE END

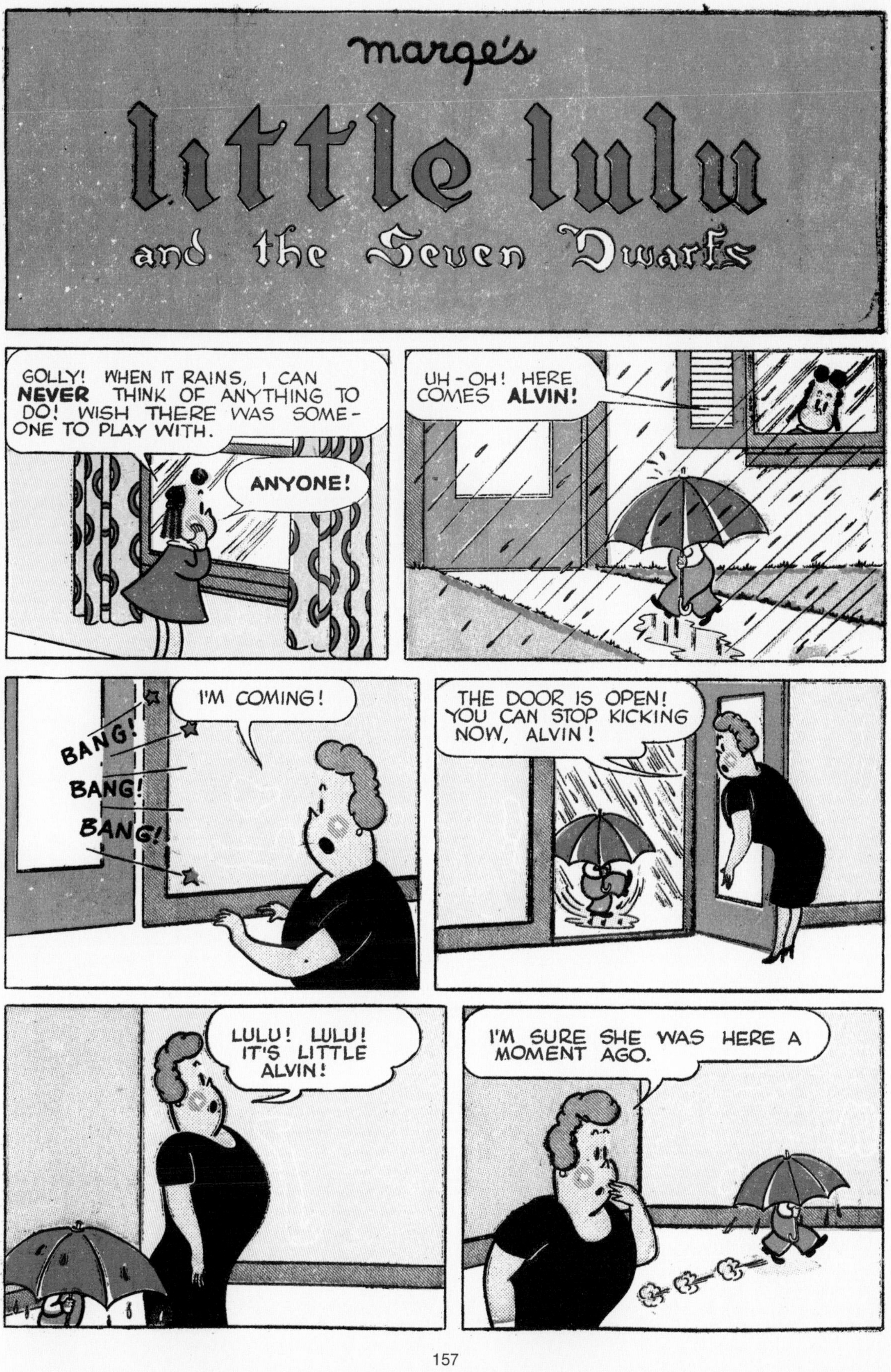
marge's
little lulu
and the Seven Dwarfs
GOLLY! WHEN IT RAINS, I CAN NEVER THINK OF ANYTHING TO DO! WISH THERE WAS SOMEONE TO PLAY WITH.
ANYONE!
UH-OH! HERE COMES ALVIN!
BANG! BANG! BANG!
I'M COMING!
THE DOOR IS OPEN! YOU CAN STOP KICKING NOW, ALVIN!
LULU! LULU! IT'S LITTLE ALVIN!
I'M SURE SHE WAS HERE A MOMENT AGO.

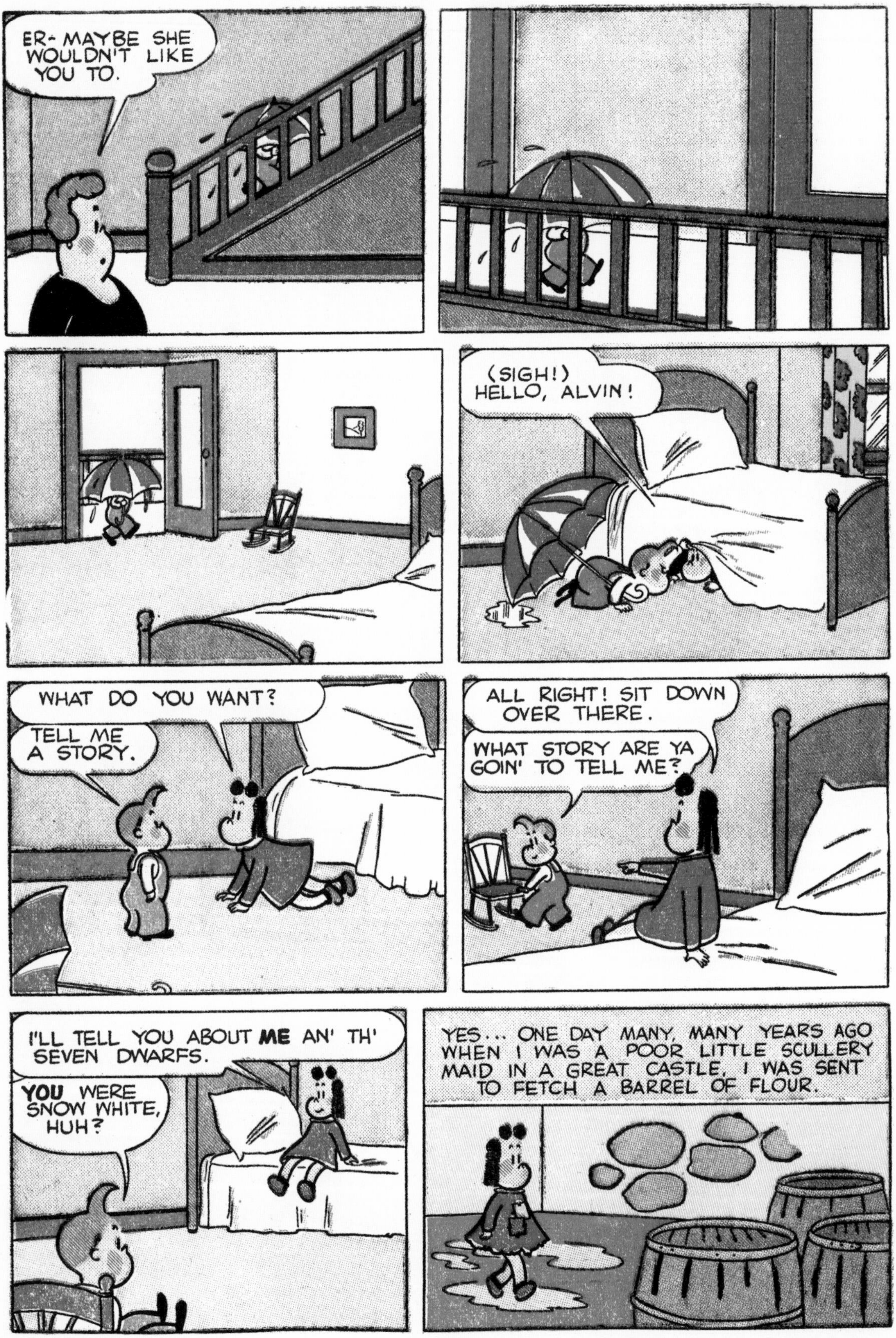
ER- MAYBE SHE WOULDN'T LIKE YOU TO.
(SIGH!) HELLO, ALVIN!
WHAT DO YOU WANT?
TELL ME A STORY.
ALL RIGHT! SIT DOWN OVER THERE.
WHAT STORY ARE YA GOIN' TO TELL ME?
I'LL TELL YOU ABOUT **ME** AN' TH' SEVEN DWARFS.
YOU WERE SNOW WHITE, HUH?
YES... ONE DAY MANY, MANY YEARS AGO WHEN I WAS A POOR LITTLE SCULLERY MAID IN A GREAT CASTLE, I WAS SENT TO FETCH A BARREL OF FLOUR.

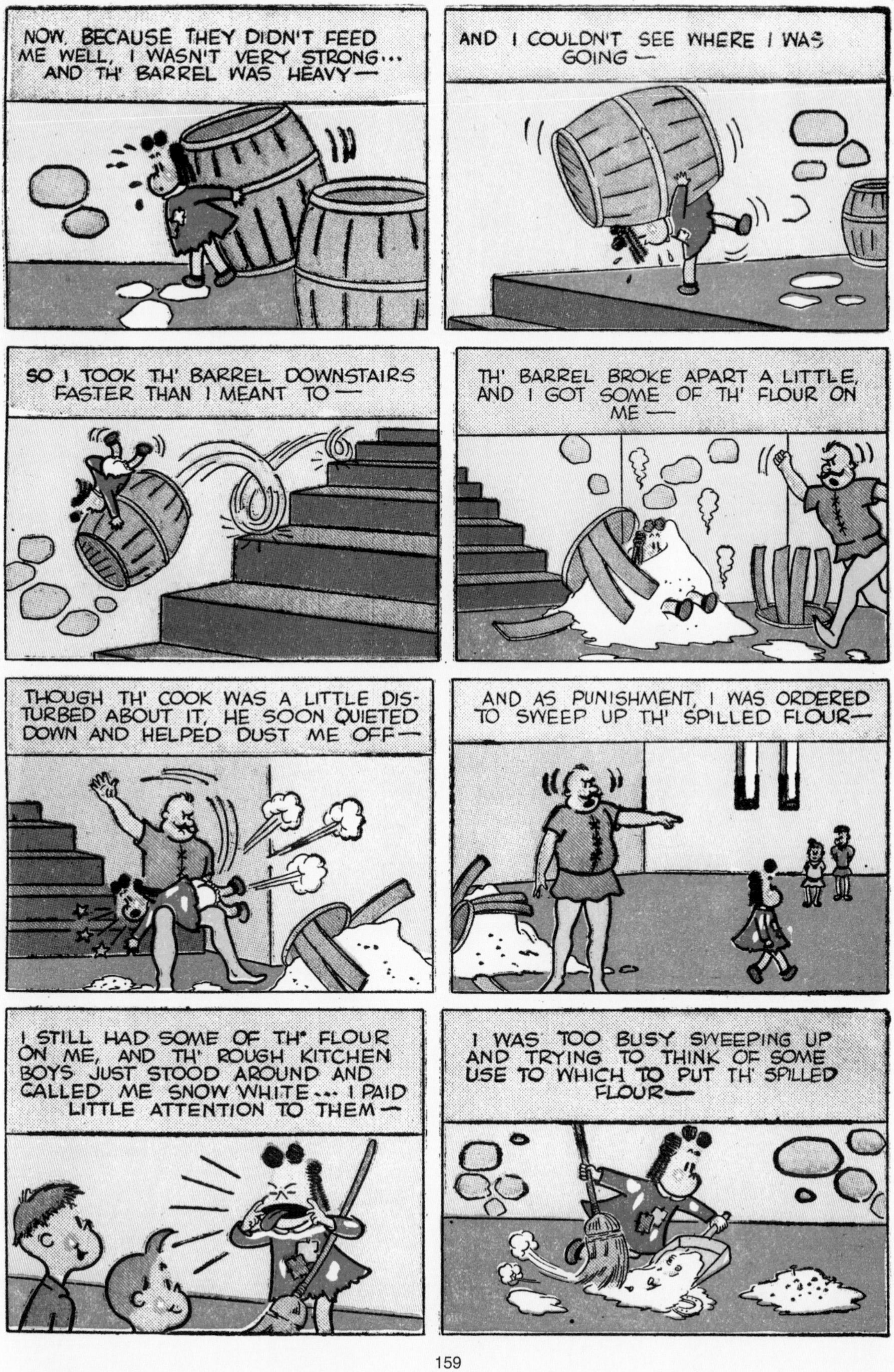
NOW, BECAUSE THEY DIDN'T FEED ME WELL, I WASN'T VERY STRONG... AND TH' BARREL WAS HEAVY—
AND I COULDN'T SEE WHERE I WAS GOING—
SO I TOOK TH' BARREL DOWNSTAIRS FASTER THAN I MEANT TO—
TH' BARREL BROKE APART A LITTLE, AND I GOT SOME OF TH' FLOUR ON ME—
THOUGH TH' COOK WAS A LITTLE DIS-TURBED ABOUT IT, HE SOON QUIETED DOWN AND HELPED DUST ME OFF—
AND AS PUNISHMENT, I WAS ORDERED TO SWEEP UP TH' SPILLED FLOUR—
I STILL HAD SOME OF TH' FLOUR ON ME, AND TH' ROUGH KITCHEN BOYS JUST STOOD AROUND AND CALLED ME SNOW WHITE... I PAID LITTLE ATTENTION TO THEM—
I WAS TOO BUSY SWEEPING UP AND TRYING TO THINK OF SOME USE TO WHICH TO PUT TH' SPILLED FLOUR—

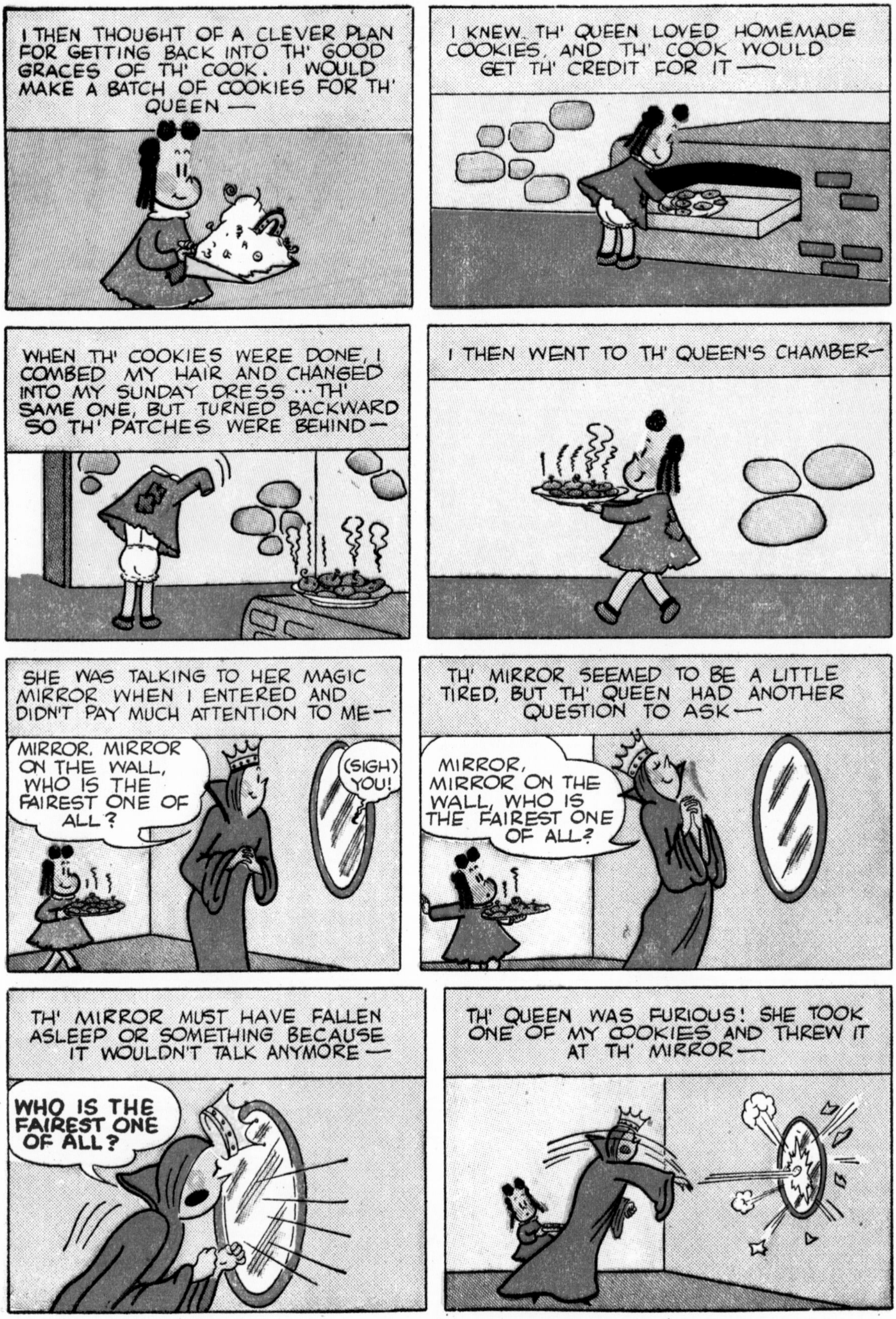
I THEN THOUGHT OF A CLEVER PLAN FOR GETTING BACK INTO TH' GOOD GRACES OF TH' COOK. I WOULD MAKE A BATCH OF COOKIES FOR TH' QUEEN—
I KNEW TH' QUEEN LOVED HOMEMADE COOKIES, AND TH' COOK WOULD GET TH' CREDIT FOR IT—
WHEN TH' COOKIES WERE DONE, I COMBED MY HAIR AND CHANGED INTO MY SUNDAY DRESS ... TH' SAME ONE, BUT TURNED BACKWARD SO TH' PATCHES WERE BEHIND—
I THEN WENT TO TH' QUEEN'S CHAMBER—
SHE WAS TALKING TO HER MAGIC MIRROR WHEN I ENTERED AND DIDN'T PAY MUCH ATTENTION TO ME—
MIRROR, MIRROR ON THE WALL, WHO IS THE FAIREST ONE OF ALL?
(SIGH) YOU!
TH' MIRROR SEEMED TO BE A LITTLE TIRED, BUT TH' QUEEN HAD ANOTHER QUESTION TO ASK—
MIRROR, MIRROR ON THE WALL, WHO IS THE FAIREST ONE OF ALL?
TH' MIRROR MUST HAVE FALLEN ASLEEP OR SOMETHING BECAUSE IT WOULDN'T TALK ANYMORE—
WHO IS THE FAIREST ONE OF ALL?
TH' QUEEN WAS FURIOUS! SHE TOOK ONE OF MY COOKIES AND THREW IT AT TH' MIRROR—

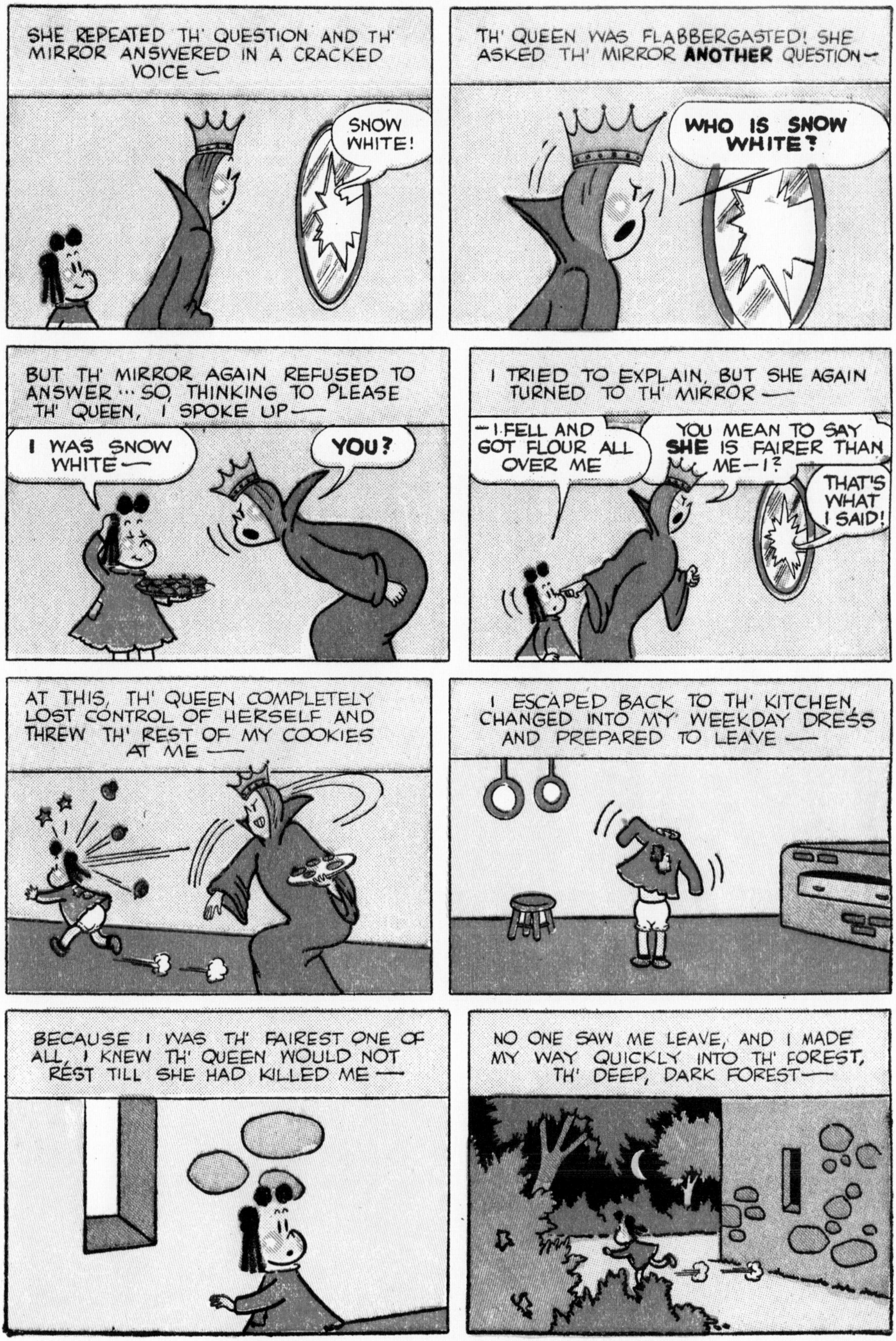
SHE REPEATED TH' QUESTION AND TH' MIRROR ANSWERED IN A CRACKED VOICE —
SNOW WHITE!
TH' QUEEN WAS FLABBERGASTED! SHE ASKED TH' MIRROR **ANOTHER** QUESTION —
WHO IS SNOW WHITE?
BUT TH' MIRROR AGAIN REFUSED TO ANSWER ... SO, THINKING TO PLEASE TH' QUEEN, I SPOKE UP —
I WAS SNOW WHITE —
YOU?
I TRIED TO EXPLAIN, BUT SHE AGAIN TURNED TO TH' MIRROR —
— I FELL AND GOT FLOUR ALL OVER ME
YOU MEAN TO SAY **SHE** IS FAIRER THAN ME — I?
THAT'S WHAT I SAID!
AT THIS, TH' QUEEN COMPLETELY LOST CONTROL OF HERSELF AND THREW TH' REST OF MY COOKIES AT ME —
I ESCAPED BACK TO TH' KITCHEN, CHANGED INTO MY WEEKDAY DRESS AND PREPARED TO LEAVE —
BECAUSE I WAS TH' FAIREST ONE OF ALL, I KNEW TH' QUEEN WOULD NOT REST TILL SHE HAD KILLED ME —
NO ONE SAW ME LEAVE, AND I MADE MY WAY QUICKLY INTO TH' FOREST, TH' DEEP, DARK FOREST —

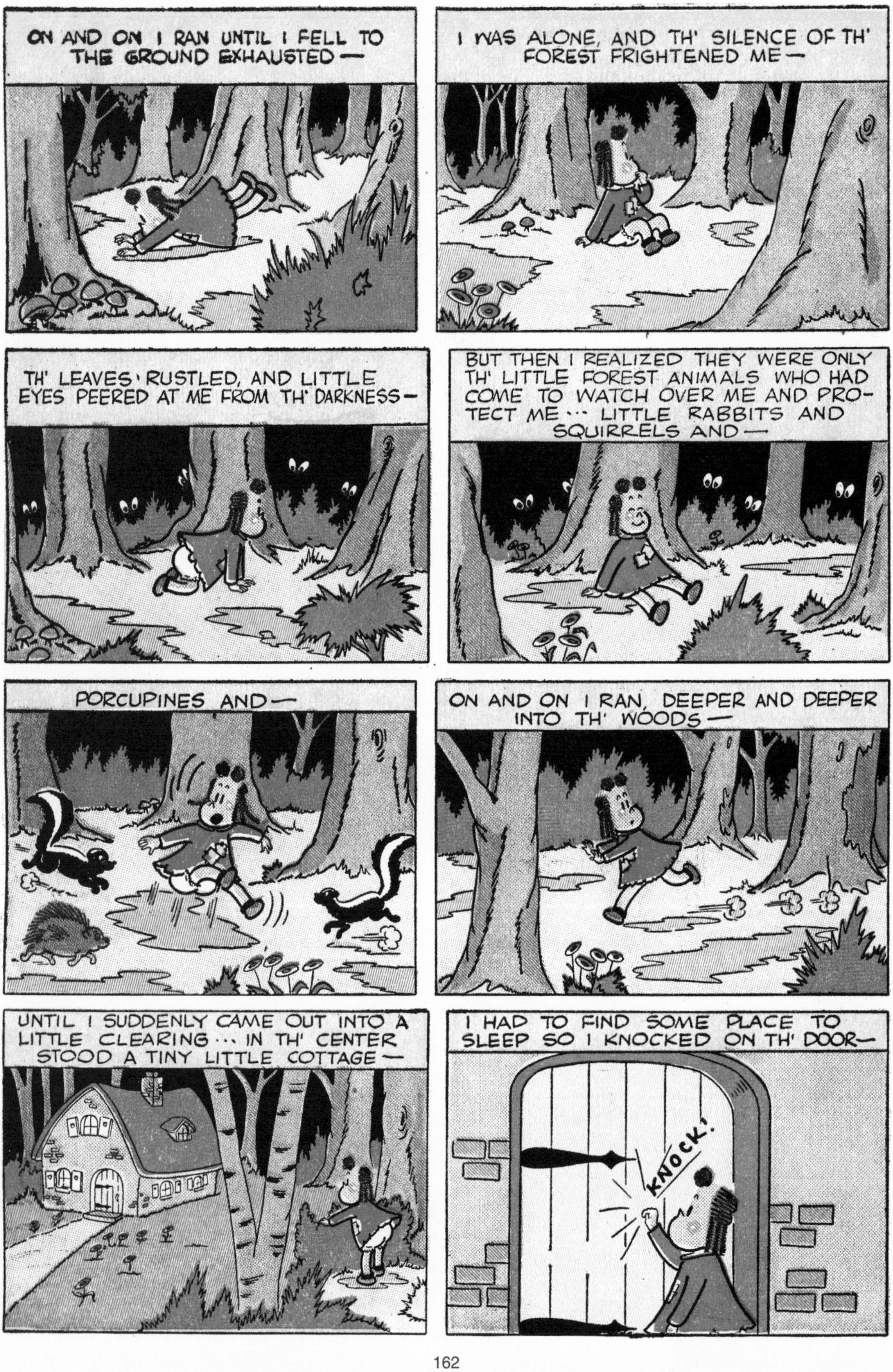
ON AND ON I RAN UNTIL I FELL TO THE GROUND EXHAUSTED—
I WAS ALONE, AND TH' SILENCE OF TH' FOREST FRIGHTENED ME—
TH' LEAVES RUSTLED, AND LITTLE EYES PEERED AT ME FROM TH' DARKNESS—
BUT THEN I REALIZED THEY WERE ONLY TH' LITTLE FOREST ANIMALS WHO HAD COME TO WATCH OVER ME AND PROTECT ME... LITTLE RABBITS AND SQUIRRELS AND—
PORCUPINES AND—
ON AND ON I RAN, DEEPER AND DEEPER INTO TH' WOODS—
UNTIL I SUDDENLY CAME OUT INTO A LITTLE CLEARING... IN TH' CENTER STOOD A TINY LITTLE COTTAGE—
I HAD TO FIND SOME PLACE TO SLEEP SO I KNOCKED ON TH' DOOR—
KNOCK!

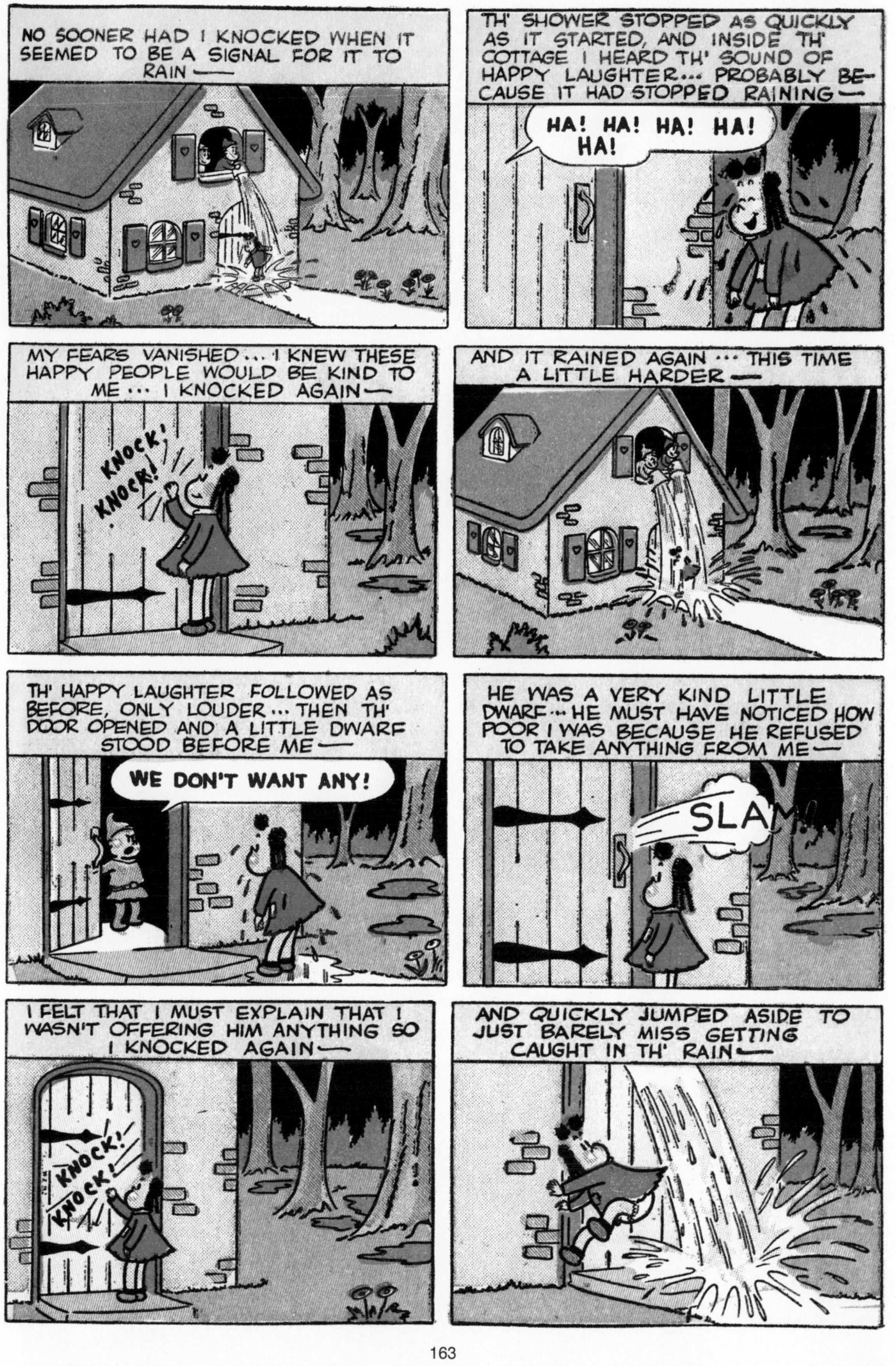
NO SOONER HAD I KNOCKED WHEN IT SEEMED TO BE A SIGNAL FOR IT TO RAIN —
TH' SHOWER STOPPED AS QUICKLY AS IT STARTED, AND INSIDE TH' COTTAGE I HEARD TH' SOUND OF HAPPY LAUGHTER... PROBABLY BE-CAUSE IT HAD STOPPED RAINING —
HA! HA! HA! HA! HA!
MY FEARS VANISHED... I KNEW THESE HAPPY PEOPLE WOULD BE KIND TO ME... I KNOCKED AGAIN —
KNOCK! KNOCK!
AND IT RAINED AGAIN... THIS TIME A LITTLE HARDER —
TH' HAPPY LAUGHTER FOLLOWED AS BEFORE, ONLY LOUDER... THEN TH' DOOR OPENED AND A LITTLE DWARF STOOD BEFORE ME —
WE DON'T WANT ANY!
HE WAS A VERY KIND LITTLE DWARF... HE MUST HAVE NOTICED HOW POOR I WAS BECAUSE HE REFUSED TO TAKE ANYTHING FROM ME —
SLAM!
I FELT THAT I MUST EXPLAIN THAT I WASN'T OFFERING HIM ANYTHING SO I KNOCKED AGAIN —
KNOCK! KNOCK!
AND QUICKLY JUMPED ASIDE TO JUST BARELY MISS GETTING CAUGHT IN TH' RAIN —

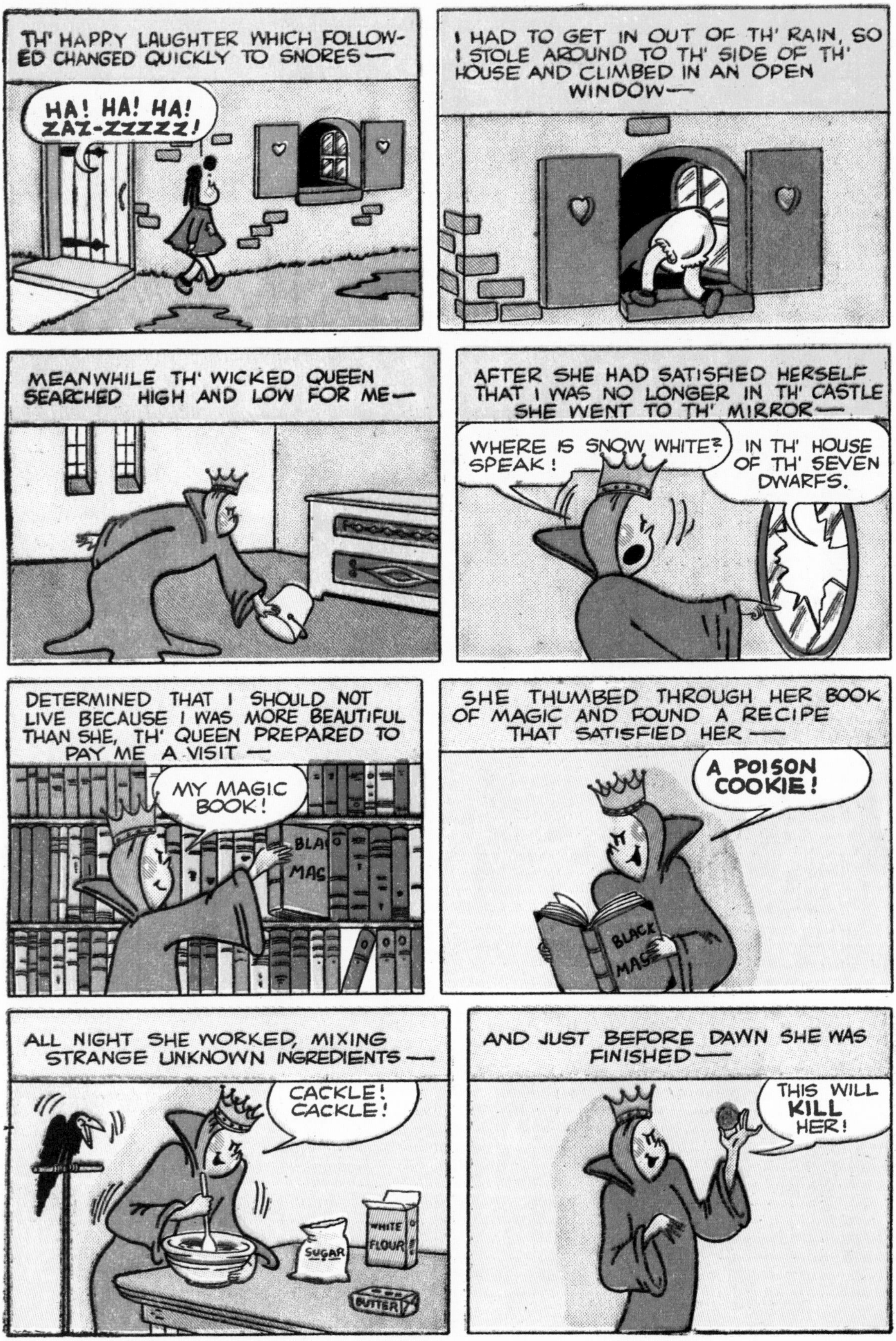
TH' HAPPY LAUGHTER WHICH FOLLOWED CHANGED QUICKLY TO SNORES—
HA! HA! HA! ZAZ-ZZZZZ!
I HAD TO GET IN OUT OF TH' RAIN, SO I STOLE AROUND TO TH' SIDE OF TH' HOUSE AND CLIMBED IN AN OPEN WINDOW—
MEANWHILE TH' WICKED QUEEN SEARCHED HIGH AND LOW FOR ME—
AFTER SHE HAD SATISFIED HERSELF THAT I WAS NO LONGER IN TH' CASTLE SHE WENT TO TH' MIRROR—
WHERE IS SNOW WHITE? SPEAK!
IN TH' HOUSE OF TH' SEVEN DWARFS.
DETERMINED THAT I SHOULD NOT LIVE BECAUSE I WAS MORE BEAUTIFUL THAN SHE, TH' QUEEN PREPARED TO PAY ME A VISIT—
MY MAGIC BOOK!
SHE THUMBED THROUGH HER BOOK OF MAGIC AND FOUND A RECIPE THAT SATISFIED HER—
A POISON COOKIE!
BLACK MAG
ALL NIGHT SHE WORKED, MIXING STRANGE UNKNOWN INGREDIENTS—
CACKLE! CACKLE!
SUGAR
WHITE FLOUR
BUTTER
AND JUST BEFORE DAWN SHE WAS FINISHED—
THIS WILL KILL HER!

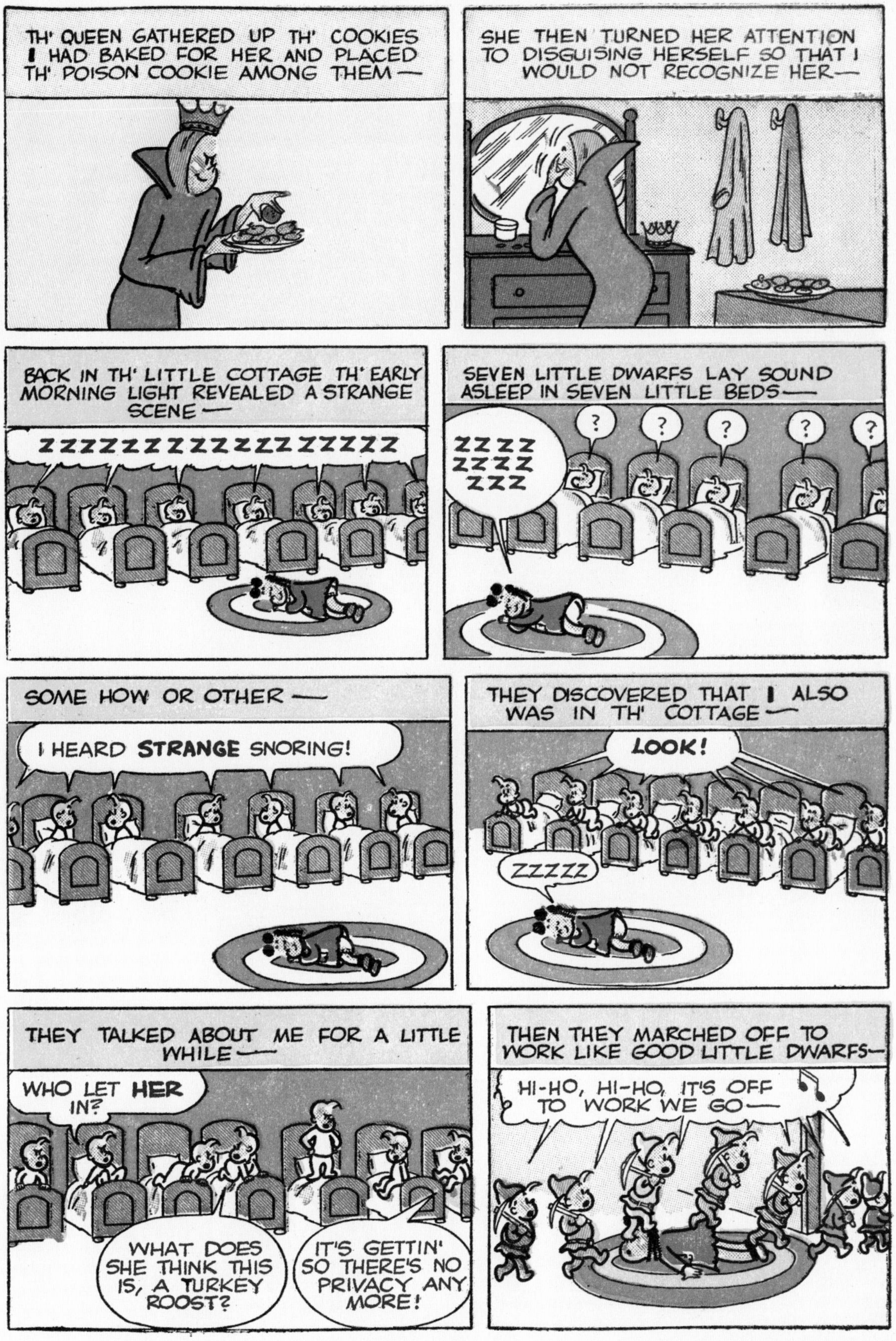
TH' QUEEN GATHERED UP TH' COOKIES I HAD BAKED FOR HER AND PLACED TH' POISON COOKIE AMONG THEM—
SHE THEN TURNED HER ATTENTION TO DISGUISING HERSELF SO THAT I WOULD NOT RECOGNIZE HER—
BACK IN TH' LITTLE COTTAGE TH' EARLY MORNING LIGHT REVEALED A STRANGE SCENE—
ZZZZZZZZZZZZZZZZZZZ
SEVEN LITTLE DWARFS LAY SOUND ASLEEP IN SEVEN LITTLE BEDS—
ZZZZ ZZZZ ZZZ
?
?
?
?
?
SOME HOW OR OTHER—
I HEARD **STRANGE** SNORING!
THEY DISCOVERED THAT I ALSO WAS IN TH' COTTAGE—
LOOK!
ZZZZZ
THEY TALKED ABOUT ME FOR A LITTLE WHILE—
WHO LET **HER** IN?
WHAT DOES SHE THINK THIS IS, A TURKEY ROOST?
IT'S GETTIN' SO THERE'S NO PRIVACY ANY MORE!
THEN THEY MARCHED OFF TO WORK LIKE GOOD LITTLE DWARFS—
HI-HO, HI-HO, IT'S OFF TO WORK WE GO—

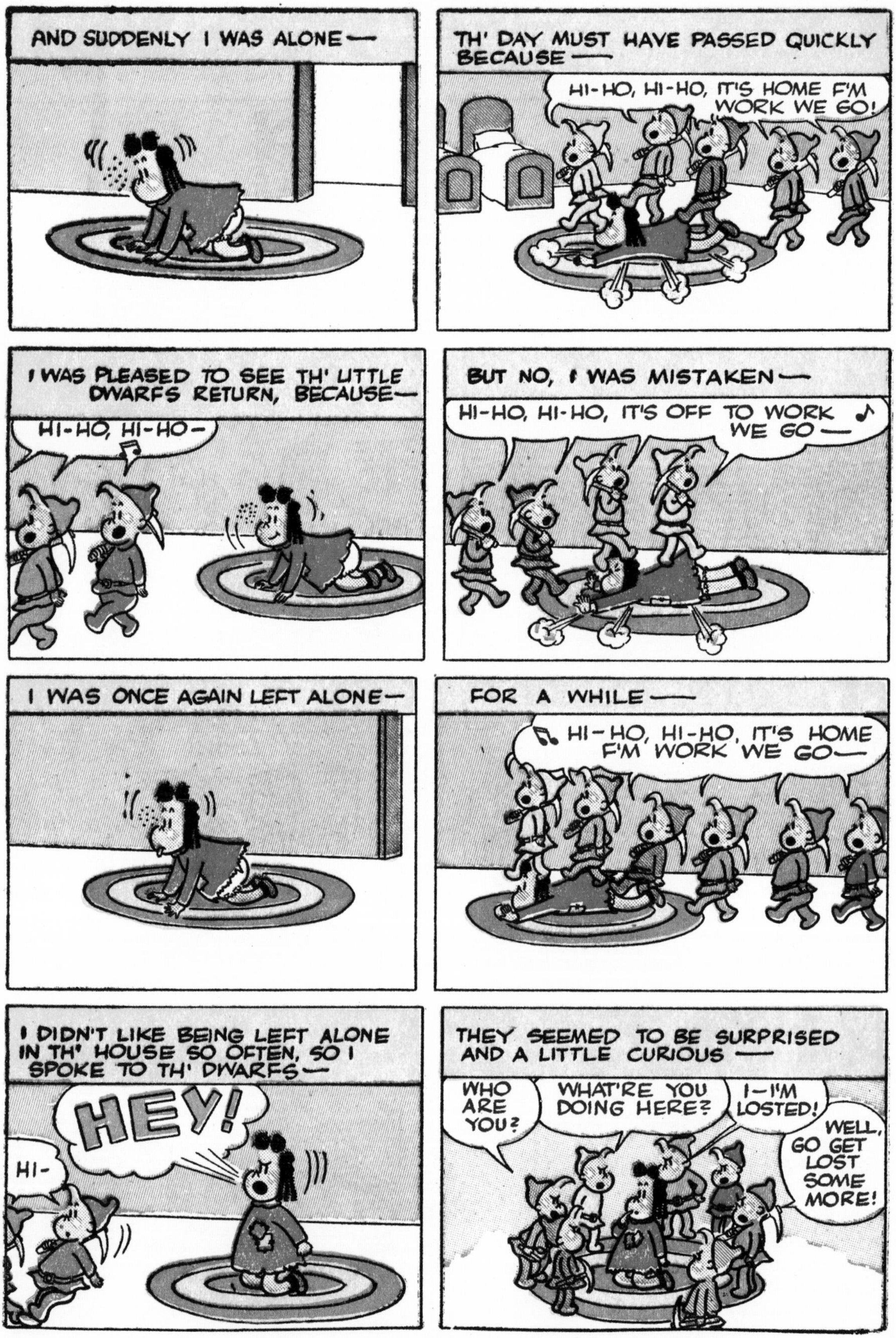
AND SUDDENLY I WAS ALONE—
TH' DAY MUST HAVE PASSED QUICKLY BECAUSE—
HI-HO, HI-HO, IT'S HOME F'M WORK WE GO!
I WAS PLEASED TO SEE TH' LITTLE DWARFS RETURN, BECAUSE—
HI-HO, HI-HO—
BUT NO, I WAS MISTAKEN—
HI-HO, HI-HO, IT'S OFF TO WORK WE GO—
I WAS ONCE AGAIN LEFT ALONE—
FOR A WHILE—
HI-HO, HI-HO, IT'S HOME F'M WORK WE GO—
I DIDN'T LIKE BEING LEFT ALONE IN TH' HOUSE SO OFTEN, SO I SPOKE TO TH' DWARFS—
HEY!
HI-
THEY SEEMED TO BE SURPRISED AND A LITTLE CURIOUS—
WHO ARE YOU?
WHAT'RE YOU DOING HERE?
I-I'M LOSTED!
WELL, GO GET LOST SOME MORE!

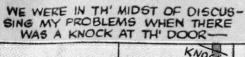

WE WERE IN TH' MIDST OF DISCUSSING MY PROBLEMS WHEN THERE WAS A KNOCK AT TH' DOOR—

I WAS ON MY WAY TO TH' DOOR ANYWAY, SO I ANSWERED IT—

A GENTLE OLD LADY STOOD OUTSIDE HOLDING A PLATE OF HOME-MADE CAKES—

HAVE ONE, LITTLE GIRL!

AT FIRST I HESITATED, BECAUSE THEY DIDN'T LOOK SO GOOD, BUT TH' OLD LADY PICKED OUT A NICE ONE FOR ME—

TRY THIS!

OOOH, THANKS!

THEN TH' DWARFS SWARMED OVER HER BEGGING FOR COOKIES—

YUM! GIMME! GET AWAY! GIMME! GIMME!

SHE DROPPED TH' PLATTER, AND TH' DWARFS POUNCED ON IT—

BUT TH' WAY IT WORKED OUT, EVERYONE GOT A COOKIE—EVEN TH' OLD LADY—

YUM! YUM! YUM! YUM!

AND WE SAT AROUND MUNCHING HAPPILY TILL THEY WERE ALL GONE—

YUM! YUM! YUM! YUM! YUM! YUM!

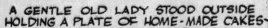

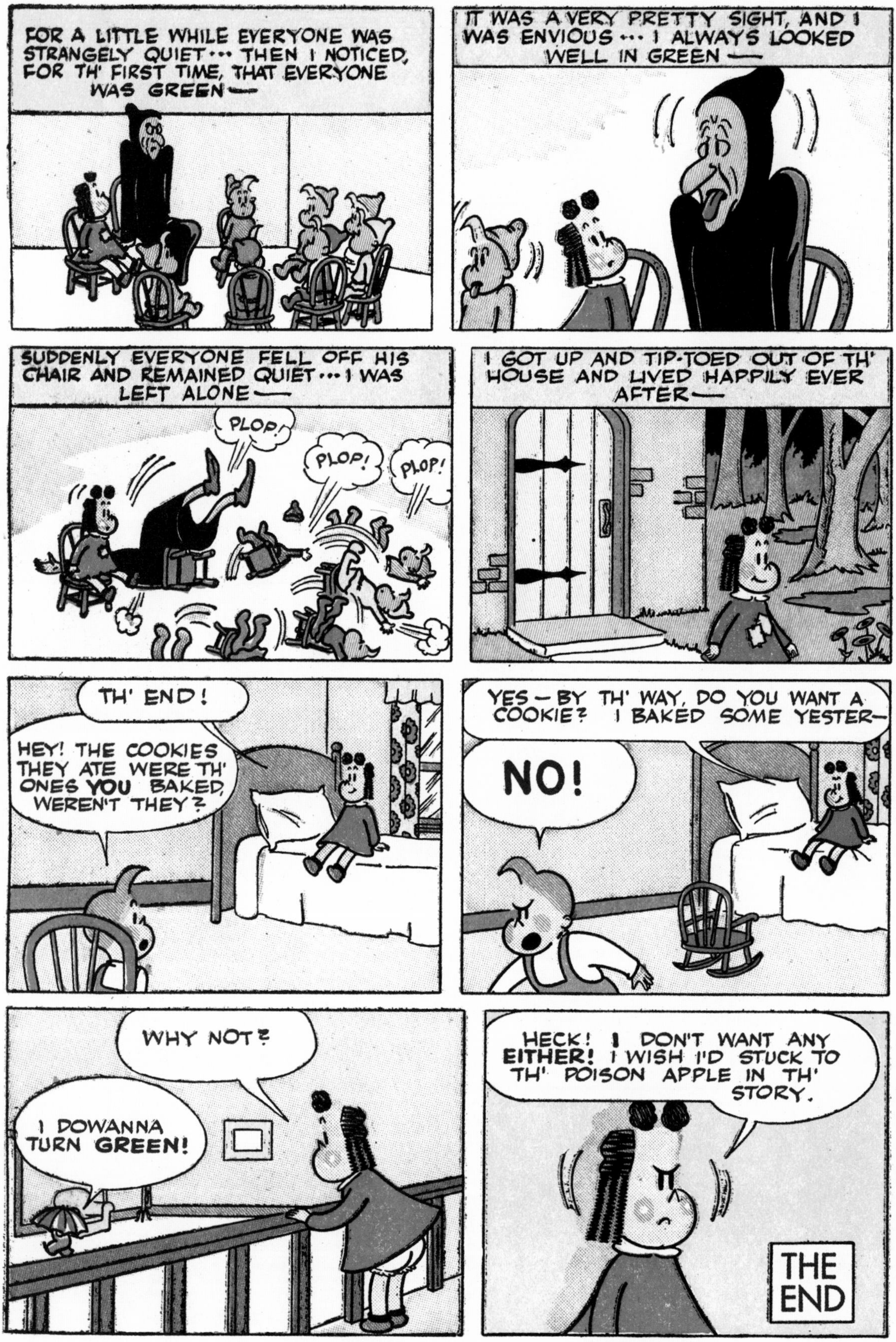

FOR A LITTLE WHILE EVERYONE WAS STRANGELY QUIET ··· THEN I NOTICED, FOR TH' FIRST TIME, THAT EVERYONE WAS GREEN —
IT WAS A VERY PRETTY SIGHT, AND I WAS ENVIOUS ··· I ALWAYS LOOKED WELL IN GREEN —
SUDDENLY EVERYONE FELL OFF HIS CHAIR AND REMAINED QUIET ··· I WAS LEFT ALONE —
PLOP!
PLOP!
PLOP!
I GOT UP AND TIP-TOED OUT OF TH' HOUSE AND LIVED HAPPILY EVER AFTER —
TH' END!
HEY! THE COOKIES THEY ATE WERE TH' ONES **YOU** BAKED, WEREN'T THEY?
YES — BY TH' WAY, DO YOU WANT A COOKIE? I BAKED SOME YESTER—
NO!
WHY NOT?
I DOWANNA TURN **GREEN**!
HECK! **I** DON'T WANT ANY **EITHER**! I WISH I'D STUCK TO TH' POISON APPLE IN TH' STORY.
THE END

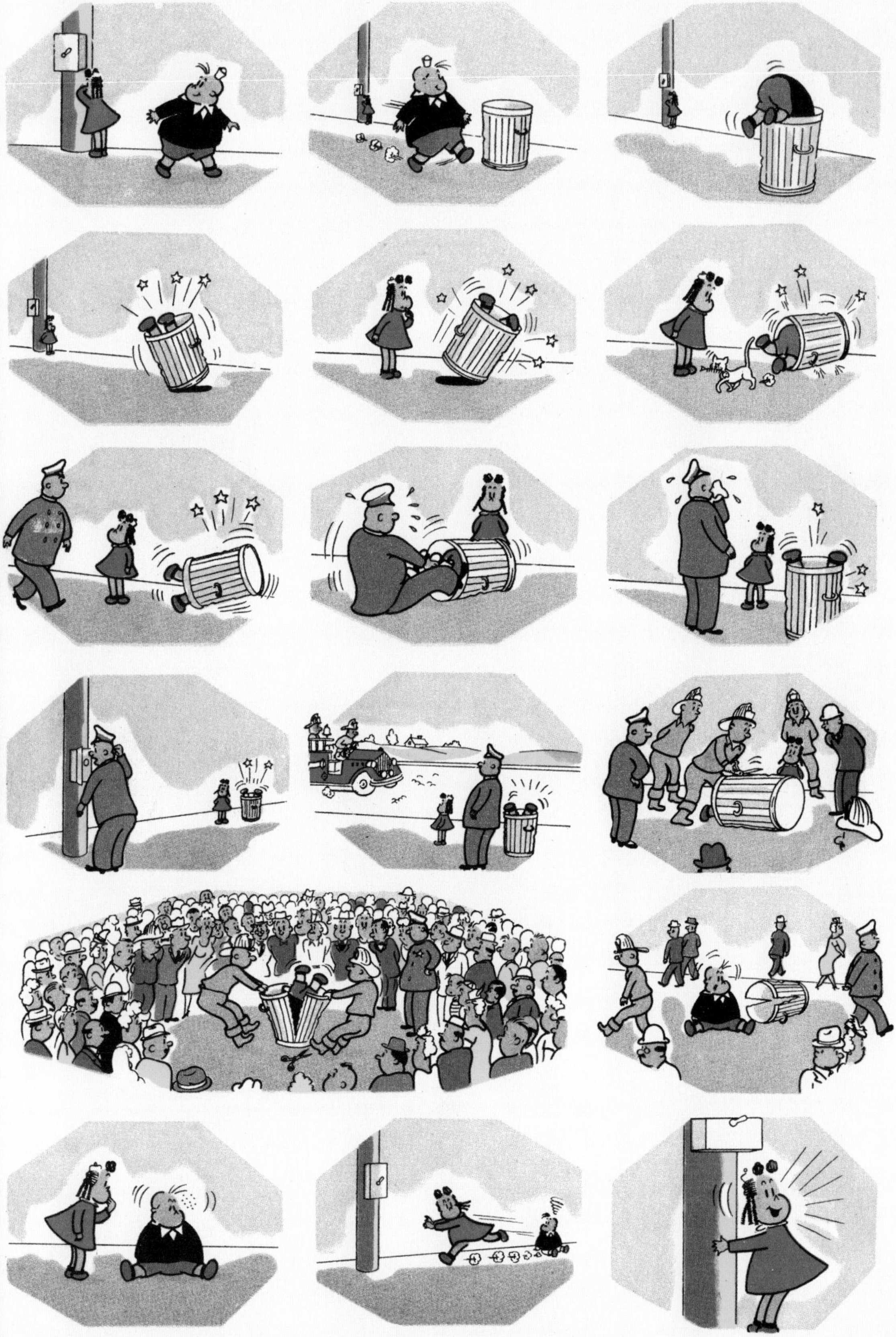

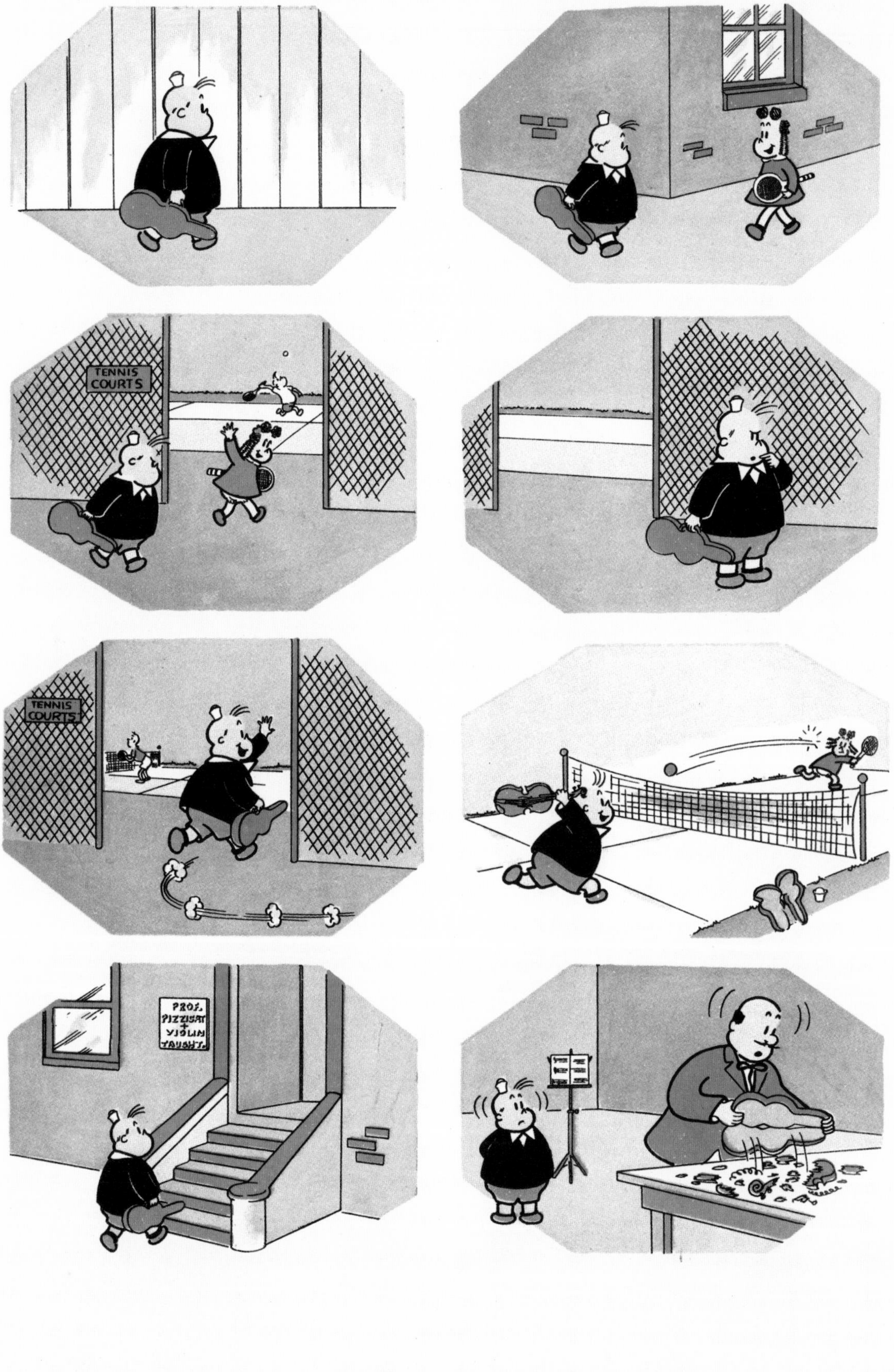
TENNIS COURTS
TENNIS COURTS
PROF. PIZZICAT + VIOLIN TAUGHT.

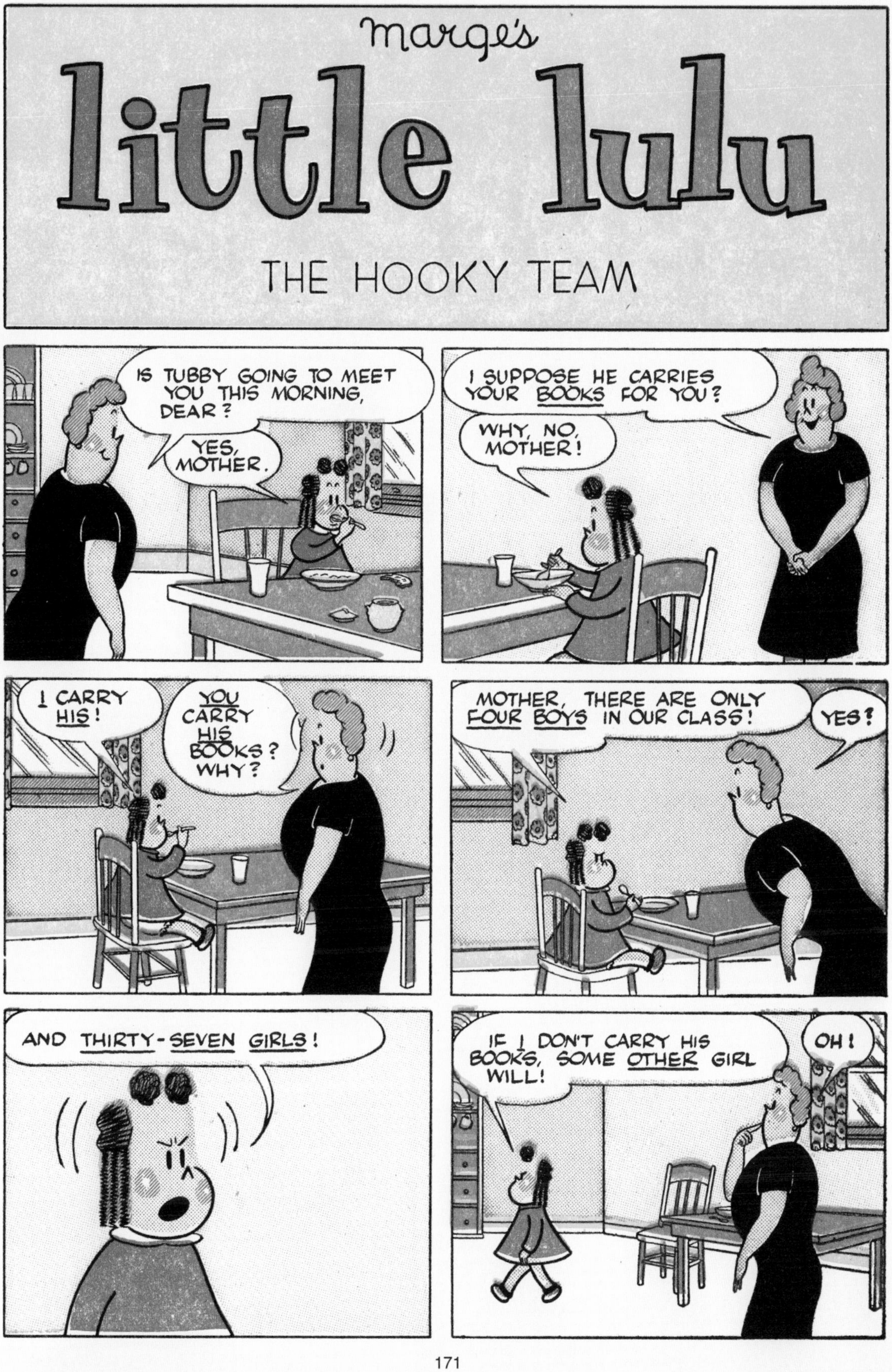
marge's
little lulu
THE HOOKY TEAM
IS TUBBY GOING TO MEET YOU THIS MORNING, DEAR?
YES, MOTHER.
I SUPPOSE HE CARRIES YOUR BOOKS FOR YOU?
WHY, NO, MOTHER!
I CARRY HIS!
YOU CARRY HIS BOOKS? WHY?
MOTHER, THERE ARE ONLY FOUR BOYS IN OUR CLASS!
YES?
AND THIRTY-SEVEN GIRLS!
IF I DON'T CARRY HIS BOOKS, SOME OTHER GIRL WILL!
OH!

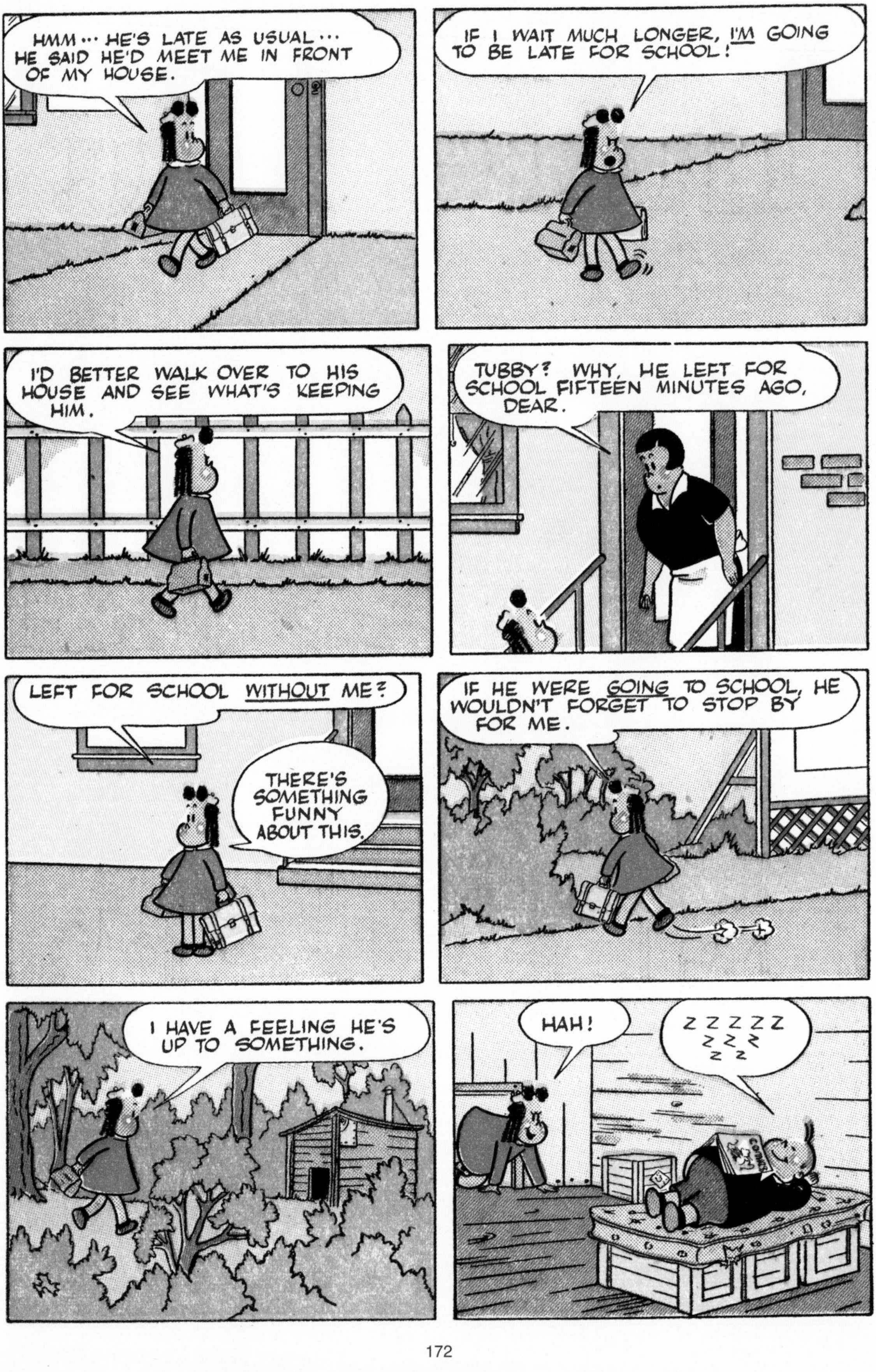
HMM··· HE'S LATE AS USUAL··· HE SAID HE'D MEET ME IN FRONT OF MY HOUSE.
IF I WAIT MUCH LONGER, I'M GOING TO BE LATE FOR SCHOOL!
I'D BETTER WALK OVER TO HIS HOUSE AND SEE WHAT'S KEEPING HIM.
TUBBY? WHY, HE LEFT FOR SCHOOL FIFTEEN MINUTES AGO, DEAR.
LEFT FOR SCHOOL WITHOUT ME?
THERE'S SOMETHING FUNNY ABOUT THIS.
IF HE WERE GOING TO SCHOOL, HE WOULDN'T FORGET TO STOP BY FOR ME.
I HAVE A FEELING HE'S UP TO SOMETHING.
HAH!
Z Z Z Z Z Z Z Z Z Z

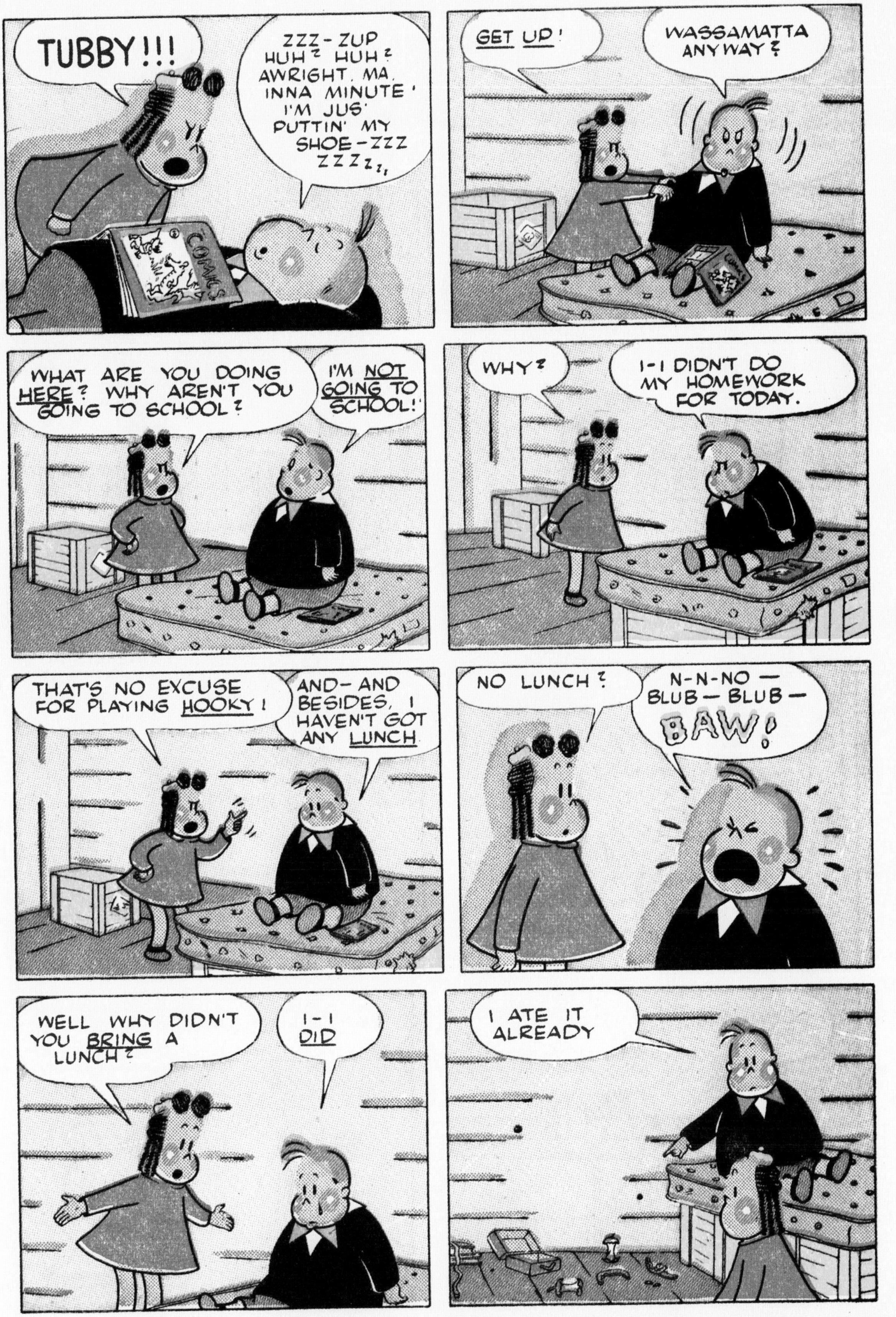
TUBBY!!!
ZZZ-ZUP HUH? HUH? AWRIGHT, MA, INNA MINUTE' I'M JUS' PUTTIN' MY SHOE-ZZZ ZZZzz
COMICS
GET UP!
WASSAMATTA ANYWAY?
WHAT ARE YOU DOING HERE? WHY AREN'T YOU GOING TO SCHOOL?
I'M NOT GOING TO SCHOOL!
WHY?
I-I DIDN'T DO MY HOMEWORK FOR TODAY.
THAT'S NO EXCUSE FOR PLAYING HOOKY!
AND-AND BESIDES, I HAVEN'T GOT ANY LUNCH.
NO LUNCH?
N-N-NO — BLUB — BLUB — BAW!
WELL WHY DIDN'T YOU BRING A LUNCH?
I-I DID
I ATE IT ALREADY

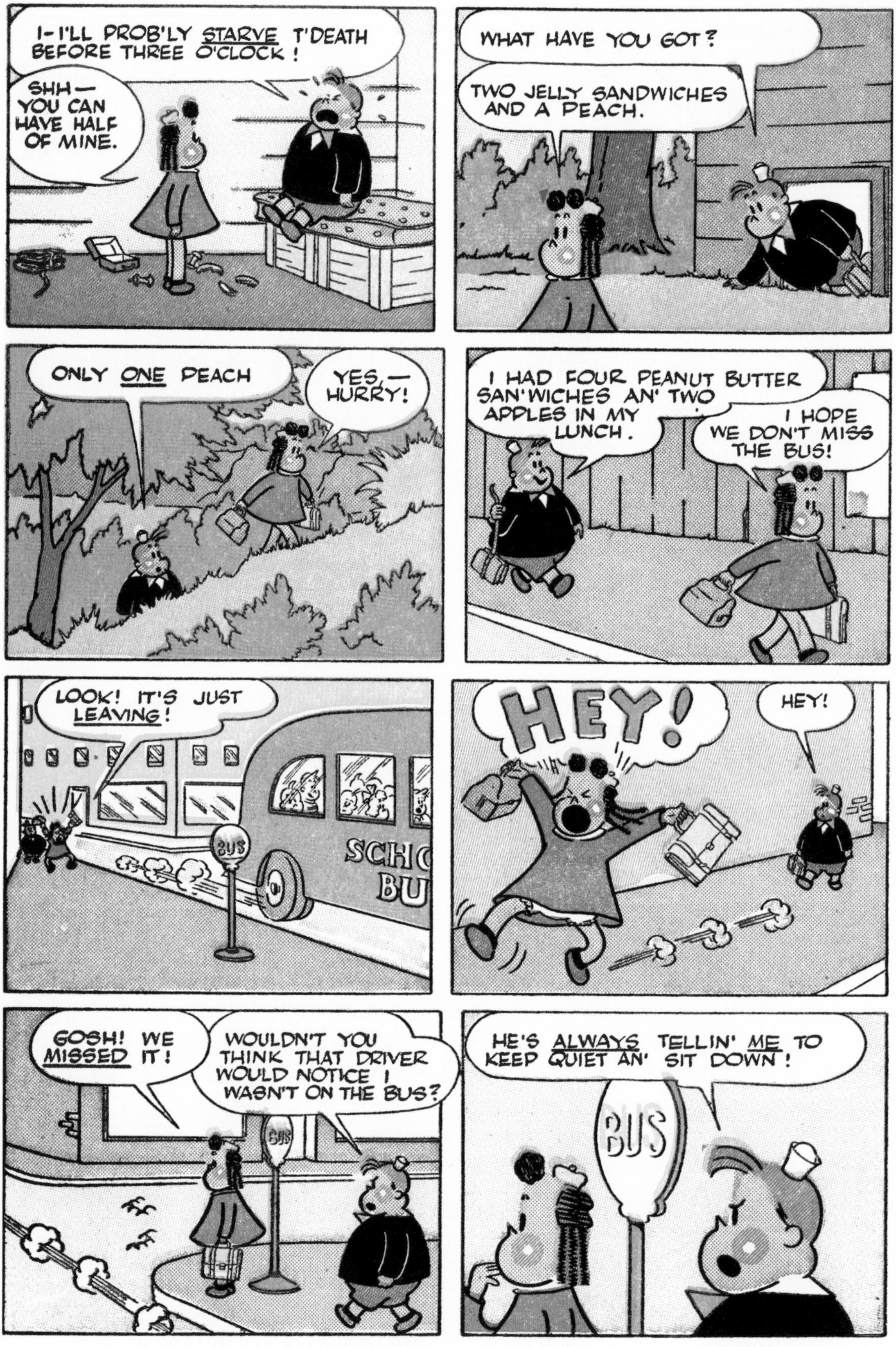

I-I'LL PROB'LY STARVE T'DEATH BEFORE THREE O'CLOCK!
SHH— YOU CAN HAVE HALF OF MINE.
WHAT HAVE YOU GOT?
TWO JELLY SANDWICHES AND A PEACH.
ONLY ONE PEACH
YES,— HURRY!
I HAD FOUR PEANUT BUTTER SAN'WICHES AN' TWO APPLES IN MY LUNCH.
I HOPE WE DON'T MISS THE BUS!
LOOK! IT'S JUST LEAVING!
SCHO BU
BUS
HEY!
HEY!
GOSH! WE MISSED IT!
WOULDN'T YOU THINK THAT DRIVER WOULD NOTICE I WASN'T ON THE BUS?
BUS
HE'S ALWAYS TELLIN' ME TO KEEP QUIET AN' SIT DOWN!
BUS

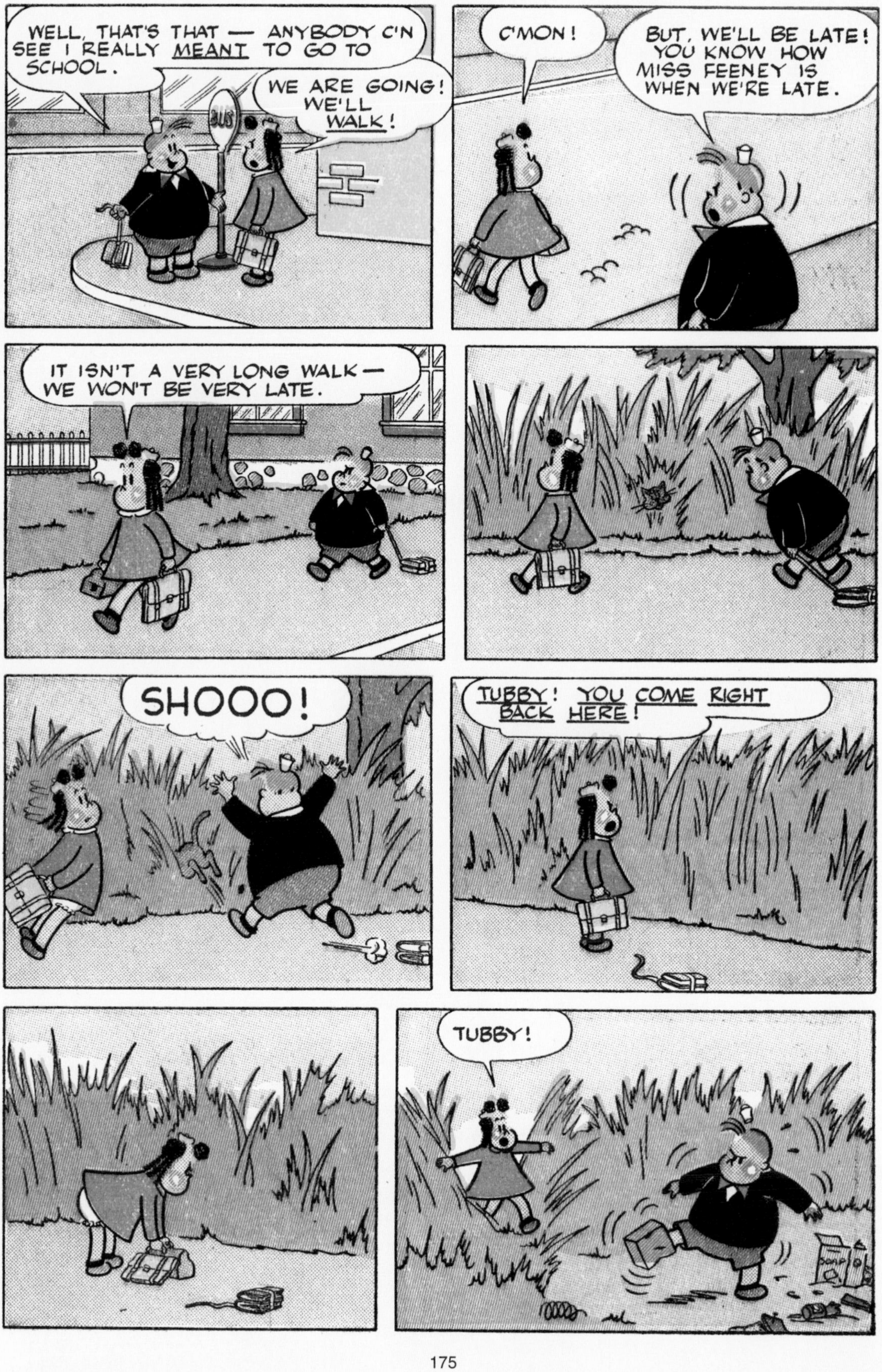
WELL, THAT'S THAT — ANYBODY C'N SEE I REALLY MEANT TO GO TO SCHOOL.
WE ARE GOING! WE'LL WALK!
C'MON!
BUT, WE'LL BE LATE! YOU KNOW HOW MISS FEENEY IS WHEN WE'RE LATE.
IT ISN'T A VERY LONG WALK — WE WON'T BE VERY LATE.
SHOOO!
TUBBY! YOU COME RIGHT BACK HERE!
TUBBY!

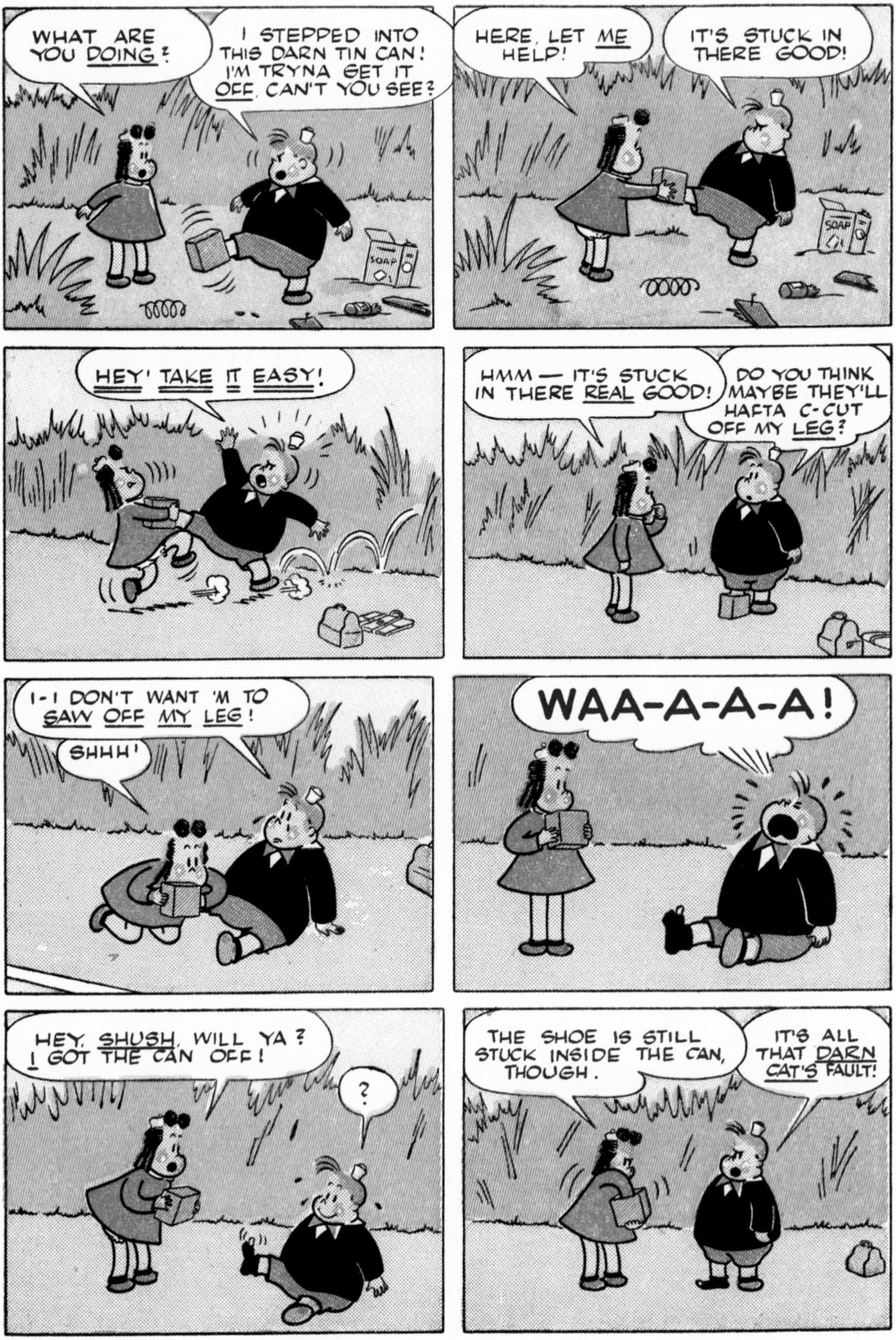

WHAT ARE YOU DOING?
I STEPPED INTO THIS DARN TIN CAN! I'M TRYNA GET IT OFF, CAN'T YOU SEE?
HERE, LET ME HELP!
IT'S STUCK IN THERE GOOD!
HEY! TAKE IT EASY!
HMM — IT'S STUCK IN THERE REAL GOOD!
DO YOU THINK MAYBE THEY'LL HAFTA C-CUT OFF MY LEG?
I-I DON'T WANT 'M TO SAW OFF MY LEG!
SHHH!
WAA-A-A-A!
HEY, SHUSH, WILL YA? I GOT THE CAN OFF!
?
THE SHOE IS STILL STUCK INSIDE THE CAN, THOUGH.
IT'S ALL THAT DARN CAT'S FAULT!

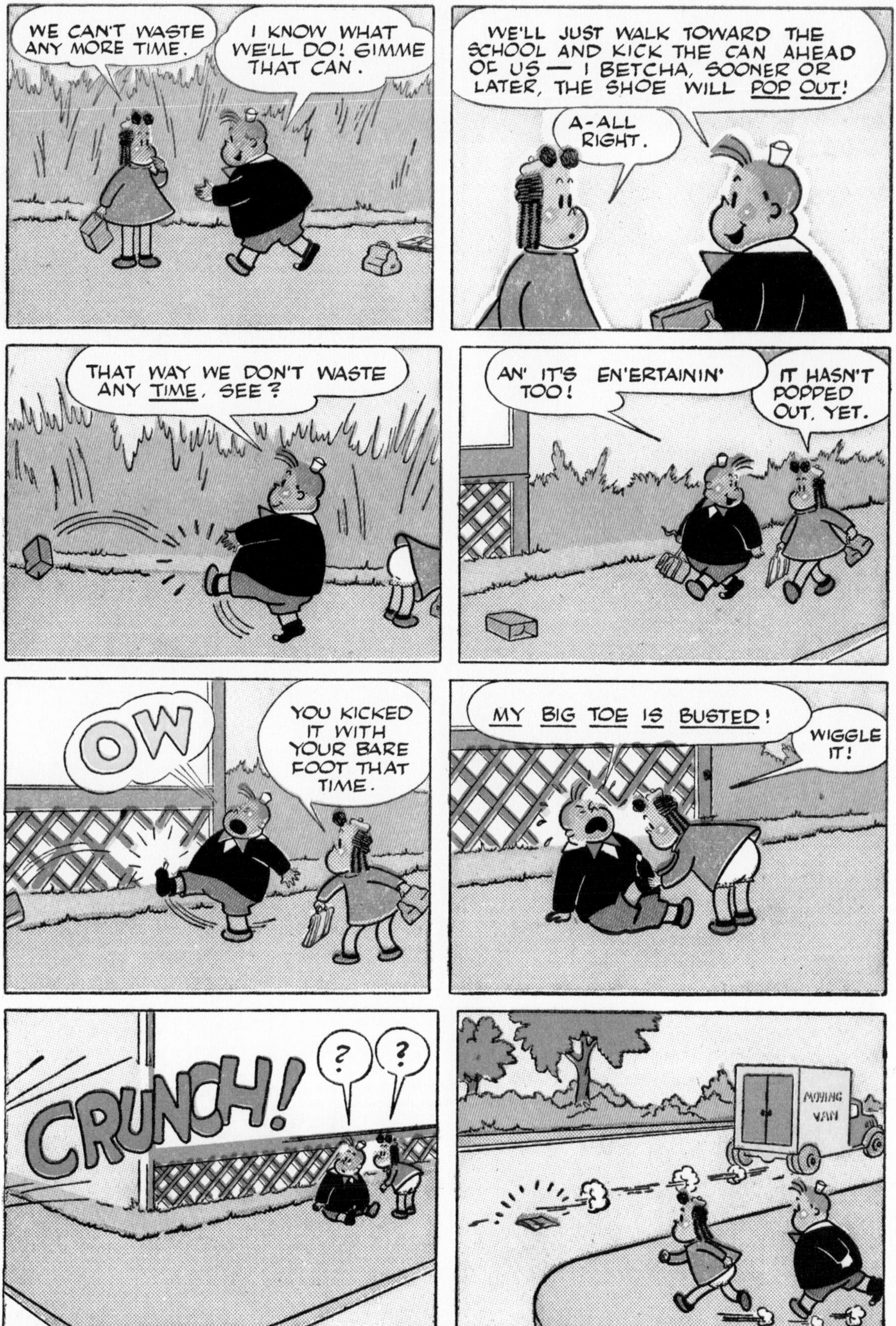
WE CAN'T WASTE ANY MORE TIME.
I KNOW WHAT WE'LL DO! GIMME THAT CAN.
WE'LL JUST WALK TOWARD THE SCHOOL AND KICK THE CAN AHEAD OF US — I BETCHA, SOONER OR LATER, THE SHOE WILL POP OUT!
A-ALL RIGHT.
THAT WAY WE DON'T WASTE ANY TIME, SEE?
AN' IT'S EN'ERTAININ' TOO!
IT HASN'T POPPED OUT, YET.
OW
YOU KICKED IT WITH YOUR BARE FOOT THAT TIME.
MY BIG TOE IS BUSTED!
WIGGLE IT!
CRUNCH!
?
?
MOVING VAN

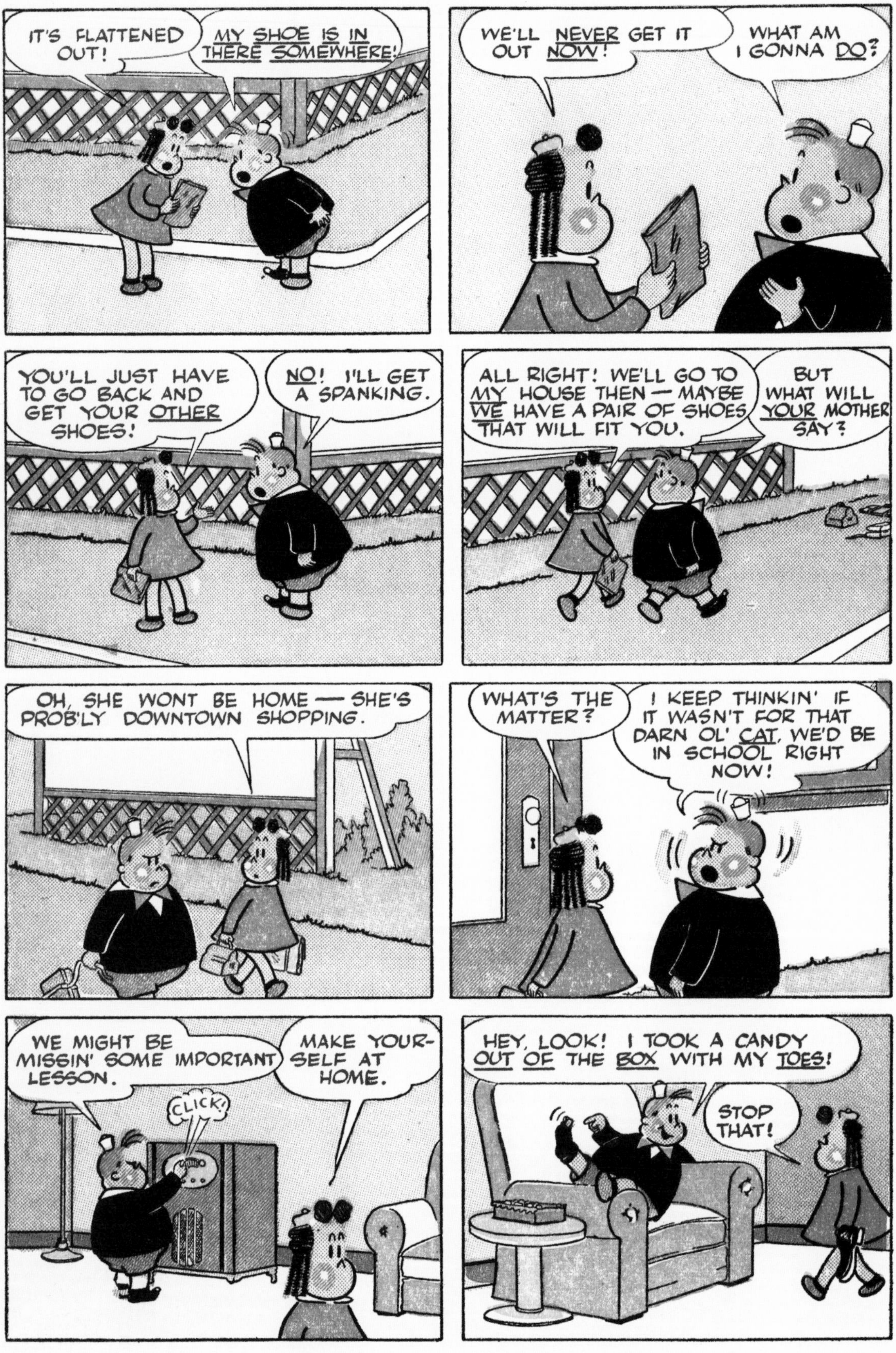
IT'S FLATTENED OUT!
MY SHOE IS IN THERE SOMEWHERE!
WE'LL NEVER GET IT OUT NOW!
WHAT AM I GONNA DO?
YOU'LL JUST HAVE TO GO BACK AND GET YOUR OTHER SHOES!
NO! I'LL GET A SPANKING.
ALL RIGHT! WE'LL GO TO MY HOUSE THEN — MAYBE WE HAVE A PAIR OF SHOES THAT WILL FIT YOU.
BUT WHAT WILL YOUR MOTHER SAY?
OH, SHE WONT BE HOME — SHE'S PROB'LY DOWNTOWN SHOPPING.
WHAT'S THE MATTER?
I KEEP THINKIN' IF IT WASN'T FOR THAT DARN OL' CAT, WE'D BE IN SCHOOL RIGHT NOW!
WE MIGHT BE MISSIN' SOME IMPORTANT LESSON.
CLICK!
MAKE YOURSELF AT HOME.
HEY, LOOK! I TOOK A CANDY OUT OF THE BOX WITH MY TOES!
STOP THAT!

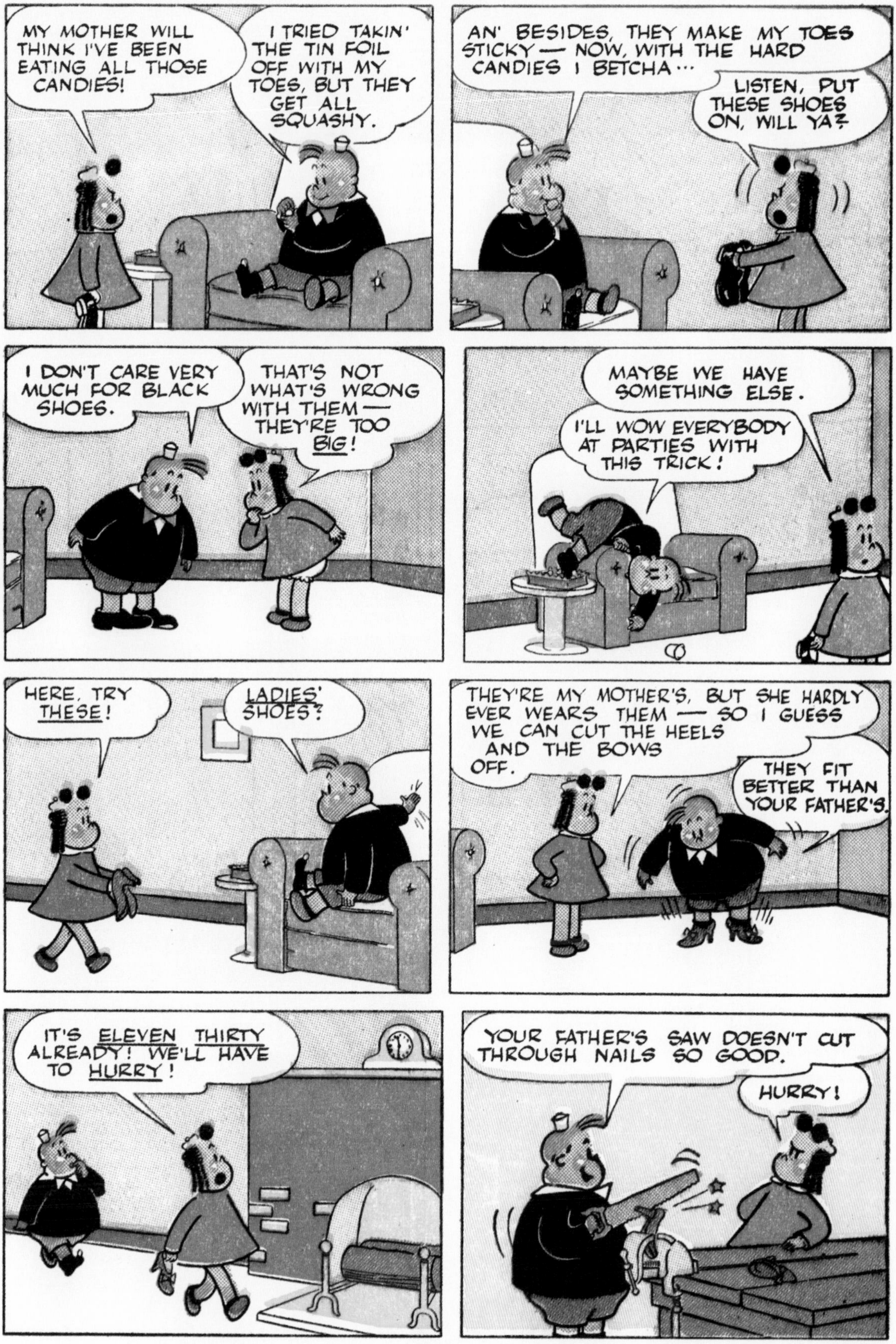
MY MOTHER WILL THINK I'VE BEEN EATING ALL THOSE CANDIES!
I TRIED TAKIN' THE TIN FOIL OFF WITH MY TOES, BUT THEY GET ALL SQUASHY.
AN' BESIDES, THEY MAKE MY TOES STICKY — NOW, WITH THE HARD CANDIES I BETCHA...
LISTEN, PUT THESE SHOES ON, WILL YA?
I DON'T CARE VERY MUCH FOR BLACK SHOES.
THAT'S NOT WHAT'S WRONG WITH THEM — THEY'RE TOO BIG!
MAYBE WE HAVE SOMETHING ELSE.
I'LL WOW EVERYBODY AT PARTIES WITH THIS TRICK!
HERE, TRY THESE!
LADIES' SHOES?
THEY'RE MY MOTHER'S, BUT SHE HARDLY EVER WEARS THEM — SO I GUESS WE CAN CUT THE HEELS AND THE BOWS OFF.
THEY FIT BETTER THAN YOUR FATHER'S.
IT'S ELEVEN THIRTY ALREADY! WE'LL HAVE TO HURRY!
YOUR FATHER'S SAW DOESN'T CUT THROUGH NAILS SO GOOD.
HURRY!

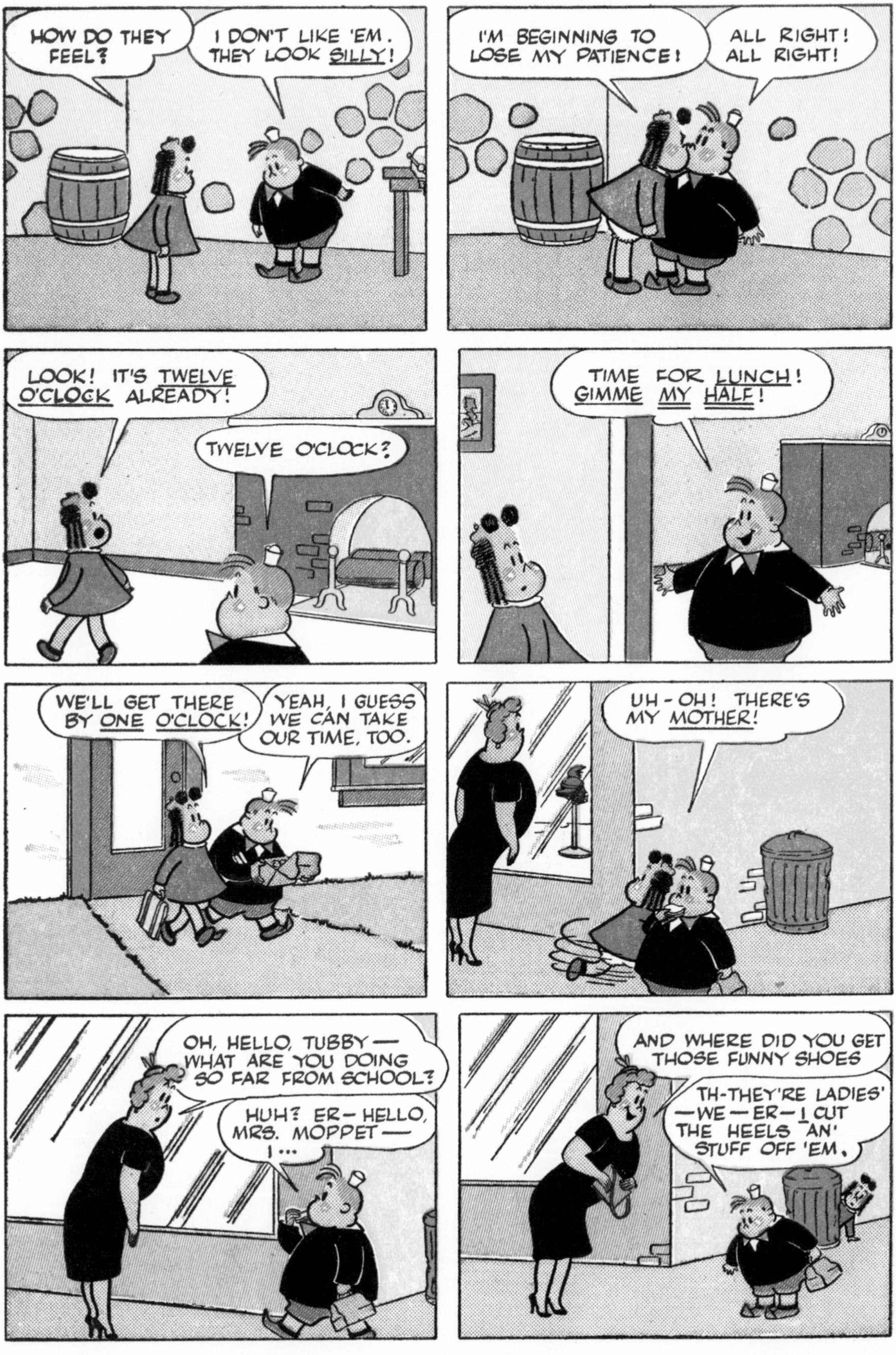
HOW DO THEY FEEL?
I DON'T LIKE 'EM. THEY LOOK SILLY!
I'M BEGINNING TO LOSE MY PATIENCE!
ALL RIGHT! ALL RIGHT!
LOOK! IT'S TWELVE O'CLOCK ALREADY!
TWELVE O'CLOCK?
TIME FOR LUNCH! GIMME MY HALF!
WE'LL GET THERE BY ONE O'CLOCK!
YEAH, I GUESS WE CAN TAKE OUR TIME, TOO.
UH-OH! THERE'S MY MOTHER!
OH, HELLO, TUBBY— WHAT ARE YOU DOING SO FAR FROM SCHOOL?
HUH? ER—HELLO, MRS. MOPPET— I...
AND WHERE DID YOU GET THOSE FUNNY SHOES
TH-THEY'RE LADIES' —WE—ER—I CUT THE HEELS 'AN' STUFF OFF 'EM.

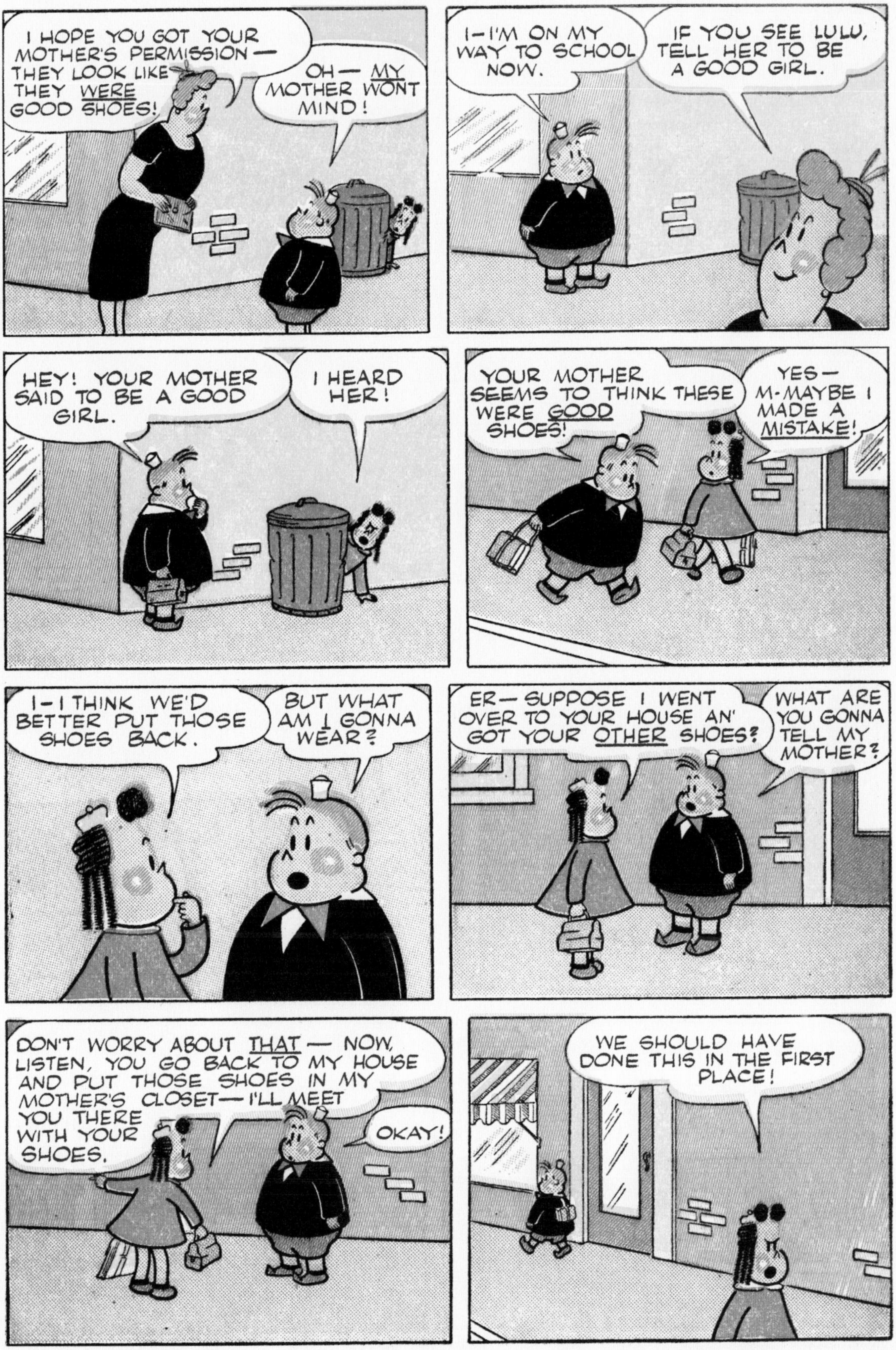
I HOPE YOU GOT YOUR MOTHER'S PERMISSION— THEY LOOK LIKE THEY WERE GOOD SHOES!
OH— MY MOTHER WONT MIND!
I-I'M ON MY WAY TO SCHOOL NOW.
IF YOU SEE LULU, TELL HER TO BE A GOOD GIRL.
HEY! YOUR MOTHER SAID TO BE A GOOD GIRL.
I HEARD HER!
YOUR MOTHER SEEMS TO THINK THESE WERE GOOD SHOES!
YES— M-MAYBE I MADE A MISTAKE!
I-I THINK WE'D BETTER PUT THOSE SHOES BACK.
BUT WHAT AM I GONNA WEAR?
ER— SUPPOSE I WENT OVER TO YOUR HOUSE AN' GOT YOUR OTHER SHOES?
WHAT ARE YOU GONNA TELL MY MOTHER?
DON'T WORRY ABOUT THAT— NOW, LISTEN, YOU GO BACK TO MY HOUSE AND PUT THOSE SHOES IN MY MOTHER'S CLOSET— I'LL MEET YOU THERE WITH YOUR SHOES.
OKAY!
WE SHOULD HAVE DONE THIS IN THE FIRST PLACE!

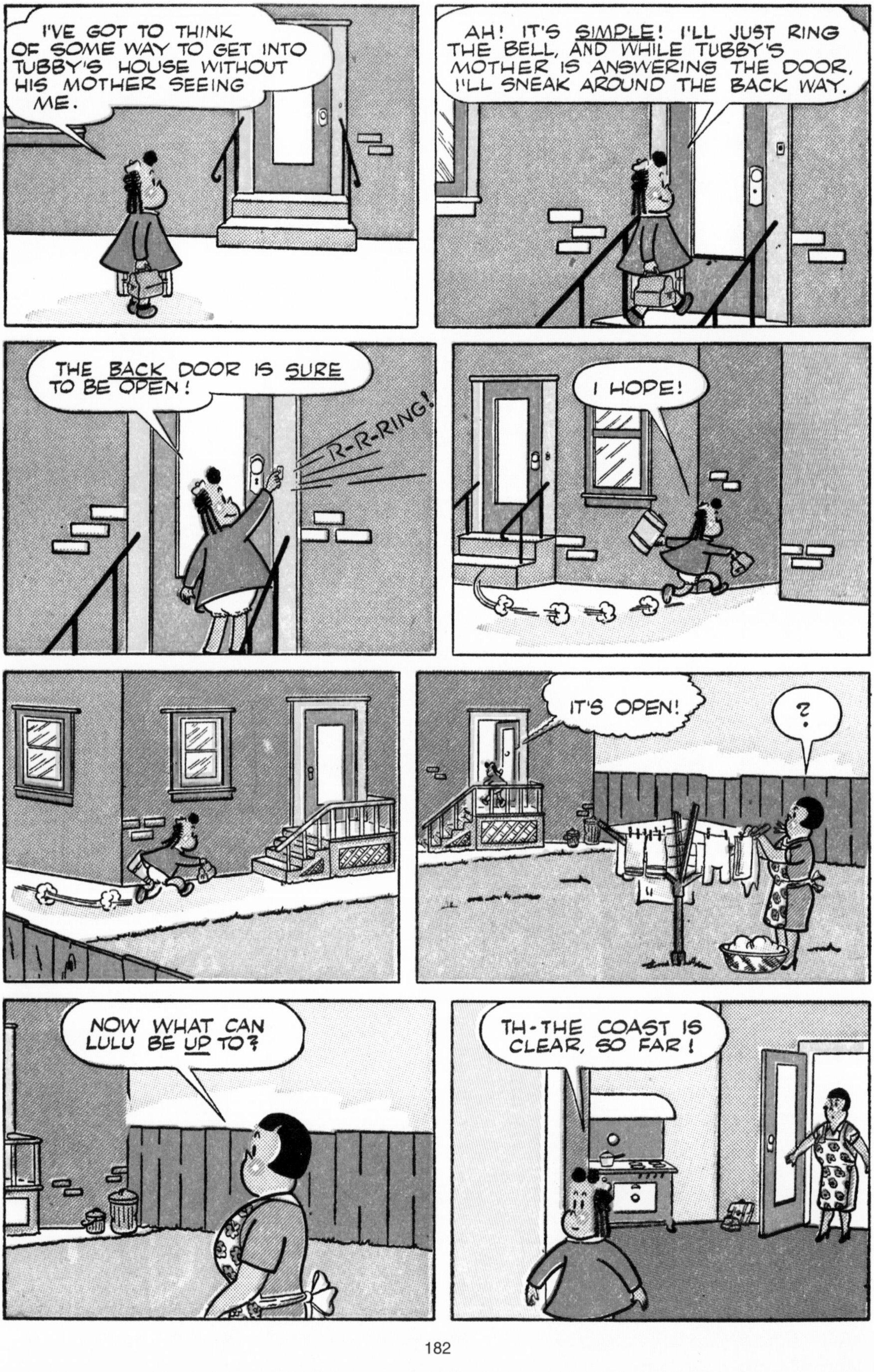
I'VE GOT TO THINK OF SOME WAY TO GET INTO TUBBY'S HOUSE WITHOUT HIS MOTHER SEEING ME.
AH! IT'S SIMPLE! I'LL JUST RING THE BELL, AND WHILE TUBBY'S MOTHER IS ANSWERING THE DOOR, I'LL SNEAK AROUND THE BACK WAY.
THE BACK DOOR IS SURE TO BE OPEN!
R-R-RING!
I HOPE!
IT'S OPEN!
?
NOW WHAT CAN LULU BE UP TO?
TH-THE COAST IS CLEAR, SO FAR!

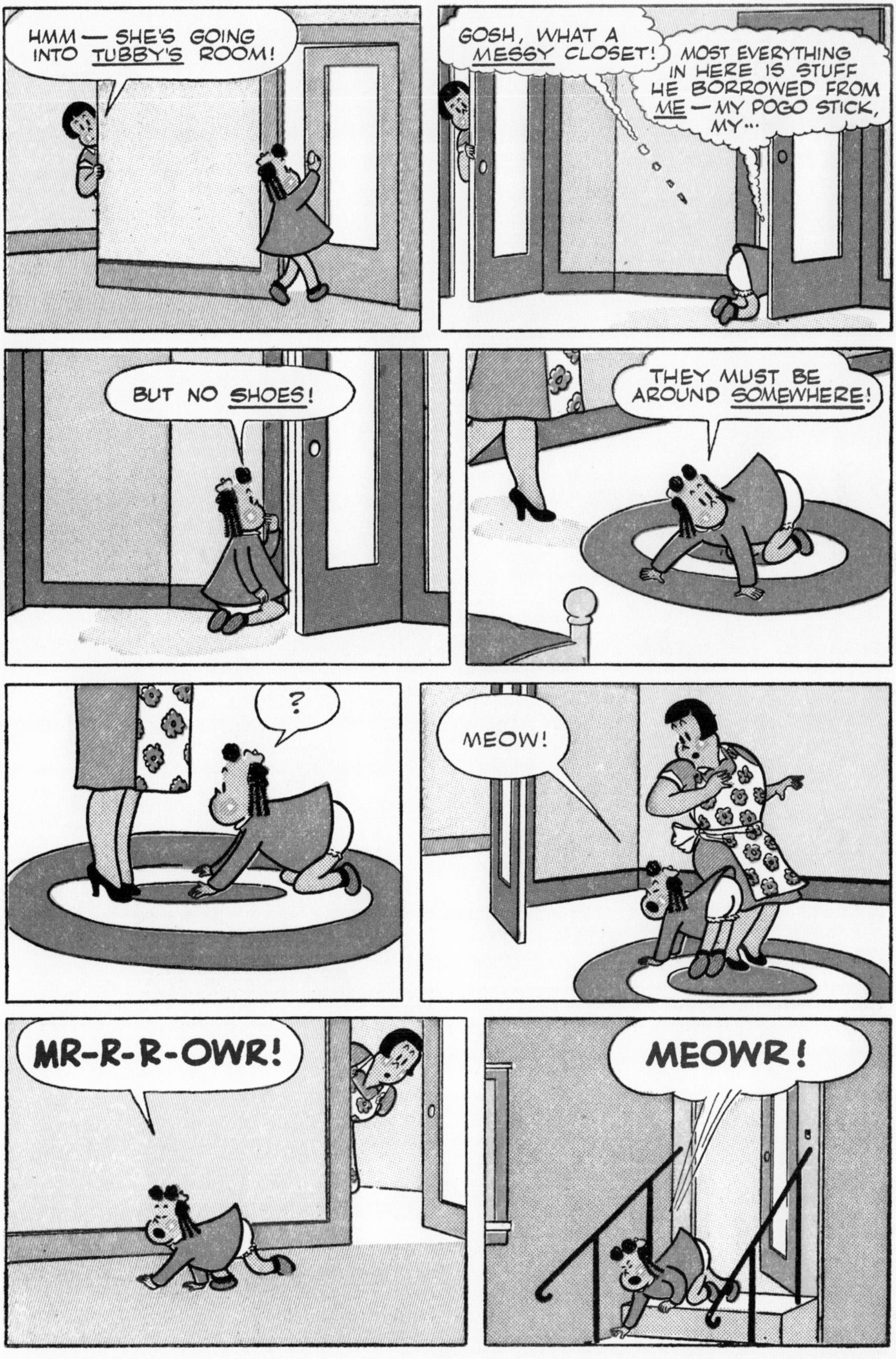

HMM — SHE'S GOING INTO TUBBY'S ROOM!
GOSH, WHAT A MESSY CLOSET!
MOST EVERYTHING IN HERE IS STUFF HE BORROWED FROM ME — MY POGO STICK, MY...
BUT NO SHOES!
THEY MUST BE AROUND SOMEWHERE!
?
MEOW!
MR-R-R-OWR!
MEOWR!

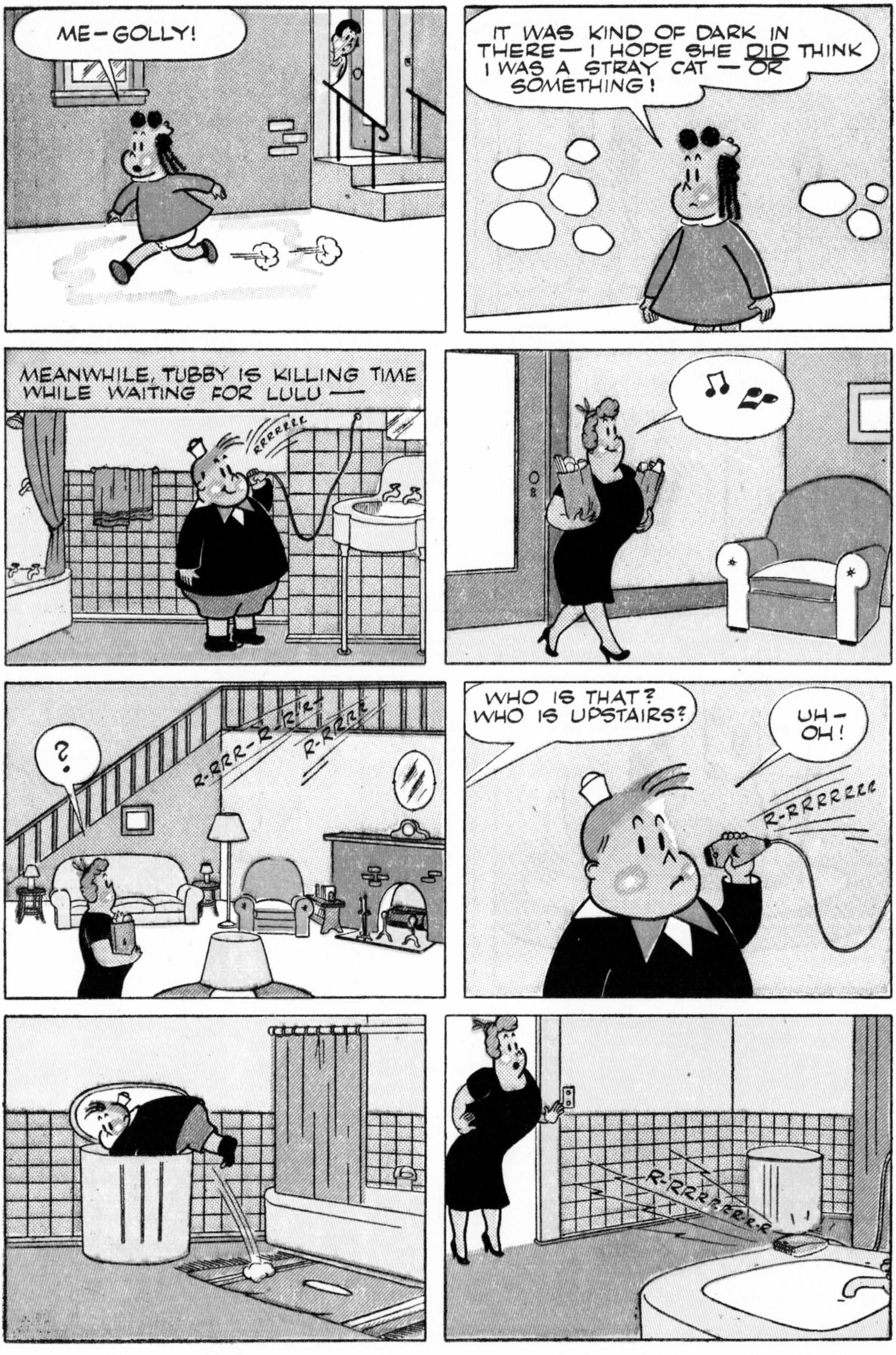
ME-GOLLY!
IT WAS KIND OF DARK IN THERE—I HOPE SHE DID THINK I WAS A STRAY CAT—OR SOMETHING!
MEANWHILE, TUBBY IS KILLING TIME WHILE WAITING FOR LULU—
RRRRRRR
?
R-RRR-R R'R'R-
R-RRRR
WHO IS THAT? WHO IS UPSTAIRS?
UH-OH!
R-RRRRRRR
R-RRRRRRR-R-R

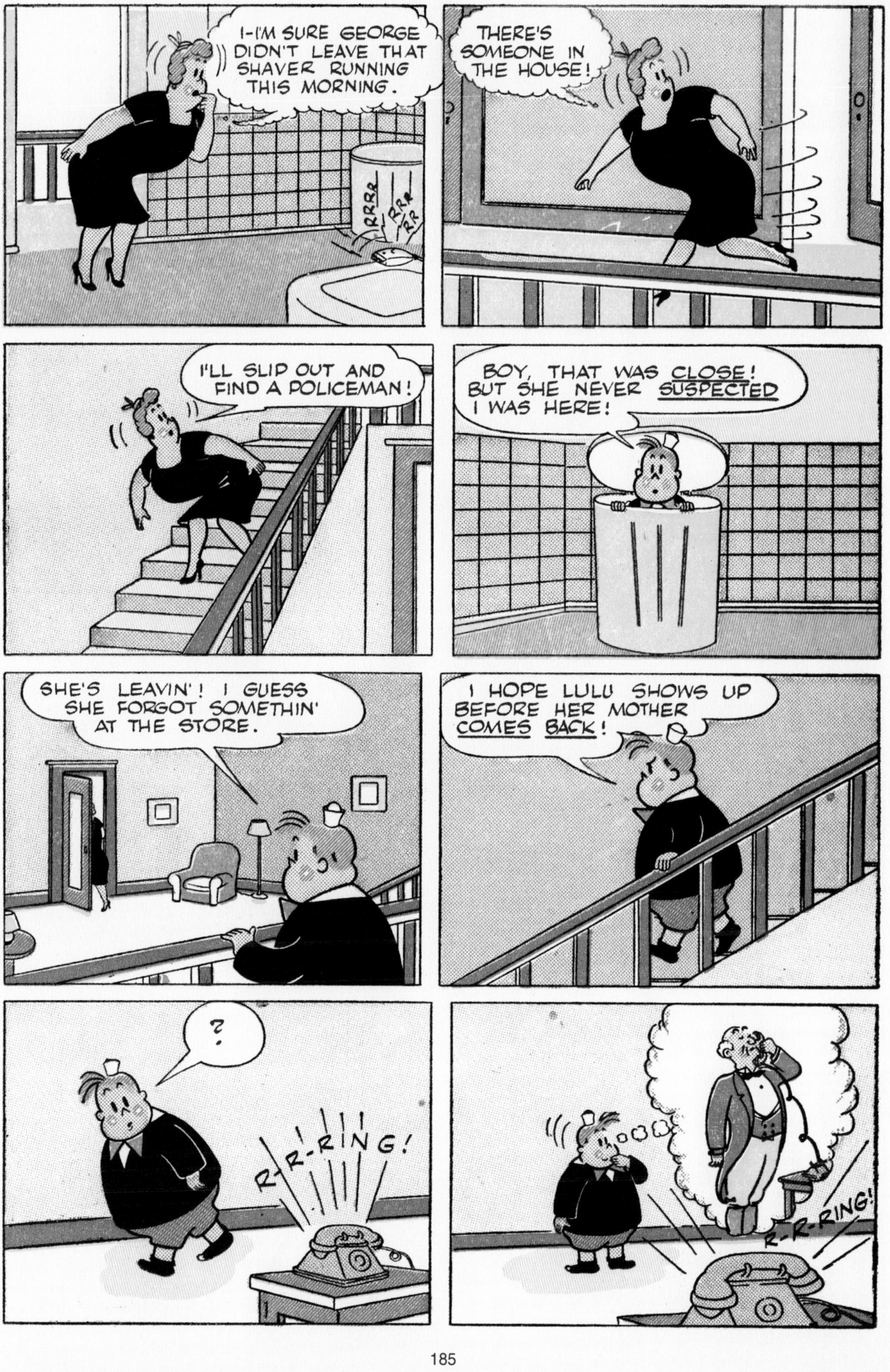
I-I'M SURE GEORGE DIDN'T LEAVE THAT SHAVER RUNNING THIS MORNING.
RRRR
RRR RR
THERE'S SOMEONE IN THE HOUSE!
I'LL SLIP OUT AND FIND A POLICEMAN!
BOY, THAT WAS CLOSE! BUT SHE NEVER SUSPECTED I WAS HERE!
SHE'S LEAVIN'! I GUESS SHE FORGOT SOMETHIN' AT THE STORE.
I HOPE LULU SHOWS UP BEFORE HER MOTHER COMES BACK!
?
R-R-RING!
R-R-RING!

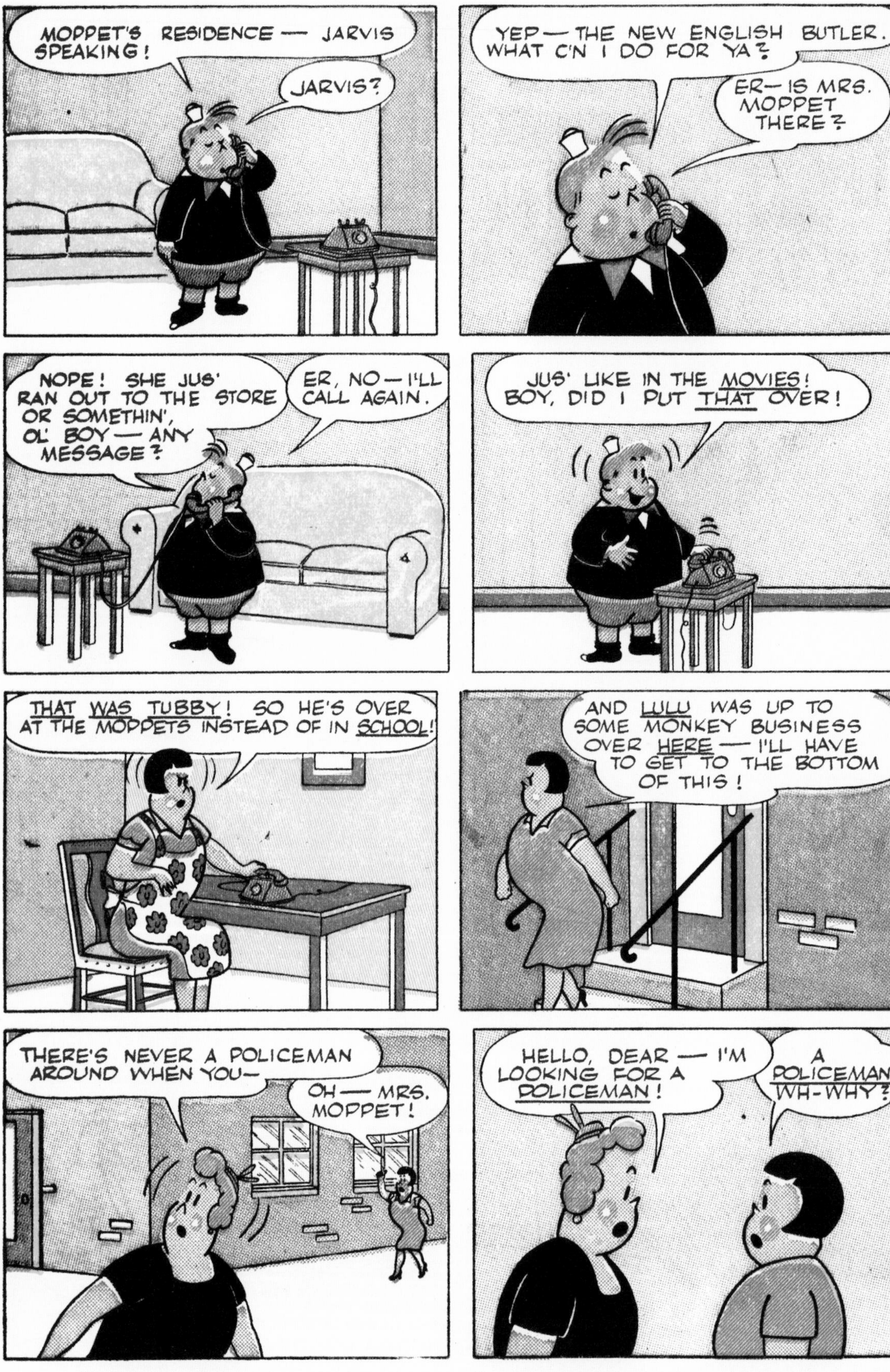
MOPPET'S RESIDENCE — JARVIS SPEAKING!
JARVIS?
YEP— THE NEW ENGLISH BUTLER. WHAT C'N I DO FOR YA?
ER— IS MRS. MOPPET THERE?
NOPE! SHE JUS' RAN OUT TO THE STORE OR SOMETHIN', OL' BOY — ANY MESSAGE?
ER, NO — I'LL CALL AGAIN.
JUS' LIKE IN THE MOVIES! BOY, DID I PUT THAT OVER!
THAT WAS TUBBY! SO HE'S OVER AT THE MOPPETS INSTEAD OF IN SCHOOL!
AND LULU WAS UP TO SOME MONKEY BUSINESS OVER HERE — I'LL HAVE TO GET TO THE BOTTOM OF THIS!
THERE'S NEVER A POLICEMAN AROUND WHEN YOU—
OH — MRS. MOPPET!
HELLO, DEAR — I'M LOOKING FOR A POLICEMAN!
A POLICEMAN? WH-WHY?

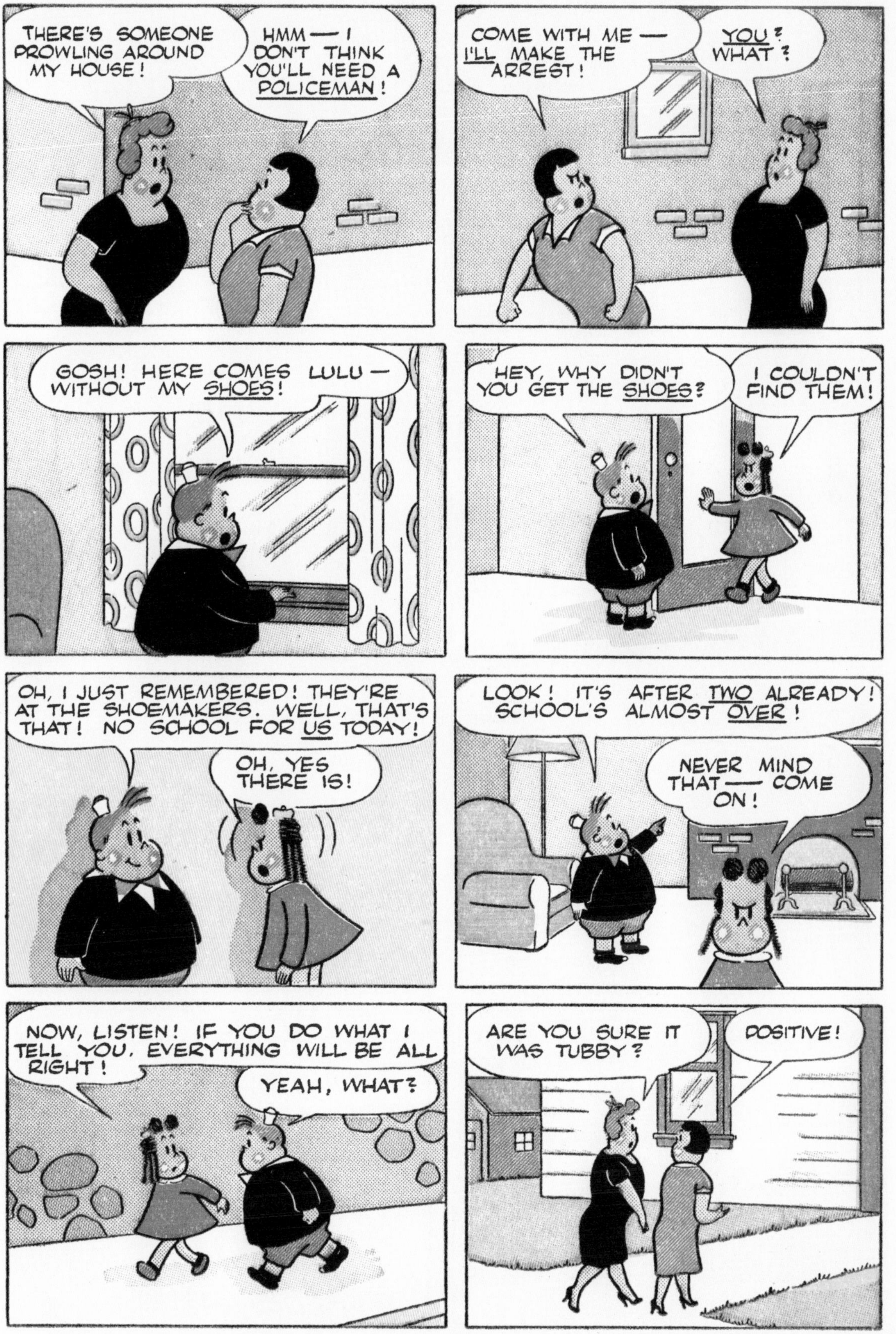

THERE'S SOMEONE PROWLING AROUND MY HOUSE!
HMM — I DON'T THINK YOU'LL NEED A POLICEMAN!
COME WITH ME — I'LL MAKE THE ARREST!
YOU? WHAT?
GOSH! HERE COMES LULU — WITHOUT MY SHOES!
HEY, WHY DIDN'T YOU GET THE SHOES?
I COULDN'T FIND THEM!
OH, I JUST REMEMBERED! THEY'RE AT THE SHOEMAKERS. WELL, THAT'S THAT! NO SCHOOL FOR US TODAY!
OH, YES THERE IS!
LOOK! IT'S AFTER TWO ALREADY! SCHOOL'S ALMOST OVER!
NEVER MIND THAT — COME ON!
NOW, LISTEN! IF YOU DO WHAT I TELL YOU, EVERYTHING WILL BE ALL RIGHT!
YEAH, WHAT?
ARE YOU SURE IT WAS TUBBY?
POSITIVE!

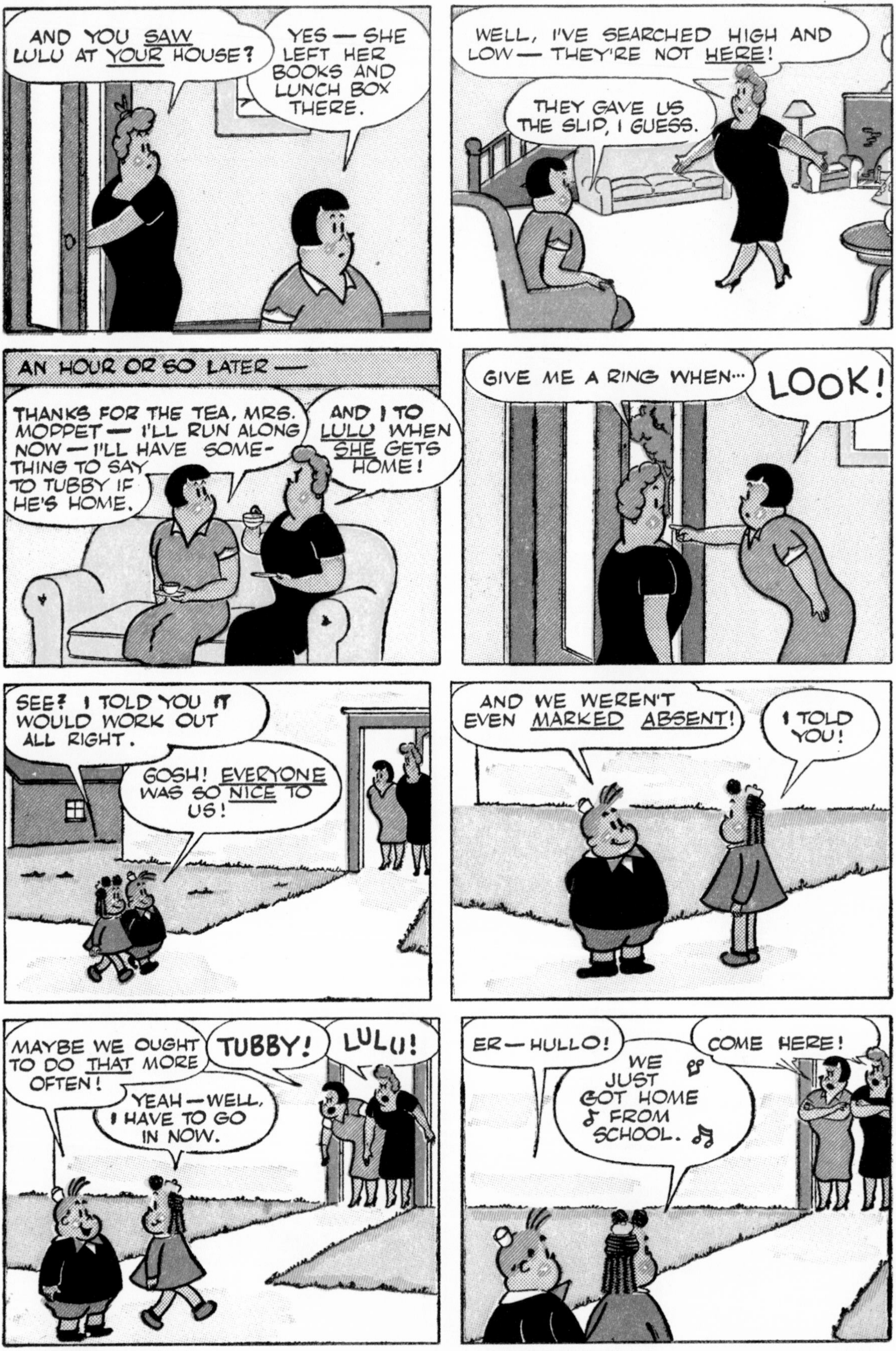
AND YOU SAW LULU AT YOUR HOUSE?
YES — SHE LEFT HER BOOKS AND LUNCH BOX THERE.
WELL, I'VE SEARCHED HIGH AND LOW — THEY'RE NOT HERE!
THEY GAVE US THE SLIP, I GUESS.
AN HOUR OR SO LATER —
THANKS FOR THE TEA, MRS. MOPPET — I'LL RUN ALONG NOW — I'LL HAVE SOMETHING TO SAY TO TUBBY IF HE'S HOME.
AND I TO LULU WHEN SHE GETS HOME!
GIVE ME A RING WHEN...
LOOK!
SEE? I TOLD YOU IT WOULD WORK OUT ALL RIGHT.
GOSH! EVERYONE WAS SO NICE TO US!
AND WE WEREN'T EVEN MARKED ABSENT!
I TOLD YOU!
MAYBE WE OUGHT TO DO THAT MORE OFTEN!
TUBBY!
LULU!
YEAH — WELL, I HAVE TO GO IN NOW.
ER — HULLO!
WE JUST GOT HOME FROM SCHOOL.
COME HERE!

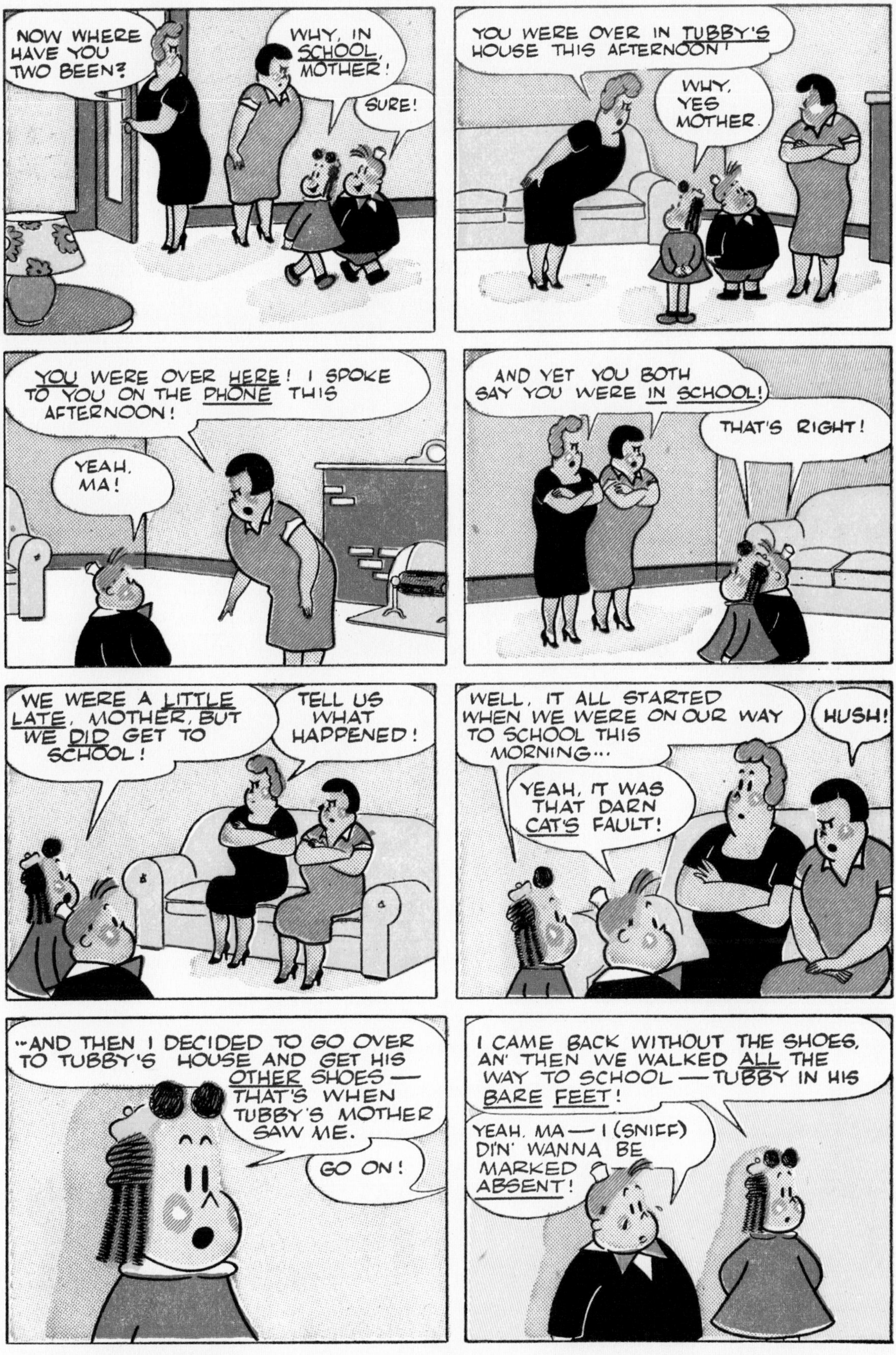

NOW WHERE HAVE YOU TWO BEEN?
WHY, IN SCHOOL, MOTHER!
SURE!
YOU WERE OVER IN TUBBY'S HOUSE THIS AFTERNOON!
WHY, YES MOTHER.
YOU WERE OVER HERE! I SPOKE TO YOU ON THE PHONE THIS AFTERNOON!
YEAH, MA!
AND YET YOU BOTH SAY YOU WERE IN SCHOOL!
THAT'S RIGHT!
WE WERE A LITTLE LATE, MOTHER, BUT WE DID GET TO SCHOOL!
TELL US WHAT HAPPENED!
WELL, IT ALL STARTED WHEN WE WERE ON OUR WAY TO SCHOOL THIS MORNING...
HUSH!
YEAH, IT WAS THAT DARN CAT'S FAULT!
...AND THEN I DECIDED TO GO OVER TO TUBBY'S HOUSE AND GET HIS OTHER SHOES — THAT'S WHEN TUBBY'S MOTHER SAW ME.
GO ON!
I CAME BACK WITHOUT THE SHOES, AN' THEN WE WALKED ALL THE WAY TO SCHOOL — TUBBY IN HIS BARE FEET!
YEAH, MA — I (SNIFF) DIN' WANNA BE MARKED ABSENT!

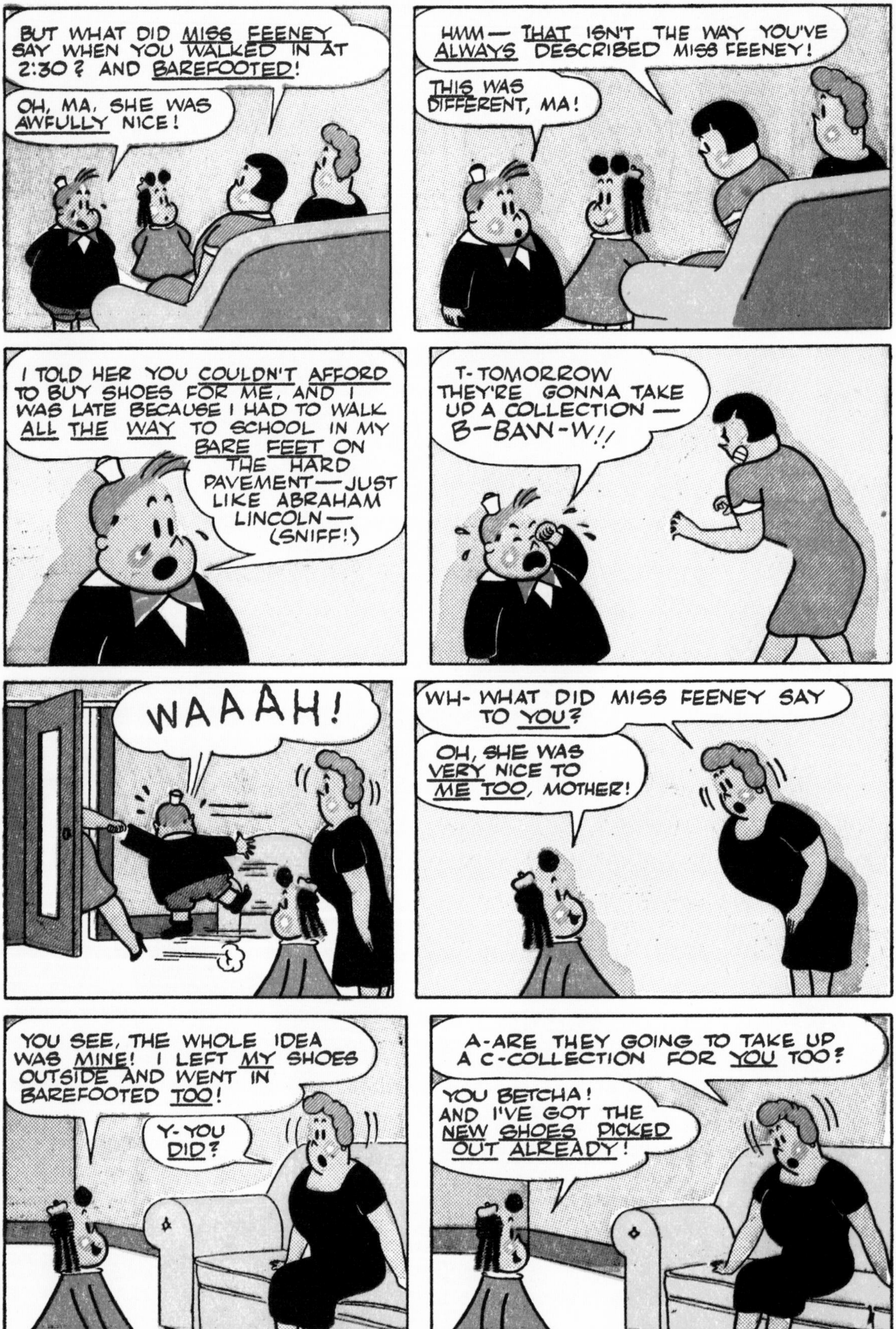
BUT WHAT DID MISS FEENEY SAY WHEN YOU WALKED IN AT 2:30? AND BAREFOOTED!
OH, MA, SHE WAS AWFULLY NICE!
HMM— THAT ISN'T THE WAY YOU'VE ALWAYS DESCRIBED MISS FEENEY!
THIS WAS DIFFERENT, MA!
I TOLD HER YOU COULDN'T AFFORD TO BUY SHOES FOR ME, AND I WAS LATE BECAUSE I HAD TO WALK ALL THE WAY TO SCHOOL IN MY BARE FEET ON THE HARD PAVEMENT—JUST LIKE ABRAHAM LINCOLN— (SNIFF!)
T-TOMORROW THEY'RE GONNA TAKE UP A COLLECTION — B—BAW-W!!
WAAAH!
WH- WHAT DID MISS FEENEY SAY TO YOU?
OH, SHE WAS VERY NICE TO ME TOO, MOTHER!
YOU SEE, THE WHOLE IDEA WAS MINE! I LEFT MY SHOES OUTSIDE AND WENT IN BAREFOOTED TOO!
Y-YOU DID?
A-ARE THEY GOING TO TAKE UP A C-COLLECTION FOR YOU TOO?
YOU BETCHA! AND I'VE GOT THE NEW SHOES PICKED OUT ALREADY!

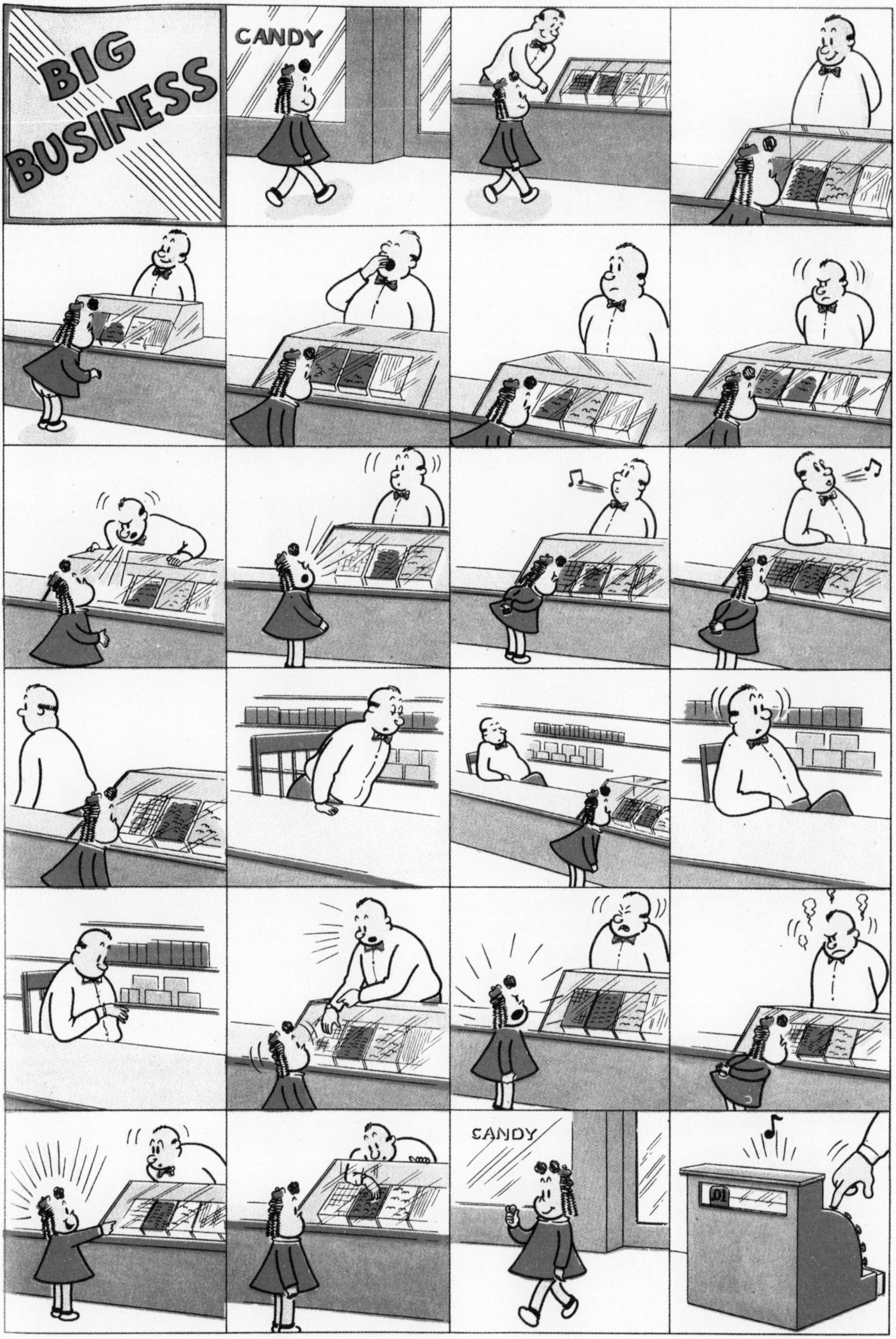
BIG BUSINESS
CANDY
CANDY
.01

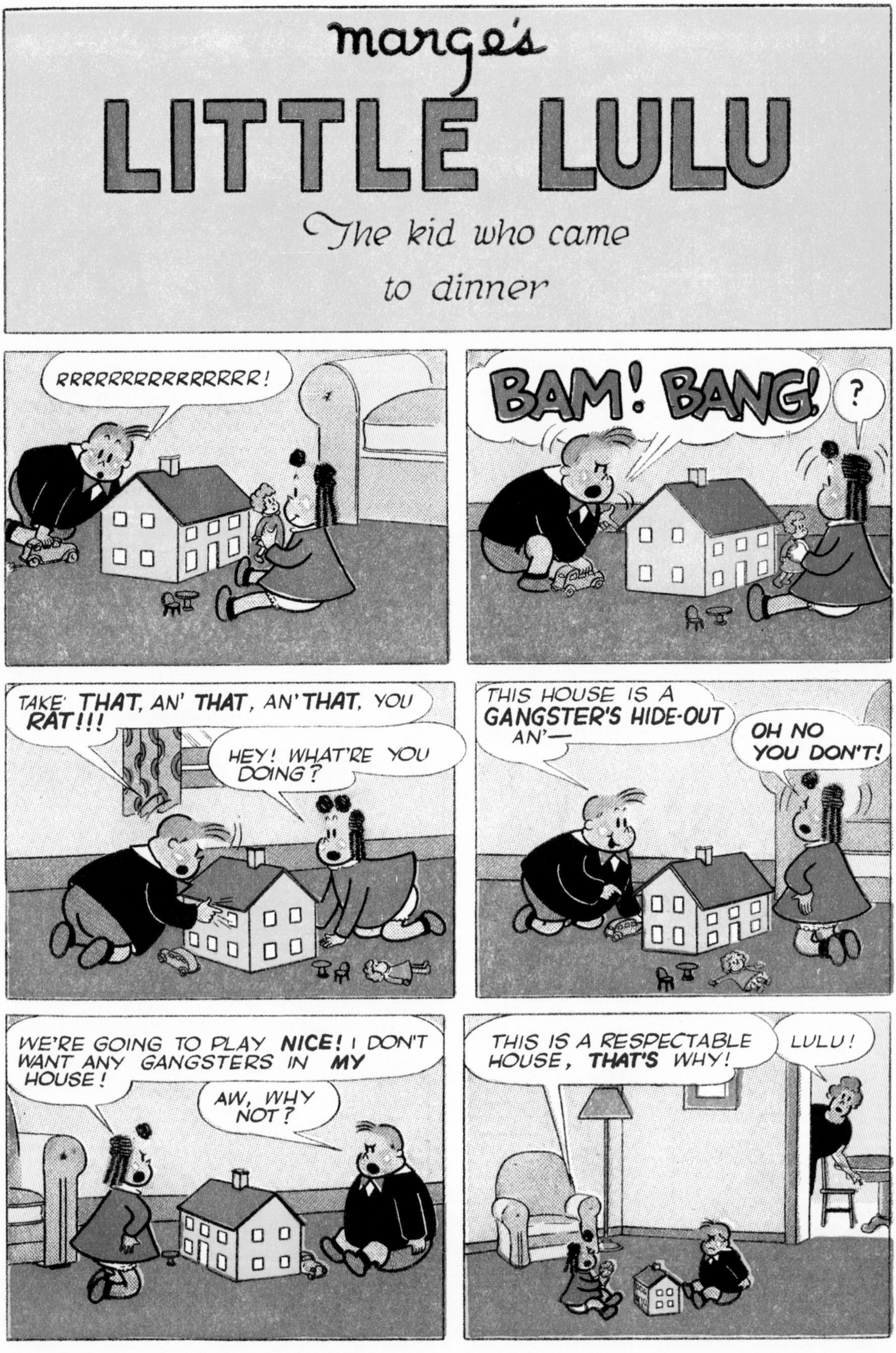
marge's
LITTLE LULU
The kid who came to dinner
RRRRRRRRRRRRRRR!
BAM! BANG!
?
TAKE THAT, AN' THAT, AN' THAT, YOU RAT!!!
HEY! WHAT'RE YOU DOING?
THIS HOUSE IS A GANGSTER'S HIDE-OUT AN'—
OH NO YOU DON'T!
WE'RE GOING TO PLAY NICE! I DON'T WANT ANY GANGSTERS IN MY HOUSE!
AW, WHY NOT?
THIS IS A RESPECTABLE HOUSE, THAT'S WHY!
LULU!

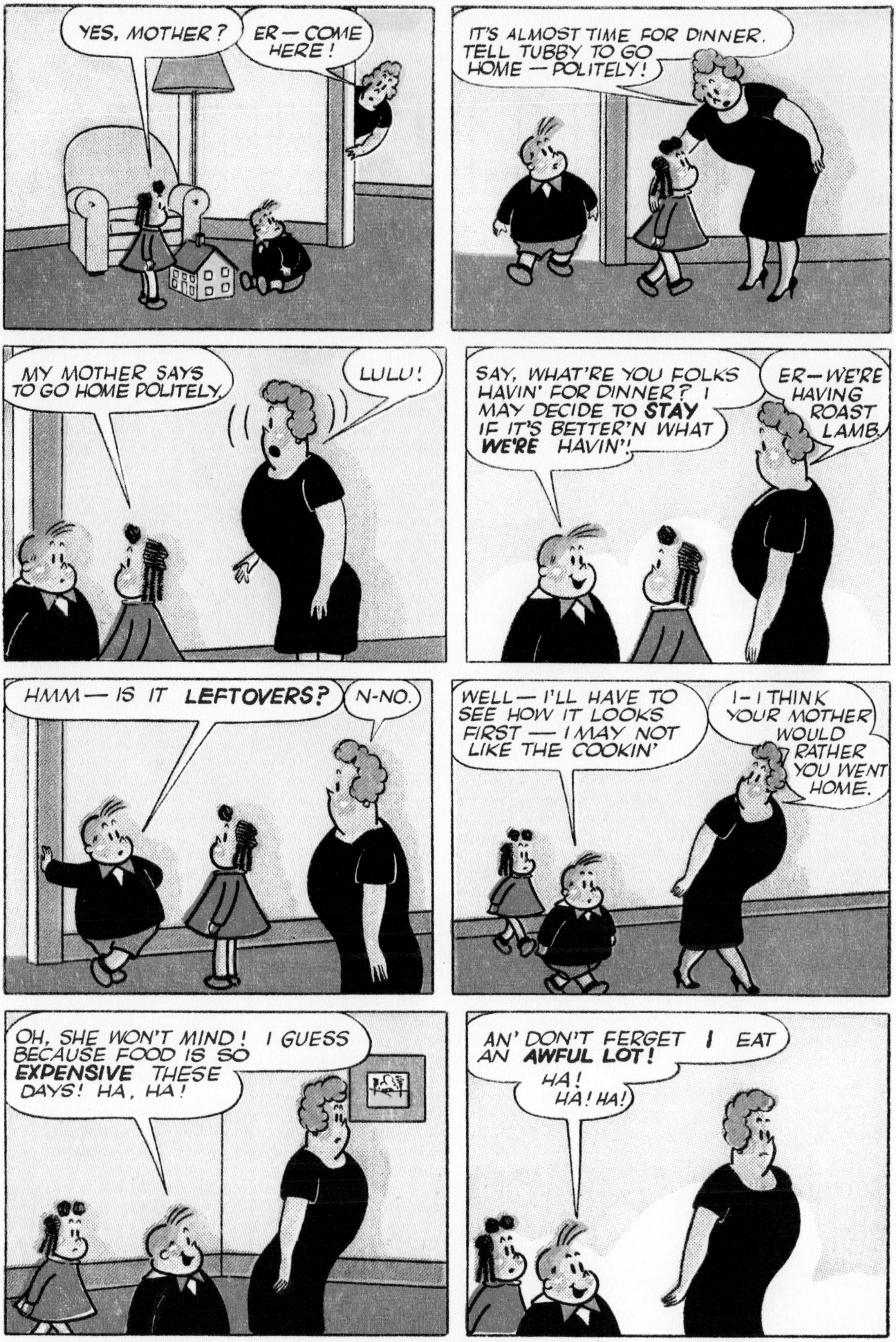
YES, MOTHER?
ER— COME HERE!
IT'S ALMOST TIME FOR DINNER. TELL TUBBY TO GO HOME — POLITELY!
MY MOTHER SAYS TO GO HOME POLITELY.
LULU!
SAY, WHAT'RE YOU FOLKS HAVIN' FOR DINNER? I MAY DECIDE TO STAY IF IT'S BETTER'N WHAT WE'RE HAVIN'!
ER—WE'RE HAVING ROAST LAMB.
HMM— IS IT LEFTOVERS?
N-NO.
WELL— I'LL HAVE TO SEE HOW IT LOOKS FIRST — I MAY NOT LIKE THE COOKIN'
I-I THINK YOUR MOTHER WOULD RATHER YOU WENT HOME.
OH, SHE WON'T MIND! I GUESS BECAUSE FOOD IS SO EXPENSIVE THESE DAYS! HA, HA!
AN' DON'T FERGET I EAT AN AWFUL LOT!
HA! HA! HA!

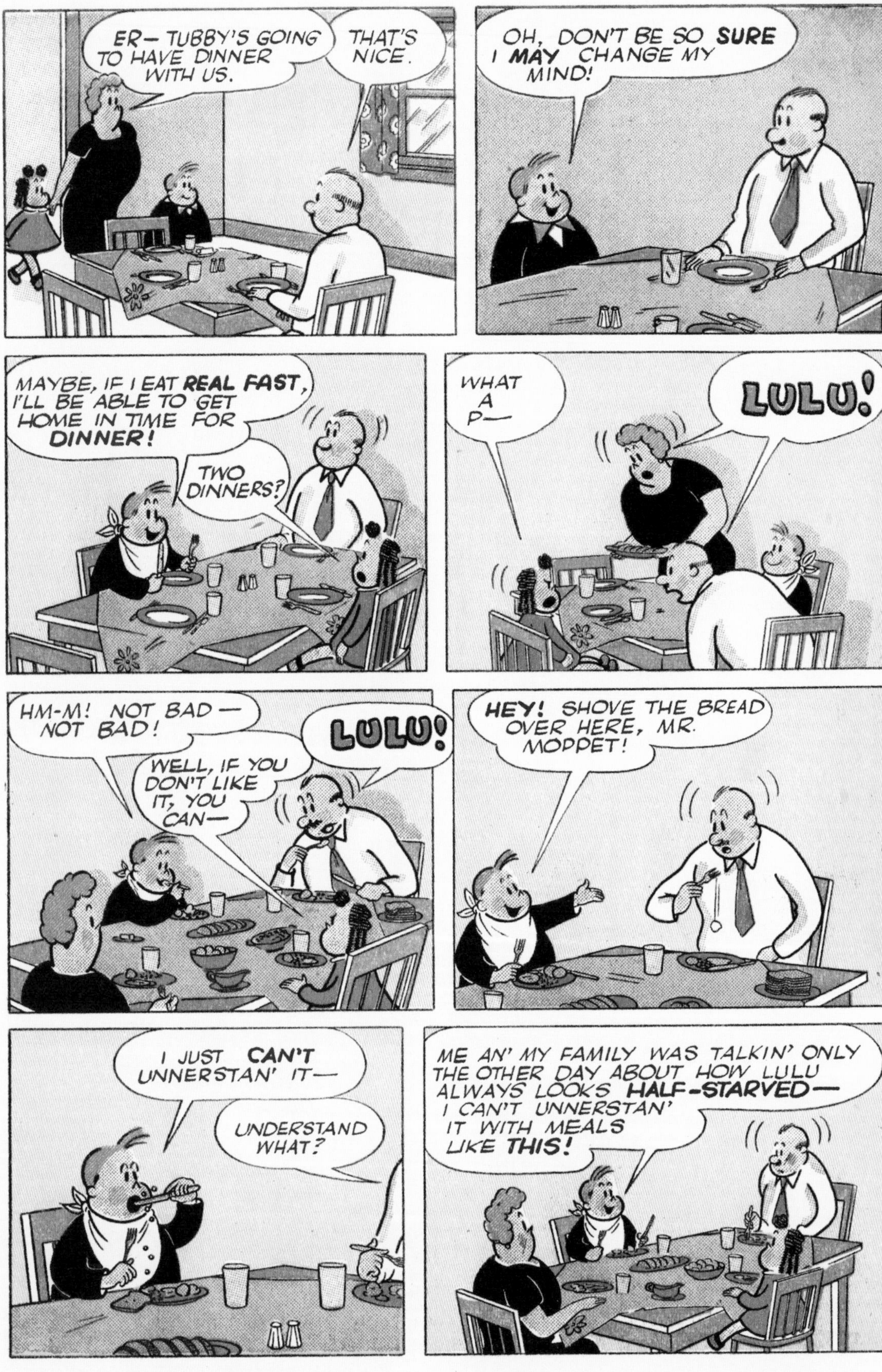
ER— TUBBY'S GOING TO HAVE DINNER WITH US.
THAT'S NICE.
OH, DON'T BE SO SURE I MAY CHANGE MY MIND!
MAYBE, IF I EAT REAL FAST, I'LL BE ABLE TO GET HOME IN TIME FOR DINNER!
TWO DINNERS?
WHAT A P—
LULU!
HM-M! NOT BAD — NOT BAD!
WELL, IF YOU DON'T LIKE IT, YOU CAN—
LULU!
HEY! SHOVE THE BREAD OVER HERE, MR. MOPPET!
I JUST CAN'T UNNERSTAN' IT—
UNDERSTAND WHAT?
ME AN' MY FAMILY WAS TALKIN' ONLY THE OTHER DAY ABOUT HOW LULU ALWAYS LOOKS HALF-STARVED— I CAN'T UNNERSTAN' IT WITH MEALS LIKE THIS!

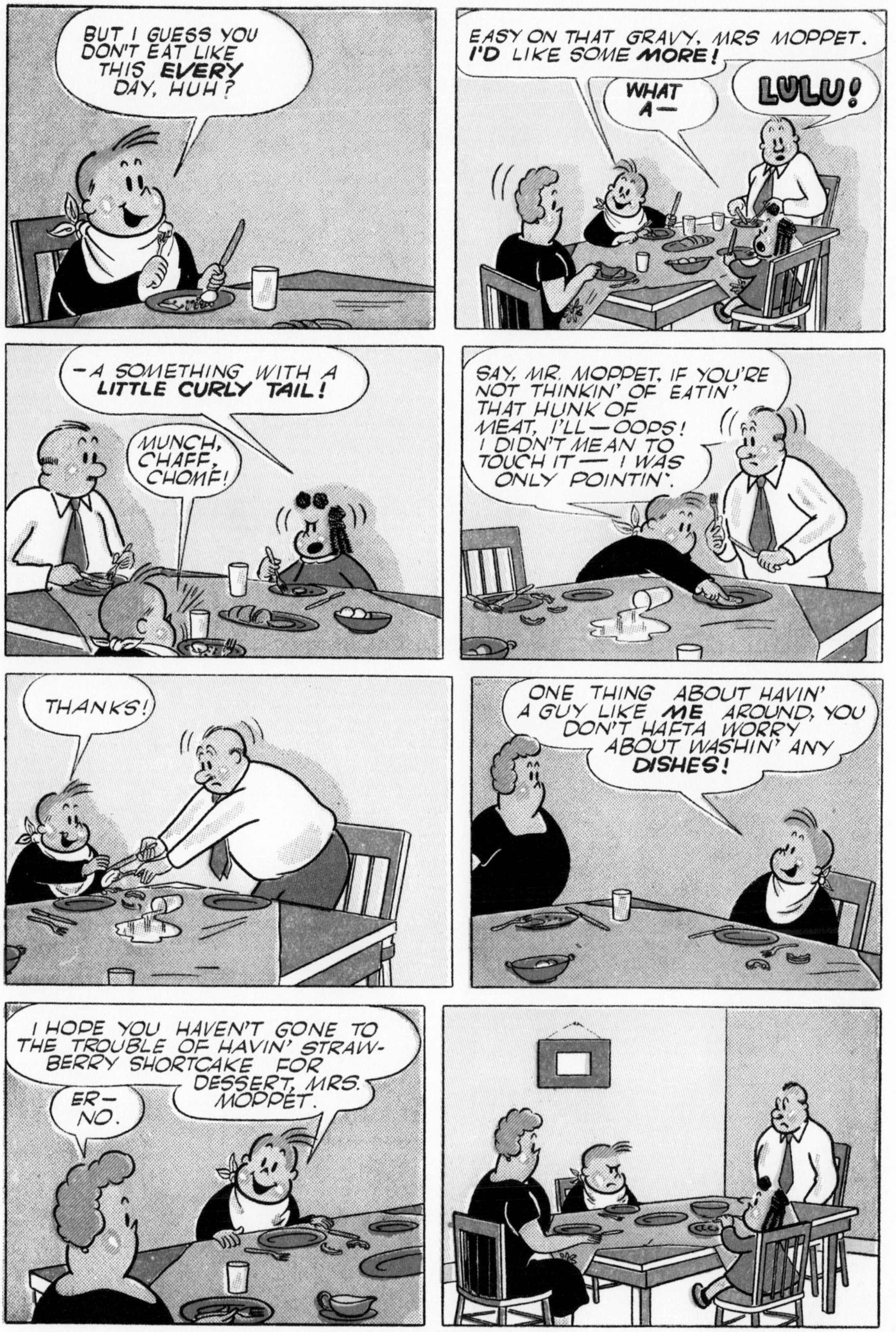
BUT I GUESS YOU DON'T EAT LIKE THIS EVERY DAY, HUH?
EASY ON THAT GRAVY, MRS MOPPET. I'D LIKE SOME MORE!
WHAT A—
LULU!
—A SOMETHING WITH A LITTLE CURLY TAIL!
MUNCH, CHAFF, CHOMF!
SAY, MR. MOPPET, IF YOU'RE NOT THINKIN' OF EATIN' THAT HUNK OF MEAT, I'LL—OOPS! I DIDN'T MEAN TO TOUCH IT— I WAS ONLY POINTIN'.
THANKS!
ONE THING ABOUT HAVIN' A GUY LIKE ME AROUND, YOU DON'T HAFTA WORRY ABOUT WASHIN' ANY DISHES!
I HOPE YOU HAVEN'T GONE TO THE TROUBLE OF HAVIN' STRAWBERRY SHORTCAKE FOR DESSERT, MRS. MOPPET.
ER— NO.

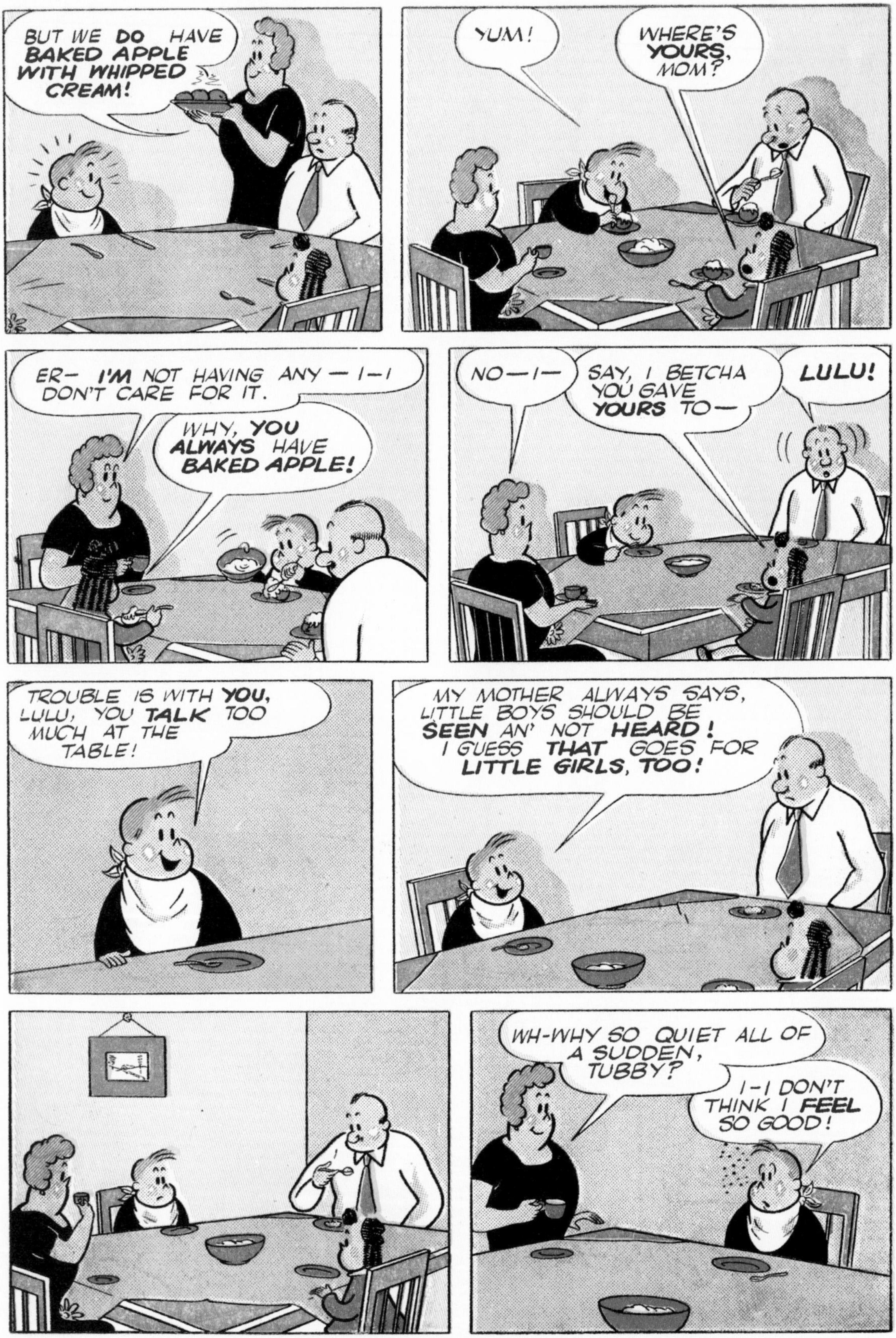
BUT WE DO HAVE BAKED APPLE WITH WHIPPED CREAM!
YUM!
WHERE'S YOURS, MOM?
ER— I'M NOT HAVING ANY — I—I DON'T CARE FOR IT.
WHY, YOU ALWAYS HAVE BAKED APPLE!
NO—I—
SAY, I BETCHA YOU GAVE YOURS TO—
LULU!
TROUBLE IS WITH YOU, LULU, YOU TALK TOO MUCH AT THE TABLE!
MY MOTHER ALWAYS SAYS, LITTLE BOYS SHOULD BE SEEN AN' NOT HEARD! I GUESS THAT GOES FOR LITTLE GIRLS, TOO!
WH-WHY SO QUIET ALL OF A SUDDEN, TUBBY?
I-I DON'T THINK I FEEL SO GOOD!

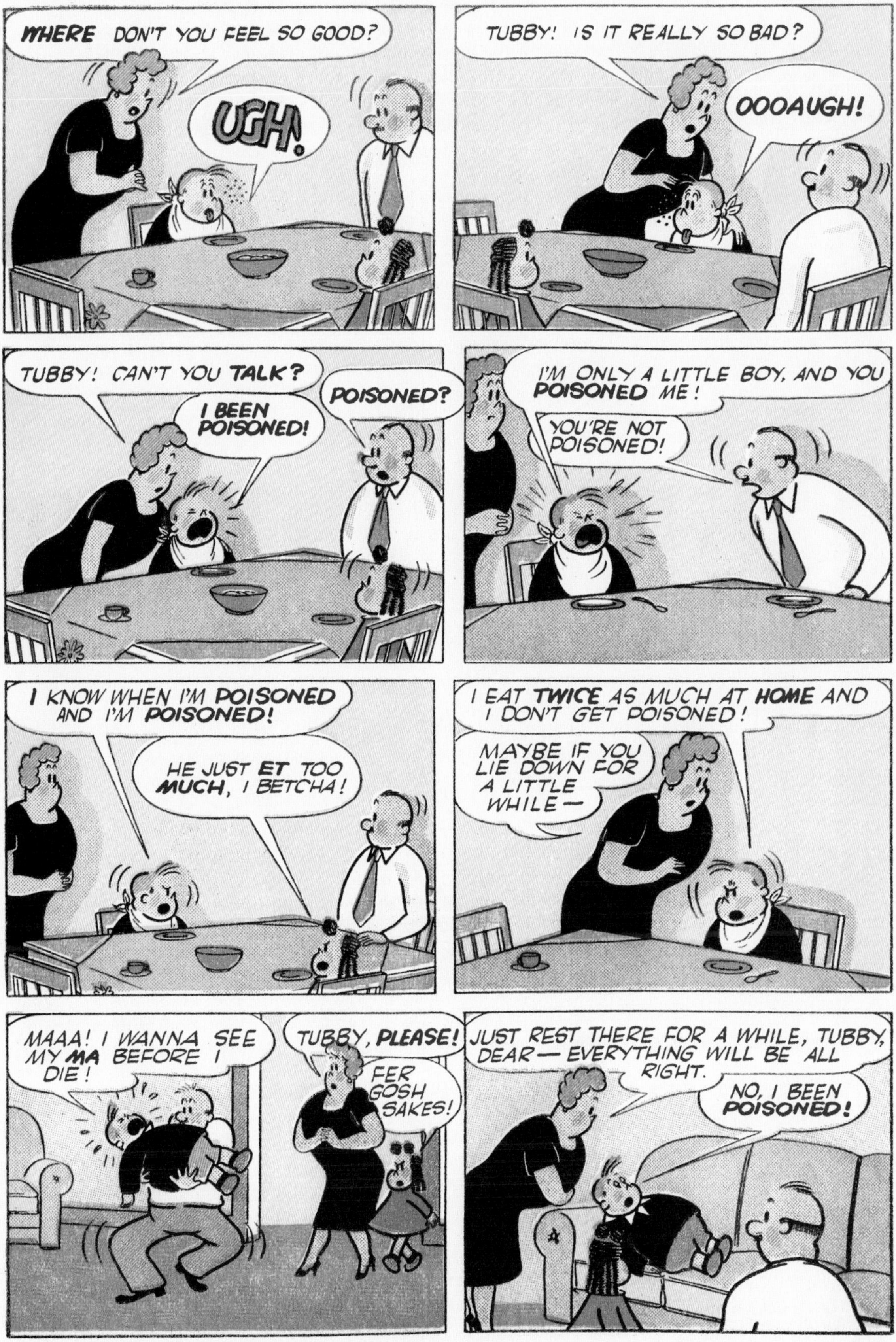
WHERE DON'T YOU FEEL SO GOOD?
UGH!
TUBBY! IS IT REALLY SO BAD?
OOOAUGH!
TUBBY! CAN'T YOU TALK?
I BEEN POISONED!
POISONED?
I'M ONLY A LITTLE BOY, AND YOU POISONED ME!
YOU'RE NOT POISONED!
I KNOW WHEN I'M POISONED AND I'M POISONED!
HE JUST ET TOO MUCH, I BETCHA!
I EAT TWICE AS MUCH AT HOME AND I DON'T GET POISONED!
MAYBE IF YOU LIE DOWN FOR A LITTLE WHILE—
MAAA! I WANNA SEE MY MA BEFORE I DIE!
TUBBY, PLEASE!
FER GOSH SAKES!
JUST REST THERE FOR A WHILE, TUBBY, DEAR— EVERYTHING WILL BE ALL RIGHT.
NO, I BEEN POISONED!

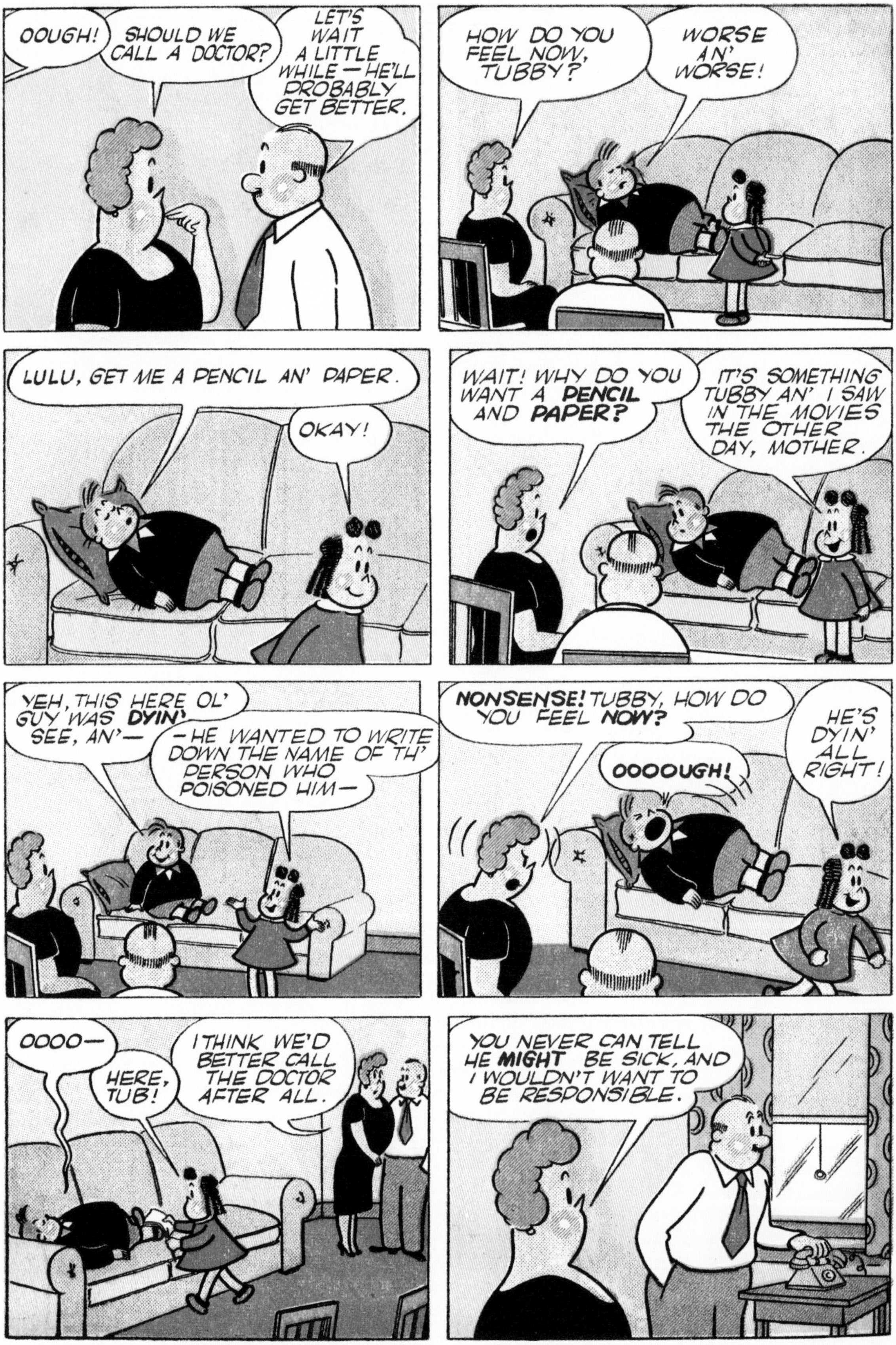

OOUGH!
SHOULD WE CALL A DOCTOR?
LET'S WAIT A LITTLE WHILE — HE'LL PROBABLY GET BETTER.
HOW DO YOU FEEL NOW, TUBBY?
WORSE AN' WORSE!
LULU, GET ME A PENCIL AN' PAPER.
OKAY!
WAIT! WHY DO YOU WANT A **PENCIL** AND **PAPER?**
IT'S SOMETHING TUBBY AN' I SAW IN THE MOVIES THE OTHER DAY, MOTHER.
YEH, THIS HERE OL' GUY WAS **DYIN'** SEE, AN'—
—HE WANTED TO WRITE DOWN THE NAME OF TH' PERSON WHO POISONED HIM—
NONSENSE! TUBBY, HOW DO YOU FEEL **NOW?**
OOOOUGH!
HE'S DYIN' ALL RIGHT!
OOOO—
HERE, TUB!
I THINK WE'D BETTER CALL THE DOCTOR AFTER ALL.
YOU NEVER CAN TELL HE **MIGHT** BE SICK, AND I WOULDN'T WANT TO BE RESPONSIBLE.

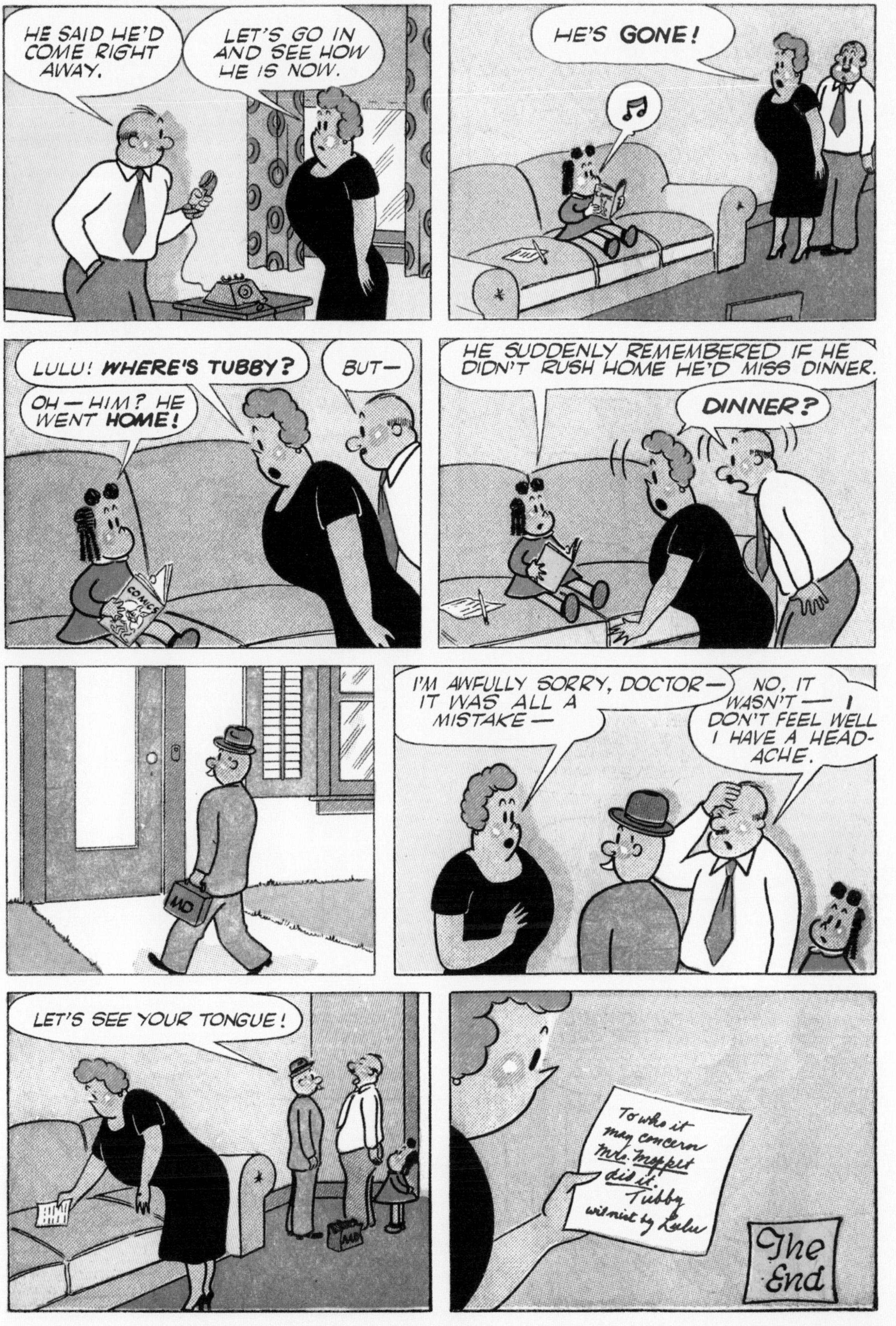
HE SAID HE'D COME RIGHT AWAY.
LET'S GO IN AND SEE HOW HE IS NOW.
HE'S **GONE!**
LULU! **WHERE'S TUBBY?**
BUT—
OH — HIM? HE WENT **HOME!**
HE SUDDENLY REMEMBERED IF HE DIDN'T RUSH HOME HE'D MISS DINNER.
DINNER?
COMICS
MD
I'M AWFULLY SORRY, DOCTOR— IT WAS ALL A MISTAKE—
NO, IT WASN'T — I DON'T FEEL WELL I HAVE A HEADACHE.
LET'S SEE YOUR TONGUE!
To who it may concern Mr. Moppet did it. Tubby witniss by Lulu
The End

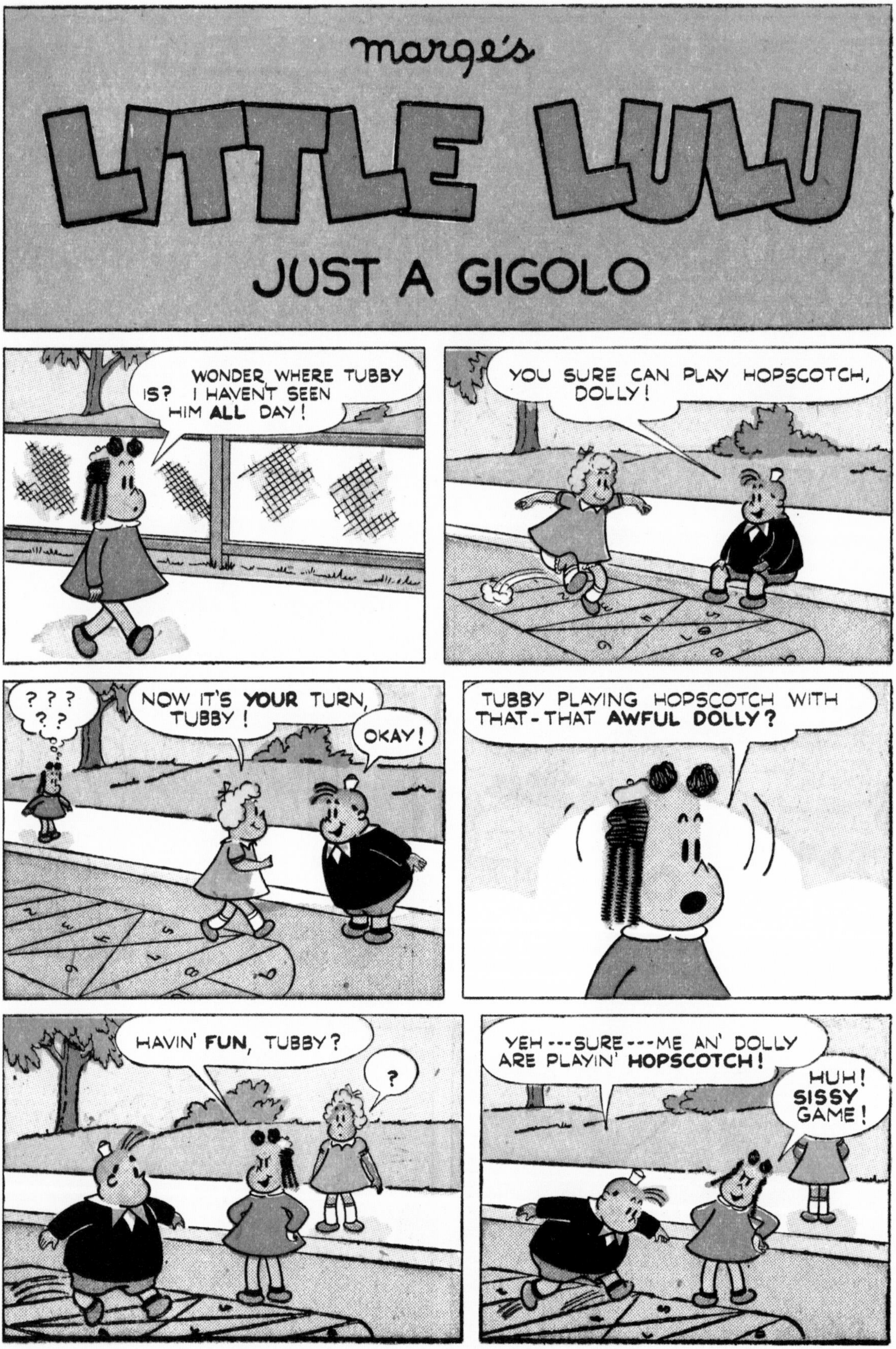
marge's
LITTLE LULU
JUST A GIGOLO
WONDER WHERE TUBBY IS? I HAVEN'T SEEN HIM ALL DAY!
YOU SURE CAN PLAY HOPSCOTCH, DOLLY!
? ? ? ? ?
NOW IT'S YOUR TURN, TUBBY!
OKAY!
TUBBY PLAYING HOPSCOTCH WITH THAT-THAT AWFUL DOLLY?
HAVIN' FUN, TUBBY?
?
YEH---SURE---ME AN' DOLLY ARE PLAYIN' HOPSCOTCH!
HUH! SISSY GAME!

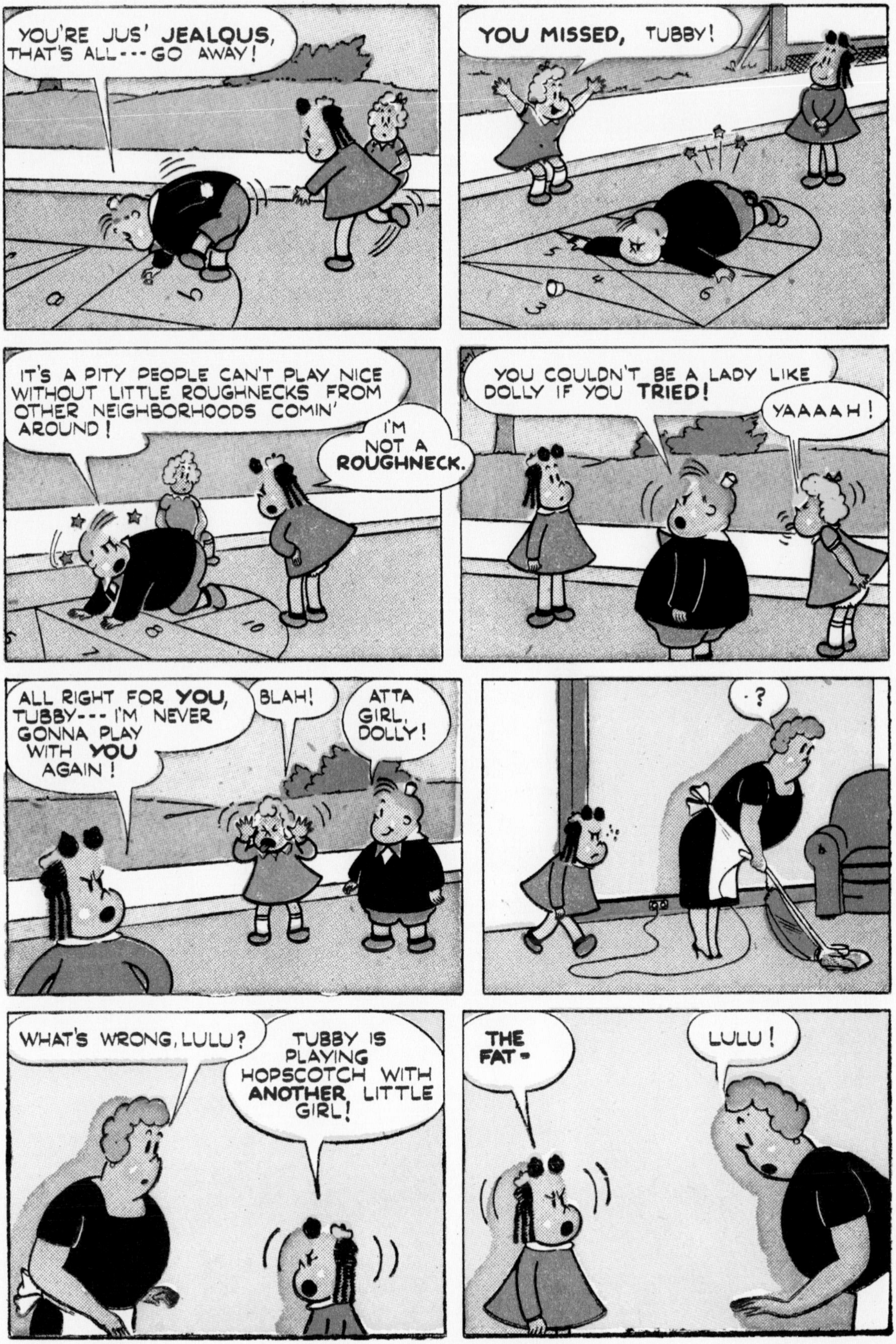

YOU'RE JUS' JEALOUS, THAT'S ALL--- GO AWAY!
YOU MISSED, TUBBY!
IT'S A PITY PEOPLE CAN'T PLAY NICE WITHOUT LITTLE ROUGHNECKS FROM OTHER NEIGHBORHOODS COMIN' AROUND!
I'M NOT A ROUGHNECK.
YOU COULDN'T BE A LADY LIKE DOLLY IF YOU TRIED!
YAAAAH!
ALL RIGHT FOR YOU, TUBBY--- I'M NEVER GONNA PLAY WITH YOU AGAIN!
BLAH!
ATTA GIRL, DOLLY!
-?
WHAT'S WRONG, LULU?
TUBBY IS PLAYING HOPSCOTCH WITH ANOTHER LITTLE GIRL!
THE FAT-
LULU!

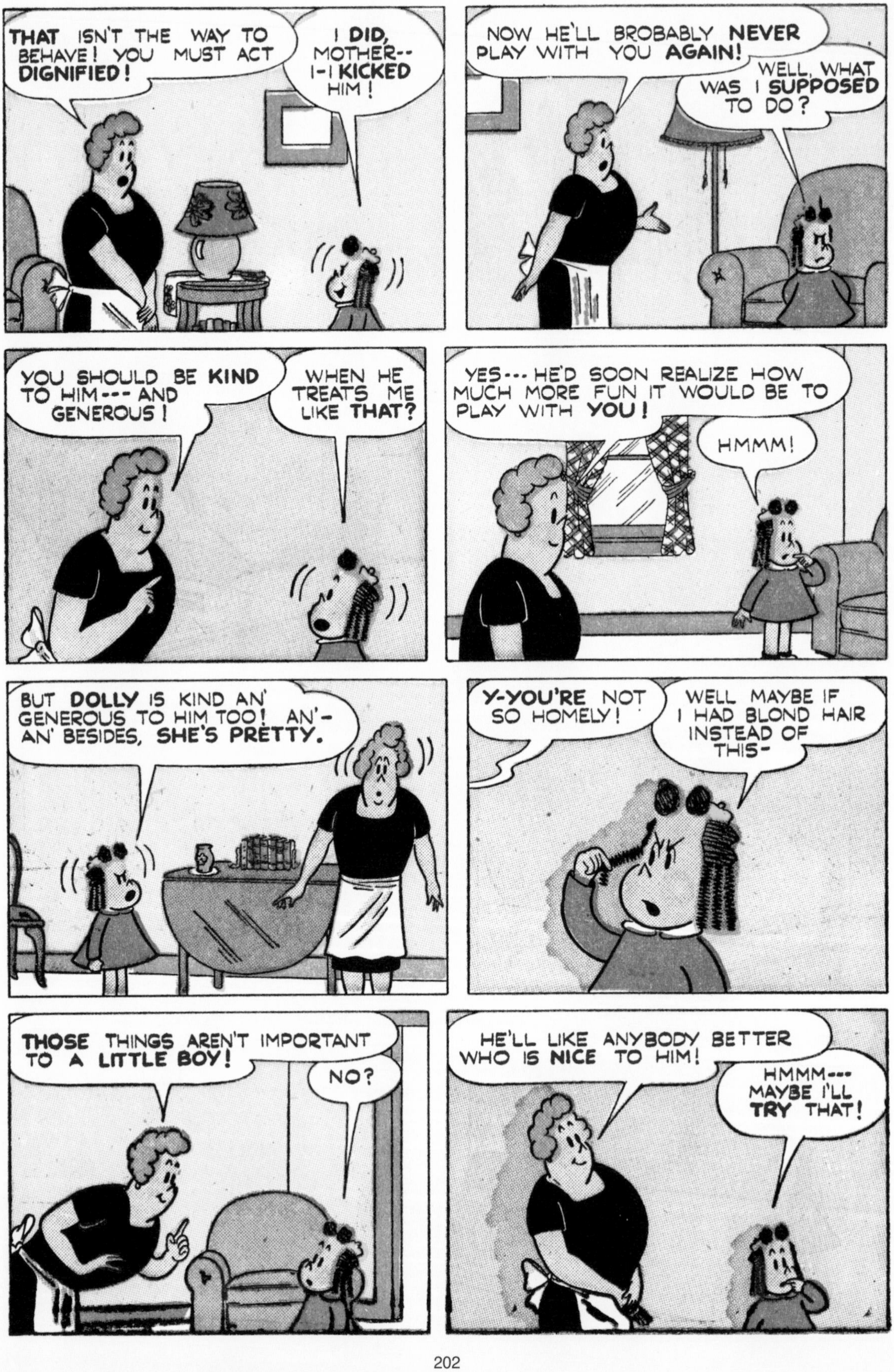
THAT ISN'T THE WAY TO BEHAVE! YOU MUST ACT DIGNIFIED!
I DID, MOTHER-- I-I KICKED HIM!
NOW HE'LL BROBABLY NEVER PLAY WITH YOU AGAIN!
WELL, WHAT WAS I SUPPOSED TO DO?
YOU SHOULD BE KIND TO HIM--- AND GENEROUS!
WHEN HE TREATS ME LIKE THAT?
YES--- HE'D SOON REALIZE HOW MUCH MORE FUN IT WOULD BE TO PLAY WITH YOU!
HMMM!
BUT DOLLY IS KIND AN' GENEROUS TO HIM TOO! AN'- AN' BESIDES, SHE'S PRETTY.
Y-YOU'RE NOT SO HOMELY!
WELL MAYBE IF I HAD BLOND HAIR INSTEAD OF THIS-
THOSE THINGS AREN'T IMPORTANT TO A LITTLE BOY!
NO?
HE'LL LIKE ANYBODY BETTER WHO IS NICE TO HIM!
HMMM--- MAYBE I'LL TRY THAT!

JINGLE! JINGLE!
SIXTY-FIVE CENTS.
HELLO, TUBBY!
HMPH!
LOOK, SMARTY--- TUBBY JUST BOUGHT ME A LOLLIPOP!

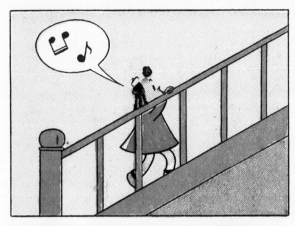

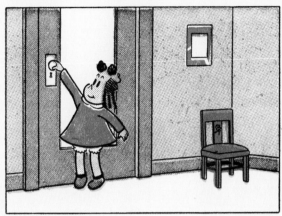

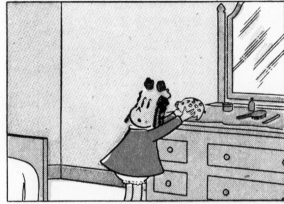

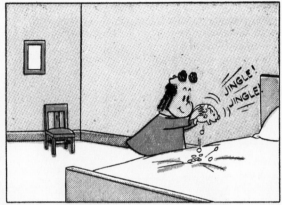

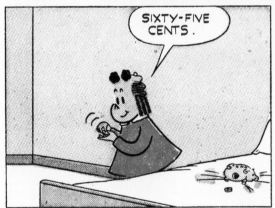

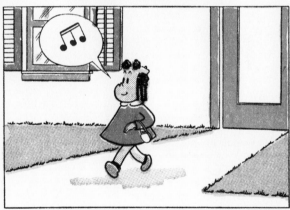

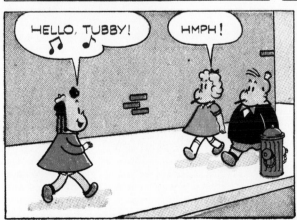

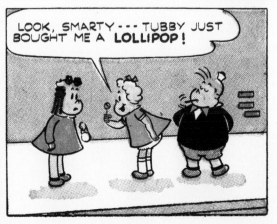

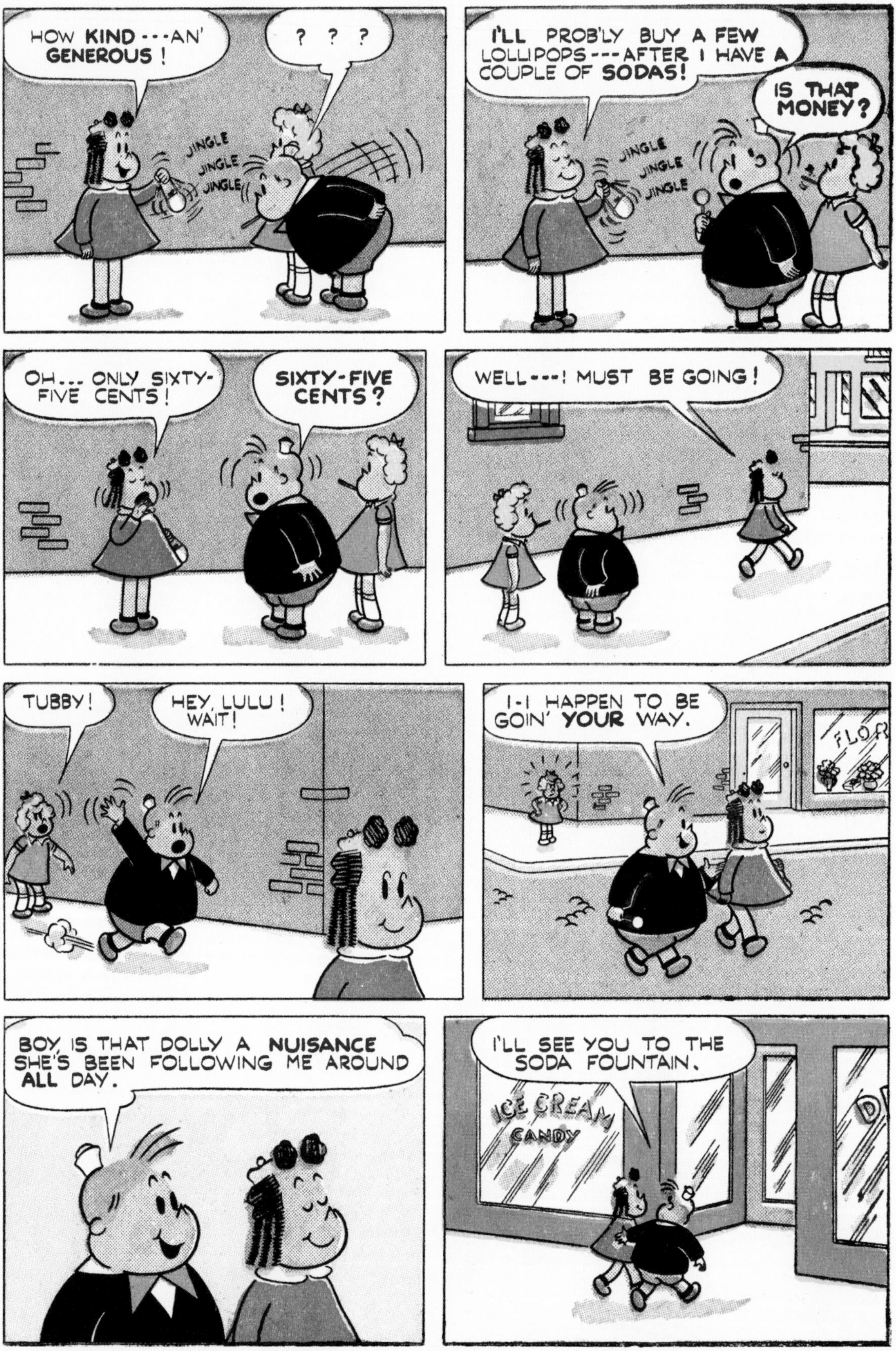
HOW KIND---AN' GENEROUS!
? ? ?
JINGLE JINGLE JINGLE
I'LL PROB'LY BUY A FEW LOLLIPOPS---AFTER I HAVE A COUPLE OF SODAS!
JINGLE JINGLE JINGLE
IS THAT MONEY?
OH... ONLY SIXTY-FIVE CENTS!
SIXTY-FIVE CENTS?
WELL---I MUST BE GOING!
TUBBY!
HEY, LULU! WAIT!
I-I HAPPEN TO BE GOIN' YOUR WAY.
BOY, IS THAT DOLLY A NUISANCE SHE'S BEEN FOLLOWING ME AROUND ALL DAY.
I'LL SEE YOU TO THE SODA FOUNTAIN.
ICE CREAM
CANDY

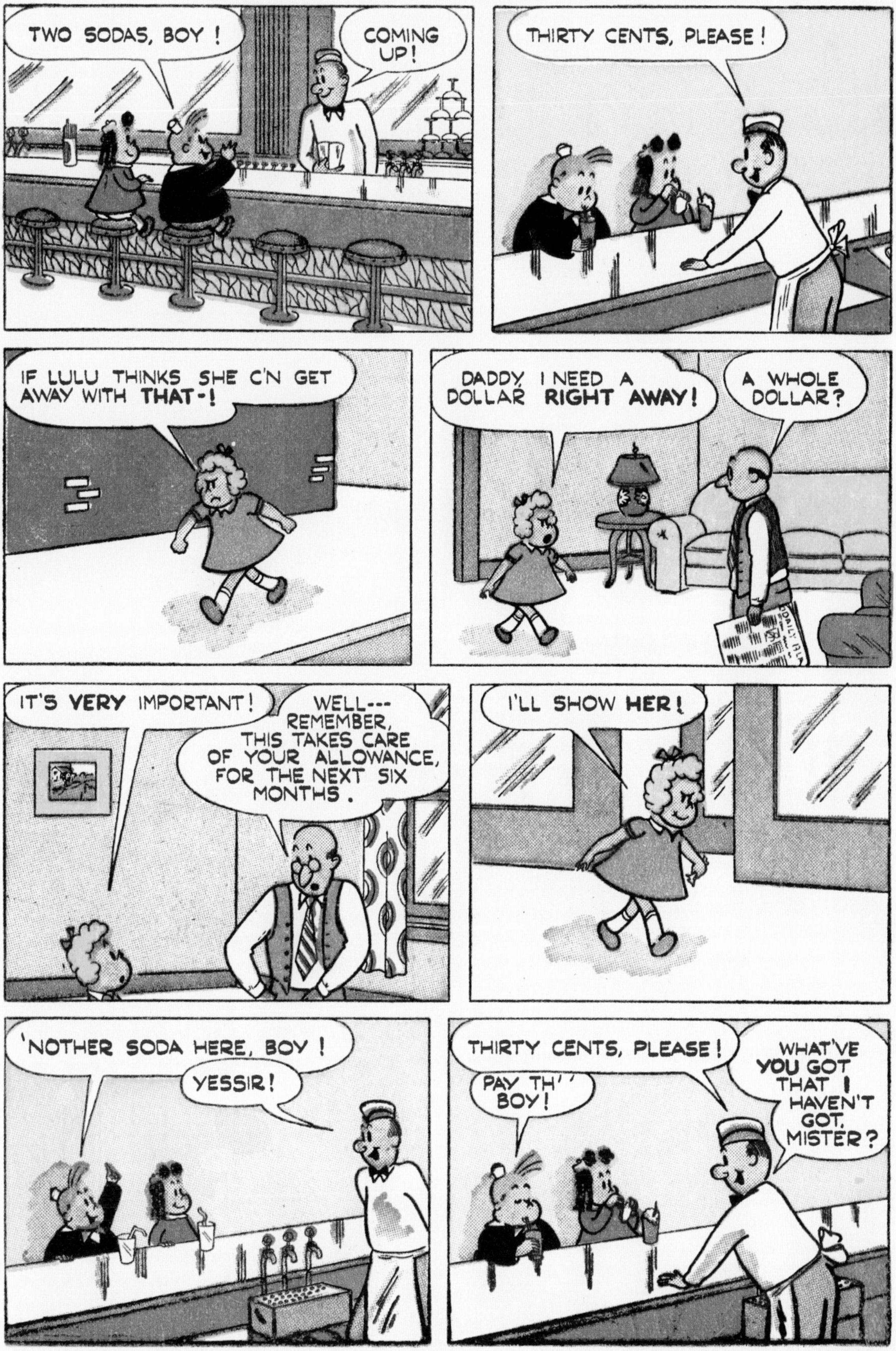
TWO SODAS, BOY!
COMING UP!
THIRTY CENTS, PLEASE!
IF LULU THINKS SHE C'N GET AWAY WITH THAT-!
DADDY, I NEED A DOLLAR RIGHT AWAY!
A WHOLE DOLLAR?
IT'S VERY IMPORTANT!
WELL--- REMEMBER, THIS TAKES CARE OF YOUR ALLOWANCE, FOR THE NEXT SIX MONTHS.
I'LL SHOW HER!
'NOTHER SODA HERE, BOY!
YESSIR!
THIRTY CENTS, PLEASE!
PAY TH' BOY!
WHAT'VE YOU GOT THAT I HAVEN'T GOT, MISTER?

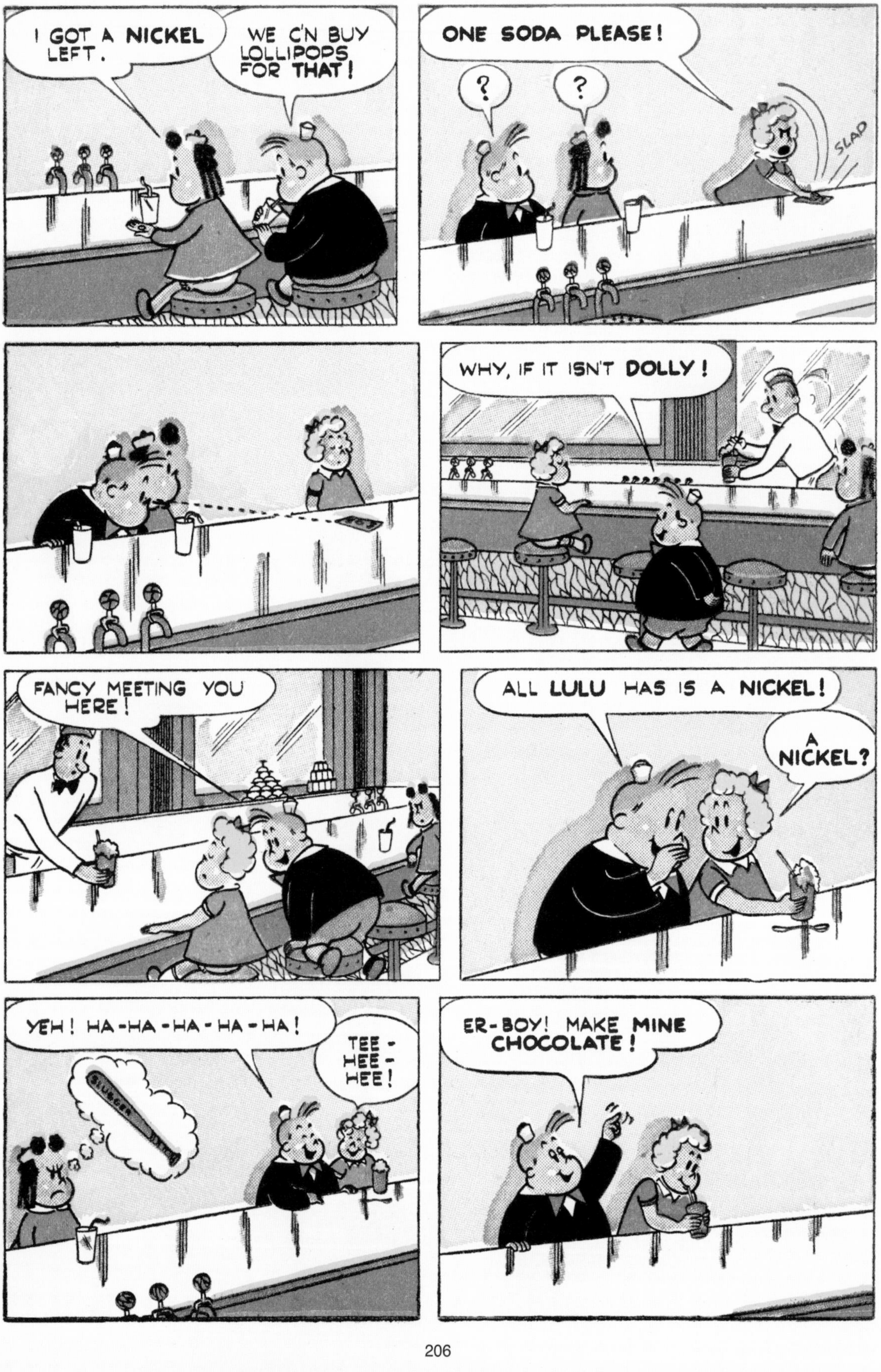
I GOT A NICKEL LEFT.
WE C'N BUY LOLLIPOPS FOR THAT!
ONE SODA PLEASE!
?
?
SLAP
WHY, IF IT ISN'T DOLLY!
FANCY MEETING YOU HERE!
ALL LULU HAS IS A NICKEL!
A NICKEL?
YEH! HA-HA-HA-HA-HA!
TEE-HEE-HEE!
SLUGGER
ER-BOY! MAKE MINE CHOCOLATE!

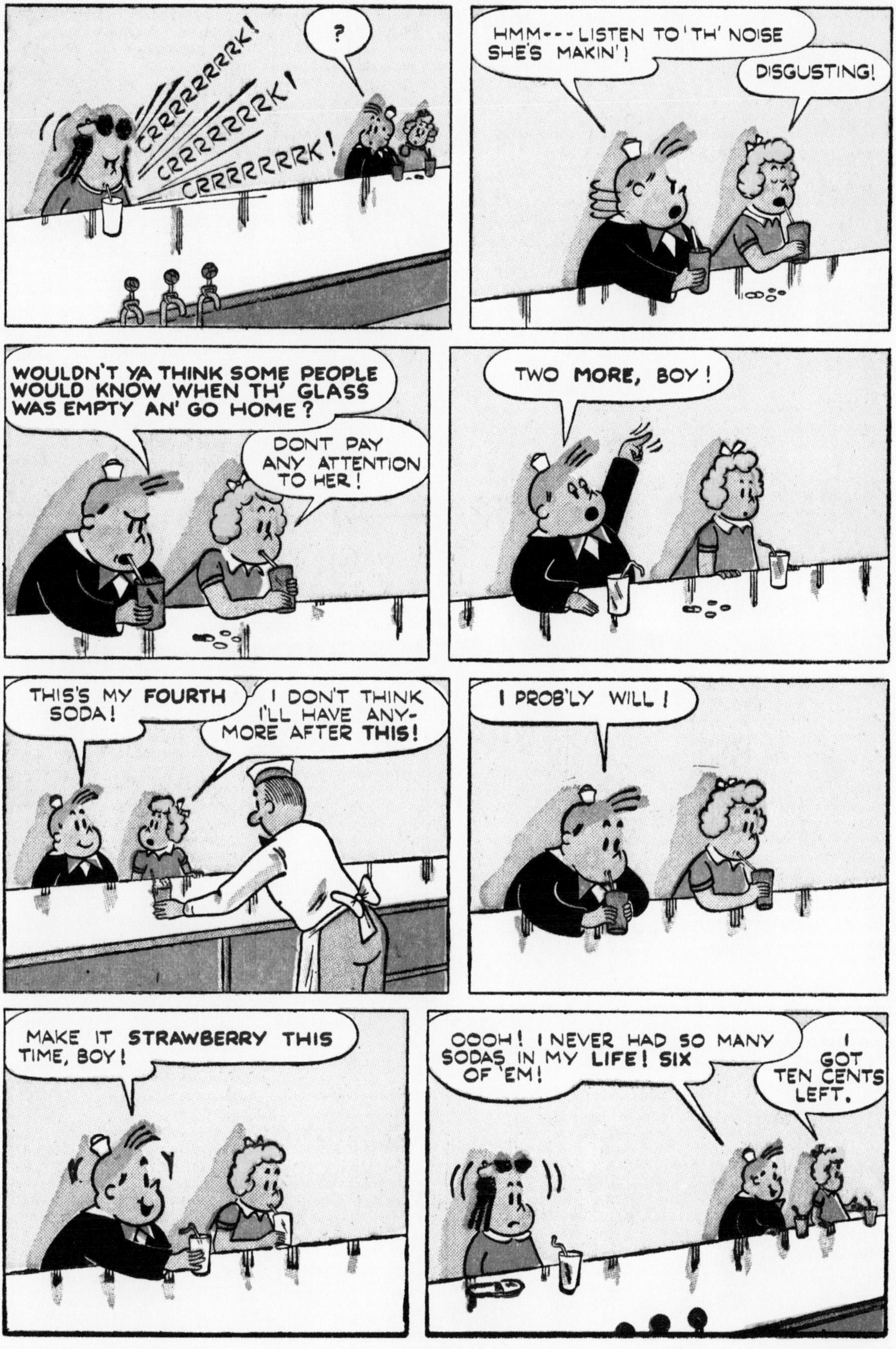
CRRRRRRRK!
CRRRRRRRK!
CRRRRRRRK!
?
HMM--- LISTEN TO 'TH' NOISE SHE'S MAKIN'!
DISGUSTING!
WOULDN'T YA THINK SOME PEOPLE WOULD KNOW WHEN TH' GLASS WAS EMPTY AN' GO HOME?
DONT PAY ANY ATTENTION TO HER!
TWO MORE, BOY!
THIS'S MY FOURTH SODA!
I DON'T THINK I'LL HAVE ANY-MORE AFTER THIS!
I PROB'LY WILL!
MAKE IT STRAWBERRY THIS TIME, BOY!
OOOH! I NEVER HAD SO MANY SODAS IN MY LIFE! SIX OF 'EM!
I GOT TEN CENTS LEFT.

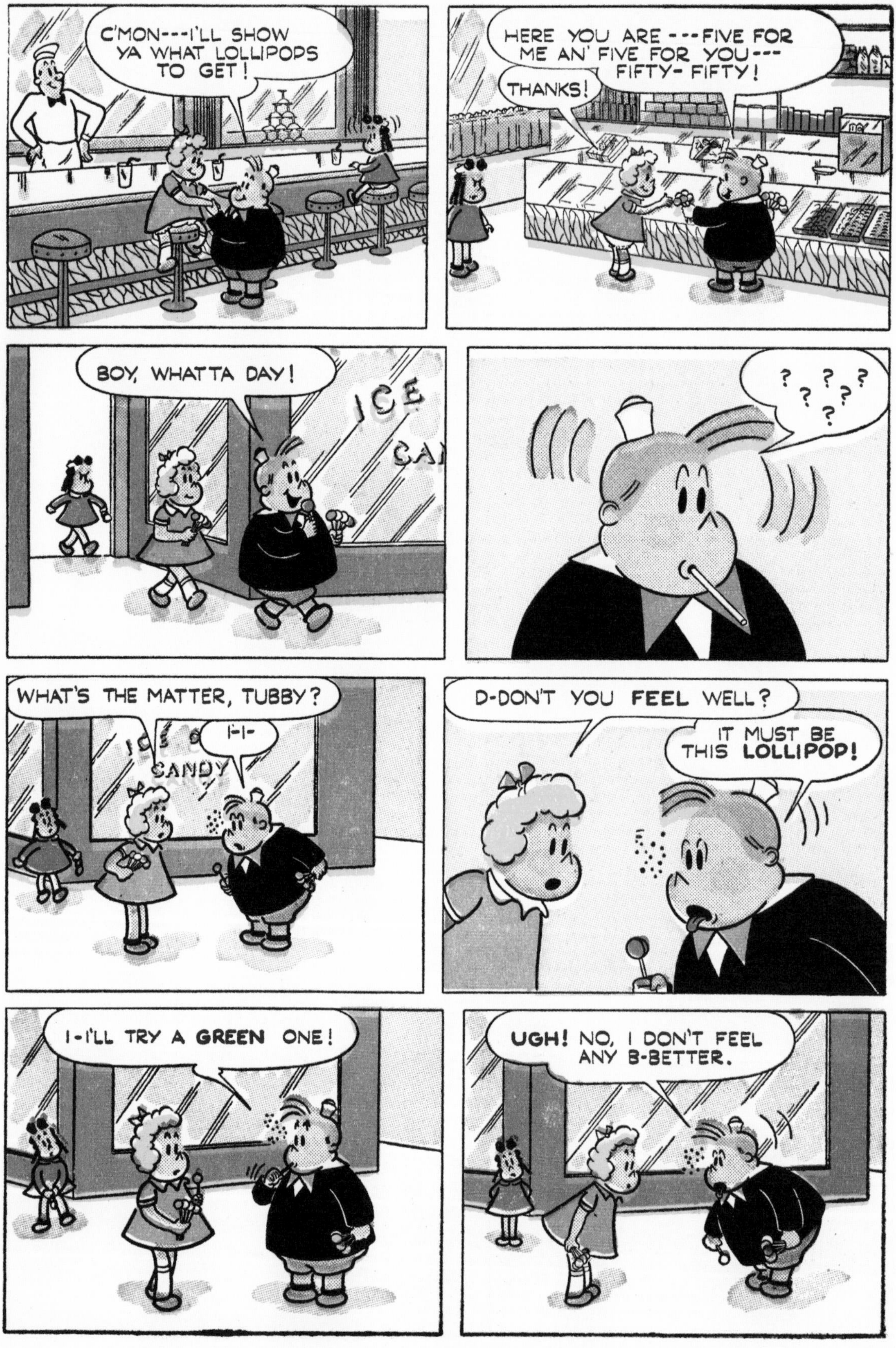
C'MON---I'LL SHOW YA WHAT LOLLIPOPS TO GET!
HERE YOU ARE---FIVE FOR ME AN' FIVE FOR YOU---FIFTY-FIFTY!
THANKS!
BOY, WHATTA DAY!
ICE
? ? ? ? ? ?
WHAT'S THE MATTER, TUBBY?
I-I-
CANDY
D-DON'T YOU FEEL WELL?
IT MUST BE THIS LOLLIPOP!
I-I'LL TRY A GREEN ONE!
UGH! NO, I DON'T FEEL ANY B-BETTER.

IT WAS THOSE SODAS!
I-I FEEL TERRIBLE! THINK I'M DYIN!!
SHE SAVED HIS LIFE
LITTLE ANGEL!
TUBBY!!
I'LL TAKE CARE OF YOU--- I'LL-
GET AWAY F'M ME!
WHY, I-
IT'S ALL YOUR FAULT! YOU STARTED BUYIN' ME THEM SODAS!

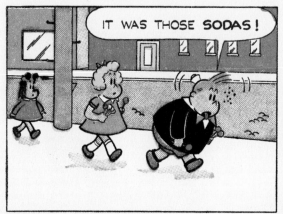

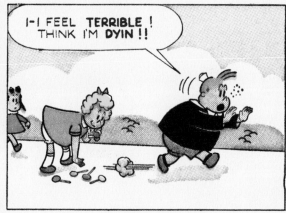

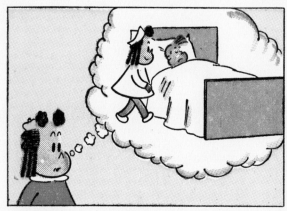

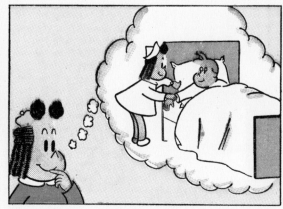

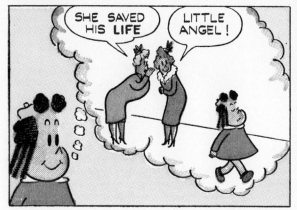

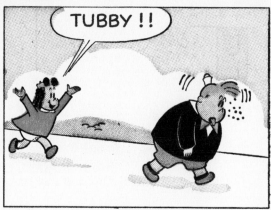

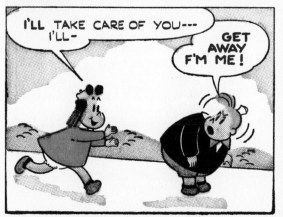

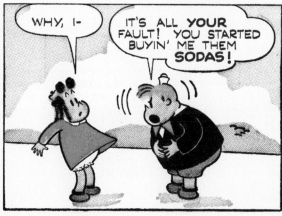

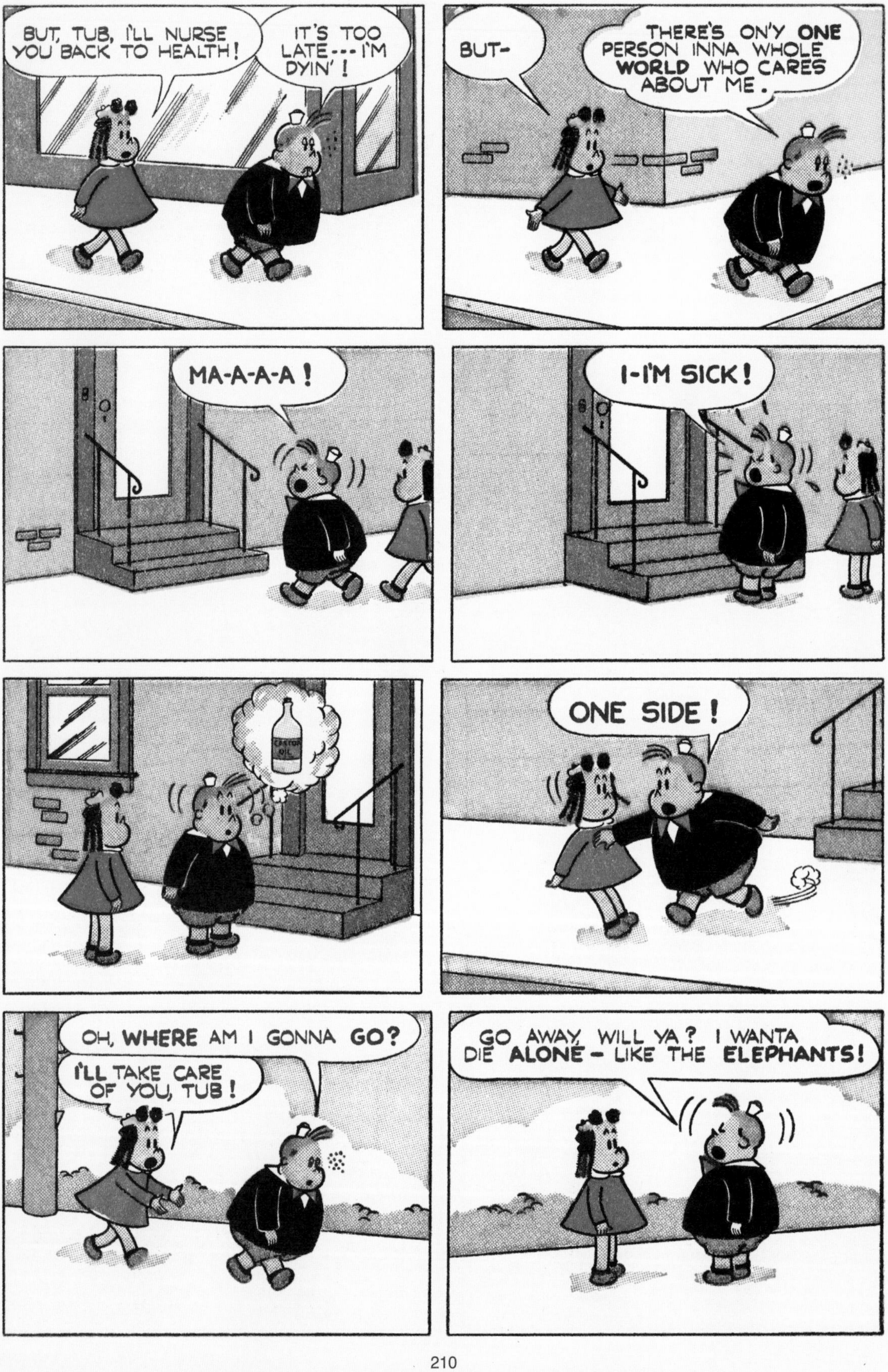

BUT, TUB, I'LL NURSE YOU BACK TO HEALTH!
IT'S TOO LATE--- I'M DYIN'!
BUT-
THERE'S ON'Y **ONE** PERSON INNA WHOLE **WORLD** WHO CARES ABOUT ME.
MA-A-A-A!
I-I'M SICK!
CASTOR OIL
ONE SIDE!
OH, **WHERE** AM I GONNA **GO**?
I'LL TAKE CARE OF YOU, TUB!
GO AWAY, WILL YA? I WANTA DIE **ALONE** – LIKE THE **ELEPHANTS**!

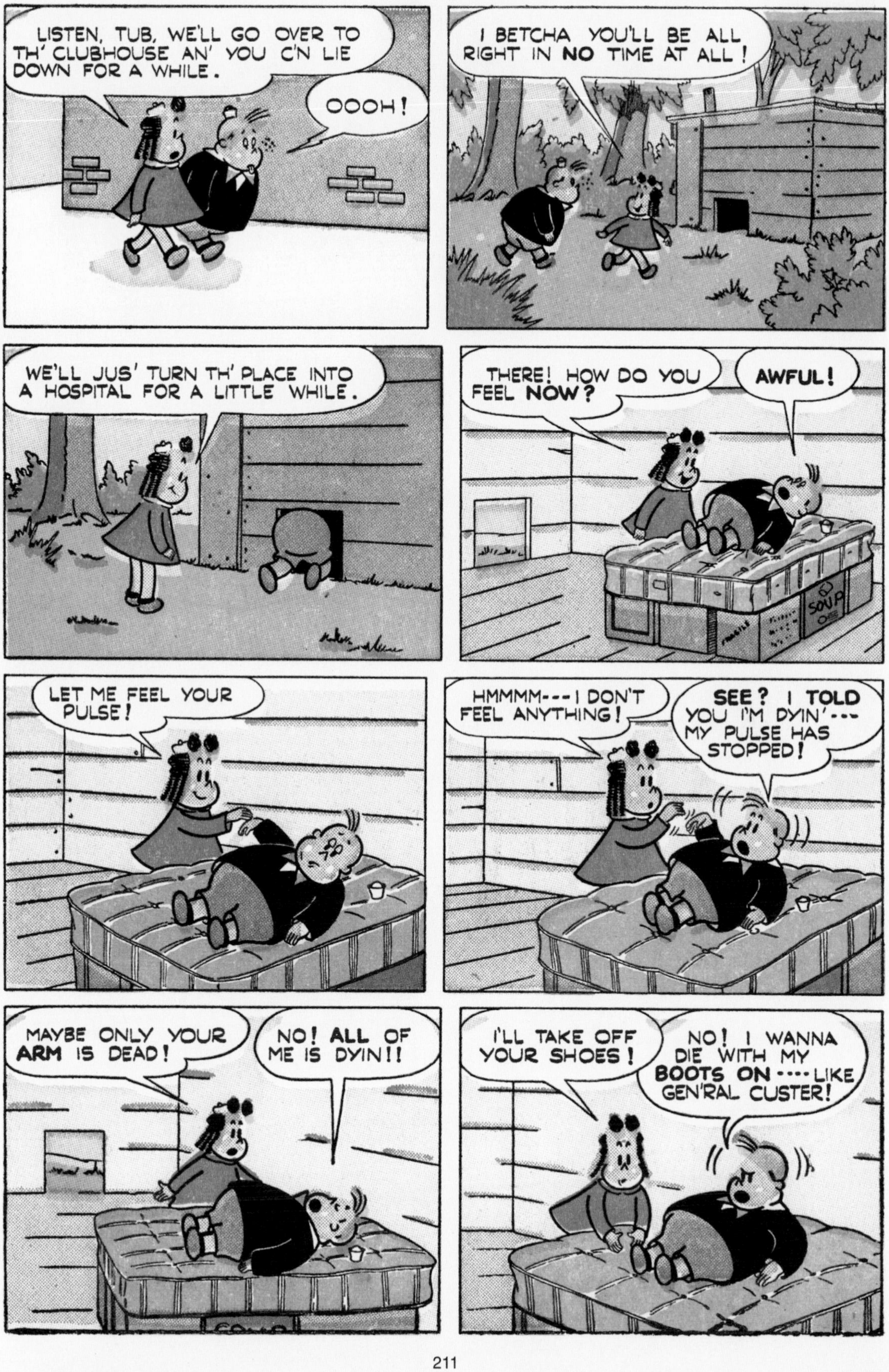
LISTEN, TUB, WE'LL GO OVER TO TH' CLUBHOUSE AN' YOU C'N LIE DOWN FOR A WHILE.
OOOH!
I BETCHA YOU'LL BE ALL RIGHT IN **NO** TIME AT ALL!
WE'LL JUS' TURN TH' PLACE INTO A HOSPITAL FOR A LITTLE WHILE.
THERE! HOW DO YOU FEEL **NOW?**
AWFUL!
SOUP
LET ME FEEL YOUR PULSE!
HMMMM---I DON'T FEEL ANYTHING!
SEE? I **TOLD** YOU I'M DYIN'--- MY PULSE HAS STOPPED!
MAYBE ONLY YOUR **ARM** IS DEAD!
NO! **ALL** OF ME IS DYIN!!
I'LL TAKE OFF YOUR SHOES!
NO! I WANNA DIE WITH MY **BOOTS ON**----LIKE GEN'RAL CUSTER!

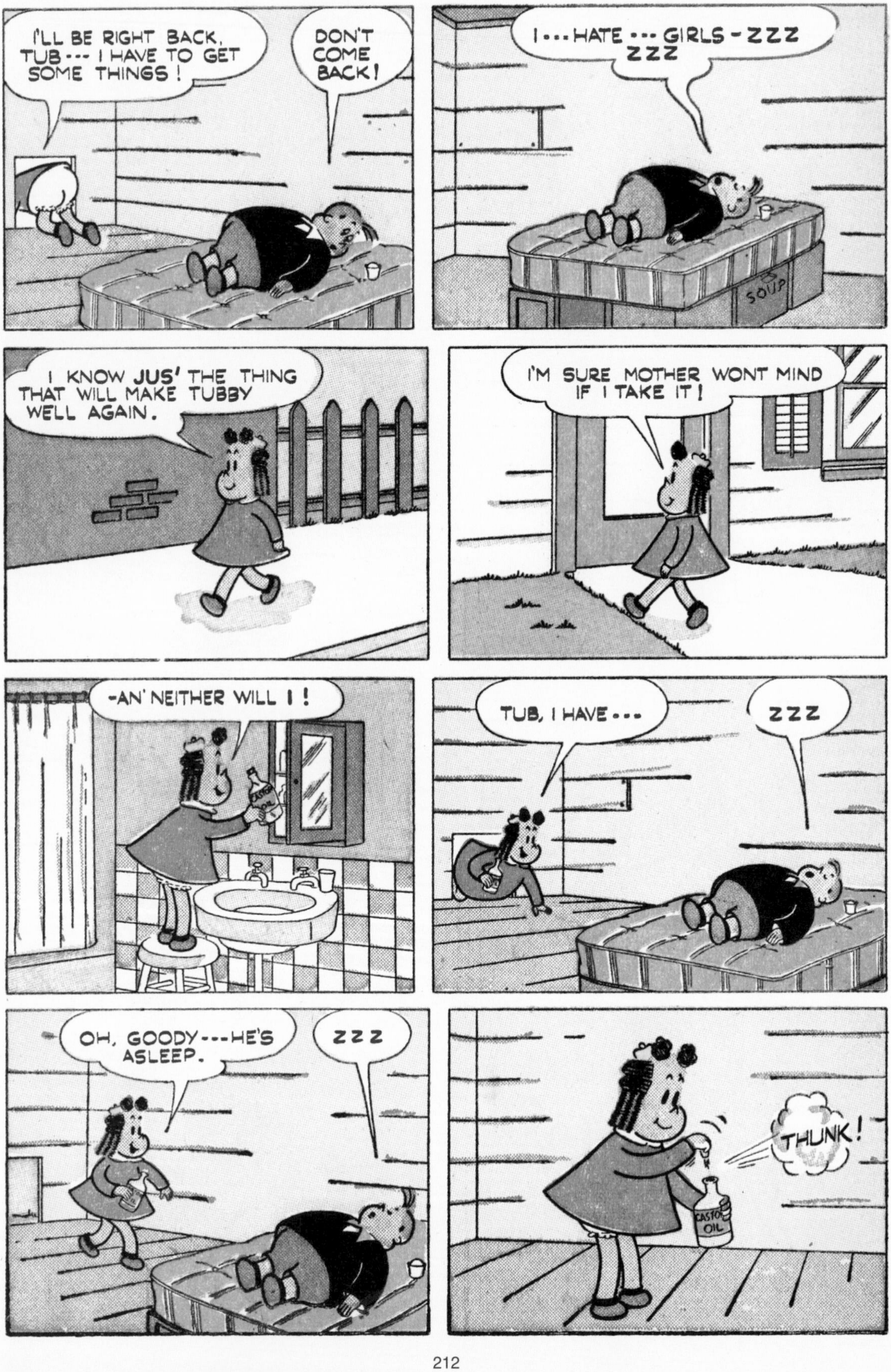
I'LL BE RIGHT BACK, TUB--- I HAVE TO GET SOME THINGS!
DON'T COME BACK!
I...HATE...GIRLS-ZZZ ZZZ
SOUP
I KNOW JUS' THE THING THAT WILL MAKE TUBBY WELL AGAIN.
I'M SURE MOTHER WONT MIND IF I TAKE IT!
-AN' NEITHER WILL I!
TUB, I HAVE...
ZZZ
OH, GOODY---HE'S ASLEEP.
ZZZ
THUNK!
CASTOR OIL

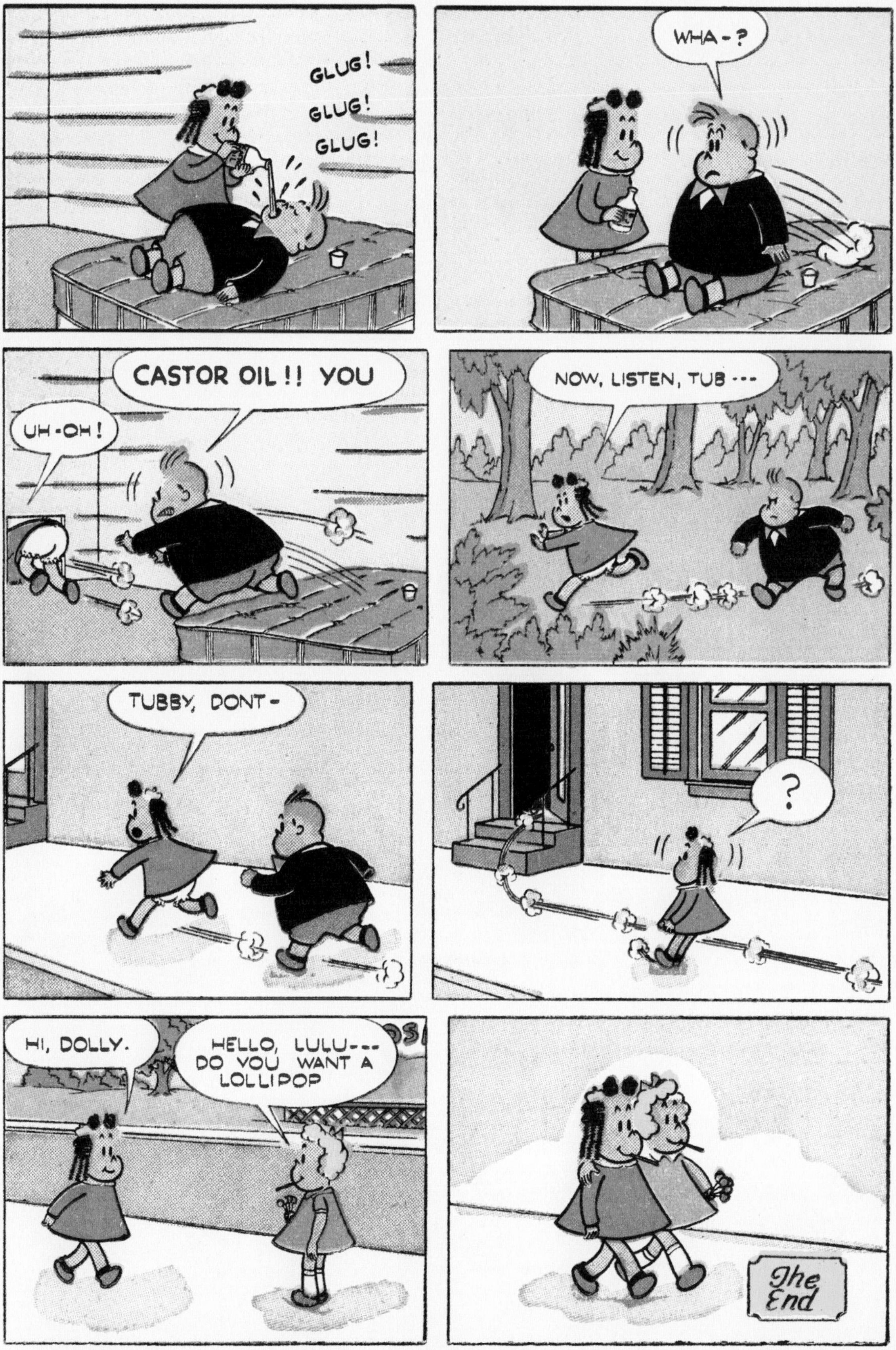
GLUG!
GLUG!
GLUG!
WHA-?
CASTOR OIL!! YOU
UH-OH!
NOW, LISTEN, TUB---
TUBBY, DONT-
?
HI, DOLLY.
HELLO, LULU---
DO YOU WANT A
LOLLIPOP
The End

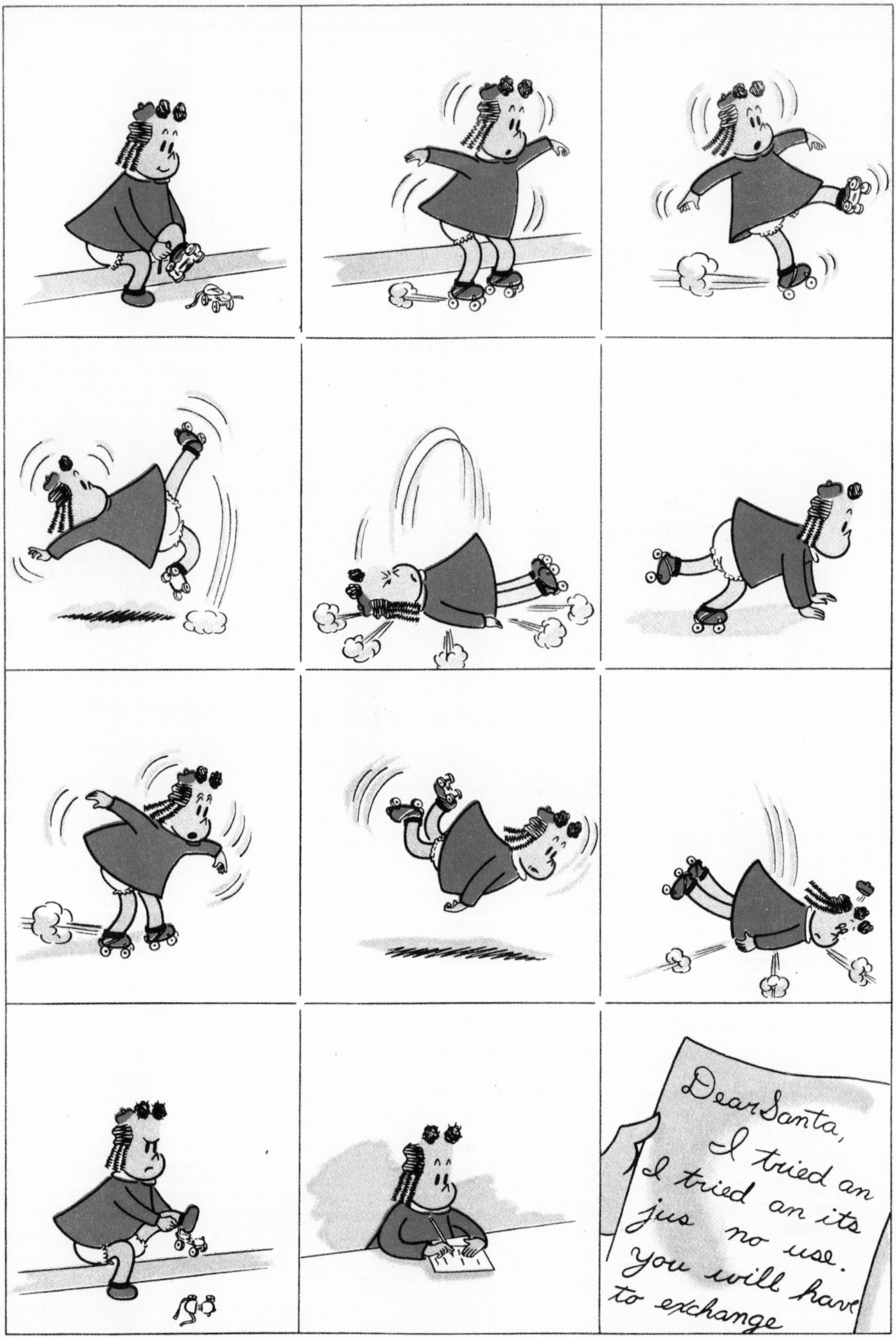
Dear Santa,
I tried an
I tried an its
jus no use.
you will have
to exchange

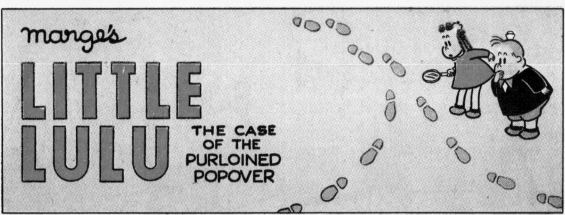

marge's

LITTLE LULU

THE CASE OF THE PURLOINED POPOVER

ZZZZ ZZZ ZZ

LULU!

ZZZZ

I'M COMING, MOTHER.

WHAT IS IT, MOTHER?

COME HERE!

LOOK!

WHAT'S THE MATTER?

DON'T PRETEND YOU DON'T KNOW! THERE WERE **SIX** POPOVERS IN THAT PACKAGE WHEN I BROUGHT IT HOME!

HMM---THERE'S ONLY **THREE** NOW!

MOTHER! YOU DON'T THINK I --

WHO ELSE? DO YOU THINK I TOOK THEM? OR YOUR **FATHER**?

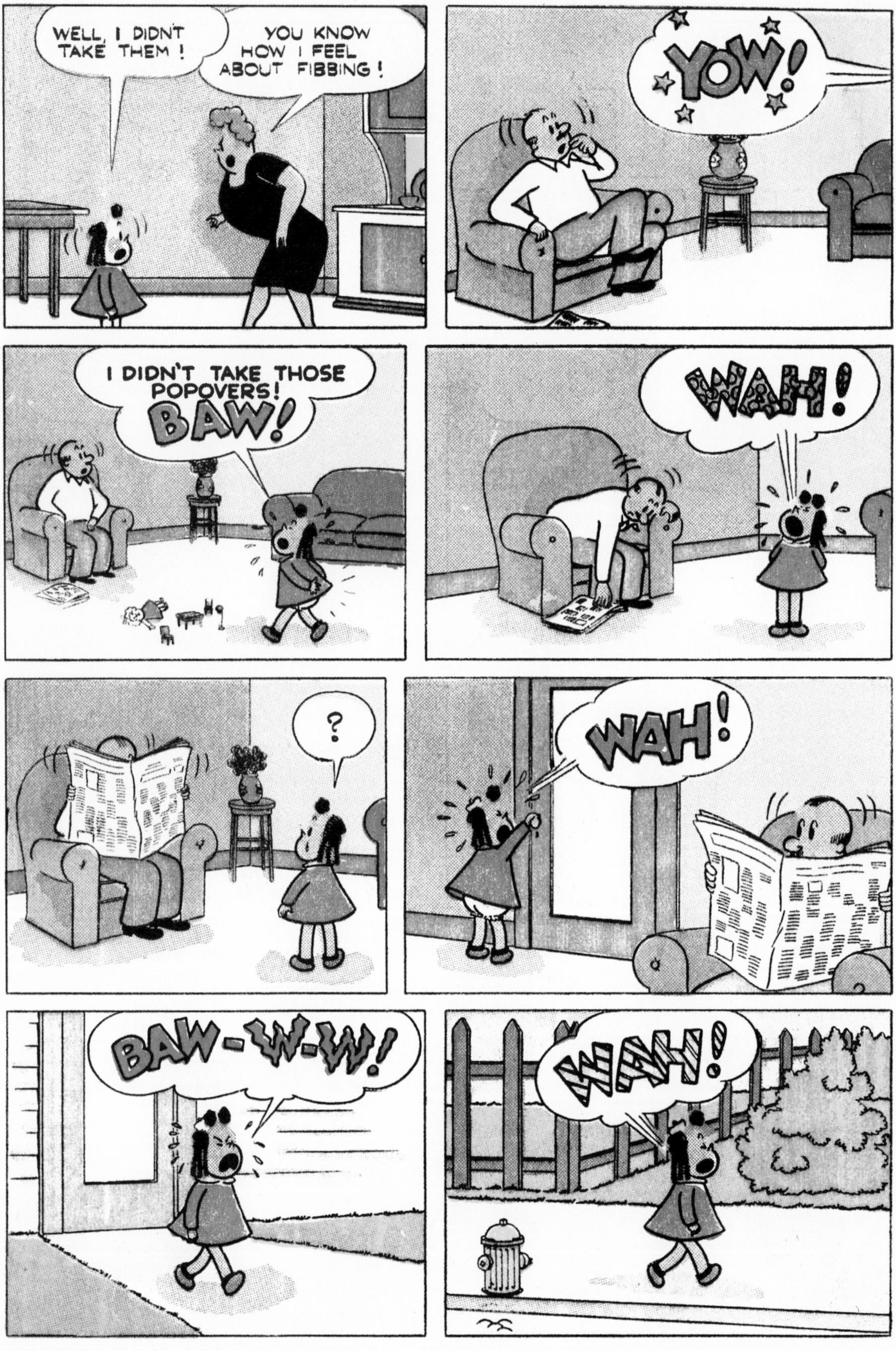
WELL, I DIDN'T TAKE THEM!
YOU KNOW HOW I FEEL ABOUT FIBBING!
YOW!
I DIDN'T TAKE THOSE POPOVERS! BAW!
WAH!
?
WAH!
BAW-W-W!
WAH!

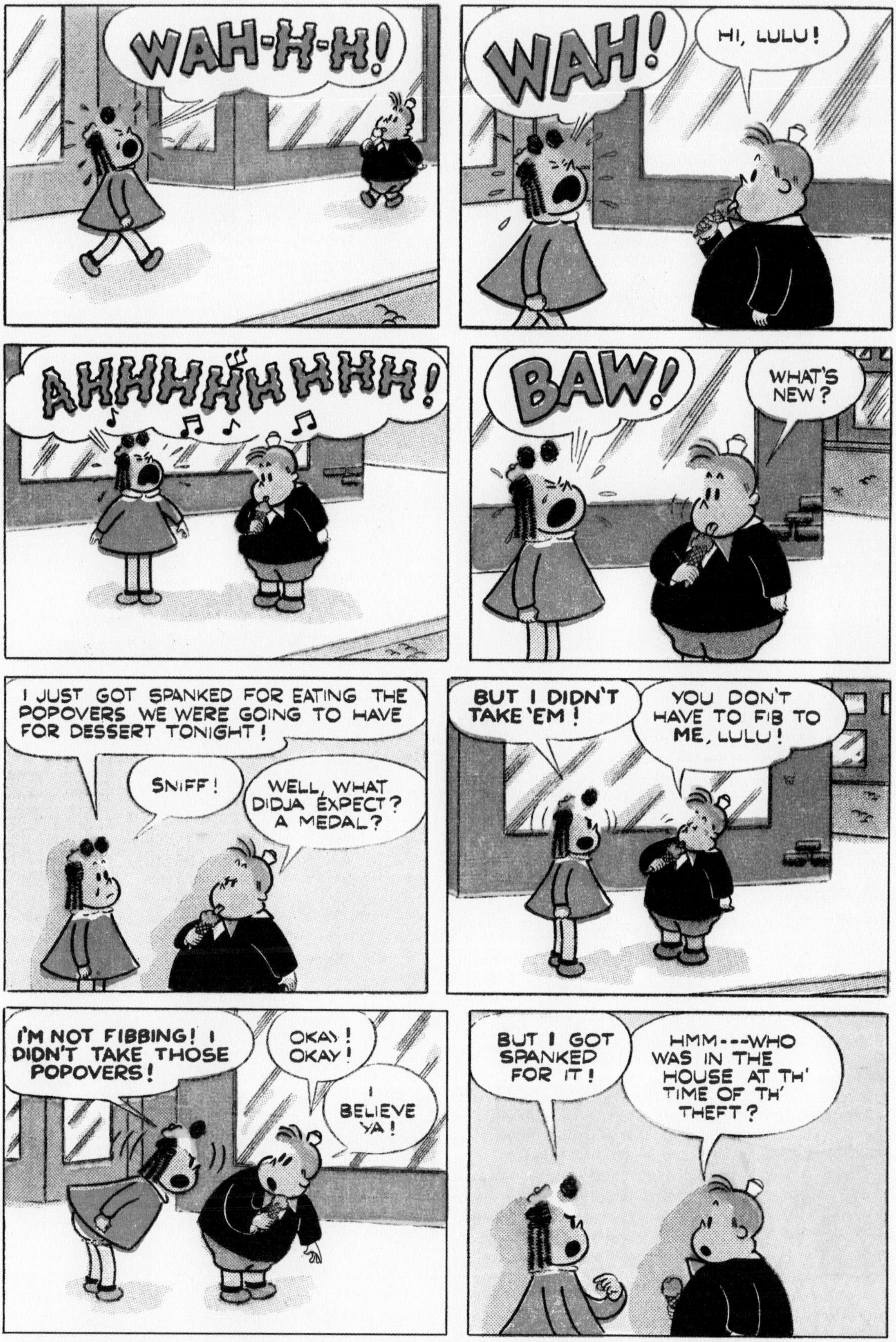
WAH-H-H!
WAH!
HI, LULU!
AHHHHHHHH!
BAW!
WHAT'S NEW?
I JUST GOT SPANKED FOR EATING THE POPOVERS WE WERE GOING TO HAVE FOR DESSERT TONIGHT!
SNIFF!
WELL, WHAT DIDJA EXPECT? A MEDAL?
BUT I DIDN'T TAKE 'EM!
YOU DON'T HAVE TO FIB TO ME, LULU!
I'M NOT FIBBING! I DIDN'T TAKE THOSE POPOVERS!
OKAY! OKAY!
I BELIEVE YA!
BUT I GOT SPANKED FOR IT!
HMM---WHO WAS IN THE HOUSE AT TH' TIME OF TH' THEFT?

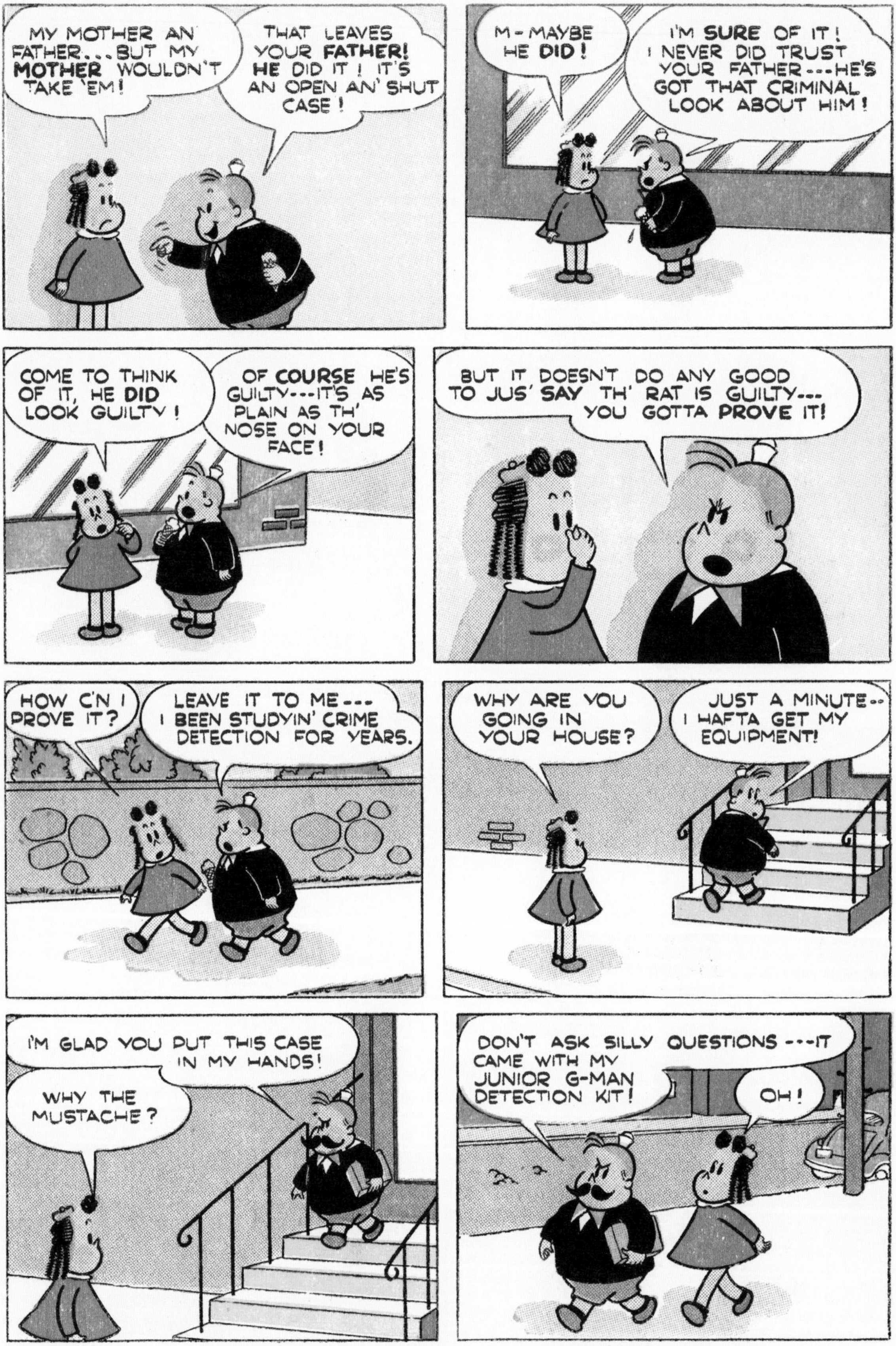

MY MOTHER AN' FATHER... BUT MY MOTHER WOULDN'T TAKE 'EM!
THAT LEAVES YOUR FATHER! HE DID IT! IT'S AN OPEN AN' SHUT CASE!
M-MAYBE HE DID!
I'M SURE OF IT! I NEVER DID TRUST YOUR FATHER---HE'S GOT THAT CRIMINAL LOOK ABOUT HIM!
COME TO THINK OF IT, HE DID LOOK GUILTY!
OF COURSE HE'S GUILTY---IT'S AS PLAIN AS TH' NOSE ON YOUR FACE!
BUT IT DOESN'T DO ANY GOOD TO JUS' SAY TH' RAT IS GUILTY--- YOU GOTTA PROVE IT!
HOW C'N I PROVE IT?
LEAVE IT TO ME--- I BEEN STUDYIN' CRIME DETECTION FOR YEARS.
WHY ARE YOU GOING IN YOUR HOUSE?
JUST A MINUTE-- I HAFTA GET MY EQUIPMENT!
I'M GLAD YOU PUT THIS CASE IN MY HANDS!
WHY THE MUSTACHE?
DON'T ASK SILLY QUESTIONS ---IT CAME WITH MY JUNIOR G-MAN DETECTION KIT!
OH!

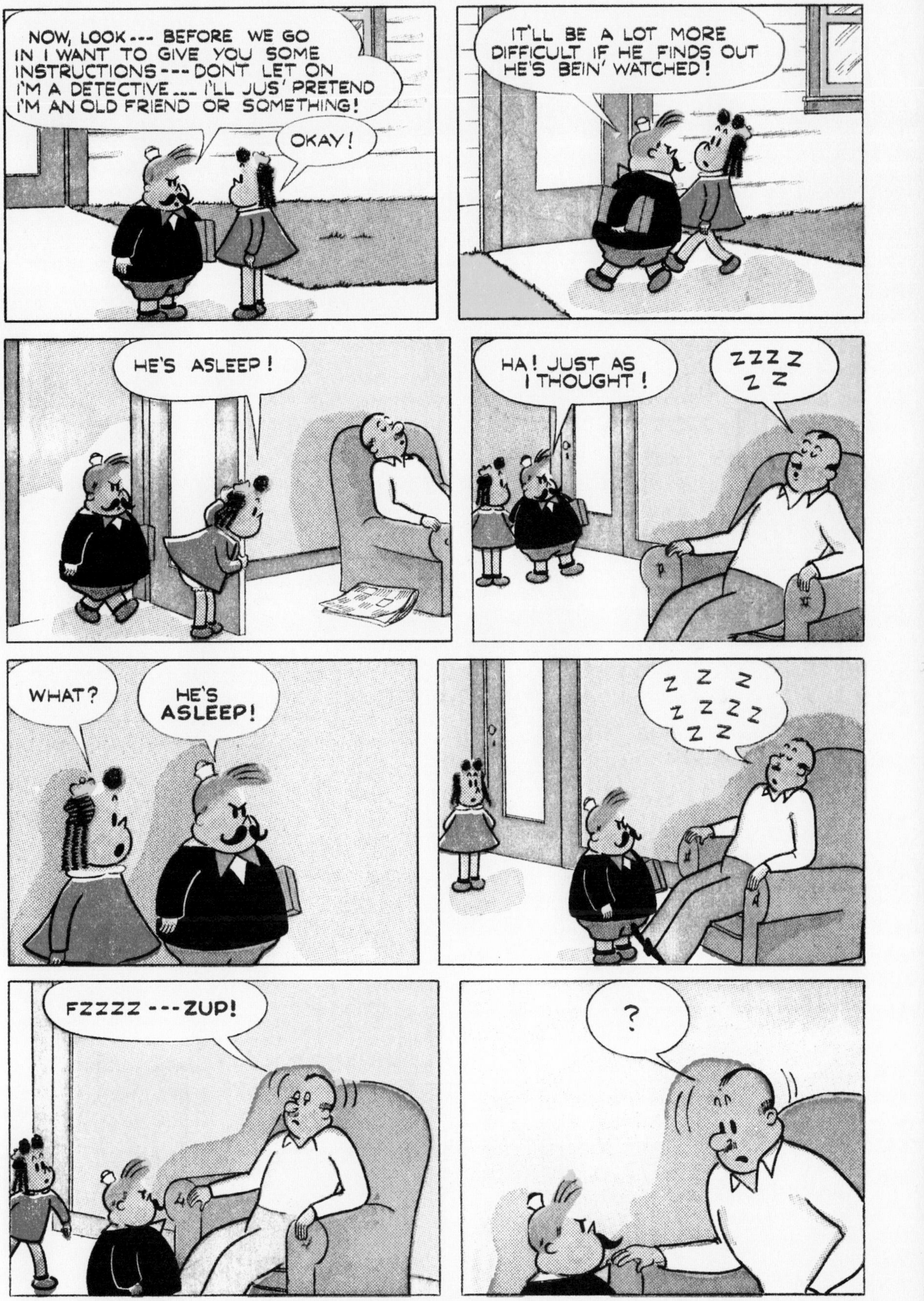
NOW, LOOK--- BEFORE WE GO IN I WANT TO GIVE YOU SOME INSTRUCTIONS---DONT LET ON I'M A DETECTIVE... I'LL JUS' PRETEND I'M AN OLD FRIEND OR SOMETHING!
OKAY!
IT'LL BE A LOT MORE DIFFICULT IF HE FINDS OUT HE'S BEIN' WATCHED!
HE'S ASLEEP!
HA! JUST AS I THOUGHT!
ZZZZ Z Z
WHAT?
HE'S ASLEEP!
Z Z Z Z Z Z Z Z Z
FZZZZ---ZUP!
?

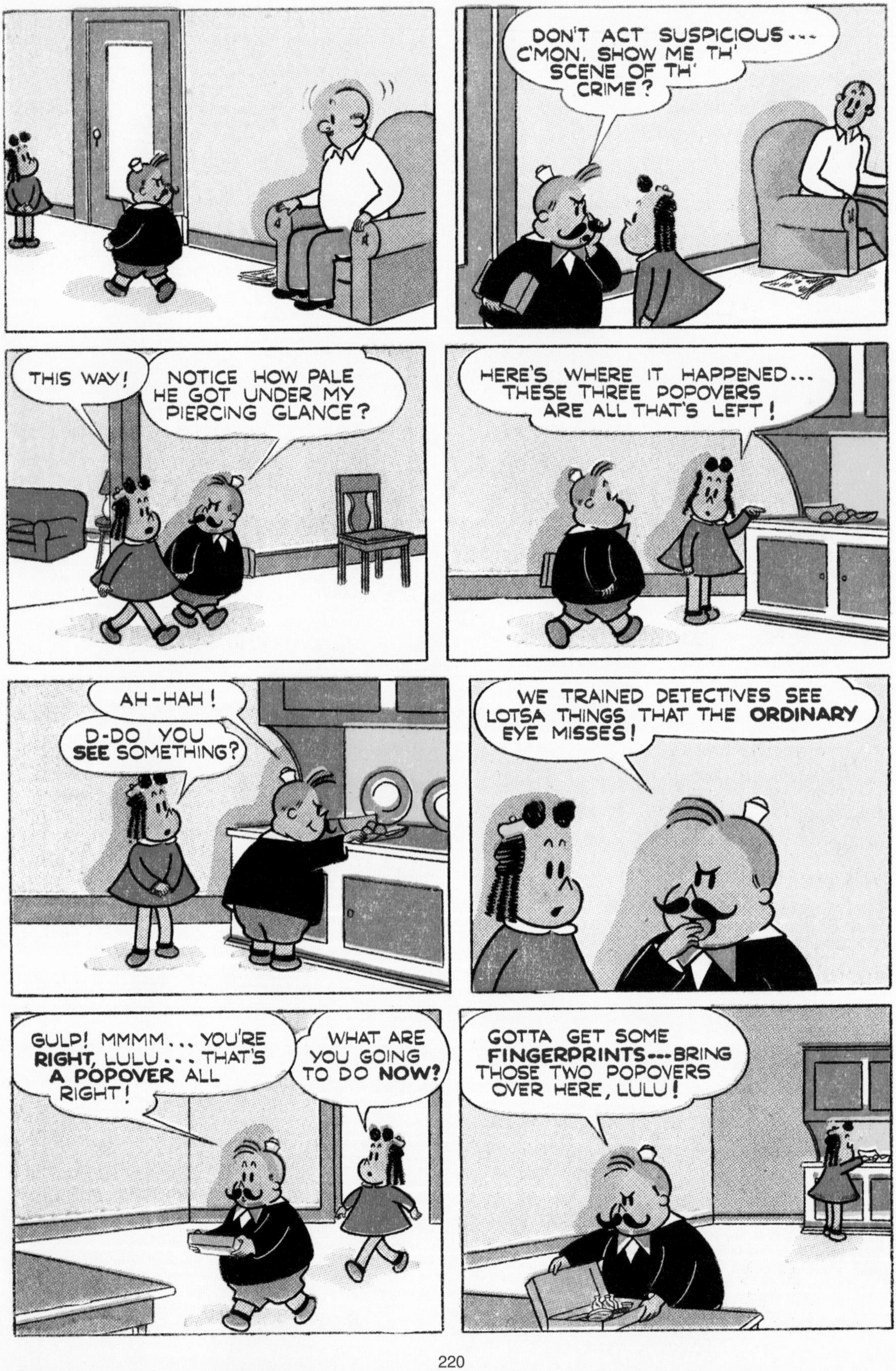

DON'T ACT SUSPICIOUS... C'MON, SHOW ME TH' SCENE OF TH' CRIME?
THIS WAY!
NOTICE HOW PALE HE GOT UNDER MY PIERCING GLANCE?
HERE'S WHERE IT HAPPENED... THESE THREE POPOVERS ARE ALL THAT'S LEFT!
AH-HAH!
D-DO YOU **SEE** SOMETHING?
WE TRAINED DETECTIVES SEE LOTSA THINGS THAT THE **ORDINARY** EYE MISSES!
GULP! MMMM... YOU'RE **RIGHT**, LULU... THAT'S **A POPOVER** ALL RIGHT!
WHAT ARE YOU GOING TO DO **NOW?**
GOTTA GET SOME **FINGERPRINTS**---BRING THOSE TWO POPOVERS OVER HERE, LULU!

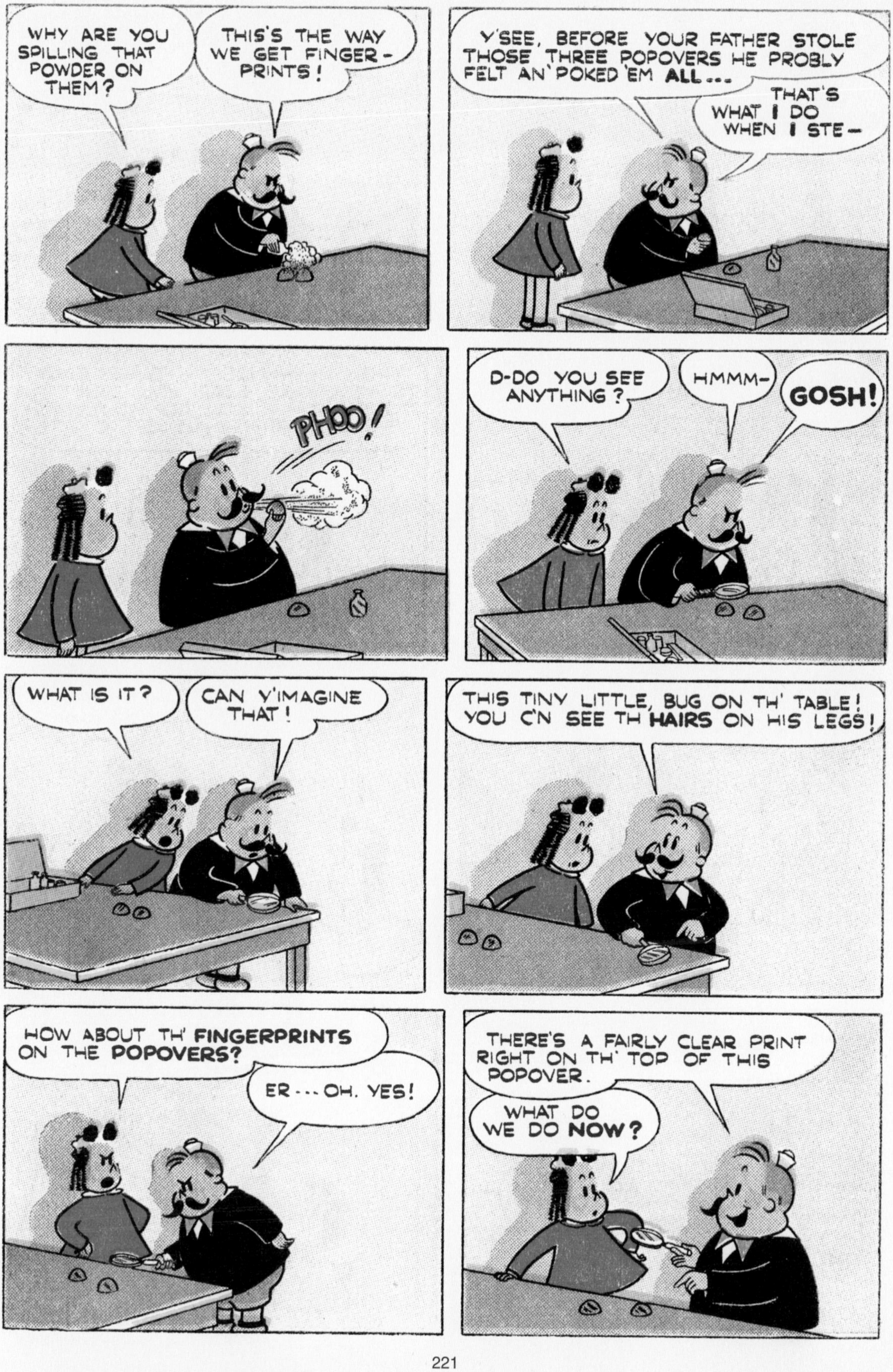
WHY ARE YOU SPILLING THAT POWDER ON THEM?
THIS'S THE WAY WE GET FINGER-PRINTS!
Y'SEE, BEFORE YOUR FATHER STOLE THOSE THREE POPOVERS HE PROBLY FELT AN' POKED 'EM **ALL**...
THAT'S WHAT **I** DO WHEN **I** STE—
PHOO!
D-DO YOU SEE ANYTHING?
HMMM—
GOSH!
WHAT IS IT?
CAN Y'IMAGINE THAT!
THIS TINY LITTLE, BUG ON TH' TABLE! YOU C'N SEE TH **HAIRS** ON HIS LEGS!
HOW ABOUT TH' **FINGERPRINTS** ON THE **POPOVERS?**
ER...OH. YES!
THERE'S A FAIRLY CLEAR PRINT RIGHT ON TH' TOP OF THIS POPOVER.
WHAT DO WE DO **NOW?**

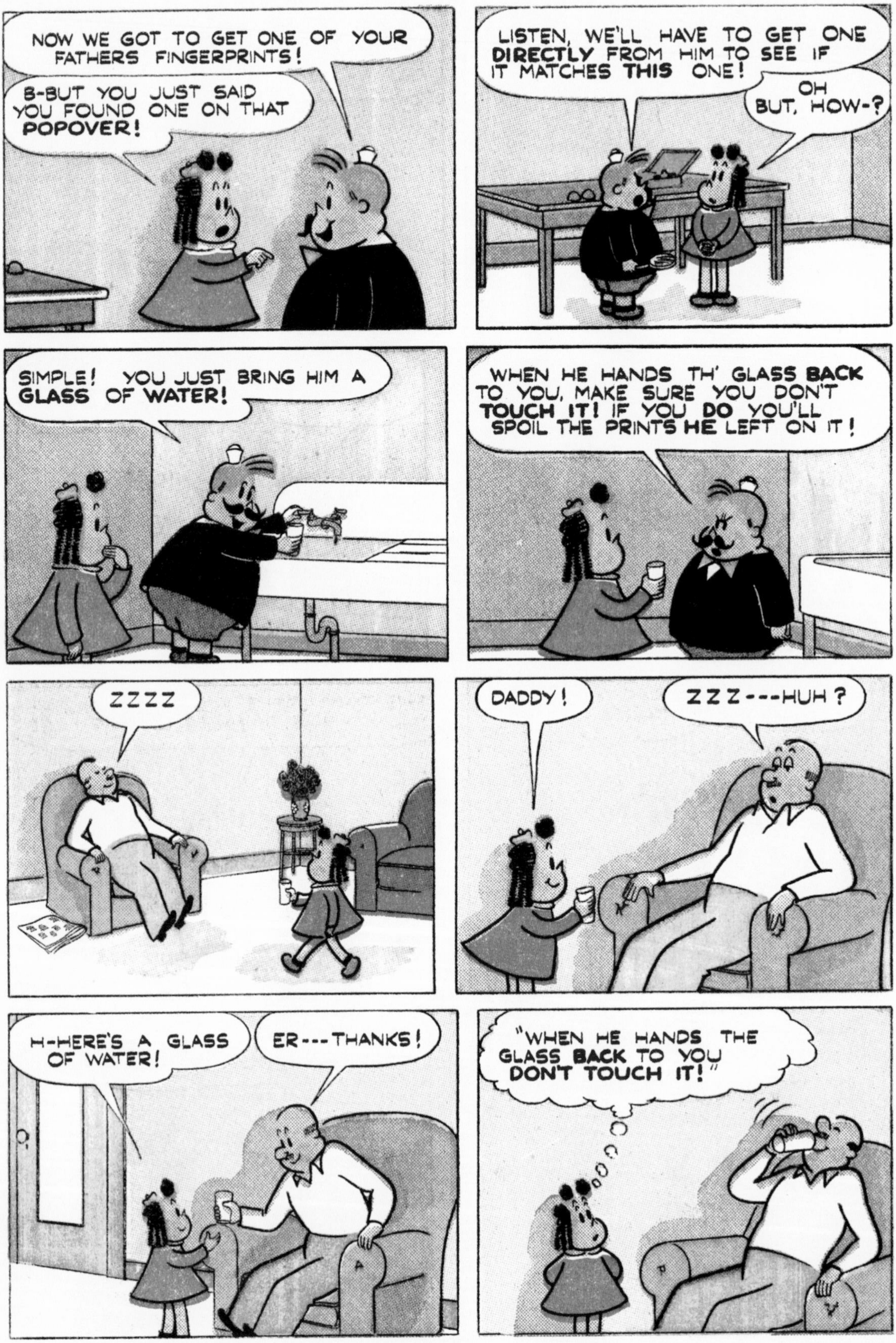
NOW WE GOT TO GET ONE OF YOUR FATHERS FINGERPRINTS!
B-BUT YOU JUST SAID YOU FOUND ONE ON THAT POPOVER!
LISTEN, WE'LL HAVE TO GET ONE DIRECTLY FROM HIM TO SEE IF IT MATCHES THIS ONE!
OH BUT, HOW-?
SIMPLE! YOU JUST BRING HIM A GLASS OF WATER!
WHEN HE HANDS TH' GLASS BACK TO YOU, MAKE SURE YOU DON'T TOUCH IT! IF YOU DO YOU'LL SPOIL THE PRINTS HE LEFT ON IT!
ZZZZ
DADDY!
ZZZ---HUH?
H-HERE'S A GLASS OF WATER!
ER---THANKS!
"WHEN HE HANDS THE GLASS BACK TO YOU DON'T TOUCH IT!"

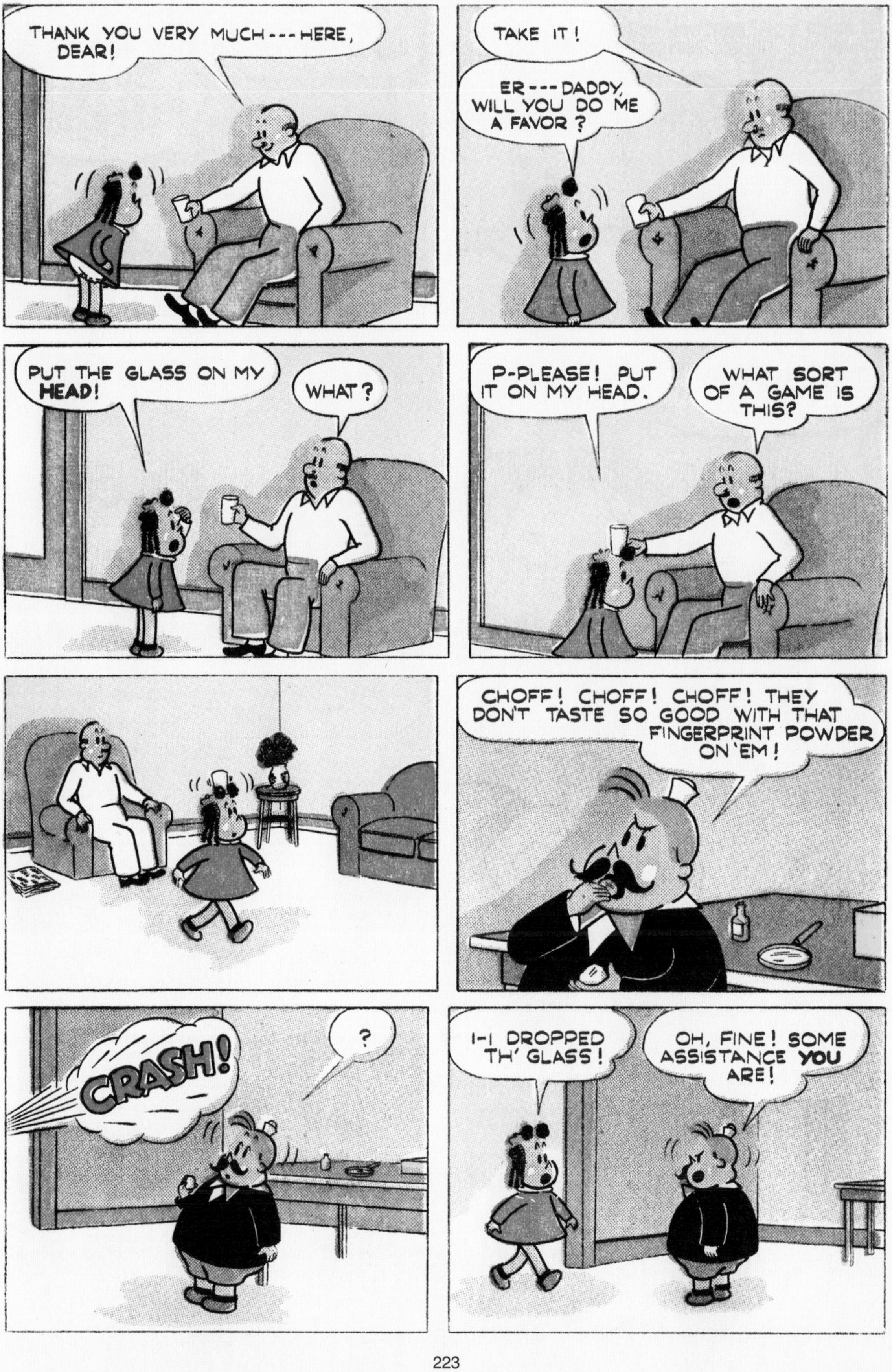
THANK YOU VERY MUCH---HERE, DEAR!
TAKE IT!
ER---DADDY, WILL YOU DO ME A FAVOR ?
PUT THE GLASS ON MY HEAD!
WHAT ?
P-PLEASE! PUT IT ON MY HEAD.
WHAT SORT OF A GAME IS THIS?
CHOFF! CHOFF! CHOFF! THEY DON'T TASTE SO GOOD WITH THAT FINGERPRINT POWDER ON 'EM!
CRASH!
?
I-I DROPPED TH' GLASS!
OH, FINE! SOME ASSISTANCE YOU ARE!

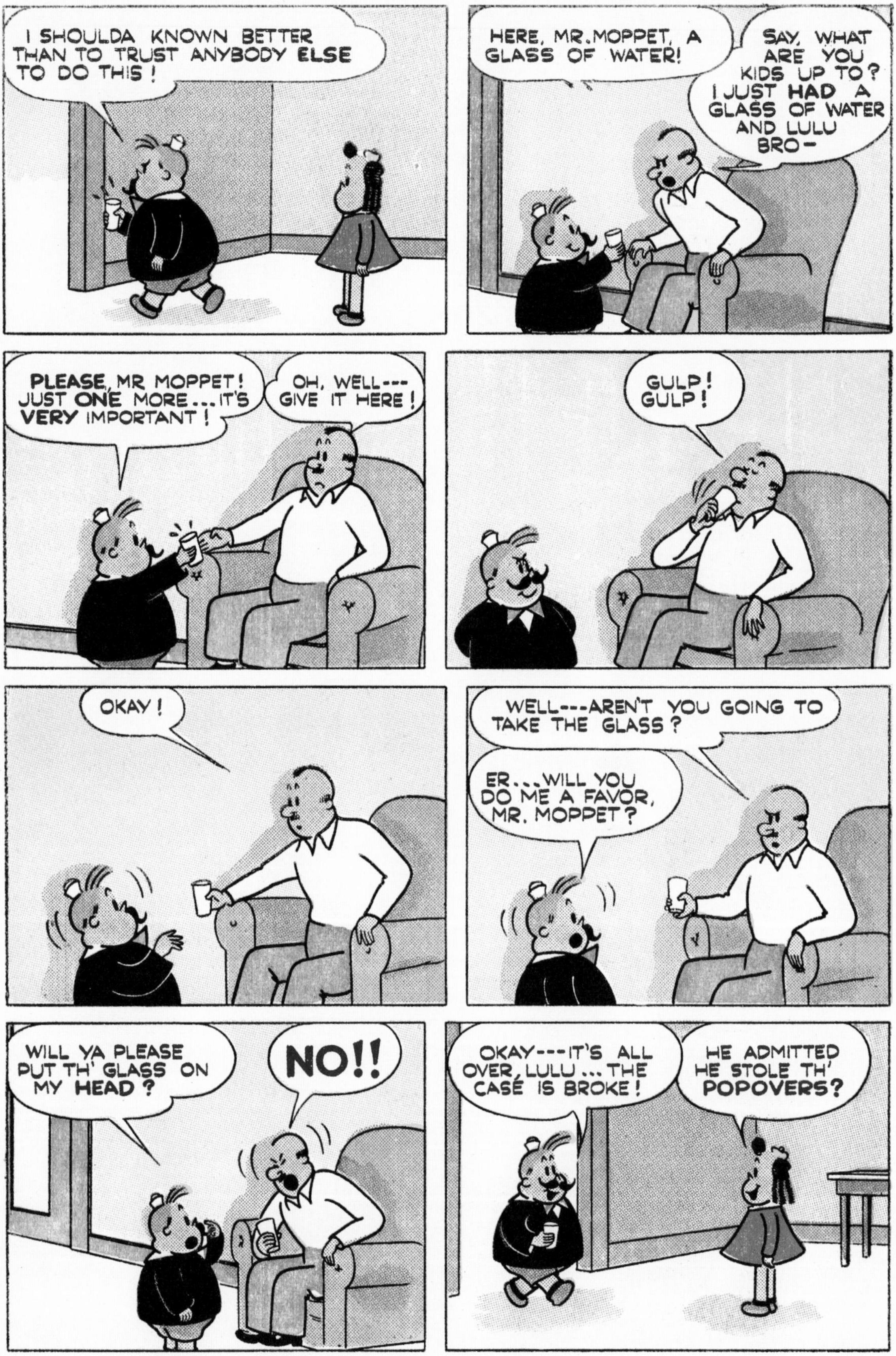
I SHOULDA KNOWN BETTER THAN TO TRUST ANYBODY **ELSE** TO DO THIS!
HERE, MR. MOPPET, A GLASS OF WATER!
SAY, WHAT ARE YOU KIDS UP TO? I JUST **HAD** A GLASS OF WATER AND LULU BRO—
PLEASE, MR MOPPET! JUST **ONE** MORE... IT'S **VERY** IMPORTANT!
OH, WELL--- GIVE IT HERE!
GULP! GULP!
OKAY!
WELL---AREN'T YOU GOING TO TAKE THE GLASS?
ER... WILL YOU DO ME A FAVOR, MR. MOPPET?
WILL YA PLEASE PUT TH' GLASS ON MY **HEAD**?
NO!!
OKAY---IT'S ALL OVER, LULU... THE CASE IS BROKE!
HE ADMITTED HE STOLE TH' **POPOVERS?**

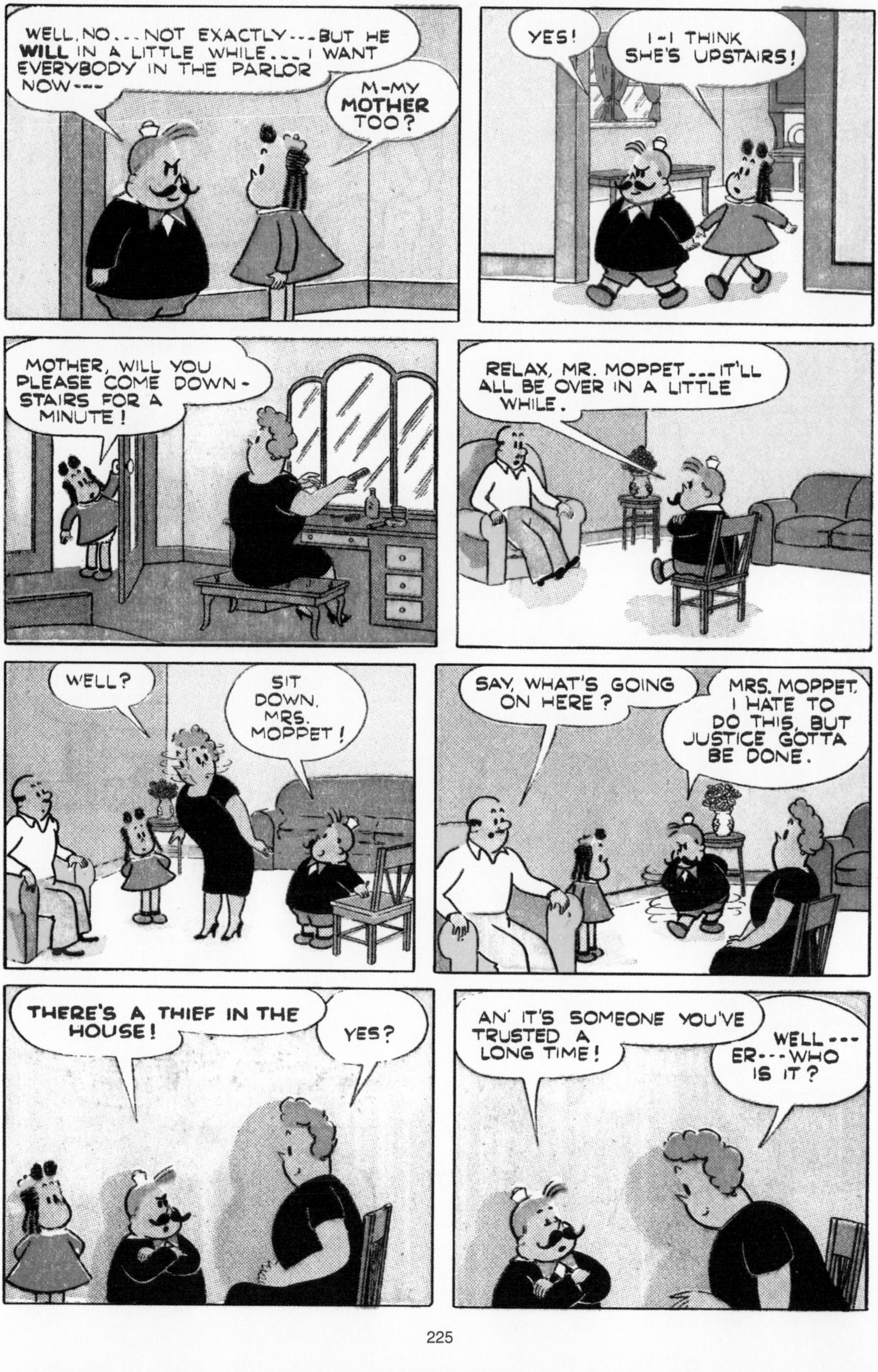
WELL, NO... NOT EXACTLY... BUT HE **WILL** IN A LITTLE WHILE... I WANT EVERYBODY IN THE PARLOR NOW...
M-MY **MOTHER** TOO?
YES!
I-I THINK SHE'S UPSTAIRS!
MOTHER, WILL YOU PLEASE COME DOWN-STAIRS FOR A MINUTE!
RELAX, MR. MOPPET... IT'LL ALL BE OVER IN A LITTLE WHILE.
WELL?
SIT DOWN, MRS. MOPPET!
SAY, WHAT'S GOING ON HERE?
MRS. MOPPET, I HATE TO DO THIS, BUT JUSTICE GOTTA BE DONE.
THERE'S A THIEF IN THE HOUSE!
YES?
AN' IT'S SOMEONE YOU'VE TRUSTED A LONG TIME!
WELL... ER... WHO IS IT?

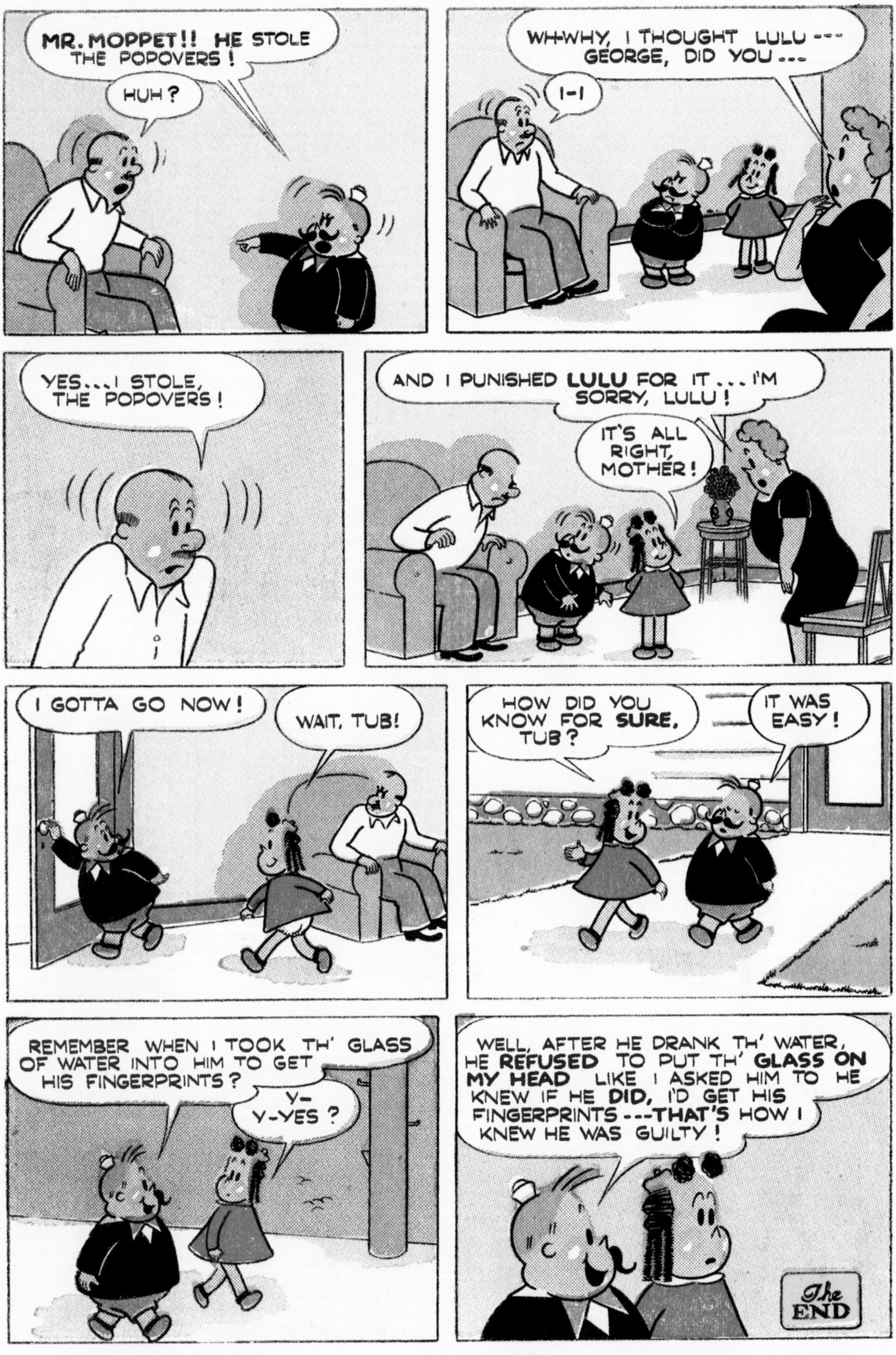

MR. MOPPET!! HE STOLE THE POPOVERS!
HUH?
WH-WHY, I THOUGHT LULU--- GEORGE, DID YOU...
I-I
YES...I STOLE, THE POPOVERS!
AND I PUNISHED LULU FOR IT...I'M SORRY, LULU!
IT'S ALL RIGHT, MOTHER!
I GOTTA GO NOW!
WAIT, TUB!
HOW DID YOU KNOW FOR SURE, TUB?
IT WAS EASY!
REMEMBER WHEN I TOOK TH' GLASS OF WATER INTO HIM TO GET HIS FINGERPRINTS?
Y- Y-YES?
WELL, AFTER HE DRANK TH' WATER, HE REFUSED TO PUT TH' GLASS ON MY HEAD LIKE I ASKED HIM TO HE KNEW IF HE DID, I'D GET HIS FINGERPRINTS---THAT'S HOW I KNEW HE WAS GUILTY!
The END

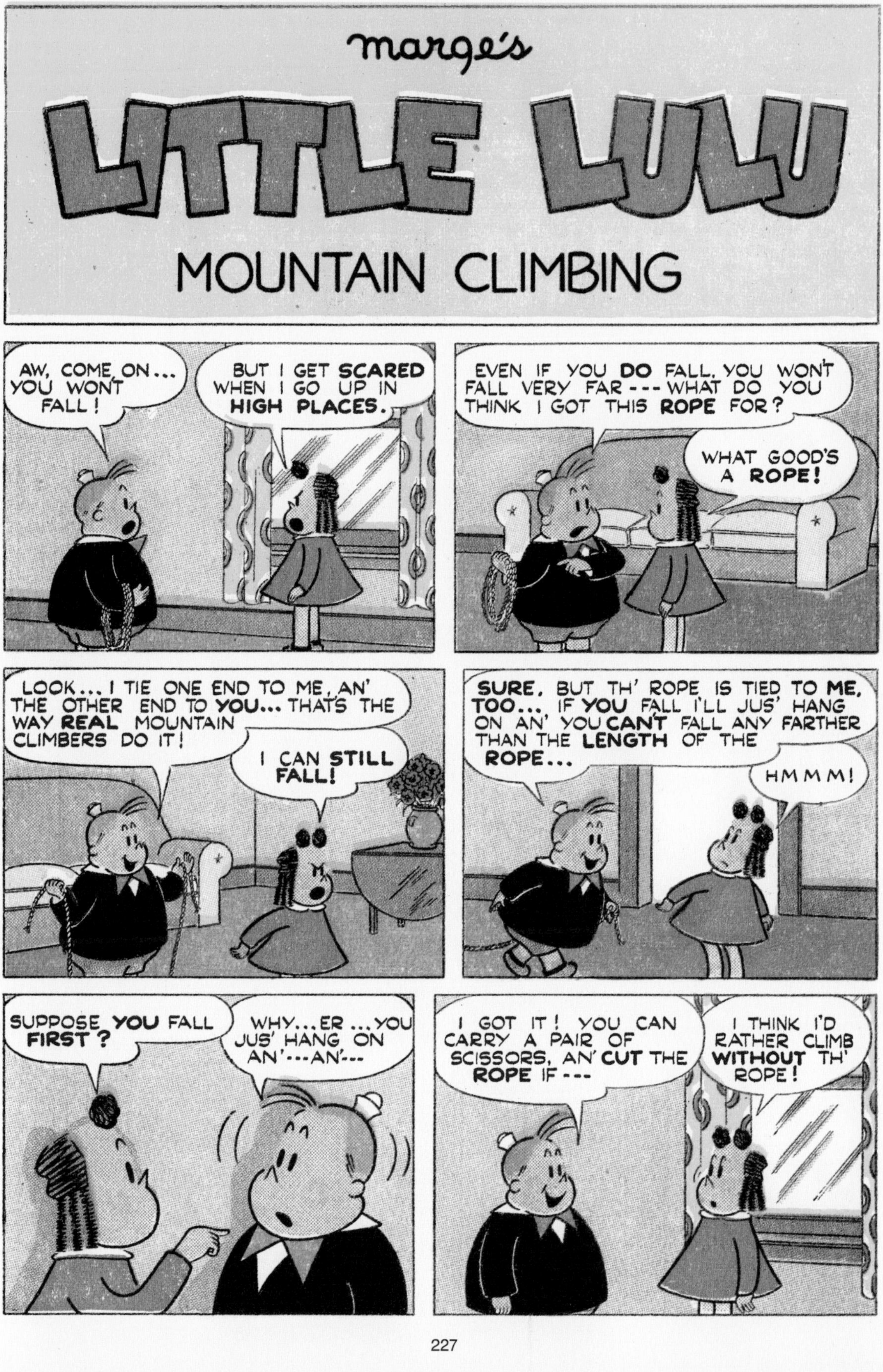
marge's
LITTLE LULU
MOUNTAIN CLIMBING
AW, COME ON... YOU WON'T FALL!
BUT I GET SCARED WHEN I GO UP IN HIGH PLACES.
EVEN IF YOU DO FALL, YOU WON'T FALL VERY FAR---WHAT DO YOU THINK I GOT THIS ROPE FOR?
WHAT GOOD'S A ROPE!
LOOK... I TIE ONE END TO ME, AN' THE OTHER END TO YOU... THAT'S THE WAY REAL MOUNTAIN CLIMBERS DO IT!
I CAN STILL FALL!
SURE, BUT TH' ROPE IS TIED TO ME, TOO... IF YOU FALL I'LL JUS' HANG ON AN' YOU CAN'T FALL ANY FARTHER THAN THE LENGTH OF THE ROPE...
HMMM!
SUPPOSE YOU FALL FIRST?
WHY...ER...YOU JUS' HANG ON AN'---AN'---
I GOT IT! YOU CAN CARRY A PAIR OF SCISSORS, AN' CUT THE ROPE IF---
I THINK I'D RATHER CLIMB WITHOUT TH' ROPE!

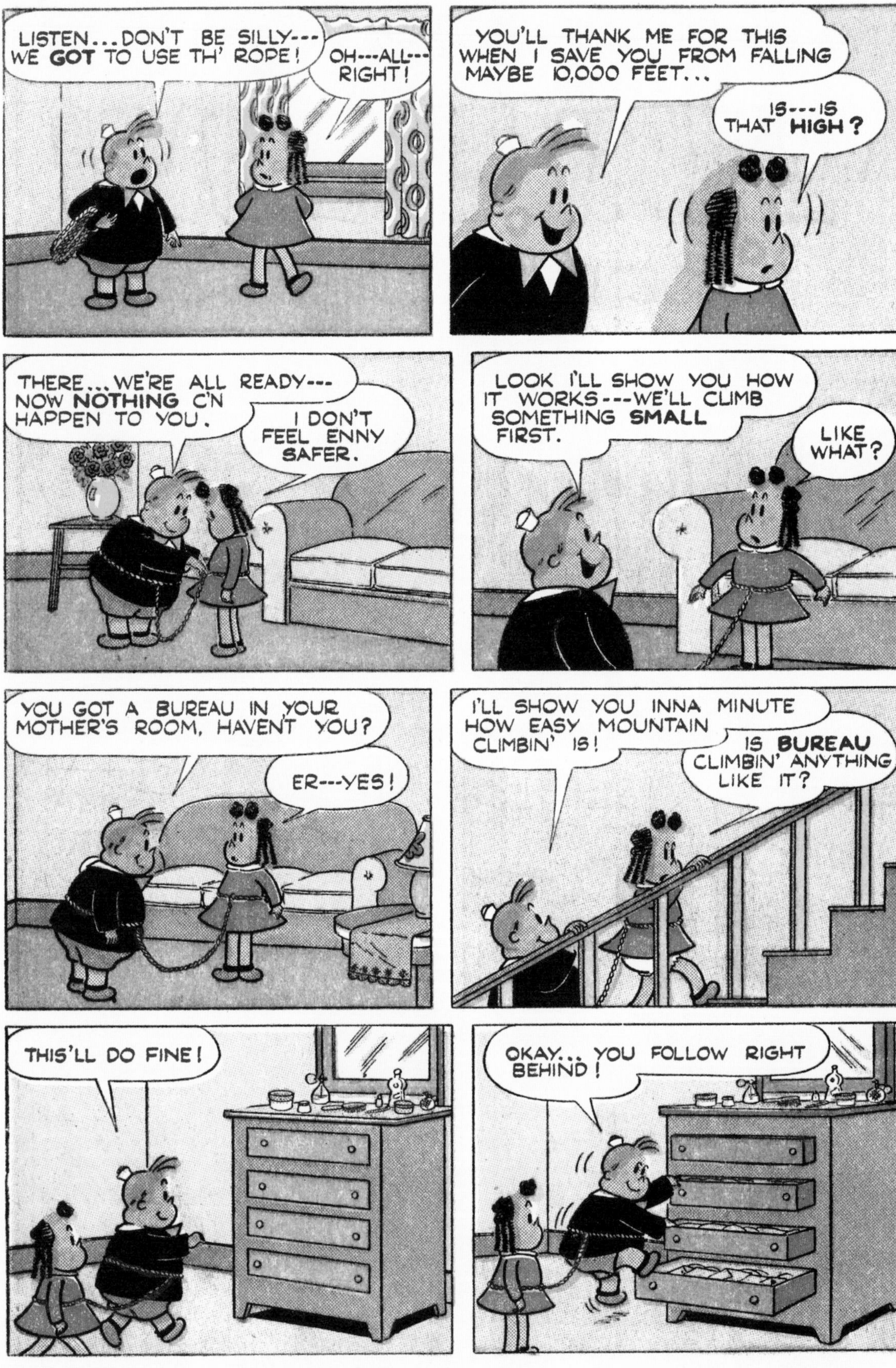
LISTEN... DON'T BE SILLY--- WE **GOT** TO USE TH' ROPE!
OH---ALL--- RIGHT!
YOU'LL THANK ME FOR THIS WHEN I SAVE YOU FROM FALLING MAYBE 10,000 FEET...
IS---IS THAT **HIGH?**
THERE... WE'RE ALL READY--- NOW **NOTHING** C'N HAPPEN TO YOU.
I DON'T FEEL ENNY SAFER.
LOOK I'LL SHOW YOU HOW IT WORKS---WE'LL CLIMB SOMETHING **SMALL** FIRST.
LIKE WHAT?
YOU GOT A BUREAU IN YOUR MOTHER'S ROOM, HAVEN'T YOU?
ER---YES!
I'LL SHOW YOU INNA MINUTE HOW EASY MOUNTAIN CLIMBIN' IS!
IS **BUREAU** CLIMBIN' ANYTHING LIKE IT?
THIS'LL DO FINE!
OKAY... YOU FOLLOW RIGHT BEHIND!

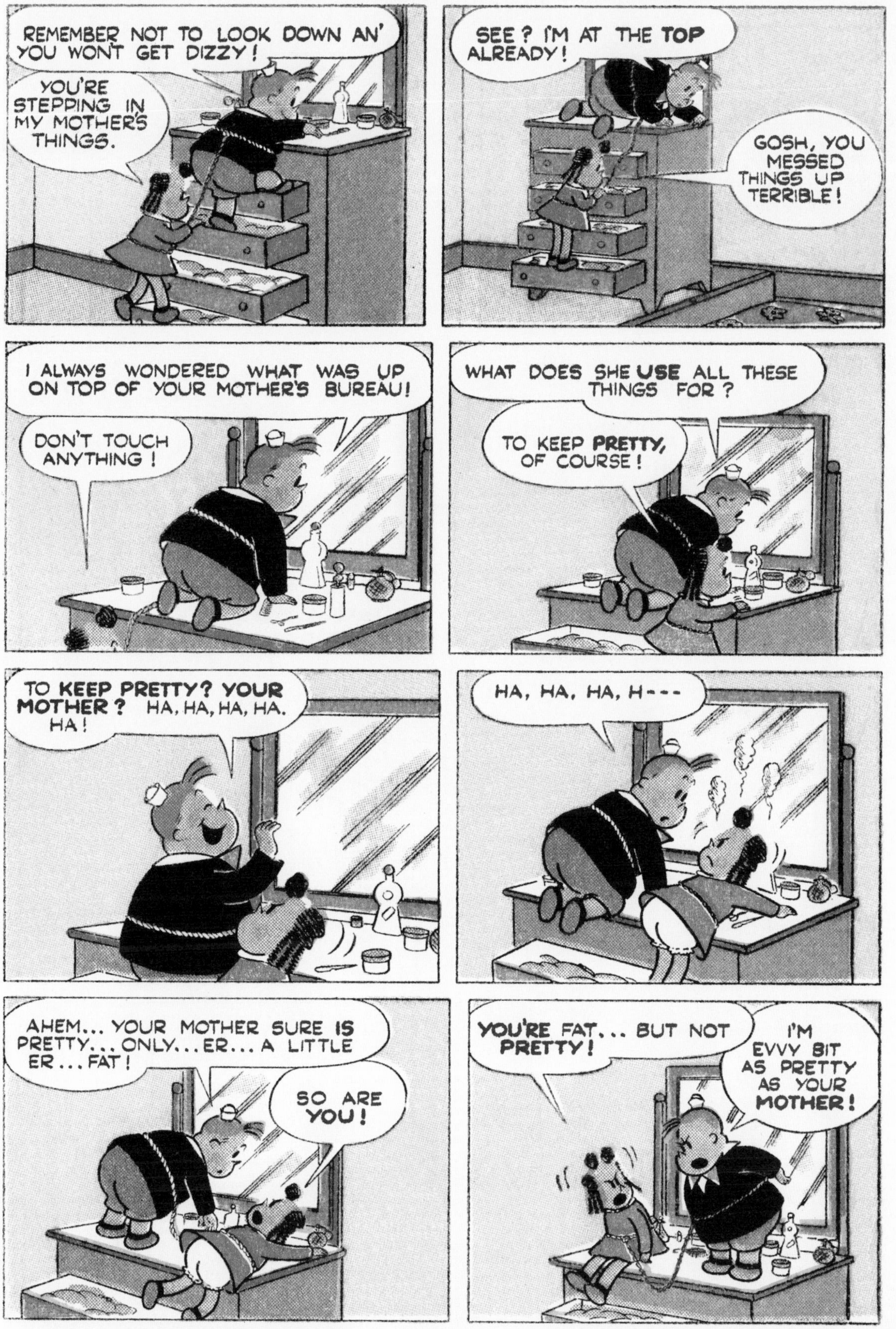
REMEMBER NOT TO LOOK DOWN AN' YOU WON'T GET DIZZY!
YOU'RE STEPPING IN MY MOTHER'S THINGS.
SEE? I'M AT THE TOP ALREADY!
GOSH, YOU MESSED THINGS UP TERRIBLE!
I ALWAYS WONDERED WHAT WAS UP ON TOP OF YOUR MOTHER'S BUREAU!
DON'T TOUCH ANYTHING!
WHAT DOES SHE USE ALL THESE THINGS FOR?
TO KEEP PRETTY, OF COURSE!
TO KEEP PRETTY? YOUR MOTHER? HA, HA, HA, HA. HA!
HA, HA, HA, H---
AHEM... YOUR MOTHER SURE IS PRETTY... ONLY... ER... A LITTLE ER... FAT!
SO ARE YOU!
YOU'RE FAT... BUT NOT PRETTY!
I'M EVVY BIT AS PRETTY AS YOUR MOTHER!

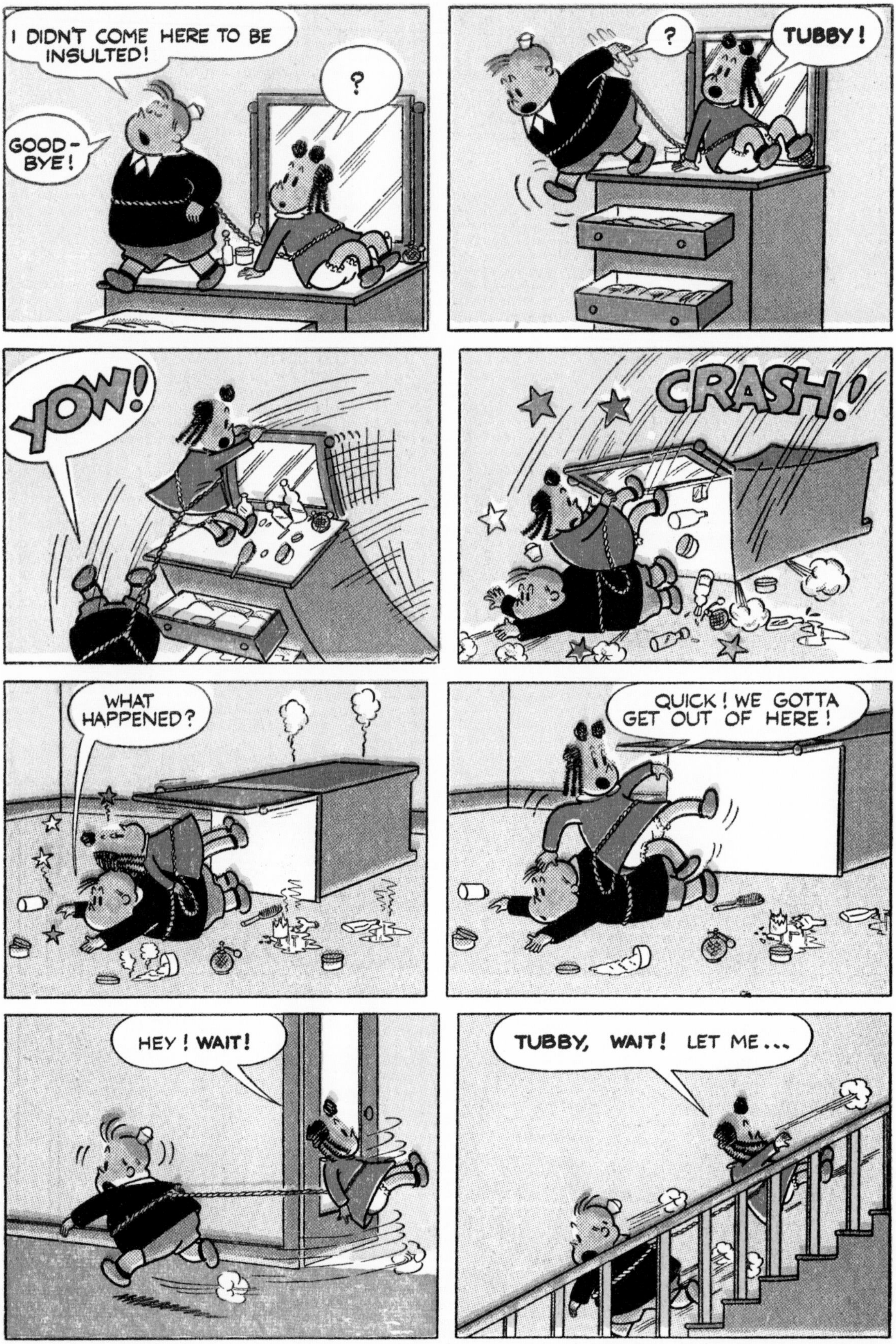
I DIDN'T COME HERE TO BE INSULTED!
GOOD-BYE!
?
?
TUBBY!
YOW!
CRASH!
WHAT HAPPENED?
QUICK! WE GOTTA GET OUT OF HERE!
HEY! WAIT!
TUBBY, WAIT! LET ME...

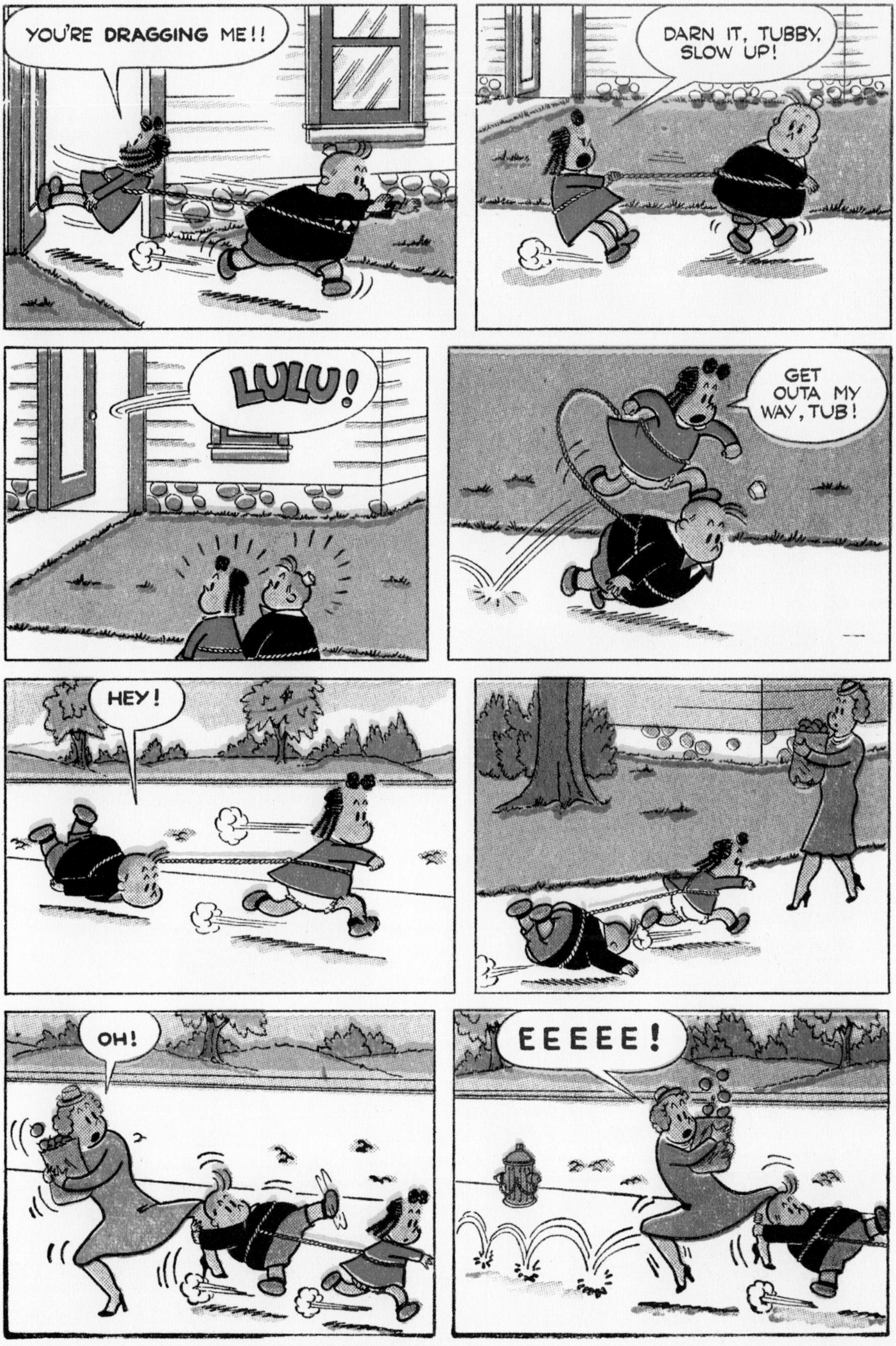
YOU'RE DRAGGING ME!!
DARN IT, TUBBY, SLOW UP!
LULU!
GET OUTA MY WAY, TUB!
HEY!
OH!
EEEEE!

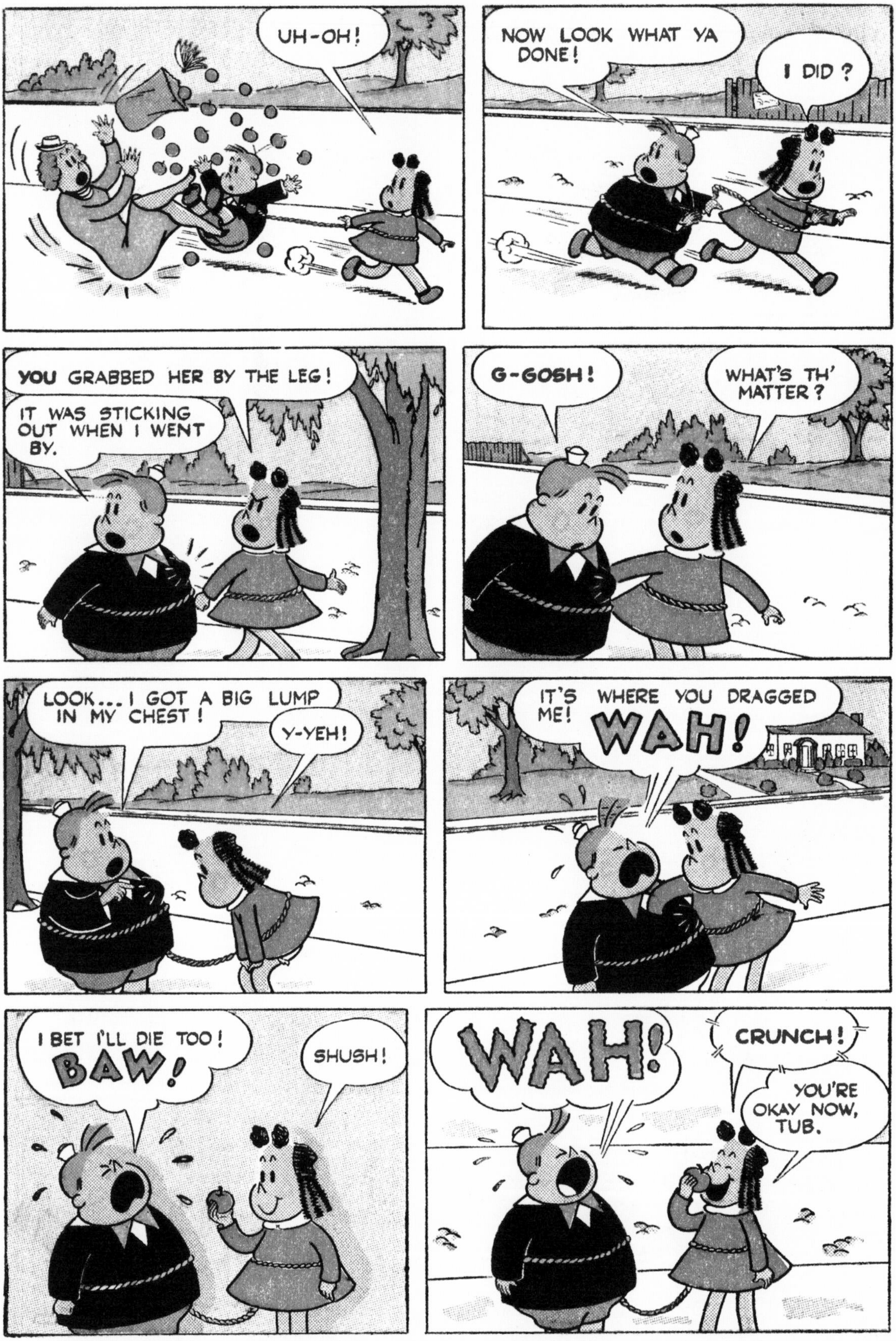

UH-OH!
NOW LOOK WHAT YA DONE!
I DID?
YOU GRABBED HER BY THE LEG!
IT WAS STICKING OUT WHEN I WENT BY.
G-GOSH!
WHAT'S TH' MATTER?
LOOK... I GOT A BIG LUMP IN MY CHEST!
Y-YEH!
IT'S WHERE YOU DRAGGED ME!
WAH!
I BET I'LL DIE TOO! BAW!
SHUSH!
WAH!
CRUNCH!
YOU'RE OKAY NOW, TUB.

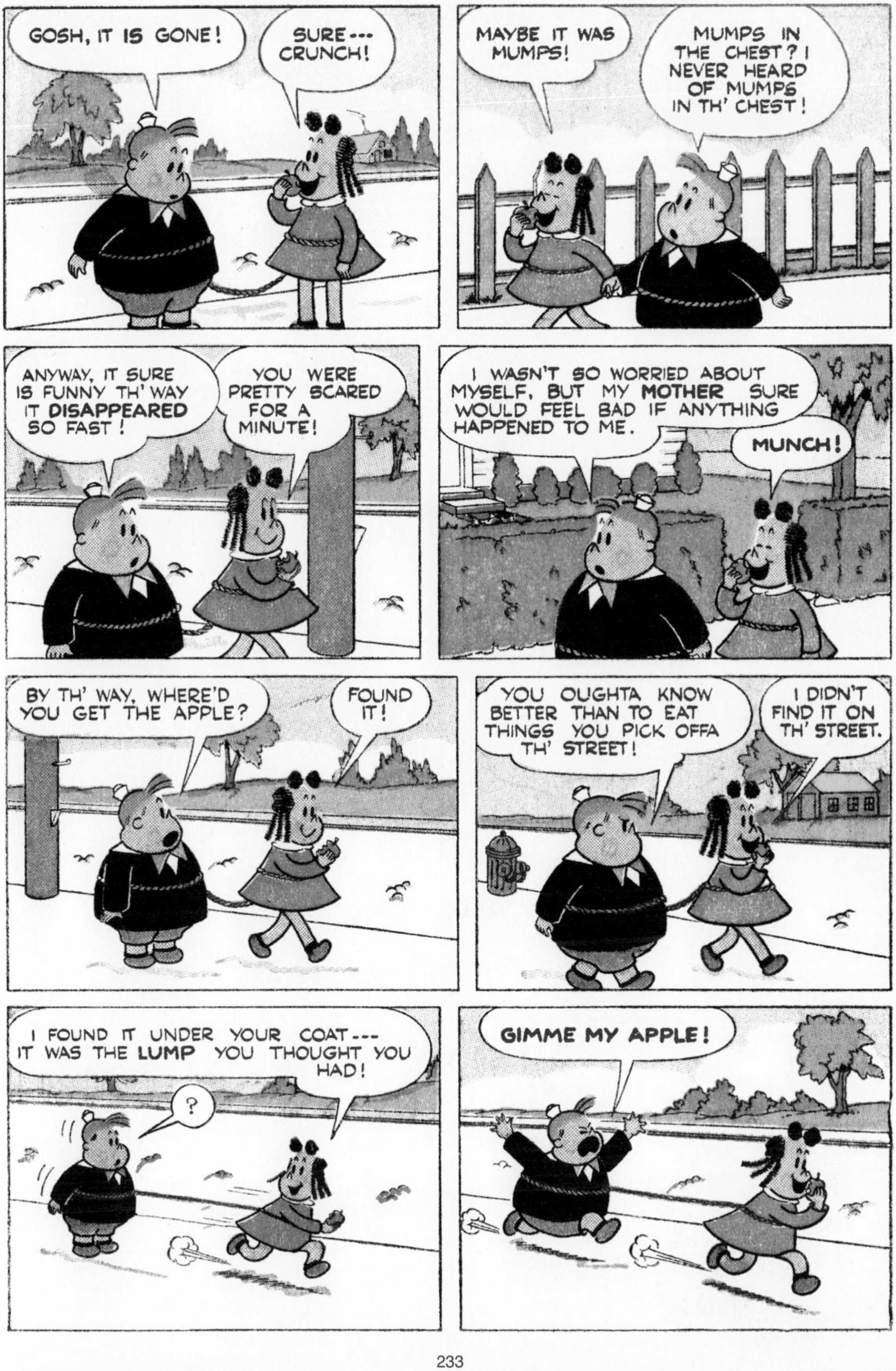
GOSH, IT IS GONE!
SURE--- CRUNCH!
MAYBE IT WAS MUMPS!
MUMPS IN THE CHEST? I NEVER HEARD OF MUMPS IN TH' CHEST!
ANYWAY, IT SURE IS FUNNY TH' WAY IT DISAPPEARED SO FAST!
YOU WERE PRETTY SCARED FOR A MINUTE!
I WASN'T SO WORRIED ABOUT MYSELF, BUT MY MOTHER SURE WOULD FEEL BAD IF ANYTHING HAPPENED TO ME.
MUNCH!
BY TH' WAY, WHERE'D YOU GET THE APPLE?
FOUND IT!
YOU OUGHTA KNOW BETTER THAN TO EAT THINGS YOU PICK OFFA TH' STREET!
I DIDN'T FIND IT ON TH' STREET.
I FOUND IT UNDER YOUR COAT--- IT WAS THE LUMP YOU THOUGHT YOU HAD!
?
GIMME MY APPLE!

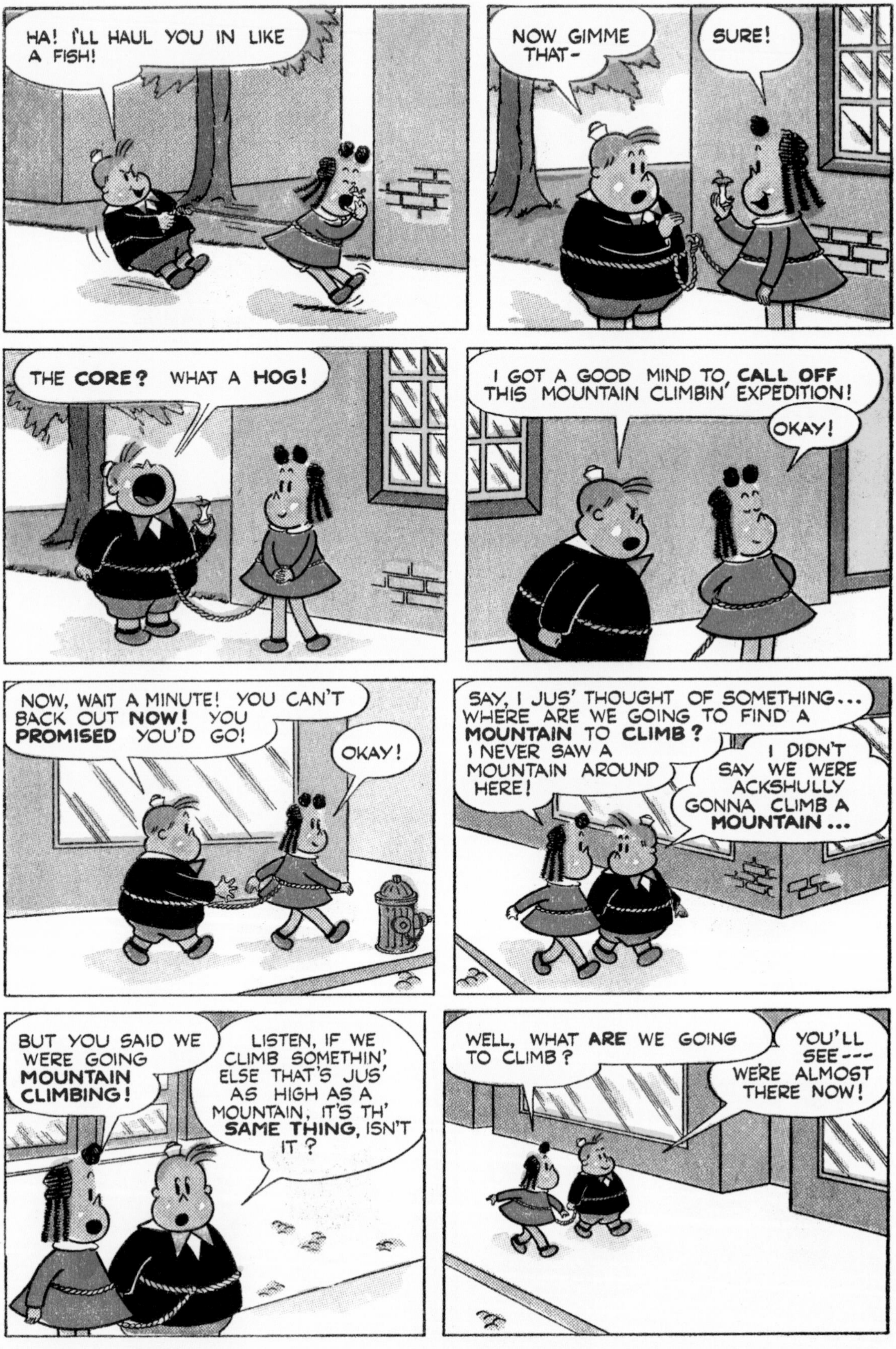

HA! I'LL HAUL YOU IN LIKE A FISH!
NOW GIMME THAT-
SURE!
THE **CORE?** WHAT A **HOG!**
I GOT A GOOD MIND TO, **CALL OFF** THIS MOUNTAIN CLIMBIN' EXPEDITION!
OKAY!
NOW, WAIT A MINUTE! YOU CAN'T BACK OUT **NOW!** YOU **PROMISED** YOU'D GO!
OKAY!
SAY, I JUS' THOUGHT OF SOMETHING... WHERE ARE WE GOING TO FIND A **MOUNTAIN** TO **CLIMB?** I NEVER SAW A MOUNTAIN AROUND HERE!
I DIDN'T SAY WE WERE ACKSHULLY GONNA CLIMB A **MOUNTAIN...**
BUT YOU SAID WE WERE GOING **MOUNTAIN CLIMBING!**
LISTEN, IF WE CLIMB SOMETHIN' ELSE THAT'S JUS' AS HIGH AS A MOUNTAIN, IT'S TH' **SAME THING**, ISN'T IT?
WELL, WHAT **ARE** WE GOING TO CLIMB?
YOU'LL SEE--- WE'RE ALMOST THERE NOW!

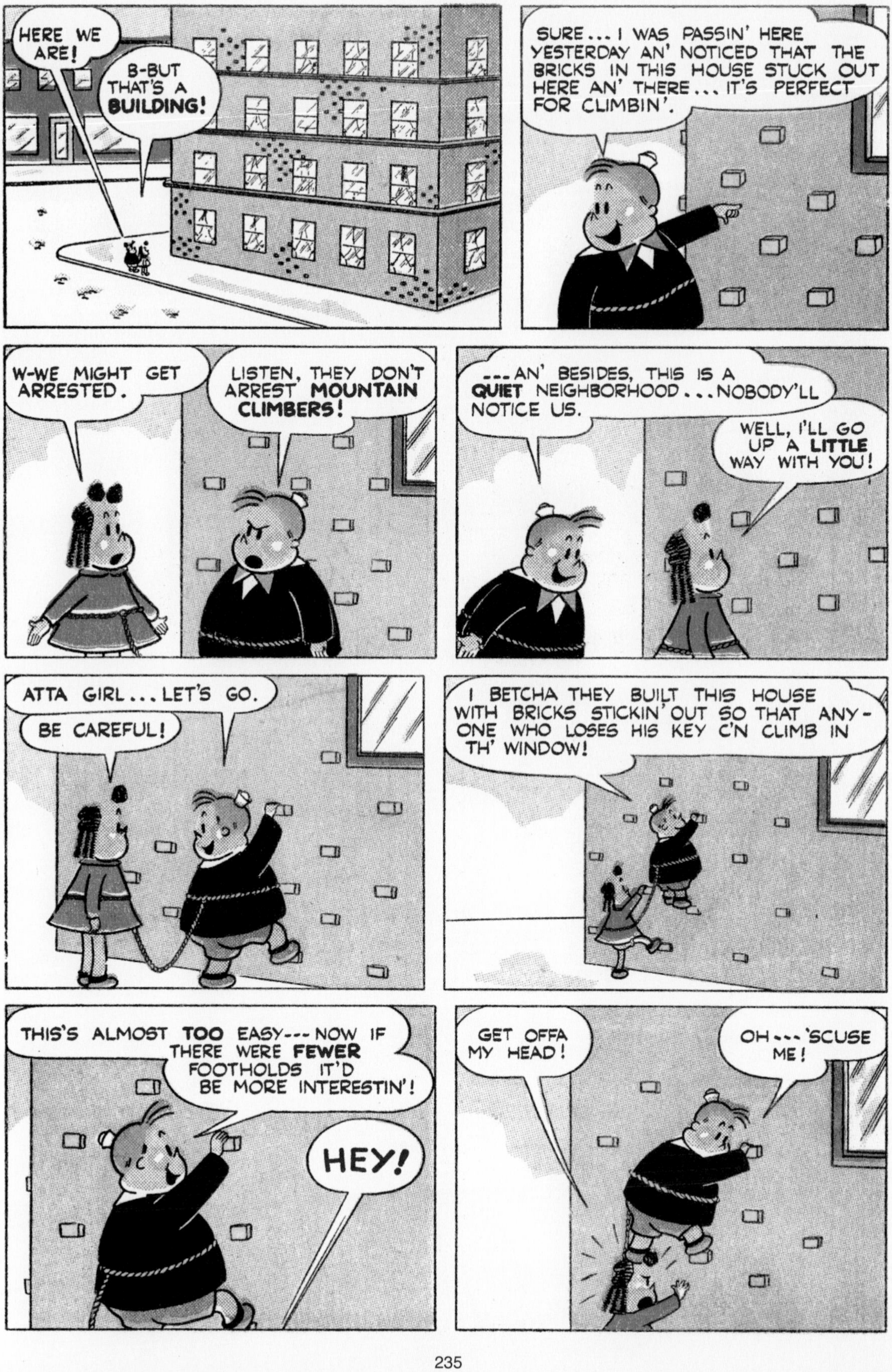
HERE WE ARE!
B-BUT THAT'S A **BUILDING**!
SURE... I WAS PASSIN' HERE YESTERDAY AN' NOTICED THAT THE BRICKS IN THIS HOUSE STUCK OUT HERE AN' THERE... IT'S PERFECT FOR CLIMBIN'.
W-WE MIGHT GET ARRESTED.
LISTEN, THEY DON'T ARREST **MOUNTAIN CLIMBERS**!
---AN' BESIDES, THIS IS A **QUIET** NEIGHBORHOOD...NOBODY'LL NOTICE US.
WELL, I'LL GO UP A **LITTLE** WAY WITH YOU!
ATTA GIRL... LET'S GO.
BE CAREFUL!
I BETCHA THEY BUILT THIS HOUSE WITH BRICKS STICKIN' OUT SO THAT ANY-ONE WHO LOSES HIS KEY C'N CLIMB IN TH' WINDOW!
THIS'S ALMOST **TOO** EASY---NOW IF THERE WERE **FEWER** FOOTHOLDS IT'D BE MORE INTERESTIN'!
HEY!
GET OFFA MY HEAD!
OH---'SCUSE ME!

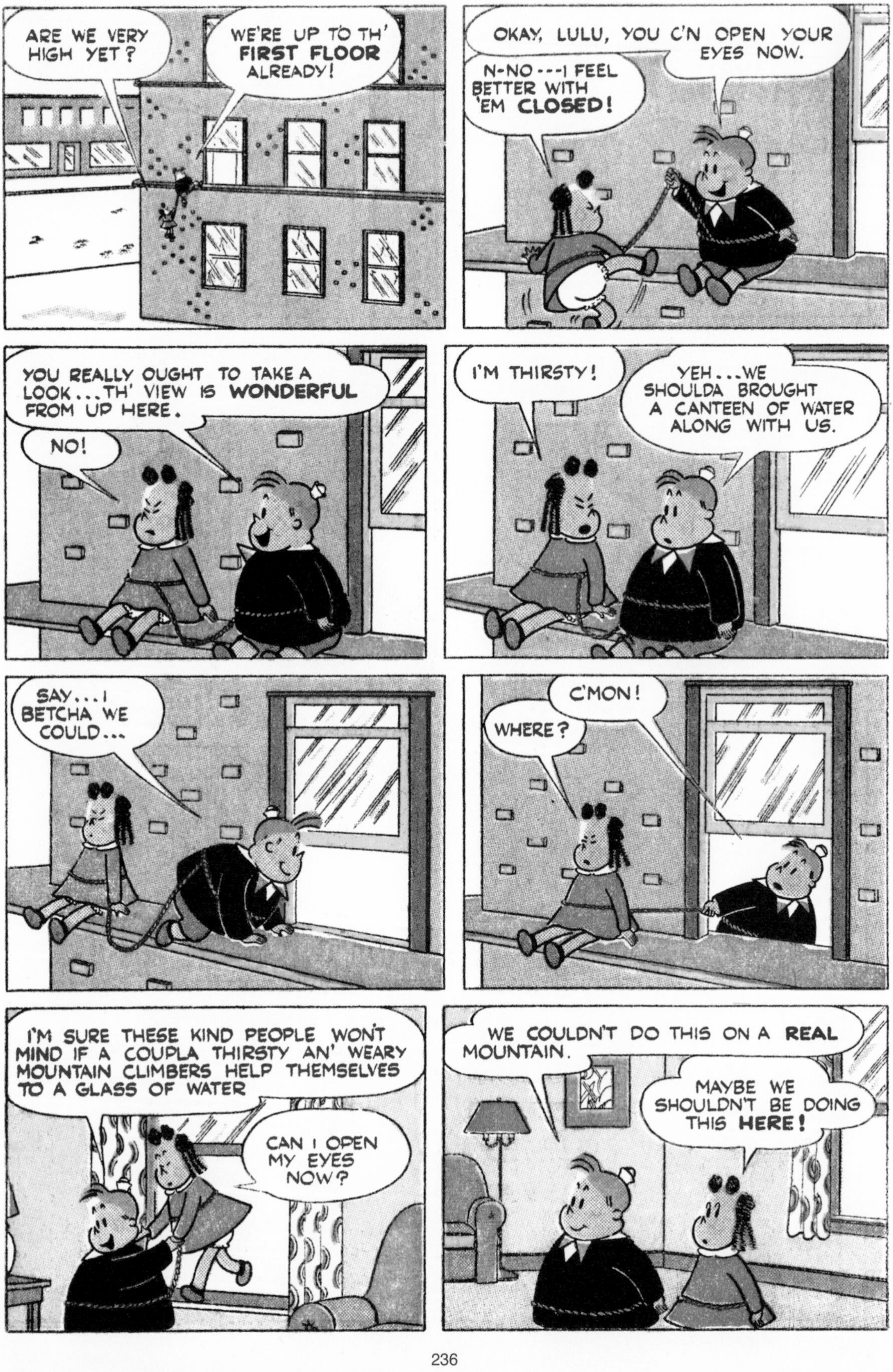
ARE WE VERY HIGH YET?
WE'RE UP TO TH' FIRST FLOOR ALREADY!
OKAY, LULU, YOU C'N OPEN YOUR EYES NOW.
N-NO---I FEEL BETTER WITH 'EM CLOSED!
YOU REALLY OUGHT TO TAKE A LOOK...TH' VIEW IS WONDERFUL FROM UP HERE.
NO!
I'M THIRSTY!
YEH...WE SHOULDA BROUGHT A CANTEEN OF WATER ALONG WITH US.
SAY...I BETCHA WE COULD...
C'MON!
WHERE?
I'M SURE THESE KIND PEOPLE WON'T MIND IF A COUPLA THIRSTY AN' WEARY MOUNTAIN CLIMBERS HELP THEMSELVES TO A GLASS OF WATER
CAN I OPEN MY EYES NOW?
WE COULDN'T DO THIS ON A REAL MOUNTAIN.
MAYBE WE SHOULDN'T BE DOING THIS HERE!

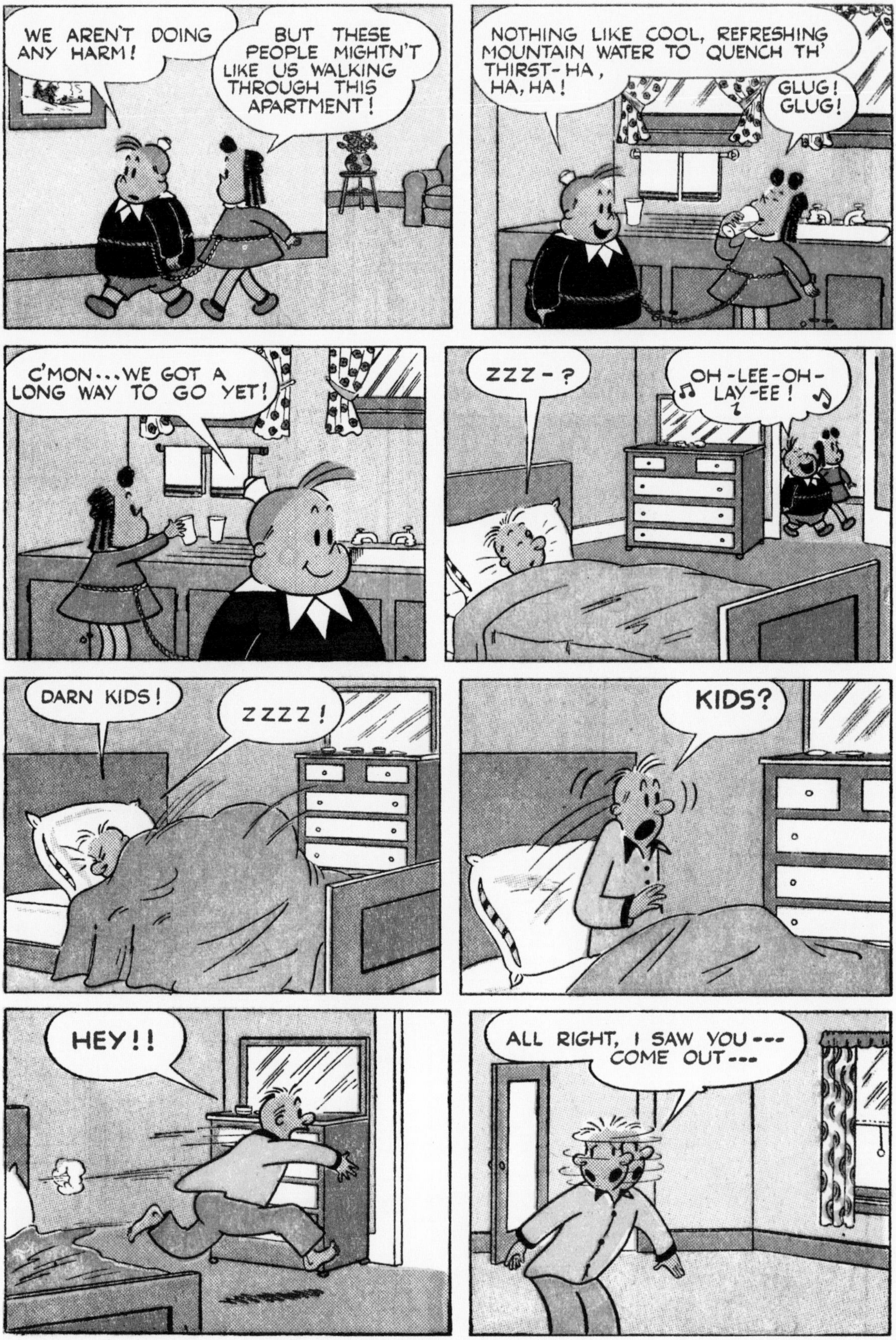
WE AREN'T DOING ANY HARM!
BUT THESE PEOPLE MIGHTN'T LIKE US WALKING THROUGH THIS APARTMENT!
NOTHING LIKE COOL, REFRESHING MOUNTAIN WATER TO QUENCH TH' THIRST-HA, HA, HA!
GLUG! GLUG!
C'MON... WE GOT A LONG WAY TO GO YET!
ZZZ-?
OH-LEE-OH-LAY-EE!
DARN KIDS!
ZZZZ!
KIDS?
HEY!!
ALL RIGHT, I SAW YOU--- COME OUT---

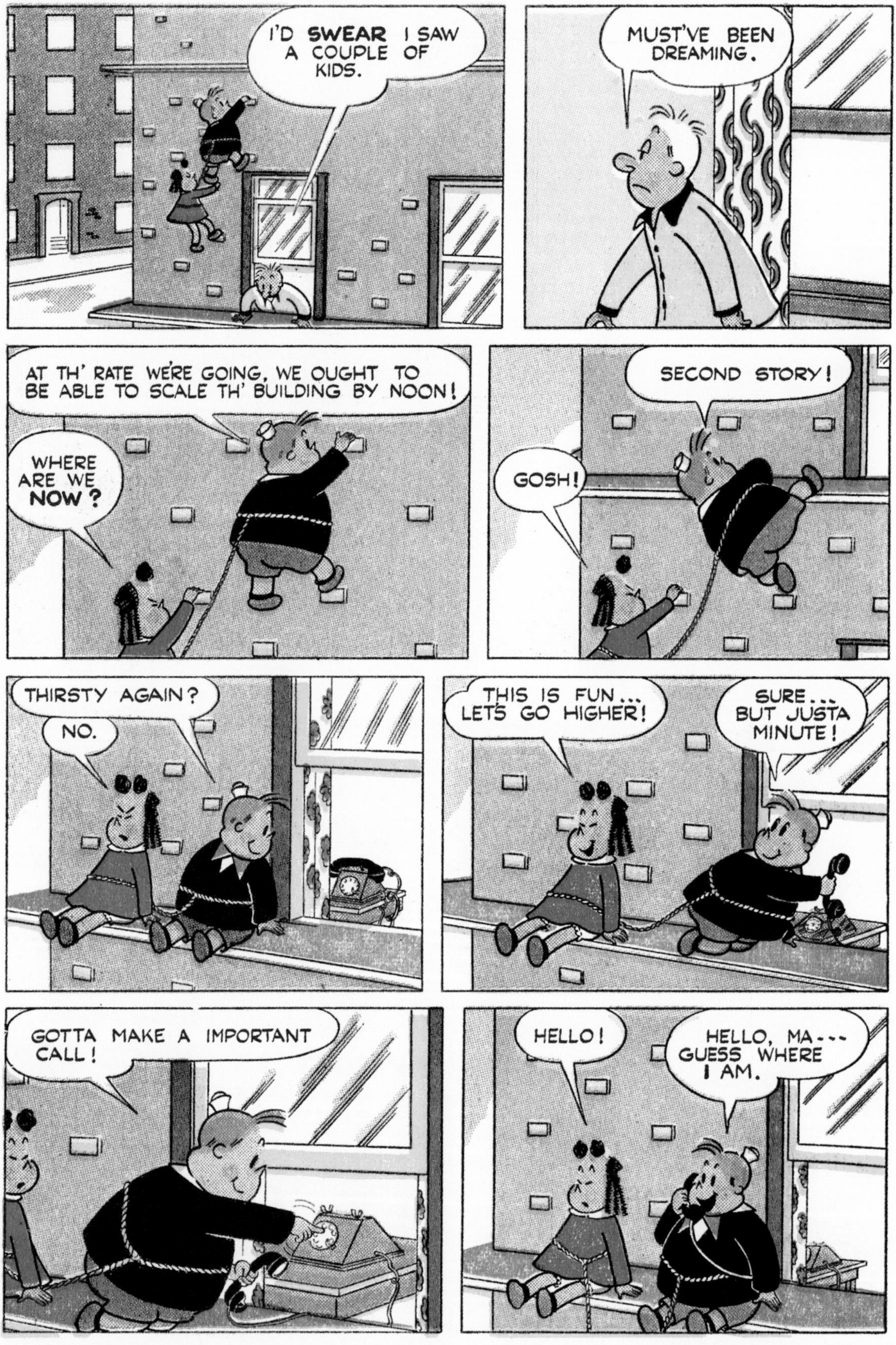
I'D SWEAR I SAW A COUPLE OF KIDS.
MUST'VE BEEN DREAMING.
AT TH' RATE WE'RE GOING, WE OUGHT TO BE ABLE TO SCALE TH' BUILDING BY NOON!
WHERE ARE WE NOW?
SECOND STORY!
GOSH!
THIRSTY AGAIN?
NO.
THIS IS FUN... LETS GO HIGHER!
SURE... BUT JUSTA MINUTE!
GOTTA MAKE A IMPORTANT CALL!
HELLO!
HELLO, MA--- GUESS WHERE I AM.

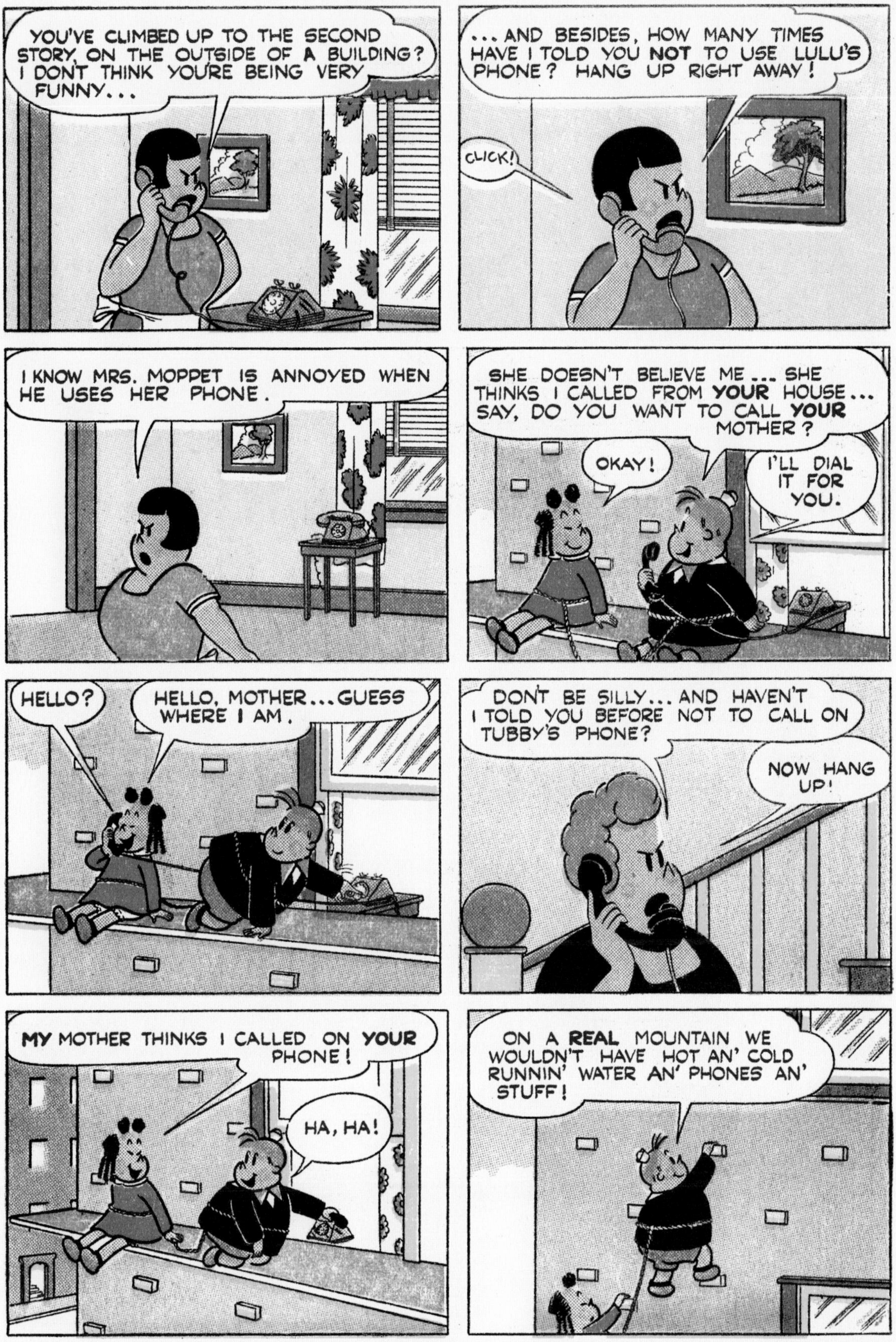
YOU'VE CLIMBED UP TO THE SECOND STORY, ON THE OUTSIDE OF A BUILDING? I DON'T THINK YOU'RE BEING VERY FUNNY...
... AND BESIDES, HOW MANY TIMES HAVE I TOLD YOU NOT TO USE LULU'S PHONE? HANG UP RIGHT AWAY!
CLICK!
I KNOW MRS. MOPPET IS ANNOYED WHEN HE USES HER PHONE.
SHE DOESN'T BELIEVE ME ... SHE THINKS I CALLED FROM YOUR HOUSE... SAY, DO YOU WANT TO CALL YOUR MOTHER?
OKAY!
I'LL DIAL IT FOR YOU.
HELLO?
HELLO, MOTHER... GUESS WHERE I AM.
DON'T BE SILLY... AND HAVEN'T I TOLD YOU BEFORE NOT TO CALL ON TUBBY'S PHONE?
NOW HANG UP!
MY MOTHER THINKS I CALLED ON YOUR PHONE!
HA, HA!
ON A REAL MOUNTAIN WE WOULDN'T HAVE HOT AN' COLD RUNNIN' WATER AN' PHONES AN' STUFF!

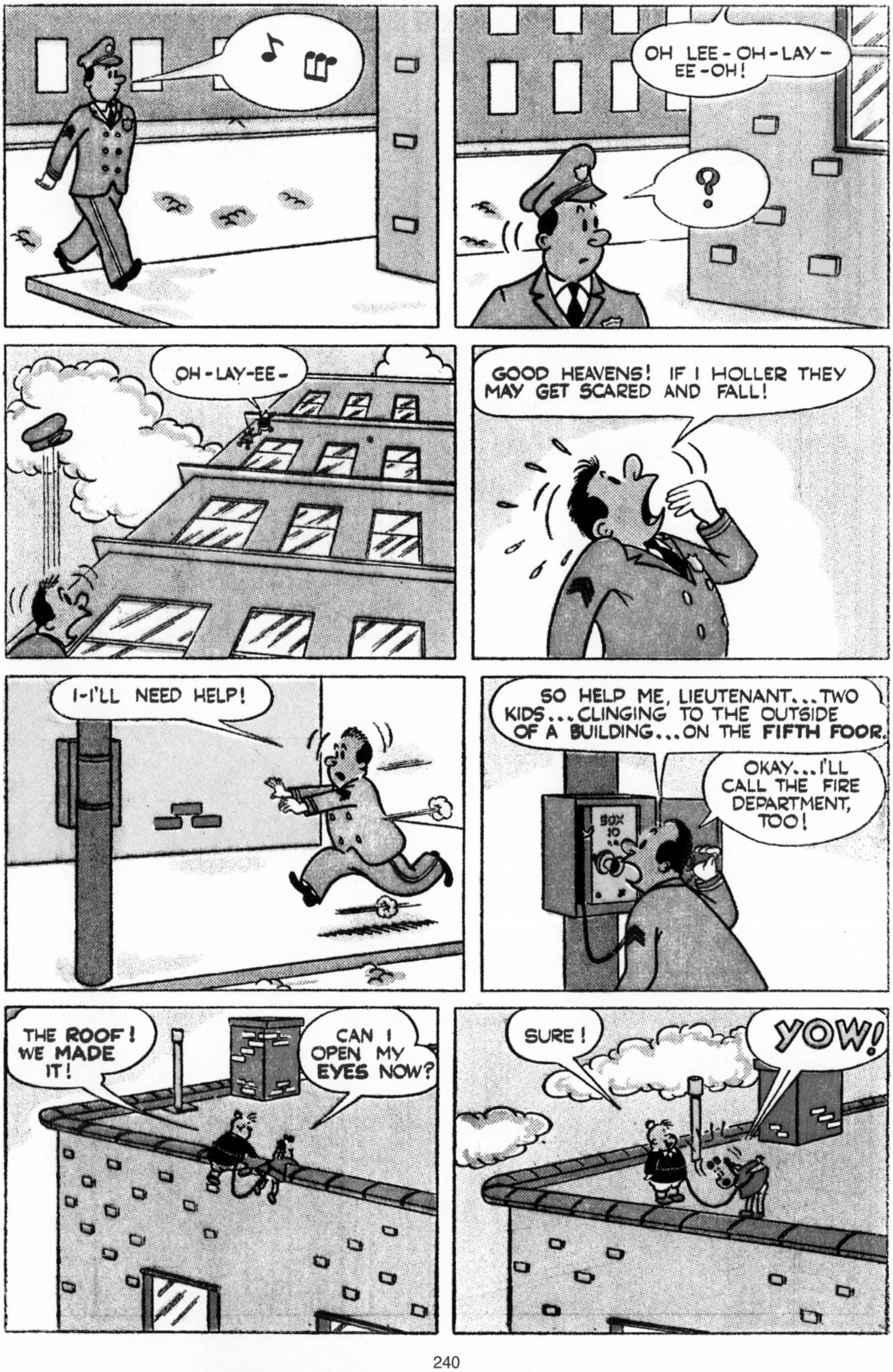
OH LEE-OH-LAY-EE-OH!
?
OH-LAY-EE-
GOOD HEAVENS! IF I HOLLER THEY MAY GET SCARED AND FALL!
I-I'LL NEED HELP!
SO HELP ME, LIEUTENANT...TWO KIDS...CLINGING TO THE OUTSIDE OF A BUILDING...ON THE FIFTH FOOR.
OKAY...I'LL CALL THE FIRE DEPARTMENT, TOO!
THE ROOF! WE MADE IT!
CAN I OPEN MY EYES NOW?
SURE!
YOW!

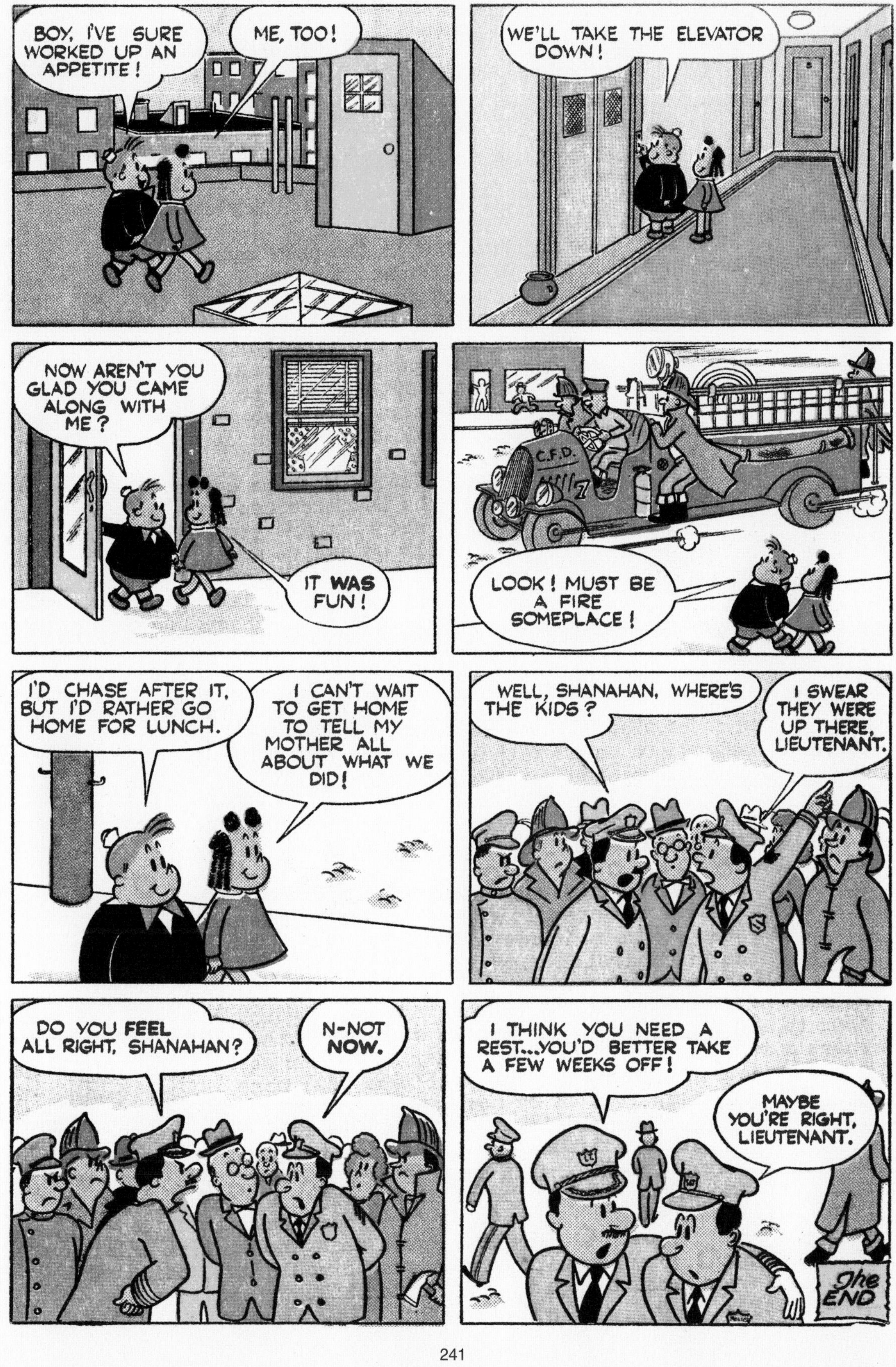
BOY, I'VE SURE WORKED UP AN APPETITE!
ME, TOO!
WE'LL TAKE THE ELEVATOR DOWN!
NOW AREN'T YOU GLAD YOU CAME ALONG WITH ME?
IT WAS FUN!
C.F.D.
LOOK! MUST BE A FIRE SOMEPLACE!
I'D CHASE AFTER IT, BUT I'D RATHER GO HOME FOR LUNCH.
I CAN'T WAIT TO GET HOME TO TELL MY MOTHER ALL ABOUT WHAT WE DID!
WELL, SHANAHAN, WHERE'S THE KIDS?
I SWEAR THEY WERE UP THERE, LIEUTENANT.
DO YOU FEEL ALL RIGHT, SHANAHAN?
N-NOT NOW.
I THINK YOU NEED A REST...YOU'D BETTER TAKE A FEW WEEKS OFF!
MAYBE YOU'RE RIGHT, LIEUTENANT.
The END

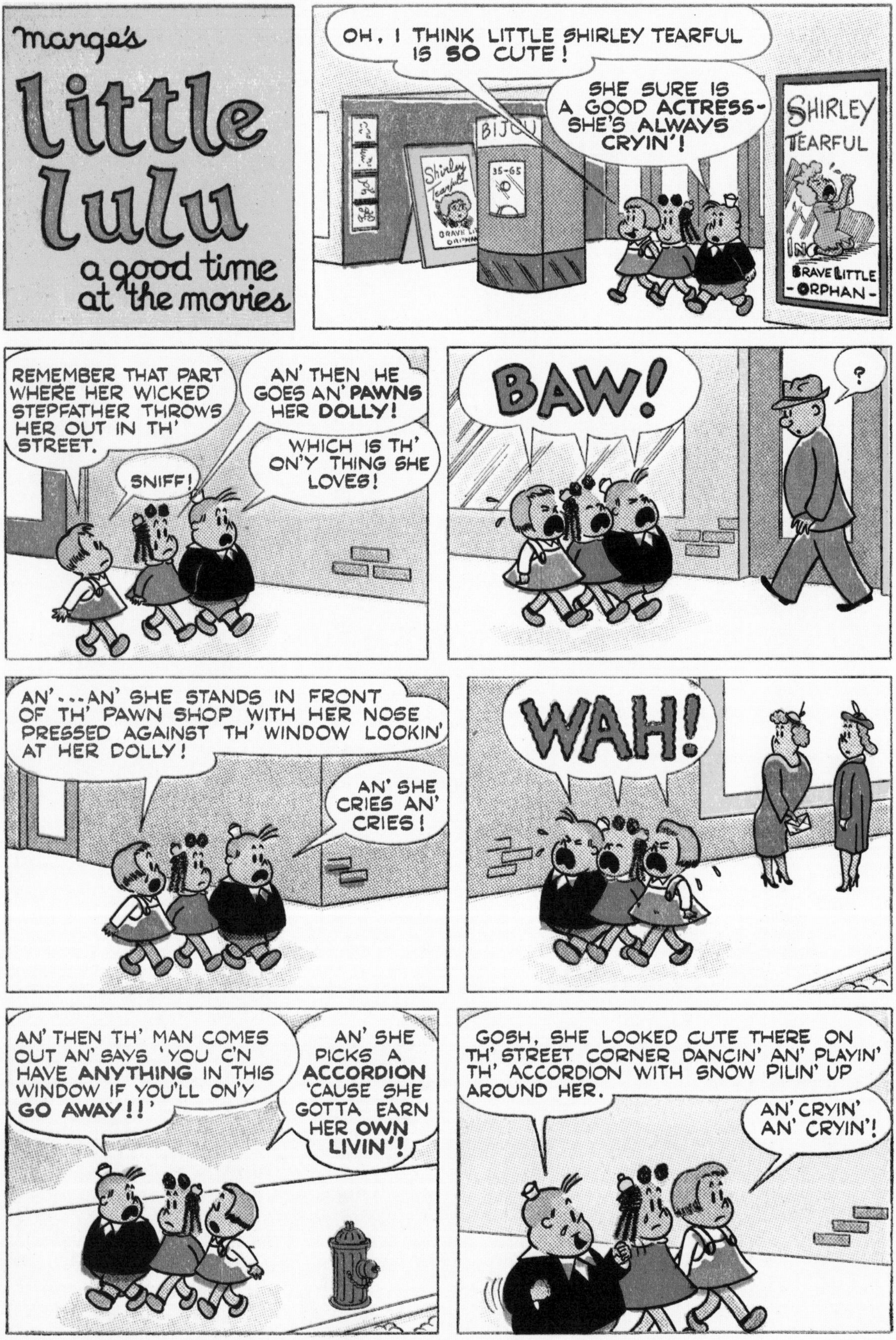
marge's
little lulu
a good time at the movies
OH, I THINK LITTLE SHIRLEY TEARFUL IS SO CUTE!
SHE SURE IS A GOOD ACTRESS- SHE'S ALWAYS CRYIN'!
BIJOU
35-65
SHIRLEY TEARFUL IN BRAVE LITTLE -ORPHAN-
REMEMBER THAT PART WHERE HER WICKED STEPFATHER THROWS HER OUT IN TH' STREET.
SNIFF!
AN' THEN HE GOES AN' PAWNS HER DOLLY!
WHICH IS TH' ON'Y THING SHE LOVES!
BAW!
?
AN'...AN' SHE STANDS IN FRONT OF TH' PAWN SHOP WITH HER NOSE PRESSED AGAINST TH' WINDOW LOOKIN' AT HER DOLLY!
AN' SHE CRIES AN' CRIES!
WAH!
AN' THEN TH' MAN COMES OUT AN' SAYS 'YOU C'N HAVE ANYTHING IN THIS WINDOW IF YOU'LL ON'Y GO AWAY!!'
AN' SHE PICKS A ACCORDION 'CAUSE SHE GOTTA EARN HER OWN LIVIN'!
GOSH, SHE LOOKED CUTE THERE ON TH' STREET CORNER DANCIN' AN' PLAYIN' TH' ACCORDION WITH SNOW PILIN' UP AROUND HER.
AN' CRYIN' AN' CRYIN'!

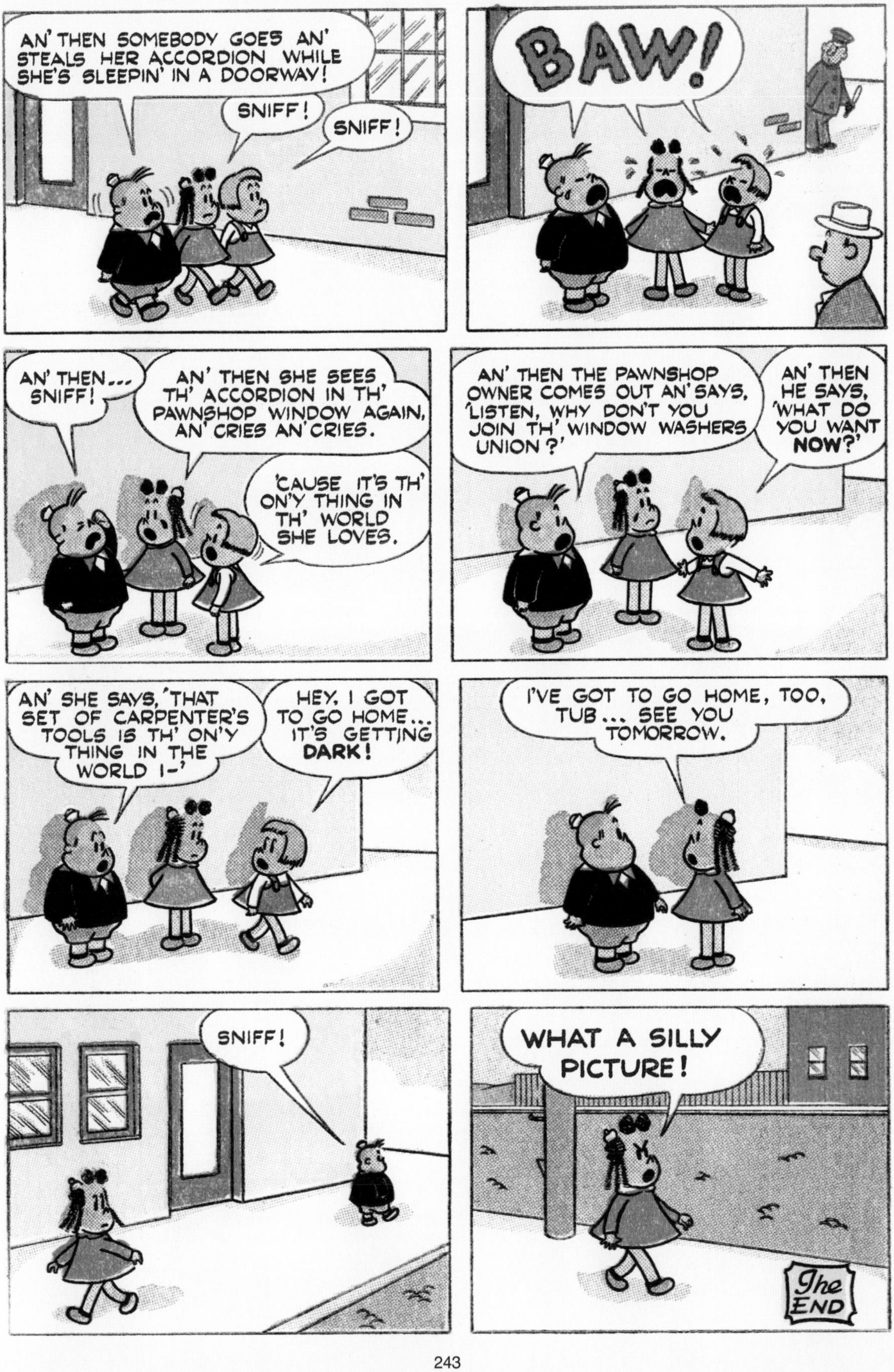
AN' THEN SOMEBODY GOES AN' STEALS HER ACCORDION WHILE SHE'S SLEEPIN' IN A DOORWAY!
SNIFF!
SNIFF!
BAW!
AN' THEN... SNIFF!
AN' THEN SHE SEES TH' ACCORDION IN TH' PAWNSHOP WINDOW AGAIN, AN' CRIES AN' CRIES.
'CAUSE IT'S TH' ON'Y THING IN TH' WORLD SHE LOVES.
AN' THEN THE PAWNSHOP OWNER COMES OUT AN' SAYS, 'LISTEN, WHY DON'T YOU JOIN TH' WINDOW WASHERS UNION?'
AN' THEN HE SAYS, 'WHAT DO YOU WANT **NOW**?'
AN' SHE SAYS, 'THAT SET OF CARPENTER'S TOOLS IS TH' ON'Y THING IN THE WORLD I-'
HEY, I GOT TO GO HOME... IT'S GETTING **DARK**!
I'VE GOT TO GO HOME, TOO, TUB... SEE YOU TOMORROW.
SNIFF!
WHAT A SILLY PICTURE!
The END

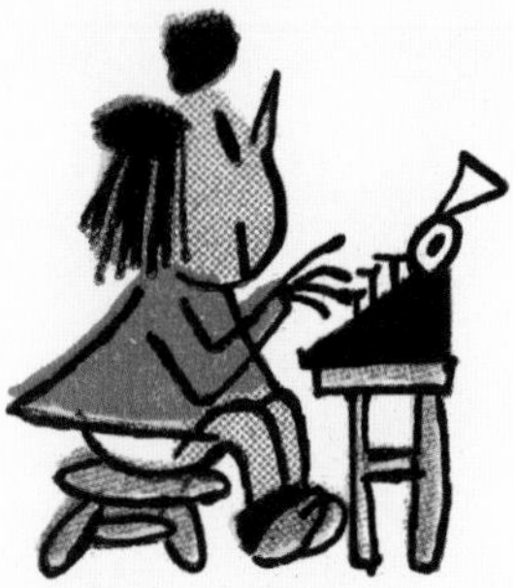

LULUS DIRY

PICTURS BY LULU TOO

Dear Diry

Hello here i am again tipriting on my tipriter. I got so much to tell you dear diry. Like what happened in school last week when our class had a drawing contest. Miss Feeny our teacher said she would give a xxxxx beautiful prize to the kid who brought in the best drawing the next day. I was sure i would win because i am the best drawer in our class because i am always drawing even when i shouldnt.

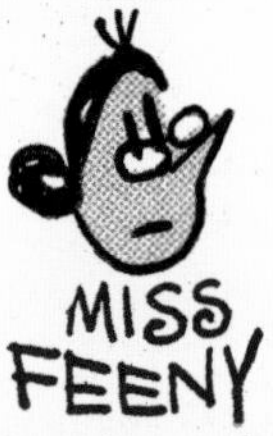

MISS FEENY

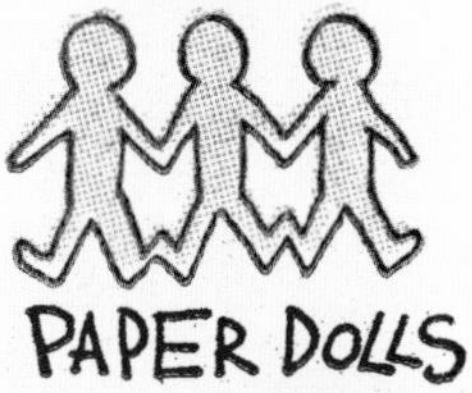

PAPER DOLLS

When i went home after school i found out that i diddnt have any drawing paper left on account of i used it all to cut out paper dolls. Then i went over to Tubbys house to ask him to lend me a piece of drawing paper. When i went in he was drawing a picture but he wouldnt let me see it and covered it up when i tried to look at it and hollered for his mother. He said i was snooping around to look at his drawing and would copy it mabe and win the prize which he was going to win himself. I wouldnt copy his ol picture which anyway was probbly a picture of a fat cowboy on a horse. Any way he wouldnt give me a piece of drawing paper because he said he needed it all for himself the selfish thing.

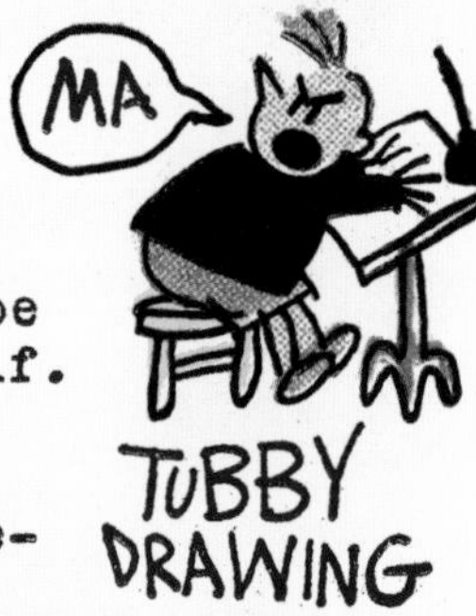

MA
TUBBY DRAWING

Then i went home again and asked mother for some money to buy a pad of drawing paper but she said no you alreddy spent your xxxxxxxxxxxxxxxxxx allowance and mabe the next time you wont waste your drawing paper cutting out paper dolls. Then i sat down and cried a litt.e because i diddnt know what to do. I was sure miss Feeny would be very mad at me if i diddnt bring in a drawing and i just diddnt have any paper at all.

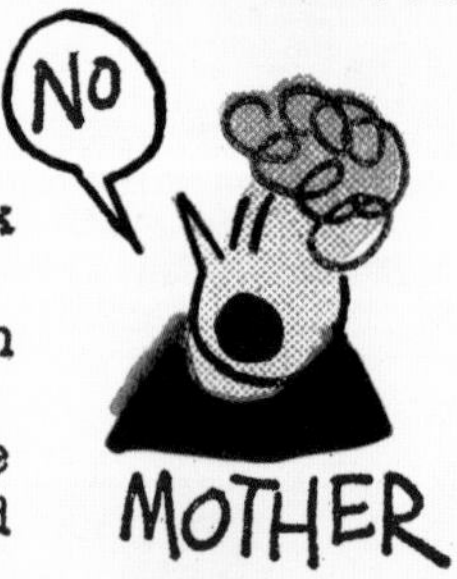

NO
MOTHER

Next morning on my way to school I was feeling very mad. Little Alvin was playing outside his house and i wished i diddnt have to go to school like him. But all of a sudden i got an idea and i asked Alvin if he would like to go to school. He said yes and i was surprised because he always says no to everything except when he is supposed to say no and then he says yes. Then i told him that first we would have to go behind a fence for a little while. After a while we

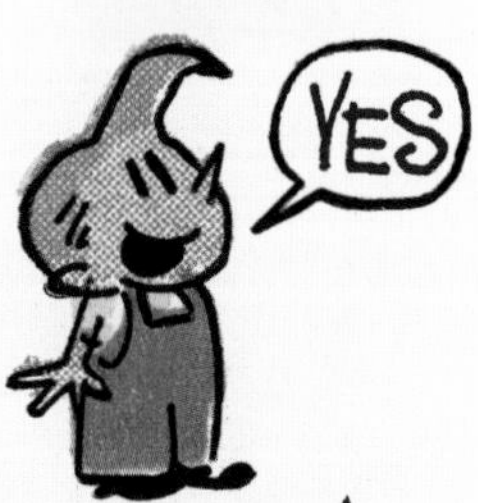

YES
ALVIN

came out and i was afriad that i was a little late for school and we ran all the way. When we got there miss Feeny was looking at everybodys drawings and she said Lulu you are late and why are you bringing a little boy with you and where is your drawing. I said here is my drawing miss Feeny and then i took off Alvins shirt. Everybody laughed even miss Feeny but they could see my drawing all right. It was a picture of a ship i drew on alvins chest with a indellible pencil just like a tattoo. I am drawing a picture here for you Dear Diry so you will know how it looked.

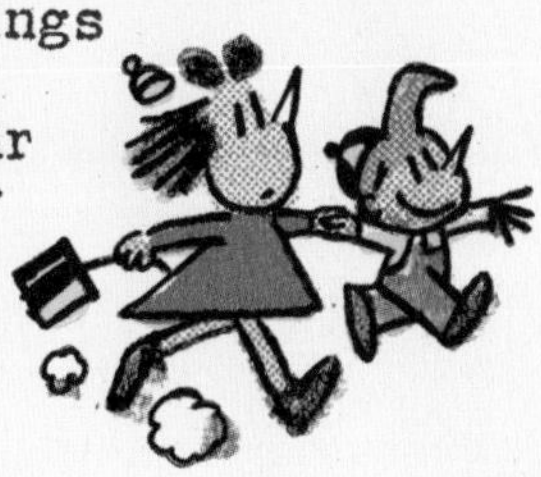

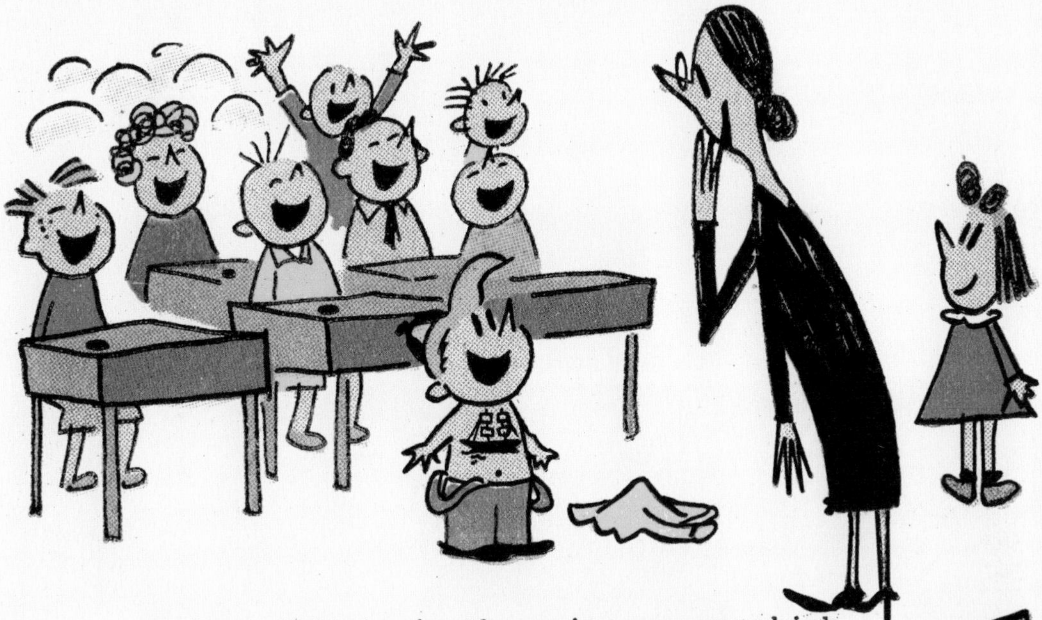

Well i diddnt win the prize anyway which was a paint box but neither did tubby because when miss Feeny looked at his drawing she said she never saw a fat cowboy in her whole life.

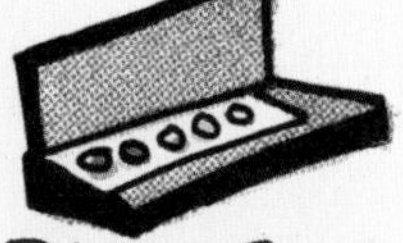

PAINT BOX WHICH I DIDDENT WANT ANYWAY

oh Dear Diry i got a new doll which my pop bought for me. It is beautiful and says mama just like a real baby. When pop brought it home he said here mabe this will keep you quiet for a while so i can read the paper in peace. Then i made my new doll say mama 496 times. I counted them. But pop said it stop it cant you see i am trying to read my paper and if that doll says mama once more i will take it away from you. i dont know how it happened but the doll slipped and said mama again and Pop jumped up and took it away from me. He said he was going to take it back and get a doll that couldnt say anything. But i cried and said i couldnt help it and Pop said well all right here is your doll but hold it up this way and it wont say mama again. But while he was showing me it said mama again and i said see.

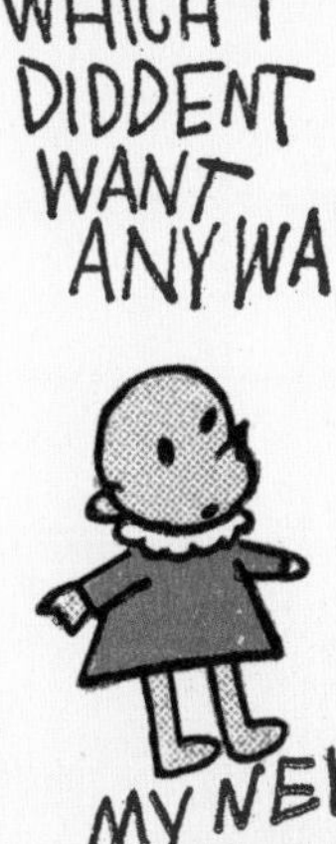

MY NEW DOLL

Thats all for now Dear Diry. See you next week.

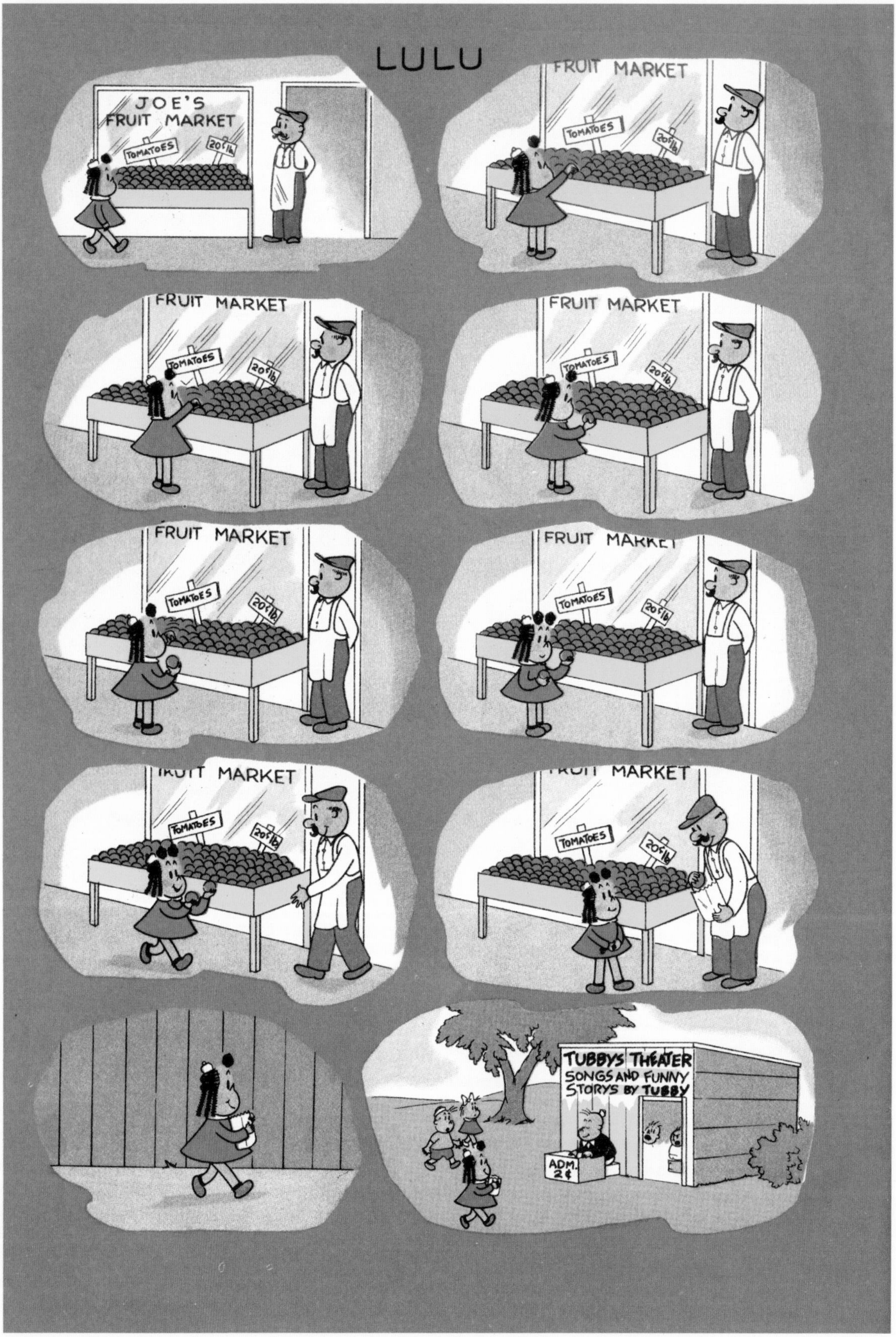
LULU
JOE'S
FRUIT MARKET
TOMATOES
20¢ lb
FRUIT MARKET
TUBBYS THEATER
SONGS AND FUNNY
STORYS BY TUBBY
ADM.
2¢

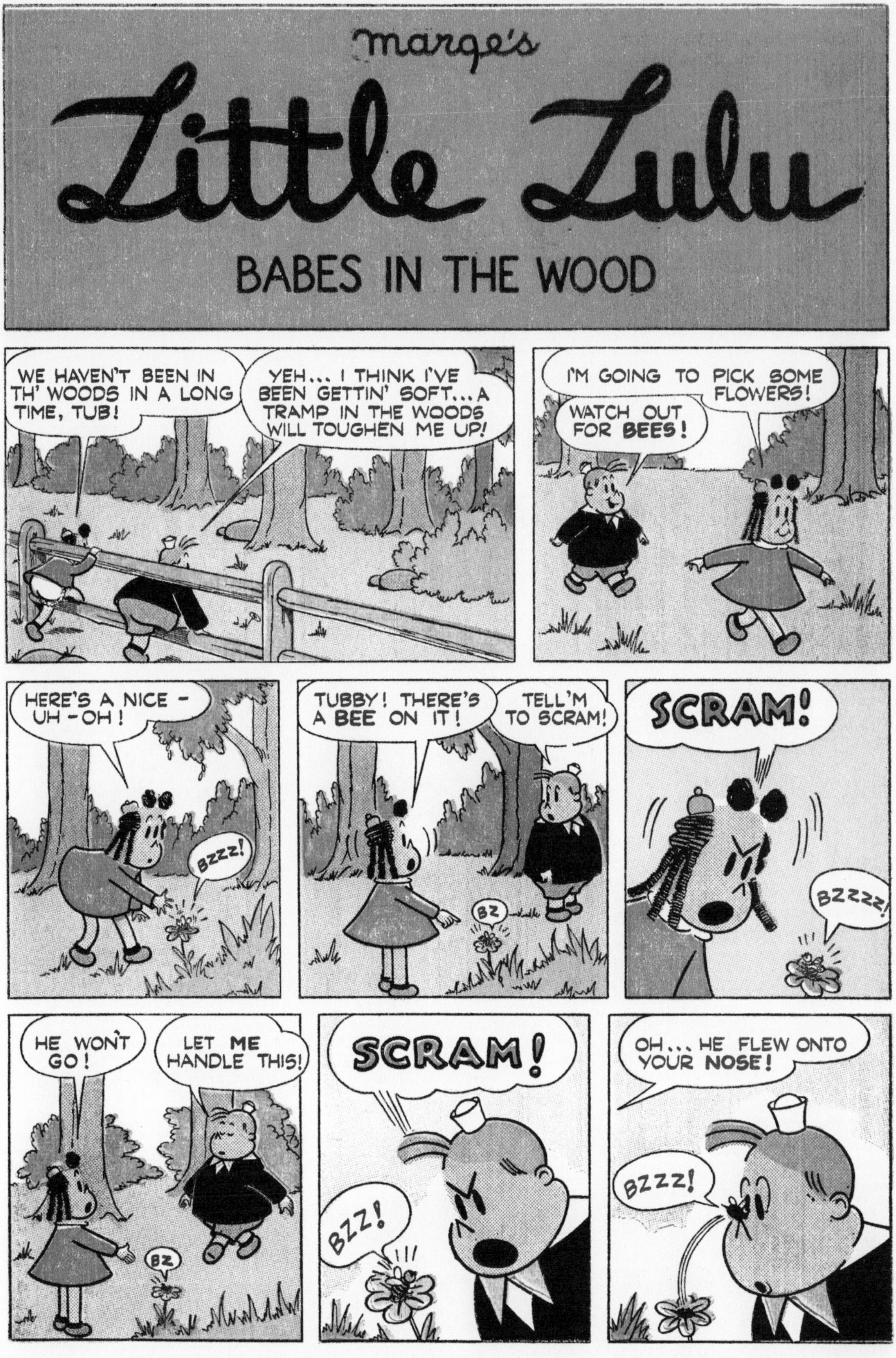
marge's
Little Lulu
BABES IN THE WOOD
WE HAVEN'T BEEN IN TH' WOODS IN A LONG TIME, TUB!
YEH... I THINK I'VE BEEN GETTIN' SOFT... A TRAMP IN THE WOODS WILL TOUGHEN ME UP!
I'M GOING TO PICK SOME FLOWERS!
WATCH OUT FOR BEES!
HERE'S A NICE - UH - OH!
BZZZ!
TUBBY! THERE'S A BEE ON IT!
TELL'M TO SCRAM!
BZ
SCRAM!
BZZZZ!
HE WON'T GO!
LET ME HANDLE THIS!
BZ
SCRAM!
BZZ!
OH... HE FLEW ONTO YOUR NOSE!
BZZZ!

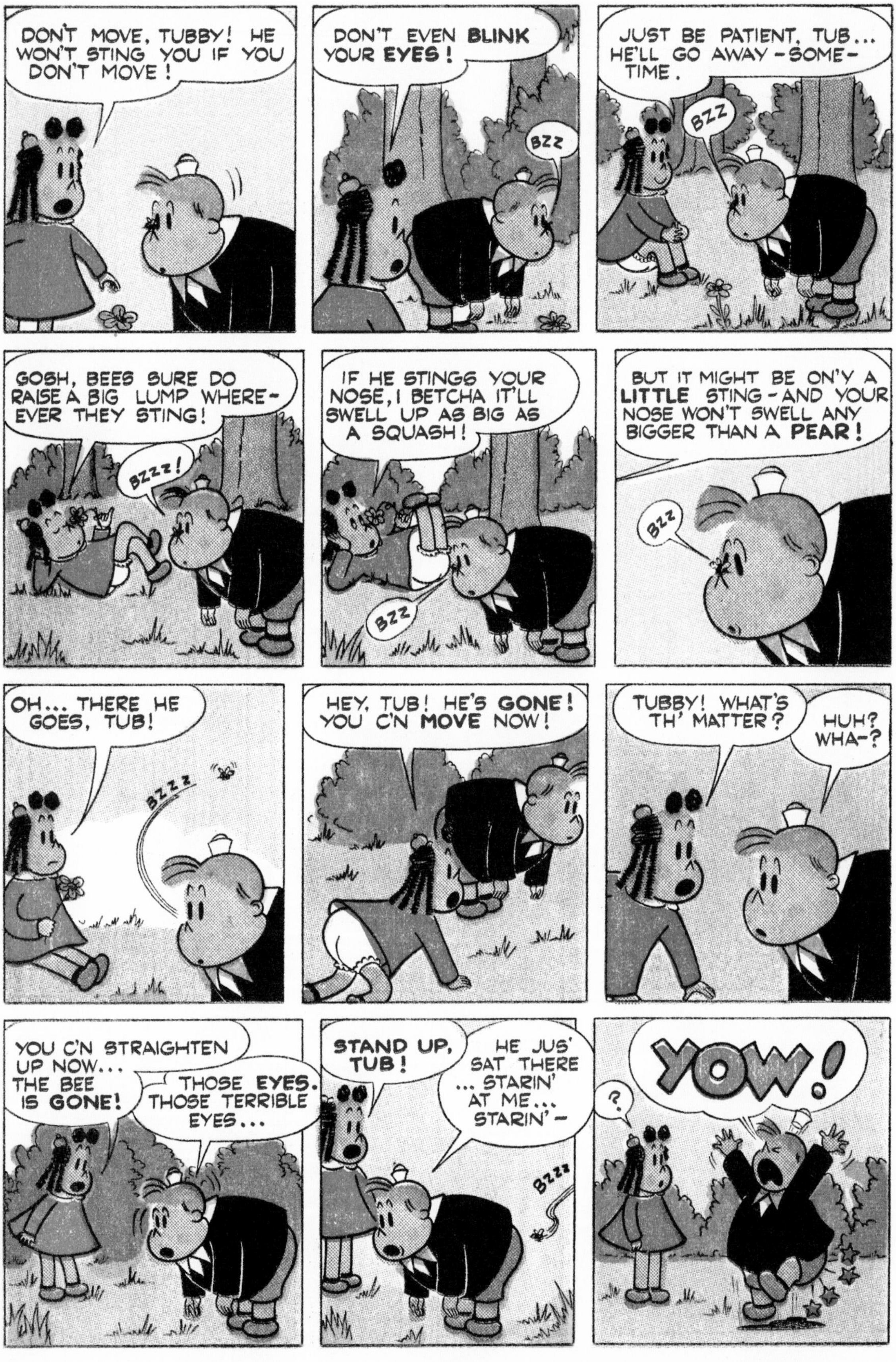
DON'T MOVE, TUBBY! HE WON'T STING YOU IF YOU DON'T MOVE!
DON'T EVEN **BLINK** YOUR **EYES!**
BZZ
JUST BE PATIENT, TUB... HE'LL GO AWAY-SOME-TIME.
BZZ
GOSH, BEES SURE DO RAISE A BIG LUMP WHERE-EVER THEY STING!
BZZZ!
IF HE STINGS YOUR NOSE, I BETCHA IT'LL SWELL UP AS BIG AS A SQUASH!
BZZ
BUT IT MIGHT BE ON'Y A **LITTLE** STING-AND YOUR NOSE WON'T SWELL ANY BIGGER THAN A **PEAR!**
BZZ
OH... THERE HE GOES, TUB!
BZZZ
HEY, TUB! HE'S **GONE!** YOU C'N **MOVE** NOW!
TUBBY! WHAT'S TH' MATTER?
HUH? WHA-?
YOU C'N STRAIGHTEN UP NOW... THE BEE IS **GONE!**
THOSE **EYES.** THOSE TERRIBLE EYES...
STAND UP, TUB!
HE JUS' SAT THERE ... STARIN' AT ME... STARIN'-
BZZZ
?
YOW!

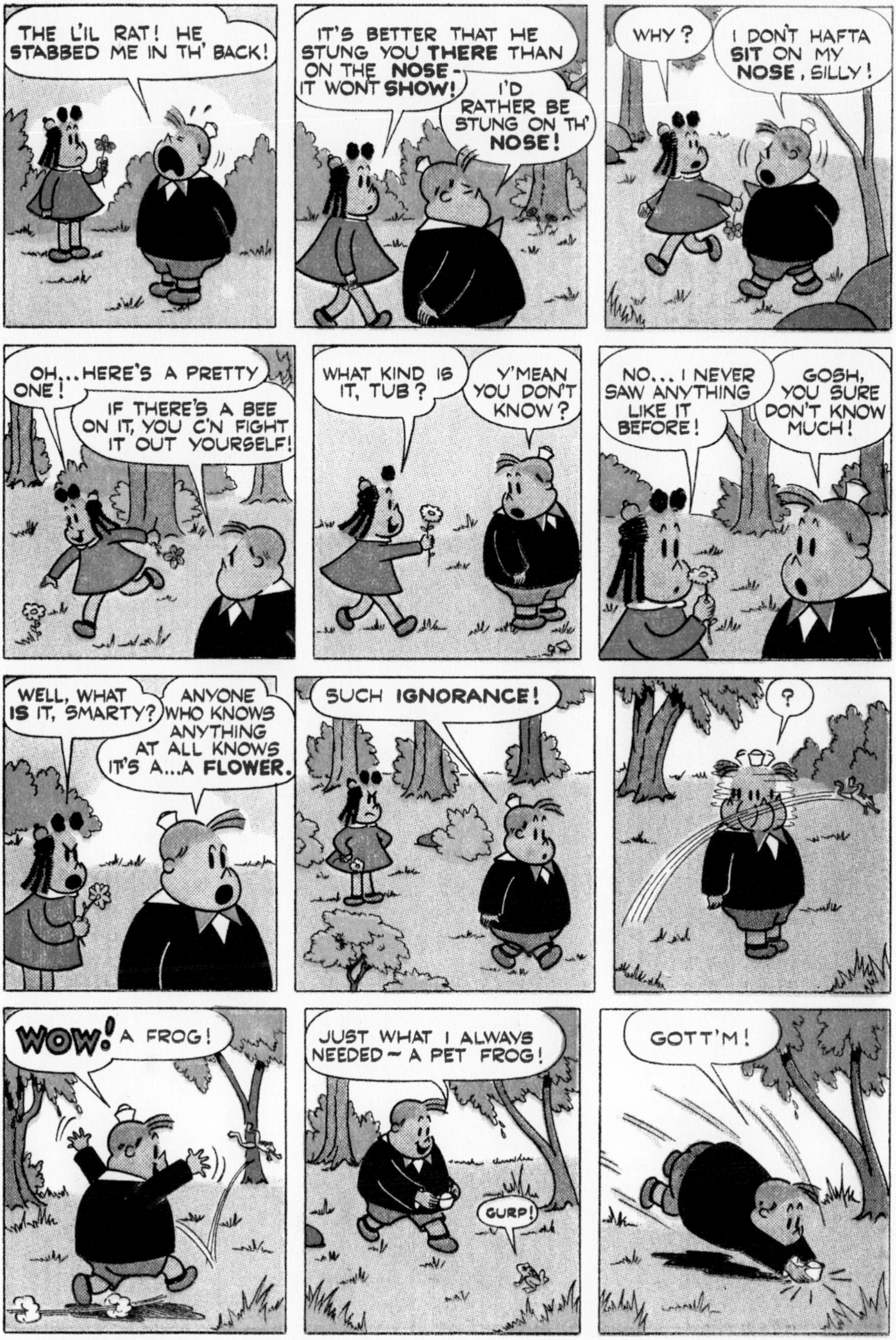
THE L'IL RAT! HE STABBED ME IN TH' BACK!
IT'S BETTER THAT HE STUNG YOU THERE THAN ON THE NOSE- IT WONT SHOW!
I'D RATHER BE STUNG ON TH' NOSE!
WHY?
I DON'T HAFTA SIT ON MY NOSE, SILLY!
OH...HERE'S A PRETTY ONE!
IF THERE'S A BEE ON IT, YOU C'N FIGHT IT OUT YOURSELF!
WHAT KIND IS IT, TUB?
Y'MEAN YOU DON'T KNOW?
NO... I NEVER SAW ANYTHING LIKE IT BEFORE!
GOSH, YOU SURE DON'T KNOW MUCH!
WELL, WHAT IS IT, SMARTY?
ANYONE WHO KNOWS ANYTHING AT ALL KNOWS IT'S A...A FLOWER.
SUCH IGNORANCE!
?
WOW! A FROG!
JUST WHAT I ALWAYS NEEDED ~ A PET FROG!
GURP!
GOTT'M!

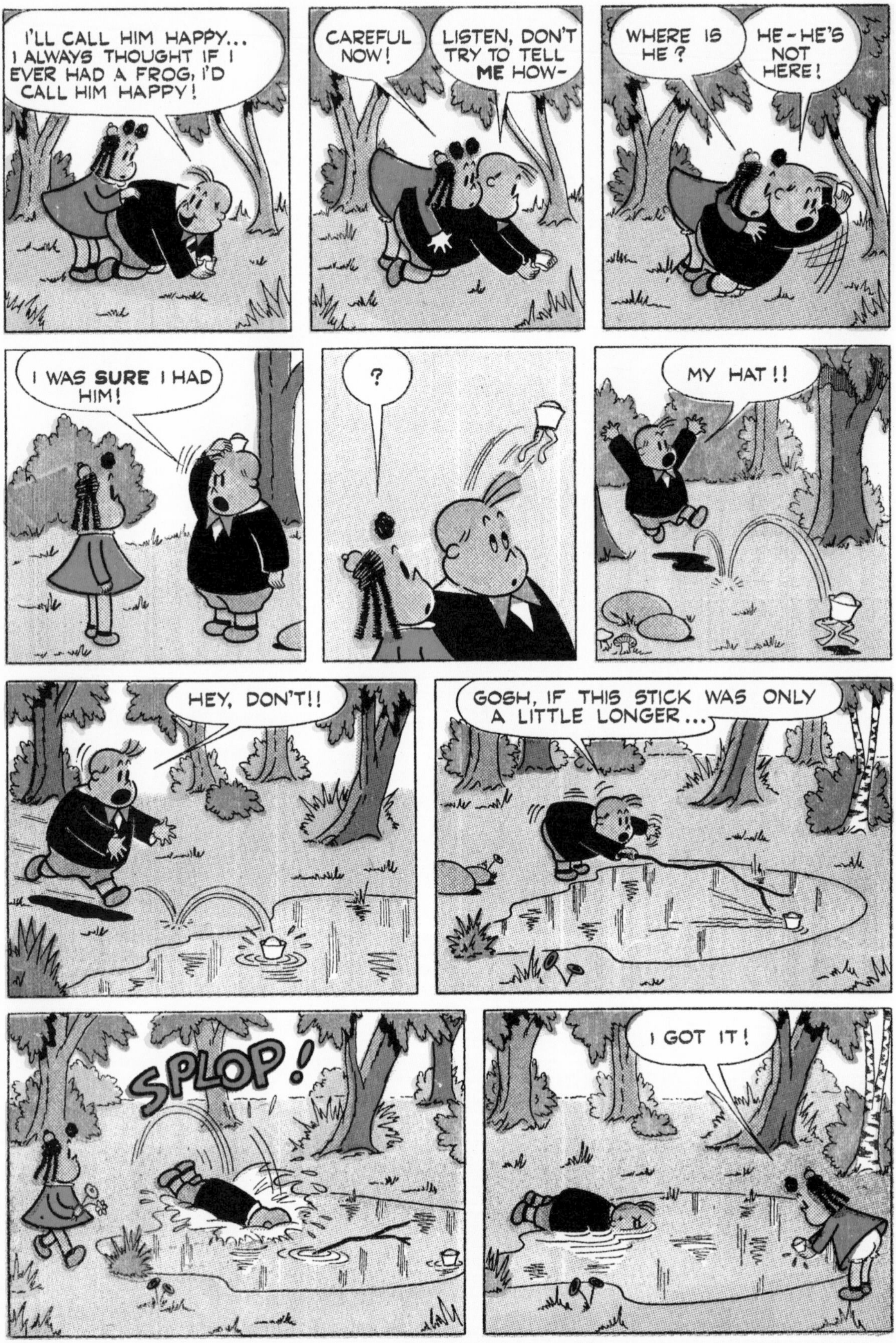
I'LL CALL HIM HAPPY... I ALWAYS THOUGHT IF I EVER HAD A FROG, I'D CALL HIM HAPPY!
CAREFUL NOW!
LISTEN, DON'T TRY TO TELL **ME** HOW-
WHERE IS HE?
HE-HE'S NOT HERE!
I WAS **SURE** I HAD HIM!
?
MY HAT!!
HEY, DON'T!!
GOSH, IF THIS STICK WAS ONLY A LITTLE LONGER...
SPLOP!
I GOT IT!

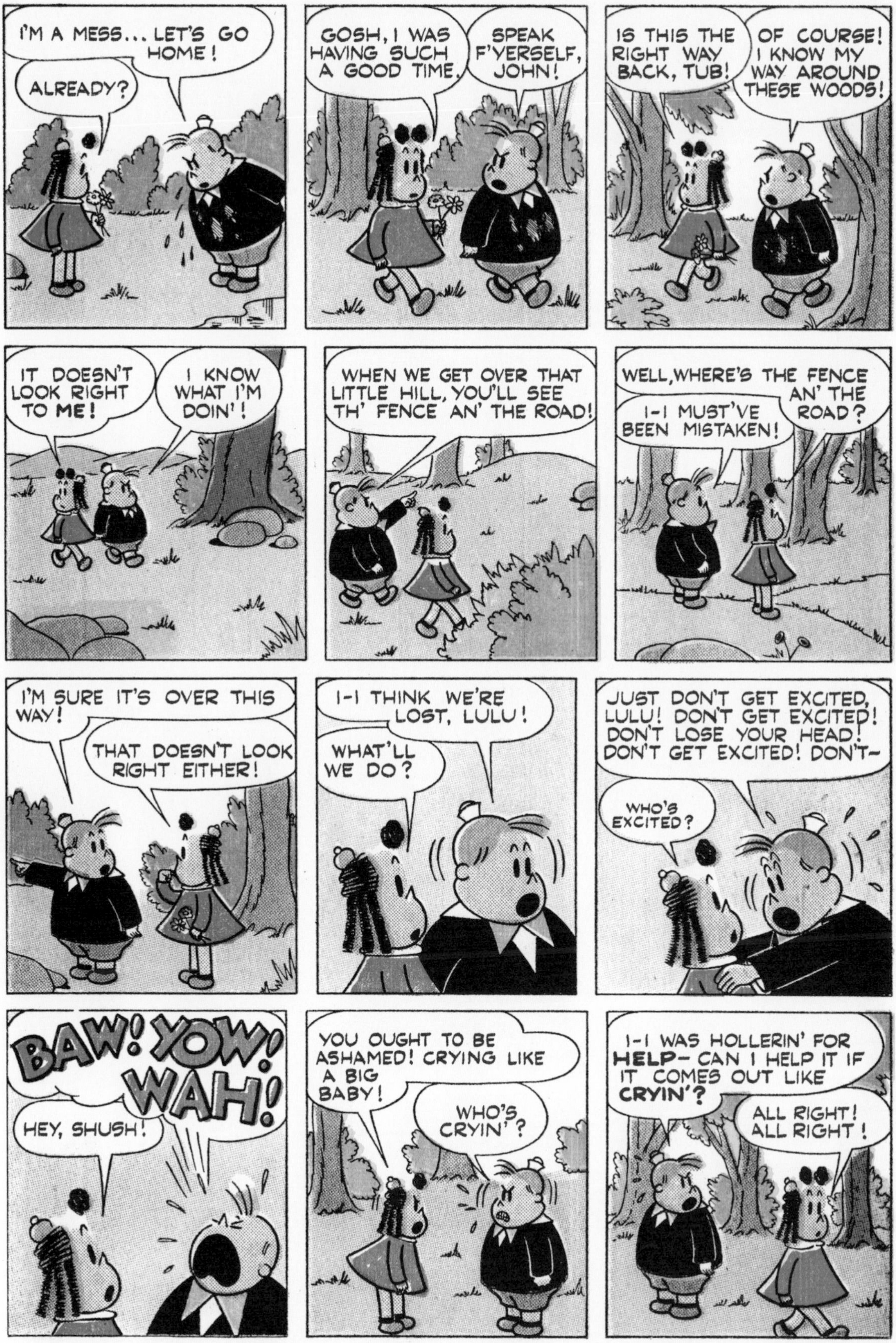
I'M A MESS... LET'S GO HOME!
ALREADY?
GOSH, I WAS HAVING SUCH A GOOD TIME.
SPEAK F'YERSELF, JOHN!
IS THIS THE RIGHT WAY BACK, TUB!
OF COURSE! I KNOW MY WAY AROUND THESE WOODS!
IT DOESN'T LOOK RIGHT TO ME!
I KNOW WHAT I'M DOIN'!
WHEN WE GET OVER THAT LITTLE HILL, YOU'LL SEE TH' FENCE AN' THE ROAD!
WELL, WHERE'S THE FENCE AN' THE ROAD?
I-I MUST'VE BEEN MISTAKEN!
I'M SURE IT'S OVER THIS WAY!
THAT DOESN'T LOOK RIGHT EITHER!
I-I THINK WE'RE LOST, LULU!
WHAT'LL WE DO?
JUST DON'T GET EXCITED, LULU! DON'T GET EXCITED! DON'T LOSE YOUR HEAD! DON'T GET EXCITED! DON'T-
WHO'S EXCITED?
BAW! YOW! WAH!
HEY, SHUSH!
YOU OUGHT TO BE ASHAMED! CRYING LIKE A BIG BABY!
WHO'S CRYIN'?
I-I WAS HOLLERIN' FOR HELP- CAN I HELP IT IF IT COMES OUT LIKE CRYIN'?
ALL RIGHT! ALL RIGHT!

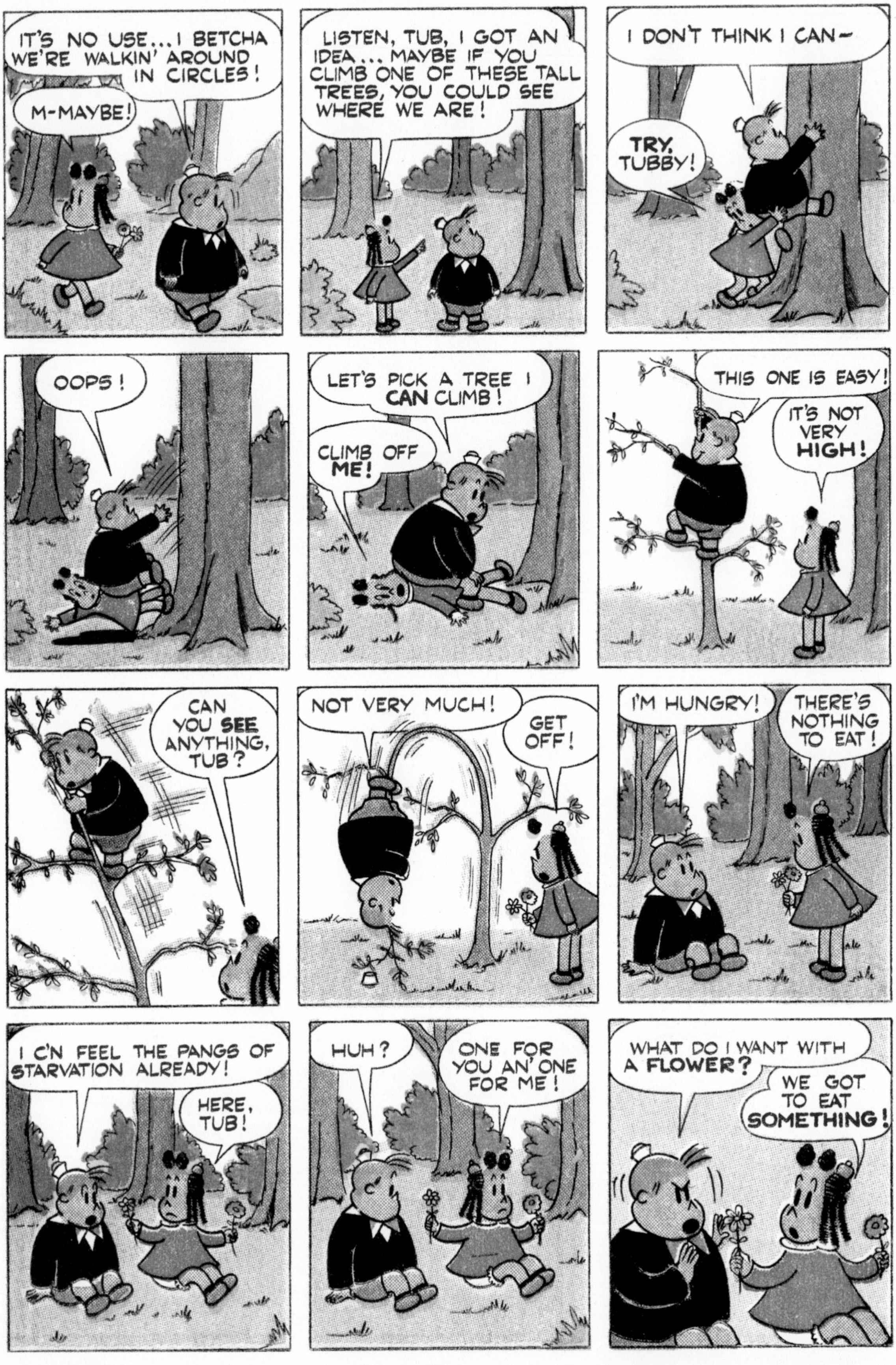
IT'S NO USE... I BETCHA WE'RE WALKIN' AROUND IN CIRCLES!
M-MAYBE!
LISTEN, TUB, I GOT AN IDEA... MAYBE IF YOU CLIMB ONE OF THESE TALL TREES, YOU COULD SEE WHERE WE ARE!
I DON'T THINK I CAN—
TRY, TUBBY!
OOPS!
LET'S PICK A TREE I CAN CLIMB!
CLIMB OFF ME!
THIS ONE IS EASY!
IT'S NOT VERY HIGH!
CAN YOU SEE ANYTHING, TUB?
NOT VERY MUCH!
GET OFF!
I'M HUNGRY!
THERE'S NOTHING TO EAT!
I C'N FEEL THE PANGS OF STARVATION ALREADY!
HERE, TUB!
HUH?
ONE FOR YOU AN' ONE FOR ME!
WHAT DO I WANT WITH A FLOWER?
WE GOT TO EAT SOMETHING!

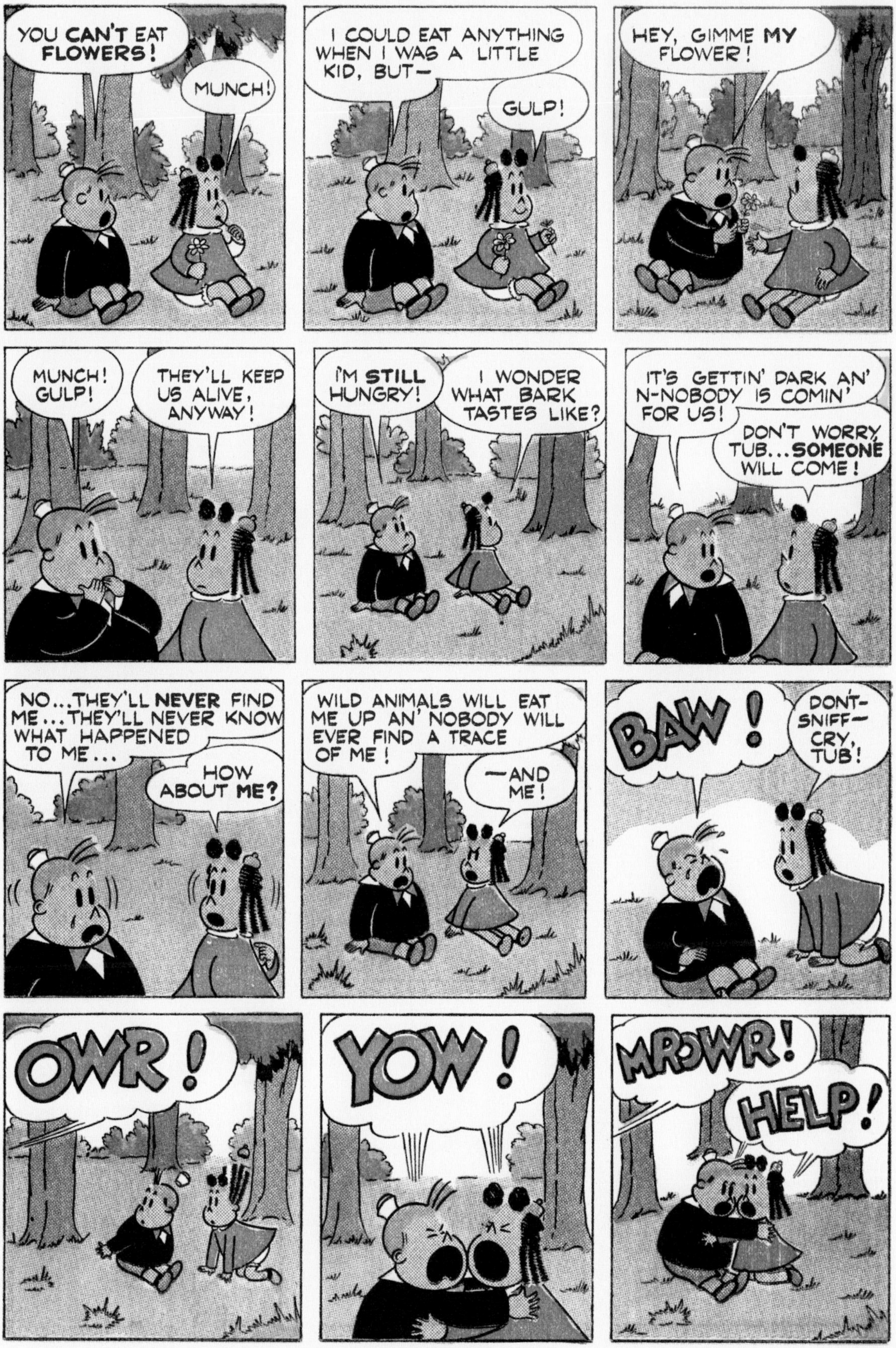
YOU CAN'T EAT FLOWERS!
MUNCH!
I COULD EAT ANYTHING WHEN I WAS A LITTLE KID, BUT—
GULP!
HEY, GIMME MY FLOWER!
MUNCH! GULP!
THEY'LL KEEP US ALIVE, ANYWAY!
I'M STILL HUNGRY!
I WONDER WHAT BARK TASTES LIKE?
IT'S GETTIN' DARK AN' N-NOBODY IS COMIN' FOR US!
DON'T WORRY TUB...SOMEONE WILL COME!
NO...THEY'LL NEVER FIND ME...THEY'LL NEVER KNOW WHAT HAPPENED TO ME...
HOW ABOUT ME?
WILD ANIMALS WILL EAT ME UP AN' NOBODY WILL EVER FIND A TRACE OF ME!
—AND ME!
BAW!
DON'T-SNIFF-CRY, TUB!
OWR!
YOW!
MROWR!
HELP!

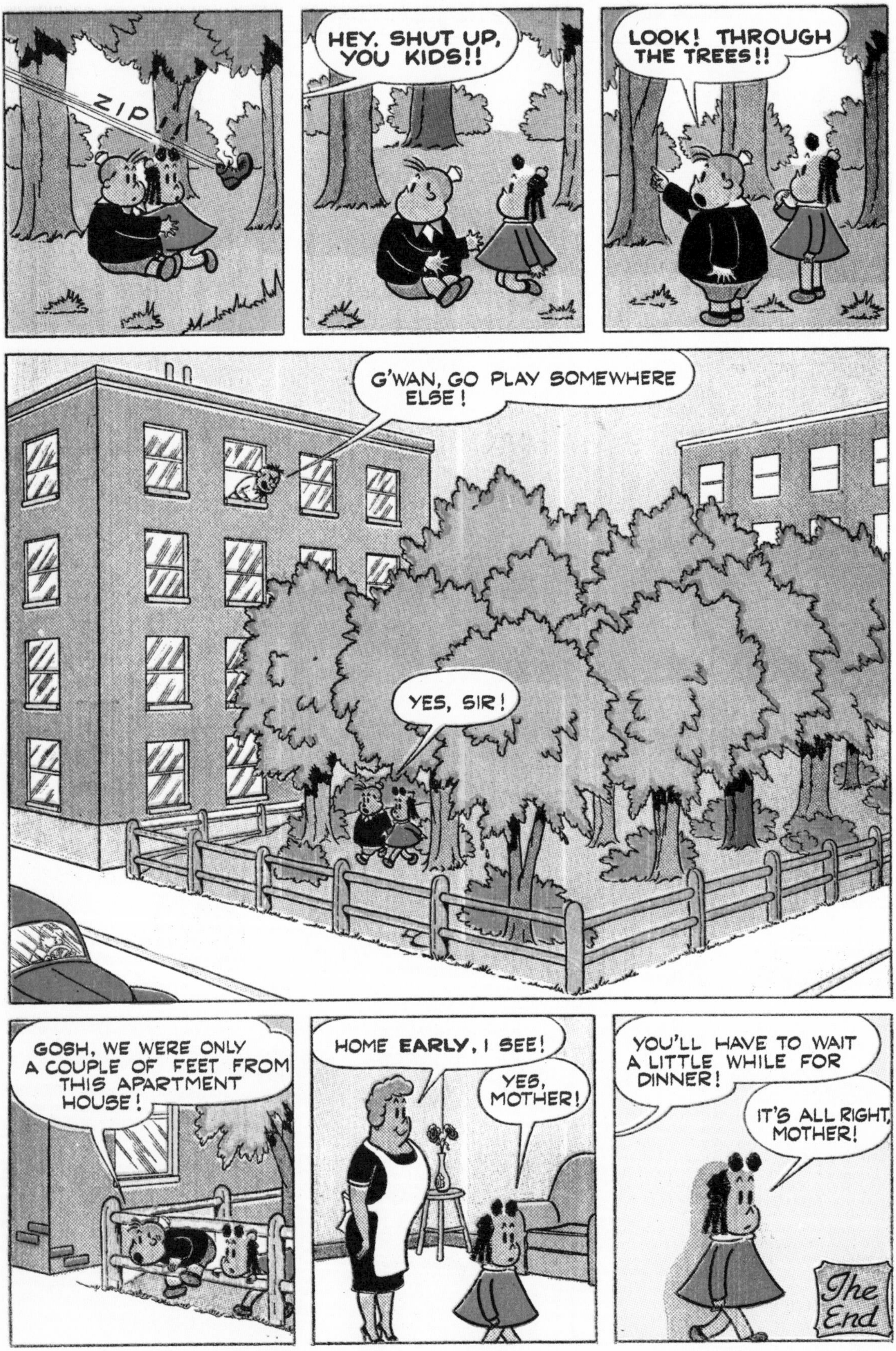

ZIP
HEY. SHUT UP, YOU KIDS!!
LOOK! THROUGH THE TREES!!
G'WAN, GO PLAY SOMEWHERE ELSE!
YES, SIR!
GOSH, WE WERE ONLY A COUPLE OF FEET FROM THIS APARTMENT HOUSE!
HOME EARLY, I SEE!
YES, MOTHER!
YOU'LL HAVE TO WAIT A LITTLE WHILE FOR DINNER!
IT'S ALL RIGHT, MOTHER!
The End

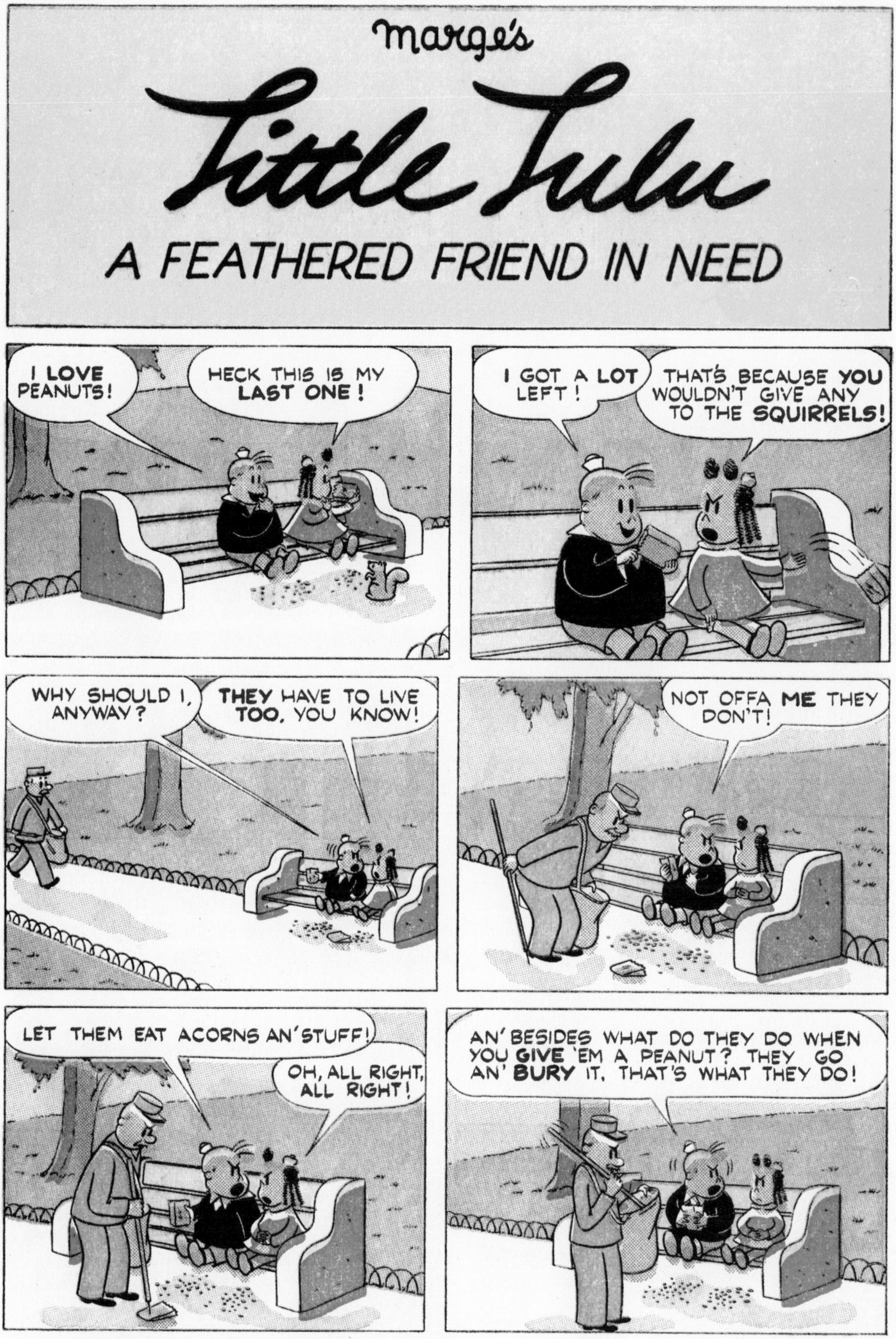
marge's
Little Lulu
A FEATHERED FRIEND IN NEED
I LOVE PEANUTS!
HECK THIS IS MY LAST ONE!
I GOT A LOT LEFT!
THAT'S BECAUSE YOU WOULDN'T GIVE ANY TO THE SQUIRRELS!
WHY SHOULD I, ANYWAY?
THEY HAVE TO LIVE TOO, YOU KNOW!
NOT OFFA ME THEY DON'T!
LET THEM EAT ACORNS AN' STUFF!
OH, ALL RIGHT, ALL RIGHT!
AN' BESIDES WHAT DO THEY DO WHEN YOU GIVE 'EM A PEANUT? THEY GO AN' BURY IT, THAT'S WHAT THEY DO!

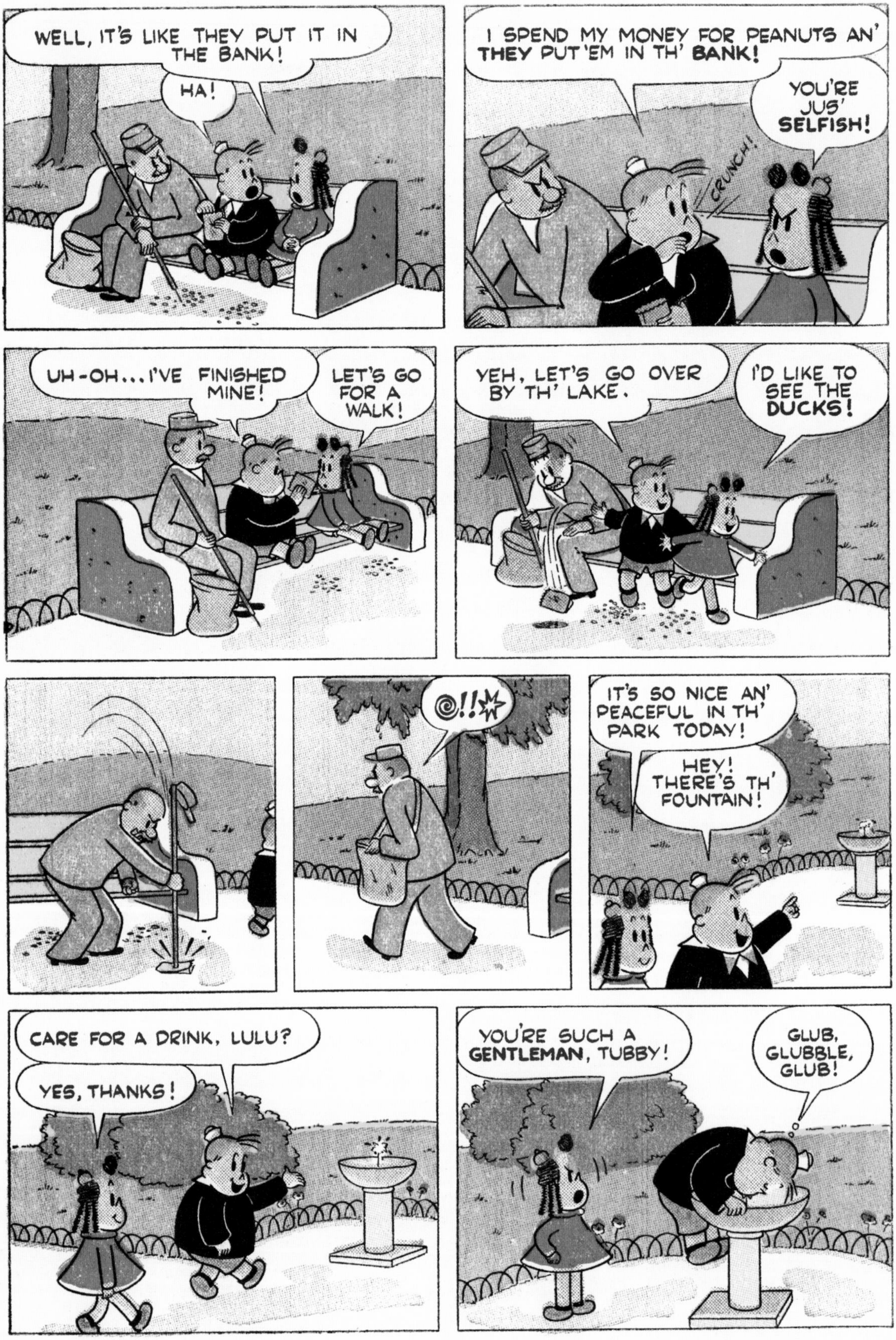
WELL, IT'S LIKE THEY PUT IT IN THE BANK!
HA!
I SPEND MY MONEY FOR PEANUTS AN' THEY PUT 'EM IN TH' BANK!
YOU'RE JUS' SELFISH!
CRUNCH!
UH-OH... I'VE FINISHED MINE!
LET'S GO FOR A WALK!
YEH, LET'S GO OVER BY TH' LAKE.
I'D LIKE TO SEE THE DUCKS!
IT'S SO NICE AN' PEACEFUL IN TH' PARK TODAY!
HEY! THERE'S TH' FOUNTAIN!
CARE FOR A DRINK, LULU?
YES, THANKS!
YOU'RE SUCH A GENTLEMAN, TUBBY!
GLUB, GLUBBLE, GLUB!

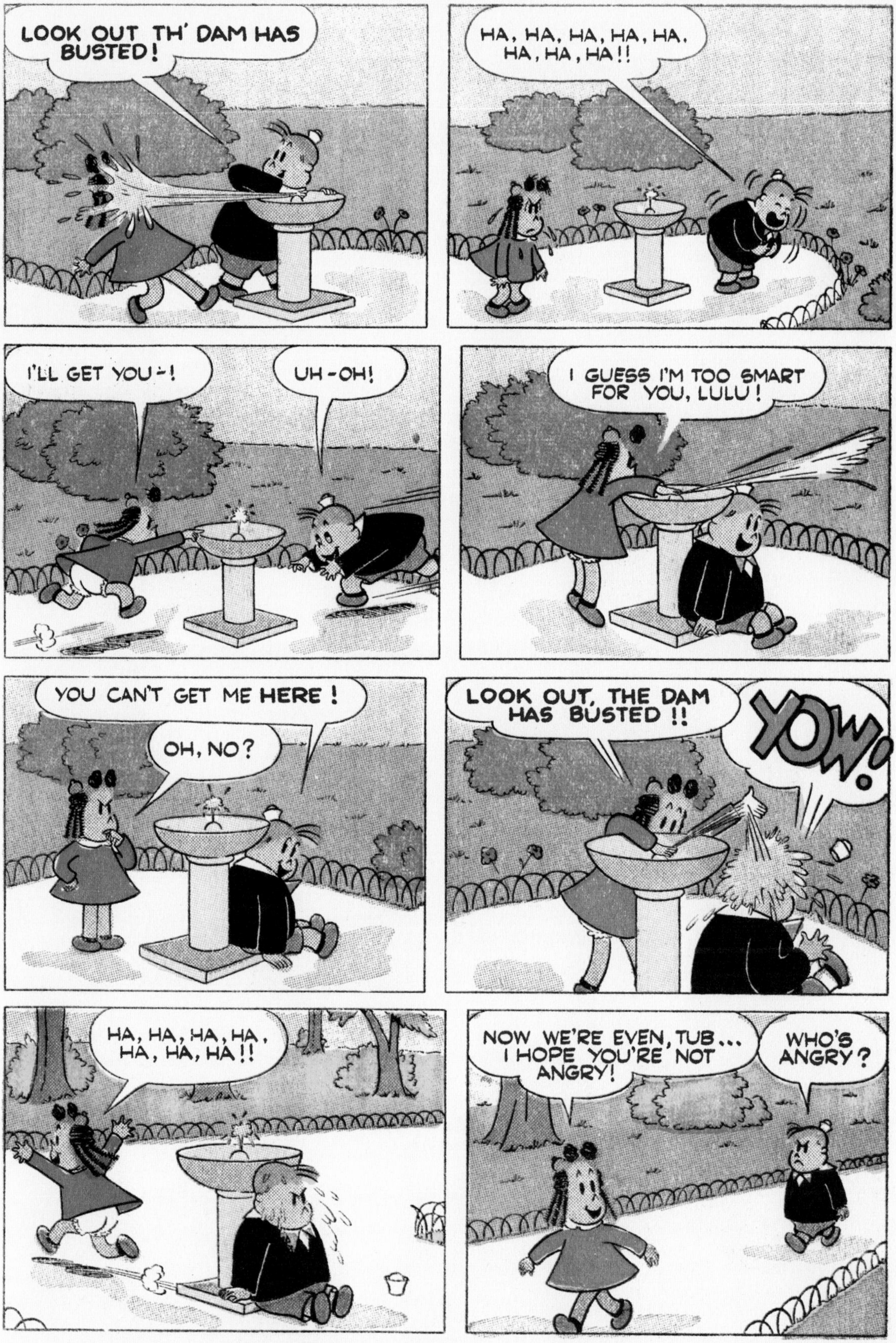
LOOK OUT TH' DAM HAS BUSTED!
HA, HA, HA, HA, HA. HA, HA, HA!!
I'LL GET YOU-!
UH-OH!
I GUESS I'M TOO SMART FOR YOU, LULU!
YOU CAN'T GET ME HERE!
OH, NO?
LOOK OUT, THE DAM HAS BUSTED!!
YOW!
HA, HA, HA, HA, HA, HA, HA!!
NOW WE'RE EVEN, TUB... I HOPE YOU'RE NOT ANGRY!
WHO'S ANGRY?

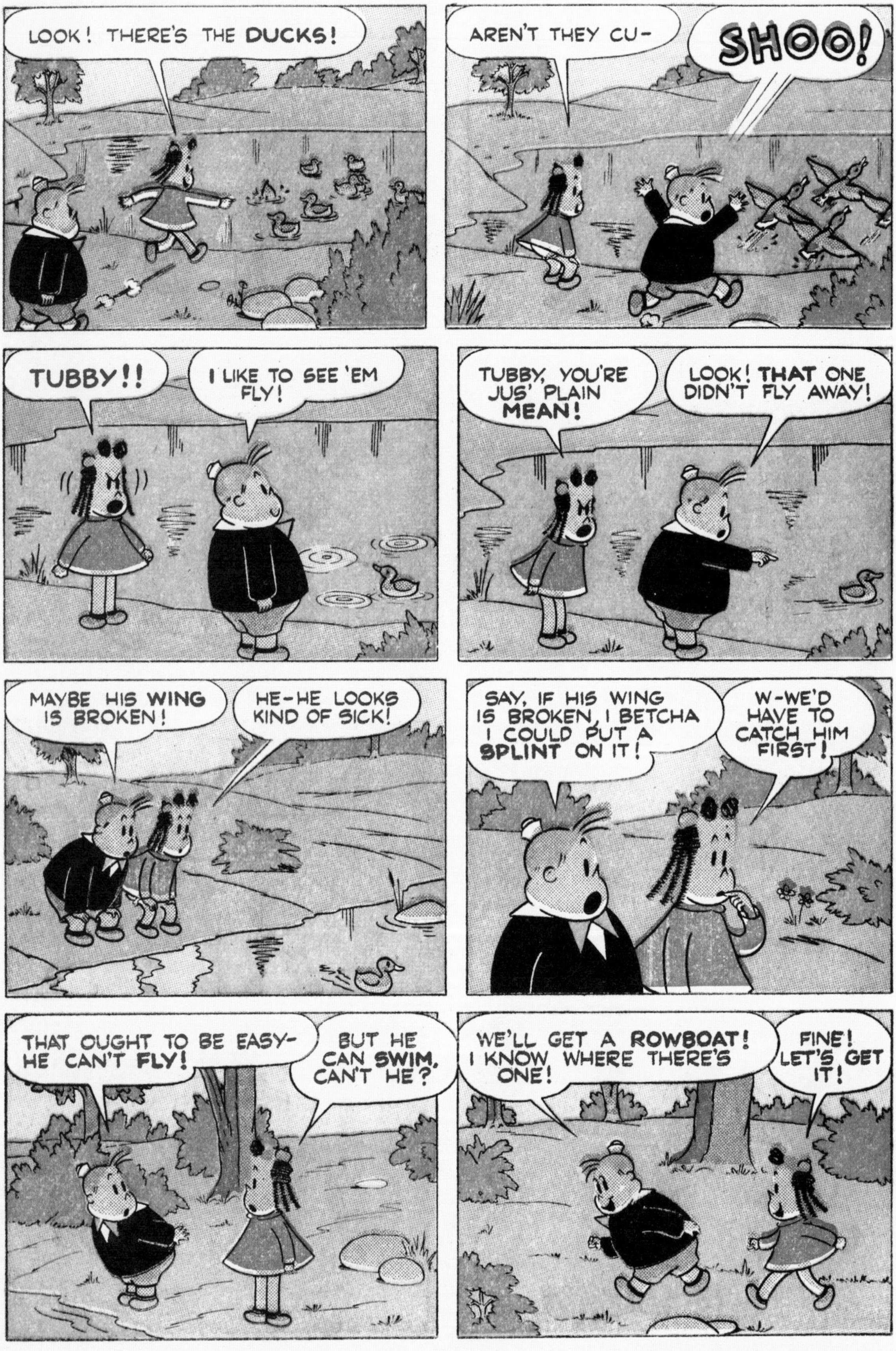

LOOK! THERE'S THE DUCKS!
AREN'T THEY CU-
SHOO!
TUBBY!!
I LIKE TO SEE 'EM FLY!
TUBBY, YOU'RE JUS' PLAIN MEAN!
LOOK! THAT ONE DIDN'T FLY AWAY!
MAYBE HIS WING IS BROKEN!
HE-HE LOOKS KIND OF SICK!
SAY, IF HIS WING IS BROKEN, I BETCHA I COULD PUT A SPLINT ON IT!
W-WE'D HAVE TO CATCH HIM FIRST!
THAT OUGHT TO BE EASY- HE CAN'T FLY!
BUT HE CAN SWIM, CAN'T HE?
WE'LL GET A ROWBOAT! I KNOW WHERE THERE'S ONE!
FINE! LET'S GET IT!

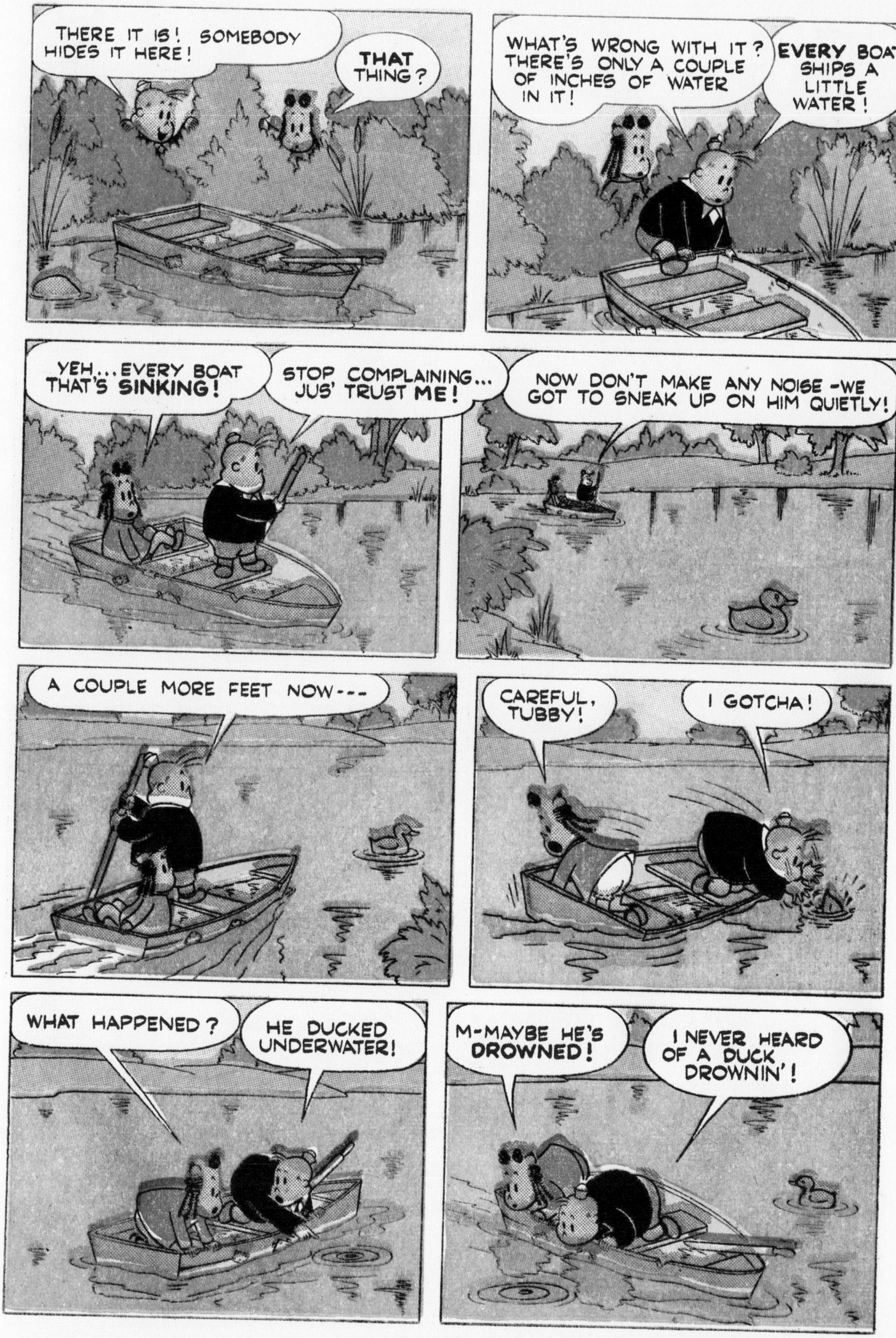
THERE IT IS! SOMEBODY HIDES IT HERE!
THAT THING?
WHAT'S WRONG WITH IT? THERE'S ONLY A COUPLE OF INCHES OF WATER IN IT!
EVERY BOAT SHIPS A LITTLE WATER!
YEH...EVERY BOAT THAT'S SINKING!
STOP COMPLAINING... JUS' TRUST ME!
NOW DON'T MAKE ANY NOISE -WE GOT TO SNEAK UP ON HIM QUIETLY!
A COUPLE MORE FEET NOW---
CAREFUL, TUBBY!
I GOTCHA!
WHAT HAPPENED?
HE DUCKED UNDERWATER!
M-MAYBE HE'S DROWNED!
I NEVER HEARD OF A DUCK DROWNIN'!

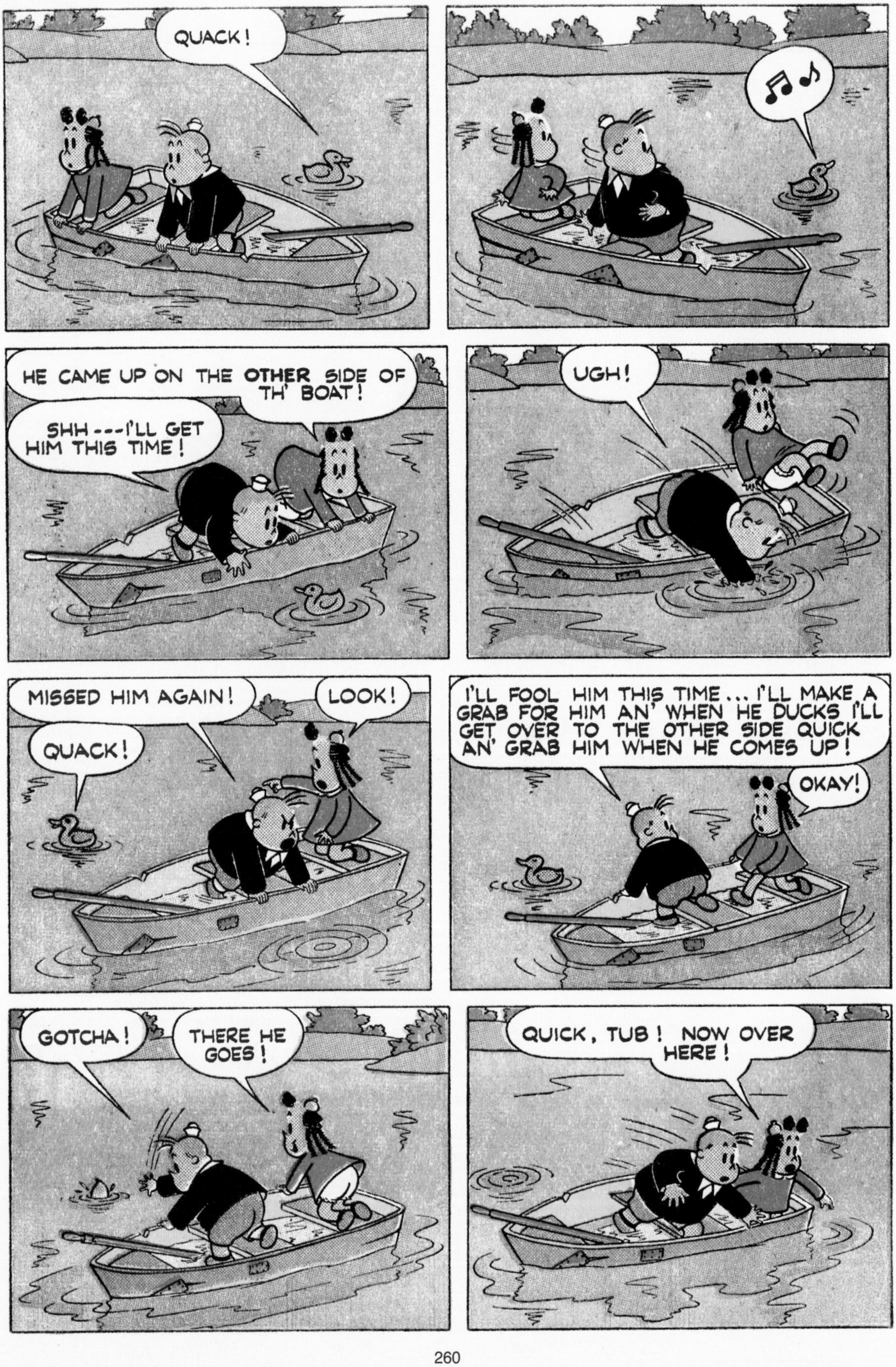
QUACK!
♫ ♪
HE CAME UP ON THE OTHER SIDE OF TH' BOAT!
SHH---I'LL GET HIM THIS TIME!
UGH!
MISSED HIM AGAIN!
LOOK!
QUACK!
I'LL FOOL HIM THIS TIME... I'LL MAKE A GRAB FOR HIM AN' WHEN HE DUCKS I'LL GET OVER TO THE OTHER SIDE QUICK AN' GRAB HIM WHEN HE COMES UP!
OKAY!
GOTCHA!
THERE HE GOES!
QUICK, TUB! NOW OVER HERE!

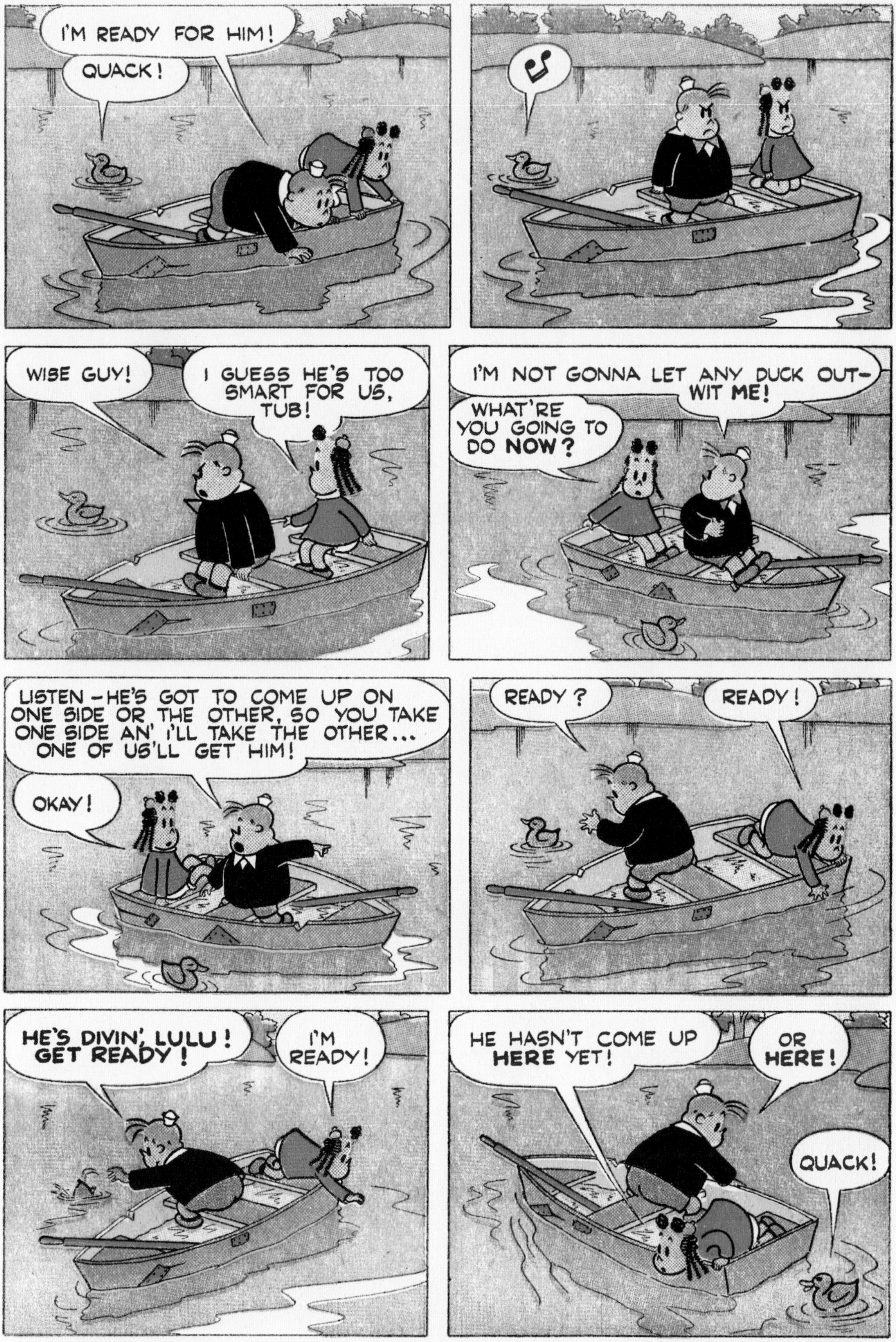
I'M READY FOR HIM!
QUACK!
WISE GUY!
I GUESS HE'S TOO SMART FOR US, TUB!
I'M NOT GONNA LET ANY DUCK OUT-WIT ME!
WHAT'RE YOU GOING TO DO NOW?
LISTEN – HE'S GOT TO COME UP ON ONE SIDE OR THE OTHER, SO YOU TAKE ONE SIDE AN' I'LL TAKE THE OTHER... ONE OF US'LL GET HIM!
OKAY!
READY?
READY!
HE'S DIVIN', LULU! GET READY!
I'M READY!
HE HASN'T COME UP HERE YET!
OR HERE!
QUACK!

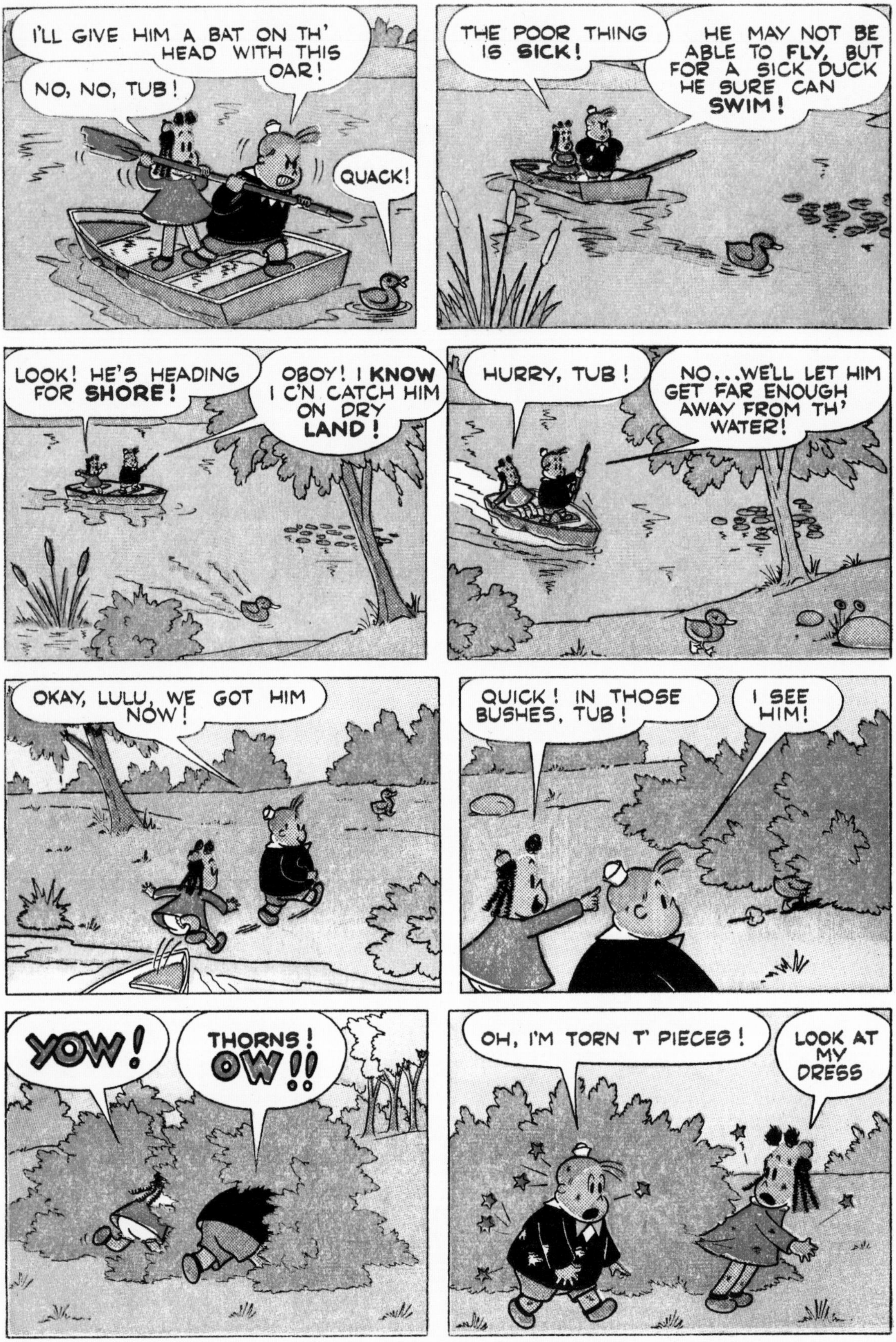
I'LL GIVE HIM A BAT ON TH' HEAD WITH THIS OAR!
NO, NO, TUB!
QUACK!
THE POOR THING IS SICK!
HE MAY NOT BE ABLE TO FLY, BUT FOR A SICK DUCK HE SURE CAN SWIM!
LOOK! HE'S HEADING FOR SHORE!
OBOY! I KNOW I C'N CATCH HIM ON DRY LAND!
HURRY, TUB!
NO...WE'LL LET HIM GET FAR ENOUGH AWAY FROM TH' WATER!
OKAY, LULU, WE GOT HIM NOW!
QUICK! IN THOSE BUSHES, TUB!
I SEE HIM!
YOW!
THORNS! OW!!
OH, I'M TORN T' PIECES!
LOOK AT MY DRESS

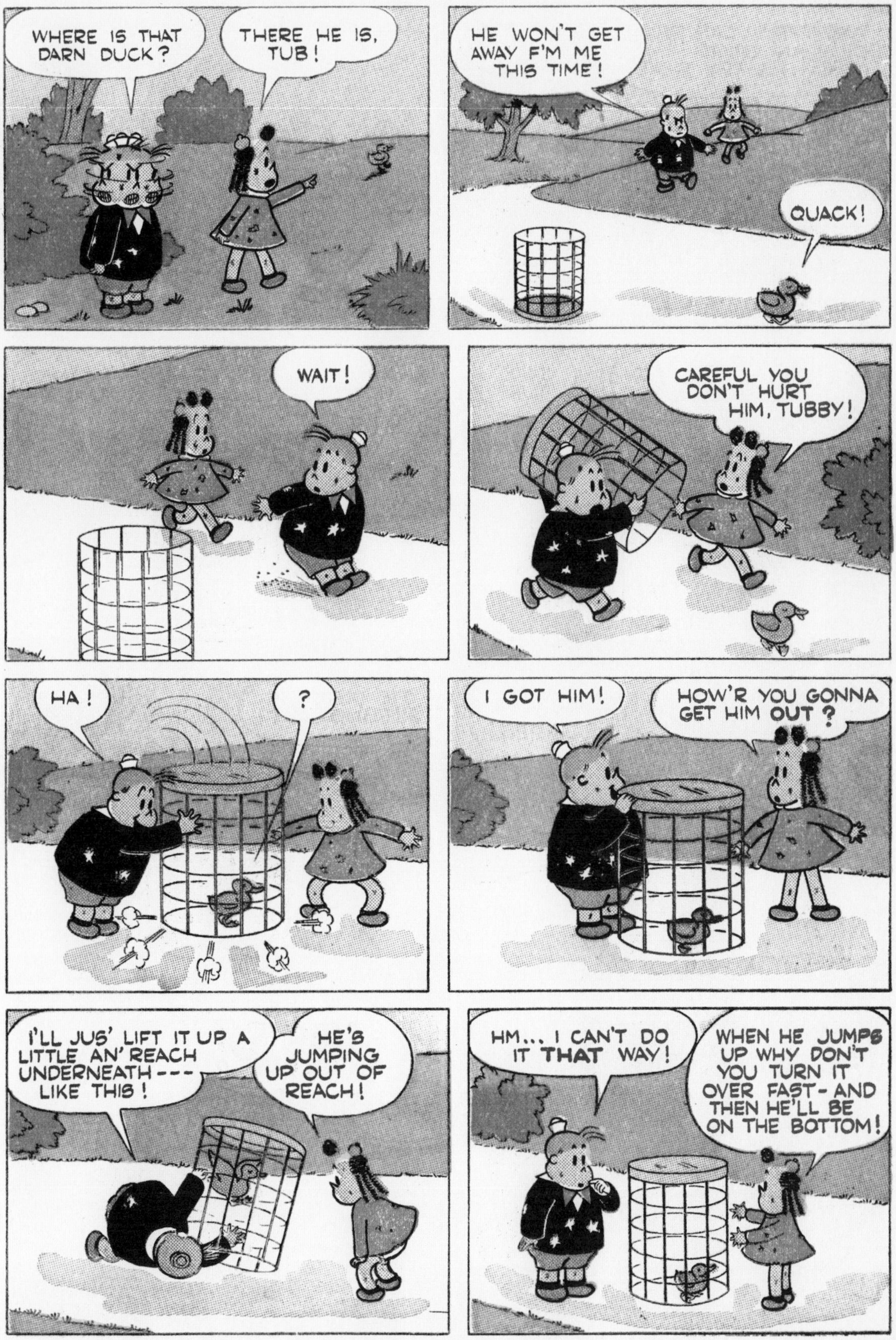
WHERE IS THAT DARN DUCK?
THERE HE IS, TUB!
HE WON'T GET AWAY F'M ME THIS TIME!
QUACK!
WAIT!
CAREFUL YOU DON'T HURT HIM, TUBBY!
HA!
?
I GOT HIM!
HOW'R YOU GONNA GET HIM OUT?
I'LL JUS' LIFT IT UP A LITTLE AN' REACH UNDERNEATH --- LIKE THIS!
HE'S JUMPING UP OUT OF REACH!
HM... I CAN'T DO IT THAT WAY!
WHEN HE JUMPS UP WHY DON'T YOU TURN IT OVER FAST- AND THEN HE'LL BE ON THE BOTTOM!

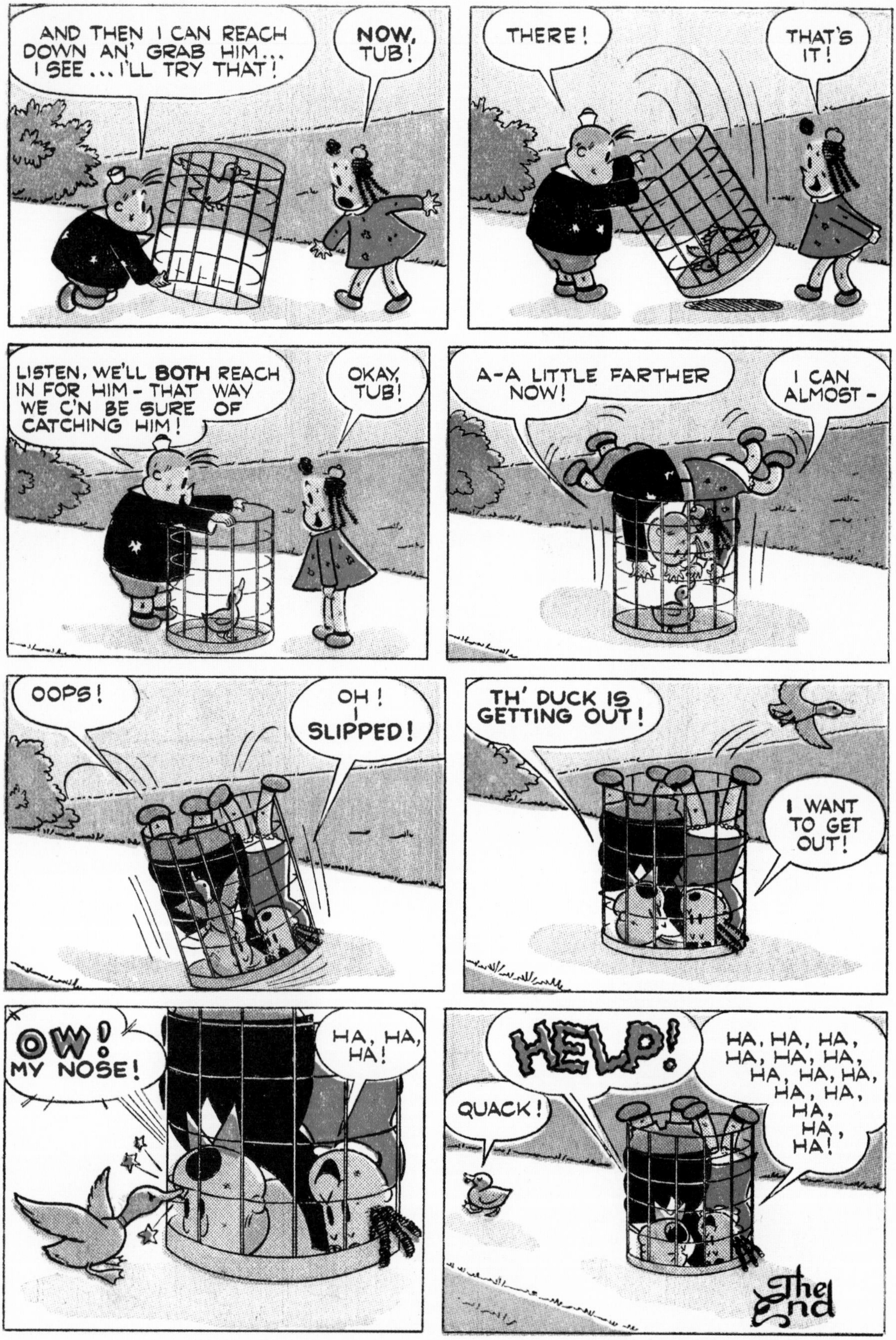
AND THEN I CAN REACH DOWN AN' GRAB HIM... I SEE... I'LL TRY THAT!
NOW, TUB!
THERE!
THAT'S IT!
LISTEN, WE'LL BOTH REACH IN FOR HIM - THAT WAY WE C'N BE SURE OF CATCHING HIM!
OKAY, TUB!
A-A LITTLE FARTHER NOW!
I CAN ALMOST -
OOPS!
OH! I SLIPPED!
TH' DUCK IS GETTING OUT!
I WANT TO GET OUT!
OW! MY NOSE!
HA, HA, HA!
HELP!
QUACK!
HA, HA, HA, HA, HA, HA, HA, HA, HA, HA, HA, HA, HA, HA!
The End

LULUS DIRY

PICTURS BY LULU TOO

Dear Diry

I had to stay in bed a whole day last week because I was very sick. I felt terrible bad in my stummik and sometimes in my head. Mother said oh Lulu you better not go to school and I will call the doctor. I said oh mother I dont feel sick enough to call a doctor I think I am only sick enough to stay home a little while from school. But mother called the doctor anyway and he came to see me.

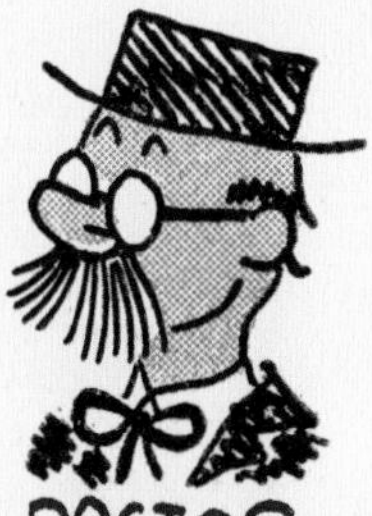
DOCTOR

He laughed and said oh I bet you are making believe you are sick little lady because you dont want to go to school. I said ha ha and mother said shush. But I reely was sick dear diry. The doctor wrote some thing on a little piece of paper and gave it to mother then he left. I said mother what did he write on that paper let me see it. Mother said it was for some medicin for me. I tried to read it but I couldnt because the doctor writes so bad, almost as bad as tubby. Maybe some day tubby will be a doctor. Mother went out and got the medicin it tasted nice and sweet like soda pop but I diddint like it anyway because it was medicin. But mother said I would have to take a little once in a while. Then I said mother can I get dressed and come downstairs but mother said no you are supposed to be sick and you have to stay in bed.

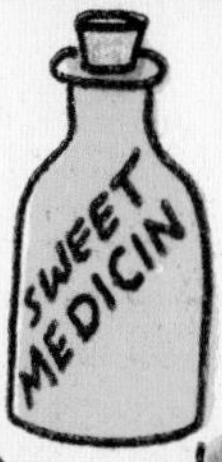
SWEET MEDICIN

When mother went downstairs I got out of bed and rocked my dolly to sleep who is crying all the time then I looked out of the window because it was such a beautiful day. Three pretty little birdies were playing in our yard and hollering and chasing each other around. they were crows I think. I woke up my dolly and took her to the window to see the birdies. I had to lean way out because the birdies were over near our tree. My dolly slipped and fell down in the grass in our yard. Gosh I diddint know what to do I couldnt leave my dolly down there because maybe some crook would come along and think it diddint belong to anybody and take it. I tip toed out in the hall and went down the stairs very quiet and went outside and walked around to where my dolly was. But my dolly wasnt there but I saw it going down the street. Oh not all by itself because my dolly cant walk. A big dog was carrying my dolly in his mouth and running along and shaking it and my dolly was saying mama. I ran after the big dog but he ran very fast and I couldnt catch him because I was running with my bare feet and I was afraid I would step on something maybe a rock.

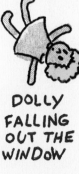

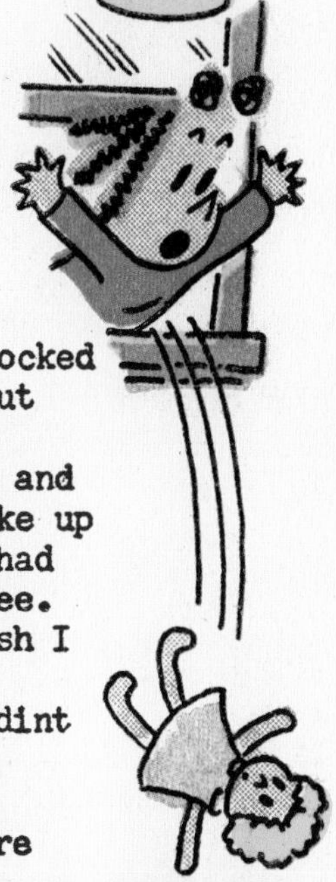
DOLLY FALLING OUT THE WINDOW

But another dog came along and tried to pull my dolly away from the big dog and they tore my dolly and all the saw dust went all over the street. Then the dogs ran away and left my dolly on the street she looked awful with no saw dust. I diddint have a broom to sweep up the saw dust to put back in my dolly so I walked over to the butcher store who has saw dust on the floor and maybe I could get some to put in my dolly. But the man said hey what are you doing in your nightie with bare feet it is cold out today go home. I felt very bad because he wouldnt give me any saw dust. I had to go home quick because mother might come up stairs and see I wasnt in bed and o boy would I get a spanking so I took the short cut through the woods.

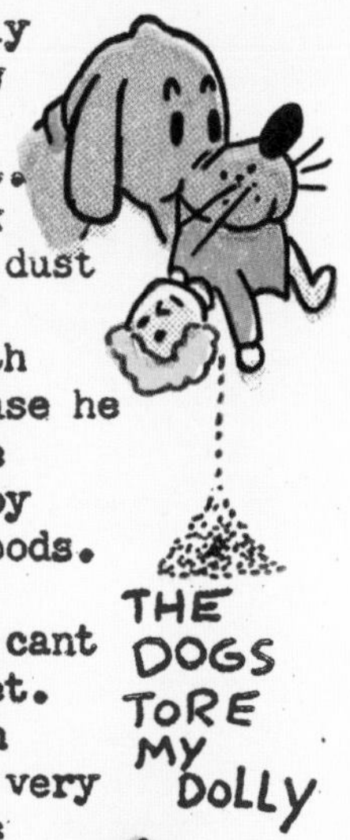
THE DOGS TORE MY DOLLY

I was walking through the grass and I said gosh why cant I fill my dolly with grass it is just as good as saw dust I bet. I was filling my dolly with grass when I found a little green apple under a tree and it sure tasted good because I was very hungry. Then I found a lot more little green apples but I was in a hurry and couldnt stay and eat them. I dumped out the grass that was in my dolly and filled her up with little apples - she was bumpy but she looked better than before. Then I went home and mother diddint see me going up to my room and I got in bed.

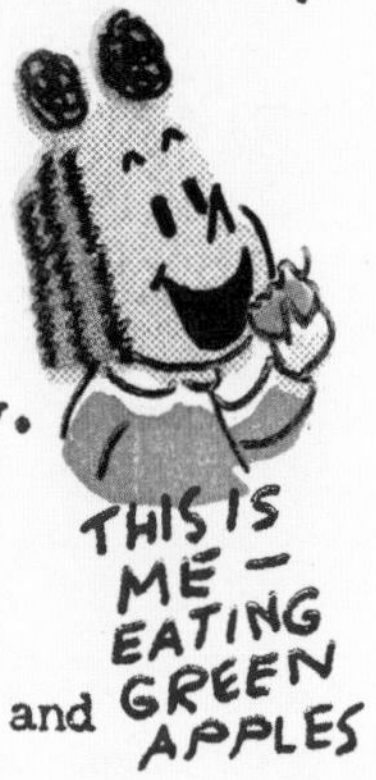
THIS IS ME - EATING GREEN APPLES

Then I ate nearly all the apples that were in my dolly. I guess it was wrong to go out doors in my bare feet because in a little while I got very very sick much sicker than before with terrible pains in my stummik. I hollered like anything and mother came up and she said oh Lulu you must be awful sick I will have to call the doctor again. The doctor came again and he said oh yes the poor little girl is very sick maybe we will have to take her to the hospital she is so sick. Then he pulled back the bed covers to put that little telaphone on my chest and when he pulled back the covers she saw all the little apple cores I hid under the covers. Then he said I think I will give you another medicin maybe I gave you the wrong medicin the first time. Mother said I think I have the medicin right here mother sure was mad. Gosh dear diry I diddint like the other sweet medicin but I like it better than castor oil.

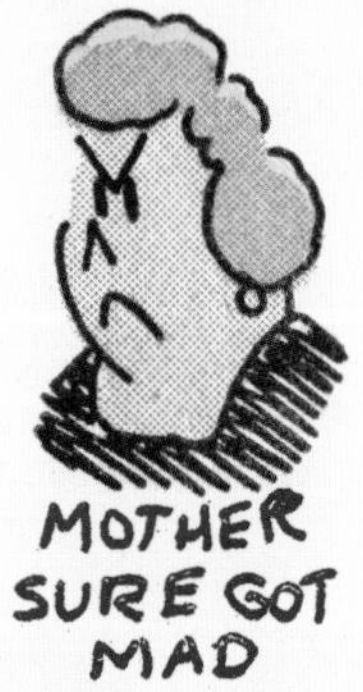
MOTHER SURE GOT MAD

Yours truly Lulu

P.S. Dear diry tubby visited me later and he ate all the rest of the little apples in my dolly then he drank the whole bottle of sweet medicin because it was sweet. He said he felt fine.

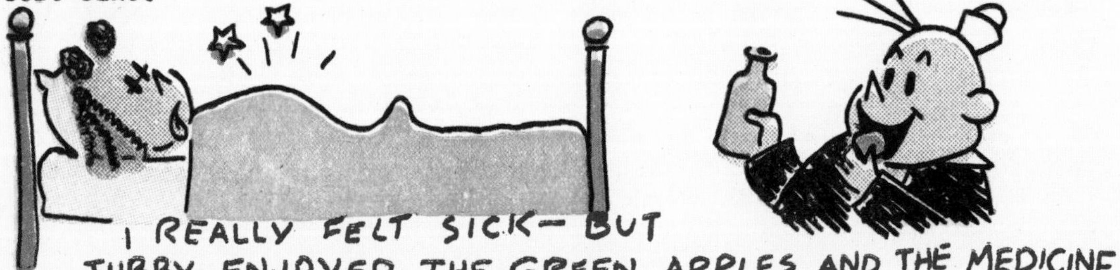
I REALLY FELT SICK- BUT
TUBBY ENJOYED THE GREEN APPLES AND THE MEDICINE

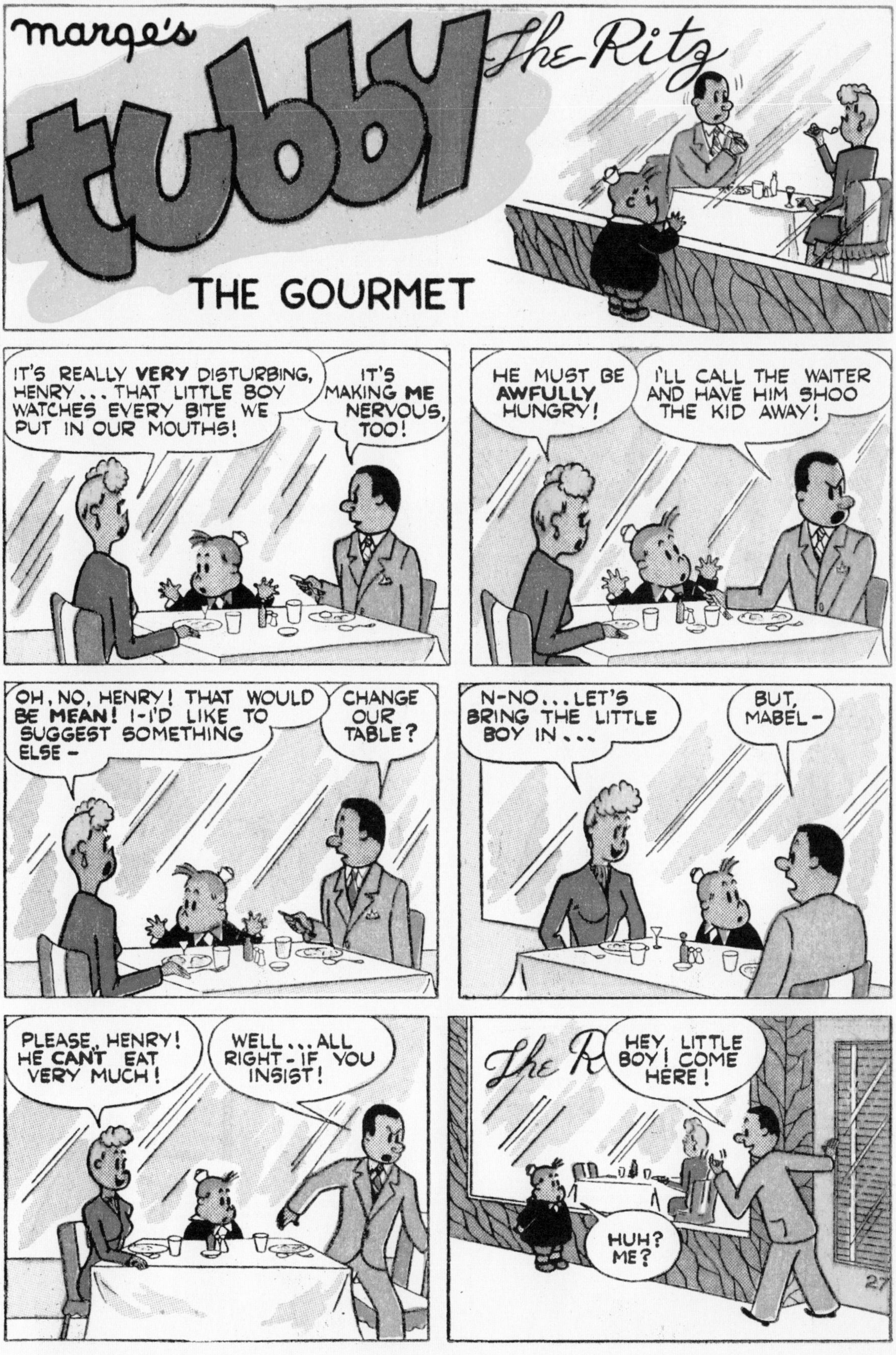
marge's
TUBBY
The Ritz
THE GOURMET
IT'S REALLY VERY DISTURBING, HENRY... THAT LITTLE BOY WATCHES EVERY BITE WE PUT IN OUR MOUTHS!
IT'S MAKING ME NERVOUS, TOO!
HE MUST BE AWFULLY HUNGRY!
I'LL CALL THE WAITER AND HAVE HIM SHOO THE KID AWAY!
OH, NO, HENRY! THAT WOULD BE MEAN! I-I'D LIKE TO SUGGEST SOMETHING ELSE-
CHANGE OUR TABLE?
N-NO... LET'S BRING THE LITTLE BOY IN...
BUT, MABEL-
PLEASE, HENRY! HE CAN'T EAT VERY MUCH!
WELL... ALL RIGHT- IF YOU INSIST!
HEY, LITTLE BOY! COME HERE!
HUH? ME?
27

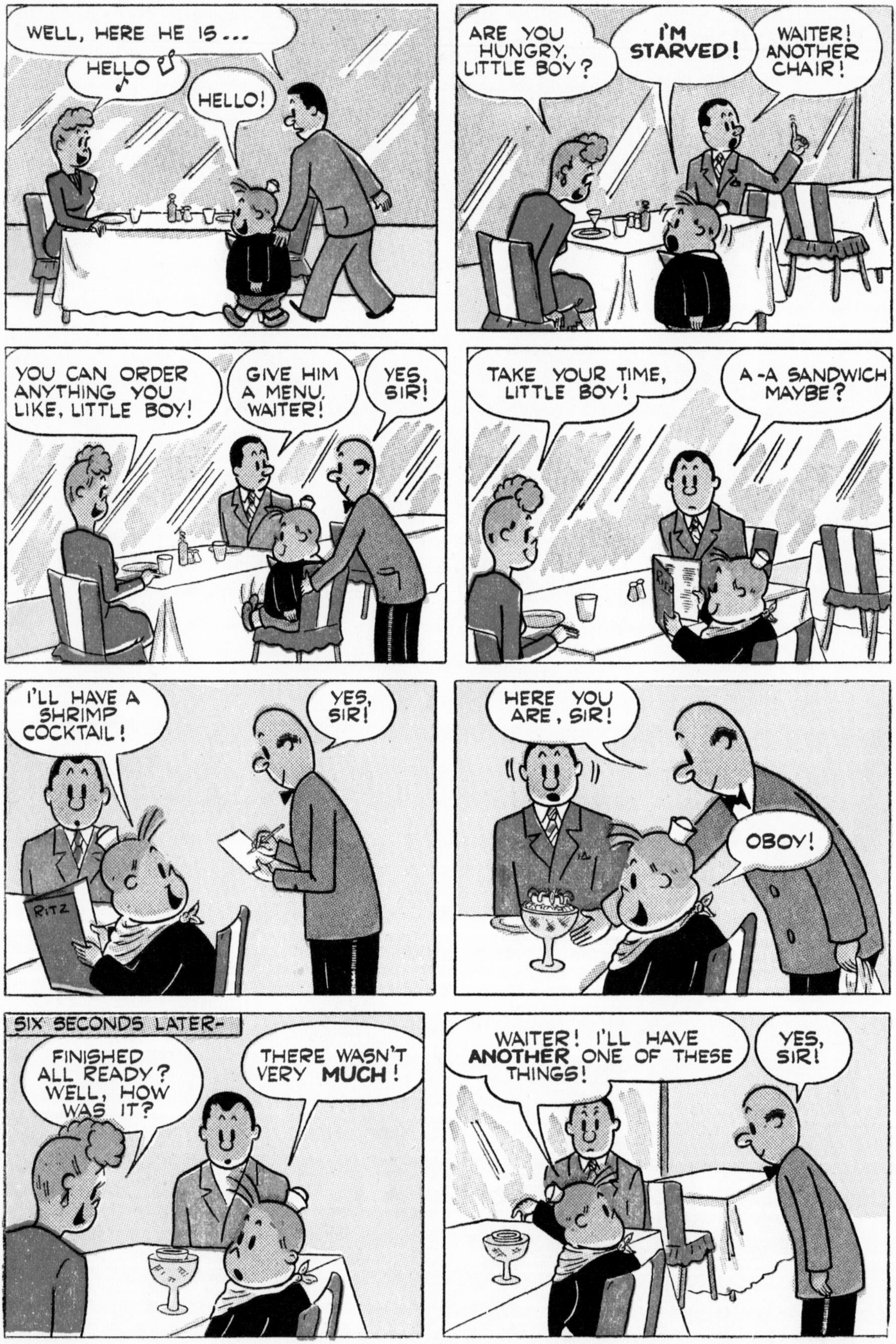
WELL, HERE HE IS...
HELLO
HELLO!
ARE YOU HUNGRY, LITTLE BOY?
I'M STARVED!
WAITER! ANOTHER CHAIR!
YOU CAN ORDER ANYTHING YOU LIKE, LITTLE BOY!
GIVE HIM A MENU, WAITER!
YES, SIR!
TAKE YOUR TIME, LITTLE BOY!
A-A SANDWICH MAYBE?
RITZ
I'LL HAVE A SHRIMP COCKTAIL!
YES, SIR!
RITZ
HERE YOU ARE, SIR!
OBOY!
SIX SECONDS LATER-
FINISHED ALL READY? WELL, HOW WAS IT?
THERE WASN'T VERY **MUCH**!
WAITER! I'LL HAVE **ANOTHER** ONE OF THESE THINGS!
YES, SIR!

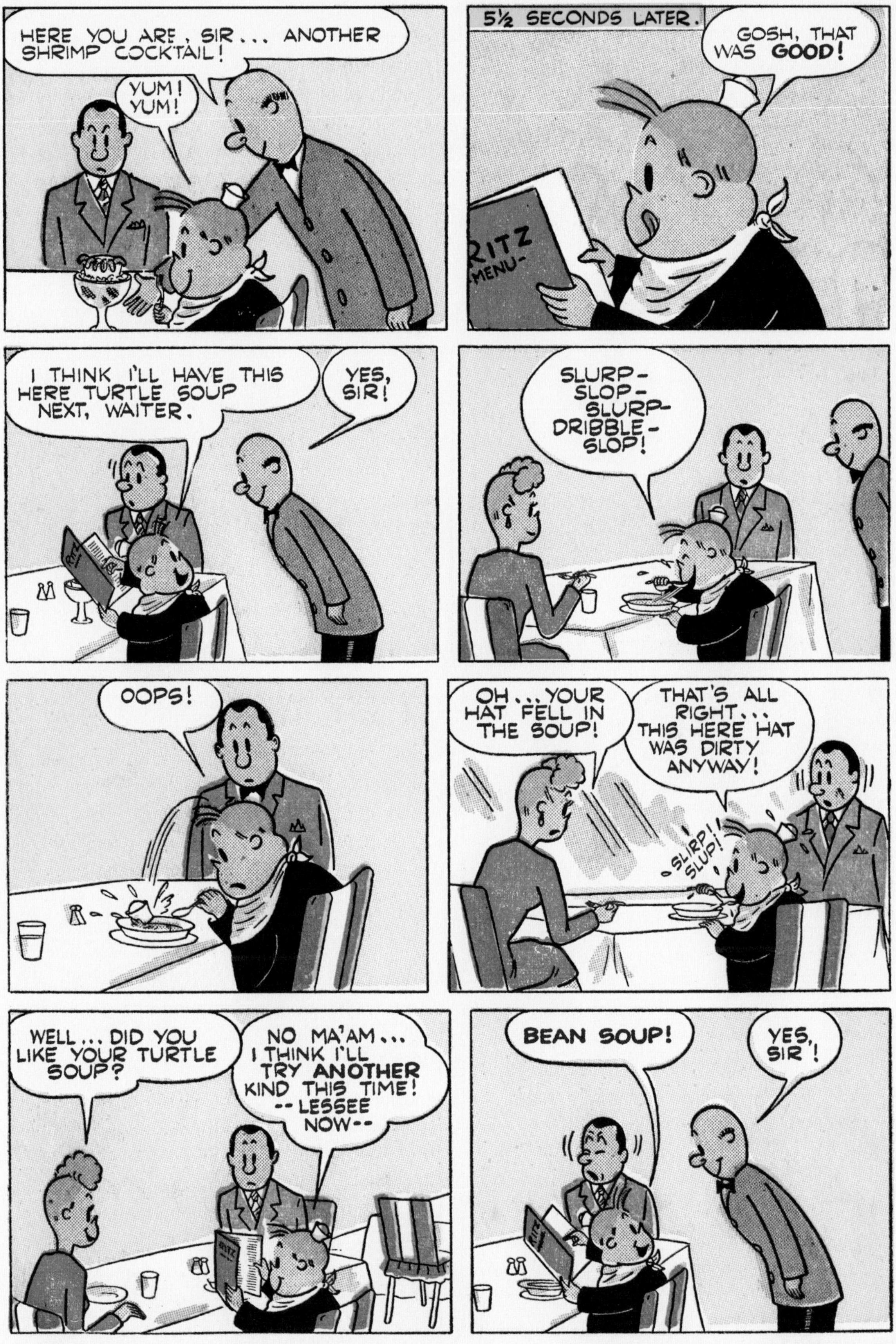
HERE YOU ARE, SIR... ANOTHER SHRIMP COCKTAIL!
YUM! YUM!
5½ SECONDS LATER.
GOSH, THAT WAS **GOOD!**
RITZ MENU
I THINK I'LL HAVE THIS HERE TURTLE SOUP NEXT, WAITER.
YES, SIR!
SLURP-SLOP-SLURP-DRIBBLE-SLOP!
OOPS!
OH... YOUR HAT FELL IN THE SOUP!
THAT'S ALL RIGHT... THIS HERE HAT WAS DIRTY ANYWAY!
SLIRP! SLUP!
WELL... DID YOU LIKE YOUR TURTLE SOUP?
NO MA'AM... I THINK I'LL TRY **ANOTHER** KIND THIS TIME! --LESSEE NOW--
BEAN SOUP!
YES, SIR!

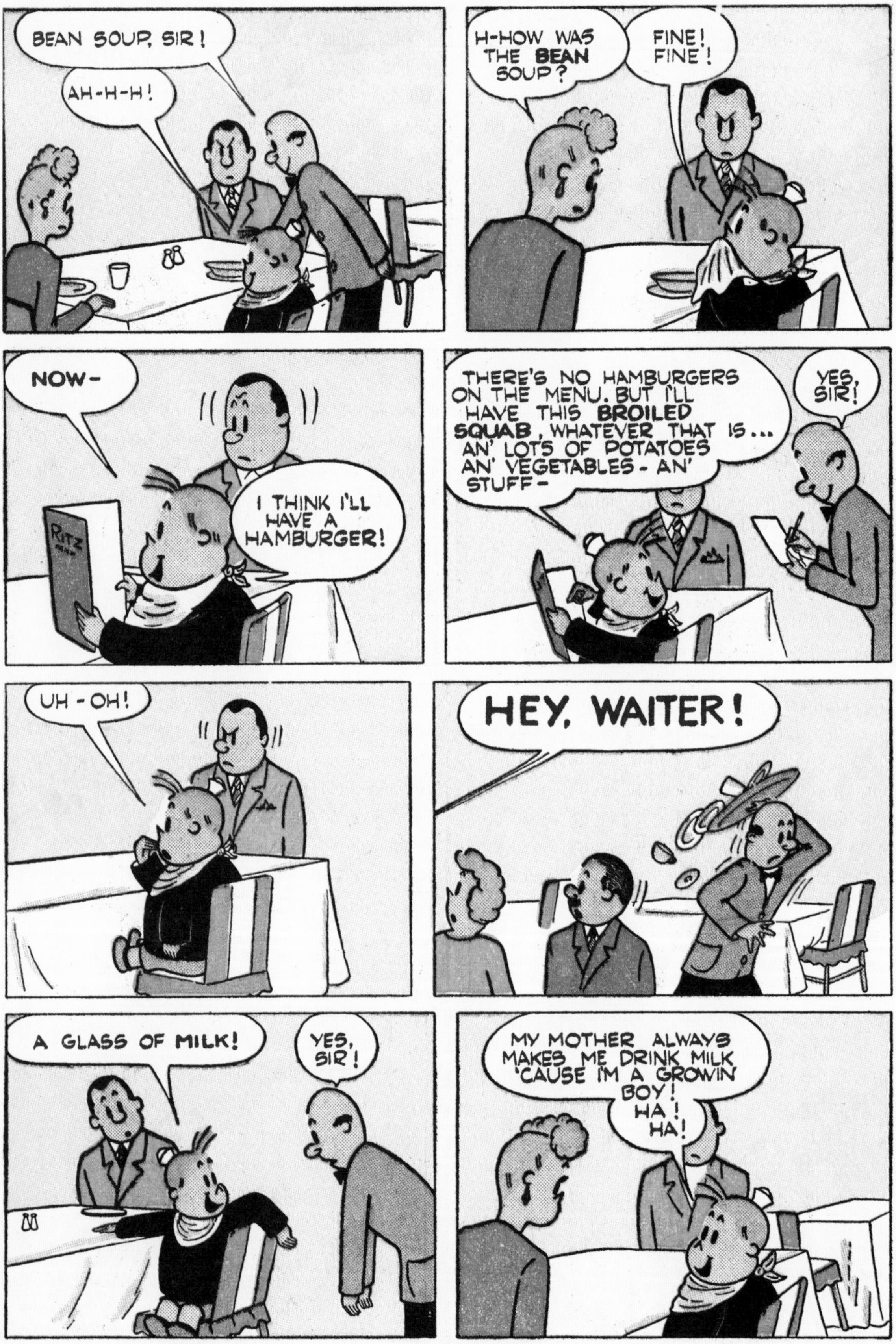
BEAN SOUP, SIR!
AH-H-H!
H-HOW WAS THE **BEAN** SOUP?
FINE! FINE!
NOW-
I THINK I'LL HAVE A HAMBURGER!
RITZ
THERE'S NO HAMBURGERS ON THE MENU. BUT I'LL HAVE THIS **BROILED SQUAB**, WHATEVER THAT IS... AN' LOTS OF POTATOES AN' VEGETABLES - AN' STUFF -
YES, SIR!
UH - OH!
HEY, WAITER!
A GLASS OF MILK!
YES, SIR!
MY MOTHER ALWAYS MAKES ME DRINK MILK 'CAUSE I'M A GROWIN' BOY! HA! HA!

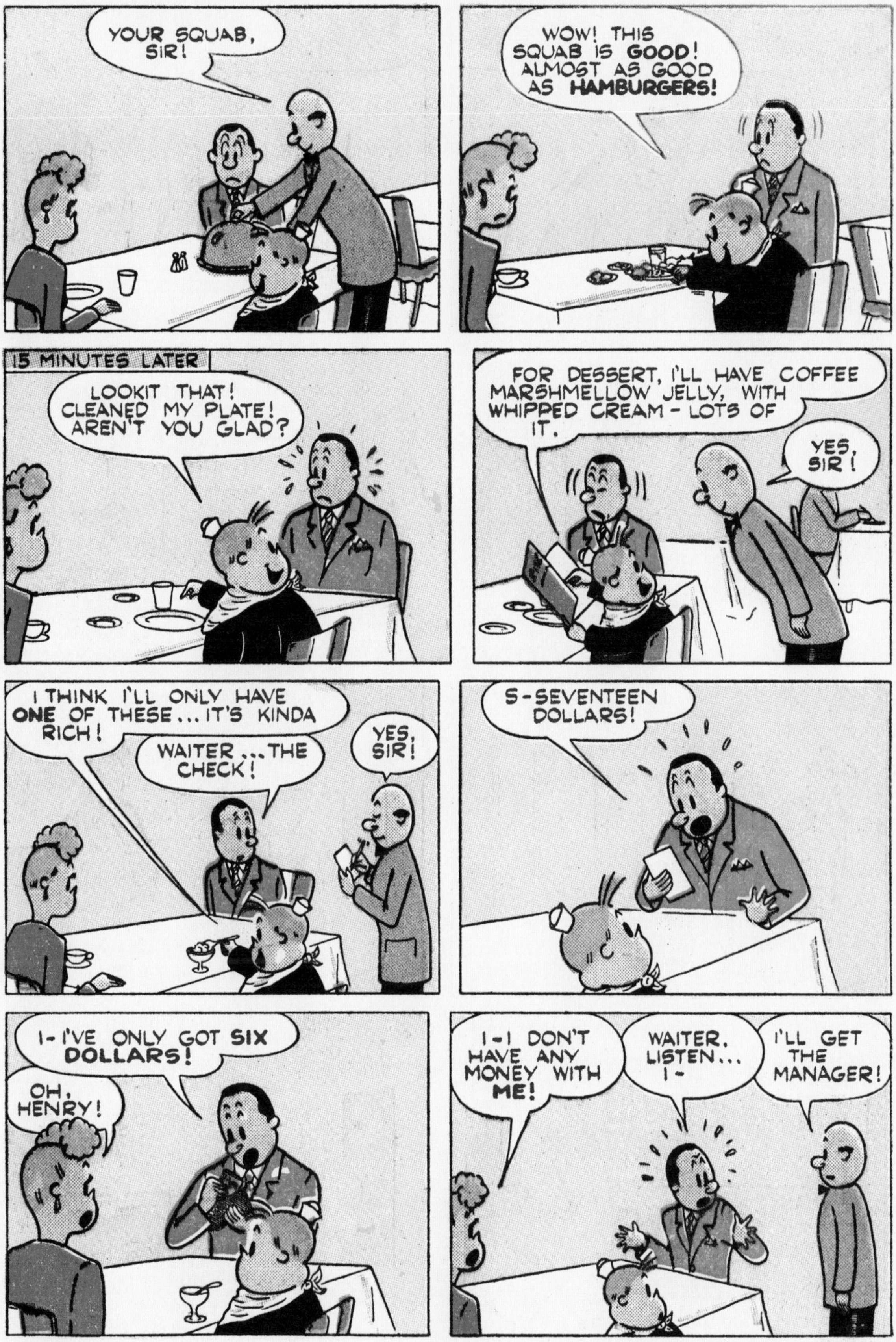
YOUR SQUAB, SIR!
WOW! THIS SQUAB IS GOOD! ALMOST AS GOOD AS HAMBURGERS!
15 MINUTES LATER
LOOKIT THAT! CLEANED MY PLATE! AREN'T YOU GLAD?
FOR DESSERT, I'LL HAVE COFFEE MARSHMELLOW JELLY, WITH WHIPPED CREAM - LOTS OF IT.
YES, SIR!
I THINK I'LL ONLY HAVE ONE OF THESE... IT'S KINDA RICH!
WAITER ... THE CHECK!
YES, SIR!
S-SEVENTEEN DOLLARS!
I- I'VE ONLY GOT SIX DOLLARS!
OH, HENRY!
I-I DON'T HAVE ANY MONEY WITH ME!
WAITER, LISTEN... I-
I'LL GET THE MANAGER!

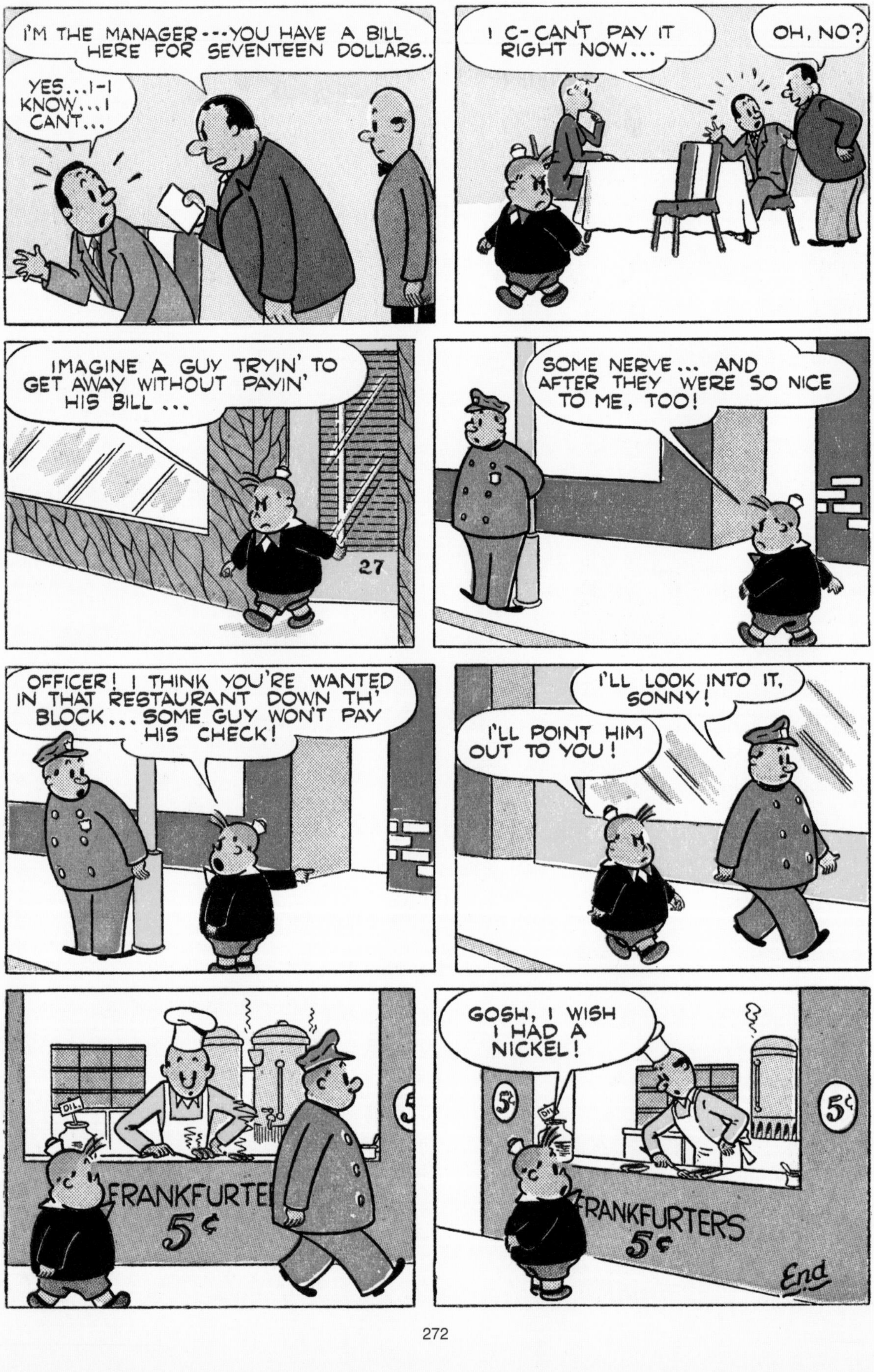
I'M THE MANAGER---YOU HAVE A BILL HERE FOR SEVENTEEN DOLLARS..
YES...I-I KNOW...I CAN'T...
I C-CAN'T PAY IT RIGHT NOW...
OH, NO?
IMAGINE A GUY TRYIN' TO GET AWAY WITHOUT PAYIN' HIS BILL...
27
SOME NERVE... AND AFTER THEY WERE SO NICE TO ME, TOO!
OFFICER! I THINK YOU'RE WANTED IN THAT RESTAURANT DOWN TH' BLOCK... SOME GUY WON'T PAY HIS CHECK!
I'LL LOOK INTO IT, SONNY!
I'LL POINT HIM OUT TO YOU!
FRANKFURTE
5¢
GOSH, I WISH I HAD A NICKEL!
5¢
FRANKFURTERS
5¢
End

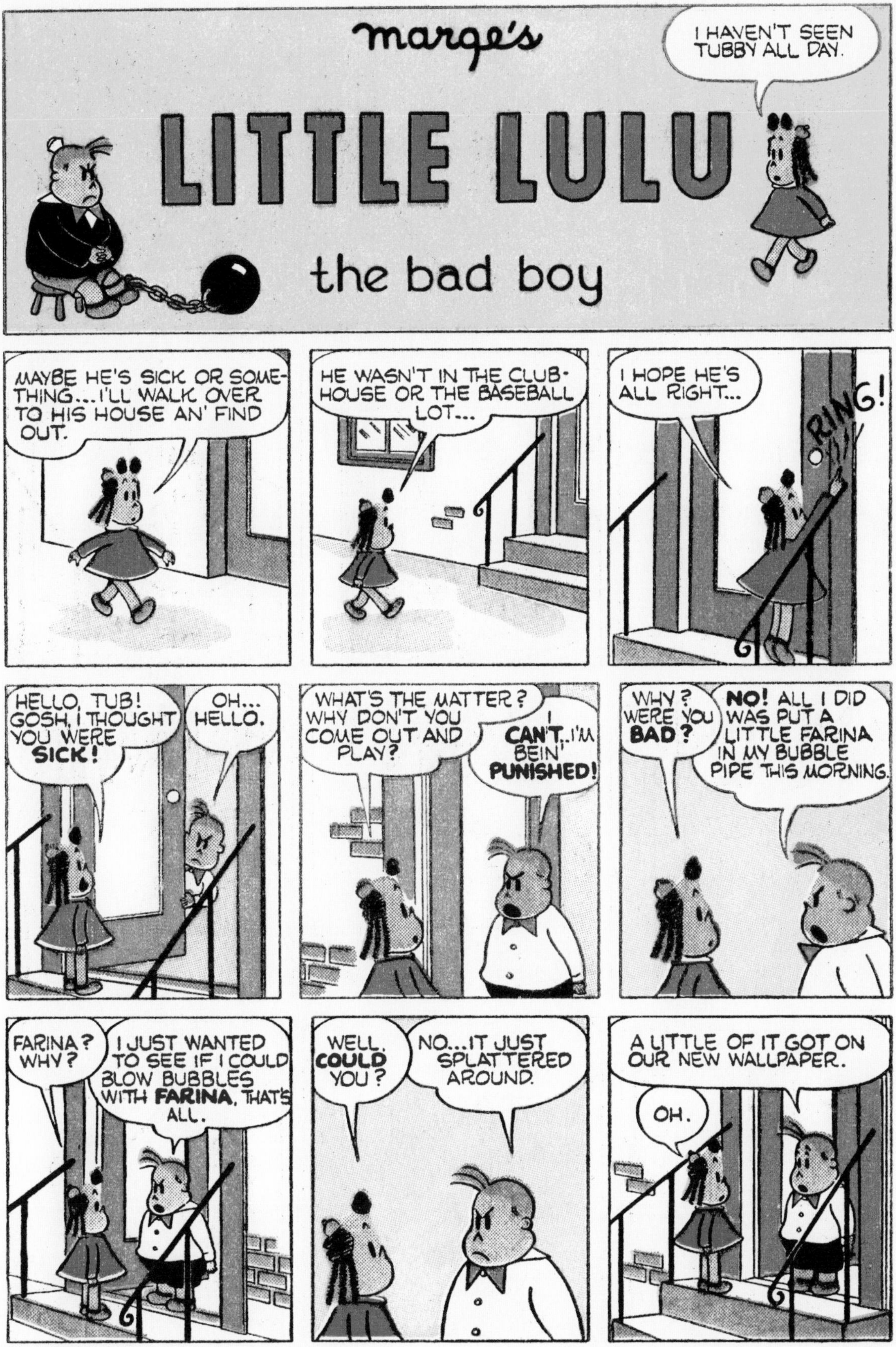
marge's
LITTLE LULU
the bad boy
I HAVEN'T SEEN TUBBY ALL DAY.
MAYBE HE'S SICK OR SOMETHING...I'LL WALK OVER TO HIS HOUSE AN' FIND OUT.
HE WASN'T IN THE CLUBHOUSE OR THE BASEBALL LOT...
I HOPE HE'S ALL RIGHT...
RING!
HELLO, TUB! GOSH, I THOUGHT YOU WERE SICK!
OH... HELLO.
WHAT'S THE MATTER? WHY DON'T YOU COME OUT AND PLAY?
I CAN'T...I'M BEIN' PUNISHED!
WHY? WERE YOU BAD?
NO! ALL I DID WAS PUT A LITTLE FARINA IN MY BUBBLE PIPE THIS MORNING.
FARINA? WHY?
I JUST WANTED TO SEE IF I COULD BLOW BUBBLES WITH FARINA, THAT'S ALL.
WELL, COULD YOU?
NO...IT JUST SPLATTERED AROUND.
A LITTLE OF IT GOT ON OUR NEW WALLPAPER.
OH.

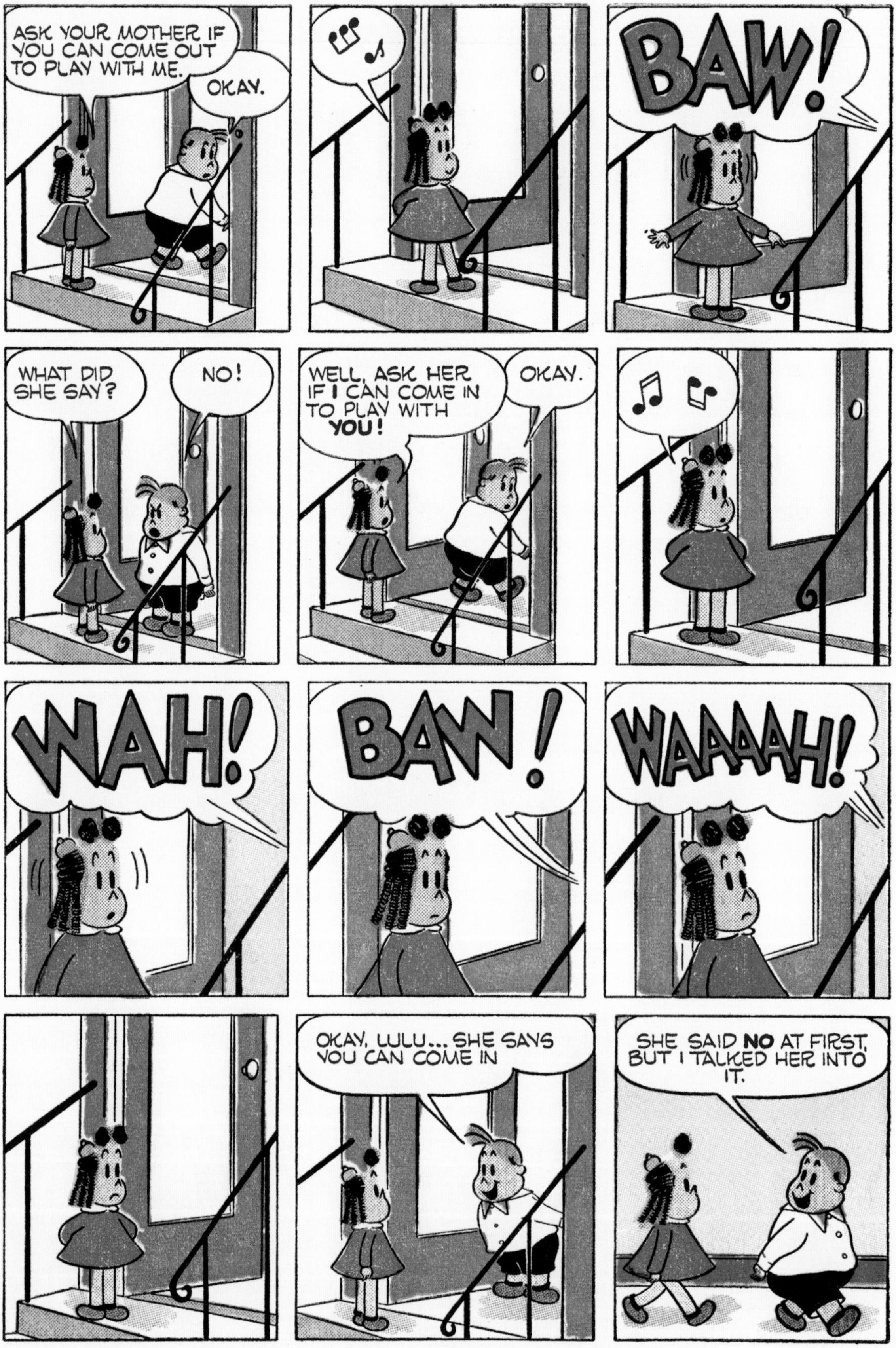
ASK YOUR MOTHER IF YOU CAN COME OUT TO PLAY WITH ME.
OKAY.
BAW!
WHAT DID SHE SAY?
NO!
WELL, ASK HER IF I CAN COME IN TO PLAY WITH YOU!
OKAY.
WAH!
BAW!
WAAAAH!
OKAY, LULU... SHE SAYS YOU CAN COME IN
SHE SAID NO AT FIRST, BUT I TALKED HER INTO IT.

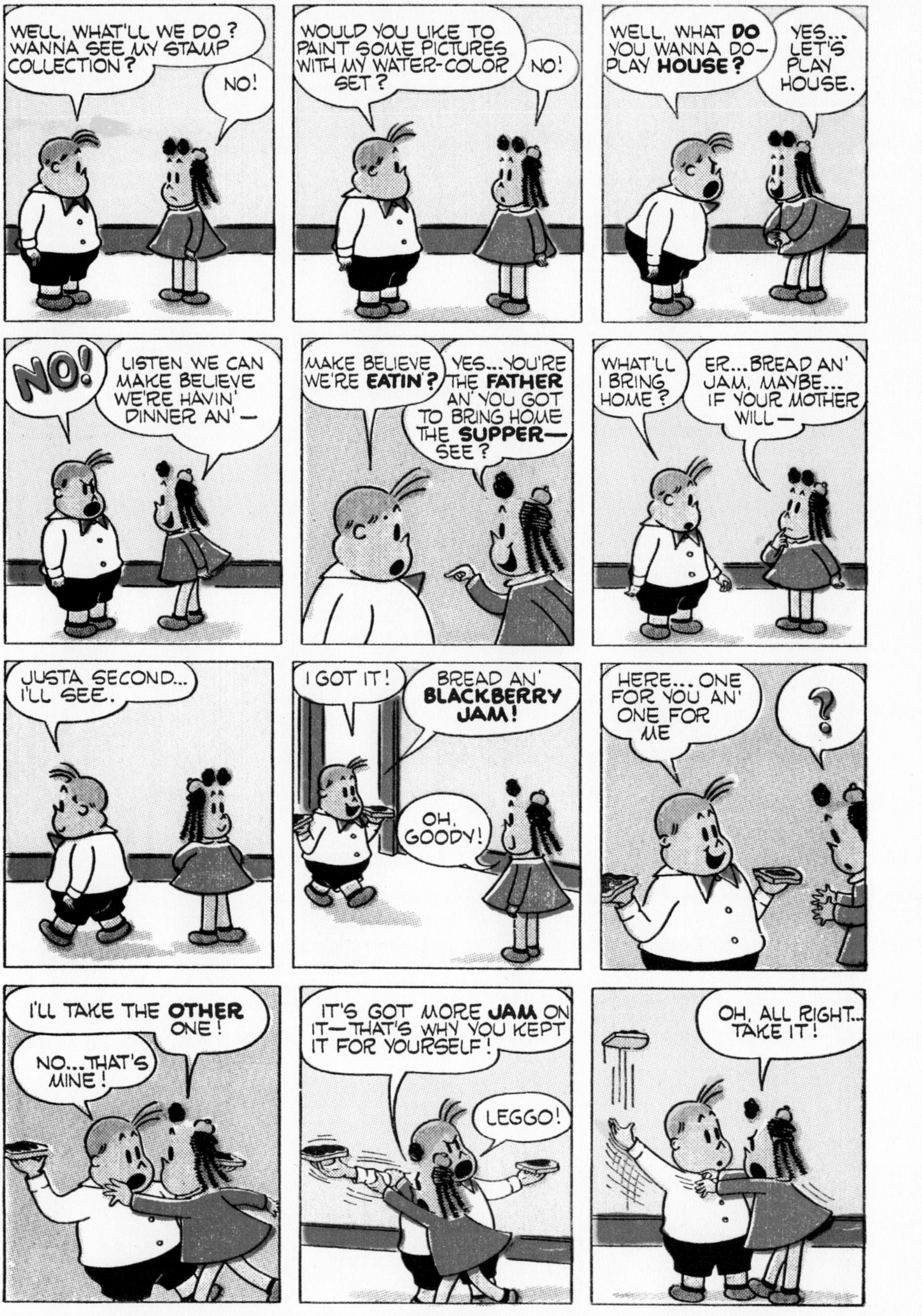
WELL, WHAT'LL WE DO? WANNA SEE MY STAMP COLLECTION?
NO!
WOULD YOU LIKE TO PAINT SOME PICTURES WITH MY WATER-COLOR SET?
NO!
WELL, WHAT **DO** YOU WANNA DO— PLAY **HOUSE?**
YES... LET'S PLAY HOUSE.
NO!
LISTEN WE CAN MAKE BELIEVE WE'RE HAVIN' DINNER AN'—
MAKE BELIEVE WE'RE **EATIN'?**
YES...YOU'RE THE **FATHER** AN' YOU GOT TO BRING HOME THE **SUPPER**— SEE?
WHAT'LL I BRING HOME?
ER...BREAD AN' JAM, MAYBE... IF YOUR MOTHER WILL—
JUSTA SECOND... I'LL SEE.
I GOT IT!
BREAD AN' **BLACKBERRY JAM!**
OH, GOODY!
HERE... ONE FOR YOU AN' ONE FOR ME
?
I'LL TAKE THE **OTHER** ONE!
NO...THAT'S MINE!
IT'S GOT MORE **JAM** ON IT—THAT'S WHY YOU KEPT IT FOR YOURSELF!
LEGGO!
OH, ALL RIGHT... TAKE IT!

?
?
GOSH! WHEN YOU LET GO OF MY ARM TH' BREAD FLEW UP AN' STUCK ON THE CEILING.
WHAT'LL WE DO?
OH, MAYBE IT'LL FALL DOWN.
YOU COULD POKE IT DOWN WITH A LONG STICK OR SOMETHING.
A **BROOM**! I'LL GET THE BROOM!
I-I TOLD MY MOTHER I WANTED THE BROOM TO SWEEP UP CRUMBS.
TSK, TSK... THAT'S A FIB!
IT WON'T REACH.
STAND ON A **CHAIR**.
I STILL CAN'T REACH IT.
HOW ABOUT **THROWING** SOMETHING AT IT?
MY MOTHER WOULD HEAR THE NOISE.
SA-A-AY HOW ABOUT YOUR **BOW AN' ARROW?**
BUT, HOW?
LISTEN, WE'LL TIE A STRING ON THE ARROW AN' SHOOT IT AT THE BREAD—
—IT'LL STICK IN THE BREAD AN' THEN YOU CAN YANK IT DOWN WITH THE **STRING**!
I-I'LL TRY IT
I GOT THE BOW AN' ARROW AN' THE STRING...
THIS IS **SURE** TO WORK.
ALL RIGHT, DON'T STAND ON THE STRING NOW.
I WON'T.

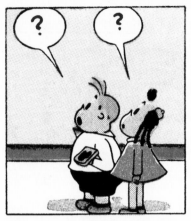

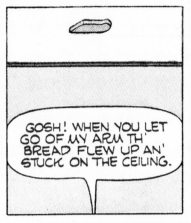

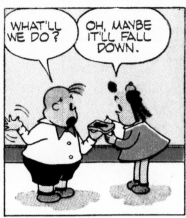

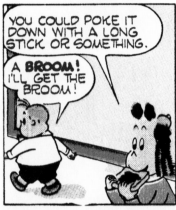

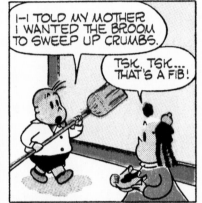

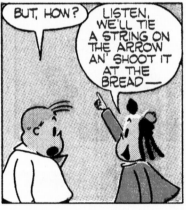

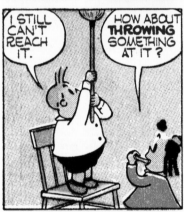

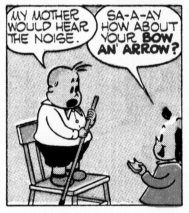

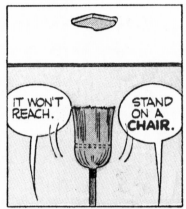

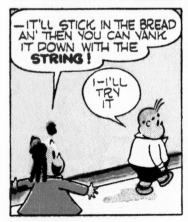

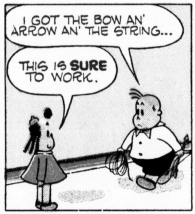

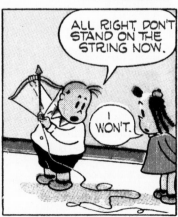

TWANG!

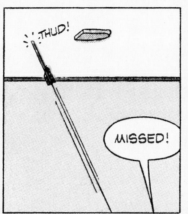

'.THUD!

MISSED!

I'LL PULL IT DOWN AN' TAKE ANOTHER SHOT.

THAT'S WHY I THOUGHT OF THE STRING!

UH-OH!

LOOKIT WHAT HAPPENED!

GOSH!

WHAT IF YOUR MOTHER COMES IN, TUB?

OH, SHE'S OUT IN THE BACK HANGIN' UP SOME WASH.

I GOTTA GET THAT BREAD DOWN BEFORE SHE COMES IN THOUGH.

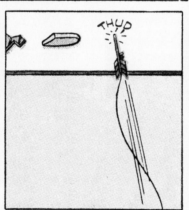

THUD

DARN! MISSED AGAIN!

YANK IT DOWN.

NOW THERE'RE TWO HOLES IN THE CEILING!

I'LL HIT IT THIS TIME!

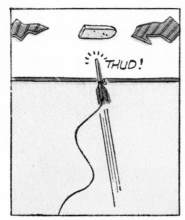

THUD!

MAYBE YOU'D BETTER LET ME TRY.

IF I MISS THIS TIME, THEN YOU CAN TRY IT.

GOSH, THE CEILING SURE IS A MESS.

OH, HELLO, MR. GREEN.

HOW DO, MRS. TRIMBLE.

DIDN'T HAPPEN TO FEEL THE GROUND SHAKING A LITTLE WHILE AGO, DID YOU, MRS. TRIMBLE?

WHY NO! WHAT HAPPENED?

I JUST HEARD ON THE RADIO THAT WE HAD A COUPLE OF SLIGHT EARTHQUAKE SHOCKS IN THESE PARTS.

REALLY? I DIDN'T FEEL ANYTHING

OH, WELL... AS LONG AS MY HOUSE IS STILL STANDING...

HMMM...WONDER WHAT THE CHILDREN ARE UP TO...THEY'RE AWFULLY QUIET.

OH! I GOT IT!

HURRY UP! PULL IT DOWN!

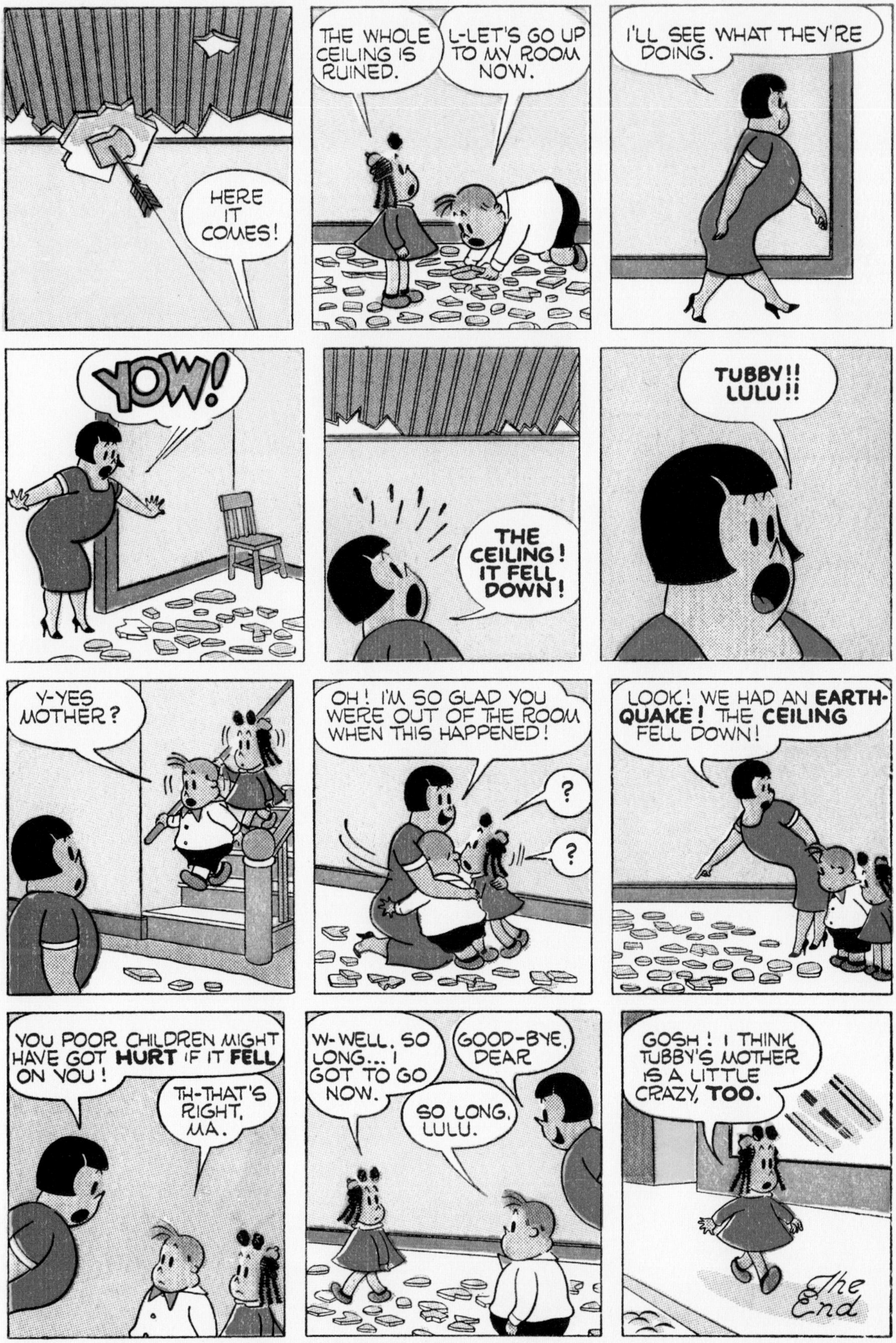

HERE IT COMES!
THE WHOLE CEILING IS RUINED.
L-LET'S GO UP TO MY ROOM NOW.
I'LL SEE WHAT THEY'RE DOING.
YOW!
THE CEILING! IT FELL DOWN!
TUBBY!! LULU!!
Y-YES MOTHER?
OH! I'M SO GLAD YOU WERE OUT OF THE ROOM WHEN THIS HAPPENED!
?
?
LOOK! WE HAD AN EARTHQUAKE! THE CEILING FELL DOWN!
YOU POOR CHILDREN MIGHT HAVE GOT HURT IF IT FELL ON YOU!
TH-THAT'S RIGHT, MA.
W-WELL, SO LONG... I GOT TO GO NOW.
GOOD-BYE, DEAR
SO LONG, LULU.
GOSH! I THINK TUBBY'S MOTHER IS A LITTLE CRAZY, TOO.
The End

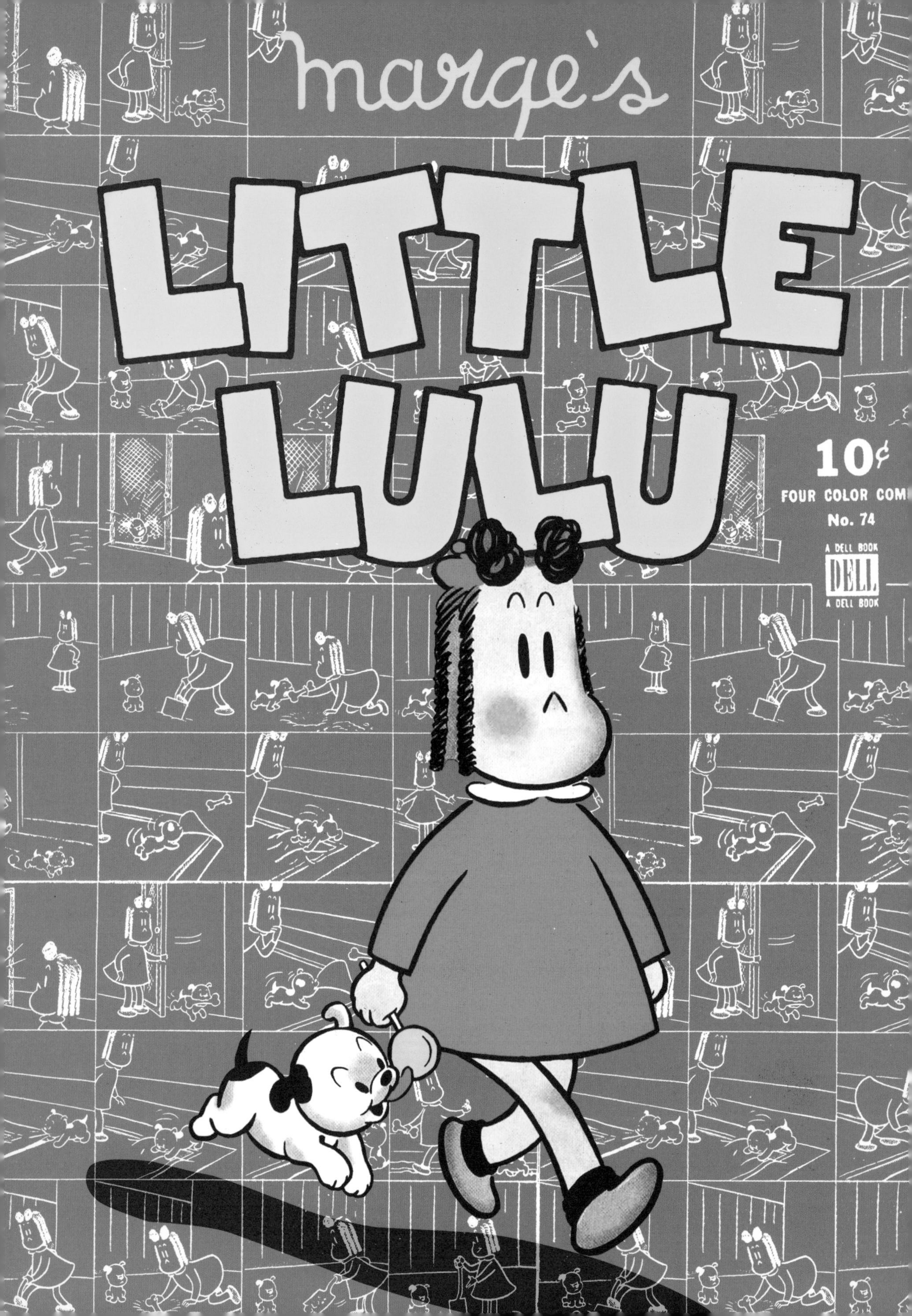

marge's
LITTLE LULU
10¢
FOUR COLOR COM
No. 74
A DELL BOOK
DELL
A DELL BOOK

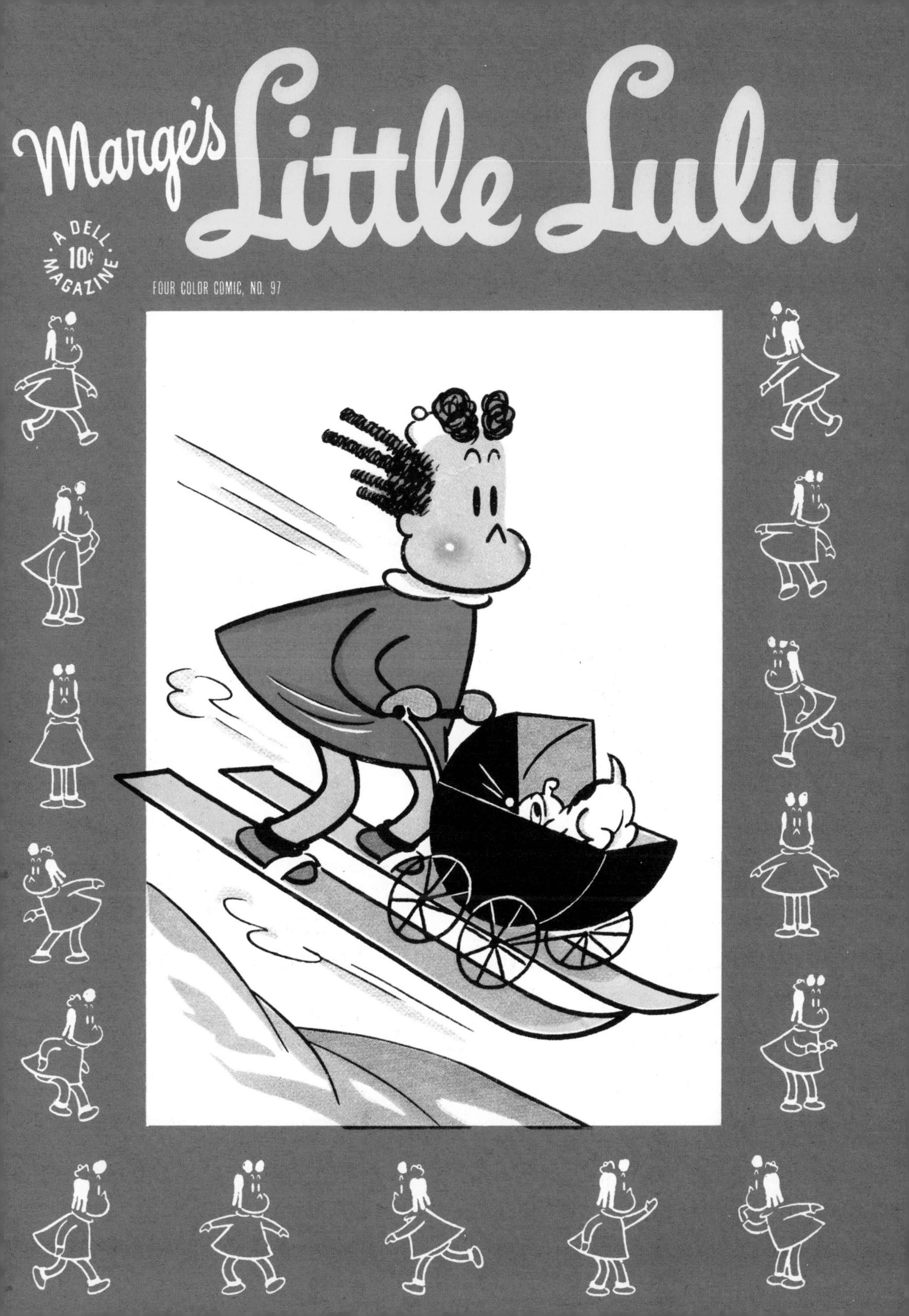
Marge's Little Lulu
A DELL 10¢ MAGAZINE
FOUR COLOR COMIC, NO. 97

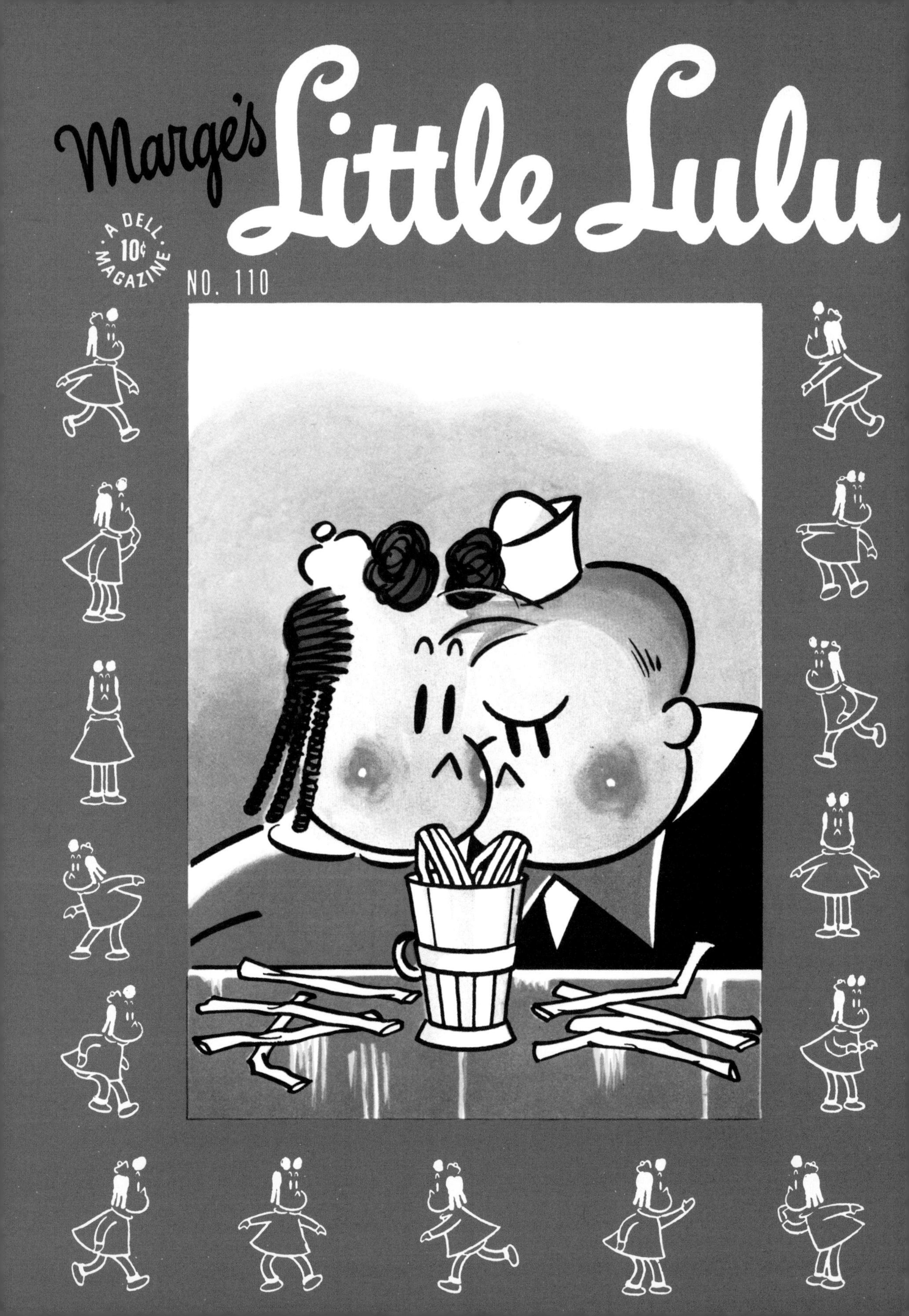
Marge's Little Lulu
A DELL 10¢ MAGAZINE
NO. 110

Marge's Little Lulu

A DELL MAGAZINE

10¢

NO. 115

$23

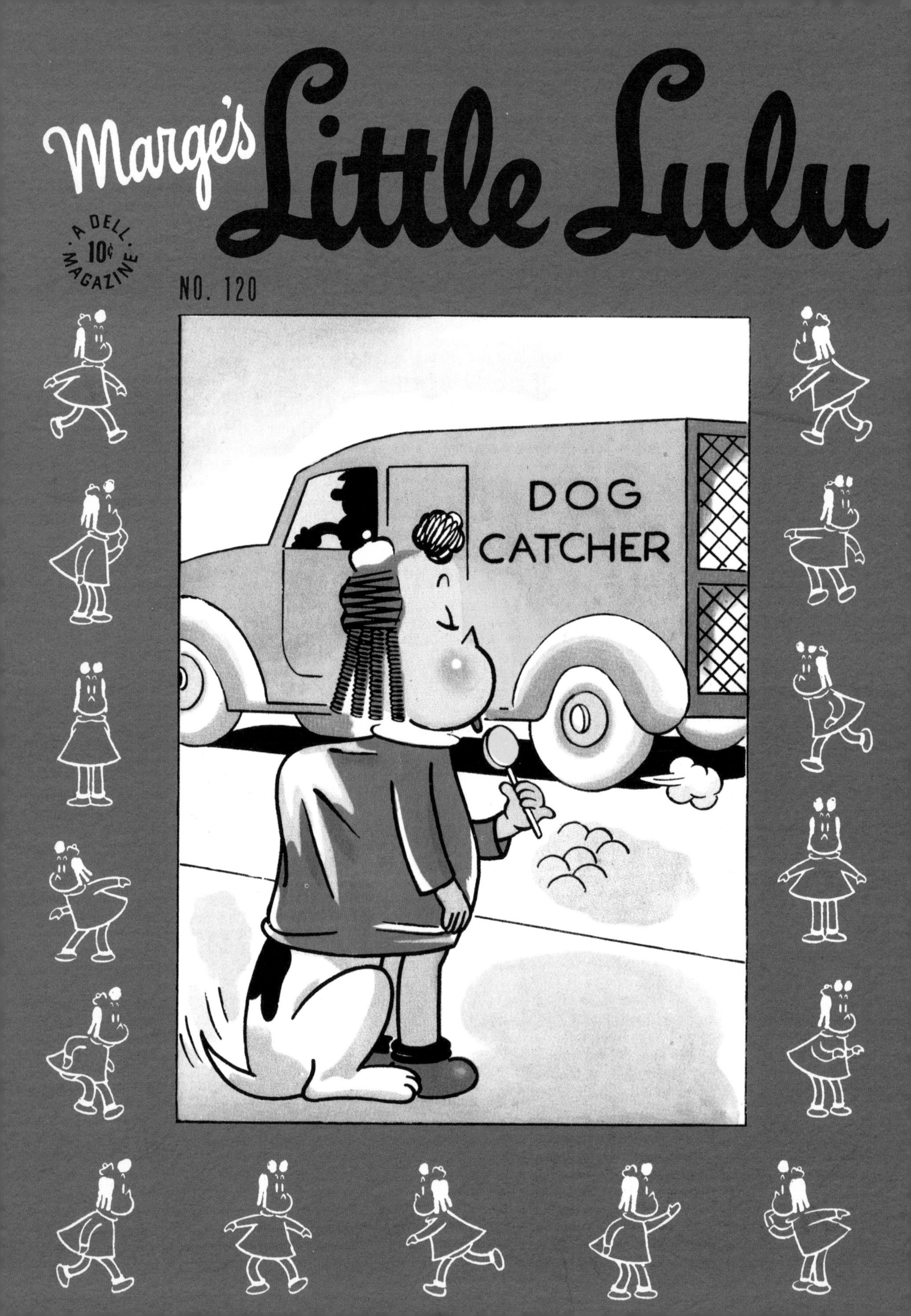
Marge's Little Lulu
A DELL 10¢ MAGAZINE
NO. 120
DOG
CATCHER

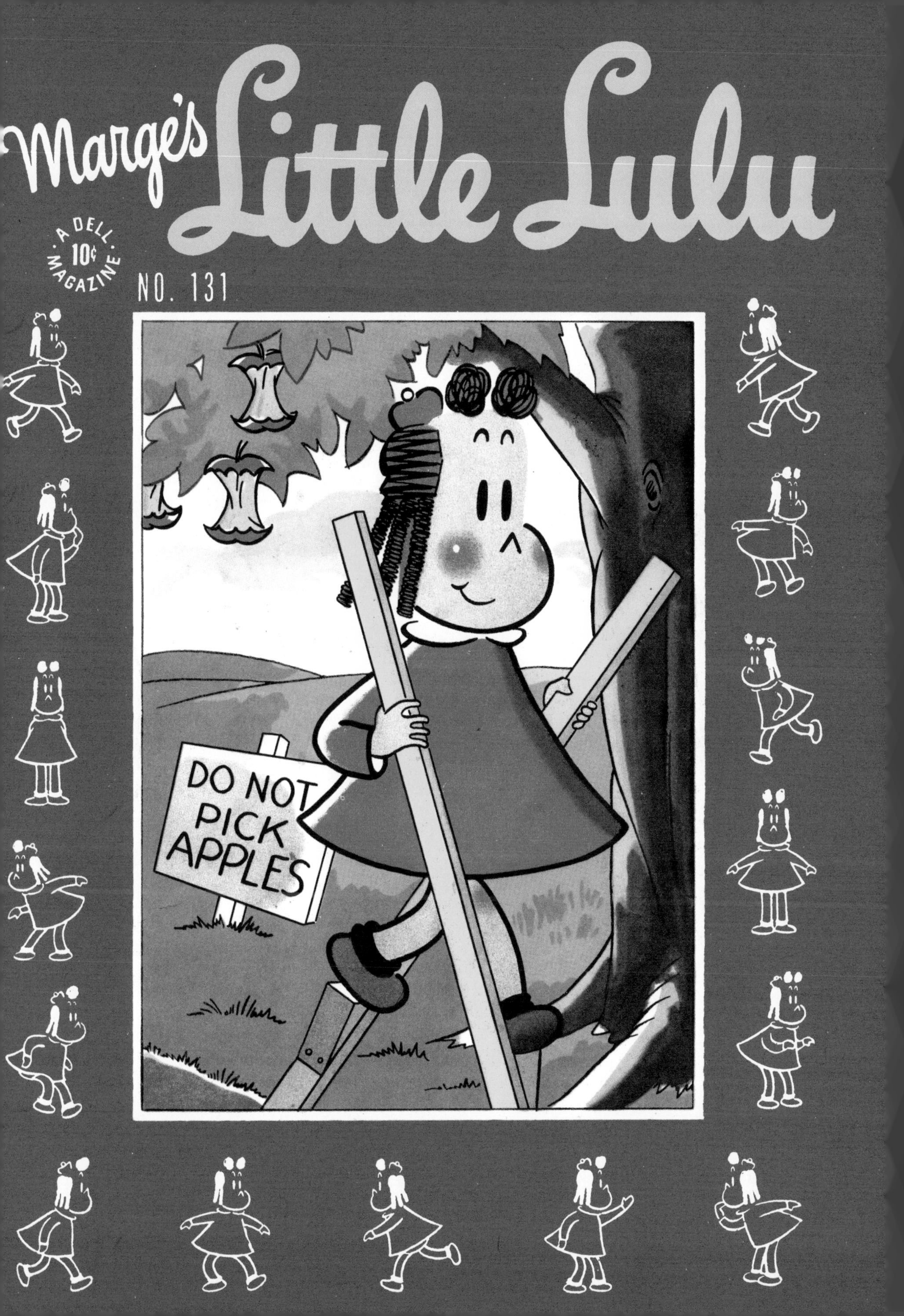
Marge's Little Lulu
A DELL 10¢ MAGAZINE
NO. 131
DO NOT PICK APPLES

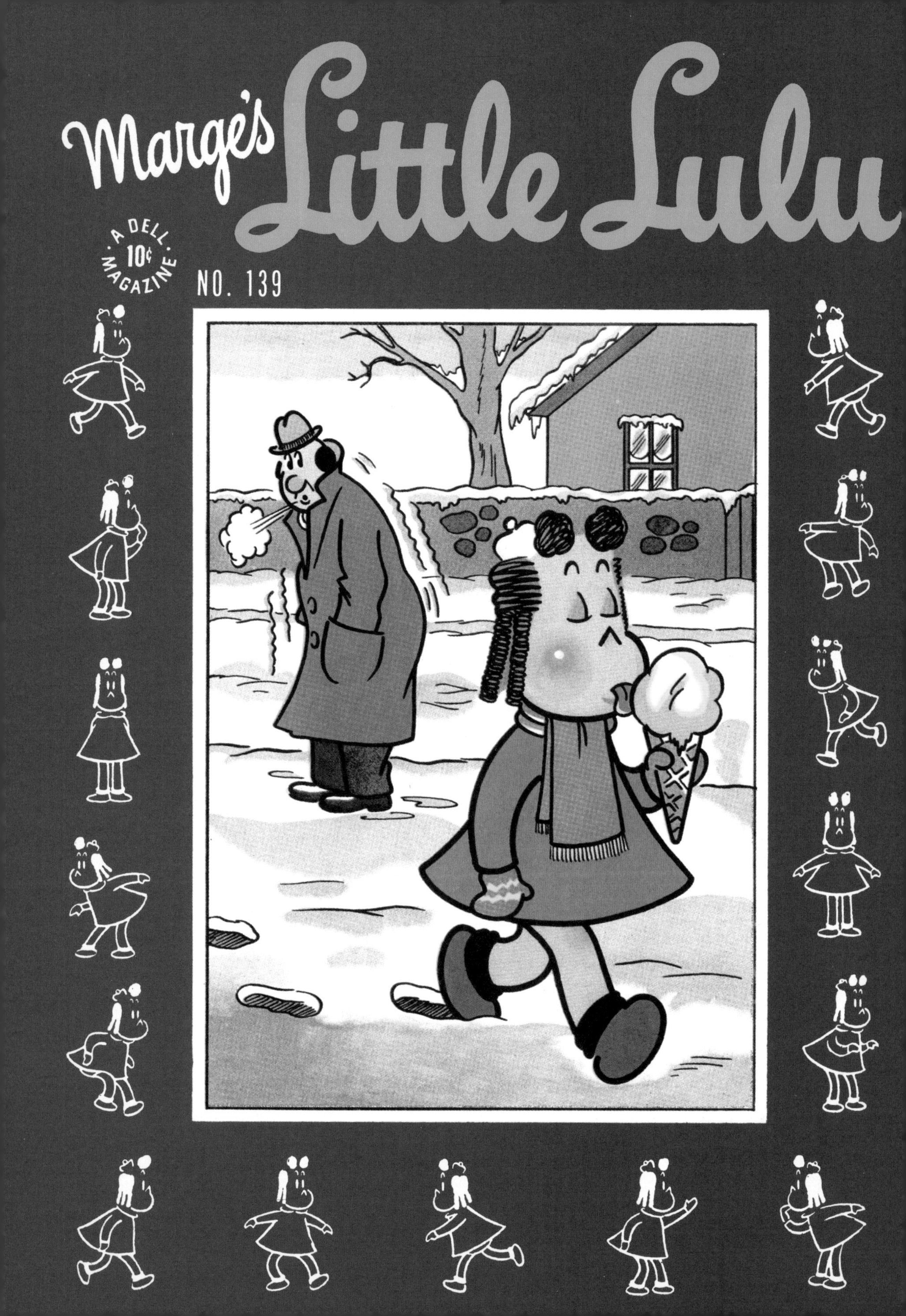
Marge's Little Lulu
A DELL 10¢ MAGAZINE
NO. 139

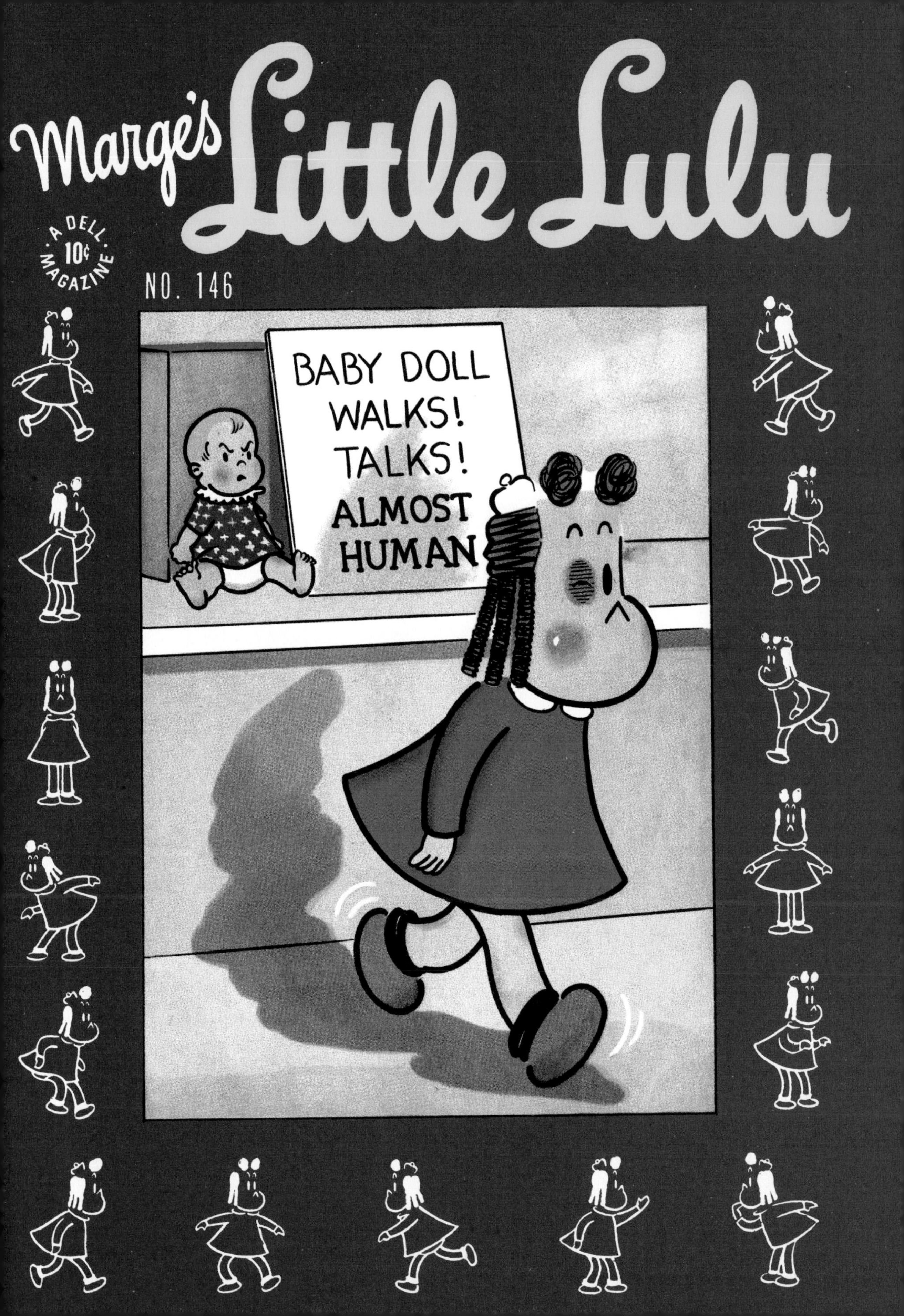
Marge's Little Lulu
A DELL 10¢ MAGAZINE
NO. 146
BABY DOLL WALKS! TALKS! ALMOST HUMAN

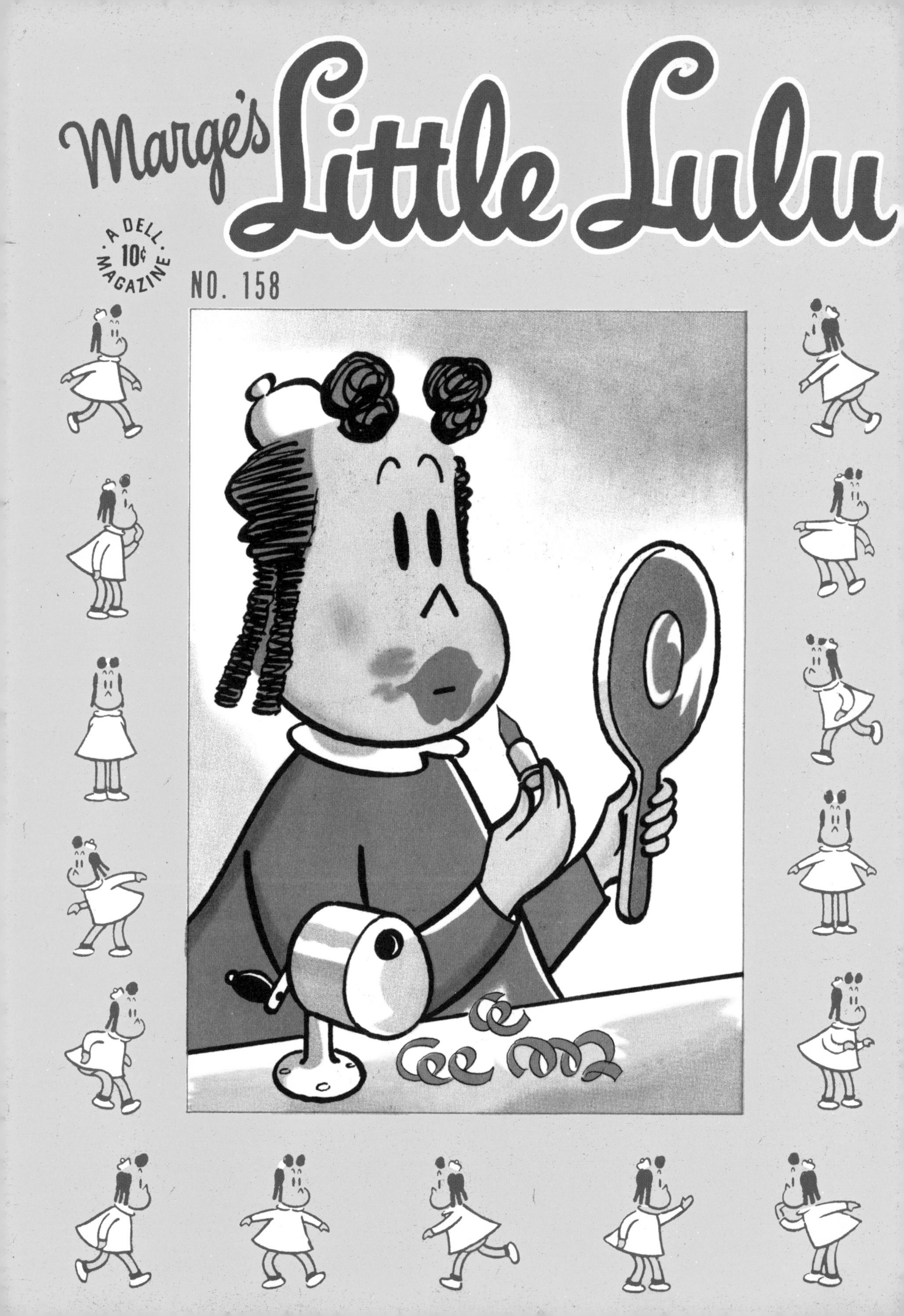
Marge's Little Lulu
A DELL 10¢ MAGAZINE
NO. 158

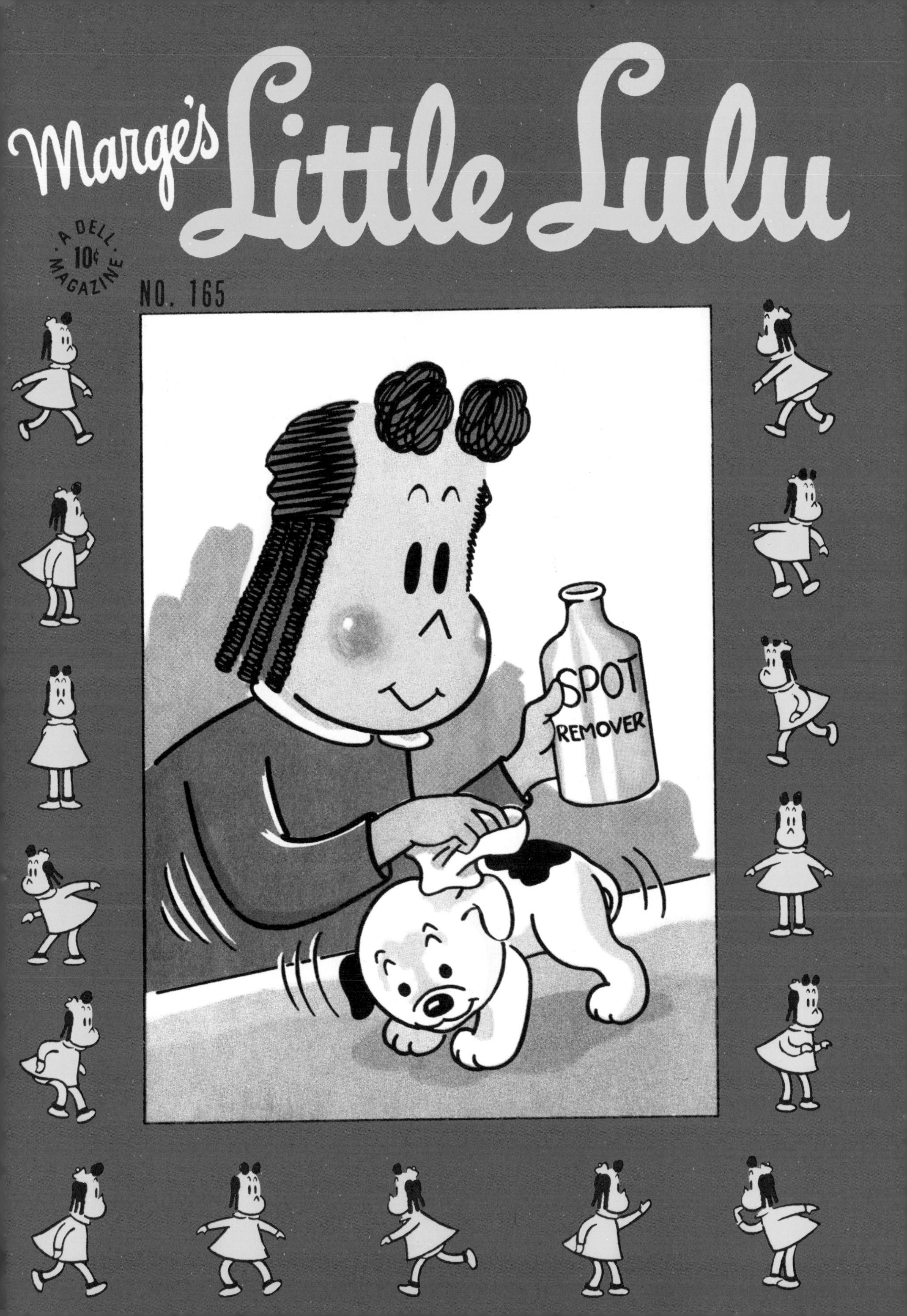
Marge's Little Lulu
A DELL 10¢ MAGAZINE
NO. 165
SPOT REMOVER

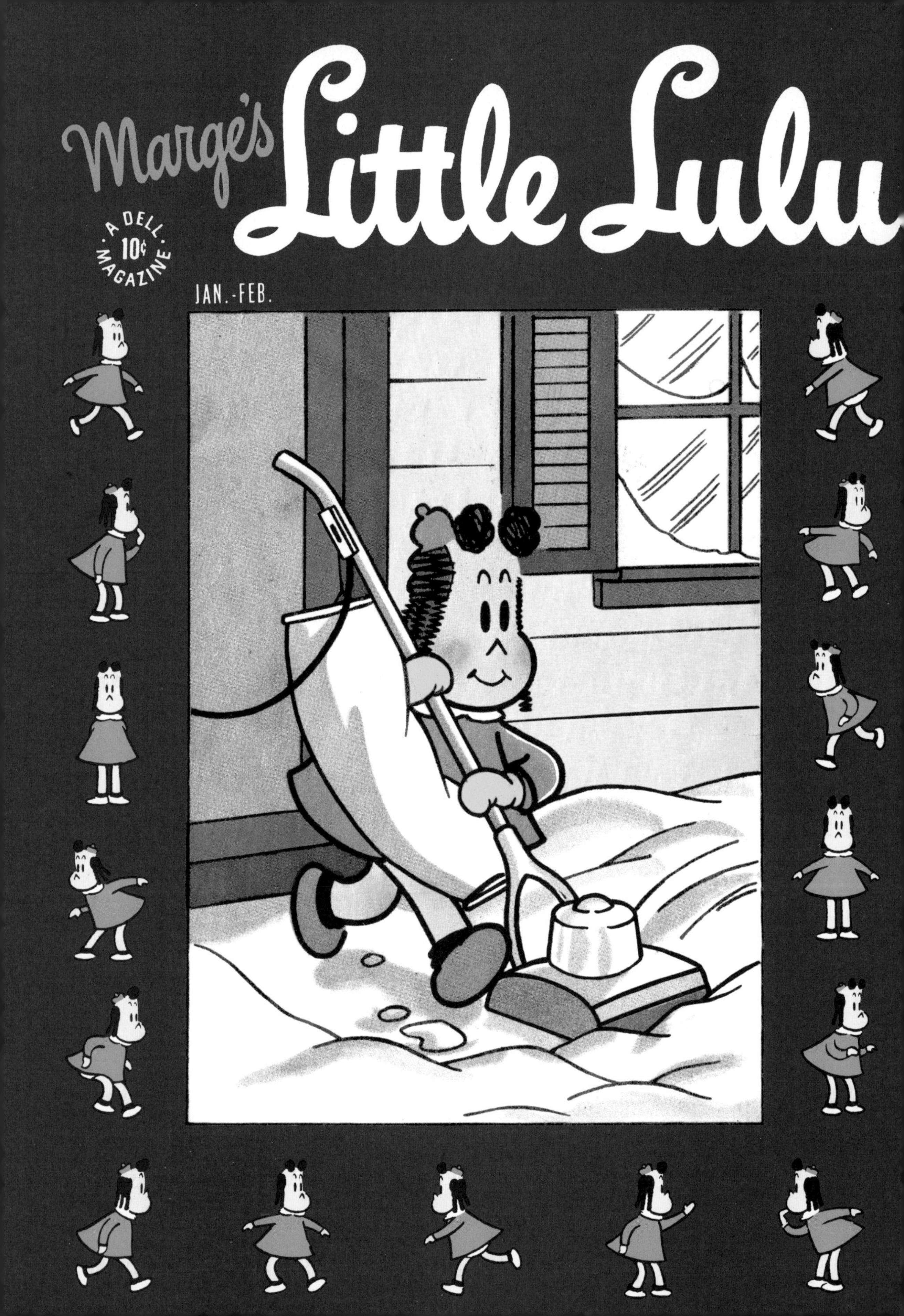
Marge's
Little Lulu
A DELL 10¢ MAGAZINE
JAN.-FEB.